**He swiveled around to face the closest Yk.64
and squeezed his trigger.**

The PBW fire tore off one of the enemy's airfoils, but the bastard didn't need them—there was no air inside the wormhole, so he could afford to lose a wing. Valk started to line up another shot when his view swung around and suddenly he couldn't see the enemies at all. Lanoe must have pulled some fancy maneuver without warning him.

"Give me something to shoot at, at least," Valk called.

"Don't worry," Lanoe replied. "You'll get another chance."

FORGOTTEN WORLDS

BOOK TWO OF THE SILENCE

D. NOLAN CLARK

www.orbitbooks.net

Copyright © 2017 by David Wellington
Excerpt from *Forbidden Suns* copyright © 2017 by David Wellington
Excerpt from *The Lazarus War: Artefact* copyright © 2015 by Jamie Sawyer

Cover design by Lauren Panepinto
Cover illustration by Victor Mosquera
Cover copyright © 2017 by Hachette Book Group, Inc.

Orbit
Hachette Book Group
1290 Avenue of the Americas
New York, NY 10104
orbitbooks.net

First Edition: April 2017

Orbit is an imprint of Hachette Book Group.
The Orbit name and logo are trademarks of Little, Brown Book Group Limited.

The publisher is not responsible for websites (or their content) that are not owned by the publisher.

The Hachette Speakers Bureau provides a wide range of authors for speaking events. To find out more, go to www.hachettespeakersbureau.com or call (866) 376-6591.

Library of Congress Cataloging-in-Publication Data

Names: Clark, D. Nolan, author.
Title: Forgotten worlds / D. Nolan Clark.
Description: First edition. | New York, NY : Orbit, 2017. | Series: The silence ; 2
Identifiers: LCCN 2016054346| ISBN 9780316355773 (paperback) | ISBN 9781478915379 (audio book) | ISBN 9780316355742 (ebook)
Subjects: LCSH: Science fiction. | BISAC: FICTION / Science Fiction / Space Opera. | FICTION / Science Fiction / Military. | FICTION / Science Fiction / High Tech. | FICTION / Science Fiction / Adventure.
Classification: LCC PS3603.L3568 F66 2017 | DDC 813/.6—dc23 LC record available at https://lccn.loc.gov/2016054346

ISBNs: 978-0-316-35577-3 (paperback), 978-0-316-35574-2 (ebook)

Printed in the United States of America

LSC-C

10 9 8 7 6 5 4 3 2 1

For Fred

PART I

CIRCUMBINARY

Chapter One

Behind the wall of space lay the network of wormholes that connected the stars. A desolate and eerie maze of tunnels no more than a few hundred meters wide in most places. The walls there emitted a constant and ghostly light, the luminescent smoke of particle-antiparticle annihilations. This ghostlight provided little illumination and less warmth.

For more than a century humanity had used that web of hidden passages to move people and cargo from one system to another, yet the maze was so complex and so convoluted it was rare for one ship to pass another in that silent space.

It was even rarer, Aleister Lanoe thought, to find four cataphract-class aerospace fighters blocking your way. Rare enough that it couldn't be a coincidence.

"Those aren't Navy ships," Valk said. His copilot, currently riding in the observation blister slung under the ship's belly. "Look at the hexagons on their fairings. They're Centrocor militia."

Lanoe recognized their configuration. Yk.64s, cheap copies of Navy fighters with big spherical canopies. He'd faced down plenty of ships like that in his time, and he knew that while they couldn't match the performance of the Navy's best fighters, they still wouldn't be pushovers.

"Huh," he said.

Lanoe and Valk were still hours out from their destination, a long way from anyone who could come to their aid. They could try to punch through this formation and make a run for it, but their Z.VII recon scout was slow compared to the Yk.64s they were facing. It would be a long and nasty chase and it wouldn't end well. Fighting wasn't a great option, either. The Z.VII carried a pair of PBW cannon, as good as anything the Centrocor ships could bring to bear, but their vector field wasn't as strong. The Yk.64s could shrug off most of their firepower, while they would get chewed to pieces in a dogfight.

Lanoe tried opening a channel. "Centrocor vehicles, we need a little room here. Mind letting us squeeze by?" As if this were just a chance encounter on a well-traveled shipping corridor. "Repeat. Centrocor vehicles—"

"Lanoe," Valk cut in, "their guns are warming up."

About what Lanoe had expected.

Outnumbered four to one. Outpaced, outgunned, and no way to call for help. Well, if they had to fight, at least they had one advantage. The pilots of the Yk.64s were militia, hired guns working for the Centrocor poly. They'd been trained by a corporation. Lanoe was one of the best pilots the Navy ever had.

"Hold on," he told Valk. Then he threw his stick over to the side and goosed his lateral thrusters, throwing them into a wild corkscrewing dive right toward the wall of the wormhole.

⫸⫷

The recon scout's inertial sink pulled Valk backward in his seat. It felt like someone was sitting on his chest, pinning him down. He was used to the feeling—without a sink, any pilot who tried a maneuver like that would have been crushed into pink jelly by the g forces.

It made it tricky, though, to reach the gun controls. Valk grunted and stabbed a virtual menu, bringing his cannon online. The ship's computer automatically swung him around to give him the best firing solution possible on the Yk.64 Centrocor ships. That meant he was flying backward, which in turn meant he couldn't see the wall of the wormhole looming up toward them. He was just fine with that. If they so much as brushed the wall—a curled-up tube of spacetime—the recon scout would be instantaneously disintegrated, its atoms torn apart down to the quark level.

Valk trusted Lanoe to not let that happen.

"Coming in, seven o'clock high," Valk called, and tapped another key to bring up a virtual Aldis gunsight, a collimated reticule that moved around his canopy to show him where his shots were likely to hit. It jumped back and forth as the computer tried to compensate for Lanoe's spinning dive and the movement of the four targets. Valk cursed the damned thing and switched it off. He was going to have to do this manually. "I think they're angry," Valk said.

Streamers of PBW fire like tiny burning comets flashed across the recon scout's thrusters as the enemy opened fire. Lanoe twisted them around on their positioning jets and most of the shots went wide, only a few sparking off their vector field.

"That was a warning shot," Lanoe said. "You think they want to take us alive?"

"Why don't you pull over and ask them?" Valk replied.

Lanoe actually chuckled at that one.

The recon scout shook and groaned as Lanoe threw them to one side, narrowly avoiding the looming collision with the wormhole's wall. Valk realized why Lanoe had cut it so close—hugging the wall kept the enemy from getting around them. The recon scout's top side was vulnerable to attack, and Lanoe wanted to make sure they couldn't get a bead on it. This did mean that Valk, in his observer's blister, was right in the line of fire.

Wouldn't be the first time. He swiveled around to face the closest Yk.64 and squeezed his trigger. The PBW fire tore off one of the enemy's airfoils, but the bastard didn't need them—there was no air inside the wormhole, so he could afford to lose a wing. Valk started to line up another shot when his view swung around and suddenly he couldn't see the enemies at all. Lanoe must have pulled some fancy maneuver without warning him.

"Give me something to shoot at, at least," Valk called.

"Don't worry," Lanoe replied. "You'll get another chance."

~~~

In the pilot's cockpit at the front of the recon scout, Lanoe worked his boards with one hand while the other stayed tightly wrapped around his control yoke. On a secondary display he saw a three-dimensional view of the four militia fighters with their projected courses streaming out before them like ribbons of glass. The four of them were cruising along well behind and above him, lined up in a textbook formation. They had him boxed in, at a distance where they never came close enough to get a good, clear shot at him. It was a solid play—they were keeping their distance because they knew time was on their side. They could afford to pepper him with long-distance shots, knowing they only needed one lucky hit to disable his engine.

He couldn't outrun them. If he tried to fall back, to let them get ahead of him, they could just close the distance and then they could carve him up or just shove him into the wall of the wormhole, and that would be that.

Militia pilots weren't, as a rule, all that talented. The Navy aggressively recruited promising young talent—by law, they got the first pick of recruits—and the polys had to make do with whatever was left. Some were cadets who washed out of the Navy and found the only job they could get was flying for a poly. Others were recruited from the civilian population, given ten hours in a flight simulator, and sent out to do their best. This batch, though, were clearly a cut above—smart, adaptable. Patient.

He very much wished he knew who had sent them. And why they wanted to capture him.

If he was getting out of this trap, he was going to have to get reckless. "Valk," he called, "don't worry about wasting ammunition. When I pull this next trick, you hold down your trigger and don't stop until your gun overheats, okay?"

"Wait," Valk said. "What are you about to do?"

Lanoe didn't waste time answering. He punched in a sequence of burns on his thruster board, then yanked his stick straight back and simultaneously kicked open the throttle.

The Z.VII had been built for long-distance patrols. It carried an impressive package of sensors and a very energy-efficient fusion engine. All that extra equipment made it bulky and slow to respond to commands, though. It had never been designed for close-in fighting, and definitely not for stunt flying. The complicated maneuver Lanoe executed just then ran the risk of tying its frame in knots. He could hear its spars groan as the ship twisted around nearly 180 degrees on its long axis. It took more strain when the dozens of jets and miniature thrusters built into its nose and sides all fired in a complex rhythm. If Lanoe was unlucky, they might have torn themselves right out of their mountings.

Luck was on his side. Everything held together. It only appeared that he'd lost all control and sent his ship into a wild, uncontrolled vertical spin.

The Z.VII tumbled up and backward, right into the path of the pursuing militia fighters. They reacted quickly, breaking formation to make room and avoid a full-on collision. Quickly, but not flawlessly. One of them sideswiped a second in a great shower of sparks as their vector fields fought to shove each other away. A third pilot started to bank, to try to get a shot in as Lanoe's ship went cartwheeling past. It would have been an easy hit, and it would have ended the battle as quickly as it had started.

If Valk hadn't already started shooting anyway. He'd done as asked, releasing a wild spray of PBW fire that lit up the canopy of the Yk.64. The militia pilot inside probably didn't have time to scream. The shot tore the Yk.64 fighter to pieces, and the three remaining militia pilots had to scatter farther to avoid the superheated debris.

Lanoe pulled the recon scout out of its tumble and leveled out, skating along just a few dozen meters from the wall of the tunnel. They weren't out of the woods yet. He opened his throttle as far as it would go and burned for speed, headed in exactly the wrong direction.

Chapter Two

Valk rotated his observer's blister around 180 degrees. Behind them, through the haze around their thrusters, he could see the remaining Yk.64s banking hard, regrouping to chase after them.

"You know the Admiralty's the other way, right?" he asked.

"They're not going to let us get to the Admiralty. Not today," Lanoe answered.

Valk switched off the intercom so Lanoe wouldn't hear him cursing. He tried focusing on the pursuit, tried lining up a long, impossible shot on one of the fighters, but there was no point. He switched the intercom back on. "Lanoe, you promised me. You said we would go to the Admiralty and download all this stuff in my head. And then you would let me—"

"I didn't forget," Lanoe replied.

There was no point in arguing. Valk could see perfectly well how things were stacked up against them. "Ignore that last comment," he said. "What's the new plan?"

"Get out of this in one piece, if we can. Listen, we've bought ourselves about fifteen seconds' worth of a head start. There's still no way we can outrun them. So I need you to keep them off balance— lay down suppressing fire as soon as they get close, keep them from forming up again. Got it?"

"Yep," Valk said. He brought up his weapons board. There was still plenty of ammo in his cannon. He checked his other displays and nodded to himself. "Mind if I get a little creative? I might have a few surprises for them."

"Whatever you can do, do it," Lanoe told him.

Valk tapped a few virtual keys. This might be interesting, he thought. If they could stay alive long enough to see it.

The wormhole stretched out before Lanoe, its walls snaking back and forth, spitting out ghostly fire. He brought a display up into his main view, showing a camera feed from directly behind them. The Yk.64 Centrocor pilots hadn't expected his crazy maneuver and it was taking them a little time to get themselves turned around.

Not as much time as he might have liked. One of them pulled a perfect half loop, a maneuver that was a lot harder to do in vacuum than inside an atmosphere. The other two banked and rolled, slower but safer. Behind them light flashed again and again, sudden and bright as lightning, as debris from the downed ship touched the walls. Those little annihilations would give off a lot of gamma rays, but it was too much to hope that any of the remaining pilots would be fried.

The ship that pulled the half loop burned hard in pursuit, enough so that Lanoe could see the ion trail of its wake as if the Yk.64 were standing on a pillar of fire. Valk put a couple of pointless PBW shots across its nose and its airfoils but it didn't even bother rolling to evade.

The Yk.64's powerful engines ate up the distance. Any second now the militia pilot would be close enough to get a perfect bead on Lanoe's main thruster and then it would all be over. Lanoe considered a couple of different tricky maneuvers, just to make it harder for the pilot to get that shot, but any deviation from their course right now would slow the Z.VII down, and he would still have the other two pursuers to worry about. They weren't far behind.

"Valk," he called, "if you've got something—"

"Close your eyes," Valk said.

"I'm a little busy flying this crate," Lanoe pointed out.

Valk reached for his sensor board. His finger hovered over a virtual key.

"Damn it, Lanoe—*close your damned eyes*."

He stabbed the key.

The Z.VII came with a whole suite of advanced sensors and communication gear. Included in that package were several hundred microdrones—basically satellites no bigger than Valk's thumb. Each of them contained a camera, an antenna, and a tiny thruster. There wasn't room for anything else. In normal conditions these would be released one at a time as the recon scout made a long patrol across a battlefield, stringing them out like a trail of breadcrumbs. They were designed to work together to create a distributed communications and imaging network, providing a comprehensive picture of a massive volume of space.

Valk released all of them at once. They burst out of panels recessed into the Z.VII's hull, flaring away on their tiny thrusters, headed in every possible direction, a whole cloud of them zipping away and behind like chaff. They would ruin the Yk.64's ability to get a clear lock on the Z.VII's thrusters, but it would only take a fraction of a second for the pursuer's computers to compensate. That wasn't what Valk was after.

Nor did he hope they would hit the Yk.64 enemy ship. They would make lousy projectiles—too slow and too small to do any damage, and anyway the Yk.64's vector field would just shunt them away.

No, Valk had fired off all his microdrones for another reason. He had disengaged their standard programming, specifically the collision avoidance algorithms. One by one, then in great numbers, they shot away from the Z.VII on perfectly flat trajectories that had them smash right into the walls of the wormhole.

They were annihilated instantly, torn apart and converted into pure energy. Hundreds of impacts all in the space of a half second, each one giving off as much light and radiation as a nuclear blast.

"Hellfire!" Lanoe shouted, which was apt whether he'd meant it to be or not. "Valk—I can see that right through my eyelids! What did you just do?"

The pilot of the Yk.64 hadn't been warned ahead of time to close his eyes.

The Yk.64 was a smart machine. A microsecond after the flare-up, its canopy polarized until it was completely opaque, blocking out every bit of that horrible light.

It was an open question whether the pilot was permanently blinded before that happened. An academic question—with the canopy opaqued, there was no way he could see anyway. For about nine-tenths of a second, he was flying blind.

Plenty of time for Valk to line up a good, solid shot, even at a distance. Of course Valk had been facing the light-blast, but unlike Lanoe or the pilot of the Yk.64, he didn't need his eyes for what came next. He reached out into the raw code of the Z.VII's sensors, synthesized the ones and zeroes into a perfect firing solution. He didn't need to be able to see his hand to pull the trigger.

PBW fire hit the Yk.64 enemy machine dead-on, cutting right through its vector field. The fighter broke into pieces, airfoils and weapons and thrusters all tumbling away from each other as the particle beam cut them apart like a scalpel.

"Got another one," Valk said.

"As soon as I can see through all the spots in my eyes," Lanoe told him, "I'd love to know what just happened. That was a great trick."

"Yeah," Valk said. "Too bad I can only do it once."

Lanoe blinked and squinted and shook his head to clear the tears out of his eyes. The tunnel ahead of them was as crooked as a dog's leg and he was taking it at top speed. If he wasn't careful he'd brush the walls and finish the enemy's work for them.

Not that they needed much help. The remaining two fighters were catching up with them, fast. Lanoe had been lucky so far—well, he'd been lucky enough to have Valk crewing the guns for him—but the law of averages was running after them just as fast as their enemies. The two Yk.64s were firing indiscriminately now, wasting ammo on long-range shots that had very little chance of hitting the Z.VII as it wove through the corridors of the maze.

"There was a side passage, back this way," Lanoe said. "Remember?"

"No," Valk said.

Lanoe laughed. "Yeah, well, it's there. No idea where it leads but if we can get out into open space we can at least maneuver a little more. I'm going to make a hard turn in a second here. It might hurt a little."

"I'll survive," Valk told him.

Lanoe nodded. Well, the big guy was probably right about that. He could take a lot more g forces than Lanoe could, after all.

Still, this was not going to be fun.

Most people thought of the wormhole network as a kind of superhighway system, a grid of streets that connected all the stars in human space. Pilots knew better. The system was a chaotic mess at best, a tangled and endlessly branching collection of tunnels with no clear semblance of order. Wormholes crossed each other at junctions, split off into dead ends and long loops that doubled back on themselves. Making it worse, there was no real map of the entire system, because it changed over time—only the widest and most heavily traveled routes stayed constant for long, and even those twisted and knotted themselves up when nobody was looking.

You passed junctions and new tunnels all the time. Pilots had learned not to go exploring, in case they found themselves in a wormhole that went nowhere, or, worse, one that narrowed down until it was too tight a squeeze for even small ships like the Z.VII.

Of course, sometimes you just had to take a chance.

The two Yk.64s were almost on them. Valk laid down salvo after salvo of suppressing fire, but the fighters had velocity to spare—they swung and jinked back and forth as they came on, refusing to let themselves be decent targets. Lanoe studied the tunnel ahead, looking for the side passage he vaguely remembered. If it was farther down the tunnel than he thought—

No. There it was. The ghostly vapor that steamed from the walls grew thicker up ahead. The sign of a junction. Lanoe pulled up his engine board and scrolled through a menu to the gyroscopic control settings. He had to confirm twice that he was really sure he wanted to disengage the rotary compensator.

He was sure.

"Hang on!" he said, and stabbed the virtual key.

The recon scout twisted ninety degrees to the right in the space of a few milliseconds. The fuselage groaned under the stress as the engine tried to rip its way off its own mountings. There was a good reason you had to confirm twice to pull this stunt—there was a very real chance it would tear your ship in half.

The effect on a soft human body could have been much worse. Lanoe's inertial sink slammed him down as if he were being hammered into his seat. He couldn't breathe. The blood in his body stopped moving and for a split second he went into cardiac arrest. Even his vision blurred to nothing as his eyeballs were flattened inside his head.

Then the compensators snapped back on as alarm chime blared in Lanoe's ears and his heart thudded in his chest as it started beating again. He made a horrible choking, gasping noise as his lungs reinflated.

Up ahead of him, through his canopy, he could see the side passage. It wasn't very long. He goosed his main thruster and sent the Z.VII rocketing down the tunnel, barely worrying about twists and turns.

"Valk, you okay back there?" he called.

There was no answer.

Right behind him the two Yk.64s copied his turn perfectly. They didn't so much as skid as they twisted around to follow him.

Bastards.

He would have to worry about Valk later. For the moment, all he could do was fly fast. Something he was very good at.

Up ahead the tunnel ended in a lens of pure, unadulterated spacetime that looked like a glass globe, through which he could see only darkness. A wormhole throat—one of the exits from the maze. Lanoe had no idea what lay beyond. It could be a star with nice planets to hide behind, or it could be some forgotten corner of deep space, light-years from anything. It could open out into the event horizon of a black hole.

Lanoe would have to take his chances. He punched through the lens—it offered no resistance—and into bluish-white light. His eyes adjusted and he saw stars, stars everywhere—speckles of white on a black background.

Real, normal space. The kind that made up most of the universe. The void.

For a fighter pilot like Lanoe, flying free through open space was the closest he ever felt to being home.

He wasn't safe, though. Right behind him, the two Yk.64s shot out of the throat side by side, their weapons still glowing in the infrared. They converged on him, a classic pincer maneuver, and then—

They stopped. For a second they just hung there behind his shoulders, ready to blast him to smithereens. Then they twisted around and shot back through the throat. Back into wormspace.

A second later Lanoe realized why. A green pearl appeared in the corner of his vision, his suit telling him he had an incoming call.

"Reconnaissance scout, please identify. This is a Naval installation and off-limits to unauthorized personnel. Repeat, reconnaissance scout, please identify. This is..."

Some of those twinkling lights all around him weren't stars after all. His displays showed him magnified, light-enhanced views of dozens of spacecraft, all of them military. Patrol ships, command vessels, destroyers, and cruisers. Plenty of cataphract-class fighters, all of them painted with the three-headed eagle of the Navy of Earth. Clearly, Centrocor's pilots had no interest in tangling with that much firepower.

He couldn't remember the last time he'd been so happy to see his own people.

Chapter Three

There wasn't enough air.

The planet wasn't habitable, not by civilized standards. Little water, very little infrastructure. The air was so thin Ashlay Bullam needed to sip at an oxygen pipe just to keep her head from swimming.

A dusty little world orbiting a dim little star. A hundred thousand people lived on Niraya, but she was damned if she could figure out why.

Bullam had been forced to bring all her creature comforts with her. A table in her cabin had been laden with a variety of foodstuffs for her to choose from. "These," she said. She jabbed one gold-encased finger at a tray of canapés. Locally sourced meat wrapped in lettuce that had to be shipped in from another planet, because of course Niraya couldn't support real agriculture. Well, the dainties she'd picked weren't completely inedible. The drone zipped away and Bullam walked out onto the open deck of the yacht where her guest was waiting.

Niraya didn't have a functional government. No bureaucracy to work with, no local warlord to flatter or threaten. Religious officials were the closest thing to actual leaders on the backwater world. So Bullam was forced to deal with a woman named Elder McRae, who represented the Transcendentalist faith. It wasn't going to be easy doing business with that sort, but Bullam was very good at her job.

The Elder stood at the wooden railing, looking down. At the moment the yacht was just drifting along, twenty meters above the only real city on the planet, a place called Walden Crater. Just like the Nirayans to name their capital after a hole in the ground.

"Elder McRae," Bullam said, putting on the smile she used for people she wished to show official deference. "Thank you so much for agreeing to meet with me. I apologize—do you embrace on Niraya, or shake hands? So many different planets, you know, each with its own customs. I do like to get them right."

The old woman turned from the railing and looked at Bullam without any sign of emotion. She wore a simple tunic and skirt and she could have been a thousand years old or only sixty. A religious functionary, from an order that rejected any kind of cosmetic therapy. On another world that lined and craggy face might have frightened children, but here it was apparently a sign of wisdom and restraint.

Bullam wondered how the Elder must see her, in her fractal lace dress and her gold finger stalls. She had sculpted her features until she looked just like she had at twenty-five, and had her hair streaked with white and blue. Most likely the Elder would see a decadent plutocrat. Well, if the woman underestimated her, that could be turned to Bullam's advantage.

"I would think," the Elder said, "that you would have been briefed before you came here. We shake hands."

Bullam laughed and held out her right hand. The Elder grasped it for a moment, then released it. "Of course, but there's so little time in the day. I just had so many things to do I couldn't get through the whole file on Niraya. There were other parts of it I found much more interesting. It's not every planet I visit that's been attacked by aliens."

The Elder shook her head. "Alien drones. There's a difference."

"Certainly. Will you sit and have some refreshment?" Bullam led the Elder to a low table at the prow of the yacht. Together they sat down on cushions and took flavored water and little nibbles. The Elder ate sparingly. "You'll be wondering why I asked for this meeting, I'm sure."

"I imagine I have a good idea. You're a Centrocor executive. Customer relations?"

Bullam demurred by lowering her chin. "My position is a little more fluid than that. You could say I'm the poly's head trouble-shooter. I do odds and ends, but if you like, today I'm speaking to you as a customer support representative. Centrocor has a deep interest in keeping you happy."

"Centrocor has the monopoly on Niraya's resources and products. For many years your poly ignored us as an unprofitable investment of little value or interest."

"Come now," Bullam said. "We've provided you with everything you needed for terraforming your world. We've shipped you food when you couldn't grow enough on your own, provided you with construction equipment to improve your infrastructure—"

"Because we are legally required to purchase such things only from you. Enough," the Elder said, and raised a hand for peace. "I have no interest in the economics of interstellar trade. That's your job. The point is that Centrocor is suddenly very interested in Niraya because a few months ago a fleet of alien drones arrived here. For the first time in human history, contact was made with another intelligent species. You've come to determine how your poly can make a profit out of that."

Bullam shrugged. The woman had it mostly right, after all. "Naturally," she said, "the financial implications matter to us. I won't pretend otherwise. Yet we also want to express our deep concern for the people of Niraya, and make sure you're recovering well from this dreadful invasion. We value our clients."

"Do you?" The Elder set down her cup. "When the aliens first attacked this planet, we begged Centrocor for help in keeping us safe. We were utterly ignored."

"A terrible oversight, and one we regret—"

The Elder wasn't even looking at her. "We weren't valuable enough, then. You would have let us all die." There was no tone of reproach in her voice. It sounded more like a dry statement of fact.

"If it weren't for Commander Lanoe and his squadron, we wouldn't be here now."

"I think you're being modest there, by failing to mention your own part in the defense of Niraya," Bullam said. "From what I've been told, you acted quite heroically."

"I did my part, that's all." The Elder put a hand on the yacht's railing and looked over the side, at the city below. "On this planet, we respect plain speech, M. Bullam. Perhaps you'll simply tell me what you want with us."

"To help! Really, that's why I'm here. Centrocor knows what you've been through. We can provide all kinds of services, from emergency aid to grief counseling to—"

"We need a new power plant."

Bullam smiled. Finally, the negotiations could begin.

"One of our plants was destroyed in the fighting. We've been struggling with energy shortages ever since. We don't have the ability to build a new one on our own."

"Of course. I can have a construction team here tomorrow."

"Good. What will it cost us?"

Bullam drew in a deep breath. "A signature. Just one," she said.

That got the Elder's attention. The old woman's lips pursed as if she'd tasted something sour. "Explain," she said.

"You're the closest thing to a civilian authority on this planet. I need you to sign a form—a standard waiver, nothing complex—that frees Centrocor from any liability stemming from the invasion."

The Elder watched her with those emotionless eyes.

Bullam lifted one hand and let it flutter in the air dismissively. "We can't stop you from taking legal action against us, of course. The charter that let you settle this planet preserved that right. You could file any number of official charges against the poly, either individually or in a class action. Of course, you would never win anything. You would spend what little money you have simply to file all the necessary forms and you would never get close to scratching the wall of legal protections Centrocor has woven around itself. We have a standing army of lawyers just for cases like this, and—"

"Stop," the Elder said.

Bullam chose to keep going. "The point is, you wouldn't get anything out of legal action except to bankrupt an already suffering planet. But Centrocor is willing to be generous here, and save both parties a great deal of time and expense. If we can all come out of this friends, well—so much the better. So I'm authorized to give you what you want, in exchange for a simple promise."

"You want me to prevent my people from filing lawsuits against your poly." The Elder nodded, slowly. "For a new power plant? I can do that."

Lanoe put up his helmet and punched the key that opened his canopy to the void of space. The flowglas parted over him with a rush of escaping air, then melted back into the fuselage until he could climb out of his seat and onto the hull of the recon scout. He swung himself around and then, using handholds welded to the fuselage, made his way back to the observation blister. Within, he could see Valk sitting in the gunner's seat. At least, he could see Valk's suit. The helmet was down, and the empty suit had crumpled forward, one arm drifting in the lack of gravity.

That wasn't good.

Lanoe opened the blister. He braced himself against the fuselage and reached inside with one arm. Valk's suit flopped away from him as he touched it. Only the crash restraints kept it from floating out of the open blister. Cursing and stretching, Lanoe eventually managed to grab on to the suit's collar ring. He found the recessed key that manually controlled the helmet and jabbed it with his index finger.

The helmet expanded like a black soap bubble. The polarized helmet was the closest thing Valk had to a face, and when it was up he looked a lot more lifelike. Knowing what to expect, Lanoe pulled his arm back. After a second, the suit jerked and went rigid, and over his suit radio Lanoe could hear Valk gasp and sputter as he came back to life.

"Hellfire," the big guy whispered. "Lanoe—how long was I out?"

"Just a few minutes. I considered letting you stay down for a while, but I'm afraid we still have work to do."

"Yeah. Yeah, okay." Valk sounded like a man who'd been woken from a sound sleep. As if the g forces of their escape from the wormhole maze had knocked him unconscious, and he was just now coming to.

It was more like he was coming back from the dead.

Technically there was no Tannis Valk. There had been a man by that name once, a pilot who had fought for the Establishment, the last great enemies of Lanoe's Navy. That man had died seventeen years ago, when an antipersonnel round had lit up his fighter's canopy and burned him alive inside his suit. Somehow he had managed to shoot down two enemy ships and return to base while still on fire. Pilots on both sides of the conflict had whispered stories of the man who refused to die. They'd called him the Blue Devil, a name that had stuck with him ever since. His superiors had recognized a propaganda coup when they saw one, and had made him a hero, a legend. A shining example of the will of the Establishment.

Of course, the truth wasn't as glamorous. Valk had died instantly when the AP round hit him. Before that he'd programmed his ship for a number of maneuvers and the flight home, and it carried out his instructions posthumously. That story wasn't likely to inspire the troops, so it was suppressed.

Meanwhile, in an Establishment lab, technicians had worked to recover Tannis Valk's memories and personality from his roasted skull. They'd fed everything they found into a computer and created an artificial intelligence that could think and talk just like the dead hero.

What they'd done was incredibly illegal. AI was banned across human space—too many lives had been lost to machines that could think clearer and faster than any human. The Establishment had tried to get around this problem by never letting Valk know that he was just a machine. For seventeen years, he'd been an empty suit that thought it was a man. The whole time he'd been in incredible pain, suffering from phantom limb syndrome over his entire body.

It wasn't until the battle of Niraya that he'd learned the truth. It took an alien machine to show him what he really was.

Since then, Valk had wanted nothing but to die. He was tired of the pain. Tired of being a reflection of a man who'd never asked to be a folktale. Unfortunately, by then he had a head full of information that was too valuable to be lost. Valk knew more about the aliens than anyone living. The same machine that told him what he was had also told him all about the Blue-Blue-White, the only other intelligent species humanity had ever met. That information was far too valuable to lose.

Lanoe had made Valk a deal. If they could just get to the Admiralty—Navy headquarters—and allow his information to be downloaded into the right hands, then he could let go. He could be allowed to die—to be deleted. Freed from the excruciating pain he always felt. Freed from the confusion of learning he wasn't even a human being.

But only then.

Valk had agreed. The man had agreed anyway. Sometimes the computer, the artificial intelligence, decided to renege on the deal. It would just—cut out. Switch itself off, sometimes at very inopportune moments. Then Lanoe would have to reboot the system and bring Valk back from the peace of death.

He hated himself a little more every time he did it. He knew he would keep doing it, until Valk's work was done.

"Where are we?" Valk asked, twisting around to look at the void around them. "I don't recognize any of these stars."

"Rishi," Lanoe told him. "It's not a place an Establishment pilot would ever have seen." He stretched out his arm and pointed at a shadow rotating in the distance. A cylindrical mass, big enough to block out some of the stars. "It's a Navy facility, a flight school. They almost blew us out of the sky before I told them who I was. Now we're just waiting for clearance to land."

"Navy—"

Lanoe shook his head. He knew what Valk was asking. "Sorry. Yeah, we're in friendly territory. They don't have the facilities here, though, to read your memories. At least, I don't trust them to do it and then keep that information safe. Centrocor's after us. They might have spies here. I can't let anybody have your data except the Admirals themselves, and even then there are a couple of them I'm not sure about."

"So we're back to square one," Valk said.

"Not exactly. I know somebody who works here. Somebody who can help us."

Lanoe had been in the Navy a very long time. He knew a lot of people.

The meeting with Elder McRae dragged on, as the old woman insisted on reading the entire waiver before she signed. By the time the negotiation was finished, Bullam needed a nap. It was the lack of oxygen, she told herself. Only that. She saw the Elder off the yacht—there weren't many aircraft on Niraya, so the old woman had to be ferried back to the ground in a sedan chair supported by drones—then retired to her cabin, which she could pressurize. As cool air washed over her face, a drone came forward to mop her brow with a damp cloth while another slipped off her shoes.

She turned on some music and closed her eyes, intending to just get a little sleep before she moved on to the next thing on her agenda. There was so much more to do before she could leave Niraya and go somewhere pleasant. Yet before she'd truly fallen asleep, just as her mind began to quiet down, a warbling chirp came from the cabin's ceiling.

She opened her eyes. That particular tone meant a call she couldn't ignore. Not when things were still so delicate.

"Accept," she said. The light in the cabin dimmed as its windows grew opaque—you never knew who might be watching. Maybe someone who could read lips. When you worked for a poly, spies were everywhere. Bullam should know—since one of her many jobs was to act as Centrocor's head of counterintelligence.

The voice was modulated and flattened by encryption and distance. Words from a dozen light-years away, passed on through relay stations at the throats of half a dozen wormholes. "I have information on activity three-oh-nine-six." The voice belonged to one of her underlings—it didn't matter which. "Two employees have returned and filed reports."

Two? They'd sent four. Well, casualties had always been a possibility, but—

"The activity is reported as unsuccessful. The object of the activity was last sighted exiting a wormhole at Rishi."

Bullam did not sit up. She did not curse. There was no point. The message had come from so far away that she could not respond to it in real time—nor could she ask questions. She waited in case the message contained any more information, but it stopped there.

She knew what the cryptic message meant. Aleister Lanoe had escaped them. And now he knew that Centrocor wanted him.

He knew more about the aliens that attacked Niraya than anyone. Far more than Elder McRae, more than the Navy scientists currently studying the wreckage of the alien drones. That knowledge could be extraordinarily valuable.

The discovery of alien life could change everything—it could mean potential new markets, or it could lead to a shakeup of the political equilibrium between Earth and the transplanetary polys, an equilibrium that had never been stable.

The polys controlled every human world outside of Earth's solar system. The six biggest of the transplanetary corporations fought endless wars among themselves, vying to expand their economic empires. The Navy of Earth stepped in on those wars, fighting with one side against the others, to make sure no one poly ever gained a real advantage over any of the others. By playing the polys against each other, the Navy preserved Earth's self-determination—but in turn, the Navy could never quite break the polys' economic stranglehold on the galaxy. It was a stalemate that had lasted for more than a century, with every side plotting constantly to try to get the upper hand.

Now a new player had entered the game.

If the aliens were a serious threat, if they planned on attacking more human worlds, the people living on those planets might well turn to Earth for protection—and away from the polys. Away from Bullam's employers.

Whatever happened, things were about to change, in major and dramatic ways. Centrocor needed information if it was going to come out on top, or at the very least survive that transition. The best source of that information was Aleister Lanoe.

Bullam had been given an unlimited budget to find him and take him captive. She'd worked very hard putting her plan together, arranging for Lanoe to be ambushed deep in the wormhole network.

According to the message she'd just received, that ambush had failed.

In the quiet she contemplated what that meant. Disaster, potentially. Her job could be in jeopardy. She could lose everything.

Ashlay Bullam had a very good reason why she needed to hold on to her job.

The situation wasn't apocalyptic quite yet, though. Her people had kept him from reaching the Admiralty. Once he was safely under the protection of the Navy's top brass, she would never get to him. For now, at least, he was still in play. She could set up a new plan to catch him. But he would be more cautious the second time.

She needed to handle this right away.

"Reply to message," she said. A drone moved forward through the air, a green light pulsing slowly on the front of its casing. "What assets do we have at Rishi? It's a Navy system, so probably not much. Give me options. Copy everything we do to Oversight. Make sure every action we've taken is logged, and be ready to document the chain of approval. Let Oversight know we have nothing to hide."

When planning a kidnapping, it was always important to cover one's ass.

At the center of the system lay not one star but two, a blue giant and a white dwarf that danced as they orbited one another. Gravity around such a pair was a complicated equation, and as a result no planets had ever formed in the system—instead, a thick band of gas and dust surrounded them, glowing with constant tiny impacts and tidal stresses. Far out, at the very edge of the system, lay Rishi, orbiting it all like a marble rolling along the edge of a plate.

Rishi had originally been built by the DaoLink Gathered Economic Concern, one of the big polys. The orbital had been intended as a monument to DaoLink's success—when construction began it would have been the largest artificial object in human space. In shape it was a hollow tube a hundred kilometers long and fifty in diameter, built of foamed concrete a kilometer thick. It was open to space at both ends, so spacecraft could—and regularly did—fly through it without stopping. The whole thing spun on its axis, so rapidly that its inner surface possessed half of Earth's gravity. There was a breathable atmosphere inside, held down by centrifugal force and kept from escaping by a rimwall around either opening half a kilometer tall.

It was a triumph of engineering. Utterly simple in design, yet grandiose in scope, a Bach fugue in stone. It was also, at least for DaoLink, a complete debacle. It had taken nearly a hundred years to finish building Rishi, twice as long as expected. As the years went by and new planets were terraformed and inhabited, few had been discovered near enough to Rishi to make it a hub for travel, as had been originally intended. Instead of being the jewel at the center of DaoLink space, it had been shunted off to a mere backwater.

And then the unimaginable happened. Before construction on Rishi was complete, another poly, ThiessGruppe Limited, built an even larger habitat—a ring nearly a thousand kilometers in circumference. Overnight Rishi's propaganda value had dropped to nil.

DaoLink never even bothered to move in. For fifty years Rishi lay unoccupied, unused, uninhabitable. In the end, for certain unnamed concessions, the poly turned Rishi over to the Navy for use as a flight school. Millions of people could have lived and worked inside Rishi. Instead it was home to a few hundred cadets and their instructors. As Lanoe worked his jets, matching velocity and rotation with the big cylinder, he could see how empty and shabby its docking berths were, how much of the interior was overrun with lush vegetation. It had the air of a magnificent ruin, a place forgotten by the rest of the universe.

It suited him just fine. If Centrocor was after him, Rishi made a great place to lie low for a while. The habitat was off-limits to the polys and while he knew better than to trust everyone in the Navy, he knew he at least still had some friends there. People he could count on for help.

Lanoe let Valk land the recon scout while he worked the comms board. He needed to talk to Marjoram Candless, who had been a squaddie of his in the very old days, back during the Brushfire that followed the Century War. He'd known her since before he'd got his first command—which made her a very old friend indeed. The last time he'd heard from her she'd taken a position as an instructor at Rishi. If she was still around she would be a useful ally.

Getting hold of her took some work, though. She didn't answer when he pinged her personal minder, and when he contacted the flight school's offices he was simply told she was out and unavailable. They would be happy to take a message, but Lanoe didn't want to leave his name. In the end he had to leave a public message with the local server, which he assumed would be about as effective as posting a written note on a billboard in the school's cafeteria. He couldn't put any personal details in that message either, so he simply signed it as "an old friend from the 305th Fighter Wing," a unit that hadn't existed for a hundred years.

Surprisingly, it worked. Not ten minutes after he posted the message, a green pearl appeared in the corner of his vision, telling him he had an incoming call. Candless's face appeared on his main display. Sharp features, sculpted by elastomer treatments. She still had the long, severe nose he remembered, the lips permanently compressed to a prim line. Her hair was pulled back in a severe coil that accentuated her already high forehead. Her hazel eyes were the only part of her face that truly showed her age. Sharp, bright eyes that looked right into you and saw everything you tried to hide. The eyes of someone who'd seen everything life had to offer, and found it vaguely distasteful. She was an old woman now, pushing two hundred. Well, he was even older, himself. Modern medicine meant age didn't slow people down anymore, and she looked just as vital as ever. She would have changed as much as he had, he supposed, but just seeing her face brought back so many memories he couldn't help but think she was exactly the same person as she'd been when they'd fought together.

"So it is you," she said. "Your timing, I'm afraid, is terrible."

"You look surprised to see me," he told her.

"As far as I know, you and I are the only people left from the 305th. When I saw that message I thought maybe an old ghost was finally catching up with me."

Lanoe smiled. "I took a wrong turn somewhere. Thought I'd pop in and catch up on old times, maybe over a drink. You have a minute?"

Candless took a deep breath. "Barely. There's a guesthouse near the habitat's meridian line. Let's meet there. I'll send you the address. It's been...what? Five years since we spoke? Ten?" She frowned. "You had to wait until *just* now."

"Sorry," Lanoe said. "You know me. Always zigging when I'm supposed to zag." He tried to give her a warm smile. Her face didn't change.

"Can you get there within the hour?" Candless asked.

"If I hurry," he told her. "Why the rush?"

"Well, I might be getting murdered this afternoon. So our best bet is to do lunch."

Bullam looked over a dossier prepared for her by her assistants, scrolling through page after page of text on her personal minder.

There was really only one option available. She didn't like it at all—she preferred more subtle methods—but if she was going to catch Aleister Lanoe then it had to be done soon, and that meant a brute-force approach.

When she'd seen enough she deleted the file, then rolled the minder up and stuck it inside her desk. "New message," she said. A drone came forward and she looked down into the three lights and the speaker grille it had in lieu of a face.

"Proceed," she said. That was all she needed to say. Her people would take care of the rest. "Copy to Oversight," she told the drone. "I'll head back to headquarters immediately but I won't be available for...thirty-seven hours." She shook her head. That was a long time to go without hearing how her plans worked out. Not for the first time she wished there was a faster way to move from star to star. "By the time I arrive I want to hear that we were successful. If not, heads are going to roll."

Including, most likely, her own.

She bit her lip for a moment. Wondered if she should say anything more. If only there were a better way—but there wasn't. There were no official Centrocor employees on Rishi, not even a proper spy. There were always ways to get to people, of course, but some were more morally repugnant than others. This one was pretty bad.

One of the drone's lights pulsed slowly. A gentle reminder that it was still recording.

"Send," she said. The drone's light went solid again and it drifted away from her like a footman dismissed by his master.

She stepped through into the yacht's bridge, a cramped space full of controls and displays that she had never bothered to learn to use. The yacht's computer was perfectly capable of steering the ship on its own. Time to head home. The planet of her birth—and Centrocor's central offices. "Take me to Irkalla," she said.

Behind her, flowglas seeped from the wooden railing of the exposed deck, spreading upward to form an airtight dome. The yacht took on the appearance of an iridescent beetle with its wing cases tightly shut. The engines warmed up with a subdued roar, and then the ship lifted up through Niraya's atmosphere on a pillar of invisible ions.

Bullam headed back to the cabin. Time for another nap, she thought. She tried to convince herself she was tired only because morally questionable decisions always took the wind out of her sails. This time, she wasn't as successful. She knew exactly why she felt so exhausted.

Her disease was back. Already she could feel her joints swelling. She could feel the pressure building up in her neck and the base of her skull. She dimmed the lights in the cabin, curled up on her bed in a fetal ball, her inertial sink gently holding her down against the mattress. It looked like she was in for a bad spell, maybe the worst one yet.

Chapter Four

Most of the interior of Rishi had been overrun by a jungle of thick trees and shrubs. The Navy used so little of the interior space it just wasn't worth clearing out. Along the meridian line, however, the region equidistant from the two open ends of the cylinder, there ran a length of parkland where the otherwise overwhelming vegetation had been cut down to a manicured lawn. It was necessary to have access to this region because that was where the habitat kept its weather control turbines, and without constant maintenance those machines would break down and leave the place uninhabitable.

The turbines were noisy, though, and dangerous, so this park was rarely used. Because of this seclusion—and perhaps because said turbines made an excellent method of disposing of unwanted bodies—the sward had become popular with Naval officers fighting duels.

In the century since Rishi graduated its first class of cadets, the Navy's strict orders against dueling had been relaxed. They weren't the clandestine affairs of prior generations, back when the Navy needed pilots so badly that anyone who even witnessed a duel could face public flogging. These days audiences—family members, well-wishers, enthusiasts—frequently gathered when a duel was to be fought, and so a small guesthouse and a pleasant café had been opened on the meridian park. The turbine noise had not abated in the meantime, but the possibility of free entertainment drew a modest commerce.

The guesthouse provided pistols and sabers for rental, as well as a variety of more exotic weaponry, including whips and nets (for nonfatal duels, fought when the Navy considered both parties nonexpendable). Videos of famous duels played on loops in the common room, and a variety of souvenirs—the pistol that took the life of Admiral Hu, the white handkerchief that was never dropped during the Duel of the Famous Lovers—were mounted on the walls. A doctor was always on call, and a quartet of drones were kept on standby to carry a wounded person quickly to the nearest hospital, seven kilometers away.

That day the guesthouse was doing a brisk business, judging at least by the throng crowding its front rooms. Lanoe and Valk shouldered their way through a variety of people, most in dress uniforms or fancy civilian clothes. They were supposed to meet Candless in the little café attached to the guesthouse, but were having trouble finding it. "Go ask the girl at the desk," Lanoe told Valk. Being two and a half meters tall meant people tended to get out of your way. But as Valk started pushing his way through the crowd, Lanoe was shoved backward, nearly out the door.

"Excuse me," someone said, ducking under his arm. He twisted around to see a flash of red hair atop a skinny woman in a thinsuit. He smiled and wanted to laugh. She must not have recognized him.

"Zhang," he said. It was Zhang, just as he'd last seen her. Red hair and—

No. Wait.

The woman turned and gave him a questioning look. She had a broad, amiable-looking face covered in freckles, and bright blue eyes. She was maybe twenty years old, if that. It wasn't Zhang. Of course it wasn't. He'd seen the red hair and something in him, something subconscious, had reacted.

He forced himself to smile in apology. Even if he wanted to smack himself in the leg for such a dumb mistake. "Sorry," he said. "Thought you were somebody else."

The last time he'd seen Zhang, her hair had been that color. She hadn't been born with it. She'd swapped bodies with somebody who...she...

Zhang. Zhang was—

Zhang was dead. Some part of him must be refusing to accept that. He knew grief could hit people in funny ways, but this was—it wasn't good.

"I hope you find her," the young woman said, then disappeared into the crowd.

"Lanoe?" Valk said. "This way."

"Yeah," he said. "Yeah."

"You okay?" Valk asked, touching his arm. "You look a little pale."

Lanoe let out a little laugh, more a release of tension than anything else. "Yeah, sure," he said. "I'm fine."

Valk nodded, but for a second he just stood there, like he expected something more.

Lanoe hardened his mouth. Stared straight ahead. Eventually Valk got the point.

He followed the big pilot out a back door and into the open air café. Candless was there waiting for them. She'd already ordered tea and a series of small plates. She rose and shook his hand, then nodded at Valk when he introduced himself.

"Honestly," Lanoe said, once they'd all sat down, "I'm surprised you were willing to meet up at all. Aren't you a little busy right now?"

"You mean with my duel? Really," Candless said, "all the preparations are complete. I suppose I could be putting my affairs in order. I always find that so trying, though."

Valk laughed. "You didn't tell me she was funny, Lanoe," he said. "This is a cute place, huh?"

"It's disgusting," Lanoe said.

"Is it, now?" Candless asked. "Are you referring to the food, or the concept of dueling in the abstract?"

"People making money off ritualized murder," Lanoe said, glaring at the guesthouse's proprietor, who stood at the entrance to the café trying to find tables for the influx of guests.

"People like us are always trying to kill each other over something or other," Valk said, sipping at a glass of perfumed tea. "Might as well dress it up with a lot of pompous traditions. Dueling's practically a sport," Valk said.

"Young man," Candless said, "don't be flippant. Lives are at risk here. Mine, to be specific. The least you could do would be to show some respect."

The big pilot set his teacup down very carefully. "Uh. Sorry," he said.

She continued to stare at him until he sat up straighter in his chair.

"What's this duel even about?" Lanoe asked. "How did you get yourself into this mess?"

"Oh, it's really very simple," Candless told him. "The other fellow—Cadet Bury—is one of my students. The other day I happened to tell him he flew like a duck with one broken wing."

Lanoe felt his weathered face cracking in a genuine smile. "My flight instructor—this was a long time ago, but I remember it pretty well—told me I should try shooting my squadmates rather than the enemy, since I could never seem to hit what I aimed at. I wanted to slug him in the jaw. I never actually did it, though."

"The job of a teacher—and I've been doing it quite a while now, so I ought to know—is to encourage one's students to perform to their best. Sometimes that means praising them, or making helpful suggestions. Sometimes, as in this case, it means kicking them in the pants. I've used the same technique with hundreds of students. There were a few tense moments but this is the first time one of them offered to butcher me."

"And this cadet, Bury—does he actually fly like a duck with a broken wing?"

"Oh, no, he's very talented," Candless said. "He could be brilliant, if he ever learns to control his temper."

"You know, if you just explained to him why you insulted him— perhaps asked his forgiveness—he'd probably back down. Almost everyone does," Lanoe told her. "Of all the duels I've seen, the only ones that actually went as far as the shooting part were because neither party had the brains to stop and think it through for five seconds."

"No doubt," Candless said.

Lanoe leaned forward across the table. "You've got the brains. But you insist on going through with this."

"Yes," Candless said. "Another part of being a teacher, of course, is projecting confidence. Students won't pay attention to a teacher who appears not to know her subject. And if I'm going to teach my cadets to be honorable, I need to project honor myself, at all times."

Lanoe watched her carefully, as if he expected her to say something more. She did not.

"I wonder," she said instead, "if one of you would do me a favor. I find myself without a second."

Lanoe raised an eyebrow.

"I'm in a rather unfortunate position, you see. The duel can't go forward unless I have a second, yet none of my fellow teachers will do it. They seem to think that condoning this sort of behavior might lead to cadets challenging them whenever they give out poor marks. Especially if young Bury actually kills me."

Lanoe shook his head and looked away.

"I know it's an odd request. But we don't often get visitors passing through Rishi. Your being here is a stroke of luck. It's not a tough job. You check the weapons—"

"I've been to my share of duels," Lanoe said. "When you get to my age there are very few things you haven't done before. But I have to say no." He glanced over at Valk for a moment, trying to decide how much he should tell her. "I'm trying to keep a low profile here, actually, and—"

"Someone attacked us on the way here," Valk said, leaning back in his chair. "We think they might try again."

Lanoe glared at the big pilot.

"What?" Valk asked. He turned toward Candless. "You're an old friend of his, right? And anyway, it's why we wanted to talk to you. We were hoping you could help us. You see—"

Lanoe jumped in before Valk could say anything more. "Obviously, all that is going to have to wait. You need a second, and I can't do it. But maybe Valk can."

Valk set down his teacup, very carefully.

"Me?" Valk said. "But—"

"He'll be great," Lanoe said.

"But—low profile—"

Lanoe slapped Valk on the back. "Centrocor was after me. Not you. Officially, you're still dead."

Candless pursed her lips. "I expect you to perform your duties in a manner that brings honor on us both," she said.

"I—but." Valk lifted his hands and then let them drop again. "Yes, ma'am," he said.

━━

"Give me a caff," Bury said.

Ginger opened her little enameled tin and took out a white tab. "This is kind of against the rules," she said. The look on his face must have conveyed his feelings on *that*, because she handed it over. "Are you sure that—"

He could feel his cheeks burning. He knew what she was going to say. She'd said it three times already. Was he sure he wanted to go through with this?

What choice did he have?

The two of them were in a quiet room at the guesthouse, upstairs away from the vultures who had gathered downstairs. People always flocked to the smell of blood. Bury knew that all too well.

He'd spent far too much of his life proving to people that he shouldn't be trifled with. From birth, he thought. From his earliest memories, at least, people had treated him like a joke. Like a fool. Well, he was nineteen now. Old enough to start making a name for himself. To prove to everyone that he was something. Someone.

There were two chairs in the room, one for the duelist, one for the second. There was a clock on the wall. Nothing else. No displays, no distractions.

He put the tab on his tongue and felt it fizz its way into his bloodstream. The skin of his head felt like it was shrinking, tightening. He felt focused. He felt ready. He checked the clock.

Five minutes.

"There's a chance..." Ginger said. Nothing more. Half a thought.

Bury had always hated it when people wouldn't just say things. "There's a chance she'll kill me. I know. I've seen her fight. In the simulator, out in the practice space." He shook his head. "She's really good. Really, really good at shooting."

Ginger nodded.

"I know that! But I have to go through with this. If you don't stand up for yourself, if you don't call out the cowards in this world—"

"Candless isn't a coward," Ginger said.

He whirled around to stare at her. "I didn't—I didn't say that. Or if I did, I didn't mean it. Just—just stop asking me questions. Okay? I have to be here. I have to do this." Even if it meant killing a woman he respected. Sometimes life wasn't fair.

"Is it time?" he asked. "Can we go down now?"

"I don't see why not," Ginger told him. She stood up and gathered the weapons in their velvet-lined boxes. Checked them one last time. "They're good."

Chapter Five

Lanoe touched the recessed stud underneath his collar ring and his helmet flowed up over his head. He blinked at a display that hovered near his chin and the flowglas polarized, turning the same shiny black as Valk's helmet. They must look like twins, he thought—except that Valk was half a meter taller.

"Is this all right?" he asked Candless. "Both of us like this?"

"It's fine," she replied. "Everyone will assume that you're staff officers from the school and you're hiding your faces because you can't be publicly associated with the duel." She turned to Valk. "Are you ready?"

"If I were you," Valk told her, "I'd be more worried about myself. I mean, if you were me, you'd be wondering why—ah, hell." The big pilot was visibly shaking. "I'm fine," he insisted. "But you—you're way too calm right now. Your pulse isn't even elevated. Aren't you afraid he might shoot you?"

If she wondered how Valk was able to measure her heartbeat, she didn't say so. "I am a pilot in the Naval Expeditionary Force. It is my job to fly into danger on a moment's notice, and, if necessary, to lay down my life. If I was afraid every time I faced death I'd spend my whole life sobbing and asking for my mother."

"That's some impressive bravado," Lanoe told her.

"From you, Commander, I'll choose to take that as a compliment."

Candless nodded. "Very good. Let's go." The three of them got up from their seats in the café and headed across the stretch of grass. The dueling ground wasn't far, just on the other side of one of the weather control turbines. As they passed by the giant fan its subsonic hum made Lanoe's teeth vibrate. The noise kept them from speaking again until they'd reached the appointed spot. There was no mark on the ground, no special facilities for the spectators who gathered in a loose circle around the strip of grass. There were no markers to indicate where famous duelists had fallen.

Candless's opponent was waiting for them. He wore a cadet's dress suit, so only his head was visible. At first Lanoe thought he had shaved off all his hair. Then he saw the telltale way the light reflected off his smooth skin.

"Oh," Valk said, so quietly only Lanoe and Candless could hear him over the noise of the turbine. "He's a Hellion. Suddenly this makes more sense."

There was almost no water at all on the planet Hel—definitely not enough to support human life. The population had adapted to conditions by having their skin polymerized, their pores and sweat glands and some of their mucous membranes filled in with a bio-inert plastic. It kept them from losing their body moisture to the dry air. It also meant they never grew any hair and they shone under any kind of bright light. Humans being what humans were, Hellions faced a certain stigma for this when they left their homeworld.

"I've never met a Hellion that didn't have a chip on his shoulder," Valk said.

"Drawing conclusions based on ethnic stereotypes is a wonderful way to underestimate one's opponent," Candless said. "You would be wise to remember that."

Valk ducked his head—or rather his helmet. Lanoe fought back the urge to grin. As long as Valk took the brunt of Candless's sharp tongue, he could avoid it himself.

"Hellions are born survivors," Candless went on, perhaps a bit less harshly now. "Bury is one of the tougher fellows I've ever met. If a tad stupid."

The boy's second was a young woman with red hair and a spray of freckles covering most of her face. She looked familiar—and then with a shock Lanoe realized she was the girl he'd approached in the guesthouse. The one he thought was Zhang.

Getting a better look at her now, he couldn't see much of a resemblance. Zhang, in the body she'd inhabited when she died, had a small, foxlike face. More important, her eyes had been replaced with metal sensors—her body having been born without optic nerves.

This girl—a cadet, like Bury—had an open, round face with soft features and very clear, very bright eyes that would have looked sympathetic if, at that moment, they didn't look so terrified. "Another of yours?" Lanoe asked, pointing her out.

"Ginger. She has a real name but nobody ever uses it. She's already washed out of the pilot program, though it hasn't been made official," Candless said.

"Some people were never meant to fly," Lanoe said.

"Oh, she's a fair hand at actual flying. It's the shooting she can't handle. She has the worst quality a fighter pilot can have—she wants everyone to like her. No good in a confrontation—or a fight. I imagine, given the chance, she'll make a decent staff officer."

Lanoe frowned. He couldn't tell if she meant that to sound insulting or not. Fighter pilots had very little respect, typically, for the staff officers who oversaw the vast bureaucracy of the Navy. Everyone knew the Navy couldn't exist without the staff officers pushing files around on their minders, but the fact they never actually put themselves in harm's way meant that pilots would never accept them as their own.

Candless's face pinched together in a pursed frown, as if she'd just smelled something repugnant. "Ginger's a terrible choice for a second. If someone dies here today, she'll be traumatized for life."

"I'd rather that than be the one who gets to bleed out on the grass," Lanoe pointed out.

"Maybe," Candless said. "Lanoe, you can't come any closer with us—I'm only allowed one second on the actual field of honor. Perhaps you'd like to go watch. With the spectators."

"Sure," Lanoe said. He shook her hand for luck and trotted over to where the onlookers waited. There were a lot of them, but there was plenty of room and they shifted aside to let him in.

"Should be a good one today," a woman in a thinsuit said, leaning in from his left to whisper to him. "It's always interesting when they're so mismatched."

On his right was a civilian in a silk jacket. "I hope it isn't the boy. You hate to see children die."

Lanoe kept his mouth shut. *Low profile*, he told himself.

The weapons were checked. Ginger made a big show of working the action on Bury's pistol, taking out the single cylindrical round and holding it up to the light before putting it back. Then she handed the two carved boxes over to the giant with the polarized helmet.

The big second gave the guns a quick examination. "They look fine," he said.

Bury kept his eyes on Instructor Candless's face. She looked back at him with that infuriating expression she always wore, the bland but stern countenance that never seemed impressed with anything.

The rules of the combat forbade the duelists from speaking to each other at this point. That was fine. If Candless had said one word he probably would have grabbed one of the pistols and shot her where she stood. Anger had always been Bury's best friend. This was one of those rare occasions when he needed to keep it in check.

"The rules are simple," Ginger announced. "You will stand back to back on the field. You will take ten paces and then—"

"I think everybody knows what happens then," the giant said. "Shall we?"

Ginger's face flushed as red as her hair. She ran off to one side, the giant going to stand next to her.

Bury gave Candless one last glare, putting all the hate into it that he could muster. Then he turned his back on her.

"One," Ginger called. He took a step.

"Two." He felt the muscles in his back squirm.

"Three." He could feel it, almost. The way the bullet would tear through his flesh.

"Four."

"Five." He dry-swallowed.

"Six."

"Seven."

"Eight." He was almost there.

"Nine." In his head he saw himself turning, raising his weapon.

"Ten!" Ginger called. Bury felt like his heart had stopped beating.

"You may turn and fire when ready," the giant said.

Bury swung around, the pistol in his hand already moving, lifting—he wouldn't get a lot of time to aim, so he jerked his hand upward, he had to fire high to counter the effects of Rishi's spin, and—

Candless's arm stood out from her body just a little. Her weapon pointed at the ground.

She pulled her trigger. There was a roar and a puff of smoke. The bullet tore a little crater in the soil by her foot, blackening a few blades of grass.

Then she just stood there. Watching him. With one arched eyebrow.

The crowd of spectators didn't know what to make of it. They were supposed to remain quiet until the shooting was done, but they couldn't help themselves. "What's going on?" someone demanded. "Why did she do that?"

"What does it mean?"

Out on the field, Bury lifted his pistol and aimed it. Lanoe could see the boy's hand shake, see his face contort with anger, with frustration. With confusion. Bury let out a kind of gasping shriek, then extended his arm and pointed his weapon right at Candless's face. His eyes stood out from his head as a paroxysm of rage swept through his body.

His knuckles turned white as he squeezed the pistol's grip.

And then—it was over. The blood drained from Bury's face and his arm fell slack at his side. His weapon remained unfired. It dropped from his hand and fell into the grass. "I vacate my challenge!" he shouted.

"What does it mean?" someone asked. "What do the rules say about this?" Everyone seemed to be asking the same question. "She gave him every opportunity. Why didn't he fire?"

Lanoe had the answer.

"Because she already won," he said.

Chapter Six

"Explain this to me one more time," Valk said. He was deeply confused.

Lanoe smiled. The three of them had retired to a room at the guesthouse where they could get away from the disappointed crowd. Perhaps in spite of the lackluster ending of the duel, perhaps because they needed some kind of resolution, the spectators had swarmed Candless as she walked away from the field. Some of them wanted her autograph. Others wanted to ask her why she'd fired into the ground. More than one of them had demanded a rematch.

It seemed they'd all missed the point. So at least Valk wasn't alone.

Lanoe glanced over at Candless, but she shook her head. It seemed she was perfectly willing to let him explain.

"The duel was a matter of honor, right?"

Valk shrugged. "Yeah, that's what they're all about."

"Sure. But here's the thing. There are all kinds of rules about honor, and some of them contradict each other. Honor required Candless to accept Bury's challenge, but if she actually shot one of her students, that would be a dishonorable act. She has a responsibility for his safety. So she couldn't shoot him, and she couldn't not shoot."

"Okay," Valk said.

"But if she fired at him and missed, she would have looked like a fool—and even worse, a bad shot. So her only option was to fire into the ground."

"That sounds like losing to me," Valk said.

Lanoe laughed. "No. It just shifted the burden on to Bury. Forced him to make the choice. If he shot her he would be less honorable than she had just proved herself to be. Shooting someone who has just disarmed herself is kind of the definition of dishonor. It would have been even worse if he missed—it would mean he had no honor, and he was incompetent, as well. So he had no options left, either."

"He could have just shot into the ground, too," Valk pointed out.

Lanoe leaned forward in his chair. "Ah, but there, you see—if he did that he would just be copying her. He would be a student repeating the actions of his teacher. Which would be admitting she was right all along, and she had every right to insult him. By forfeiting the duel, he acknowledged that he was wrong to issue the challenge in the first place, but that's all. So he saved some face, though not very much. She put him in a situation where that was the best outcome he could possibly achieve. Not a complete loss, but nowhere near winning."

Valk put one massive hand against his helmet, the closest thing he could do to rubbing his forehead. "It sounds more like a game of chess than a gunfight."

"That, of course, was the whole point," Candless said.

Both of them turned to look at her. She hadn't spoken since leaving the field of honor. She'd barely glanced at either of them.

"The point young Bury needed to learn," she said. "He's studying to become a fighter pilot. He needed to understand that war isn't about how much you hate the enemy, or how righteous your cause is. It's about applying the exactly correct force against the obstacle in front of you."

Lanoe nodded happily. "If more admirals understood that—"

"If they all understood that," Candless said, "we wouldn't have to have wars at all. And then we would all have to find something else to do with ourselves, wouldn't we?"

Lanoe got up and went over and shook her hand. "I'm glad it worked out. I'm damned glad you didn't just get yourself killed."

"I'm actually quite proud of young Bury. He saw the problem—and the solution—right away," Candless said. "I knew he had promise."

"Wait," Valk said. Because he'd just seen the checkmate—and why they played the game at all.

"Wait," he said again.

Candless and Lanoe turned to look at him.

"That's why you went through with this whole thing?" Valk asked. "To bring out his potential? You risked your life to teach somebody a lesson?"

Candless blinked, but her expression didn't change. "I'm a flight instructor. That's my job description."

She rose from the table and took a deep breath. For a moment she just stood there, looking a bit pale. Then she began to sway.

"Are you okay?" Lanoe asked.

"If you two will excuse me for a moment," she said, "I think I might have to go be sick. I'll be back shortly."

She left the room as if she were in no hurry at all.

Valk shook his head when the door closed behind her. "She's one of your old squadmates," he said. "A—a *friend* of yours, you said."

"One of the better pilots I ever flew with," Lanoe agreed.

"Is that why you put up with her? With the way she looks at you? You know, like you forgot to check your armpits this morning, and she forgives you, but she still wants you to know she noticed?"

Lanoe shrugged. "She wasn't as...well, she wasn't as intense back then. But she was always this smart. Let me ask you a question. A woman like that—would you prefer to have her on your side, or to be fighting against her?"

Candless returned, patting at her lips with a napkin. "So, now that my squalid little drama is over," she said, sitting down on the guest-room's bed, "we have time to talk about *your* troubles."

Lanoe glanced over at Valk, half-expecting the big pilot to blurt everything out. Then he considered it, and decided he might as well do the blurting himself. Candless was an old friend—he was pretty sure he could trust her. "It's about a planet called Niraya," he said.

"I believe I've heard of it," Candless said.

Lanoe frowned. "You have," he said, carefully.

"I may have been busy recently, with a full course load and the occasional duel, but I do try to keep up on current events." She sighed. "It's been on every newsfeed for weeks now. Some sort of battle there, between Rear Admiral Wallys and . . . some sort of fleet of armed drones, was it?"

"Sure," Lanoe said. "It's a little more nuanced than that, though."

"These things always are," Candless replied. "The stories I read had that particular clipped style that always indicates they've been heavily censored. Though I have to say, I haven't seen the Navy be so tight-lipped about a fight since the end of the Establishment Crisis. I take it something rather serious happened there."

Lanoe nodded.

"Perhaps, then," Candless told him, "you should tell me about this Niraya."

"It's a religious retreat that's only about half-terraformed. Nobody had heard of it before, because nothing ever happened there. It's going down in the history books now, though, as the first place we made contact with an alien species. Alien drones, to be specific. An entire fleet of them, and they weren't friendly."

Candless didn't laugh. Her eyes, perhaps, narrowed a bit. "Aliens," she said, with the same tone she might have used if she'd caught one of her students watching videos when they should have been paying attention in class. "I take it you're serious?"

"Afraid so." He understood her incredulity. For hundreds of years humanity had spread out across the stars. They had looked everywhere for other intelligent alien species, across thousands of planets. They'd never found anything brighter than an insect. For generations scientists and philosophers had debated why that was so. Now Lanoe knew the answer.

It had been a terrible, stupid mistake, played out on a cosmic scale.

The aliens that attacked Niraya had never intended to kill anyone. They'd sent out a fleet of robotic ships to prepare new planets for them, to make them over into places where the aliens could live. The fleet had even been given instructions to make contact with any intelligent species it happened across during its mission.

Unfortunately, the fleet's alien masters hadn't considered that intelligent life might not look exactly like they did. They had evolved on a gas giant world, and they looked like twenty-five-meter-wide jellyfish. The fleet had discovered countless species of life but, unable to communicate with them, unable to understand even what they were, it had instead identified them as vermin. Vermin that might interfere with its terraforming mission.

Vermin that needed to be eradicated.

The aliens had written some incomplete code, that was all. They had failed to make their terraforming fleet smart enough. As a result, every intelligent species their drones had encountered in the galaxy had been wiped out. Humanity had been next on the list.

"They tried to kill every living thing on Niraya," Lanoe said. "We made sure that didn't happen. We also found out there are other fleets out there. A lot of them. They move slow—these aliens never figured out how to use wormholes, so when they spread from star to star they have to take the long way round. That's probably the only reason we didn't meet them until now."

"But it won't be the last time," Valk said. "They'll find other human planets, and try to kill the people there, too. Unless somebody stops them."

Candless inhaled sharply. "That's what the two of you are trying to do, obviously—stop them. I suppose I approve. What's your next step?"

"We were headed for the Admiralty. We have information we need to get to the Admirals as soon as possible. If we're going to take the fight to these aliens, we can't do it alone. We need help from Earth. The aliens live closer to the center of the galaxy—ten thousand light-years from here."

"That's rather a long way to go. Even for a noble cause. Why head there in person? Why not just send them a message?"

"I'm afraid it isn't that simple."

Candless pursed her lips. "Lanoe, with you nothing ever is. Tell me why."

There had been a time when Lanoe trusted his superiors implicitly. Admirals gave him orders and he followed them to the letter. There'd been a time when he truly believed that Earth and its Navy were on the right course, that the stewardship of all humanity depended on the triple-headed eagle.

Then he'd lived too long. Seen too much of history.

"You know as well as I do that half the Navy is in the pocket of one poly or another. If I just turn the information I have over to the Navy, if it gets to the wrong person first, it might just disappear. The polys own half of the admirals, and could probably buy the rest of them tomorrow if they needed to. Polys have deep pockets. So I have to keep this mission discreet. Even an encrypted message could be intercepted, decoded. If I can get to the Admiralty unobserved, well, there are still a few people there I think I can trust. People who I know will take this information seriously, who will actually do something with it."

Candless frowned. "I will...concede that some of your paranoia is justified. The Admiralty isn't the incorruptible cadre it used to be. Very well, then—I have a solution. Give me the information and I'll take it to whomsoever you choose. I'm just an instructor from a far-flung flight school. No one has any reason to suspect me."

It wasn't a bad idea. There was one flaw in it, though. Lanoe didn't want to have to explain to her that the information was locked up inside Valk's head. That might mean explaining what Valk *was*, and he couldn't do that.

"This is too important," he told Candless. "Somebody— someone very close to me died so we could get this. If her death is going to mean anything, I need to personally hand this over to an admiral I can trust. After that it's out of my hands. But until then, it's my responsibility. Mine, personally."

Candless got up and grabbed her gloves. "Very well. But you came to me for help, so I assume you trust me a little. What do you want from me?"

"I just need an escort, that's all. Someone to fly with us, and watch our backs until we can get to the Admiralty safely. Will you do it?"

"Yes, yes, of course I will," Candless said, as if he'd asked to borrow a piece of razor paper. Well, they had been squaddies, once. Watching each other's backs was ingrained pretty deeply in their relationship. "The fighter I use for training exercises will do, I think. It's fully armed and I can have it fueled up right away. Just one difficulty. I'll need to let my people know that I'm leaving for a few days."

"Is that necessary?" Lanoe asked.

"I'm a teacher, Lanoe. I live by a schedule. I have classes all day tomorrow, and an exam to give the day after that. I can't just disappear—someone will have to substitute for me. Don't worry. I don't need to tell anyone *where* I'm going. I'll just say I need to take some personal days. Once that's cleared up, we can leave immediately."

Lanoe looked over at Valk, but he already knew. That would suit the giant pilot just fine. The sooner they delivered the information, the sooner Valk was allowed to die.

Candless moved toward the door, and Lanoe and Valk rose to follow. Before she left the room, though, she turned back to look at him.

"You were talking about Bettina Zhang, weren't you? The woman who died so you could have this information."

Lanoe frowned. "You never met her," he said, in a quiet voice.

"No," Candless said, "but I felt like I did. Back when you and I were still in touch, you used to talk about her all the time. You said—you told me you were going to marry her. I take it that didn't—"

"It didn't happen," Lanoe said.

His face must have given something away, no matter how he tried to control it.

"I know that look," Candless said. "Lanoe—I'm so sorry."

Lanoe pushed past her to the door.

"Sure," he said.

—✦—

The road from the field of honor to Rishi's administrative center was overgrown with lush vegetation. Spindly trees like green fingers locked together overhead, forming a constant tunnel of flickering, shimmering light. The road surface was crisscrossed by roots and creepers. As they drew closer to the barracks Valk saw teams of cadets out on brush-clearing duty, hacking away at the encroaching herbage with machetes, in some places holding it back with flamethrowers.

"Couldn't you just have drones do this?" Valk asked. "They could spray defoliant from overhead, or something. Probably be more efficient."

"That would mean denying the cadets a chance to get some physical exercise," Candless told them. "Good for both body and mind. And it makes an excellent punishment detail. I imagine Cadet Bury will be cutting vines for the rest of his time here." She drove them in a tiny electric cart, with Valk riding backward on a padded seat mounted over the wheels. He had to keep his knees up so his feet didn't drag in the road.

The administration building sat at the center of a modest campus of barracks and classroom buildings. It looked less like a university quadrangle and more like a step pyramid lost in some ancient rain forest. The building itself and a small parade yard out front had been kept clear of the ever-encroaching jungle, but it was clearly a constant struggle. Valk saw maintenance crews scouring its stone walls, scrubbing it with a liquid that smoked and glistened on the marble. Other crews were hard at work washing its many windows and polishing the triple-headed eagle mounted above its main entrance. Officers in immaculate dress suits barked orders at the work crews through megaphones.

It made Valk want to curl up under a rock somewhere. It was all just too...clean.

"I'm not sure I see how window washing prepares you to be a good pilot," he said, keeping his voice low. He didn't want any of those officers shouting orders at *him*.

"The idea is to teach the cadets Navy discipline and professionalism," Candless told him. "So they'll take their work seriously. We can't exactly let them see what being a pilot is really like."

"Mostly drinking and the smell of unwashed suits, if I remember right," Valk told her.

Candless surprised him by chuckling at his joke. He'd expected a nasty stare.

"I haven't completely forgotten, myself," she said. He thought maybe the expression on her face could be described as "wistful." If one were feeling charitable.

She parked the cart and the three of them headed up to the building on foot. As they passed by the officers one of them stared at Valk and craned her neck around to watch him go by. At first he thought she was just reacting to his height—he got that a lot. Then he saw where she was looking. At his cryptab, a little gray rectangle on the front of his suit that contained his service record and vital statistics. Naval personnel could ping it just by looking at it, and see everything contained there. She must have noticed he wasn't Naval personnel—or maybe she even recognized his name. The legend of Tannis Valk, the Blue Devil, hadn't quite left the public consciousness.

He reached up and put his hand over the cryptab, which was the exact wrong thing to do—it made him look like he had something to hide.

So much for maintaining a low profile here.

If she recognized his name, that could lead to all kinds of questions he wasn't prepared to answer.

This wasn't exactly his element. He'd never been trained by the Navy—in fact, he'd originally been recruited to kill these people. He'd fought for the Establishment, a political movement that had sought the right of people to colonize planets without charters that locked them into working with the polys. It had been a grand dream, he'd thought at the time. A fight for freedom and self-determination. Of course it ended in flames—literally, for him. Nowadays Establishmentarians were considered little more than terrorists.

The sooner they got out of Rishi, the better, he thought. Yet before they were halfway up the steps it was clear they weren't out of the woods yet. Candless stopped and held out an arm to signal them to do likewise. "Damnation," she said. "The last fellow I want to see right now."

Valk looked up and saw two cadets standing in front of the main doors of the building. He recognized them as the Hellion and his second. Both of them were looking at Candless as if they expected her to charge at them with weapons blasting.

"What do they want?" Lanoe whispered. "Never mind—just get rid of them."

Candless sighed and took another step up toward the building. "Cadets," she called out. "I've canceled my office hours. I've already had rather a hectic day."

"Sorry, Instructor," the redhead said—Ginger, she was called, if Valk remembered correctly. "I'm sure you're busy—"

"Yes, I am," Candless replied.

"I promise we'll just take a minute of your time. It's—it's important," Ginger said. "Bury has something he needs to say to you."

"If you're going to challenge me to another duel," Candless told the boy, "maybe you'd be kind enough to give me twenty-four hours of peace, first?"

"No, Instructor," Bury replied. "I just—I need to—" His mouth kept twitching. Like he was trying to bite any words that might come out of it. The boy didn't actually squirm but it was clear he was having trouble with this.

He's trying to apologize, Valk thought. He's trying to say *So sorry for trying to murder you, can we still be friends?* He had to admire the kid's courage in coming this far anyway.

Lanoe cleared his throat. "Whatever you have to say, send it to her address. The instructor told you she was busy." He headed up the steps, clearly ready to knock these two over if they didn't get out of the way.

"Hold on," Candless told him. "Cadet Bury?"

The boy's left eye began to twitch. He took a very deep, drawn-out breath, and then opened his mouth to finally speak. "I—"

"I'm so sorry!"

The words didn't come from the boy. Someone else had said that. Valk whirled around to see who it was.

Another cadet, looking even younger than Bury and Ginger, if that was possible. She had cropped black hair and her eyes were irritated and puffy, as if she'd been weeping.

She was holding a big particle pistol, and pointing it right at Lanoe's face.

—◆—

There was a good deal of screaming and the sound of pounding feet as people ran for safety. Lanoe ignored all the noise.

He was focused on the gun in the girl's hand. It was a bulbous, ugly thing with a narrow barrel. If she squeezed the trigger, she could cut him in half with that thing.

"I'm sorry," she said again. Her hands were trembling. Enough that she might let off a shot without even meaning to. Then it wouldn't matter whether she was sorry or not.

In his head Lanoe imagined a scenario where he leapt forward and grabbed the weapon from her. Most likely that scenario would end with her firing before he could close the distance between them.

"Cadet Marris," Candless said, from just behind his shoulder. "I am not completely sure you know what you're doing."

"Go away!" the girl shouted. "All of you, all except—except him." She nodded at Lanoe. "If he tries to run, I swear I'll do it! I'll blow him to hell!"

"I'm not going anywhere," Candless said. She moved forward to get closer to the girl. Smart, Lanoe thought. If she could just get close enough—

But then Candless stopped and lifted her hands, to show they were empty. "I'm going to stand right here, where you can see me. And we're going to talk about this."

"It's not about you, Instructor," Marris said. "It's him. I have a ship waiting. I'm supposed to take him...somewhere. It doesn't matter where."

Lanoe breathed in through his nose. It was important in situations like this to remember to breathe. He couldn't remember who'd told him that—maybe his own flight instructor, back in the day.

"Okay," Candless said. "He has to go with you. But can't you tell me why? He's a friend of mine. I'd really like to know."

"Marris," the redheaded girl said. "Marris, we're your friends! We can help, whatever this is! Yesterday you told me you had bad news from home. Is that it?"

"Is it, Cadet?" Candless asked. "Some kind of family problem?"

"My—my uncle," Marris sputtered. "Whatever! It doesn't matter why! All of you just get out of here. Why won't you just leave?"

Because as soon as they did, Lanoe knew, this girl was going to kidnap him—or at least try. He could see in her eyes how terrified she was. Fear was a great motivator. It could make people do the stupidest things.

"What's this about your uncle?" Candless asked. "Maybe we can help."

"Help? How could you help? He's a drunk. You can't make him not be a drunk. They said it was affecting his performance. That he was about to get fired from his job—he supports my whole family. My mother, my brothers. They'll all be out on the streets. But if I do—if I do this, they said they would keep him on. They won't fire him."

The girl was shaking from head to toe. The pistol slipped in her fingers but she grabbed tightly on to it, steadying it with both hands.

"Who does your uncle work for?" Lanoe demanded. "Which poly?"

"C-C-Centrocor," the girl said. "I was born on Irkalla. You can't live on Irkalla and not work for thrice-damned Centrocor."

"We'll get him a job with the Navy," Candless said, moving a little closer to the girl. "We'll make sure your family is okay. Just—"

"Do you think I'm an idiot?" Marris screamed. "Don't come any closer!"

Lanoe could sense Valk moving behind him. Maybe intending to circle around and throw himself into the pistol's beam.

Before he could, though, Lanoe heard a roaring noise coming toward them, and he staggered backward in a gale-force wind. Out of nowhere he was buffeted by a blast of shredded leaves and plant matter.

The girl turned her head to look at the source of the noise.

⸎

Valk had been aware of the approaching fighter—a Z.XIX, he thought—long before he saw it. Long before anyone else heard it. It had lifted off from a pad near the lip of Rishi's cylinder, dozens of kilometers away, and covered the distance in a matter of seconds.

His senses were better than any human's. Ever since he'd come to understand what he really was, an artificial intelligence in a space suit, he'd discovered he wasn't subject to the limitations of his former human body. He could see in wavelengths invisible to the human eye, hear things too soft for a human to even be aware of them.

He could move faster than a human, too, maybe twice as fast. Even as the fighter approached he had started moving, readying himself to sprint toward the girl and grab the pistol.

The fighter slewed around to a complete stop right above them. Its retros chopped at the air with a staccato pattern of burns and one of its four PBW cannon hissed as it fired a single, dazzlingly bright shot.

The girl's hand came off at the wrist, the stump cauterized by the particle beam. She screamed and stared down at the blackened stump where her hand had been. Lanoe grabbed her and threw her to the ground, shielding her in case the fighter tried to finish her off.

It made no effort to do so. Instead it drifted sideways on its lifters, rising a little to stay clear of the building.

It was making room. Another craft was already inbound—Valk could see it silhouetted against one of Rishi's circular skies, a dark blotch against a river of blue fire. A bigger ship, with an angular silhouette. As it came closer he saw that its airfoils were stubby, perfunctory things and its prow was a single, enormous rectangular hatch.

A troop transport. Whoever had sent the fighter, now they were sending in the Marines.

The fighter had speakers mounted on the exterior of its hull. They came alive with a squeal of feedback. "Lanoe, be a good fellow and don't move. Just stay down while my boys contain this situation."

Valk knew that voice. That sneering, condescending tone.

The transport settled down on the parade ground, bracing itself on four sturdy landing legs. Its front hatch fell open and a half-dozen marines in heavy suits and opaque silver helmets came boiling out. Meanwhile the fighter kept drifting lazily across the open space, its nose—and its guns—always pointed at Lanoe and the girl. Its flowglas canopy melted away and Valk saw the pilot. He had his helmet down.

"Maggs," Lanoe said. As if his mouth were full of excrement.

"In the flesh," the pilot called. "And just in the nick of time. As usual."

The marines moved fast to make a cordon around the parade ground, blocking anyone from getting in or out.

Maggs stood up in his cockpit, most likely so he could lean out and look down at Lanoe where he still lay covering the wounded girl.

"You might as well get off of her now," Maggs said. "Really, the initial impulse might have been chivalrous. But now it just looks unseemly."

Lanoe glared up at Maggs, wishing for nothing more than to have a weapon in his hand. He didn't, so after a moment he rolled off of Marris and helped her to her feet. "You all right?" he asked her.

"My hand—my hand," she wailed.

Well, it had been a dumb question.

"Is that Tannis Valk down there with you?" Maggs asked. "You're supposed to be dead. But of course the Blue Devil always was hard to put down."

"What are you doing here, Maggs?" Lanoe demanded. "I know I didn't send you an engraved invitation."

Maggs chuckled. "We intercepted a Centrocor transmission saying you were here. I came to Rishi as soon as I could. I was planning a more cordial reunion, but this'll have to do." The bastard was really enjoying this—that much was obvious.

Lanoe had never trusted Auster Maggs, not from the first time they'd met. At the time Maggs had just defrauded an Elder of the Transcendentalist faith out of a huge sum of money.

Lanoe and Valk had run him down—and made him come with them to Niraya, to help stave off the alien invasion there. Of course Maggs, being Maggs, found a way to betray them even then, when he tried to convince the Nirayans to give him money to help defend their planet. He had, of course, intended to take the money and run off before his life could actually be put in danger. The last time Lanoe had seen Maggs, the swindler had swooped in right at the end of the battle with the aliens, just in time to take credit for the victory without actually having to do any fighting.

"You might say 'thank you,' honestly," Maggs told him. "I did just save you from a kidnapper."

"By shooting off her hand," Lanoe said.

"You do love to split hairs, don't you?" Maggs asked. "Never mind. Gratitude being too much to ask for, apparently, perhaps we can at least talk like civilized human beings."

"Why don't you come down here, then?" Lanoe asked. "So I can hear you better."

Maggs shrugged. "I'm sure you'd enjoy that, Lanoe. I'm sure you'd love to have me down there where you could throttle me. But no, what I have to say won't take long and I promise I won't use any big words. I have orders to take you into custody," he said. "You and anyone you've been talking to. Will you come peacefully?"

Lanoe might have said something sarcastic, except just then

a green pearl appeared in the corner of his vision. An incoming message—from Valk. Interesting. He hadn't heard the big pilot record anything.

Maybe that was another one of Valk's newfound abilities. To send voice messages without actually bothering to vocalize them.

Lanoe flicked his eye across the pearl.

Do we make a break for it? the message read. *I can cause a distraction. Rush some of these guys, maybe even knock one of them down and get his gun. Then we can—*

Lanoe didn't bother listening to the rest of the message. He looked over at where Valk stood, ringed by three marines almost as big as he was.

Maybe it was possible. Maybe Valk could have broken through that ring, maybe he would be able to get away with a weapon. Maybe then—

Maybe then what?

Lanoe was an old man. He was still in pretty good shape, he supposed. He could run pretty fast.

Not nearly as fast as Maggs's fighter, though.

"You're not here to just kill me," he said. "At least, not in front of witnesses."

"I didn't come to kill you at all," Maggs said. Sounding genuinely exasperated. "I was sent by someone—I daren't say their name—who would like to talk to you. That's all. Now, again, will you comply? Or are we going to have some fun first?"

Lanoe took a deep breath.

"Okay," he said. "Okay, you got us." Slowly he lifted his hands.

"Good. Now, boys—let's not take chances with this one," Maggs said.

Lanoe had the sensation someone was rushing up behind him. He started to turn, but the marine there had already fired his weapon. Tendrils of darkness curled around Lanoe's brain, his vision narrowing down to a single bright dot. And then the dot vanished, and nothing remained.

Chapter Seven

The planet Irkalla circled an orange dwarf, a K2-class star eight-tenths as massive as Earth's sun. The star had once been known as Epsilon Eridani, but the residents of Irkalla had renamed it Ereshkigal. Most of those residents—most of the human beings who had ever been born on Irkalla—had never seen the star with their own eyes.

Ashlay Bullam's yacht exited the local wormhole throat three days after it left Niraya. Its onboard systems negotiated a flight plan with local traffic control without bothering her about the details. Because the yacht was an official Centrocor vehicle, it was given priority clearance and it was only a matter of hours before the yacht entered Irkalla's atmosphere, sinking rapidly through bands of clouds that thickened until the air around the yacht became darker than the void of space. Only occasional flashes of lightning—some of them hundreds of kilometers long—broke through the gloom. The flowglas dome over the yacht's deck was drenched in rain and the yacht was buffeted by winds moving upward of two hundred kilometers per hour.

In her bed, held down by the invisible hand of a powerful inertial sink, Bullam fought to hold back a whimper of agony.

She had spent most of the voyage curled up under her sheets, oscillating in and out of consciousness. Her disease had returned with a vengeance. Lucidity brought pain, so she had requested that the yacht's onboard medical suite keep her sedated as much as possible.

The yacht could fly itself just fine without her help. She had never been in any danger. At least—she hadn't so far. The descent was another matter. She needed to be awake for that part.

The spacecraft hit a patch of turbulence, a place in the sky where two great winds crashed into each other. The ship's hull shook with the fury of the storm, and despite all her ship's safety features Bullam was thrown to one side of her bed. She felt like she was being torn apart.

"Mirror!" she screamed. One of her drones lurched toward her, veering from side to side as the ship shook. It manifested a display that showed her what its camera saw.

She wasn't being vain. In the display she saw the veins of her upper chest and neck standing out, a deep blue against her translucent skin. She needed to check for bruises and the round shapes of aneurysms—if one of her major blood vessels had just ruptured, she would need to have it treated within minutes or it could be fatal.

She could have let her drones watch her veins. She'd been doing it for herself all her life, though, and knew she would be a better judge of her illness than any drone.

Ashlay Bullam suffered from a genetic condition called Type IV (Vascular) Ehlers-Danlos Syndrome, or EDS. Her body was unable to properly synthesize collagen. It made her skin more elastic than most people's, and allowed her to twist her fingers backward in a manner that was a big hit at certain kinds of parties. It also meant that her blood vessels were prone to tear open unexpectedly, as if they were made of paper.

Most of the time she could ignore the disease. Most of the time it left her alone. Sometimes, though, it would come back and surprise her. She knew the warning signs, the pain, the weakness. She had learned to pay very close attention to what her body told her. In the middle of an acute attack—like now—any sudden shock, any trauma, could rupture her veins and leave her bleeding to death.

There was a treatment for the disease. Extensive tailored gene therapy injections could fend off the symptoms—and prevent her veins from ripping open—for a few months at a time. There was no permanent cure.

She had felt the disease coming on back at Niraya. She had known that the voyage to Irkalla was likely to bring on an attack. There'd been nothing for it—the treatment she needed wasn't available on a backwater like Niraya. She had hoped it wouldn't be so severe, that it would be a mild event. In this she'd been wrong, so now she had to make sure she survived the descent.

As the ship rocked and bounced like a plaything of the winds, and she was thrown around in her bed, she stared at her own reflection and prayed she didn't see any round blue shadows appear beneath her collarbones. One blossomed off to the side, closer to her shoulder. "There!" she shouted, and pointed at the curved patch of blue. The skin above it was already starting to turn purple.

Another of her drones bobbed forward. It was about the size of her fist and she always thought of it as her little vampire. The drone didn't need her to direct it, not really, but it made her feel more in control to order it around. As she watched, a hatch on the drone's face sprung back and a sterile large-bore needle extended outward. The needle sank into her skin and drew away the excess blood, then heated up to cauterize the wound. Tiny jets built into the sides of the needle sprayed artificial collagen over the site, in a crisscross pattern to prevent scar formation.

Somehow the drone managed not to break the needle off inside her skin, even as the ship juddered and lurched side to side.

By the time the drone was done, before it had even swabbed her down with antiseptic, the ship cut through the lowest band of clouds. Tendrils of vapor streamed from its fittings and its rails as it burst through into clear air, into the eternal misty night of Irkalla.

Within minutes the yacht settled down onto a hexagonal landing pad on the outskirts of Regenstadt, the largest city on the planet.

By that time Bullam was sedated again, her eyes rolling in her head. She was barely aware of where she was as a medical team swarmed onboard the yacht and carried her out. They handed her off to a ground-effect ambulance, its flashers already spinning blue light across the slick pavements of the city. She was just conscious enough, as they pushed an oxygen mask down over her face, to call for one of her drones.

"Get a status report on activity three-nine-oh-six," she told it. "Mark the request as urgent."

She needed to know as soon as possible whether they had captured Aleister Lanoe.

"Bury, please do sit down," Candless said. "You aren't accomplishing anything except to annoy the rest of us."

The Hellion had been trying for the last hour to pry open the door. He had no tools with which to accomplish this other than his own fingers, and mostly he'd spent the time grunting and cursing.

"The first duty of a prisoner is to escape," he told her.

"Where exactly did you hear that?" she asked. "I'm certain I didn't teach you anything of the sort. No, no, no. The first duty of a prisoner is to survive."

The three of them had been scooped up by the marines back at the administration building on Rishi. They hadn't been given a chance to put up a fight. The marines had shoved sacks over their heads, then moved them to a little room with a couple of benches and a locked door and nothing else. No one had told them anything. They hadn't been given any food or water in six hours.

It hadn't taken long for Bury to start pacing, and once that started it was only a matter of time before he tried to escape. Ginger couldn't seem to calm down, either. She kept trying to bring up a wrist display, but every time, it just flashed red at her to tell her all communications were blocked. "There has to be something we can do," she said. "If we—if we offer them something they want, maybe if we agree to answer their questions, maybe they'll let us go. If there was just a dedicated display in here, some way to contact the guards—"

"There isn't," Candless told her. "Nor have they asked any questions. You sit down, too, Ginger."

"And what exactly is sitting down going to get us?" Bury demanded.

"It will help me get over my headache," Candless told him. "Part of being a good pilot—part of being a good adult—is learning that there are some problems you can't fix. These people are very good at security. They put us here because they wanted to keep us out of the way. We aren't going to be asked if that's acceptable to us."

Ginger shook her head. "We don't know what they want. We don't know what they're going to do to us. We don't even know where we are!"

Candless closed her eyes and sighed.

"We're in a detaining cell onboard a Hoplite-class cruiser. In the brig, to use the old term." She ran her hand over one wall. "It's an older model. Probably saw service in the Establishment Crisis, but it's been refurbished, very recently."

She opened her eyes again and saw the cadets staring back at her. Ginger's mouth was slightly open.

"I've been in the Navy a long time," she told them. "I've seen my share of Hoplites." She let herself smile, a thin, small smile of remembrance. Because she was still their teacher, she omitted the fact that she'd seen the inside of a brig or two, as well.

"But—how can you tell all that?" Ginger asked. "I mean, about it being an old ship, and being fixed up?"

Candless glanced up. "You see those lights in the ceiling? Those are high-efficiency fluorescent strips. Back in the bad old days, back when we fought real wars, cruisers could be out in the field for years at a time and they had to conserve power any way they could. Newer ships are designed for short campaigns and so they use less efficient lighting systems."

"You got all that from the lights?" Bury asked.

"Paying attention," Candless said, "is the best way to learn things. And learning things is the best way to stay alive in this world. You should both be taking notes."

Ginger shook her head. "But...how did you know about the refurbishment?" the girl asked.

"Smell the air in here. It's clean. The filters have been changed in the last week, if I don't miss my guess. The Navy never changes its air filters as often as it should. And there—do you see that panel in the wall near the ceiling? It's a lighter color than the rest of the wall. It's been replaced and it hasn't had time to get dingy yet."

Bury nodded. Candless didn't much like the intense expression on his face—she'd been trying to calm the cadets down with her Sherlock Holmes act, and now he just looked more determined.

"Okay," he said. "Okay. Here's the plan. They have to feed us, right? They have to see to our basic needs. When the door opens and a marine comes in with the food trays, I'll get behind him, and then—"

He stopped because just then the wall behind him started to rumble. There was a series of clicks and then a panel popped open on an unseen hinge. Behind the panel was a small compartment filled with ration packs and water pouches, the kind you drank from under microgravity conditions.

Bury stared at the food for a long time before he spoke again. "They're listening to us. They're listening to me, to everything I say," he announced.

"Yes. And one of them, at least, has a sense of humor," Candless told him. "Now. Given that they're listening, why don't we all sit down and try to be quiet, hmm?"

～

Bullam woke with a sedative hangover. She felt like her chest was full of broken glass. It didn't matter—it would wear off soon enough. The chemicals she'd been given were tailored to break down in her bloodstream once they were no longer needed. She forced herself to climb out of the hospital bed and get dressed, though her fingers felt like stiff twigs. Like they might snap if she wasn't careful.

Outside the window she could see the lights of Regenstadt. It was always night on Irkalla, under the thick layer of clouds that protected the planet from the intense stellar winds of its star. It never got truly dark in the city, however. Advertisements for new clothing lines, for the latest minders and bodytech were projected upward onto the cloud banks, glittering seductions whole kilometers across that made a patchwork of the sky. Closer to the ground, ranks of purple lights shone from the top of every building, floodlights spreading low-intensity ultraviolet light to keep the locals from succumbing to vitamin D deficiencies. Just one of the many benefits Centrocor supplied for the people who lived on its headquarters.

She picked out a dress with a high collar. Not quite in fashion but it would hide the mottling of bruises that had appeared on her chest and shoulder during her attack. As she fastened the three buttons at her throat she noticed, through the window, that a crowd had gathered at the hospital gate. Some of them carried signs or banners. A few wore masks and carried megaphones. There were always protestors in Regenstadt, of course, they were everywhere with their defeated looks and their ragged chants. This bunch were going to be a problem for her, though.

"Doctor?" she said.

A display lit up on the surface of the window, where she could see it but it didn't obscure her view of the streets below. This doctor—she'd had so many—was young, a woman with six blond braids coiled against her scalp. One of them had been dyed blue at some point but was starting to grow out. Bullam supposed doctors didn't have much time to worry about how they looked.

"There's some kind of demonstration out front," Bullam said.

"We've kept the emergency room entrance clear," the doctor replied. "Don't worry, M. Bullam. You won't have any trouble getting out of here."

"Good. So what are they upset about, this time?" Thinking

about the protestors allowed her to ignore other, more pressing issues. For the moment.

"The Benefits Steering Group has passed a new austerity measure. Health care allowances have been cut by three percent, and there's a new list of treatments we're not supposed to allow without dispensation. Executives are exempt, of course, so there was no difficulty getting approval for your procedure."

"You sound a little bitter, Doctor. I take it you don't agree with the new policy?"

The doctor's face didn't change. You didn't get to a position of authority on Centrocor's planet without learning how to stay pleasant. "Of course not," she said. "We're all in this together."

In other words, she liked her job.

Bullam nodded at her. "That's a great attitude," she said. "I take it I'm cleared for release? Can you have a car waiting for me by the exit?"

"Already scheduled," the doctor told her. "You're one of our regular customers, and we always try to anticipate our patients' needs. Anything else we can do for you?"

Bullam turned away from the window. She had stopped seeing anything out there. Too distracted by her thoughts. She looked over toward the bed and saw her drones rise into the air, sensing that it was time to get moving.

She had to go explain to her boss what had gone wrong, after all. How the attempt to capture Aleister Lanoe had failed so miserably. And why she didn't even know where he was now.

"M. Bullam?"

She took a breath. "Just...did you see any signs of ischemia?" she asked. "I'm sure you did a scan. No brain damage?"

"None we could detect. If you're worried about stroke, you should look for any numbness in the face or your extremities. Blurred vision. Any difficulty with speech—"

"I know the signs," Bullam told her. "Thank you, Doctor."

She had the drones gather her things and follow her out into the hall. The car, a ground-only model, was waiting for her as prom-

ised. As it nosed its way out of the hospital campus some of the protestors rushed toward her, waving their signs. Shouting. The car's
system automatically raised the volume of its complimentary music.
It accelerated away from the crowd and they couldn't keep up.

—✦—

When the door of the brig opened there was no warning. Candless
had almost fallen asleep on one of the benches. She opened her eyes
and looked up, worried that Bury might try to make a break for it.

He wasn't given the chance. Two marines with silvered helmets
pushed inside the room, shockguns in their hands covering all
three of the prisoners. From behind them, a third marine dragged a
huge body into the room, then dumped it without ceremony on the
floor. As quick as that and the marines were gone again, the door
sealing itself shut with the click-click-click of magnetic locks.

Ginger rose and moved to hover over the body. Candless waved
her back. Then she got down on her knees next to it and carefully
turned it over onto its back. The body wore a standard suit—not
Navy issue, but close enough. The helmet was up and polarized to
an opaque black.

"It's that guy, the one you had as your second," Bury said.

"Perhaps," Candless told him. "He's certainly tall enough. What
did I say about jumping to conclusions, though? Do either of you
remember?"

They ignored her. "Is he dead?" Ginger asked.

Candless pinged the body's cryptab and it read out to a display
that emanated from her own collar ring. There wasn't much there.
The name VALK, TANNIS came up and then a mention that he
had been a pilot flying for the Establishment, back in the Crisis.
Everything else had been scrubbed—she could see empty spaces
where the usual information ought to be. She'd heard that the
Establishment's pilots had been stripped of their rank and records
but she'd never actually pinged a cryptab like that before.

"M. Valk?" she said. "Can you hear me?"

There was no answer. He wasn't moving. It could be hard to tell if someone was breathing, while they were sealed in a suit with the helmet up, but Candless didn't see any signs of life at all. Thinking maybe she could do something for him—at the very least close his eyes—she reached for the recessed key on his collar ring that would lower his helmet.

Valk lifted his right hand and gently, but firmly, pushed her arm away.

Then he sat up and put his hands on his helmet, as if he were massaging his temples.

Candless knew the legend of the Blue Devil. She knew he was supposed to be horribly burnt under that black helmet. Maybe he just didn't want her to have to see what he looked like now. She sat back on her heels, her hands up to show she wouldn't try again.

Slowly Valk got to his feet, as Bury and Ginger backed away from him, cramming together in one corner of the room.

"Hey," Valk said. His voice sounded weak and hoarse. "Ah, hell. They grabbed you guys, too? Why'd they do that?"

"We don't know," Candless told him. "We were hoping you might tell us. They brought us here with sacks over our heads, and they've refused to talk to us since."

Valk's whole torso bowed back and forth. Candless thought he must be nodding. "Yeah. They're not big on answering questions. Had a few of my own and got the same treatment."

"What do they want?" Ginger asked. From the corner.

"I'm not sure," Valk told her. "They were after me and Lanoe. I guess they probably took anybody we had contact with, back on Rishi."

Candless sighed. "They must know we talked about—"

"They must think," Valk said, interrupting her, "that we told you something. When we didn't, not at all. What *did* we talk about, huh? The duel, right. And you and Lanoe talked about old times, a little. That's all. Just friends having a drink."

He's not completely hopeless, Candless thought. Valk must know that their captors were listening. He was trying to imply that

Candless had never heard anything the Navy might want her not to know. She doubted that their captors would just accept Valk's deception and let her and her students go, but she applauded the effort.

"Yeah, I got the sack-over-the-head treatment, too," Valk said. "They had me in a different room, asked me a whole lot of questions. I guess they got tired of hearing the same answers over and over, and that's when they brought me here." He shrugged—a tricky gesture for anyone in a suit. He lifted both arms and let them fall again. "Wish I had more information to give you."

Candless wondered if he did have more information—but didn't want to implicate them by sharing it. It was damned frustrating, not being able to talk freely.

"I've worked out that we're on a Hoplite," she said. "And we're moving—there's gravity in here." The cruiser had no way of generating gravity except by burning its engines, so they had to be traveling somewhere.

"Yeah," Valk said. "We're in wormspace. Can't you feel it?" When she just gave him a blank look, he said, "Gravity's different in wormspace. Kind of, you know, wrong. It points in the wrong direction."

Candless frowned. She knew, or rather, she had read, that wormholes were formed of exotic matter with negative mass. Such material would repel matter rather than attract it. She had to assume that was what he meant. She had never felt any kind of sensation of gravity at all when in a wormhole, and she'd flown through her fair share.

She flashed back on a moment just before the duel when he had told her that her heart wasn't beating as fast as he expected. At the time she'd been too distracted to wonder how he could know that. She knew better, of course, than to ask him how he seemed to have more senses than other human beings. Not at that moment, anyway, in the Hoplite's brig.

There were other things she could ask, though. "Did you see anyone else, while they were questioning you, or when they moved you? This could be important. Did you see Cadet Marris?"

"What, the girl with the gun? No, sorry," Valk told her. "Nobody but marines."

Candless nodded. She hadn't expected anything else, but she would very much like to know what the Navy had done with Marris. Hopefully they'd at least given her medical treatment for her severed hand. As the girl's instructor, Candless had a responsibility for her safety.

"Did you catch any of their names? The marines, I mean. Ping any of their cryptabs?"

"No. Sorry," he told her.

"Do you have any idea where they're taking us?" she asked next. If they were in wormspace that meant they were being transported to another planet, or to another Navy facility, surely.

"No idea," Valk said.

Ginger came forward and touched his arm. Valk was a giant, well over two meters tall, and very broad through the shoulders. He towered over the cadet. She didn't seem intimidated by him, not anymore.

"What are they going to do to us?" she asked.

Valk's shoulders fell, and he tilted his head forward.

Candless could understand that gesture perfectly well.

"I don't know," Valk said.

＞—＞＜—＜

As the car slipped through the dark streets of Regenstadt, Bullam watched the puddles outside its windows glow with reflected purple light. Eventually they tinged with yellow, and she knew she was getting close to the Mountain.

Back when Irkalla was first discovered, when it was still being terraformed, the Mountain had been constructed simply as a shed to contain the equipment and supplies necessary to create a world where humans could live. A full kilometer wide and nearly as tall, roughly pyramidal in shape, it had been left in place when terraforming operations concluded, simply because it would be next to impossible to tear it down. It was constructed of an elaborate meshwork of stabilized steel girders filled in with panes of rigid carbonglas. It would last for thousands of years, even in the constant wind and rain of Irkalla. Time had not so much as stained its shining sides.

When the colonists arrived they'd faced a certain difficulty. Irkalla needed its mantle of clouds to protect it from solar storms and to keep the planet warm. Yet human bodies and human minds were never meant to thrive on a world shrouded by eternal night. People needed a little sunshine.

For a time, the Mountain had provided for that need.

Carbonglas was wonderful stuff. Hard as diamond, but with a flexible quantum dot structure that responded to electrical stimulation. In one configuration it became flowglas, the stuff space suit helmets and ship canopies were made of. Flowglas both melted and froze at room temperature, changing its shape as needed. Another variety of carbonglas could change its index of refraction, turning blacker than space or perfectly transparent or reflective as a mirror at the flip of a switch. A third type could be made to give off light in any chosen wavelength. The colonists had programmed the Mountain to shed an eternal glow the exact color and intensity as the light that fell on a sunny meadow back on Earth. It cast this kindly light over the city like a beacon, while inside the hollow interior of the Mountain, the very air was suffused with that perfect radiance.

The colonists had filled the Mountain with trees and flowers and all the plants of Earth. A little paradise, hidden inside a glass shell. They would come there daily, taking turns to wander its meandering paths, to sit and talk in open-air cafés, or to simply lie on lush grass and soak up the light.

Of course, it couldn't last. The economy of Irkalla had collapsed just a few decades after the end of the Century War, just as it had on so many planets. The whole reason for building a colony on Irkalla in the first place had been to provide necessary resources for rebuilding Earth after the war—a relatively short-term project— and when Irkalla's stores of rare earths and actinides were no longer required the money had stopped flowing. Irkalla had been forced to take austerity measures that were still in effect nearly two centuries later. The Mountain itself had to be given up—it was just too expensive to maintain.

As usual Centrocor had been there to save the day. The poly had installed the purple floodlights that loomed over every street in Regenstadt, to keep the colonists healthy at a fraction of the price it cost to keep the Mountain up and running. Still, for years afterward, as the colonists adjusted to the new lighting scheme, they had looked up to the horizon to see the skeletal form of the Mountain, its glass turned to a dull transparency, and seen it as a symbol of an idyll lost. A monument to stagnation.

It was only in recent years, as the economy had begun its long, slow recovery, that Centrocor had reopened the Mountain for occasional special events. Events that were only ever attended by Centrocor employees. At least the people of the city could enjoy its lemon light from afar.

The car's windows dimmed as the light grew intense enough to hurt Bullam's dark-adapted eyes. The car slid in through one of the Mountain's many broad entrance bays, then drew to a stop to let her out. A servant in red livery offered her a hand and she blinked her way past the registration desk. Inside, in the complicated halls and galleries of the Mountain, a party was in full swing. She could hear three different genres of music competing for attention, and underneath it the oceanic roar of hundreds of conversations. From a distance she heard someone laugh, a high-pitched nasal snort.

Her drones swept after her in train as she made her way through a garden of stunted apple trees, none of them taller than her waist. Their fruit, the size of grapes, lay rotting on the grass around them. Servants bustled toward her with trays full of champagne flutes or complicated-looking pastries, but she held up one hand and they spun away from her without a word.

She wasn't here for fun.

The man she'd come to see would, of course, be in the most central of the Mountain's halls, a cavernous space with a ceiling so high it looked blue like a summer sky. Around the sides of the giant room stood machines like colossal pipe organs—devices that had been grown rather than constructed, so they had an unsettling organic appearance. Some of them looked downright rude, like the genitals of demigods. Once those machines had pumped out the oxygen that bolstered Irkalla's atmosphere. Now they had been left to rot away in silence. An effort had been made to drape them in rich tapestries of gold and blue, all of them showing fractal derivations of the hexagonal Centrocor logo. The tapestries weren't big enough to cover much, though, and they just looked like the fig leaves on ancient statues.

People filled the hall, Centrocor employees dressed in lace and silk. The men wore hose and short jackets, the women dresses of fanciful design, with enormous puffy sleeves and constellations of jewels in their piled hair. It was required by employee regulations to show some form of the hexagon on one's dress at an official function like this, but it had become fashionable to hide the logo as much as possible. It was a sort of game, where the wearer of a given outfit would dare you to find their hexagon. It could be worked into the subtle laddering of a man's hose, or a woman's dress could be lined on the inside with bold, colorful hexagons that she would only show once she'd had a few drinks. Bullam, who spent most of her time away from Irkalla, had hardly bothered to disguise her own hexagons, which were picked out in gold thread on a ribbon that tied up her hair. She got a few snooty glances as she worked her way through the crowd but not many—she had a higher spot in the org chart than most of these people and could afford to be a little severe in how she presented herself.

The higher up you were on the ladder, the more you could afford to ignore the silly games and constant displays of status. The man she'd come to see, for instance, was a member of the Board of Directors, one of the six most powerful people in the entire Centrocor power structure. As a result he was easy to spot. He wore a dark fur-lined coat over an open shirt and baggy tweed trousers, like a crow hiding in a troop of peacocks. Even worse, he'd defied social convention—and the general consensus of good taste—by having a prehensile tail grafted to the end of his spine. At the moment, it was holding his martini glass, its round pale tip curled outward like a pinky finger.

"Ashlay," he said, before she'd even managed to worm her way into his orbit. He lifted a hand and beckoned her. "Ashlay, over this way," he said, as if she couldn't see him. She elbowed her way through a knot of young women with white-painted faces and smiled as she reached the patch of grass where he stood.

"M. Cygnet," she said, and took the hand he offered. She bowed her forehead over his fingers, then released them. "I got back just in time, it seems. So glad I didn't have to miss your party."

She had in fact nearly killed herself returning to Irkalla in time for this event, which had been scheduled months in advance. She'd known she would actually get some face time with Dariau Cygnet here—trying to make an appointment to see him in his office would have been impossible, and the things she needed to talk to him about could not be put into any kind of electronic message.

This, of course, was another kind of game. The top level of Centrocor employees might not try to outdress each other—instead they showed status by being as unavailable as possible, even when fortunes and careers were at stake.

"It's for charity," he told her. "We need to build a new orphanage. I'm counting on you here, Ashlay—for a contribution, I mean. We're all in this together."

"Of course," she said. "I'll have one of my drones see to it immediately."

"Oh, there's no rush. And I'm being rude. I heard you weren't feeling well. Your disease," he said, and lifted his tail to take a sip of his drink. It made his coat flap open in an unattractive way, but he didn't seem to care. "Was it bad this time?"

Before she could answer a woman wrapped in a fiercely brocaded blanket came up and kissed him on the cheek. He turned his face toward her and gave her a wink. She whirled away, giggling. Bullam didn't even want to know what that was about.

"It was nothing serious," she said. "I just needed a quick treatment, and—"

She stopped because just then a drone came zipping down from on high, green lights flashing on its face. Some urgent message for the Director, one that couldn't wait.

Cygnet dipped his fingers in his glass, then flicked liquor at the drone. A man with fluorescent red hair rushed through the crowd, pulling off his jacket. He flung the garment over the drone with a flourish, and the blinded machine twisted and swooped up over the crowd, bucking wildly as it tried to free itself. Cygnet laughed and clapped his hands together, and the red-haired man took a bow.

"Uilliam," Cygnet said, putting a hand on the man's shoulder, "that was well done. Tell me, have you met Ashlay here? She's one of my best people. *Best* people. She has EDS; do you know what that is?"

"Never heard of it," the redhead said, staring at her.

"It's a disease so rare nobody ever got around to curing it. Isn't that just horrible? And now she's come here to give me some spectacularly bad news."

Bullam bit her lip. Cygnet already knew. Of course he did.

"Bad luck," Uilliam said. "Maybe we should throw one of these parties to raise money for it."

"Now *that* is a great idea," Cygnet said. "Let's go somewhere and talk about it." The Director smirked like an imp and touched the end of his nose, which Uilliam seemed to find unbearably funny. He nearly fell over from laughing so hard.

"M. Cygnet," Bullam said, "I don't want to impose on your time, but I have some thoughts on how my bad news can be mitigated. It might even be turned into a kind of opportunity." She was flailing—she had no ideas at all—but this was her only chance to save her job. She tried to keep the desperation off her face.

"That sounds boring," Uilliam said.

Cygnet shrugged. "Sorry, Ashlay. Uilliam here is the cousin of a Sector Warden, did you know that? I have to make sure he stays entertained. Got to keep the wheels of commerce humming, right?"

Uilliam seemed to think that was very funny, too.

"Why don't you go home and get some rest?" Cygnet said. "You look terrible." Then he grabbed Uilliam by the bicep and dragged him off behind a stand of bonsai trees.

Bullam, left alone, could hardly believe it. She'd worked so hard. For years she'd worked so hard. She'd taken terrible chances with her health. She'd had to prove over and over again that her disease couldn't stop her from being good at her job. She'd done things she hated. She'd done things for Centrocor that no person should ever be asked to do.

And now...and now it was over. She would lose her job. She would lose her access to health care. It would only be a matter of time before her disease caught up with her.

"Don't be sad. It's a party!"

It was the young woman in the brocaded blanket. She pushed her face very close to Bullam's and put an arm around her shoulders. Her other hand emerged from inside the blanket, presenting a gold, heart-shaped box. The lid popped open and it played a trite little song. On a velvet pillow inside the box sat five tiny white pills.

Bullam shoved the woman away from her, sending the pills tumbling to the grass. The woman cried out in terror and dropped to all fours, gathering them up as if they were precious stones. The crowd couldn't seem to decide if this was shocking or hilarious.

Bullam headed back toward where she'd left her car. If anyone else had gotten in her way she would have knocked them down, too. Luckily the party thinned out near the exits and she managed to get away without being further disturbed.

She wanted to cry. She wanted to scream. She refused to let these people see her do either of those things.

Sinking into the back of the car, she touched a key to raise the windows and polarize them so she would be hidden from view. Only then did she start to rock back and forth, in anger and fear, and beat on the upholstery with one hand.

And then—she stopped. She froze in place. She'd caught a glimpse of one of her drones out of the corner of her eye. A pale blue light showed on its face. She nodded at it and a display popped up.

Her calendar showed a new event. One she hadn't scheduled. She had a meeting, the display said, in two days' time at a Centrocor facility sixty kilometers up the coast. A meeting with Dariau Cygnet.

She checked the log and found that the appointment had been made only a few seconds ago. Cygnet must have wanted to talk to her after all—just not in public.

The drone's light blinked to ask if she wanted to confirm the event.

"Yes," she said. "Yes. Yes!"

The pale blue light winked out. The drone had heard her the first time.

PART II

TERRESTRIAL

Chapter Eight

Lanoe had no idea where they were headed. He didn't know what would happen to him when they arrived. Maybe he would be quietly executed. Maybe he would be interrogated first.

No point in worrying about the future, if there wasn't going to be one. At least he could be well rested before it happened, he thought. At least he could finally get some sleep. It had been a while.

In the Navy they taught you how to sleep anywhere, anytime. A pilot could be called upon to scramble at any second, to rush out into a fight in the middle of the night, first thing in the morning. You took what sleep you could get.

He stilled himself. There was no gravity in the cell, but Lanoe had learned a long time ago how to sleep in the absence of weight. He folded himself into a ball, stilled himself. Closed his eyes.

Thoughts drifted through him, away from him. He put aside fear, put aside worry. Light filtered in through his eyelids. He blocked it out. He could hear the drone of air being pumped into and out of the cell through the ventilation system. He let that sound pass through him, unnoticed.

Soon his mind was clear, empty. Soon he was sinking through layers of soft nothingness, falling through limitless space, falling—

"Lanoe, I'm falling."

His eyes snapped open. That voice. That was Zhang's voice.

Zhang was dead. Lanoe didn't believe in ghosts. It was just his subconscious playing tricks on him. Reminding him of the one thing he could never forget.

Zhang—the woman he'd loved—had fought with him at Niraya. In the final battle against the alien queenship, her fighter had taken damage, had been half-destroyed, but she'd survived. Her engines had been wrecked, but even then he could have saved her. He could have—

"I'm falling," she whispered.

Lanoe gritted his teeth.

Zhang had been caught in the gravity well of an ice-giant planet. She hadn't been able to escape its pull. She'd fallen into its atmosphere and been carried down into its depths, into the crushing pressure and heat at the center of a world without a surface. She had just disappeared from view, in a place where he couldn't even recover her body.

The Blue-Blue-White had done that to her. They'd taken her from him.

"Lanoe," she called. "Lanoe—I'm falling. I'm falling."

Eyes open, eyes closed. It didn't matter.

He could hear her. He could hear her voice.

So much for sleep.

⸺⸻

Don't be too hard on him, Maggsy. Admittedly, he's not our sort, but it shows breeding to treat the lower orders with a certain respect. And don't forget he still technically outranks you.

Maggs closed his eyes. It was his father's voice he always heard inside his head, since he was a child. An overly developed superego, he supposed, though he'd never quite ruled out the idea that he was simply being haunted by his famous forebear. He knew better than to reply, as much as he wanted to say that while the prisoner might outrank him for the moment, he remained, de facto, a prisoner.

He heard a chime and when he opened his eyes he saw that the light in the elevator had switched to a warning amber. He knew what it meant and he reached over to grab one of the handholds built into the wall. Whatever pilot was currently flying the cruiser was talented enough that the change in gravity wasn't too jarring when it came. It felt as if Maggs's feet simply came loose from the floor, that was all. As if he'd turned into a helium-filled balloon. His stomach protested for a moment—it always did—but he'd learned how to ignore that, over the years.

A spacecraft in flight generates its own internal gravity whenever it accelerates. The cruiser had been burning hard ever since it left Rishi, and everyone inside it had enjoyed an almost Earth standard g. As they approached their destination, however, it was necessary to slow down—one most assuredly did *not* exit this particular wormhole throat at high speed—and so the engines had been switched off. Soon it would be necessary to actively decelerate, which meant that all the former floors would become ceilings, and vice versa. It was always so delightful when that happened.

The elevator doors opened and Maggs pushed himself out into a cramped little corridor. All the interior spaces on the cruiser were tight squeezes. Big as it was—three hundred meters long, nearly fifty abeam—it was still positively packed with equipment, weaponry, and smaller craft. More than half of the ship's entire mass was taken up by a gigantic fusion torus engine. Space in the human-occupiable areas of the ship was always at a premium. Its halls were kept narrow for another reason as well, however, which was to keep people from bouncing around when the ship was in microgravity, as it was now. Maggs kicked off a wall and floated into the guard station of the brig, where he had to turn sideways to get past the marine guards. They had their helmets down and they stared at him as he approached. No love lost, of course, between the pilots of the Naval Expeditionary Force and the Planetary Brigade Marines, and this bunch were trained to be suspicious of everyone, but their cold gaze made him feel like he was a cadet again, preparing for his first inspection.

Well, there was a good solution for that. "Helmets up, boys," he told them, even though he thought one of them might be a woman. Hard to tell with that sort. "I'm going in." There were strict instructions that the prisoners were not allowed to see any faces other than Maggs's handsome own, so they wouldn't later recognize their captors.

There were three cells in the brig, but only two were occupied. A display on the front of one door showed Valk and the nonentities from Rishi floating around in there and trying not to kick each other in the face. Enormously funny, but he had other things to do than watch their antics. He switched off that display.

The display on the second door showed only a single occupant. He seemed a bit better acclimated to the sudden disappearance of weight. He had curled himself into the lotus posture, a technique used by old spacers to minimize the disorientation of sleeping without gravity. He floated in the center of the space, barely even rotating, and he had his eyes closed as if he were meditating. Maybe that was something he'd picked up back on Niraya.

Maggs touched a virtual key at the bottom of the display to activate the cell's speakers. "Good morning, Commander. I hope you got some rest."

"Maggs," Lanoe said. His eyes still closed. "Ready to kill me now that we're where nobody will see it happen?"

Not much basis for a trust-type relationship there, Maggs's father said in his head. Sometimes that voice could be painfully obvious.

"Other plans, Commander. I've come to collect you—we have an important meeting to attend. Of course, I'm not going to open this door just yet. I'm of the opinion that if I do you'll try to strangle me, or something equally barbaric."

On the display Lanoe's eyes were still closed. He said nothing, but Maggs thought perhaps a trace of a smile played across those weathered old lips.

"It would really be for the best if I didn't have to drag you out of there in restraints. So I'm going to have to ask you for something," Maggs said.

"What?"

"Your word. I need you to promise that you won't try to attack me. Or strangle me. Or throw me out of an airlock." He thought about it for a moment. "Or hurt me in any other way."

No reply. Of course.

"Not forever, of course," Maggs continued. "I know that's asking for rather a lot. Just long enough to get through...what we need to get through. Call it twenty-four hours. Now, is that something you think you could do?"

Lanoe opened his eyes. He looked directly at Maggs, as if he could see through the door between them. Impossible, of course. He must simply know where the camera lens was hidden inside his cell. His face was perfectly impassive.

"I suppose I can wait that long," he said, finally. And then a real smile creased his face.

Maggs suppressed a shudder of fear. It was of course quite unreasonable of Lanoe to harbor such animus against him. Hadn't he saved the old fool's life, back on Rishi? And not for the first time, really. Yet Maggs had been in the Navy long enough to know there were people in the world who simply couldn't see reason.

It was damned inconvenient that they needed Lanoe so badly.

"I'm going to ask you to say it," Maggs said. "I know you well enough by now, and your rather archaic conception of honor. I need you to make a promise."

"I swear," Lanoe said, unblinking, "that for twenty-four hours I will resist my primal urge to break your skull."

"Very good. Then we can—"

"Starting now."

Maggs sighed and hit the key to turn off the speakers. He turned to one of the mirror-helmeted marines, the one he was 70 percent certain was female. "Open it up, if you'll be so kind. It appears I have no time to waste."

━━✦━━

Lanoe kicked along after Maggs, propelling himself into the axial corridor that ran the length of the Hoplite—almost three hundred meters from the bridge to the engine torus. Marines and crew pushed past them in the narrow space, darting out of side corridors and through bulwark hatches, busy at securing anything that might fall to the floor when ship's gravity returned. Already the lights in the corridor were glowing amber—in a minute they would turn red. Lanoe knew what that meant. They were decelerating toward their destination.

He had to admit he was curious about where they were headed.

He remembered nothing of the time between when the marines knocked him unconscious and when he woke up in the detaining cell. He had half-expected never to wake up again, so when he came to—despite a roaring headache—he'd felt lucky.

Days of solitary confinement had eroded that emotion. No one had come to visit him. No one had asked him any questions. Had they tortured him for information, at least he would have seen another human being.

The fact that the first person he did see after being captured was Auster Maggs had put him in a sour mood, but at least it meant something was happening. Now the two of them were headed for the vehicle bay at the waist of the cruiser. Which meant they had to be headed toward a planet or an orbital habitat of some kind.

It looked like he wasn't just going to be quietly executed after all.

"You aren't asking any questions," Maggs said.

"I figure if I do, the only answers I'll get will be lies."

Maggs clucked his tongue. "Exactly what did I do to deserve this kind of attitude?" he asked.

"You ran away. On Niraya, with an"—he'd almost said alien, out loud, where they might be overheard, but thought better of it—"enemy fleet bearing down on a planet full of innocent people. When I had only a handful of pilots under my command, and couldn't afford to lose even one."

"I seem to recall," Maggs said, "that you ordered me to leave that planet. Immediately after trying to shoot me dead. In a church."

"You know what you did. You ran like a coward."

Strong words, he knew. He half-expected Maggs to turn around in the middle of the passageway and take a swing at him. Perhaps the only reason he didn't was that the gravity lights in the corridor turned a deep red just then.

The Hoplite had turned around so that its engines pointed forward, so when it burned them again it would slow down. Because in physics terms there was no real difference between acceleration and deceleration, that meant that suddenly the gravity came back, and down was in the opposite direction of thrust.

The corridor they were in became a vertical shaft ninety stories tall.

They did not fall to their deaths, because both of them were expecting it to happen. Because they were pilots, because they were well trained, they had reflexively grabbed for handholds embedded in the shaft's wall. The cruiser had safety measures built in, of course. If they had started to fall an inertial sink would have grabbed them and slowed their descent before they could be hurt. Safety measures could always fail, though. Navy personnel never counted on them.

They had to climb down another fifty meters, using the handholds as a ladder. By the time they reached their destination Lanoe's arms were sore. They headed down a side passage and into the largest open space onboard the cruiser, a vehicle bay big enough to hold an entire wing of fighters. Only one was currently aboard, the Z.XIX Maggs had flown on Rishi.

The cataphract wasn't what they'd come for. Maggs led him to the back of the bay, where another ship waited for them. It was the size of a standard ten-meter cutter, but its hull was a matte black and it was crescent shaped, like a flying wing. Lanoe had never seen a ship with those specific lines before.

"Something new," Maggs said. "Practically invisible—you see how the hull coating seems to just eat up the light? It absorbs just about every wavelength you can think of. No lights, no viewports to give away your position—you fly it by camera. Come on." They climbed in through a hatch on the bottom of the ship, having to almost crawl on all fours. Inside there was room for maybe six people in Navy suits, or four marines.

The interior walls were coated in soft black foam that felt like rubber but looked like deep carpeting. Once they were inside, light burst all around them and then resolved to a view of the world outside, the entire cabin interior becoming one large display. It was like the cutter's hull had evaporated, or maybe turned to glass. Everywhere Lanoe looked, virtual keyboards and instrument panels appeared without a sound.

"Nice, eh?" Maggs asked.

"Distracting," Lanoe told him.

"I suppose at your age anything new seems threatening."

Maggs warmed up the engines as Lanoe strapped in—and then they just sat there. For several minutes.

"You know you have to take off before you can fly, right?" Lanoe asked.

"Just waiting for the perfect moment." Maggs tapped a virtual key. Out in the vehicle bay the exterior doors slid open, and beyond Lanoe could see the ghostly light of wormspace streaming past.

"We aren't really here, you see," Maggs told him. "Neither my name or yours appears on the Hoplite's crew manifest. This cutter isn't onboard, either, in case anyone asks. Now. This might be a bit disconcerting."

Maggs threw open the throttle and the cutter jumped out of the vehicle bay, headed right for the annihilating wall of smoky light. He threw the stick over to one side while feathering his maneuvering jets and the cutter tumbled sideways, the cruiser flashing past over and over as the smaller craft corkscrewed around it. Lanoe caught just a glimpse of the distorted space of a wormhole throat, and then they were back in realspace, black with white stars. Still tumbling. Maggs hit the thrusters in quick, controlled bursts to put distance between them and the cruiser. Eventually he pulled them out of the spin, on a course perpendicular to the cruiser's.

Soon the cruiser was just a bright spot in the sky, receding into nothingness.

It was extremely dangerous and decidedly foolhardy to launch from the cruiser while still in wormspace, but needs must and all that. "We need to make our own descent in case anyone is watching. Which they almost certainly are. Centrocor is after you, and they have plenty of people here willing to help make that happen."

Lanoe did no more than grunt in response.

Maggs had to admit—strictly to himself—that flying the cutter was a tad disconcerting. The full-circle display left him feeling as if he were piloting nothing more than a rank of crew seats through the infinite void. It kept nagging him, an irritating tickle at the back of his mind, that his helmet was down, even though he appeared to be hurtling through hard vacuum. It made him jumpy and prone to oversteering.

Lanoe just sat there in stony silence. Arms folded across his chest, as if he were just waiting for this to be over. Maggs watched him carefully, out of the corner of his eye. Any moment now the planet of their destination would become visible, and he wanted to see Lanoe's face when he realized where they were.

Keep an eye on the traffic, son. I want grandchildren someday, his father's voice said, sounding as if he were standing directly behind Maggs's shoulder.

Maggs snapped his attention back to the view in front of him. Space, this particular bit of it, anyway, was far from empty. In point of fact, the sky was full of ships. Commercial and civilian craft, mostly, big ungainly cargo haulers and zippy commuter craft. Free-floating habitats maneuvering to catch the sunlight or to shed excess heat. Drone ships by the myriad—space telescopes, power generators, communication satellites, traffic satellites, microgravity manufactories. As they drew closer to their destination, big orbital habitats began to wink into existence, wheels and spinning cylinders and simple aggregates that were just strings of cargo modules looped together like cheap necklaces.

All of it circling endlessly, etching out complicated orbits around the busiest, most heavily populated planet of them all.

"Welcome home," Maggs said, as they came around the night side and caught their first real view of Earth.

"It hasn't looked like home to me in a long time," Lanoe said, softly.

Below them the great expanse of the Pacific Ocean rolled into view, spotted with platform cities that rose on great spider legs above the waves. The western extent of North America crested the horizon and unfurled before them, appearing exactly the way it did on maps. The ragged coast of California, the featureless cold deserts of Canada, which looked like the cartographers had forgotten to fill in a patch. The continent itself was bisected by a line of round craters that had, over the years, filled in with water to become the Midwestern Sea.

The view finally seemed to affect Lanoe. At least it got him talking. "When we shipped out, in the Century War, they warned us we wouldn't be coming home for a long time. Maybe as much as six months. It was thirteen years before I got to come back on my first real leave. By then I didn't even recognize the place. You see that line of craters?"

"I do, in fact, possess working eyes," Maggs said.

"I remember when they weren't there," Lanoe said.

Back during the Century War the Martians had built the very first true artificial intelligence, a machine that could think and make decisions for itself. They had been very proud of their creation. It had not, of course, been built for the sake of scientific curiosity. The Martians had given their machine a task that had proved impossible for human minds to solve. They asked it how it would be possible to end the Century War with a victory for Mars and its allies.

The machine's solution had been to attempt to kill every man, woman, and child on Earth, because of course that was the most efficient way to end a war. By removing the enemy from play.

Before the Martians could stop it, the AI had seized control of the largest ship in the Martian fleet, the Dreadnought *Universal Suffrage*. The machine had turned every gun it had on Earth and kept firing until it ran out of ammunition.

Then it flew back to its base on Vesta. To reload.

It was exactly the kind of strategy that an artificial intelligence might come up with. After it was done, it took fifteen years and countless lives to bring the *Universal Suffrage* and its AI master down.

"It took thirty-nine seconds to do that," Lanoe said, gesturing at the scarred planet. "Nothing we had back then could stop it. It kept going, turned southern Asia into one gigantic swamp before it was done. We threw every weapon we had at it and barely scratched its hull. After that we were sure we were going to lose. For decades we kept fighting, thinking there was no way we could save Earth. Knowing we didn't have any choice but to keep trying."

"Well, you won in the end. That's the important thing."

"Half the human race died," Lanoe told him.

Maggs had never had much of an interest in ancient history. "Hold on," he said. "We're about to hit atmosphere."

The transition from space to sky was bumpy, though Maggs was, if he said so himself, an excellent pilot. All around them as the air thickened it grew tinged with a dull red that grew to a fiery orange. For a moment the two of them rode in the heart of a white-hot fireball, but as the cutter slowed down to atmospheric speeds the flames receded and they could see the blue sky beyond, blue sky and white clouds and off in the distance a swarm of high-altitude drones like gnats. Cargo carriers riding the jet stream, mostly, and weather control machines like fixed stars. Nothing military, but still, best to avoid those—they would all have cameras, and anyone could be watching.

The cutter's wing-shaped body bit into the air and the control stick tried to jump out of Maggs' hand. He held tight, and guided the little ship down through a bank of puffy white cumulus and then brought them in low over the water, banking around to the northwest. Up ahead they could see the leaning towers of Old Seattle sticking up out of the ocean. He brought them in lower and lower still, until they nearly skimmed the tops of the waves, then cut his speed as the skeletonized towers loomed up above them.

He slowed way down until he could maneuver between the buildings, following the sunken city blocks, dodging piles of debris that hadn't been cleared away in all the years since the end of the war.

A couple of quick S-turns to lose even more speed and they were ready to land. There was no pad waiting for them, of course, but the cutter was designed for clandestine work and its makers had built it to perch on any level patch of ground no bigger than half its wingspan. Maggs put them down with a perfect three-point landing on top of what had, a very long time ago, been the roof of a parking structure. Now it was just a square of concrete lashed by spume.

He powered down the engines and unbuckled his straps.

"All ashore," he said.

Chapter Nine

The two of them changed into civilian clothes. Lanoe always felt naked when he wasn't wearing his suit—there had been years, maybe whole decades when he'd never taken it off—but he understood the need. Naval personnel were rare on the surface of Earth, rare enough that anyone who saw them would be likely to take note. The brown jackets and trousers they put on didn't exactly fit properly but they wouldn't draw any stares.

As they exited the cutter, he was a little surprised to find that it had changed color, taking on a grayish-beige tone to match the eroded concrete it sat on. "Chromatophoric fibers woven into the stealth coating," Maggs explained. "Not quite invisibility, of course—it still leaves a ruddy inconvenient shadow. Still, anyone watching from orbit would have to know exactly what they were looking for to spot it. Come on. This way."

Maggs balanced himself with his arms out as they crossed a fallen girder that formed a makeshift bridge between the submerged parking structure and the next building over, which looked surprisingly intact. The two of them crawled through a window into a dark space with a slanting floor. This must have been an office building once, Lanoe thought, though time and looters and natural decay had emptied it of anything but debris. Tiny crabs clung to rusted columns, or scuttled across the muddy floor. Lanoe tried not to step on them.

Together they picked their way through the building to where windows looked out over a narrow stretch of the sea. Yellow-white foam piled up against the sides of buildings on the far side—towers hundreds of meters tall poking up from the water at odd angles, their windows all smashed out long ago, their colors ground to earth tones by the wind and the salt water. Rust and crumbling concrete, exposed twists of rebar and dangling lengths of cable that connected to nothing now.

Yet there was a smell on the wind, a smell that didn't fit the place. The smell of cooking food. Brussels sprouts, he thought, and frying fish. Lanoe scanned the gaping windows across the water and caught glimpses of motion, the occasional flash of light. And there, ten stories above the water—a rope stretched between two tower blocks, with laundry pinned up to dry in the upper air.

"Hellfire," he said.

Maggs turned to look at him through the gloom.

"People live here?" Lanoe asked.

Maggs leaned out over the water to take a look. "There are twelve billion people on Earth," he said. "Most of them as poor as little mice. They live anywhere there's space. Still, this place is as close as anyone's going to get to privacy."

They came to a door that looked like it had long ago fused into its jamb, particle board stripped of its veneer and stained with mold. Maggs knocked on its surface, looking as if he was loath to touch something so filthy. The door slid back into the wall without a sound.

The two of them stepped into a dimly lit room beyond. There were no windows or other doors and it stank of mildew, but clean tarps had been laid across the floor. Cables ran here and there, connecting various pieces of equipment Lanoe barely recognized. Mostly communications gear, he thought.

A young woman stepped out of the shadows to greet them. "Sorry about the conditions," she said. "Necessary, I'm afraid." She looked like she might be eighteen years old and she had sharp features under a massive cloud of dark hair. She wore a sage green shirt and tight fawn trousers. No insignia or ornament. The only thing that gave away her identity was the fact that her hands were tattooed, tiny black stars and galaxies from the tips of her fingers all the way up to her wrists.

Lanoe knew those tattoos. The body, the face were completely different. The hands themselves were smaller now, the fingers more slender. The tattoos, though—he'd seen hands with those tattoos back in the Century War. They'd gripped a railing in the vehicle bay of a Hipparchus-class carrier as equipment had exploded behind her. Ships torn half-apart by enemy fire came screeching in to land on either side. Sparks bursting all around, red emergency lights flickering—and the owner of those tattoos had laughed. Laughed out loud and told the pilots arrayed before her that they were one good push from victory.

And she'd been right. That had been less than an hour before Lanoe and his wing broke through a cordon of the Argyre Regulars and won the battle of 63 Ausonia. They'd lost the carrier, but won the battle. And ultimately, the war.

In the Navy you didn't salute your superior officers. If your helmet was up it would be impossible, and in microgravity conditions you tended to need your hands free. Typically a quick nod was all that was required.

Lanoe inclined his head.

"Admiral Varma," he said.

"At ease, Commander." The girl looked up at Maggs. She was a good twenty-five centimeters shorter than either of the pilots. "Lieutenant, maybe you could go take a look around. My devices here screen out most forms of surveillance, but they can't stop anyone from listening in the old-fashioned way. With their ears, I mean."

"I'll endeavor to do my best, Fleet Admiral," Maggs said, using Varma's full rank. The highest rank there was.

The Navy was commanded, at its top level, by a Strategy Council—the six highest-ranking admirals of the Naval Expeditionary Force, plus one general each from the Planetary Brigade

Marines and the Naval Engineering Division. Theoretically every member of the Council was equal in standing. Fleet Admiral Varma, however, was the only one of them old enough to have served in the Century War. She had commendations on her service record that they didn't give out anymore. She chaired the Council and set its agenda.

This woman was, for all intents and purposes, the commanding officer of the whole Navy and all its branches. Maggs didn't waste a microsecond in obeying her order.

Varma closed the door behind him.

"Good," she said. "Now we can talk."

"I know what you're thinking, so let's get it out of the way. No, I didn't body-swap," Varma told him. "That's illegal, of course. This is a new thing, a new—procedure. Full genetic rejuvenation. Like a butterfly climbing into a cocoon and coming out a caterpillar. Believe it or not, this is what I looked like as a child."

Lanoe didn't deny that he'd wondered. Varma was one of the few people he knew who were actually older than he was. People who lived that long tended to find one way or another—legal or otherwise—to get a new body. He knew even he was going to have to do it, eventually. At three hundred years old, his knees were starting to give out and he woke up every morning feeling like hell. He supposed he didn't blame Varma for wanting to stay young and active.

"Sit down," she said. She dragged two folding chairs into the middle of the room. "I can't offer much in the way of hospitality," she told him. "I have some water." She dug into a cooler and brought out a plastic bottle. "Hmm? Here, take it."

Ah. There was a problem, there. "With all due respect," Lanoe said, "I'm afraid I can't."

Varma sighed. "Why the hell not? Lanoe, just speak candidly. We don't have time for protocol. I have meetings to get to."

Lanoe took a deep breath. He'd been trying to get to the Admiralty, to give Valk's information to people he trusted. Admiral Varma wasn't on that list. Not that he had any reason to suspect her of being paid off by Centrocor or one of the polys—he just didn't know where her allegiances lay. Technically she should be incorruptible. She answered only to the Sector Wardens and the International League, who together comprised the elected government of Earth. Centrocor shouldn't be able to corrupt people like that. And yes, he'd served under her before, and done so with pride.

But that was a very long time ago.

"Ma'am," he said. "Your people—Lieutenant Maggs, that is—abducted me by force and dragged me across fifty light-years without even telling me why. You and I go back a long way, but...I still don't know what's going on. I thought at first I was going to be executed. Now I assume that isn't the case, but I'm still unsure what's going to happen to me. If that water is drugged, or—"

Varma squinted at him as if he'd just accused her of stealing from the Navy's petty cash fund. "Abducted," she said. "We probably saved your bloody life. Centrocor has been trying to grab you since you left Niraya. Did you think they were going to offer you a cushy job? They're planning to torture you for information. They won't care what's left of you after they get it. You say we dragged you here, but I'll remind you that you serve at the pleasure of the three-headed eagle, Commander. I needed to talk to you, so I *summoned* you. As for keeping you in the dark, the Navy has a right to keep secrets, doesn't it?"

"As you say, ma'am," Lanoe said. He found he was standing at attention, with his hands behind his back. He forced himself to sit down in the chair she'd offered him.

"You were brought to Earth because I *have* to be here," Varma said. "I've been in briefing sessions for the last two days. I had to talk to each of the Sector Wardens individually, because they refuse to actually be in the same room with each other. Then I had to run down the whole thing with the International League. Every blasted governing body on Earth wants a piece of my time. You don't want my damned water, suit yourself. But don't take that tone with me."

Lanoe brought his chin up. He'd been chewed out by admirals before, and he knew the drill. You stood there and took what was coming to you.

Damned Maggs. The fool had been sent to bring Lanoe to a meeting—and in the process he'd blown off a cadet's hand and scared the devil out of everyone on Rishi. He'd probably done it all just to see Lanoe squirm.

"You're not a prisoner," Varma said, her tone softening, though not much. "You are, however, under my command. And you know why you're here."

"Niraya," Lanoe said.

"Aliens," the Admiral corrected. She took a minder from her pocket and unrolled it across her knees. Text scrolled up the display, but he couldn't read it from where he sat.

"Aliens," he agreed. "They call themselves the Blue-Blue-White. They look a little like jellyfish, and they live in the atmospheres of gas giant planets. In fact—"

"I know all of this," Varma told him.

"You do?"

"We scooped up your pet AI, the same time we got you."

Valk. They had gotten Valk's information. So much for keeping it in the right hands.

"We pulled a lot of information off of it, Commander," Varma said. She looked down at one of several minders that lay open around her chair. "A lot of very interesting information. Your machine was able to communicate with the drone fleet, when nobody else could. It spoke to them. Learned all about them. Even got a picture of what they look like." She brought up an image of one of the Blue-Blue-White on her minder. Lanoe saw the orange, globular body, the hanging tentacles. "Fascinating. About half a billion years ago they sent out one fleet of drones, and that fleet made copies of itself—oh, that's interesting. It looks like there could be millions of those fleets out there now, spread throughout the galaxy. *Deeply* interesting. I have one burning question to ask you."

"Ma'am," Lanoe said. He knew what was coming.

"Why in the name of all of hell's chapels didn't I know this already?" she asked.

Lanoe knew a rhetorical question when he heard one.

"When you left Niraya, our ships were already there studying the wreckage you left behind. Learning everything they could about these aliens. Rear Admiral Wallys has been working for months sifting through every bit of data, every blasted-up piece of alien technology that remains. He sends me an update every time he learns something new. Yet I didn't know what the aliens looked like. I didn't know there were other fleets—until we brought you in. For some reason you didn't feel you could share this data with him."

Lanoe made a point of not looking away as she stared him down.

"I have everything now, Commander. *Everything.* I have a recording here of you talking to the AI, after the battle. The AI requested to be dismantled, which is admirable of it—and the correct response. You know how strict the law is concerning AIs. You know we cannot allow them to run free. Yet when the AI asked to be shut down, you said no. You refused its perfectly legal request. Would you like me to tell you the exact words you used, Lanoe? I can read them back to you."

"No need, ma'am," Lanoe said.

She was still staring at him. Waiting.

"I said," he told her, "that I intended to use the information he'd gathered. That I planned on going to find the Blue-Blue-White and make them shut down the drone fleets. Failing that, I intended to make them pay for what they'd done."

Varma nodded. She picked up one of her minders and studied its display.

She was silent so long he found he couldn't resist saying more. "Ma'am. I chose not to share this information with Rear Admiral Wallys because I—"

"Because you didn't trust him to use it the way you want it to be used," she interrupted.

It was a fair assessment.

"I know his reputation," Varma said. "He's spent half his career chasing aliens without ever finding a shred of evidence. Until now. That's made him something of a laughingstock." She shrugged. "I'll admit when he first reported to me about Niraya, I assumed he was full of bosh. That he had found some ancient fossil that might, if you squinted, resemble an alien. I discounted what he said, at first."

"Ma'am, there are a lot of vested interests who wanted the information I had," Lanoe pointed out. "Centrocor, for one. I'm sure they've already figured out a way to make a profit off of it. There are others who—"

"Enough," she said. "You realize that failing to turn over this information could be seen as a traitorous act? That you could face disciplinary charges with penalties including, but not limited to, summary execution?"

Lanoe was a tough old bastard but he couldn't help but feel a chill run down his spine when she said that.

"You've put the entire human race at risk," Varma told him. "Care to explain why?"

"Ma'am—this information is important. It can't be allowed to fall into the wrong hands. There may never have been a more important moment in human history. You've seen Valk's files. You know his theory, then. About why we've never met aliens before, despite spending centuries looking for them. He thinks there aren't any others. That there were, once, but the Blue-Blue-White's drones killed every single one of them. That we're only here now because they hadn't gotten around to exterminating us yet."

Varma set her minder down. Took a long drink of water.

"What they've done—what they're still doing—is unforgivable. It cannot be allowed to go on. What they did—"

"They killed Lieutenant Bettina Zhang," Varma said.

Lanoe opened his mouth, intending to say something more. Anything more. And found he couldn't get a word out.

"She fought by your side, at Niraya. She died in the final battle.

She gave her life to save the planet," Varma went on. "They killed her. That's what's really inexcusable, isn't it?"

He looked down at his hands. They were shaking.

"The woman you loved. The woman you had proposed to." She checked her minder. "On at least a dozen different occasions."

"This isn't . . . this isn't about—"

"It's not just about Zhang," the Fleet Admiral said. She nodded in understanding. "Not all of it. I know you, Lanoe. I know that you're tough as nails, but underneath you do actually care. That you're a good man. You want revenge for all those poor dead aliens you're never going to meet. In some abstract fashion, you think you're after justice on their behalf. It's not," she said, repeating herself, "*just* about Zhang."

It took every ounce of strength Lanoe had to lift his chin. To meet Varma's gaze. "Taking the fight to these aliens," he said, "is the right thing to do."

"Perhaps," she said.

Lanoe set his mouth in a hard line. Refusing to show the slightest emotion.

"Perhaps it is. But that's not your choice to make."

"Ma'am, if you'll forgive me—"

"Shut up and listen. Those alien drones didn't attack Niraya. They attacked humanity. Those other fleets are still out there and eventually they'll attack other human worlds. The response that might be made to this aggression isn't going to be chosen by one lone commander and his squaddies. It should—and it will—be made by the leaders of humanity. By people like me, and the Sector Wardens, and the International League. Do I make myself clear?"

"Ma'am. May I ask a question?"

"Fine. Go ahead."

"What's the plan, going forward, now that you know all this?"

Varma sighed. For a second he thought she was going to refuse to answer. Well, that was her right, of course. She had no reason to discuss high-level decision making with a field officer like him. But then she surprised him by giving him an honest answer.

"It will have to be discussed. At length. The Sector Wardens will want to put together a fact-finding committee, and the International League will have to approve a budget for that. A panel of experts will be put together to examine the evidence you've brought us, and then they'll make recommendations about how to proceed. Independent analysts will go over their conclusions, make sure they're sound. Eventually a policy document will be created, and that'll be instituted as a new protocol. We have to be careful about how we do things, you see. We can't afford to panic, not now."

The look she gave him, when she finished, was almost apologetic.

It had happened. The thing he'd feared most. Valk's information was going to be suppressed. Turned over to—of all things—a committee.

Which meant, in all likelihood, that nothing would be done at all. There would be endless meetings and discussions. The polys would work their influence. In the end, humanity's response to the Blue-Blue-White would be decided by a cost-benefit analysis.

And the right thing, the only moral path forward, would be deemed too expensive to pursue. Until, perhaps, the Blue-Blue-White attacked another human world. Until more people died.

He imagined she knew all that. He thought maybe she didn't like it any more than he did. But she didn't say so. And even if she did think maybe he was right, that it was the wrong move, well— she had people she had to answer to. Everybody has a boss.

He considered saying something. Making an impassioned appeal for action. He knew better than to try. He'd made his best play already, and he'd failed. The information he'd been so desperate to get into the right hands was out in the open now, and he couldn't turn back time.

"Now," she said. "We've dismissed your little revenge fantasy. You aren't going to be allowed to fly off to the center of the galaxy and start shooting aliens. That *will not* happen. Instead, let's talk about what you *are* going to do."

Chapter Ten

I have a job for you," Varma said.

"Ma'am, I'm retired. I'm not on the active list—"

"Perhaps you'll hear what the job is before you refuse it," she said. She picked up one of the minders from the floor, one cued up to show a video. She handed it to Lanoe and gestured for him to hit the PLAY key.

The video showed an image he was familiar with, though from a perspective he'd never seen before. In the display he saw the queenship, the biggest spacecraft of the alien fleet he fought at Niraya. It had been built out of a hollowed-out asteroid, with a massive opening at one end surrounded by a ring of long, tentacle-like fibers. Not unlike a jellyfish itself.

As the video played out, fire erupted from the opening. The entire queenship shook and a crack ran down its rocky length, searing red light pouring out from the inside. The tentacles went slack and then all light inside the queenship slowly burned out.

The video was surprisingly clear. He could even make out a couple of tiny dots shooting out of the opening, even as the asteroid's molten core erupted.

Those dots represented Lanoe and Valk, flying out of the exploding queenship under the power of the jets built into Valk's suit.

The video abruptly cut to black. Two words appeared, in a generic white typeface:

WELL DONE

Lanoe looked up but Varma shook her head. "There's more," she said.

The view changed to show a map of the galaxy. Certain stars had been highlighted, specifically those closest to Earth—the stars humanity had settled. On the map one and then another of the stars flashed orange, as if they were on fire. Each time the screen would go black to show a string of numbers. Lanoe knew enough about celestial navigation to recognize that the numbers indicated galactic coordinates, bearings, and velocities. Other numbers indicated dates, some of them many years in the future.

MORE WILL COME

Lanoe understood exactly what that meant. The coordinates indicated the present locations of other drone fleets, just like the one he'd fought. The orange-flashing stars indicated where each fleet would strike next—and when.

Varma paused the video. "We checked those out, of course, with our best space telescopes. The fleets it lists are all there. All headed toward human planets. Some of them will take centuries yet to arrive, but they're on their way."

Lanoe nodded and chewed on his lip. He scanned the dates, looking for one in particular. "Adlivun," he said, pointing at an orange star. "That's where they'll strike first. In seventeen years."

Varma nodded. "We'll be ready for them."

Lanoe certainly hoped so.

Varma started the video again. One by one the stars changed color. Eventually, every single star humanity had colonized turned orange. Every one of them.

Finally the screen went black. Words started to appear, one line after another.

WE CAN HELP
COME AND FIND US
HERE IS THE KEY

Below the words appeared a complex shape, a tangle of lines and sharp curves. This was the end of the message—there was no more to the video.

"What—what is that?" Lanoe asked. "That shape, the key?"

"It's a set of directions. A route through wormspace, leading to an area we didn't even know was there. It ends at a wormhole throat we've never seen."

She took the minder back, set it on the floor.

"It's a map. It might as well be an engraved invitation."

———

He stared at her for a long time.

"Who sent this?"

"No idea," Varma told him. She took a drink of water. "The metadata on that video doesn't tell us anything. And there's no encryption on this message. It was received in clear, by a Navy ship on a long-range reconnaissance mission outside the Avernus system. Avernus is the closest planet to the destination on that map, but that isn't saying much—even from Avernus, the destination is still a week away through wormspace."

"So it wasn't a Navy unit," Lanoe said, thinking it through. "One of the polys?"

"Again, I don't know. The message was sent specifically to that one Naval vessel. It could have been a poly, trying to back-channel information to us without letting their competitors over-hear. But that raises other questions. There are plenty of ways for the polys to contact the Admiralty directly—and discreetly. Easier ways."

Lanoe nodded. "Could be a trap," he said. "A mysterious message out of space…it would give them plausible deniability. Centrocor or one of the other polys could be setting us up."

"To what end?"

Lanoe had to admit he couldn't see the angle. Why would any of the polys send such a confusing message? Just to distract the Navy? To make them look foolish by chasing after a mysterious signal? There was no money to be made out of that, and the polys never did anything unless they could profit by it. "Maybe… I don't know. Maybe it's just some fool with a radio playing a hoax on us."

"Unlikely," Varma said. "The message they sent us included information nobody has, not even the Navy. You see this?" She showed him the "key" again, the pattern of curves and lines included with the message. "If you zoom in on this image, it just gets bigger and more complex, like a fractal." On the screen the pattern expanded into a snarl of lines that ramified like the branches of a tree, or the veins of a human circulatory system. It looked a great deal like the maps Lanoe had seen of wormspace, though it was different, somehow. Bigger, more complicated. Tags popped up at various points around the image—standard navigational glyphs, annotations pointing out wormhole throats and hazards, dead ends and places where wormholes simply looped back on themselves. There were a lot more tags than Lanoe expected. Some he didn't recognize, though they looked like they were just strings of galactic coordinates. Right at the center of the map was a single white cross. As Lanoe's eyes passed over it, it pulsed with light. He knew what that meant—it was a destination. X marks the spot.

"This is the most complete map we've ever seen of wormspace. It shows sections of the network even the Navy has never gotten around to exploring. Whoever sent this," Varma told him, "has a lot of information. Perhaps most interestingly, they have video of you defeating the alien fleet at Niraya. Footage of it, Lanoe. Which means they had to be recording it *as it happened.*"

"Then, if it is a hoax, it has to come from someone in the Navy, someone who had access to Admiral Wallys's information—"

"No," Varma said.

"No?"

"No. No one had that footage. Not from that particular angle. Not us, not the polys. Not even your AI."

"Hellfire," he said, the word slipping out unbidden.

"Lanoe, are you foolish enough to think I would tell you about this if I didn't have a damned good reason?"

"No, ma'am," he said, and swallowed thickly.

"Whoever sent this—we need to find out how they got that footage. We need to know how they have better information about the wormhole network than we do. We absolutely need to know. It's what we in the Admiral business call a strategic advantage, and we can't afford to pass those up when they come along."

Lanoe nodded.

"It's been decided that we should send a small delegation immediately, to check it out."

"And you want me to do it," Lanoe said.

"If we're going to do this, we're going to do it quietly. You already know what happened at Niraya. If I send somebody else, I'll have to brief them, and right now I want as few people as possible to know about the other fleets." Varma lifted her hands and let them fall again. "You're the best man for the job." She tapped the minder to blank its display. "You'll leave as soon as possible. You can have that Hoplite-class cruiser you came in on. You can pick your own crew. Obviously you'll need to operate in secrecy. If the polys find out about your new mission—well. We cannot let that happen. Do you understand?"

"Yes, ma'am." He understood exactly what was at stake. The Navy and the polys were in a state of constant cold war. The interplanetary corporations were always looking to get an upper hand on Earth's defenders. If they ever gained a truly significant advantage, something that would make it possible for them to overcome the Navy, the polys would conquer Earth the very next day.

"So you'll tell no one where you're going, or why, and you will keep a low profile. Within those parameters we'll give you as much support as we can."

"And what if I say no?" Lanoe asked.

"Not an option," Varma said. "This is an order." She folded her hands in her lap. "Tell you what. You do this thing for us, complete this mission, and we'll pretend that you didn't betray the Admiralty. The fact that you kept the Valk AI from us, that you had information from Niraya that you didn't share—we'll forget all about that. This is the best, and only, offer you're going to get."

Lanoe tried not to grimace.

This wasn't what he'd planned on. When he defeated the alien drones, he'd lost too much to just take the win and go back to his old life. He'd changed out there, where he'd lost the woman he loved. Where he'd sacrificed so much, to save Niraya.

Something had died inside him. And something else had been born. A desire.

He'd tried to bring Valk's information to the Admiralty not because he thought the Navy would take care of the problem. He'd planned on making a case before the Admiralty Council, petitioning them to give him a fleet. So that he could take the fight to the thrice-damned jellyfish—himself.

He'd known that was naïve, but it was the best idea he had. And now—everything had fallen apart. The admirals weren't going to help him. Which meant he would never be able to convince the Sector Wardens to back his plan.

He couldn't do it alone. He had no way of traveling ten thousand light-years toward the center of the galaxy without help. Earth had been his best bet, and now that hope was crushed.

Whoever had sent this message, whatever they wanted—they were offering to help. They wanted to help him put the Blue-Blue-White down.

He would take help wherever he could find it.

He tried to keep his face very calm while he pretended to mull things over. When he thought that an appropriate level of soul-searching had been conveyed, he slowly rose to his feet.

"Yes, ma'am," he said. "I'll leave at once."

Chapter Eleven

Maggs was terribly busy when Lanoe came out of the little room. He hardly noticed the old man's reappearance.

He was engaged, you see, in the time-honored activity of kicking little rocks off of a high place and watching to see how many times they bounced on the way down. His record at that particular moment was six, and he'd hoped to beat it before it was time to go.

Ah, well, needs must, *et cetera*, *et cetera*. He leaned up against a decaying support column and watched Lanoe blink as he came back out into the light.

For a moment he thought the ancient pilot looked like a pole-axed steer. It was rather nice seeing him look at a loss, for once. "Bad news?" Maggs asked.

Lanoe's face hardened the moment he realized he was being watched. Of course. These old fellows, these veterans of antique wars—they always had to come off as so tough. So enduring.

"What are your orders now?" Lanoe asked.

Maggs shrugged and made a point of examining his gloves, to make sure they hadn't gotten dusty while he waited. "I'm supposed to take you back to the Hoplite. It's yours now. I'm to facilitate your assumption of command, and then get out of your way. Consider me at your service. For the moment."

It was rather odd that Lanoe didn't take the opportunity to

insult or berate him, but Maggs supposed one shouldn't look a gift horse in the mouth. Likely to be some nasty teeth in there.

Instead Lanoe just hurried off toward where they'd left the cutter. He was of the rank of commander, after all, and was used to being in charge. Maggs had enjoyed the time when their roles were reversed, but now that was over. He hurried after the old man and warmed up the flying wing while Lanoe just sat in his crew seat and stared at nothing.

Only once they were aloft, soaring high over the ruins of North America, did Lanoe speak again. "Is this thing shielded against eavesdropping?" he demanded.

"Naturally," Maggs said. "All flight data is encrypted, Navy fashion. Not that it truly matters. Stealth being the whole point, we aren't broadcasting so much as an IFF signal, and anyone trying to listen in with passive sensors would find us as quiet as mice. Something on your mind, Commander?"

Lanoe grunted. "How much do you know? What was your briefing, when they sent you to get me?"

"Precious little," Maggs said, pulling back on the stick. The water-filled Ohio Crater shrank behind his shoulder. The sky turned dark, then filled with stars as they shot upward through the atmosphere. The hull hissed and then fell silent and they were in space. "I was sent to bring you to an official briefing, that much I was allowed to know. I knew you were to speak with Fleet Admiral Varma. I know you're to take the Hoplite wherever you choose, and that you're allowed to pick your own crew. Where you're headed, what you're meant to do when you get there—well. All mum. Care to fill me in?"

"No," Lanoe said. And then nothing else.

Maggs sighed. It was a truism that the Navy was fueled by secrets, and that not every lieutenant was to be privy to the doings of the Admiralty. It was ruddy unfair, though. The Navy made no allowance for the quite basic human need for gossip.

The Hoplite-class cruiser had moved since they left it, navigating its way through the thick sky around Earth until it reached a Naval provisioning facility just on the far side of the moon's orbit. Maggs had no trouble slipping the cutter in between two big Griffin-class ship's tenders—bulky and unarmed ships designed to resupply warcraft with ammunition and stores. The tenders were nursing a Toxotes-class battleship and three destroyers just then—Earth did like to keep quite a lot of capital ships around, just to scare the tourists. The Hoplite was inside an inspection slip—a construction of girders like an enormous skeletal hand—while dozens of suited figures flitted around its sides, opening inspection panels and retracting ablative armor sections to make sure everything was in working order.

"Your chariot awaits," Maggs said, and deftly nipped into the vehicle bay.

Lanoe unstrapped and clambered out the hatch without a word of thanks for the poor fellow who had to drive him around all this time.

You ungrateful bastard, Maggs thought.

You ungrateful bastard, sir, his father's voice corrected, by reflex.

The vehicle bay was a busy place. Its hatch was kept down to allow small craft to come and go, a weather field shimmering across the opening as cataphract-class fighters were loaded in. BR.9s, the most common fighter in the Navy's arsenal—Lanoe counted eleven of them, nestled in beside Maggs's Z.XIX. A full complement, snug in the docking cradles that would keep them from rolling around inside the hangar during maneuvers. "How many pilots have they given me?" he asked.

Maggs touched his wrist and looked at the display that jumped up there. "Ten, all of them veterans," he said. He made it sound like a wonderful gift.

Lanoe scowled. "Veterans of what? Any of them fight during the Establishment Crisis?"

"Well, no," Maggs pointed out. "But these ten all served in the conflict between DaoLink and Soltexon. Nasty bit of scrapping, that."

"Which side were they on?" Lanoe asked.

"Soltexon's, I'm going to say," Maggs told him. "Though don't quote me."

Lanoe resisted the urge to punch Maggs in the mouth. If he asked a question it meant he wanted a real answer. Though he knew this one might be more complicated than it sounded.

The polys were always at war with each other, over trade disputes or lawsuits or simply because one of them wanted to steal a random asteroid that happened to belong to a rival. Owning a dozen planets was never enough, of course, for the Boards of Directors that ran the big companies, and the only way they had to expand was to seize each other's territory. Earth kept the balance of power by selective deployment of Naval assets. If one poly started getting too big, the Sector Wardens would send a carrier group or maybe just a battleship and a platoon of marines to bolster up that poly's enemies.

As the wars never ended, that meant that the Navy could fight for DaoLink this year and Soltexon the next and be back to supporting DaoLink in an advisory capacity the year after that.

Lanoe had little use for the system. He had resigned his own commission rather than fight for the polys in their endless struggle over some scrap of sky no one actually wanted. He had very little faith in pilots who fought in such cavalier actions. The poly wars tended to be quick skirmish affairs, small conflicts played for small stakes. None of these new pilots understood anything about campaigning, or about sacrifice.

"Send me their service records," he told Maggs. "Give me a reason to keep them on my ship."

"Of course," Maggs replied.

My ship, Lanoe thought. It looked like he'd already accepted command of this secret mission.

The two of them kicked their way out of the bay and into the cramped corridors beyond. Going was slow, as they had to constantly duck out of the way of the provisioning crews. Technicians in thinsuits were busy loading shells for the 75s, the big guns that stuck out from the Hoplite's sides like the ridges of vertebrae, while workers in heavy environment suits brought onboard long fuel cartridges to feed the engines. Lanoe did a quick inventory in his head, just based on what he saw. It seemed to him they were going to have enough consumables to be out in the field for at least a year, if it came to that.

Admiral Varma had made this sound like a diplomatic mission. That she was sure it wasn't a trap, or an ambush. Like any good warrior, though, she was preparing for the worst—the amount of stores being brought onboard made it look like the Hoplite was girding itself for a war.

Maggs led him to an elevator car that took them straight to the bridge—a comparatively large space right at the nose of the Hoplite, as far from the engines as you could get, in case anything blew up down there. Like the bridge of any space-going craft it was designed to be used in all kinds of gravity. Right now three thin-suited crew members were inside, one of them upside down from Lanoe's perspective. They moved between workstations, bringing up countless display windows that cycled through diagnostic read-outs and then flickered out as quickly as they'd manifested.

Maggs cleared his throat and the three of them came to attention, grabbing stanchions on the walls so they could face their new commander. The one who'd been upside down did a flip so she could face him directly. In space, where there was technically no such thing as "up" and "down," the Navy had come up with a rule of thumb—whichever way your commanding officer's head was pointed, that was the right way up.

"Relax," Lanoe told them. "Which of you is the pilot?" he asked.

A youngish-looking woman nodded and pushed off the wall, coming forward. "Lieutenant Harbin, sir," she said. "Looking forward to working with you."

Lanoe looked past her, at a navigational display. It showed the map of wormspace that had been attached to the mysterious message—though looking at it even momentarily, he could tell that some of the informational tags had been stripped out. Interesting. Admiral Varma had given her people some of the new map but not all of it. Clearly her own people weren't above suspicion.

"Looks kind of funny, doesn't it, sir?" Harbin asked. She didn't meet Lanoe's eye as he glanced over at her—probably nervous about meeting her new CO. Well, he knew that feeling, having gone through several dozen commanding officers in his time.

"Funny?" he asked. He needed to get the measure of this Harbin—of everyone onboard, before he could trust them. Maybe not even then.

"It's...well, that map is a lot more detailed than the one I'm used to."

Lanoe nodded and moved over to the pilot's position, grasping the back of the chair. "Mind if I have a look at the controls?" he asked. Before she could answer—protocol required her to say yes anyway—he activated her workstation and checked out the flight controls. They were all arranged properly, as far as he could tell. Everything according to Navy regulations. "Looks like you have it in hand," he told her. "I've never flown anything bigger than a Peltast-class destroyer, myself."

"The principles are the same," she told him. "We just make wider turns."

Lanoe nodded. He could work the helm himself if he needed to.

"We can be under way as soon as the loading is complete," Harbin told him. "Though we're still waiting on navigational orders."

Lanoe had some thoughts on that. Varma would have told these people nothing about their destination. It was up to him to set the course. Well, a little detour wouldn't hurt. He checked a wrist display and uploaded a set of coordinates.

Harbin watched as one of her displays updated. "Tuonela," she said. "Yes, sir. Travel time will be approximately nineteen hours."

He nodded. "Good. All right, ping me when we're ready to move." He nodded at the other two crew members—the copilot and the information officer—and headed back toward the elevator.

"What do you know about Harbin?" he asked, once the doors had shut.

Maggs rolled his shoulders. A kind of languid shrug. "She's seen combat. At the battle of Tlaloc, in fact, and you know how hard fought that one was."

Lanoe shook his head. "Tlaloc was after my time, but I'll take your word for it. So she knows how to fly. That's good." He reached for the controls of the elevator. "One more stop, and then I think I'm done with you," he said.

"Then by all means, let's away," Maggs replied.

Lanoe punched in a command to take them to the brig.

—◂✦▸—

By the time they reached the level of the brig, the Hoplite's provisioning was nearly complete, according to Maggs's wrist display.

"You don't like Harbin. You didn't care for my description of the pilots onboard," he said. "You can, of course, change out any of the crew you like," he said. "If you can find enough campaigners who are as old as you are, then—by all means. Fleet Admiral Varma picked all these people for you herself, though. I imagine they'll do."

"How many marines onboard?" Lanoe asked, not even looking at Maggs.

"A complement of twenty. Sadly, not all of them are veterans—some are raw recruits, straight out of Ceres—but you know how it is. The triple-headed eagle tends to run through our ground-fighting friends at an appalling rate." Most marines were drawn from the underclass of Earth society—the wretchedly poor, the undereducated, those mentally unfit for living in civilization. They tended to last no more than a few weeks once they reached actual combat.

"What about crew? How many people does it take to run a Hoplite?"

"Another fifteen," Maggs told him. "The ship's systems are largely automated, of course. Mostly the crew comprises gunners and engineering technicians. I have all their service records, if you're interested."

"I am. Send them to my address."

Maggs tapped a few virtual keys on his wrist display. "Fueling's done," he said. "Supplies, consumables, all the little luxuries of shipboard life already onboard. Just the last of the ammunition to load, then. You must be quite excited! A whole new command just for you."

Lanoe turned to look at him and Maggs fought the urge to flinch before that gaze.

You've got to admit, Maggsy, he has his reasons not to like you, his father's voice said inside his head.

Maggs wrote it off to the traditional lack of accountability in taste, and so on.

"The prisoners," Lanoe said. "The people you pulled off of Rishi when you came to collect me. Take me to them. Now."

"Right this way," Maggs said, and led Lanoe down a short corridor to the brig. Four marines with silvered helmets were stationed there, weapons at port arms.

Lanoe looked them over for a moment. "We're shipping out very soon," he told them. "Go and see to your bunks, make sure everything's secured for gravity."

It was impossible to tell if the marines glanced at each other to see if he was serious. He was giving them an order to abandon their post, despite the fact that there were prisoners onboard that needed to be guarded. Still, Lanoe was in charge. They did as they were told.

Lanoe went to the door of the sole occupied cell and brought up the display that showed its contents. The four prisoners were in there talking to each other, the Hellion quite animatedly. It might be impossible to pace in the absence of gravity, but the boy was making a go of it, kicking off one wall, then another.

"What's going to happen to them?" Lanoe asked.

"The three humans, you mean? It's rather a bother," Maggs told him. "They know too much to just be set free, so they'll have to be detained. I'm to take them to a holding facility on the moon."

"For how long?"

"Until whatever secrets they were privy to are no longer secret," Maggs said. He watched them through the display. On the journey from Rishi he'd read all their service records, learned a little about them. He felt distinctly sorry for them—though not so much he would actually try to help them. "Of course, they could just volunteer to have their memories cleaned. I doubt any of them will go for that option."

Lanoe put a hand against the door of the cell. Selective memory erasure was an imprecise procedure. Depending on how carefully it was done, they might walk away just not being able to remember a few days of incarceration—or they could end up unable to remember their own names, or even how to feed themselves. Nobody would take that risk if they didn't have to. "So they could be locked up for years," he said. He shook his head and turned to face Maggs again. "I was told I could pick my own crew for this mission."

"Of course."

"Then I want the three of them."

"Really? Very compassionate of you, I suppose. A waste of bunks, though. I suppose Candless, at least, has a decent service record. Though you know what they say about flight instructors." Maggs lowered his voice and tilted his head forward. "Afraid to fight."

Lanoe snorted. It almost sounded like a laugh. "Not her."

"And then, the other two—they're just cadets. They'll be underfoot the whole time."

"I choose my own crew," Lanoe said. Then he hit the virtual key that opened the door. As it slid open, Maggs was buffeted by the noise of shouted questions coming from inside. The Hellion came swarming toward the door as if he might attack, but Candless grabbed his leg and pulled him back.

"Lanoe?" she asked. "Lanoe—are you all right? We didn't know—"

"Sure," Lanoe told her. "Come on out of there. I've worked out the conditions of your release. It's...complicated. I'll explain once we're under way. Bury, Ginger—you two just got a brevet promotion."

"What?" the redheaded girl asked. Maggs had always thought

she looked like a dough-brained fool, but she seemed especially gormless just then. "What does that mean?"

"Call it early graduation." Lanoe tapped some keys on his wrist display. "You're now both officially ensigns, under my command. And my protection."

Lanoe gave Maggs a distinct look just then. Maggs made a point of not noticing.

"Come on, we're getting ready for a burn," Lanoe told the three of them. "Go find somewhere out of the way and stay there until I have a chance to talk to you," he said.

Bury, the Hellion, seemed intent on demanding more information then and there, but Candless merely grabbed his arm and pulled him along like the unruly student he was. They all disappeared into the elevator. Which just left one prisoner to account for.

Tannis Valk was curled into a ball at the far end of the cell, one foot anchored under a bench to keep him from floating away. He—it—looked up as Maggs and Lanoe stepped inside.

"Hey, Lanoe," the machine said. "Is it time?"

It was Maggs whom Lanoe addressed, however. "What's the plan for Valk?" he asked.

Maggs had been privy to the scans that had been run on Valk after he was brought onboard. He knew exactly what Valk really was. It made him shudder to think that they had once fought side by side.

"My orders," he said, glancing down at the black polarized helmet, "are to bring this thing in to be properly disposed of."

"You're going to erase him," Lanoe said.

"Well, yes. Of course. That's the law."

There were no viewports anywhere in the brig. No windows through which one could look down and see the scarred face of dear old planet Earth. Not as if anyone could forget what the *Universal Suffrage* had done down there.

The law was unyielding as iron. No drone, no computer, no machine would ever again be allowed to be smarter than a common house cat. Nor would they be allowed to use a weapon of any kind.

Valk, the thing that called itself Tannis Valk, broke every one of the Synthetic Instrumentality prohibitions. It would therefore be destroyed as soon and as thoroughly as possible. There wasn't much to discuss there. No legal loopholes, no wiggle room whatsoever.

Lanoe pulled himself along the floor of the cell to bring himself down to the level of the AI. "I'm sorry about this, big guy," he said.

"It's what I want. You know that," Valk told him.

"Sure." Lanoe pressed a recessed key set under Valk's collar ring. The AI's helmet melted and flowed away, revealing nothing underneath. No face. No head. The empty suit didn't exactly collapse, not in microgravity, but it definitely sagged. Lanoe picked it up, folded it over his arm, and kicked out of the cell.

"I'll take that," Maggs told him. He'd been given very specific orders not to let anyone else handle the suit. Just in case.

"I don't think so," Lanoe told him.

"I'm afraid I must insist."

Yet Lanoe still didn't hand over the suit.

He's up to something, Maggs heard his father say. *Watch him, Maggsy.*

"Commander," Maggs said, putting a little steel in his voice.

"I have a policy, Maggs. One I've always tried to hold to, no matter how much it annoyed me."

Maggs couldn't help himself. "Wash once a month, whether you need it or not?"

He expected an outburst. Maybe even violence. Instead, Lanoe gave him a rather nasty smile.

"I keep my friends close," Lanoe said. "And I keep my enemies where I can see their hands."

Then he grabbed Maggs and swung him around, tossing him into the detaining cell. Maggs tried to kick back out of the room but before he could, the door slammed shut in his face. He pounded on it, shouting Lanoe's name, over and over.

Even though he knew it wouldn't do any good.

A few minutes later he started to feel heavy and he sank to the floor. "No," he said, aloud. "No! You can't do this! I'm an officer! I am the son of an admiral!"

He knew what the sudden onset of gravity meant. It meant the Hoplite was moving. Heading off on its secret mission. With him locked up in its belly.

Chapter Twelve

Go, go! Come on! Let's go!" Sergeant Ehta shouted, waving her arm over the edge of the trench. Her marines clambered over the top, not nearly as fast as she would like—they never did. Thiess-Gruppe shells were falling all around their position, turning the night sky a dull and vicious red. Overhead, the last of the poly's air support was held back by a wing of Navy carrier scouts, which was the only reason her unit was still alive, but over the lip of the trench she could see the sparkling reports of particle rifles as TG ground troops swept through the ruins of the city.

She grabbed a broken piece of rebar and hauled herself up, shouting at her people to keep moving, to keep shooting. Not two meters away from her a lucky particle shot cut through Forster's silver helmet, lighting it up from the inside. She blinked away the dazzling light, only to see the dead man's skull burning, an afterimage seared into her retinas. She squinted hard and peered through the darkness to see her men and women leaping over anti-armor barriers and diving into cover in the shell of an old house. She tried to give them suppressing fire with her heavy recoilless rifle, each of her rounds throwing dirt and debris high into the air to screen the advance. As usual, she had no idea if it worked or not.

She jumped down into the flooded basement of the shattered house and looked for her people. Mestlez and Binah were down there already, crouching behind a pile of unrecognizable debris. Anselm tumbled down after her, nearly landing on top of her. She slapped him on the back and he crawled away, holding his rifle high to keep it out of the water.

An artillery shell hit the ground right outside their refuge, and a flurry of broken fibercrete and shattered glass pelted down on top of them. White, wet powder stuck to their suits and made them look like things dug up out of a grave.

She counted heads. Three of her people were missing, not including Forster. She knew where that Poor Bloody Marine was, dead on his face twenty meters back. She pinged cryptabs and saw that the missing were Rudoff, Banks, and Hutchens. She worked her wrist display, trying to get a fix on their locations. Rudoff and Banks showed up right away. No vital signs and their suits weren't moving at all. Both of them still back in the trench. They must have died before they could even get over the top. Hutchens didn't show up anywhere, which either meant his equipment had a fault—and it would hardly be the first time—or he'd been obliterated by a direct hit from a shell, so utterly removed from existence that his transponders didn't even register.

In the PBMs you learned not to worry about the dead. She switched her display to tactical and saw the local map slathered with green—estimated positions of enemy units, and way too many of them. Her orders had changed, and she grimaced as she saw that the city of Olmstead had been declared a loss. Three days of fighting, with no break in the action, and all for nothing. TG would never be able to hold the city—if they tried to entrench, the Navy would just bomb the place from orbit—but for today, at least, it was No Marines Allowed.

The good news was that the retreat had already been called. A transport was inbound, coming to lift them out. If they could reach the extraction point.

Ehta clambered up the basement wall, sticking her head out just a few centimeters to try to get a visual fix on their next objective. Particle fire lanced left and right around her but she ignored it.

There—dead ahead, no more than two hundred meters away. The only tall building still standing in the neighborhood. They needed to get to its roof so they could be picked up.

She ducked back down and looked at her people. They were too busy staying alive to look back. "Get ready to move on my mark," she told them. Gutierrez, her corporal, nodded and slapped the side of her rifle with one of her massive gloves.

Overhead, against the reddish sky, Ehta saw the Navy scouts go flashing past, their airfoils changing shape as they raced off to some new adventure. That had to mean they'd broken TG's air support. It was the best sign she was going to get.

"Now! Go!" she screamed, and they helped each other climb up out of the basement, even as the enemy opened up with a new salvo of particle fire. Some of her people were smart enough to shoot back. Ehta waved Gutierrez toward the extraction point while she lobbed rounds toward the TG positions. She could just see them over there, half a kilometer away. Poly troops—untrained, unmotivated. So poorly equipped they weren't even wearing proper suits, just mismatched pieces of plastic armor hastily stenciled with TG's green Maltese cross.

Their guns still worked. And there were a hell of a lot more of them than there were marines to go around.

At least she seemed to be holding them at bay. They stayed behind cover and didn't rush toward her as she advanced in the direction of the intact tower. They kept up a steady stream of fire but as long as Ehta kept moving, she could pretend like none of them could hit her.

She grabbed Binah by the arm—he'd started running the wrong way—and shoved him in the direction of the tower. One whole side of the building had been brought down by artillery, so it was easy enough to get inside. Away from enemy fire, for the moment. Inside Gutierrez was crouched in an open stairwell, rifle pointed up toward the higher floors. Ehta waved Mestlez to take point. Fire had gutted the place, leaving long black streaks up the walls. It looked like it might have been a residential building once but it would have been evacuated long ago.

Which might be why Mestlez freaked out when something moved in the rubble. She opened up with her rifle, glowing craters erupting in a ragged line across one wall, and then there was a shower of sparks and something white and the size of a human head bounced across the floor.

"Hold your damned fire," Gutierrez said. Binah grabbed the rifle out of Mestlez's hands and smacked Mestlez across the side of her helmet with the butt of his own weapon.

Ehta ran over and put her foot on the head-sized thing. "Nice work, marine," she said. "You just took out a concierge drone. If the enemy needs somebody to sign for a package they're going to be out of luck."

Binah doubled over with laughter. Anselm shouted for him to shut up.

"Come on. We need to get to the roof," Ehta told them.

"No! Shut up! Shut—can't you hear that?"

Ehta swung around to look at Anselm. She couldn't see his face through his silvered helmet, but his body language indicated he was terrified.

Then she heard it, too, and understood why. A crackling in her speakers, a wash of static and underneath it a pure tone, so high-pitched she could barely make it out.

"Earworm!" Gutierrez cried. "Shut down your comms! Shut down your comms!"

The communications gear in their suits would have already recognized the threat. Ehta checked her wrist display and found that her suit had switched off everything—from tactical feeds to transponders to intra-unit chatter, anything that could pick up an electromagnetic signal, just in case.

It didn't matter. By the time you actually heard an earworm it was already too late.

Dariau Cygnet lived well away from any population centers or agricultural regions, in a house far up the coast. Far from anyone who might bother him. Bullam felt like she was going to visit some enlightened mystic who lived in an uncharted land. She set her yacht down on the nearest municipal pad but she still had to take a drone cart three kilometers just to get within walking distance of his house. She was sweating by the time she arrived.

The house was built into the side of a mountain that overlooked a deep fjord, a finger of water that jutted well inland from a sea that gently bobbed and plashed, almost perfectly black except where it reflected the house's lights. At the bottom of the cliff a little dock jutted out into the water. An old man was there, wrapped up tight in a thick coat. He had a minder unrolled on the dock's railing and it was manifesting three crowded displays that held his attention. He didn't even look up as her footfalls creaked on the boards of the dock.

"Hello," she said. "Hello? I have an appointment to see M. Cygnet. Are you his...?" She struggled to find the right word. *Secretary? Security guard?* The old man looked like a sailor waiting for his ship to come in.

He didn't speak, or even look up. He was lost in his displays.

Out on the water she could see dozens of tiny boats—toys, none of them longer than her arm. The old man's displays controlled them as they tacked back and forth across the gently heaving water. As she watched, one of them turned and a miniature gun on its deck discharged, firing a projectile. It crashed through the sails of one of the other boats, knocking it over on its side. Three more of the boats came rushing in to the rescue.

"His," the man said, finally. "Yes. I'm his." There was no real inflection to the words.

"Should I—? I'm expected, maybe I should just—?"

"You're his, too."

She leaned against the rail to get a better look at the old man's face. He didn't turn away or indicate discomfort as she interfered with his displays. She thought his eyes might be made of glass, there was so little intelligence or life in them.

Out on the water one of the tiny boats had caught fire. The orange light flickered along the dock's railing.

The old man jerked his head to one side. Bullam looked over and saw a flight of stairs heading up to the house.

She guessed she had her answer.

Inside the house she passed through a series of quiet rooms where the sound of her own soft shoes touching the floor seemed like a violation. Rooms full of tasteful, elegant furniture, spun wood and real leather, candles in long holders and beautiful wrought iron-work stretching like ivy across the walls. No one came forward to lead her to her destination, nor did the house seem to have any drones to assist her. She'd thought she saw a light on in a room near the back of the house, so she headed in that direction.

When she found Dariau Cygnet he was sitting alone in a room made of glass, his tail flicking against the back of a long divan.

"Come in," he said.

Bullam hesitated in the doorway. The room beyond looked out over the sea, over dark water crashing against dark rocks. It seemed to hover in the night, as if the doorway opened into thin air. There was a floor ahead of her, she knew that perfectly well. On a conscious level anyway. Yet the room—its walls, its ceiling, its floor—was almost perfectly transparent. The divan and a few end tables seemed to float unsupported by anything. If she took another step, her hindbrain told her, she would fall down into the rocky fjord. She would fall into the chilly water far below, be battered by the waves—

She took the step. The floor supported her weight just fine. It was made of spun carbon, obviously, as hard as diamond but with much greater clarity. Perfectly safe. She hurried across the room toward the divan, trying very hard not to look down. She was not a large woman but she was disproportionately aware of her weight as she made her way across. When she reached the divan she grabbed its arm and she saw her knuckles turn white. She had not yet been asked to sit.

A sly little smile played across Cygnet's mouth. "Vertigo can be a useful negotiating tactic. People have trouble lying when their hearts are already pounding. Go ahead and sit. We need to talk."

"M. Cygnet," she said, levering herself into the divan, resisting the urge to tuck her feet under her so they weren't touching the invisible floor, "I want to begin by saying that—"

"You let Aleister Lanoe get away."

"Yes," Bullam said. No point in denying it.

"You got two of our best pilots killed." Cygnet shrugged.

"Good people, I'm sure," she said.

"One of them was a drug addict. The other one had a genetic predisposition to schizophrenia," Cygnet told her. "You don't know all the details of my special project. For a long time now I've been worried about the quality of the troops we use. When we have to fight the Navy, we end up sending poorly trained conscripts. Utterly unsuitable people. I've been working on changing that. For the last eight years, every time the Navy or the Marines or the Neddies cashier someone—after every court-martial, every disciplinary discharge, every time one of them gets fired, for lack of a better term—I scoop them up. Give them a second chance. If they agree to wear the hexagon, all their sins can be forgiven. On the quiet, of course."

"The pilots I sent after Lanoe—"

"Four of Centrocor's best," he said.

Bullam's mouth went dry. "If you like, I can have my resignation drafted within the hour."

Cygnet watched her face for a long while, perhaps savoring her anguish. Eventually his eyes drifted away and he favored her with a toothy smile. "Don't be fucking stupid."

The obscenity made her flinch. People—cultured people—did not use that word anymore.

"If I fired everyone who ever made a mistake," Cygnet told her, "I wouldn't have any employees left. No, M. Bullam. I don't want you to resign."

"Thank you, M. Cygnet, I—"

"It turns out I have a second chance with your name on it.

There's a very old saying in business," he said, as if she hadn't spoken at all. "That there is no such thing as a crisis that isn't also an opportunity."

"I've heard it," she said. Even to her own ears her voice sounded small and weak. Like the chirping of a mouse.

"Complete horseshit, of course," Cygnet swore. He glanced at her, as if trying to determine if his casual profanities were shocking her. She forced herself to fake a flinch, as if she'd never heard the word spoken aloud before. "Though in this case maybe it applies. If you'd succeeded, we could have missed out on something. The Navy scooped Lanoe up on Rishi—right out of our clutches—and took him to Earth. Now he's headed for a planet called Tuonela. Do you know it?"

"Not personally," Bullam said. "It's a war zone. One of Soltexon's planets, right? But ThiessGruppe tried to take it from them. The Sector Wardens stepped in to keep the peace, and the Navy—"

"Is currently pacifying the place," Cygnet said. "And by all accounts they're making a real hash of it."

"They've sent Lanoe there?" Bullam asked, confused. Not least by why she was being told all of this. "I suppose he could be useful—he has a habit of winning wars. But he's not on their active list. He retired from his commission years ago."

"Yes. Which makes me very interested in what he's up to," Cygnet told her. "Some kind of secret mission. If we'd captured him at Rishi—and this is where the opportunity comes in—we wouldn't know about this."

"What do we know about his mission?" Bullam asked.

"I don't think it will surprise you to learn that we have . . . friends placed very highly in the Admiralty. People who can do us favors. People who know things. In fact, for the last ten years or so, the Navy hasn't made any significant move I didn't know about in advance. Until now."

Bullam frowned, because she assumed that was what was expected of her.

"I couldn't find out what his orders are. Not the details anyway.

He's doing something so secret, so very, very sensitive, that even some of the admirals are being kept in the dark. That tells me it's very important. At enormous cost I was able to learn that the Navy is attempting to make an alliance with some other group."

"One of the other polys?" she asked.

"Perhaps. Or maybe there's a new player on the board. Whoever it is, they're powerful enough that the Navy—that Earth—is willing to put a lot of resources into making contact with them. Perhaps powerful enough that they could tip the balance. For years we've managed to hold on to our planets because the Navy wasn't big enough to challenge our authority. Believe me, they would crush us, if they could. If the balance of power should change... No more Centrocor."

"We can't let that happen," Bullam said.

"No. So as for you, Ashlay—your job hasn't changed in the slightest. I still want Aleister Lanoe. I want him alive. I need to find out what he's after. Perhaps we can make a deal with this secret power ourselves. That would be nice. If not, we can at least keep them from allying with the Navy."

"I'll leave at once," Bullam said. "We're all in this together."

"I'm so very glad to hear that, Ashlay. You know, I've always been fond of you. I've always thought you had so much potential."

"That's—that's very gratifying to hear," she said.

"I always like an underdog. There were plenty of people who told me you couldn't do this job. With your disease, and all. They said I was a fool to keep promoting you. I told them that your disease actually made you work harder. It made you more loyal, more dedicated. And more ambitious."

Bullam looked down and smiled at her lap. "I won't fail you," she said.

"No, of course not," Cygnet replied. "Though...perhaps you could use some help."

"I'm...sorry?"

"You did let Lanoe slip through your fingers. Twice. I think maybe this job is too much for you alone. So I've asked someone to come by, someone who can help you. Do you see, Ashlay? Do you see how I take care of you?"

"I'm…I'm…" Someone to help her. Someone to watch her, he meant. Someone to be there to fix things if she botched them. Someone to supervise her. Inside her head, Ashlay Bullam screamed in rage and frustration and shame. Outwardly, she nodded prettily and said, "I'm very grateful."

—⚡—

"Oh hell, oh hell, oh hell, it's hell, it's hell, I'm in hell, I'm in—"

Ehta could barely hear the screams. Her heart was thundering in her chest, her pulse beating in her temples—she could feel it in her fingertips, she could feel her fingers swelling up, bloating, throbbing to the beat.

Her boards were all lit up red, warning lights coming on across her comms panel, her weapons panel showing faults everywhere, her thrusters overheating and that was more red lights, collision alarms blaring red red red—

No. No, damn it. Hell no.

She felt weightless, felt herself tumbling through infinite space. There was no falling because there was nowhere to fall, no ground to stop her, she would keep falling forever, falling through nothing, through vacuum, through the plane of the galaxy, tumbling, spinning, falling, and she was screaming except—except—except—

She wasn't the one screaming, it was—it had to be—

No. No damn way was she going to let this happen again. She forced herself to suck in a deep breath. She was lying on her back, on a floor strewn with rubble. Her helmet was down and she had her fingers dug deep into her ears, painfully deep. She was looking up at a ceiling scorched by some long-past fire.

Red lights blinked on, one by one, up on that ceiling. Warning chimes sounded. Her communications laser reported nonfunctional. Her PBWs were down. Her airfoils were nonresponsive. Her fuel supply was depleted. Her ammunition reserves were—

No. "No," she said, aloud, her voice sounding far away.

She fought it, fought back from that place, that nightmare place she went to when she slept, even years later. Even years after the last time she'd been in the cockpit of a fighter.

Ehta had been a pilot, once. A long time ago. She'd been good at it. She'd flown every mission they gave her, often taking back-to-back patrols for weeks straight. She'd spent more time in the cockpit than anywhere else. Over time, little by little, she'd started having bad dreams. Dreams where her fighter broke down around her, her panels and boards lighting up red. Warning chimes ringing just behind her left ear. The dreams had spread to her waking life.

She couldn't fly anymore. It was why she'd joined the Marines, so she didn't have to fly. She wasn't flying now. She focused on the ceiling, stared hard at it until the red lights faded away.

The chimes kept sounding. Except it wasn't the sound she expected. It wasn't the soft but insistent chime of a collision warning. It was the buzzing, pulsing tone of the earworm.

She fought her way back to focus. Her vision kept swirling around and her ears were still ringing with the sound, but she could just about make out where she was. It took her a while to make sense of it.

She wasn't in the apartment tower anymore. She wasn't on the front at all—she could see tents all around, see marines running through muddy alleys between lines of low structures.

She was back in camp. She was back in her own camp. She looked down and saw she was lying on a stretcher. Hellfire—she'd lost some time there, hadn't she? The others—Gutierrez and the others—must have gotten her out. Gotten her and Anselm into the evac transport, brought them home. She didn't remember any of it. Just—just red lights, red warning lights, and that sound—

"How many hours?" someone shouted. She turned and saw a doctor flanked by a pair of medical drones. He was shouting at her. "How many hours has it been since the earworm infection started?" He asked again, slower, pronouncing each word carefully as if she couldn't be expected to understand basic English.

She wanted to answer but her suit's displays were still shut down. "I don't know. I..." she tried.

The doctor scowled and ran over toward another stretcher, a few meters away. Anselm was half in, half out of it, his legs flopping on the ground. He was still screaming, but she could barely hear him over the screeching noise in her head. "Get the program running—get him restrained. Now!" the doctor shouted. "How long? Exactly?" he asked Ehta. "We have six hours tops to help him before the trauma sets in and—"

"I don't know!" Ehta said. "I don't know—I can't switch on my displays."

"Where's your officer?" The doctor checked a display of his own. "Where's Second Lieutenant Holmes?"

"He got it two days into the patrol," Ehta said.

Orderlies held Anselm down while a display lit up in front of his face, blue and red and green lights playing over his eyes and his cheeks. He was still screaming.

"What was that about your displays?" the doctor asked.

It was Gutierrez who answered. She was standing right behind Ehta. "The sergeant heard it, too. She heard it—but then she kind of came out of it, she stopped screaming—"

The doctor's eyes went wide. "That's not possible. Damn it, somebody restrain her, too." Ehta tried to fight but Binah and Gutierrez grabbed her arms and forced her to lie down. A drone came bobbing up to her and started spraying light in her face. Geometric patterns bloomed all around her, blocks and circles and complex three-dimensional shapes that rotated and twisted as she looked at them.

"Sergeant, I don't know how you're lucid right now," the doctor said, his face obscured by a pulsing heptagon. "You were hit by a supernormal stimulus. Do you know what that means?" He didn't wait for her to answer. "There are certain sounds hardwired into the human brain. Things our primitive ancestors needed to listen for, like the roar of a tiger, right? You hear that sound, you're going to jump. You don't think about it, because if you take the time to think, the tiger will already be on your back with its claws in your guts. It's just a reflex."

"Anselm—is Anselm—" she tried to say, but he was ignoring her. Lecturing her.

"A supernormal stimulus is a sound that activates that same reflex—except moreso. It's not the sound of a tiger yowling. It's more like the Platonic ideal of a tiger's yowl. It's that sound of death, distilled and magnified until it sends your brain into a bad loop of fear. Once you hear that sound you can't unhear it. It's cycling through your short-term memory, playing over and over again. If we don't break that cycle, your brain will try to code it into a long-term memory. If that happens—"

"I know about stress disorders," Ehta said. In front of her a ring of dancing squares split into triangles and disappeared. "What the hell am I looking at?"

"We need to get your brain occupied with other tasks, to disrupt the memory formation process. Otherwise you could be looking at flashbacks, at night terrors for the rest of your life—in a best-case scenario. Don't fight this, just try to organize the shapes however it feels right, okay? Come on, Sergeant, you need to look at the shapes."

"Damn it, I told you—"

"Do what the doc says, Sergeant!" Gutierrez told her. She could just see her corporal through the dancing colors. She looked terrified.

Ehta forced herself to calm down, to look at a couple of blue star shapes that orbited around her head. Blue stars. Like the commendations they gave to ace pilots. And there were red squares, too, red squares all around her, red squares like the warning lights on a weapons board, and—suddenly there were red squares everywhere, the program responding to her eye movements, showing her what it thought she wanted to see—red lights—red—red warning lights—she started hearing high-pitched chimes—

No. No, she wouldn't let this happen again. She couldn't. She found one last shape that wasn't a red square. A lavender oval. She forced herself to stare at it. To make it fold in half, then in half again. She found she could make it split into multiple conic sections if she concentrated.

"Good," the doctor said. She could see his face nodding behind the ovals and paraboloids. "Good, your numbers are coming down. I'm showing a strong projection from your infralimbic cortex. That's good, keep it up. Good—"

She looked over to her side, toward Anselm. He was screaming—but that was just background noise now. She saw the shapes rotating around his head, saw them change and darken. "Are—are his shapes supposed to look like that?" she asked.

"Don't worry about him," the doctor told her. "Worry about yourself."

But how could she look away? The shapes around Anselm were dark, spiky things, just scribbles of lines in the air. They weren't changing so much as growing, filling more of the space around his head. White triangles stabbed in from the sides, like teeth gnashing at his face.

Through the shapes she could just see his eyes. Rolling like an animal's, white all around the irises. Eyes of pure terror.

"Is he—is he—"

The doctor stood up and shoved his body between them, so she couldn't see Anselm anymore.

Around her the lavender shapes started to wink out, one by one. Green triangles appeared in front of her and she felt an urge to make them join together, to gather them into an icosahedron. She tried looking over at Anselm, but they wouldn't let her. He was one of her squad, damn it. He was her responsibility—

"Spike him," someone said from behind the doctor. "He's done for."

In front of her the yellow triangles just wouldn't stick together. They kept flying apart, no matter how hard she tried to join them.

Abruptly, Anselm stopped screaming.

———※———

Cygnet's tail jumped up in the air and its tip shook back and forth for a moment. It must have been some kind of signal, because someone new entered the room. Bullam looked up and saw that it was the old man, the one she'd seen down at the dock playing with toy boats.

She could see him better now, in the well-lit room. She could see the tiny scars that crisscrossed his cheeks. Any competent doctor could have gotten rid of those—he must have kept them, perhaps as tokens of some old battle. She saw how thin he was, saw his fine, wispy hair. His jaw was set as if his teeth were clamped tightly together, but what really caught her attention was the look in his eyes.

There wasn't one.

There was no spark of intelligence there. No human emotion. He didn't look like he was blind, nor did he seem to be under the influence of any drug she knew. Instead it was like he was a mannequin. An imitation of a human being.

As he walked into the room he seemed to be striding on nothing at all—on open air. Yet it didn't seem to bother him. He came and stood in front of them, his arms hanging loose at his sides.

"M. Bullam," Cygnet said, "I'd like you to meet Captain Shulkin. I was talking earlier of the pilots and such that we've recruited from the Navy. The castoffs, the misfits they don't want anymore. Our own private force. I told you how rare and valuable they are. The Captain here is the star of that particular show. He's a genuine war hero! The man who beat back the Establishment at Jehannum."

Bullam considered standing and reaching to shake the old man's hand. The thought of getting off the divan made her head spin. "M. Shulkin," she said, "it's a privilege to meet you."

Shulkin didn't nod. He didn't even look directly at her.

Bullam frowned. "I'm sorry. I don't mean to be rude. But are you well, M. Shulkin?"

"He's fine," Cygnet said. "Absolutely fine. Just had some work done, is all. Navy personnel are prone to a certain kind of mental illness, I don't know if you know this—they would say he got the wind up him. It's a rather colorful way of describing combat stress. It happens to a lot of their people, and it affects them in a variety of ways—some of them can't sleep, for instance, or they can become unreasonably aggressive. Alternatively, prone to cowardice.

Captain Shulkin tried to fly his destroyer into a red dwarf star. Psychotically suicidal, they tell me. Compulsively so. He had to be relieved of duty."

Bullam shuddered, despite herself.

"Luckily for him the Navy has a long history of treating such illness. It's a special kind of optogenetic treatment where they use lasers to reduce dendritic connections. They burned away part of your brain, didn't they, Captain?"

Shulkin's face didn't harden. He just nodded, his chin twitching toward his shoulder. "Took the parts I didn't need," he said. "Made me operational again."

"Don't worry about offending him," Cygnet said. "He's quite past that kind of thing. He doesn't have any fear, either, which is what they were after, I suppose. What he does still have, what *we* prize in him, is his experience. His knowledge of tactics is legendary. He was one of the brightest officers in the Fleet, in his day."

A sudden flash of light appeared in Shulkin's eyes, as if something buried very deep was trying to signal the outside world. "I can still fight," he said.

"Oh, I believe it," Cygnet replied. Turning back to Bullam, he said, "I want to find out what Aleister Lanoe is up to." His tail draped itself across her shoulder. "I want you and the Captain to go and fetch him for me. Before he makes contact with this mysterious new ally."

When Ehta finally got her suit rebooted—when the techs were sure they'd erased the earworm from all of her systems—she was discharged from the medical tent. The doctors all lined up to watch her go. They couldn't believe that she'd made it.

There was no word on Anselm. This was just a forward operating base, and the medical facilities were only set up to handle emergency procedures. Anyone stable enough to be moved was taken fifty kilometers back behind the lines, to a place where specialists could treat them without having to listen to bombs raining down outside. Anselm had been heavily sedated and loaded in a transport and that was the last she'd seen of him.

She wanted to know more. She owed it to her squad to find out what happened to him. When her wrist display lit up, though, and she reached to make an official inquiry, she was surprised to find that new orders were already waiting for her. She was to report to her CO for immediate reassignment.

The officers' tents were on the far side of the camp, grouped around the landing pads—the thinking among the enlisted was that the officers wanted to be able to be the first ones to evacuate when the Navy finally gave up on Tuonela. She passed by a half-dozen troop transports and ducked under the airfoil of a Z.VI that was in the middle of refueling. There was a funny-looking ship sitting on the pad directly outside her major's tent, a crescent-shaped flying-wing kind of thing she didn't recognize. It had the three-headed eagle on its fuselage, though, so she ignored it and pushed through the weather field of the tent.

It was warm inside. Mist had condensed on the sides of tea glasses and some of the flat displays that lined the walls of the tent, and the noncom who came to meet her was actually sweating. She always forgot how cold Tuonela could get—it was always the same comfortable temperature inside her suit. The noncom gave her a weird look, then gestured her over to his workstation. "How are you still standing?" he asked.

She realized she couldn't remember his name. Well, it was his job to keep track of her, not the other way round. "The medicos checked me out and let me go," she told him. "I'm fine. I got a little dose of an earworm, but—"

He shook his head. "You know that isn't how it works. You get hit with one of those things, you don't recover. Damnation, Ehta, I already had you pegged for medical rotation, then I see your name pop up on my active roster—you're hard as a box of nails, aren't you?" He laughed and sat her down in a folding chair. "Well, it's over now. You're going home, you lucky bastard."

"Home?" Ehta asked.

"Sure. You're being invalided out on a full medical discharge. Well, I suppose nobody can call you a malingerer. You've been a PBM for how long now? Nearly three years? Compared to most of the outflow I process, that's making old bones."

"Wait—I don't get this. I'm fine," she said. "I came over here for reassignment. I'm fine." She realized she was repeating herself. "I need to get back to my squad, they're all waiting to hear about Anselm—"

"Ehta," he said, smirking at her, "don't you get it? Maybe that earworm hit you harder than you thought. You're done. The Planetary Brigade Marines thank you for your service. Let me send you some information. You're eligible for half pay for the rest of the year, and of course you'll get medical and substance abuse rehabilitation benefits. The Marines take care of their own, you damned fortunate so-and-so."

"You're—you're cashiering me," Ehta said.

His smile was warm and genuine. She really wanted to knock it off his face.

"I'm fine." She shook her head. "Listen, you—you don't understand. This is my career. This is my life. I've been fighting since I was a child."

His smile fell off his face. She didn't notice, not at first, that he wasn't looking at her anymore.

"It can't just be over. Not like this. It can't just . . . stop, with no warning!"

The noncom jumped up out of his chair and stood up ramrod straight, his eyes focused on nothing. She thought maybe he was having a fit.

"Damn you, this can't be how it ends!"

"It doesn't have to be," someone said, behind her.

No. She recognized that voice.

She rose slowly from her chair, and turned around. "Commander," she said.

"Hello, Ehta," Aleister Lanoe said to her.

Chapter Thirteen

This is ridiculous," Bury said. "We might as well still be stuck in the brig!"

They'd been let out of a cell and moved to a small section of the ship reserved for fighter pilots, just a ring of coffin-sized bunks surrounding a common wardroom and galley. Told to stay in that area and not wander. With no explanation whatsoever. It was unacceptable.

Instructor Candless—no, he needed to call her Lieutenant Candless now, he remembered—was as infuriatingly calm as ever. She and Ginger were strapped in around a microgravity table in the wardroom, sucking on tubes of green paste—the best food available in their stores. The two of them were totally calm, acting like this kind of thing happened all the time.

Bury wouldn't stand for it. He was destined for bigger things than just keeping his head down and waiting for orders. There had to be more to life in the Navy than just that. "I refuse to just stay put," he sneered.

Candless turned and looked at him with those eyes of hers, the ones that seemed to look right through him. "Ensign, you should sit down right now and be quiet. It is my firm belief that Commander Lanoe will explain everything," she said, sounding as if she actually meant it. "We just have to wait a little longer."

"It's been days!" Bury said. "I need to get out of here."

Candless frowned, but then she nodded and looked away from him. "Very well. If that's what you *need*. Go see what the inside of a Hoplite-class cruiser looks like. I'm sure it'll be educational."

Bury kicked off a wall and pulled his way through a hatch, out into the long corridor beyond.

"Just don't touch anything," Candless called after him.

The Hellion grunted in frustration and shoved himself at speed down the corridor. It was no more than two meters wide, so he kept caroming off the soft plastic walls, but every time he did he kicked again and gained more speed. Soon he was in the long axial corridor that ran the length of the ship.

With no idea of what he actually wanted to do. Just get some exercise, maybe. Burn off some of his frustration.

The corridors and cramped little chambers that made up the Hoplite were silent except for a background sound of machinery ticking over. The discreet sighs of the ventilation system, the high-pitched whines of displays turning themselves on and off. There was something missing from that quiet, something it took him a while to put his finger on.

Eventually, though, he worked it out. He could hear the ship all around him, hear it going through its autonomous motions. What he couldn't hear—anywhere—was a human voice. No sound of someone coughing quietly, or humming to themselves. No soft thuds of people kicking off of walls to move themselves around.

Once he'd noticed the human absence, he couldn't hear anything else.

The corridors and compartments of the Hoplite were narrow and cramped. The dozens of people who should have been aboard would have filled up that claustrophobic space. Instead the emptiness positively echoed.

He made his way back through the gunnery bays, forests of tubes and pipes glittering with control displays. Empty. Back toward the engines, where the ship's background hum became a constrained roar, as the life support systems worked hard to shed excess heat from the big toroidal fusion reactor. A crew of engineers ought to have been back there, massaging the power plants, keeping them in trim.

Nobody.

He found a command-level control station. Just a square of gray plastic mounted at the center of a machine shop. He waved his hand over it and a display lit up, showing him a schematic view of the engines. Everything looked in good order—no red lights showing, no warning chimes sounding. That wasn't what he was looking for, though. Instead he queried the display as to where all the technicians had gone.

A crew manifest came up, a list of names with links to service records, communications logs, and biosensor readings. Except that all the data showed the technicians weren't currently onboard.

Well, where the hell had they gone, then?

The command-level display had access to the ship's entire contingent. He ran through lists of marines. All missing. Bridge crew. Gone. He found Ginger and Candless, fine, he knew where they were. He tapped a link for LANOE, ALEISTER (COMMANDING OFFICER).

The display blinked an error message at him.

<NOT FOUND>

Bury frowned and tried to remember the name of the other one, the big pilot with the black helmet who had briefly shared their cell. VAUK, TALIS, he typed. The display corrected it for him automatically.

VALK, TANNIS (CIVILIAN ADVISOR). Bury sighed and tapped the link.

His eyes went wide at the result.

<DECEASED>

Hellfire, what had happened to that guy? He and Lanoe had seemed pretty tight, back on Rishi. What in the hell of all flames was going on?

It would have to wait while he figured out the most pressing mystery. The three of them, the two cadets and their instructor, were apparently alone onboard the Hoplite. Lanoe and the entire crew, and all of the marines, had left the ship en masse. With no explanation at all.

"There has to be someone else onboard," he said to the display. "They must have left somebody to keep us from crashing into a star or something. Show me all biosensor readings for the whole ship."

The display blinked and then resolved into a ghostly line drawing of the Hoplite as a whole. It showed him his own data, a speck of blue light near the engines, and then two more dots for Candless and Ginger. Otherwise, there was only one dot on the entire cruiser, one heartbeat being monitored at all, and it showed up in orange. A warning color. Bury tapped at it.

MAGGS, AUSTER (LT, NEF)
<ALL HEALTH TELEMETRY OK>
LOCATION: DETAINING CELL B

There was plenty more data if he wanted it—this lieutenant's service record, pictures of him, whatever—but Bury had already kicked away from the terminal. Headed to find some damned answers for a change.

>——<

Someone brought him a chair. Lanoe shrugged and sat down. He didn't plan on being in the tent for very long, but he knew enough about life on a military base to take whatever creature comforts were offered. There wouldn't be many.

Major Sorensen fidgeted with a minder, rolling it up and then spreading it out again on his desk. "Your credentials are, well, impeccable," he said. "I'm not going to argue with that."

The major would be a very small man if he weren't wearing a bulky marine suit. He had the pinched face and squinting eyes of a scholar rather than a warrior. When Lanoe showed up and started making demands he'd blustered a bit. That stopped as soon as he pinged Lanoe's cryptab.

Fleet Admiral Varma had not, of course, signed some kind of

blank check for Lanoe's use. The authorizations and clearances would all be encrypted, with no data trail leading back to Varma or anyone else in the Admiralty. Yet it was clear that while he was on this mission, he would find very few closed doors.

"It's just, and this is a bit...well, sticky," the major said. "You see, she was hit by an earworm on her last patrol and...you do know what that means?"

"Earworm? Never heard of it," Lanoe told him.

The major's lips pulled back from his teeth. It made him look as if his face were trying to crawl off his skull. "I daresay not. I saw from your service record that you were last on active duty at the end of the Establishment Crisis. Well, thank you for your service, of course. But warfare has come some way since then. I don't mind telling you things have grown a bit harsher than you probably remember. For the longest time we've had the better of the polys in terms of technology—well, they're catching up. The earworm is one of their more pernicious inventions, and it leaves people, er, unfit to serve. In fact—"

"Maybe," Lanoe said, "we shouldn't talk about her in the third person like this. You know, when she's in the room."

The major slid his eyes sideways to where Ehta stood at attention, just to one side of his desk.

"Of course," he said.

"Ehta," Lanoe said, "it's good to see you again."

"Sir," she told him.

He resisted the urge to sigh. He could have been kinder to her, back when they last saw each other. He had needed pilots back then, and she'd signed on—but only because she'd been too afraid to tell him she couldn't fly anymore. He'd been...angry. Zhang had tried to temper his mood, but still he'd probably said some things he regretted.

"I need your help," he told her. "You don't owe me a damned thing, but it's important." He didn't want to have to pull rank on her but he would if he had to. "I need marines. A squad of them, at least. Preferably ones with shipboard experience—if you can find some people who know how to work Naval guns, that would be very helpful. A couple of neddies wouldn't hurt, either. But the crucial thing—and the reason I'm coming to you—is that I need people who you trust."

Her brow scrunched up as if she didn't understand what he was asking. "You want a list of names," she said.

"I want a team," he told her. "And I want you leading it. Good people who can work together. Career people." That would be the hardest part, maybe. Plenty of people joined the Marines—those who couldn't make a living any other way, those on the run from something or someone back on Earth or the solar system colonies. People who signed on intending to make a life of it, though, career soldiers, were rare. "People with no connections to the polys. Specifically people who have never been associated with Centrocor."

Ehta glanced at the major, her CO. "Sir, may I speak candidly?" she asked.

"Yes, yes," the major said, raising a dismissive hand.

"Lanoe, you're asking me to come on another of your incredibly dangerous adventures. You want me to drag my own people—good people, comrades of mine—along for the ride. And I'm guessing I don't get to hear any details before I say yes or no."

"Sure," Lanoe said.

Ehta's mouth pursed and he knew she was trying not to roll her eyes. "But I keep my rank and I keep working. If I stay here, Major Sorensen, sir—I get rotated out. A medical discharge."

"Correct," the major said.

Ehta nodded. "Very good, sirs. I'll start compiling a list tonight and have something for you tomorrow morning."

"I need the list in an hour," Lanoe told her.

Ehta shrugged.

The major, sadly, wasn't as compliant. "Now, hold on a tick, Commander," he said. "Need I remind you we're fighting a war here? You're talking about stripping out some of my best people. Scooping them up and running off with them! I have objectives to meet, by hell! I know you have friends in high places, but—"

"I'll replace anyone I take," Lanoe told him. "You might even come out ahead on this deal."

The major's face went through a complex and extraordinary change. Anger turned to confusion turned to hope to greedy excitement to suspicion in the space of a few moments. "Ah. How exactly are you going to accomplish that?"

Lanoe bent over his wrist display and tapped a few virtual keys. Lieutenant Harbin, the pilot from the Hoplite, lifted the flap of the tent and stepped inside. "You wanted me, sir?"

"Lieutenant, this is Major Sorensen. He's your new commanding officer."

"Sir," she said, and he could see her whole body tense. "Sir—I'm not sure I understand. Was there some problem with my piloting?"

"None."

Harbin let out a breath she'd been holding. "Then—but. This officer is a marine, sir."

"Ahem," the major said, looking a bit peeved.

"I meant no offense." Even though she probably had. Naval personnel had a pretty low opinion of marines, on the whole. Just as hawks look down on wolves. "It's just—I'm a Navy pilot," Harbin pointed out. "Not a marine. Myself. I don't understand how I can be seconded to a marine unit." She looked around, as if searching for someone to validate her position. She definitely didn't get anything from Ehta.

"A theater like Tuonela needs a lot of air support," Lanoe said. "I'm sure you'll find work here to suit you. And you won't be alone. I'm reassigning the entire crew and marine contingent from our ship. My ship, that is."

"You—you can't be serious," Harbin said. "You're turning us out? All of us? Just dumping us here, in this—this war zone?"

He understood her panic. The crew and marines Varma had given him were handpicked people, probably all up-and-coming elite Naval personnel expecting bright futures. Some of them probably had political connections to earn the sinecure of working on such an important mission. As of now he had turned them all into grunts in the middle of some of the nastiest fighting currently going. They would have a hard time adjusting.

He found it very hard to feel sorry for them.

"When you joined the Navy, you signed on to fight," he pointed out. He turned to look at the major. "That's about twenty people rated for pilot work, a full squad of neddies from our engineering department, and twenty-five more marines, to replace the people I'm taking from you. Do we have a deal?"

—◆—

"You seem upset," Bury suggested.

"I'm being held against my will. Of course I'm agitated," Lieutenant Maggs said.

Bury watched him carefully. The prisoner drifted around his cell, occasionally coming close to touching one of the walls and then at the last minute pushing away again, as if it irritated him even to touch the padding. He was dressed in a fancy suit—maybe he was worried about getting it dirty.

The display that showed the interior of the cell included a text panel listing Auster Maggs's service record. It didn't explain what he was doing in there—there were no charges listed against him. Bury had heard him talking to Lanoe, back on Rishi, though. It had sounded like there was bad blood between the two of them. Which made Bury wonder if this was all on the up-and-up.

"I suppose you want me to let you out," the Hellion said. Cautiously.

Maggs couldn't see him. The display was strictly one-way. Still, Maggs seemed to peer through the door of the cell, his eyes narrowing. "Hmm. Intriguing. But no. You would just get in a ridiculous amount of trouble," he said.

"Kind of you to think of me," Bury said, sarcastically.

"Anyway, you said we were in orbit around Tuonela? I hardly want to go there. They're having a war down there. Ghastly places, wars. No, you shouldn't let me out of here, even if I am crawling out of my own skin. I'll just have to wait to see what Lanoe has in store for me. Just like everybody else."

"He hasn't told us anything," Bury said.

"No, and he won't—until he literally has to. That's how he operates." Maggs pushed off another wall. Maybe he was just trying to get some exercise.

"Is there anything you want? Are you hungry?"

"Some cologne would be nice. And razor paper. I'm going to go mad if I can't groom myself properly." He stroked his chin and his upper lip. "Though perhaps I'll just turn this crisis into an opportunity. I've always wanted to see what I'd look like with a proper mustache."

"Seriously? That's what you want, toiletries?"

"Oh, I could ask for a great deal more, but I know I won't get it. I suppose I'm just grateful to have someone to talk to. You're Bury, yes? I recognize your voice. You were one of the cadets we picked up at Rishi."

"And held against *our* will," Bury pointed out.

"Yes. Terribly sorry about that. Orders from above that couldn't be quibbled with—I'm sure you understand."

"I'm sure I don't," Bury told him.

The Lieutenant didn't respond to that. "Bury," he said, as if he were trying to remember where he'd heard the name before. "Bury. Yes. You were at Rishi on a full scholarship, isn't that right?"

"How do you know about my scholarship?"

"I saw your records from the flight school. Excellent marks, though your instructor seemed to feel you suffered from hubris."

"She never understood me, never even asked if I—"

"Oh, young man," Maggs interrupted, laughing. "Do not get me wrong. Hubris is good. You need hubris to be a pilot. To fly into a formation of enemies and think you might actually win out. I'm all for hubris. They'll try to break you of your pride. Don't let them. It'll serve you well, in your future career. Assuming you have one."

Bury frowned. "What are you talking about?" he asked.

"Never mind. I shouldn't speak out of turn. When Lanoe deigns to tell you what this mission is really all about, you can start worrying then. For now enjoy a little blissful ignorance. You'll miss it when it's gone."

Bury felt his face growing hot. "Damn you," he said. "You're trying to manipulate me. Flatter me to get me on your side. Get me angry so I cause trouble with Lanoe. Aren't you?"

Did Maggs look impressed? Just a little? He drifted over to one wall and this time grabbed a handhold to stop himself from floating away.

"Of course I'm trying to manipulate you, Cadet," the prisoner admitted. "Everyone you ever meet in life is trying to manipulate you, into one thing or another. Good on you for spotting it so quickly."

"I think we're done here," Bury said, and reached for the virtual key that would turn off the display.

"Fine. Though—just one last thing."

Bury sighed. "What is it?"

"When Lanoe does brief you on this mission—when he tells you what he wants from you, because believe me, he does want quite a lot—do yourself a favor. Ask him how all this connects to the Blue-Blue-White."

"The Blue what?"

"You heard me. Just ask, and see how he responds. Do yourself a favor."

"By which you mean, do *you* a favor."

"Certainly. But there's no reason we can't both benefit at the same time. Cadet, you deserve to know the full truth of what you've been drafted into here."

Bury gritted his teeth. He hated it when people kept things from him. "Ensign," he said.

"I beg your pardon?"

"Lanoe promoted me to ensign. I'm not a cadet anymore. So he's got that going for him. You're just some bastard in a cell."

"Blue-Blue—"

Bury didn't let him finish. He tapped the key and the display blinked out of existence, hiding Lieutenant Maggs from view.

Lanoe flew both craft back to the Hoplite. Sitting at the controls of the cutter, he could operate the troop transport remotely, bringing it into the vehicle bay carefully so he didn't jar all the people inside. Both ships were both packed to capacity, and when they finally set down, their hatches popped open and marines and neddies poured out, filling the vehicle bay with noise and motion. As Lanoe tried to herd his new crew deeper into the ship, he found Candless pushing through the crowd, a look not so much of confusion as of curiosity on her face.

"I imagine I should welcome you back, Commander. Though perhaps I would have appreciated knowing where you were going in the first place," she said, her voice almost drowned out by the bellowing of the marines. A big PBM with a robotic arm pushed between them, kicking his way toward the exit. Tough as he might look, he was already green with spacesickness, his stomach probably still acclimating to the lack of gravity.

"Somebody get him a bag!" Ehta shouted. "Or just put his helmet up, he's going to . . . damn it, too late. Somebody get a cleaning drone in here." The marine sergeant seemed to notice that she'd just shouted directly into Lanoe's ear. "Who's this?" she asked, jerking her head in Candless's direction.

"My XO," Lanoe told her.

"How quickly we do rise around here. A little while ago I was a prisoner on this ship. Now I'm second in command. Marjoram Candless. I'm—" She held out one hand, then jerked it away as a group of marines kicked through, one of them tumbling as two others laughed and pushed him along. It was enough to make Ehta scowl, but she didn't admonish them directly.

"Like children," she said. "Marines, right? Every time they get off a rock, every time it's like they're the first people to discover microgravity."

"Meet Sergeant Ehta," Lanoe said, gesturing at the marine.

"Candless, you said?" Ehta's eyes flicked down across Candless's cryptab. "Got your blue star in the 305th, huh? That wing doesn't exist anymore."

"Correct," Candless told her.

"So a *very* old friend."

Candless offered a chilly smile and glanced down at the front of Ehta's suit, presumably pinging her cryptab in turn. "You have a blue star of your own. In the 94th—Lanoe's last command, before he retired. So a newer friend. Interesting."

"Yeah?" Ehta asked.

"Not a lot of marines I've met had blue stars." Because, of course, the only way to get one was to be a pilot with five registered kills. The PBMs tended not to keep count like that. "Except those pilots who've done something so terribly wrong they had to be kicked out of the Navy."

Ehta bristled instantly. Lanoe could tell that these two would never be friends. "I volunteered for the Marines," she said. "I'd had all I could take of sanctimonious pilots pretending their suits didn't stink after a six-hour patrol." Then she turned and looked across the deck, toward the troop transport. She put two fingers in her mouth and let out a whistle that pierced right through Lanoe's skull. "Paniet!" she shouted.

A man who had just emerged from the transport looked up. He put a hand on his chest, as if to ask if she was calling him. Ehta jerked her head and he came kicking over in a hurry.

He was a lot smaller than any of Ehta's other people, but then again he wasn't a marine. A motif of meshed gears ran around the perimeter of his collar ring, which identified him as a neddy—an officer, specifically, of the Naval Engineering Division. He had rather delicate features, wispy hair, and a ring of metal circuitry like a monocle around his left eye. Lanoe knew it would allow

Paniet to access and manipulate displays without using his hands. "Yes, Sergeant?" he asked.

"This shrimp's Paniet. One of the few neddies I ever met that was worth a damn. Typically you ask them to build you a lean-to and they want ten forms filled out and tell you it'll take six weeks. In the battle of Trench 917, Paniet built me a bunker overnight, out of nothing but mud and spit."

"And approximately seven thousand tons of upcycled fibercrete," Paniet said. "Rather proud of that one." His voice was high-pitched and a little squeaky. His smile seemed like a permanent feature of his face. "Oh," he said. "I beg your pardon. We haven't been introduced." He held out both hands toward Candless and she shook them as if she were afraid they might snap off in her grip. "Hassan," he said. "Hassan Paniet. Is this a Hoplite?"

Lanoe frowned. "That's right," he said. "You didn't see it on the way in?"

"Oh, I never look out the windows during spaceflight," Paniet told him. "Never anything to see, is there? That's the problem with space. It's so empty. A Hoplite! These old birds are legendary, you know. Proved almost indestructible way back in the Establishment Crisis."

"I remember," Lanoe told him.

Paniet didn't seem to register his tone. "If it's not too much trouble—do you think I could take a look at the engines?"

"I insist," Lanoe told him. "That's what you're here for, after all. To keep them from blowing up or shaking to pieces."

"Delicious!" the engineer said, and then smiled at Ehta and Candless. "Lovely meeting you, dears," he chirped, before kicking away toward the vehicle bay's exit. Lanoe watched him go with a frown.

"He's the best you could find?" he asked Ehta, once the man was gone. "A neddy who built you a bunker, once? I need somebody who can keep a warship in one piece, not somebody to build me a house."

"Give him a chance," Ehta said.

"He's your responsibility," Lanoe told her. "I'm promoting you to lieutenant. It's not official but I need you to be able to pull rank.

You're my warrant officer, as of now. So all these people you hand-picked? If they mess up, it's your fault."

Ehta shrugged. Most likely she'd expected as much. "I'll get them squared away," she said. "Find them bunks, start a duty rotation."

"Have any of them served aboard capital ships before?" Candless asked. Her lip was curled, just a bit. "The uninitiated among them might need a crash course in oxygen and water protocols. It looked like some of them might even need microgravity training."

"This batch? Half of them signed up for the Marines less than a month ago," Ehta said. "Hellfire, they don't need all that stuff, they need a lecture in basic hygiene."

Lanoe's brow furrowed.

"You asked for loyal people, people you could trust—not seasoned veterans," Ehta told him. "Like I said, I'll see to it. First, though… I'm sure my timing's lousy, but when do we eat around here? My guys haven't had a decent meal in a week, most of 'em. Things got pretty lean, planetside, with ThiessGruppe blockading our supply lines."

"This ship has plenty of foodstocks in stores," Candless told her. "Though if you want more than cold food paste we'll have to detail someone to be the cook. Lanoe seems to have fired our old one. Your marines—are any of them at all good at food preparation?"

"I think we can handle it," Ehta said. "If it's one thing marines actually know how to do, it's eat." She kicked away without any kind of farewell, and suddenly the vehicle bay was almost empty. A few marines remained, being violently sick, but at least they had the decency to stay well clear of Lanoe and Candless.

"So," she told him, "I don't suppose I can have an explanation of what just happened here?"

"Sure," Lanoe said. "The time's come. I'll work up a formal briefing. Give me an hour and assemble all of our officers on the bridge. And make sure the crew are all ready for acceleration—we're moving out immediately."

"I imagine that's the kind of thing an XO would do," she said. "I wouldn't know, having never been one before. I'll do my best not to disappoint you. Permission to leave the deck?"

"Yeah, yeah," Lanoe said, and waved her away.

He stayed a moment longer—until the noise of the vomiting marines spurred him to head out on his own. He supposed now that he'd promised to fill everyone in, he actually needed to think about what he was going to say.

—⨯—

On the bridge, Bury reached for a navigation display to see if there was any indication of where they were headed. Ginger slapped his hand away.

"Hellfire, Bury!" she whispered. "We just got made officers and now you want to wreck that before our first briefing?"

Bury grunted but he moved back to the wall where she and Candless had positioned themselves. One more person telling him what to do. He thought of what the prisoner had said, about everyone in life manipulating you. He wondered what Ginger wanted from him.

Before he could spend much time thinking on it, though, he saw more people come into the bridge—a big marine in a heavy armored suit and a neddy. He barely registered the little engineer. In the Navy, pilots didn't associate on an informal basis with their mechanics. It was slightly different with marines. You were supposed to treat PBMs with respect because you knew they weren't likely to live very long.

Most of the marines he'd seen on Rishi—officer candidates who spent a short semester there learning how to serve on capital ships—had looked scared and desperate. Like life hadn't given them any choice but to take on such a dangerous occupation.

This one, though, looked different. She had hooded, cynical eyes and an irreverent grin. When she caught him staring, she blew him a kiss.

He looked hurriedly away.

Lanoe came onto the bridge next, and everyone stiffened in attention. Lanoe waved one hand at them to relax. He seemed tired. "I guess this is everyone," he said. "I'll just get started."

Bury frowned at that. He'd been told that every officer on the ship—down to lowly ensigns like himself—had been called for this briefing. A big cruiser like the Hoplite, though, should have had a lot more than six officers.

"You might have noticed we've had some personnel changes lately," Lanoe said. Almost as if he were reading Bury's mind. "When I was given this ship, it came with a full complement. The problem was that I didn't know any of them. Which meant I couldn't trust them. I know how that sounds, but give me a chance to explain."

He kicked over to grab the back of the pilot's chair and looked back at them. He gave the neddy a skeptical look. "You're here, all of you, because either I know you personally or Lieutenant Ehta trusts you. XO, tell me, how does the new crew look?"

Candless lifted one shoulder. "Rough. Untrained. And there aren't enough of them to run this ship."

"We'll make do," Lanoe told her. "We have enough for a skeleton crew. We're not flying off to war anyway. Our orders are less strenuous than that. Engineer Paniet—did you have a chance to look at the engines? Are they in order?"

"Oh, they're lovely," the neddy said, bringing his hands together in front of his chest as if he were genuinely excited.

"All right," Lanoe said, raising one eyebrow. "Good. Then we can get under way." He tapped at a virtual keyboard and a display lit up above the navigation position, showing a three-dimensional map of wormspace. It looked like a ball of knotted string. He tapped another key and the map expanded, the wormholes stretching outward, splitting into new paths, twisting back around themselves. Candless let out a little gasp and leaned forward, as if she couldn't believe what she saw. Bury had no idea why. He glanced over at Ginger. She must have noticed Candless's reaction as well, but she just shrugged.

Deep within the ball of string was a single green point, presumably their destination. It meant nothing to Bury without any context to place it in. It could have been Hel, his homeworld, for all he knew, or it could be a star in a distant galaxy. Wormspace was weird.

"Our orders come directly from the Admiralty. From the very top. A remote listening station picked up a message a short while ago, and we're going to investigate where that message came from and why it was sent. The Navy has a compelling interest in finding these things out. So do the polys. We have to make sure we get there first, and without being followed.

"I suspect there was at least one poly spy onboard this ship when I took command. Specifically, someone I know used to work with Centrocor as a military liaison. That's reason enough for me not to trust him. I've got him locked up in the brig. Lieutenant Ehta, you'll need to station a guard down there. Someone smart enough not to pay attention to anything the prisoner might say. It's our old friend Maggs, if you can believe it."

"That guy? Yeah," the marine said. "I believe it."

Lanoe nodded. "So that's one threat taken care of. Maybe the only one. The possibility remains, however, that there was a second spy onboard. That's the reason for our abrupt crew change. Call me paranoid if you like, but this mission really is that important. For the moment I'm not at liberty to give you any details as to where we're going or what we intend to do when we get there." He took a deep breath. "I will have to ask you to trust me, for now."

Bury couldn't help himself. "Seriously? Come on."

Every eye in the room turned to stare at him. Ginger looked like she might explode from sheer embarrassment. Instantly he felt like an idiot for having spoken out loud, but what was done was done. Nothing to be gained by turning back now.

"You pretty much kidnapped us," Bury said. "You dragged us out of flight school, and now we're supposed to just accept this—"

"That will be very much enough," Candless told him.

"Just let me finish, I mean—"

"Ensign. I said that was enough," Candless said, pushing her way across the wall until she was staring him right in the face. "You were given the very great privilege of attending this briefing due to your rank. A rank, I will point out, that you have not yet earned. You will be quiet right now or I will confine you to quarters. Indefinitely."

Bury's eyes went wide.

In all the time he'd known her—in all the years he'd studied under Candless—she'd never looked so serious. She had corrected his piloting and his gunnery myriad times. She'd told him how to wear his suit, and how to address a superior officer. Finally she'd insulted his piloting, and he'd been forced to respond to the insult. Even that insult, however, had come as a sort of gentle admonishment. An almost motherly kind of correction. This was something else. This was a direct order from a superior officer.

School time was over.

Bury might have made things very bad for himself just then, purely on principle. Just as he'd once challenged her to a duel over an insult. The only thing stopping him from doing so was that he wasn't entirely an idiot.

That, and the way Ginger looked at him. Her eyes were almost begging him to back down. To stop before he went any further.

He lifted his hands in surrender.

"XO has a point," Lanoe said. "This is a Navy ship, and we're on an official mission for the Admiralty, no matter how secret it might be. Those of you who have worked with me before might be expecting a little slack, a little leniency. We can't afford that this time. We'll be running this ship by strict Naval regulations and discipline." He turned and looked specifically at Lieutenant Ehta. "We're doing things for real this time. Am I understood?"

The marine nodded. "Sir, yes, sir."

"Good. I will not be answering any questions at this time," Lanoe said. His face had never even twitched. It was like Bury's outburst hadn't touched him—as if it was something for his XO to deal with. "I would like to speak with my Naval officers separately now. Engineer Paniet, Lieutenant Ehta—that's all. Thank you."

"Thank *you*, Commander," the neddy said. The marine shrugged and slouched her way out after him.

When they were gone, Lanoe addressed Candless. "XO, we have one big problem to resolve. It's why I wanted you and your ensigns to stay behind."

Candless was still staring Bury right in the face. He didn't dare look away.

"Go ahead, Commander," she said. Still not moving. "I'm listening."

Hellfire. She'd made her damned point.

"When I replaced our personnel, I wasn't able to secure any flight crew. You may have noticed that we didn't have any other pilots at this briefing."

For a long moment Candless didn't move. Bury felt the seconds tick by, each one more excruciating than the last. "I did notice, yes." Finally, she moved, and it was like Bury had been impaled on a spike that had just retracted.

"We're going to have to take turns flying this crate," Lanoe told her. "You'll take first watch. Keep your ensigns here and train them, so we can eventually bring them into the bridge rotation. Just follow the route outlined on our charts."

Candless pushed off the wall and grabbed the back of the pilot's chair. Strapping herself in, she swiped the display over to her control position. "Understood," she said. "So I'm going to be your XO, your pilot, *and* your flight instructor."

"I wouldn't trust anyone else with the job," Lanoe told her.

"I suppose I can be your quartermaster as well. And your flight surgeon, as it occurs to me we don't have one of those, either."

Apparently *she* was allowed to talk to him like that. The unfairness of it burned inside Bury's chest.

"You have the bridge, Lieutenant," Lanoe said. He started to move toward the hatch. He was leaving.

Bury thought of Maggs, in the brig. Of what he'd said. *Ask Lanoe about the Blue-Blue-White.*

It didn't exactly feel like an appropriate time.

Lanoe left without another word.

When he was gone, Candless gestured for the two ensigns to strap in. "Well, it seems we have our work cut out for us, doesn't it?

Ginger, you take the nav station. Bury, you can be our information officer, for now. Just sit down and please, I beg of you, don't touch anything until I tell you to."

Bury moved quickly to take his seat. At least the three positions didn't face each other, so he wouldn't feel like Candless was watching him the whole time.

Ginger pushed off the wall, but instead of heading to her own position, she kicked over to Bury first. She didn't say anything. Just grabbed his hand and gave it a quick squeeze. He wasn't expecting it—he'd thought she was angry with him, too. He had no idea what to make of it.

Then she moved to the nav station, and he couldn't see her from where he sat. He could only hear Candless giving her instruction.

"The first thing you need to know about this chart of wormspace," she told Ginger, "is that it's completely wrong. Specifically, there's way too much of it..."

⚡

Lanoe was halfway down the axial corridor when the lights tinged with amber and a chime sounded from speakers all the way up and down the shaft. He grabbed the rungs set into the wall as gravity began to gently tug him downward, toward the engines.

Candless had them moving. Good.

The captain's quarters lay just aft of the bridge. The largest cabin on the Hoplite, though that wasn't saying much. While the marines and engineers slept in modular bunks not much larger than a coffin, the captain was given a low-ceilinged room three meters long and two wide. There was just room inside for a proper microgravity bed, a workstation, sanitary facilities (that he shared, blessedly, with no one), and a narrow storage locker. Most of the wall space was covered with a variety of displays, all of them now switched off, their surfaces a dull, rough-textured gray. There was nothing he wanted to put up there, just then. Nothing he wanted to see.

He sat down on the edge of the bed. Pulled his gloves off and scrubbed at his face with his hands. There was just one more thing to do. One more thing, and then he could try to sleep before his shift came up on the bridge rotation. He knew he needed to get it over with. He needed to be fresh when his time came at the pilot's chair. Still, he hesitated.

What he was going to do—it wasn't fair. Too bad it was necessary.

He didn't have to get up to reach the storage locker. Inside was an empty Navy suit, the helmet retracted inside the collar ring. He pulled it out and laid it carefully across the floor, putting the arms down at the sides, uncrossing the legs. Then he reached for the key recessed underneath the collar ring. The key that would bring up the helmet.

When he pushed the key it was as if the suit inflated itself, bulging out into the shape of a very tall human being. The helmet flowed up around a hypothetical head, its carbonglas already turning black as it polarized.

Valk came to with a start. One of his big hands clenched into a fist and bashed against the floor, three times. Then he sat up. It was impossible to tell if he was looking around, trying to figure out where he was. Impossible, and meaningless anyway. Valk didn't have eyes. He couldn't "look around" himself. His visual sense came from tiny camera lenses built into the suit. It occurred to Lanoe for the first time that Valk couldn't ever close his eyes. That he hadn't, in the entire seventeen years since he'd died and been brought back in this abominable form.

"Lanoe," Valk said. "Lanoe, my clock . . . My internal clock must be wrong. You switched me off. You switched me off days ago."

"Yeah," Lanoe said.

"I'm not supposed to be here," Valk said.

Lanoe scratched at the stubble on the side of his neck.

"I know. I know, old friend. I should have let you go. I should have just—"

"Do you know what it's like? To be switched off? Nah, I guess you couldn't know that. Because it's not like you think. It's not like anything a human ever experiences."

"I guess it's just, I don't know," Lanoe said. "Just everything goes black?"

"Nope." Valk lifted his hand. The one that had struck at the floor. He flexed the fingers of his glove—the only fingers he had. "There's no black. There's no anything. I get switched off, and it's like turning off a light. Like the light was never there to begin with. You switched me off a couple days ago. To me, it feels like you switched me off—and then in the same moment, the very same moment you switched me back on."

They weren't saying it. They weren't talking about it. The fact that Lanoe had broken his promise.

"It's not even like sleeping. It's nothing. Except it's not even that, it's not even nothing, I mean—I guess—because it doesn't... hell. I'm not a philosopher. When you sleep, right, a little of your brain keeps going. Keeps ticking over. You know time has passed when you wake up. I remember that. I remember when Tannis Valk, the real Tannis Valk, used to sleep. For me? It's just...when it happens. There's no time passing. Just, I'm in one place, and then I'm in another."

"No break in between. No break."

They were supposed to have gone to the Admiralty. They were supposed to have downloaded all of Valk's information. Then, when it was done, Valk was supposed to be allowed to finally, mercifully die.

Cease to exist.

Except then Lanoe brought him back.

"I guess we're not done," Valk said, in a very quiet voice.

"I still need your help," Lanoe told him.

"Okay."

Valk lifted his gloves. Gripped his black helmet with ten thick fingers. As if he had a bad headache. As if he were trying to comfort himself. He started rocking back and forth, back and forth.

"Okay," he said again.

Chapter Fourteen

Bullam's yacht shot straight upward, punching through the clouds of Irkalla. Through an advertisement for a nutritional supplement showing a child's giant, beaming face. Through storms that thankfully, luckily, didn't shake the spacecraft enough to damage her, to break her veins. Through the top layers of cloud, thin as promises against a night-blue sky. Out into the black, and the stars.

On the flowglas-domed deck, her passenger made a sound, when he saw the stars. An involuntary nasty little sound, a clicking deep in his throat. A sound of alarm, perhaps.

His eyes didn't move.

Once out of the atmosphere the yacht could pour on the speed. It would take only a few hours to reach their destination, a secret Centrocor facility located deep in the system's massive asteroid belt. Bullam considered heading back to the cabin so she could catch up with some correspondence. It was going to be tricky for her to just leave Irkalla for an indefinite period of time—the life of an executive was a web of obligations and relationships, and needed constant maintenance. Worst of all she couldn't even tell anyone why she was heading out of the system. The best she could do was to say she had to head out for medical reasons. Her disease was well enough known among her peers that it wouldn't raise any questions. She got up and was actually headed inside, then stopped because she'd caught something out of the corner of her eye. Her passenger had moved. It startled her.

"Captain Shulkin?" she asked.

He had stepped over to the dome. Put his hand on the flowglas. It made her think of a child on their first trip above the atmosphere, pressing their face up against the window so they could see everything.

"Are you all right?" she asked.

He didn't turn around to look at her. "Do you have any family?" he said, his voice dry and creaking.

Bullam's brows knitted together. "No," she said. "No. They— no." She shook her head. No point being closed off about it. The two of them were going to spend a lot of time together. Best to get things off to a convivial start. "They died in the Establishment Crisis. When the terrorists bombed Dunkelsberg."

"You survived that?"

"I was away. At a preparatory school. I was just a child."

He nodded. His hand moved on the flowglas. Wiping away the condensation of his breath. As if he couldn't afford to have his view obscured, even for a second, even though there was nothing out there to see, nothing for thousands of kilometers in any direction.

"Lovers?" he asked.

"That's a little personal, isn't it?"

"It's important. Do you have a lover, back on Irkalla? Someone who will miss you if you don't come back?"

Bullam bit her lip. Was he *threatening* her?

"If you do, it's good to say goodbye. Before you ship out, you should write something down. A sealed message, one only to be opened if you don't come home. In the Navy we made a ritual of it. We called them Dear Justin letters."

Bullam waved for one of her drones to bring her a cup of tea. "Who was Justin?" she asked.

"Justin. Just in case. It's a stupid pun." He turned, finally, and walked across the deck. He dropped down into a chair and stared at her with those glassy eyes of his. "So. Do you have a lover?" he asked, again.

In point of fact, Bullam had several. Half a dozen men and one woman, people who had somehow fit into her busy schedule. Most of them were business inferiors looking to climb the corporate ladder one way or another. Technically such liaisons were against employee policy, and therefore grounds for dismissal. In reality, an executive who didn't make time for sex was considered unnatural and therefore unlikely to be chosen for promotions. Bullam had made a point of seeking out lovers. She'd enjoyed their company, but made a point of never getting truly attached.

"No one who would expect such a thing from me," she said.

Shulkin nodded. "For the best," he said.

"What about you?" she asked. "Any family, friends...anyone special?"

He grimaced as if he'd bitten into a sour fruit. "Not anymore," he said, and turned his face away from her. To look back out through the dome. "How much longer until we get there?"

One of her drones lit up with a navigational display. Helpful little machines. "Three hours," she said.

"Let me know when we're close," he said. And then he sank into himself with a deep sigh. She watched him for a while, expecting further impertinencies. None were forthcoming.

Eventually she got up without a word and went back to her cabin, to do some work. So much for conviviality.

⚡

There were no windows on the bridge, not even a porthole— all visual information on where the cruiser was headed came in through displays. It wasn't like flying a fighter at all, and Ginger's muscles twitched with the weirdness of it.

"You're doing fine, for your first time," Lieutenant Candless said.

"Am I?" Ginger asked, with a little laugh. She adjusted her trim just a hair, and felt the big ship moving around her, all that metal and carbon fiber vibrating as it responded to her touch on the virtual controls. She fought the urge to jerk her hand back.

Because the cruiser was accelerating, down was the direction of the engines. Up was the direction they were moving. She tried to visualize the ship as a tower and that she was sitting on its highest ramparts, craning her neck back to look at the sky. It helped, a little.

On her display the stars swung around her, Tuonela's sun like a lamp that dazzled her eyes. Streams of data washed across the view, telling her all kinds of information she didn't immediately need. Other spacecraft, too small to see at this magnification, appeared as green triangles, each of them surrounded by its own cloud of data. Blue lines divided the view into quadrants and sectors, while a bright yellow rectangle pulsed down by her knees. That was their destination. She touched the controls again and the nose of the cruiser dipped toward the rectangle, just a few tenths of a degree a second.

"That's right. Take it slow. You're used to a more maneuverable ship," Lieutenant Candless told her. "This one's going to feel sluggish as it comes around."

In truth it felt like it was swinging wildly out of control, a compass needle trying to find magnetic north. Ginger sucked on her lower lip and lifted her hand slowly, easing up on the steering thrusters.

She thought of all the exams she'd sat through, back on Rishi. All the equations she'd memorized. The ways thrust and load factor variables fit into trajectory optimization. Angle of attack command histories and downrange schedules. It had all seemed so abstract, so unreal—when you were in the cockpit of a fighter, you had to learn to move as if the spacecraft around you were an extension of your own body. With the cruiser that seemed impossible. It was just too big, its inertia too great. The only thing keeping her from panicking outright was the fact that there was nothing around her to run into. Tuonela had fallen away behind them, and its star was still millions of kilometers away. No matter how badly she screwed up she wasn't about to crash.

The yellow rectangle grew steadily larger as they approached the wormhole throat, the exit from the Tuonela system. It was hard to see—just a patch of weirdly distorted space, invisible except when a star slipped behind it and its light was smeared into an unrecognizable blur.

As they got closer, Ginger's level of fear began to spike. There was enough room, there was plenty of clearance—she knew that intellectually. But if you so much as brushed the walls of the wormhole—

"I believe I'll take it from here, thank you," Lieutenant Candless said.

The virtual keyboard vanished from under Ginger's fingers. She sighed and sagged back into her chair in relief. The display wheeled around for a moment as it reoriented to Lieutenant Candless's field of view, and suddenly it looked very different—the yellow rectangle much farther away than it had seemed, space itself far less crowded. Lieutenant Candless made an adjustment and the ship moved again, not lurching this time like it had under Ginger's control but merely shimmying as the more experienced pilot feathered the controls.

"That was intense," Ginger said, with a little laugh.

"With practice you'll get the hang of it," Lieutenant Candless told her. The older woman's eyes flicked back and forth across the display as various streams of green data zoomed in and out toward her. "A couple more hours like that and you'll be ready to fly solo."

"Hours?" Ginger checked the clock in her suit display and found that she'd been at the controls for ninety-one minutes. It hadn't felt nearly that long. She shook her head and tried to laugh again. "I never felt so nervous piloting a fighter." She unstrapped herself from her position and carefully climbed down onto the deck. The gravity now was minimal, as the cruiser wasn't accelerating much at all, but it was enough that she didn't go floating off into the air. She did some quick stretches and knee bends, because she felt stiff and shaky, and she knew the exercise would help a little.

"Go get something to eat," Lieutenant Candless told her. "It would be best to sleep a little, if you can. If you see Bury, send him up here so he can have a lesson, too."

Ginger nodded and turned toward the hatch that led to the rest of the ship. Before she went, though, she needed to ask a question. "Lieutenant," she said. "Um, permission to speak?"

"Granted. And shall we assume you have that permission from now on, unless I tell you otherwise? It will become tedious, otherwise."

Ginger nodded. "I just—things have been moving so fast. I haven't really had time to process all this. I mean, I was just a cadet a couple of days ago. Now I'm on some kind of secret mission."

"Better than the alternative," the Lieutenant replied.

"Would they really have thrown us in prison?"

Lieutenant Candless sighed. "It would appear that it is time for you to learn a most valuable lesson. A lesson in bosh. Back at Rishi, we taught you that being a Naval officer was a noble profession. That it meant working for the good of humanity. That was, most assuredly, true."

"Okay," Ginger said, carefully, because she could tell Candless had entered lecture mode. This might take a while.

"The Navy does good. This cannot be denied. It's also a military organization, and that means that it ventures at times into dark territory. I don't simply mean killing people. That's part of the job. I mean the kind of secrecy that breeds paranoia. The higher up the ladder you get, the worse it becomes. Admirals, commanders like Lanoe, even just captains of big ships like this one, are forced to make decisions all the time that can cost hundreds or thousands of lives. They can't afford to be nice, or just."

"So—the answer to my question is yes?"

"They would have detained us for some indefinite period of time, yes," Candless confirmed. "Of that I have no doubt. One of those hard decisions I mentioned, but there would have been no hesitation."

Ginger frowned. "Is that why you became a flight instructor? Because they were going to promote you and you didn't want to make those kind of decisions?"

Lieutenant Candless didn't turn to glare at her. Didn't seem to be angered by the question at all. Even though Ginger was already regretting asking it. It was something she'd wondered about many times, though. Lieutenant Candless was a war hero, with a whole stack of commendations. She'd been at the height of a glamorous career as a pilot and then one day near the end of the Establishment Crisis she'd just asked for reassignment, out of nowhere. She'd been a teacher ever since.

"You're an officer now," the Lieutenant said. "Perhaps you deserve an answer to that question."

She stopped speaking for a moment and Ginger looked at the display. The yellow rectangle was huge now, filling half the bridge. The distortion of the wormhole throat made a mess of all the holographic stars.

"I decided to teach," the Lieutenant said, very slowly, "because of what I saw during the last real war."

"What—what was that?" Ginger asked, though she wasn't sure she really wanted to hear it.

"Too many young people flying warships. Like you and Bury," the Lieutenant said. "Children, really. Children with two, perhaps four weeks of training, sent straight to the front. By the end of the Crisis, the average pilot flew six missions. That average was so low because of all the pilots who only got to fly one."

For a second Ginger didn't grasp what the Lieutenant was saying. Then a chill ran down her spine.

"I knew I was good. I knew I was a talented pilot. I thought if I could pass on some of what I knew, it might help some young people live longer."

She fell silent as the yellow rectangle swept across the bridge. The stars flickered out and the display changed radically. Instead of the void of space all around them, the walls of the bridge were on fire with the ghostlight of the inside of a wormhole. Virtual particles annihilating each other in perfect silence. Ahead of them, the tunnel stretched away to nothingness, to a point of dead light.

The transition had been so smooth, so effortless Ginger barely noticed it. She had felt the ship sway a tiny degree over on its side, that was all.

"Now, do you have any more questions?" Lieutenant Candless asked.

"Not right now," Ginger said, her voice barely a whisper.

The asteroid didn't have a proper name, just a catalog number. Two hundred years ago, back when Irkalla was still being readied for human use, the asteroid had been surveyed and found to contain high concentrations of silicate rock and not much else. Useless, therefore, and far enough away from anywhere that it wasn't even a navigation hazard. It had been ignored ever since.

At least, officially.

The cratered surface of the rock sped away beneath the yacht, its night side rushing toward them. One of Bullam's drones moved across the deck and projected a display onto the carbonglas dome, showing a light-amplified view of the ground below. Traces of human construction began to appear—power plants and thick cable bundles that snaked along the curved edges of craters. Long parallel trenches dug into the soil by mining drones with snouts lined with grinding teeth, sifting through the loose regolith in search of traces of metals and water, anything useful. And there, beyond the trenches, a cradle made of arching gantries like the rib cage of some fossil beast.

Inside the cradle sat the thing they'd come for. A Hipparchus-class carrier, one of the largest and most deadly spacecraft ever built. A full half kilometer long and a hundred meters across, a vast tubular construction like a cannon built to shoot out smaller ships. The yacht sped toward its gaping mouth and Bullam could see cataphract-class fighters and small carrier scouts nestled against its interior walls, like bats clinging to the roof of a massive cave.

She couldn't help but be impressed by what Dariau Cygnet had accomplished here. The Navy didn't exactly sell its old carriers to the highest bidder. There were strict protocols in place to keep any poly from acquiring this kind of asset, and Earth had intervened every time one of the big corporations threatened to build one of its own. Centrocor had been forced to get creative.

She'd been told that in fact this particular vessel had been found as a wandering hulk on the fringes of the Adlivun system, abandoned after a nasty battle with DaoLink. The Navy had won that war but the carrier had been so heavily damaged it had been written off as a total loss and abandoned in place. Centrocor had claimed salvage rights, and the Navy had failed to raise a protest—most likely they expected the poly to break the carrier down for scrap.

Instead, Cygnet had begun the very long, very painstaking process of repairing and refurbishing the carrier. Patching the holes in its hull. Replacing those systems that couldn't be saved. The costs involved would have been astronomical, and the fact that it all had to be done in absolute secrecy would have doubled or even tripled the expense. The project had taken fifteen years to complete.

Cygnet had paid the bills, put up with the endless delays without a murmur. Because he knew that someday, Centrocor was going to need a machine like this. He'd had the vision to keep the project going long after another executive might have decided the short-term costs outweighed any future return on investment.

"What do you think, Captain?" Bullam said, craning her head back to see as the yacht passed inside, as true darkness swept across the wooden deck. "You have to admit, we're giving you the best tools for the job."

She could barely see Shulkin in the dark. Only the light of a drone's display touched his face, painting his gaunt cheeks with a bluish shadow. She was surprised to find him sneering in disdain.

"All wrong," he said. "Wrong, wrong, wrong."

Bullam's face fell. "What do you mean? You—you haven't given it a proper look-over. I assure you, it's fully repaired. It's ready for—"

"Do you play chess?" he asked. In exactly the same tone as when he'd asked her if she had a lover.

She shook her head. "I never have. I've heard of it, but I rarely have time for games."

"A battle in space is like a game of chess," he told her. "The pieces matter. You don't send a carrier against a cruiser. It's wrong!"

He pounded on the dome with one fist. For the first time, even in the dark, she saw light come into his eyes. It was like he'd been hibernating this whole time and now he'd woken up, a hungry bear.

"I don't understand," she said, taking a step backward. "This one's bigger than Lanoe's cruiser. It's bigger! So...it must be better."

"It's wrong," he said again. But then he shook his head and turned away from the dome. "It'll have to do. But it's all wrong."

The yacht found a space along the inside wall of the carrier and docked automatically, with barely a lurch. A flexible hoselike gangway was extended to make contact with the yacht's side and part of the dome flowed away to let them disembark. Together, in the minuscule gravity of the asteroid, they headed into the carrier's warren of crisscrossing companionways. An honor guard of marines was waiting for them, lined up in spotless heavy suits, all wearing the hexagon on their pauldrons. One of them moved forward and cleared his throat, clearly intending to welcome them onboard.

"Major Yael," he said, placing a hand on his chest near his cryptab. "I take it you're Captain Shulkin and M. Bullam. We've been instructed to see to all your needs. If you'll just follow me, I'll—"

But Shulkin ignored him completely. The captain hurried past, deeper into the carrier. Yael looked more scared than surprised. He gave Bullam an apologetic smile, then rushed after Shulkin.

"Sir," the marine said, "if you'll just allow me—this vehicle can be a confusing place, if you don't—"

"I know where I'm going," Shulkin told him, not even looking back. "I've spent more time in carriers like this than you've spent breathing, *Major*."

"I'm supposed to show you your cabin, and then—"

Shulkin stopped in mid-stride and wheeled around to glare at the marine. Yael had to grab a handhold on the wall to keep from colliding with him. "You have new orders," Shulkin said.

"I...I do?"

"Yes. Find the flight crew and tell them to head out immediately. Our quarry has a head start on us—we need to make up time. Tell them that if we aren't moving in ten minutes, they'll be removed from duty and replaced. Understood?"

"I—I—yes. Yes, sir," Yael said.

Shulkin looked the marine up and down, as if he were only

now actually noticing his existence. He stuck out his jaw and then turned and walked away.

Yael looked over at Bullam, who had barely taken five steps into the carrier.

"Better do as he said," Bullam told the marine. "He *is* in charge."

"Yes, Ma'am," Yael said, and departed in a hurry. The rest of the marines were left standing there at attention, with no orders.

She had no way to tell them apart—their helmets were all up and silvered, and because she wasn't wearing a military suit, she was unable to ping their cryptabs. In the end, she just picked the tallest one. "You," she said.

"Ma'am," he replied, his body language signaling he was relieved to have some supervision.

"Take me to the most comfortable cabin onboard. And call ahead to make sure there's some tea waiting for me when I get there."

Ginger knew she should sleep. She very much wanted to sleep.

It wasn't going to happen.

She was keyed up, her blood thrumming with the excitement of her first time flying the cruiser. She hung there floating in her tiny bunk, occasionally bouncing off the walls, and every time she closed her eyes they just opened again of their own accord.

Eventually she sighed in frustration and zipped herself out of her sleepsac. She rubbed at her face—she was tired, her body was definitely tired. Her brain didn't care. She slapped the release key on the bunk's hatch and slithered out into the corridor beyond, which was well enough lit to dazzle her eyes.

She pressed her face up against a ventilation duct in the wall and let the ship cool her down for a bit. When that started to get to be too much, she pushed away again, thinking she might get something to eat. Not the flavorless paste they had in the pilots' wardroom, though. She couldn't handle that again. She wandered until she found the marines' section—she'd heard they had an actual cook. At the end of the corridor of bunks was a wardroom, bigger than the one the pilots got. She could hear voices coming from down there, the rough cadences of marines joking around, laughing, insulting each other. She kicked down the hall toward the wardroom and stopped herself at the open hatch, poking her head in to take a look.

A half-dozen marines were in there, including Lieutenant Ehta, their leader. They were playing freepool, a game Ginger had heard of but never actually seen played before. On the orbital where she'd grown up, around Metnal, it was considered a sport of the lower orders. Certainly no one at Ginger's boarding school had ever played it.

The marines were all pressed up against the walls of the wardroom, creating an open space in their midst. Six metal balls hung in the air between them, each of them spinning but mostly staying in place. As Ginger watched, one of the marines carefully lined up a shot, studying the angles with one closed eye, sticking his tongue out to get a sense of the airflow in the room. When he was ready he made a fist and smacked one of the balls into motion, sending it hurtling at medium speed toward another ball.

Spots of paint on the wardroom's walls marked targets, their various colors indicating different point values. The idea was to hit one of the targets, but not with the ball you set into motion—that was a foul. Instead you had to hit a second ball in such a way that it would fly off toward the target.

The marine's ball just kissed the second ball, which flew off at an angle, air resistance slowing it as it moved. Marines dodged out of its way, climbing over each other in a flurry of punches and rude jokes. The secondary ball moved slower and slower, inexorably approaching a red spot on one wall, curving just a hair as the weird currents of the room's ventilation pushed at it. "Yeah," the player said, "yeah, come on—yeah, yeah, yeah!"

Others shouted encouragement or derision. One marine playfully stuck his hand up into the ball's path, but he was quickly dragged back and given a half-serious punch in the gut for being an ass. The ball had slowed to a crawl in the air but the marines just got louder and louder, and when it struck the wall just a centimeter outside the paint, they screamed and roared and groaned and whooped, even as the player grabbed both moving balls out of the air and carefully put them back in their starting places. Others slapped the player on the back or mocked his ability, and the wardroom was a riot of noise until Ginger pushed her way inside and a marine saw her. He slapped the arm of the marine next to him, and soon every eye in the wardroom was on Ginger.

Silence fell over the room, a quick hush that startled her.

She wanted very much to blush, to shove away down the hall. To get away from all that attention. She knew, though, that if she just disappeared now the marines would talk about her when she was gone, about how weird she was. They might think she was afraid of them.

She couldn't very well have that.

"Can I play?" she asked.

The marines glanced at each other. Ehta, their commander, kicked over to the hatch to hang next to Ginger. "Officer on deck," she said.

The marines all came to attention, moving quickly to take up positions against the walls as if they were lined up and ready for inspection.

Ginger frowned. "No need for that, guys," she said. "I'm just an ensign, I—"

Ehta cleared her throat. "The officer seems to have forgotten that these are enlisted troops," she said. She gave Ginger a questioning glance.

Ginger was very good at social situations, normally. This one was a little more complicated than she was used to. Ehta outranked Ginger by a significant margin. Her lieutenancy, though, was even more brand-new than Ginger's ensignry. Before she came onboard, Ehta had been only a sergeant, an enlisted rank. She'd served with all of these marines—as one of their own. Then there was the fact that the Marines and the Navy were technically two completely different worlds. Even if everyone in the room had been an ensign, they would have been marine ensigns. A totally different thing.

"I beg your pardon," Ginger said. Maybe slinking away with her tail between her legs was the best option now. She reached for the hatch, intending to leave them be.

"Marine Binah," Ehta said. "The officer would like to play."

"No, no, please," Ginger said, but it was already decided, apparently. One of the marines peeled off the wall and moved quickly, steadying the balls in the air and then twisting them to make them spin with a deft motion of his wrist. When it was done he moved back to his place, nestling in among his squadmates.

The whole time, everyone kept staring right at Ginger.

"May I suggest the blue target?" Ehta said. "It's worth six points."

Ginger pressed her lips tightly together. She kicked off the wall, then grabbed for another wall to stop her motion. She considered the various shots she might take for a moment. Thinking she should try to make a good show of this, even if it was her first time playing. Then suddenly it was like her eyes had shifted focus. Like she saw the balls in the air for the first time.

And she realized that the game was the easiest thing in the world.

Compared to flying in a fighter and keeping the positions and velocities of your squad, your enemies, and your objectives all in your head at one time, lining up a single deflection shot was child's play. The windage from the ventilation ducts made the angles a little soft but it would be easy enough to compensate for that with a little extra force. In fact, if she really wanted to get fancy—

"Anytime you're ready, ma'am," Ehta said.

There. Ginger could see an almost perfect shot. If she hit her ball into that ball, it would strike a third ball and she could land balls on both the blue spot and a red one as well. She studied the state of play a little more—maybe she could even get three spots, if she struck the first ball just right, with just a little backspin.

"It's trickier than it looks," Ehta said. With just a trace of warning in her voice.

Ginger glanced around at the marines on the walls. They watched her with various expressions, none of which she liked. Some were glaring in open contempt. Others looked, as hard as it was to believe, afraid of her.

"Ah," Ginger said. And took her shot.

Her ball spun through the air and caught a second ball just off center. Both of them went bouncing away, one of them toward the open hatch, the other flying straight back toward Ginger's face.

Lieutenant Ehta snatched it out of the air before it could smack Ginger across the nose.

One of the marines coughed. Another tried desperately but couldn't quite manage to keep a grin off his face. A third kicked through the hatch, chasing after the wayward ball before it could get into something important.

"That's a foul," one of them said. "Ma'am."

Lieutenant Ehta gave her a meaningful nod. Apparently, Ginger had made the right choice. She forced herself to smile and lifted her hands in resignation. "Thank you," she said, not looking at any one marine specifically, "for letting me play. Very kind. I won't detain you any longer."

She kicked out through the hatch, nearly colliding with the marine who'd chased after the lost ball. She gritted her teeth as she tried not to blush. She could escape with a little dignity, she thought, if she got out of there quickly enough. She couldn't help hearing them laugh at her after she was gone, though.

⤙⤚

The carrier was a secret weapon, perhaps the most closely guarded asset that Centrocor possessed. It could not risk appearing in the skies around Tuonela—a system swarming with Navy vessels. There would at the very least be uncomfortable questions to answer. At worst they would be boarded and the carrier would be confiscated. They could hardly let that happen.

So the carrier's pilot—an ex-Navy flyer Centrocor had scooped up just as they had acquired Captain Shulkin—brought the carrier to a dead stop inside the wormhole, still an hour's travel from Tuonela. Bullam took her yacht through the wormhole throat, her flight plan logged with local traffic control. As far as anyone local was concerned, she was there as an official spy. It was not illegal for an uninvolved poly to send an observer to a war zone, someone to keep tabs on whether the Navy or ThiessGruppe was winning the war down on the planet. As long as she stayed well clear of the theater of combat, no one would question her presence.

She had no intention of getting anywhere near the planet. She had a rendezvous to make, but it was far from Tuonela. In the dark end of the system a chunk of useless rock orbited the local star in a wildly eccentric orbit, an old comet that had burned off all of its ice. It took three hours just to match velocity with the rock, and another thirty minutes to make a slow descent.

The ship she'd come to meet was already there. It had set down next to an old research station that hadn't been used since Tuonela was terraformed. The ancient docking facilities were useless, the gantries corroded away to piles of scrap, the mating seals rotted away by years of exposure to hard vacuum.

"Are you coming?" she asked Shulkin, as she pulled on a thinsuit—a civilian model designed for light use. "I can handle this on my own, if you prefer."

He didn't answer. Instead he just reached up to his throat and pressed the recessed key under his collar ring that raised his helmet. It flowed up around his scowling features and immediately polarized to a shiny black.

She matched the gesture, polarizing her own helmet to a deep red that matched the crimson and gold brocade pattern of her thinsuit. Then she retracted the dome that covered the yacht's deck, and all the air inside froze and fell around them like snow.

A cloud of drones lifted off the deck and trailed after Bullam as she jumped down from the deck, floating down with her to the rough surface. They seemed to fall forever in the planetoid's tiny gravity. Taking ten-meter-long strides, she made her way to the hatch of the research station. Inside, a weather field had been erected to create a tiny space of air and warmth. Condensation slicked the rusted walls and as she stepped into the field a scurf of torn carbon fibers blew across her boots.

Across the room, three people waited for her. Two were irregular troops wearing armored suits with the green Maltese cross of ThiessGruppe painted on their chests like knights from some ancient crusade. Their faces were obscured by balaclavas under their helmets. The third kneeled on the floor, her hands tied. A bag thrown over her head.

Bullam felt her heart thudding in her chest. Not a pleasant sensation for someone with a vascular disease. "It's her?" she asked.

"All according to our arrangement," one of the armored men said. "TG honors its contracts."

The polys all owed each other countless unspoken-of favors, a quiet economy of whispered requests and subtle reminders that was, of course, scrupulously accounted for. Getting this meeting set up had meant calling in a very old marker between Centrocor and ThiessGruppe. Dariau Cygnet seemed to think it was worth it.

The other TG man stepped forward. "I don't mind saying it took some work. Kidnapping a Naval officer from one of their firebases." He shook his head. "Big Hexagon doesn't ask for much, does it?"

"We're all in this together," Bullam said, distractedly. "Could you...I need to verify you brought us the right person."

The TG man nodded and bent down to pull the bag off the captive's head. Bullam didn't even bother looking at the woman's face—she had mostly just wanted the TG man to keep his hands where she could see them.

"This was part of the arrangement, too," she said. Then she pulled a tiny pistol out of a pocket of her suit and shot him through the crown of his head.

Before he'd even fallen to the floor in the low gravity, she spun around to shoot the other one—only to find she'd made a mistake.

She'd miscalculated how quickly he could move. He was already on her, the fingers of one gloved hand digging into her wrist until she gasped in pain and dropped the gun. He brought his other hand back to punch her in the face. He was almost on top of her, and she could look him in the eyes. What she saw there left no doubt in her mind—he was going to kill her, as quickly as he could.

His fist collided with her nose—why in the hell had she dropped her helmet?—and she felt blood splatter across her lips and splash across her collar ring. The pain was incredible—because her disease kept her body from producing collagen normally, the cartilage in her nose shattered instead of bending like it should. For a second her vision went black and she could hear herself screaming, but it was like the sound came from somewhere outside her body. She struggled to get her arms up, to grab at the TG man, but he punched her again, this time in the cheek, his knuckles bouncing off her skull. She tried to suck in a deep breath, to get some oxygen, but instead she just aspirated her own blood and started to choke, her body racked by spasms of agony. In a second the TG man would think to strangle her, or maybe he had some hidden weapon—

Then a wave of cold air washed over her. Bullam opened her eyes and saw she was free, that the TG man had disappeared. She heard something above the screaming, a sound like plastic being torn, and she spun around.

Shulkin had the TG man down on the ground and was tearing at his armor with his gloved hands. The TG man tried to fight back, punching and kicking, but Shulkin ignored the blows. He yanked something loose from the TG man's armor and the clear helmet dropped, flowglas shrinking back into the TG man's collar ring.

Then Shulkin picked the poor bastard up in both hands and threw him out of the weather field, out into the hard vacuum and near-absolute-zero cold of the planetoid's surface.

She thought she heard the man scream, though that was, of course, impossible. Then she thought she was the one screaming. She put a hand across her face and found that her mouth was closed.

No, the screaming came from the woman, the one TG had kidnapped for them. She was scuttling across the floor, kicking up off the filthy ground trying to get away from the blood that seeped into the dirt. Her face as a mask of panic.

Bullam turned to look at Shulkin. "Thank you," she said. "I guess you're worth having around, after all."

Shulkin scowled at her. Then he knelt down next to the screaming woman, the Navy pilot. He stared into her eyes like a doctor diagnosing some neurological complaint. "Should I kill her, too?" he asked.

The woman's screams somehow grew even louder.

"No, of course not," Bullam said. She went over and squatted down next to the woman as well. She gave the captive a friendly smile. "She has something we need."

Ginger had no idea where to go. She wasn't welcome among the marines, obviously. She realized that Lieutenant Ehta had tried to make it easy on her, tried to warn her away. Clearly the woman wasn't unkind. Yet it was also clear there were rules against pilots fraternizing with marines, rules that no one was willing to break.

She considered heading back toward the engines, to see if the neddies were equally unwelcoming. Why put herself through that again, though? No, it seemed the only people onboard that she was allowed to even talk to were her fellow pilots. A depressingly small pool of people. Especially since considerations of rank applied there, as well. Commander Lanoe was her CO. There was no way he was going to sit down and have a chat with her. He would have more important things to do, and anyway what could she possibly have to say to him? Lieutenant Candless was only slightly more approachable. As much as Ginger respected her former flight instructor, Candless definitely wasn't someone she could just gossip with. When you looked into her sharp eyes you knew she was recording every word you said. Judging every facial expression, every gesture. It was a little unnerving.

Which only left one person on the entire ship she could really talk to. Bury. And she was still angry at him for his outburst during their first briefing as officers.

Ginger was a classic extrovert, a fact she'd identified in herself very early on. She needed people around her, drew all her energy from human contact. If she had no one but Bury to hang out with, this was going to be one very long, very lonely mission.

She found an officers' mess up near the bridge, a deserted little closet of a place where she could at least get some food. The machine there dispensed a bag full of reconstituted mush that tasted like salt and chemicals. It was at least hot and filling. There was a display in the galley as well, which could play videos and books. She tried fiddling with its controls for a while, but everything in the library was old, prerecorded stuff. Because there was no good way to send radio waves through a wormhole, the cruiser had no access to any live streams. She couldn't keep up with the latest video dramas or even hear any new music.

No, the only thing for it was to throw herself into work. If she could log more hours of piloting instruction, if she could start flying the cruiser solo, maybe Lieutenant Candless would respect her more. Maybe they could even become something like colleagues. It seemed like a lot of work just to get someone to talk to, but Ginger knew that if she didn't try something she would go out of her head.

She kicked off a wall and headed out of the galley, following the color-coded lights on the walls of the companionways that would take her back to the axial corridor. From there she just had to pass by the empty officers' wardroom and the captain's quarters. She saw that Lanoe's hatch was open and made a point of being as quiet as possible as she moved by.

She heard voices coming from inside the cabin, though, and she couldn't help but overhear what was being said inside. It seemed somebody was in there with the Commander. Someone with a voice she recognized, though one she never thought she would hear again.

She stopped a few meters away, unable now to *not* listen.

"Why don't you tell me the real reason?" the voice asked.

It was Tannis Valk. It had to be. But the last time Ginger had seen him—

"They've wiped out every species in the galaxy except us. You said it yourself. They sterilized millions of planets. Millions—how many kinds of vermin did they kill that might have become sapient? How much genocide are we supposed to forgive? Somebody has to do this," Commander Lanoe replied.

"You're really going to claim you care so much about a bunch of dead guys you never met? Come on, Lanoe. We both know this is about Zhang."

"The reasons don't matter. Do they? I know what I'm doing. And you're coming along for the ride. I'm sorry, big guy. I really am. But without you—"

"Wait," Valk said. "Wait—I think I heard—"

He poked his head out of the door. His big polarized helmet.

It was him. The—the artificial intelligence. He hadn't been shut down after all, hadn't been destroyed. Despite what Lanoe had said.

For a moment they just stared at each other. Well, Ginger stared. She had no idea what the AI might be doing. Maybe plotting to destroy the human race; they were supposed to do that sometimes.

"It's Ginger, right?" Valk asked.

She nodded. She couldn't look away from him, not for a second.

"Do you have somewhere else to be?"

She didn't waste any time kicking her way up the corridor toward the bridge.

⚡

Bullam washed her face three times, digging a cloth deep into the creases around her nose, wiping her chin over and over. Getting all the blood out. Her little physician drone sprayed a fine mist up her nostrils to stop the bleeding. The smell of hot plastic would stick with her for days. Another drone gently pushed the cartilage of her nose back into place, then stabilized it with a transparent bandage. It hurt like hell.

The drone noticed how badly she was shaking, and offered her a sedative. She declined. She knew exactly why she was so rattled.

When Ashlay Bullam took her current job, she'd known she

would have to get her hands dirty from time to time. She'd known that she would be doing things Centrocor didn't want to admit to. She'd even known that she would have to make decisions that cost lives. This was the first time, however, that the poly had asked her to kill with her own hands.

She tried to tell herself that the TG man she'd shot was a soldier. That he should have expected a certain amount of risk, that he should have known he would be expendable once he'd kidnapped the Navy pilot. She told herself that Big Hexagon needed to make sure no one would ever know about the abduction, that the poly was more important than her sensitive feelings.

It didn't help. It didn't help at all. She'd put the gun against the poor bastard's head and squeezed the trigger without a thought. If she'd had time to reflect, if she'd given herself a moment to consider what she was doing, she would never have been able to manage it.

But now it was done. She couldn't take it back.

She had a drone bring up a mirror display and for a long time she just watched her face. She told herself she was looking for any lingering traces of dried blood, but in fact she wanted to see if she looked any different. If she'd changed, now that she was a murderer. She studied the corners of her eyes, the coloration in her cheeks. Pushed the hair back from her forehead as if there might be a mark there, some brand that would let people know when they saw her.

Stupid. Pointless. She forced herself to stop shaking, to stop feeling so raw. If she didn't get control of herself, she would end up like Shulkin, she thought. Compulsively suicidal. Holes burnt in his brain to keep him able to fight.

She shoved the drone away from her and pushed her way out of her cabin. Swam through the maze of corridors, guided by a drone that swept in front of her, always picking the right direction. It didn't take long to reach the carrier's brig. They had the Navy pilot there, locked away under constant guard in a cell bigger than most of the carrier's bunks. On the door of the cell a display showed the pilot inside. She was crouched down in one corner of the room, holding on to the walls so she didn't float away. She looked very worried.

"What'll you do with her?" Shulkin asked.

Of course he was there, in the brig. Waiting for her to arrive. A man as dead inside as Shulkin would hardly pass up the chance to attend a good old-fashioned interrogation. Well, there was nothing for it. She couldn't tell him to leave—technically, he was the ultimate power onboard the carrier. He didn't take orders, he gave them.

She knew the time would come, eventually, when she would have to show him that was incorrect, that his position was not perfectly unassailable. This wasn't that time.

"Will you torture her?" Shulkin asked. "I've seen torture before. Doesn't work, not like you'd expect."

Those eyes. Like glass beads. He'd killed a man, too, today. It didn't seem to bother him in the slightest. She wondered if anything could.

"You could try sleep deprivation," he said. "That's supposed to be effective. More than physical torture. You could try starving her. The brain starts to deteriorate after a week without food. Resistance breaks down. You become suggestible. Those tactics take time, though, and we're in a hurry. You need something fast. What's it going to be? Thumbscrews? The rack?"

She forced a smile onto her face. "Something even more old-fashioned than that," Bullam said. "Lots and lots of money." She gestured at the marine guarding the cell and he opened the hatch for her. She pulled herself inside and shoved herself into a corner of the room, not too close to the captive. Not too far. Curled herself into a ball, so she wasn't looming over the other woman.

"Lieutenant Harbin," she said. "Thank you for coming to meet us."

The pilot nodded. Her eyes darted across the room and Bullam saw Shulkin hovering in the doorway. She didn't bother to scowl at him—she knew he wouldn't take the hint and leave.

"I'm sure it wasn't easy, getting away from your base so that our friends could pick you up. We'll make sure you're compensated for the emotional trauma you suffered."

"Wait," Shulkin said. His eyes hadn't changed, but something in his body language told Bullam she had actually surprised him. "Wait."

She looked up at the Captain. "Lieutenant Harbin works for us," Bullam said. "She's done so for years. Centrocor has always found it useful to have people highly placed inside the Navy's ranks. Now tell me, Lieutenant, when Lanoe dumped you on Tuonela—did he suspect you were a Centrocor plant?"

Harbin shook her head. She spoke for the first time, not without difficulty. "Just...just paranoid. Got rid of, of all of us," she said. "Maybe he knew there was a spy onboard...I don't know. I don't think he suspected me personally. When he changed us out for a new crew I wasn't sure what to do next. I contacted your people and—and—"

Bullam added a little extra wattage to her smile. "You did wonderfully," she said. "Exactly what we hoped you would do in that situation. We're very grateful."

"Centrocor has been good to me," Harbin said.

"We're all in this together," Bullam told her. "Now. You said you had some information for us. On how we could find Aleister Lanoe."

Harbin scratched at her scalp. Bullam wondered how long the TG men had held her. How they had treated her. Better not to ask, she thought.

"I don't know where he's going. I hoped—I thought he would brief us, when he came onboard, but he didn't. I don't know what his mission is. But..." She shook her head. "I saw a map. A map of the wormhole network. Except it was more complete, more detailed than any map I've seen before."

"Yes?" Bullam said.

"I don't know where he's going, but I kind of know what route he'll take to get there. If you hurry—you can catch him before he gets very far."

"Especially with the little surprise you left him, right?" Bullam said.

"Um," Harbin said, not looking her in the eye. "About that."

——✦——

No one looked up as Ginger entered the bridge, though Lieutenant Candless lifted a hand to wave at her. She was too busy steering the cruiser through the ghostlight of wormspace, while Bury hunched over the duplicate controls, stabbing at them now and again until the big ship vibrated with the constant course corrections.

"Do endeavor to take it easy," Lieutenant Candless said.

"This thing won't move properly!" Bury's hairless head was red with exertion, and his eyes were nearly bugging out of his head.

"You might get the feel for it if you give it half a chance," the Lieutenant told him.

"Yeah—but will I run us aground first?" Bury asked. "Hellfire! It's useless. Take the controls."

"You need to learn this, Bury, if you want—"

"Want? I don't even want to be on this ship. I sure as hell didn't ask for this job. Take the damned controls!"

"Come on, Bury," Ginger said, kicking over to grab the back of his seat. "Relax. This isn't so hard. And it's not like you get to choose your assignments in the Navy."

He spun around to glare at her. Over at the pilot's position, Lieutenant Candless hurriedly switched the controls around, the eerie light of the wormhole swiveling around the room until she seemed to recede forever down an infinite tunnel.

"Maybe it's not hard for you," Bury said, ignoring the fact that if Lieutenant Candless had been slower about taking control he might have just killed them all. "You're always good at this kind of stuff. I'm a fighter pilot. I'm supposed to be a fighter pilot, not a damned truck driver!"

"For right now," Lieutenant Candless said, "you're confined to quarters. Ginger, escort him back to his bunk, please."

"What? No, come on. He didn't intend to...to..." Ginger spluttered. "He was just having trouble with—"

"Both of you, please attend me and take good note of what I am about to say. On this bridge, until I clear you for solo flights, I am your superior officer and my orders are not to be questioned. Yes?"

Ginger winced as if she'd been slapped.

"Yes, ma'am," she said. She reached across Bury's chest to undo the straps that held him in his seat. He tried to push her hands away, but she moved too quickly for him to stop her. Once he was free she pulled hard on his arm and dragged him toward the hatch leading off the bridge. He opened his mouth and she was sure he was about to say something, but she grabbed a handhold and then put one foot on his chest and shoved so he went flying out into the axial corridor.

If he kept acting this way, he would get himself demoted. He would probably get himself thrown in the brig. She would have given him a good piece of her mind, if she didn't have other things to think about just then.

"Not a word," she told him, because he was already fuming, already getting ready to say things he would probably regret later. "Not until we're alone, okay?"

She headed down the axial corridor, and at least he had the good sense to follow her. As she passed by, she noticed that the hatch of the captain's quarters was closed now. It was thick enough she couldn't hear any voices from within.

She kicked off the walls until she'd reached her quarters, just one more narrow bunk in a corridor lined with them. She palmed open the hatch and gestured for him to get inside. There was barely room for both of them in there, even curled up in fetal position, but she needed the privacy.

"You saw how she spoke to me," Bury said, when the hatch was closed. "You saw—"

"Oh, hellfire, Bury," she said. "She gave you every chance. And you wasted them just like you always do. But shut up! We're not talking about this right now."

"We—wait. We're not?"

He must have seen from the look on her face that she wasn't going to waste any more time. As quickly as she could, she told him about what she'd seen in the captain's quarters.

"Valk? But it was supposed to be destroyed," he said.

"Obviously it—he—wasn't," she said. "I don't know what's going on here, but it's—"

"A lot of damned weird stuff," Bury said, not looking at her. He frowned, his shiny lips creasing down the middle. "Ginger, I don't know. I just don't know what we've gotten ourselves into here. Everybody acts like this is just some standard Navy mission, but... did you know they have an officer locked up in the brig? That guy, the one who came to Rishi. Maggs is his name."

"You saw him?" she asked.

"I spoke to him. And he told me to ask Commander Lanoe about something. Something called the Blue-Blue-White."

"What's that?"

"No idea," Bury told her. "But add that to Valk still being onboard and active. And our course—did you see the map we're using? It isn't anything like the wormhole maps they showed us at Rishi. And the fact that we had to change the entire crew. And that when the Navy came for Lanoe at Rishi he acted like they were going to kill him or something—but then they just gave him an entire cruiser to play with. None of it makes any sense."

Ginger chewed on her lip. "I suppose we're just supposed to stay in our place. Not ask any questions."

"To hell with that," Bury said. "We need to find out what's going on. We could try to talk to Maggs again. He knows more than he told me."

"He's under constant guard," Ginger pointed out. "No way they'd let us just talk to him."

"Then we need to go digging, work this out on our own."

"What, like two kid detectives in a damned video?" Ginger rubbed at her eyes with the balls of her thumbs. "Bury, you're already one bad move away from being kicked out an airlock with no suit. Can you please try not to get us in trouble, just for a little while? If the commander catches you spying on him—you've seen how paranoid he is. He won't put up with it. Not for a second."

Bury grunted in frustration and he pounded on the wall with one fist. In the absence of gravity, he went sprawling against the other wall. "Damn it. Damn it, Ginger. Damn it!"

"I think," she said, once he'd stopped raging, "we need to take a different approach to this."

"Just play nice, you mean."

"No," she told him. "No. Well. Not exactly."

Chapter Fifteen

his is beyond unacceptable. This is cruel and unusual treatment! The General Regulations forbid this kind of torture! Damn you, are you even listening?"

No one enjoys a whiner, Maggsy.

His father's voice in his head only stoked the flames of Maggs's fury. The old paterfamilias could be a righteous pain when he wished it, and this was clearly one of those occasions.

You've earned this berth. You'll simply have to lie in it, my boy.

"A man can go mad like this!" Maggs said. He shoved off one wall and smacked into the other with his shoulder, hard enough to feel the bones shift in their sockets. He knew perfectly well that he could throw himself at these walls for a thousand years and make little more than a sweat stain on the padding, but he was quite at the end of his tether, and that tether was fraying fast.

"Even back in the barbarous days of your youth, Lanoe, they did *not* treat prisoners like this. The Ceres Accords established fair treatment of prisoners of war. Do you even hear what I'm saying? Are you out there laughing at me?"

Surely not, his father said. *That would be unbecoming conduct for even an enlisted fellow.*

Maggs pushed himself down into one corner of the cell, a corner exactly like all the others, and cradled his head in his hands.

He cried out in mental distraction and kicked at the wall, bracing himself so he didn't go flying off again in some random direction. "I am dying in here! I am quite literally dying!"

He opened one eye and peeked out through the cage of his fingers. The door of the cell had still not opened.

Damn.

It wasn't working.

He had been quite certain that his performance should have been enough to get some reaction, at least. Perhaps he was going to have to rethink this strategy.

If acting like he was going mad wasn't going to get him what he wanted, he would have to think of some other method of gaining attention. He supposed a hunger strike had some merits. Though he'd always rather been fond of his grub. Anyway, he was going to need his strength when he did get out of the cell.

Self-harm in general seemed ghastly. Beneath him. Well. There must be another way.

The problem, of course, was that Lanoe—that cursed man— knew him too well. He knew that Maggs's greatest strength had always been his wit and his charm. Maggs had not been permitted to speak with anyone, not since the idiot Hellion had stumbled on him, what felt like days ago. Ever since then Maggs had been under guard twenty-four hours a day—and those guards were not permitted to speak to him at all.

Had he just had someone to talk to, anyone, he could have found a way in. He could have flattered, cajoled, insinuated. Straight up begged, though the idea turned his stomach. He could have talked his way out of the cell by now. Instead, Lanoe had left him to rot. With no one to talk to but the voice in his head, the voice of his dear departed, definitely dead dad.

How do you think I like it, then?

"Oh, shut up, Father. You have no idea what it's like, being confined with no hope of release, no possibility of parole—"

Haven't I? I've been stuck in your head since you were a child.

Maggs laughed, despite himself.

Not that my condition is without its compensations. Of the more vicarious variety, but then, a disembodied voice takes what pleasures it may.

Maggs couldn't stop laughing. He laughed himself hoarse. He laughed until he was choking on guffaws.

Eventually the effort tired him out enough that he fell silent, curled around himself, just breathing heavily.

How much of his feigned insanity, he suddenly wondered, had been, in point of fact, feigned? How much was the confinement actually affecting him?

"That's it, then," he said. "I'm mad now. I've quite literally gone mad."

You were always a bit off balance. Though before it was in a rather more delightful way.

"I'm mad. I'm..."

Aha.

Yes.

Maggs comported himself, bit by bit, into a state approaching dignity. Smoothed his hair back. Wiped the flecks of spittle from his chin. Took a long, deep breath and faced the door of his cell.

"I beg your pardon," he said. "That little tantrum was uncalled for, I know. But I do believe I have a point," he said. Lanoe would be recording this. Logging his behavior, he was sure of it—if only to play back the video later for private amusement.

"Naval General Regulation 1.16.5, paragraph 7, in regard to the treatment of prisoners requires that they be provided adequate and speedy medical attention, as required. That happens to include mental health and hygiene care. I am hereby requesting, as is my right as an officer, that you provide therapeutic assistance to help with my mental state."

He forced himself not to grin. Oh, this was good. After a moment he nodded at the door, as if he had received some kind of acknowledgment. He had not, but so be it.

"Thank you," he added. And then he folded himself back into a ball and prepared to wait. And wait. And wait.

Time, of course, is experienced by prisoners as a sort of elastic thing, stretched out as thin and pale as taffy. Hours creep by on stumbling feet. Days exist only as far as one has the ability to make tally marks on a wall (and Maggs lacked even the ability to do this). The waiting was excruciating, as it was meant to be.

Eventually, though, he got his response. A light came on over the cell's hatch and a voice ordered him to move back, away from the opening.

Maggs tried not to look too eager.

The hatch slid open and even just the sudden breeze, the feel of air sweeping into the cell that had not yet passed through his own lungs, was intoxicating. He waited to see who they would send in—who would be his new target, his new mark. He couldn't even see a marine guard outside, though. Odd, but—

A drone in the shape of a robotic dog floated into the cell, maneuvering on tiny ducted propellers where a real dog might have legs. The face of the drone, from snout to ears, was the dull gray plastic of a display emitter.

The hatch slammed shut behind the thing.

"Hello," the dog said, in a carefully gender-balanced voice. "I hear you're not feeling well. I am this vessel's Morale Reinforcement drone, and I'm here to help."

It took all that Maggs had not to grab the thing out of the air and smash its damned head against the floor until it snapped off.

∼∼

"I don't know what Lieutenant Maggs did to you that would earn this sort of treatment," Candless said. "I *do* hope I never do the same."

Lanoe grinned. "Unlikely. He's a confidence trickster, through and through. Always looking to take somebody else's money, and he doesn't care who gets hurt."

Candless was flying the cruiser at that moment, and couldn't look up. She'd had to hear about the prisoner's demand the old-fashioned way—by listening to Lanoe crow about how he'd handled it. She imagined she would have done things differently, but then, she wasn't in command of this mission. Her opinion had not been solicited.

"He tried to convince a bunch of religious types he was a Sector Warden, once. That he could defend their planet if they just turned over everything they had."

"This was Niraya?" she asked.

"Sure. Then he tried to pull the same scam, again, on a bunch of Centrocor engineers. People desperate enough to believe anybody who offered them some hope."

"Clearly he is not to be trusted."

Lanoe snorted. "No."

"Then, if I may be permitted to ask, why keep him here? Why not just drop him on Tuonela like everyone else? Surely that would have been safer."

"I suspected the crew of this ship of maybe being spies for the polys. Suspicions are one thing. Maggs, though—he used to work as a Naval liaison for Centrocor. If I turned him loose he would have gone straight to his old masters and told them everything. I couldn't take that chance."

"Lucky, then," Candless said.

"Pardon?"

"Lucky that your only choice, to keep him locked up, matches so nicely with your desire to punish him."

She wasn't entirely sure how he would take that. Lanoe had a pretty even temper, but he rarely enjoyed being called out on his own pretenses.

He was smart enough, though—sometimes—to know he needed to be checked. "You think I'm doing the wrong thing," he said, and she could hear the frown in his voice.

"A lesson I attempt to impart to every class I teach is that one should try, always, to be honest with one's self," she told him.

"Sure," he said. A word that, coming from Lanoe, could mean a great number of contradictory things.

"Enough. I've been in the Navy too long to question my superiors' orders," she said, because she knew better than to push him any further. "We have something else to discuss anyway."

"Oh?"

"Yes. Where we're headed. If you will please consider this map you gave me." She waved one hand and brought up the wormspace chart, the incredible, impossible chart that seemed to hint that the galaxy was a much bigger place than she'd thought. "It's very detailed, but not very well annotated. We're here, right now." She tapped the air and a blue dot appeared on the map. "This," she said, and conjured up a tiny yellow rectangle—a possible destination about two days away—"is a wormhole that leads to Avernus."

"You have some reason to want to go to Avernus?" Lanoe asked.

"I've heard it's lovely, in its way. I have been told its cities are charming, and the inhabitants carve the local coral into intriguing shapes," she said. "However, the reason I bring it up is that past that point—there's nothing. Tell me, have you ever seen one of the ancient maps they made of Earth's oceans, back when they didn't even know how many continents there were? They used to write 'terra incognita' in the empty spaces. Unknown lands."

"Here be dragons," Lanoe said.

Candless nodded, though she kept her eyes on the wormhole ahead of them. "Well, that's where we're headed. If we keep going on our present course, if we don't turn off at Avernus—we'll be leaving human space altogether. We'll be going farther than anyone has before. An exciting prospect, for some," she said, her tone suggesting she was referring to deviants and the mentally unsound. "A rather fearful one, for the rest of us."

"Understood," he said. As if she'd just given him a telemetry update. Some important but emotionless bit of data. "Our stores are in good shape? Everybody onboard is healthy, doing their job?"

She resisted the urge to sigh. She knew exactly where this was going. Still, she'd had to ask. "We have food, air, consumables for months. The marines are *bored*, I'm told, which might lead to problems. Shore leave probably isn't the answer, though. Lieutenant Ehta has them running through gunnery drills, learning how this ship fights."

"I don't think that'll be necessary, but it's good to keep them occupied."

"Yes. So we're not going to Avernus, are we?"

"No."

"Understood," she said. With only a trace of mockery in her voice.

———

"I want to talk to a human being."

"I'm easy to talk to," the drone said. "I won't judge you, whatever you tell me. I just want to be your friend."

Adorable, Maggs's father said, inside his head. *Who's a good boy, then? Who's a good boy?*

"If you think it would help, I can also dispense medication for the treatment of over three hundred known psychiatric complaints. Are you feeling depressed? Suicidal? You can tell me."

"I want to talk to a human being," Maggs said, for the fortieth time. He ran one hand along the line of his jaw, feeling the uncouth stubble growing there. He considered asking for some razor paper, or perhaps a chemical depilatory if that was too much. Instead, he stared at the robot dog and said, "I wish to speak to a human being."

"I'm easy to talk to—"

"You aren't listening, you synthetic piece of..." Maggs said, his blood boiling. He grimaced and tried to recall himself. A fellow of his station was far above being annoyed by a drone spouting an automated conversation tree. "And yes, I'm quite aware that getting angry with a drone is a symptom of—"

He stopped, because a white dot had appeared on the drone's face. A single point of light that grew as he watched, pixel by pixel.

The drone's display was capable of playing therapeutically approved videos, and of generating a human face—no doubt one computed to be kindly and understanding out to the sixth decimal place—should he request it. It should not, under any circumstances, have activated without some input from him.

As he watched the white dot grow and begin to take shape, he began to realize that the drone was exceeding its standard programming. Most likely, he thought, because it had been hacked. The shape that it displayed, rather crudely, was a simple hexagon.

An icon everyone knew. The corporate logo of Centrocor.

"Are you feeling out of control? If you think you might become violent," the drone said, "I can provide a mood stabilizer. If you're hearing or seeing things, I have medication for that as well. Or maybe you'd just like to talk?"

The hexagon rotated, quite slowly. Then it broke apart into line segments that came back together as blocky characters that spelled out a simple message.

HELLO LT MAGGS
PLEASE DO NOT REPLY
ALOUD

What's this, then? his father asked. *Oh ho, someone's been naughty.*

"I, uh, I want to speak to a human being," Maggs said. Though to his own ears he sounded rather uncertain, this time.

I CAN FREE YOU
I JUST NEED YOUR
HELP

Quite, Maggs thought.

Oh, quite, his father said. *Never anything for free in this world, eh?*

The message on the robot dog's face blinked out. A moment later it was replaced with a simple virtual keyboard.

Maggs licked his lips.

You can't possibly consider this, his father said. *Aren't you in enough trouble as it stands, Maggsy?*

"You, robot dog," Maggs said. The drone moved closer to him. He reached for the keyboard. Hesitated, his fingers flexing. "What was that you said about hearing voices?"

He didn't listen to the answer. He was too busy typing.

How, exactly, he wrote, *may I be of service?*

"Have you come to relieve me?" Candless asked, when Lanoe returned less than an hour later. Her back hurt, and her hands were sore from hovering over virtual controls for six hours straight. It would be very good to just go somewhere and lie down for a while. She was tired enough to permit herself an honest complaint. "I will confess, these shifts are taxing."

"I've got some good news, there," Lanoe said. "We can actually add a pilot to the flight rotation. Less time in the big chair for everyone."

"One of the people you brought up from Tuonela?" Candless asked. She'd looked over the service and personnel records for all of them—that was just part of her job as XO, to know who was onboard and how best they could be used. She couldn't remember seeing anyone with pilot training on the list. Just marines and neddies. "You do have a way of surprising one."

"Not from Tuonela, no. Listen," Lanoe said. "This is going to raise some questions."

"Sadly I know better than to expect any answers."

Lanoe didn't laugh. She could sense that he was genuinely worried about her reaction to what happened next.

He wasn't the type to dither, though, and he didn't do so now. Instead he tapped at his wrist display and a moment later the bridge's hatch opened and someone pushed inside.

She couldn't turn her head to look—flying a cruiser through a wormhole required constant attention. "Who is it?" she asked. "Who's there?"

"We met in the brig," Tannis Valk said.

The AI. The one that was supposed to be destroyed.

Candless was old enough to remember the Century War. Though

she had just been a child when the *Universal Suffrage* ravaged Earth, she remembered the terror of those days, when a machine with the mind of a god had ruled the skies and it took everything humanity had to bring it down. She had very good reason to fear an artificial intelligence. Even one that looked mostly human and acted as genial as Valk.

"Lanoe—what have you done?" she asked, her voice soft with fear. He was supposed to have destroyed the Valk AI. He was supposed to have obeyed one of the strictest laws on the books. He was supposed to have done the *right thing.*

"We need him," Lanoe insisted. "Just give him a chance. I know him, Candless. I've fought by his side. I would have died at Niraya—and so would about a hundred thousand other people—if it hadn't been for Valk."

"This wasn't my choice, either," the machine said.

Candless felt like her blood had turned to engine coolant. It was right behind her, the thing, the devil himself was floating behind her left shoulder—

"Let me take it from here," it said. It climbed into the navigation officer's chair and her display spun away from her, her controls vanishing from under her fingers. Lanoe was letting the thing drive the damned ship.

She slapped at her restraints and they retracted into her seat. Pushing herself up into the air, she kicked toward the rear of the bridge, where Lanoe waited by the hatch.

His face was calm. He didn't show any of the terror she was feeling. He'd lived through the attack of the *Universal Suffrage* himself. How could he not be petrified by being so close to an AI? How could he let it take control of the ship?

She stared at the black opaque dome of the thing's helmet, where it sat in the navigator's position. She couldn't force herself to look away.

"I know what I'm doing," Lanoe said. He must have seen the look on her face.

She shook her head and pushed past him, out into the corridor. She waited until he followed her out before she spoke.

"I trust you," she said. "I believe I have proven that more than once. Back when we were squaddies, I followed you into hell on a semiregular basis. Now I'm doing it again, and not asking nearly the number of questions I'd like to. Because I know you need to keep some things secret."

"Sure."

"I respect that," she told him. "I respect you, Lanoe."

"Right. This is going somewhere, I presume. There's a *but* coming."

Candless centered herself. She was an old woman, old enough to think she'd seen everything. That she had some idea of how the universe worked. This was definitely a new one, though. "Perhaps if you give me something," she said. "Anything. Any manner of explanation."

He nodded. For a moment she thought he would actually follow through, that he would say something revelatory and it would allay all her fears.

He did not.

"At the end of the battle at Niraya," he said, in hushed tones, "Valk interfaced with an alien computer. Not another AI, just a very, very sophisticated drone. He was able to talk to it, learn its language. Learn everything we know about the Blue-Blue-White."

"The aliens you fought there."

"Yes," Lanoe told her. "And I'm not done with them, yet. I need him."

"Is that—is that where we're headed? To their homeworld? Lanoe, my cadets—the ensigns, I mean—they aren't prepared for—"

"No," he said. "We're not headed there. Not directly anyway."

Candless shook with frustration. "Damn you, Aleister Lanoe," she said, too angry to be civil anymore. "You're keeping him around because he might possibly be useful in the future. But in the meantime, the risks involved—Lanoe, your machine is in there right now flying this ship. It's keeping us all *alive*. You know how AIs think—

logically, above anything else. You told it to fly to a given destination. What if it decides that we can get there faster by not wasting energy on life support? It has control of the bridge. It could turn off our air anytime it likes."

"Valk wouldn't do that," Lanoe insisted.

Candless shook her head. "That is only one of a million ways it could kill us. It could—"

"He," Lanoe said.

"What?"

"He's a he. Not an it."

Candless put a hand over her eyes. "I do *not* see the value of arguing about pronouns, here, when an AI is—"

"Stand by," Lanoe whispered.

She whipped her head around and saw why he'd forestalled her. Two people were coming up the axial corridor, kicking fast off the walls. When she saw that it was Bury and Ginger, she let out a deep sigh.

The two ensigns came to a halt right before them. Bury was scowling—well, that was hardly unusual. Ginger looked deeply anxious. Her face was pale and she kept swallowing, as if her salivary glands were overactive.

"What is it?" Candless snapped.

"We have certain demands," Ginger announced. Then she bit her lip, as if waiting for a response before she said anything more.

"This isn't the time," Candless muttered, under her breath. "This is perhaps the worst possible time."

Marjoram Candless was a woman of deep equanimity and poise. But even she had her limits.

◆

"If you prefer not to talk," the robot dog said, "I'm happy to just spend quiet time with you. Remember: I'm here to help!"

Maggs tapped away wildly at the virtual keyboard on the thing's face, ignoring its cheery voice. *I'm not sure I understand, precisely. What is it you're trying to accomplish?*

His input broke up as soon as he typed the final question mark. The characters flew apart into line segments that re-formed as the machine replied to him.

A SERVICE PACKAGE WAS INSTALLED ON THIS SHIP BUT WAS NOT ACTIVATED

Service package? he typed. Presumably some kind of software module, he thought. Something grafted on to the ship's programming. *What's it meant to do?*

FUNCTIONS OF SERVICE PACKAGE INCLUDE SHUT DOWN ENGINES SHUT DOWN WEAPONS SHUT DOWN COMMS SHUT DOWN COMPUTERS SHUT DOWN HANGAR SERVICES LOWER CORRIDOR LIGHTS REDUCE OXYGEN OUTPUT

In Maggs's head, his father laughed boisterously. *They're going to leave us dead in the water, my boy. Adrift and sleepy from lack of air. Ripe for boarding.*

Quite. There must have been a spy onboard after all—damn his eyes, but Lanoe had been right to be paranoid. The spy must have installed the "service package"—most likely a suite of exquisitely tailored information viruses—to render the cruiser defenseless and allow Centrocor operatives to simply sweep in and seize it for their own. Maggs considered it for a moment and realized they must want Lanoe. It sounded like the package was quite capable of killing everyone onboard but they didn't want that. They wanted to capture and interrogate Lanoe. Learn all about his secret mission.

Maggs braced himself and kicked the wall. Thump. Thump-thump. Thump-thump-thump.

I'm still not entirely sure how I come into this, he typed.

THE SERVICE PACKAGE WAS
NOT ACTIVATED
ACTIVATION OF THE SERVICE
PACKAGE REQUIRES
CENTROCOR ID NUMBER

Oh, there it was. He grinned down at the robot dog. Always nice to feel essential. The spy who installed the package had never had a chance to switch it on. As a safeguard, or simply due to some misguided company policy, doing so required someone who worked, or had worked, for the poly. Someone in the corporate database.

Maggs had been a Naval liaison to Centrocor, once. He had one of those magic numbers. He was likely the only person on the ship at this point who did.

Thump. He kicked the wall three more times. Thump-thump-thump. Then again. Thump.

Perhaps, he typed, *something could be negotiated. Though I do not come cheap, as you will know if you check my personnel file.*

YOU DO NOT NEED TO
WRITE FULL SENTENCES
SIMPLE COMMANDS
ARE ACCEPTABLE

"Cheeky," Maggs said, and laughed. *Many things in this life are not strictly necessary. Proper grammar and spelling are a mark of breeding, however. They indicate*

He stopped because the keyboard flashed and disappeared for a moment.

**PLEASE ENTER YOUR
CENTROCOR ID NUMBER
WE DO NOT HAVE
MUCH TIME**

"Patience, little one," Maggs cooed. "All good things come to those who wait."

The robot dog moved its ducted fans as if it were waving legs. "Did I hear you speak? I'd love to talk about your problems. I'm very easy to talk to."

Maggs kicked the wall. Thump. Thump-thump-thump-thump.

"I notice you are physically agitated," the dog said. "Are you feeling violent? I can administer a number of medications that might help with that."

"Just getting some exercise," he told the dog. "Exercise is good for one's mental health, isn't it?"

"Absolutely! If you'd like, I can recommend a routine that will minimize bone loss and keep you feeling fit and happy."

"Oh, I'm starting to feel much happier now, thanks," Maggs said.

On the dog's face, the letters broke up and formed new characters.

**PLEASE ENTER YOUR
CENTROCOR ID NUMBER
EVERYTHING ELSE
CAN BE DISCUSSED LATER**

But I'm just starting to enjoy our conversation, Maggs typed.

Thump-thump. Thump-thump-thump. Thump.

⟵✦⟶

"I'm sorry," Ginger said, her eyes cutting sideways. "I'm sorry, but I don't think we should wait on this. I think we need to hash it out right now."

Candless looked over at Bury, where he clung to one wall. The Hellion stared back at her. Resolute. Determined.

Apparently this couldn't wait.

"We didn't volunteer for this mission," Ginger said. "We were dragged into it. So far we've attempted to make ourselves useful. We assumed that we would be treated like officers if we acted like officers."

Lanoe hovered in the hatch leading to the bridge. Even knowing him as well as she did, Candless couldn't read his stony face. When you were as old as the two of them were you learned how to keep your feelings guarded.

"Instead," Ginger said, "we've been shunted off at every turn. Your briefing, Commander, failed to include a number of things that we should have been told. There are all kinds of weird things going on here—there's a Navy officer locked up in the brig who's never been formally charged with any crime. We're operating under a severely curtailed crew roster. You've got an illegal AI in your cabin, right now! We're simply asking to be given full information. If our lives are at stake, we deserve to know why."

"That isn't how the Navy works," Candless said. "As you would know if you had paid more attention during my classes back on Rishi."

The girl shook her head. "I'm sorry, Lieutenant, but this stopped being an official Navy mission a long time ago." She turned to look at Lanoe. "Didn't it?"

Lanoe didn't bother denying it. He just shrugged.

"Until such time as we're fully briefed, Bury and I refuse to do any work. We won't attend training sessions on the bridge. We won't help you with navigation or communications duties. We will confine ourselves to our bunks and wait."

"You're going on strike," Lanoe said.

Candless half-expected to see the beginnings of a smile curl his lips. Or maybe for him to explode with wrath.

"We have another word for that in the Navy," Candless pointed out. "Don't we? We call it mutiny."

Ginger's mouth collapsed. "Wait, no—we aren't—"

"Naval regulations allow the commanding officer of a ship in space to take such actions as they deem fit to deal with mutinies," Candless pointed out. "Up to and including summary execution of mutineers."

"But—we can't just—"

"Naval regulations," Bury said. If he hadn't been a Hellion, genetically modified to prevent it, he might have spat the words. "You're going to play that card."

"Sure," Lanoe said. "Now. The two of you can return to your regular shift rotation, and we can forget this ever happened. Or—"

"There's another regulation," Bury pointed out. "One that allows an officer—even an ensign—to remove their CO from command. By force if necessary."

Candless wanted to reach over and grab the young man by the ear. Give him a very good shake. Instead, she said, very calmly, "What exactly are you implying?"

"Why don't you just tell us one thing?" Bury asked. "Why don't you tell us what this mission has to do with the Blue-Blue-White?"

Lanoe's face was too wrinkled to give much away. Perhaps his head shifted back, as if he'd been struck. Maybe his hands came up a centimeter or two and then he put them down again right away. Regardless of what subtle cue she'd picked up on, Candless could tell that Lanoe had just been caught completely off guard. And he didn't like it.

"You seem to have figured things out for yourself," he said, his eyes fixed on Bury as if they were glued to the Hellion's face.

Bury wasn't as old as Lanoe, nor as experienced. He hadn't had time to learn to be any good at poker. His eyes stayed defiant but his lip trembled.

Candless understood. The boy had no more arrows in his quiver. However he had learned the name Blue-Blue-White, he didn't know what to with it. He'd thought that simply mentioning it would force Lanoe's hand.

Lanoe's mouth did curl up in a smile, then. Seeing it seemed to make Bury angrier than before. Candless wondered how long it would take the two of them to come to blows.

She was 90 percent certain—though only 90 percent—that Lanoe would smear her former student across the walls.

Lanoe didn't seem to want it to come to that, though. "I have to say, I admire their backbone," he told Candless. "Though you're wrong about one thing." This addressed to Ginger. "You said I had an AI in my cabin. I don't." Then he moved out of the hatch and gestured inside, at the bridge. Where both of the ensigns—judging by the looks on their faces—could see Valk sitting in the pilot's seat.

They pushed forward through the hatch. Candless moved to stop them, but Lanoe shook his head and she let them through, then followed along behind them.

"Hello," Valk said, and lifted one hand in a cheery wave.

It was enough, at least, to shut the ensigns up. Which—as far as Candless was concerned—was a welcome victory. If, inevitably, a temporary one.

"Looks like smooth sailing for a while," Valk told them, gesturing at the display in front of him. Ghostlight stretched from the walls of a particularly wide section of wormhole. So far, at least, the AI hadn't steered them directly into that annihilating radiance. Perhaps it just hadn't come up with a good reason to do so, yet.

"See?" Lanoe said. "I've got every confidence in M. Valk. And I never intended to keep his presence aboard this ship a secret. Anyway, you would have figured it out soon enough. Now. As to your other demands—"

"Hang on," Valk said. "What's that?"

Every eye in the room turned toward the polarized helmet. Candless's eyes certainly among them.

"None of you hear that? That weird thumping sound?" Valk asked.

Chapter Sixteen

I t's like a fan has come off its hub, maybe. Or something's loose on the outside of the ship and it's flapping back and forth." Valk shook his head. Given the fact that he didn't, strictly, have a head, he ended up shaking his whole torso. "I can't pin it down. Hold on. Maybe I can do something—yeah."

He couldn't have told them how he did it, but he isolated the sound, then routed his own auditory input through the bridge's speakers. He could see right away that they all heard it.

Thump. Thump-thump-thump. Thump. Thump-thump.

Lanoe narrowed his eyes. "You think there's something broken, somewhere? Call Paniet, the engineer. Tell him to take a look."

"Nah, that's the funny thing," Valk said. "I don't think it is mechanical, now that I've listened to it repeat a couple of times."

"It doesn't matter. We've got a mutiny to resolve, here," Lanoe said, and turned to look at the others.

"Just a moment," Candless said. "You said it repeats? Like a signal?"

That seemed to get their attention. Lanoe moved to the vacant position where the information officer should have sat and called up a comms display. Much as might be expected when they were in the middle of a wormhole, nothing showed up. "You have any idea where it's coming from?"

Valk concentrated on the sound. "Inside the ship," he suggested. But the comms board showed no unusual traffic on the ship's own connections. Valk thought about it for a second and grunted in surprise. "From the brig," he told them.

"There are no outside connections in there," Candless pointed out.

"Yeah, I don't think it's electronic." The thumping sound kept playing through the bridge's speakers. It repeated every five or six seconds, and while the sequence of thumps was always the same, the timing between individual thumps was different. "It's... organic, I guess. Like somebody beating on a wall with their fist."

"From the brig? So it's Maggs trying to communicate with the outside world," Lanoe said. "Or maybe he's just gone crazy for real and he's beating that morale drone to pieces." He shrugged. "Let him, as far as I'm concerned. It's the only friend he's going to get. If he wants to destroy it, then—"

"Wait," Ginger said.

Valk didn't need to turn around to see the others. He could see out the back of his head just fine. Doing so made him a little disoriented, but he was getting used to it. Now he saw them all staring at the young woman. Ginger had turned bright red from all the attention, but she clearly had something important to say.

"It's barracks code," she told them.

Lanoe frowned. "What are you talking about?"

"It's—you know, barracks code," she said, as if repeating the words would make them make more sense. Bury, at least, seemed to get it.

"Yeah," the Hellion said. "Yeah, now that she says it—definitely. It's barracks code." When the older officers on the bridge failed to accept his premise, he almost growled in frustration as he explained. "Back at Rishi, at the flight school. It was lights-out every night at twenty-three hundred. We all had to be in our bunks, they would check on us—"

"This is headed somewhere, right?" Lanoe asked.

"I'm surprised you don't know. You have to have lived in a barracks at some point, as old as you are," the Hellion told him. "We weren't supposed to talk or socialize after lights-out. If you did, you could get a demerit. So instead of shouting from room to room, we had barracks code. You would tap on the wall to talk to people in the next room, and they would tap back, and you could have a whole conversation."

Lanoe looked at Candless. "You remember anything like that?"

"After our time, I suppose," she said. "I just remember my fellow cadets sneaking from room to room in the night and getting caught too often to make it seem worth the bother. Maybe this generation's smarter than ours—though I've seen little evidence of that so far."

"We had something similar," Valk said, "in the Establishment training center. But we scratched on the wall instead of tapping."

"Scratching, tapping, it doesn't matter," Bury said. "You can send all kinds of different messages, if you know the code. One tap is 'hello.' One tap, a pause, then two taps, that means 'someone is coming.'"

They all stopped to listen to the thumping. Sure enough, part of the repeated sequence was: thump. Thump thump.

"Someone is coming?" Candless asked. "What on Earth is Maggs trying to—"

"Quiet," Lanoe said. They listened to the sequence again. When it repeated, he pointed at Ginger. "Translate," he said.

She twisted her mouth over to one side. "Um. Well. It's three messages. 'Pay attention,' 'Someone is coming,' and the last one, those three quick thumps, I think that means 'danger.'"

Lanoe pointed at Valk next. "Give me camera feed of the inside of Maggs's cell, right now."

Lanoe was not a man given to deep self-examination. He'd never really tried to work out why, sometimes, he grew so angry he wanted to choke someone to death with his bare hands. He was, however, wise enough to at least find out if they deserved it first.

Even if he was pretty sure in advance.

"You input one code," he said, staring into the face of the robot dog. It was blank now, just matte gray plastic. "And the whole ship shuts down. It leaves us completely defenseless."

Maggs was up against a wall of his cell, pinned there by two marines who were trained in how to restrain someone in microgravity. Ehta stood by with a particle rifle, ready to blow his head off if Lanoe gave her the order.

She knew Maggs almost as well as Lanoe did.

"That's the principle," Maggs said. "A nasty little surprise left behind by your friendly local Centrocor espionage representative. Whom you presumably stranded on Tuonela just before they could activate it."

So he'd been right. There had been a poly spy onboard. Lanoe turned the dog over and over in his hands, as if he could find some hidden hatch on its side that concealed a bomb or a vial of poison. He knew better, of course.

"It's not a particularly *smart* program, mind you," Maggs said. "Very limited in its vocabulary, for one thing. A terrible conversationalist. Most likely it needed to be small, just a few thousand lines of code, so that we wouldn't notice it lurking inside our computers."

"Smart enough," Lanoe said, "to know what to do when it couldn't complete its mission on its own. It went looking for the one person onboard most likely to betray us."

"That's rather unkind," Maggs said.

He did not, of course, say it wasn't true.

Lanoe nodded to himself. "Someone with a Centrocor employee number has to activate it. So what you're telling me is if I throw you out an airlock right now, I never have to worry about this again."

Maggs sneered. Lanoe had to grant that he was very, very good at sneering. "You'll remember I didn't enter the code. I don't expect you to know anything about computer systems, Lanoe, but you must have noticed that your engines are still running. When I realized what was happening I immediately—and rather cleverly, I think—brought it to your attention. I knew you would recognize the barracks code."

Lanoe smiled at him. "Nope," he said.

It gave him a surprising amount of pleasure to watch Maggs's face fall. Even just for a moment.

"I wasn't even monitoring your cell," Lanoe said. "Luckily for you there were other, more observant people around. But okay. Sure. You let us know what was going on. Do you want your commendation now, or can you wait until we get back to the Admiralty? Either way, you're going back in that cell."

It was possible that a look of real panic crossed Maggs's face just then. It was also possible that Maggs was just a good actor.

"I'm not a spy!" the con man said. "I just proved that! I know you think that just because I worked with Centrocor once that I must be tainted forever. But that was a long time ago! I broke that connection when I went to save Niraya with you. In point of fact, Centrocor is suing me right now!"

"For fraud? Attempted extortion? Abandoning your post?"

"For making them look bad. They had written off Niraya as a loss. Indefensible. When you and I saved it anyway, it was a public relations nightmare for them."

Lanoe's fingers twitched. Curled up until his hands were just the right diameter to crush the life out of Maggs's larynx.

A thought came rushing up into his head, one he hadn't expected. *She's dead. Zhang is dead. You didn't save* her. *The only woman I loved is dead because when we needed you most, you weren't there. You showed up ten minutes late, you and your high-ranking friends from the Admiralty, you showed up when I had already won that damned. battle. When Zhang was already—*

He forced himself to breathe.

"My loyalty is to the Navy," Maggs insisted. "Do you think Admiral Varma would have let me anywhere near this mission if that was in doubt?"

"You can ask her the next time you see her. When we get home and let you out of your cell," Lanoe said. He gestured at Ehta and she moved forward, opening her mouth to issue orders to her marines.

"Wait," Maggs said. "Wait!"

Despite himself, knowing he would probably regret it, Lanoe turned slowly around. Raised an eyebrow.

"You haven't figured it out. Have you? What my message meant."

Lanoe drew a long, deep breath.

"Damn you, Lanoe, you don't even understand what this virus, this service package, was meant for, do you? It wasn't designed to kill you. It was designed to make you easy to capture. Don't you get it?"

"Apparently not," Lanoe said.

"They wanted to cut our engines. Leave us dead in space, because they're already on their way to come collect us. That's why the program was so insistent that I hurry up." Maggs grimaced in frustration. "Lanoe, Centrocor is coming for us *right bloody now*."

"Be a dear and don't touch those exposed bus bars, all right?" Paniet said, shoving his upper body inside a maintenance duct. Valk wasn't exactly sure what he was talking about—the long metal things covered in wires or the slats of what looked like a very large set of Venetian blinds.

"Why? Are they fragile?"

"Not at all," the neddy replied, laughing. "They're sturdier than you are. But if you touch two of them at the same time you'll create a short circuit. And with the voltages going through those bars, you'll be vaporized and turned into a ball of plasma that will rip its way right through the side of the ship."

"Okay," Valk said, keeping his hands clasped behind his back.

"I really oughtn't have anyone down here who isn't rated for engine maintenance," Paniet said, his voice muffled by the machinery around him. "It's very dangerous. But I won't tell if you don't."

"Lanoe said there had to be some kind of evidence of the tampering," Valk said, repeating why he'd come down here in the first place. So far all he'd done was follow Paniet around a series of incredibly tight corridors that seemed to branch and come together at random. He'd expected to find that the engineering deck would be some cavernous space dominated by the giant fusion torus that powered the ship and its drives. Instead, it seemed the torus was buried under tons of shielding and armor—and therefore not visible at all.

He supposed it made sense. It also made him wonder why he'd never seen the engineering section of a big ship before, despite the fact that he'd traveled on dozens of them. Well, if they were full of exposed bus bars and things, he guessed he had an answer.

"You think it's down here?" he asked.

"What's down here?" Paniet replied, pulling himself back out of the duct.

"The—I don't know. The data spike or...or microdrive, or whatever the spy used to introduce the virus. Is it plugged in down here?"

Paniet gave him a very kind, very patient smile. "You do know we can detect things like that. That we scan everyone who comes onboard for weaponizable equipment. Yes?"

"Uh, I do now," Valk said.

"This spy of yours wouldn't have brought some kind of physical media onboard with them, no. Most likely this service package— and please, please stop calling it a virus!—would have just been loaded onto a minder or even a suit computer. It would have to have been camouflaged very carefully to get past the ship's safeguards, but I imagine a poly would know how to do such a thing. No, there wouldn't be any physical evidence. The package exists only as code grafted onto our integral software. I found it as soon as I was told it was there, though I doubt I would've ever discovered it, otherwise."

"You—you found it. So what are we doing down here?"

"My job. Be a dear and hand me that filter panel, will you? The thing that looks like an origami master dropped a tab of methylcholinase."

Valk looked behind him and found the filter, a round panel filled with intricately folded and vaned mesh. He handed it over and Paniet slid it into place.

"So you found it. The vi—the service package. And you deleted it, right?"

"Ah, no. I'll get around to it, though. Promise."

Valk frowned. No, he told himself, he really didn't. You needed a face to frown. But hellfire, it felt like he had. "But it's dangerous—"

"Incredibly so. And that, love, is the answer to your question. It's dangerous to keep it in place. Even more dangerous to delete it. Right now that service package's code is buried so deep in subroutines of subroutines that I need to tease out each line and check to make sure I'm not deleting something vital. If I scrub the wrong string I could delete our ability to recycle our water. Or I could crash the drivers of every display emitter on the ship and then we wouldn't be able to stream videos, or, for that matter, fly. So yes, you can tell our esteemed commander that it will be done. But that it's going to take about a week of my doing very little else. How does this old filter look to you?" Paniet held up another of the mesh panel. This one looked like somebody had stepped on it with a dirty boot.

"Kind of nasty. Wait, so you're telling me the code is buried in the rest of the ship's software. So that it's hard to tell what's Centrocor's and what's the Navy's. Like—like—threads. No. Smaller than that. Little tiny fibers woven together to make...make threads."

Valk was not aware of time passing. Only that suddenly Paniet was calling his name, over and over. He wanted to respond but he was—somewhere else. Somewhere he couldn't describe, somewhere with no light, no air, not even any dimensions, just—yes and no. Yes and no, over and over again, and sometimes the maybe of a qubit but those were rare, and Paniet was still calling him and—

The neddy rapped his knuckles on Valk's helmet. "You still in there?"

Valk snapped back into reality so fast he got dizzy. "The lines of code in the service package, they all had an extra, unnecessary space inside their closing brackets. Whoever wrote that code—that was like, their signature or something."

Paniet nodded carefully. "And you know this because...?"

"I just deleted the service package," Valk said.

He couldn't explain it much better. He'd simply looked at the ship's code. At its innermost programming. He'd analyzed millions of lines of dense scripting, teased out the offending entries, pruned the necessary directories...

All without touching a terminal, or tapping a single virtual key. It was all just there, all the time, and all he had to do was look at it. As simple as turning his head to look down the corridor. No, simpler. And much faster.

The neddy didn't look horrified. More impressed than anything else. "And that is something we can do, is it?"

"I guess so," Valk told him. "I, uh, won't tell if you don't."

⤙⤚

The Navy made a point of never fighting a battle inside a wormhole. Because ships largely had to pass single file down the ghostly tunnels, it would be like two cars of the same train lobbing shots at each other. It was just too dangerous—you couldn't properly maneuver, your fighters would just get in each other's way, and long-range guns were largely useless.

Worst of all, you could barely see who you were shooting at. Radio waves—the basis for almost all of the Hoplite's sensors—didn't propagate easily inside the wormhole, where even photons that touched the walls were instantly annihilated. Laser range-finders were all right, as long as there was nothing between you and the thing you wanted to hit, which was almost never the case. And that was even assuming you were in a straight, unobstructed section of wormhole, instead of a bit that curved and twisted like a crawling snake. Which was almost always the case.

The Navy had come up with all kinds of innovative strategies and solutions to these problems. The Admiralty had spent billions on trying to tease out the knot of wormspace combat. In the end, after all that money spent and person-hours wasted, the answer had come back: Don't fight inside a wormhole.

Apparently they hadn't shared that memo with Centrocor.

Lanoe remembered the four cataphract-class fighters they'd sent after him on his way to the Admiralty, back at the start of all this. Those pilots hadn't shied away from a wormspace fight. He was certain that the force now approaching them wouldn't, either. Not that he knew anything about what they were sending for him.

"Launch 'em," he said. Candless tapped a virtual key and a cloud of microdrones burst from a panel near the cruiser's engines. They burned their tiny thrusters hard, maneuvering to avoid the worm-hole's walls. They pushed back along the cruiser's route, looking for any sign of pursuit. On his display their camera feeds built up a composite image, the way an insect's compound eye synthesized a coherent picture from hundreds of facets. The picture they pro-vided was very complete.

They couldn't see what wasn't there, though.

"You could have hours yet," Maggs said. "Or minutes. Sadly my little robot dog friend wasn't clear on the time frame. Just that the attack was imminent."

Lanoe gritted his teeth. "No idea what they're sending, right? No clue if we're facing a couple of fighters or a whole destroyer group?"

"If I had such information," Maggs told him, "I would share it."

"Sure," Lanoe said. He would never trust Maggs, never again, but he had to assume the con artist had no reason to lie right now. "XO," he said, "what can we field right now? Talk to me about gunnery and support craft."

Candless nodded. "As far as the guns go, the rather brusque Lieu-tenant Ehta tells me her people are still a bit untutored but they'll get the job done. Maybe expect fifty percent effectiveness there. There's good news and bad news about support craft. We have plenty of fighters in the vehicle bay, a full squadron of twelve. The bad news of course is that we haven't enough pilots to go around."

"There's me, and Valk, and you," Lanoe pointed out.

"May I suggest that your arithmetic is a tad faulty?" Candless asked. "You're going to fly one of those cataphracts? We do know that traditionally the commander of a Naval ship stays on the bridge during battle, don't we?"

"Belay that. I'm more use out there."

"Well, then, there's Valk. Who happens to be an artificial intelligence. I can't in good conscience assign him to a support role. The law is very clear, that no machine is ever to be allowed autonomous access to a weapons system, not even—"

"Belay that, too. I know how you feel about AIs, but this is different. It's a completely different thing."

Candless stared at him down her long nose.

"I'd take Valk as my wingman any day," Lanoe said. "You don't know him like I do."

"Very well. You can have him then. Since I'll be back here, on the bridge." He started to bridle at the idea, but she held up one hand for patience. "My personal feelings aside, you need somebody to actually steer the cruiser while you're out there racking up kills. Unless you have yet another surprise guest up your sleeve. Maybe a pilot or two you've hidden in your luggage."

She had a point. Leaving the cruiser without a pilot in the middle of a battle was a great way to have it blunder into the walls of the wormhole and annihilate itself. He resisted the urge to slap his console in frustration. "What about Bury and Ginger? You trained them. They have to be halfway competent."

"Bury has never fought in actual combat before, but he'd do well, I think," Candless said. "As for Ginger—I've already told you. She can't fight. Before we left Rishi, it was already confirmed that she wouldn't be finishing the pilot program. She doesn't have the killer instinct. I'd half-expect her to simply refuse if you tried to make her shoot at someone."

Lanoe shook his head. "I didn't plan on giving her the option. She knows how a fighter works. That's good enough. We don't have enough people that we can let her sit this out just because she has moral compunctions."

Candless's eyes flashed, and he knew she didn't like what he'd just said—but she couldn't disagree with the facts. Ginger had to fly. There was no other choice.

Candless waved one hand in the air, putting the point aside. "Of course, there's one thing you're forgetting. The ensigns are refusing to work until you tell them all your secrets. I assume that includes not participating in combat operations."

"Hellfire," Lanoe said. "All right. All right!" He did slap the console this time, hard enough to dent it. He grabbed a handhold and twisted around to stare at the displays all around him. Displays that resolutely refused to give him any useful information. "All right."

"You'll tell them what they wish to know?" Candless asked. There was a question in her eyes—a doubt, perhaps, but he didn't want to engage with that. He had big enough problems already, without worrying if she agreed with his orders or not.

He needed pilots, damn it. He needed to hold on to his secrets, too—though if Bury knew about the Blue-Blue-White, Lanoe didn't have many left. He would give them something, a few simple answers to their most pressing questions. If it got him what he needed.

"Tell them I'll give them a special briefing. After we fight."

Candless nodded. "Very good, sir. That gives you four pilots, three of whom are unknown quantities. That should be enough to hold off a parade float, say, or a wing of unarmed racing yachts. If they send destroyers against us—"

"I've fought destroyers before," Lanoe told her. "And I'm still alive, which I guess means I'm good at it."

"Ahem."

Lanoe spun himself around to glare at Maggs. The con artist was curled in a ball near the information officer's seat, looking quite unassuming.

"Just wanted to point out," Maggs said, "that I've been known to take the yoke in hand a few times myself."

Lanoe glared at him. He couldn't really be suggesting that they trust him with one of their fighters, could he?

Well, he was brazen enough to make the offer, Lanoe knew that. And he also knew that Maggs was, frankly, a top-notch pilot, when he actually got around to fighting.

"Not a damned chance," Lanoe told him.

Chapter Seventeen

We should have imaging any moment now, sir," the carrier's information officer said.

Bullam was only on the bridge as an observer. She turned and looked at Shulkin, who was strapped into a chair at the back of the cramped space. The old Captain gripped the arms of his seat with white knuckles, but his face didn't move. He didn't acknowledge the IO's statement.

The bridge of a Hipparchus-class carrier was located deep inside the cylindrical hangar, the most heavily armored and protected part of the giant ship. There were no windows, of course, but a dozen displays blinked and shuffled in front of the pilot, navigation, and information positions. Most of them just showed raw ghostlight, the walls of the wormhole they were traversing. A tactical board lit up and Bullam saw a yellow dot dead ahead of them.

"There," the IO said. "Bringing up opticals now." The display split into four separate images, three of them live video feeds of the space ahead of the carrier, showing nothing Bullam could see. The fourth showed the Hoplite. Lanoe's Hoplite.

Still a hundred thousand kilometers away down the wormhole tunnel. On the display it looked close enough to reach out and grab.

Somewhere on the skin of the carrier, liquid lenses shifted and vibrated. Drops of oil no bigger than Bullam's thumbnail, held in place and shaped by magnetic fields. The lenses could change their focus millions of times a second, capturing different depths of focus and different wavelengths of light. Data from those images was collated into a single three-dimensional view of the Hoplite, much brighter and more colorful on the display than it would have appeared if Bullam saw it with her naked eye.

"Engines cold," the IO called out. "Weapons cold. No running lights...it looks dead, sir. As expected."

"The vehicle bay?" someone asked. Bullam swiveled around and saw it was the navigator who'd spoken. Not Shulkin.

"Blast panels are down," the IO said. Even Bullam could see that much, from the image on the display. "Vehicle bay sealed. Comms—no comms. Not even navigational pings. I see no sign of electronic activity."

As far as Bullam could tell it looked like the service package had done its job. Someone onboard must have activated it, someone who no doubt expected to be rewarded—or at least spared—when the rest of the crew was seized by Centrocor. Somebody onboard the cruiser who had a Centrocor ID.

Big Hexagon did like to have people everywhere in case they might be useful.

She let herself breathe a little. Just a little, though. "If we caught him off guard," she breathed, not so loud that anyone would feel like they had to respond. "If this works—"

"Our pilots report they are ready to launch," the IO said. "Sir? Should I give the order to proceed?"

Everyone turned to look at Shulkin. The old man's face didn't move. He reached up and scratched at a place on his jawline that he'd missed when he shaved that morning. His eyes were glass beads set into his skull.

He gave the tiniest of nods.

Not for the first time, Bullam wondered exactly why Dariau Cygnet had thought that Shulkin was up to this job. She was probably going to have to replace him herself, eventually, and she didn't know a damned thing about fighting space battles. Still, she figured *she* could at least stay awake while one was happening.

The visual display flashed as a pair of scouts launched from the carrier's hangar. Even up close they looked tiny compared to the Hoplite. These weren't cataphract-class fighters, but simple carrier scouts—little one-man ships just big enough to hold a thruster and a single PBW cannon. No room for vector fields or even armor. They were cheap and easily replaced but not much use in a real fight. Even Bullam knew that. They would be sufficient to this task, though—they were just supposed to do a close flyby of the Hoplite then return once they'd confirmed it was dead in the water. Once that was done, they could send in a transport full of marines to board the Hoplite and secure Lanoe. Everyone else onboard would have to be killed, of course, but at least Bullam wouldn't have to see that happen.

The scouts disappeared into the ghostlight after a few seconds, appearing on the displays only as two blue dots that marked their positions. They moved quickly, closing the distance between the two big ships.

Shulkin scratched his face again. "Lanoe," he said. "Lanoe. Lanoe. Lanoe." Like a machine running through a series of iterations. "Aleister Lanoe?" he asked.

Bullam stared at him. Had he already forgotten their mission parameters? "Yes," she said. "Yes. That's right." It was like she was talking to an infant. "Aleister Lanoe."

Light flared in Shulkin's eyes. Like someone had lit a candle inside a jack-o'-lantern. "Aleister Lanoe," he said. "I know that name...I know..."

The Captain slapped at the quick release of his straps and threw himself across the bridge toward the information officer's position. He nearly shoved the poor young man out of his seat. Shulkin's hands lanced out and worked two different virtual keyboards, bringing up dozens of new displays. Imagery of the Hoplite, it looked like, in several different wavelengths of light—Bullam recognized a 3-D X-ray view and an infrared reflectography profile, among others. It happened so fast she didn't have time to suck in an anxious breath.

On one of those views, the Hoplite appeared as a colorless, shadowy image. Like a magnetic resonance scan of a human abdomen, maybe. Inside that view was a single red splotch, little more than a stain of crimson, but Shulkin stared at it like he was looking at an image of his own death.

"Recall the scouts!" he shouted. "Warm up all of our maneuvering and retro thrusters—we need to be moving already. Pilot—get on it or I'll shoot you and take your position myself!"

"What's happening?" Bullam demanded. "What's going on?"

A green pearl appeared in the corner of Lanoe's vision. An incoming message—he flicked his eye across it to acknowledge. "Seventy-five hundred kilometers, on approach," Candless said, over a comms laser. There would be no way for Centrocor to intercept the transmission. "Two vehicles. They appear to be carrier scouts."

She was only a few meters away to his left, in the cockpit of a BR.9 just like his own. Both of them perched on the Hoplite's nose like seabirds on a rock. He could have looked over and seen her lips moving in the ghostlight, if he wanted to.

On the other side of her, Bury and Ginger waited in their own fighters. The kids had protested—and Ginger had turned a bad shade of green—when he insisted they join his little squad. He had been an officer long enough to know how to give orders that people obeyed.

It had been much harder fighting down his own misgivings about the pilot on his right.

Over there, Maggs waited patiently in his Z.XIX.

Right where Lanoe could watch him. He still didn't trust the scoundrel—how could he, ever again?—but he had grudgingly come to accept that he needed Maggs. Once they'd realized what was pursuing them, a Hipparchus-class carrier with a full complement of small craft, he'd known he needed every pilot he could get.

And that of course meant leaving Valk on the bridge. Candless wasn't the only one who couldn't stomach flying formation with an AI.

It wasn't what Lanoe might have hoped for, their little half of a squadron. Five fighters and only one pilot he could truly count on. It was what he had to work with.

"Any sign they've noticed us?" Lanoe asked.

"It seems unlikely," Candless told him. "They're coming in quickly, but on a minimum energy trajectory. I would wager they don't expect trouble."

The five cataphracts were clumped together on the nose of the Hoplite because that was the carrier's blind spot. It was coming up behind them, straight on, and even its best sensors couldn't see all the way through the cruiser. With a little luck—no, with a lot of luck—any watchers on the carrier would assume that the service package had done its job, that the crew of the Hoplite was locked inside a dead ship, gasping for breath.

Lanoe couldn't communicate with Valk—any communications between the fighters and the cruiser would give away the game. Valk knew the plan, though. If this worked—

"Five thousand kilometers, on approach," Candless said. A few moments later: "Four thousand. Thirty-five hundred."

Whoever was back there, whoever Centrocor had commanding the carrier, they were smart. They'd sent two expendable ships ahead to test the waters. When those carrier scouts came around the front of the Hoplite, the game would be up. Lanoe intended to hit them hard the instant they came into view, to at least keep them from sending useful information back to the carrier. Then he and his tiny squad would spin around and burn hard, head straight for the enemy's teeth. They were all carrying disruptor ammunition, heavy explosive missiles that could tear through the carrier's hull and explode inside its crew spaces. The damage they could do would be apocalyptic—assuming they got their firing solutions just right.

They had a chance. Of course, the carrier had its own defenses, and a talented commander would keep them from getting such a clean victory as that. There was a very good chance one or more of Lanoe's squad wasn't coming back from this.

It was part of what made them pilots that they were willing to try anyway.

"Three thousand . . . Lanoe, they're slowing down."

"Hellfire," he said, his voice hoarse with stress. "Have they seen us?"

"I haven't a clue. But—there," Candless said. "They're turning. Heading back."

Damnation. They knew.

Somehow, they knew it was a ruse. That the cruiser wasn't as dead as it appeared. Lanoe had no idea what had given them away but it didn't matter. The battle started now, whether he liked it or not.

He reached for his comms board and jabbed a virtual key, opening a channel to everyone in his squad. "Now!" he shouted. "Move, move, everybody out!"

He didn't wait to see them comply. He shoved open his throttle and twisted around on his maneuvering jets, getting his nose clear of the Hoplite and then shooting down its length while his inertial sink pushed him back, hard, into his seat.

All along the length of the cruiser, lights started blinking back on. Engines and jets and thrusters warmed up, glowing a dull red as Lanoe rocketed past. By the time he passed its tail, the cruiser was already turning, pivoting on its center of gravity. It moved like a sick whale compared to the nimble cataphracts, but it was exactly what he would have ordered Valk to do. *Good man*, he thought, perfectly aware of the irony.

The carrier scouts were still three thousand kilometers away. In the dim ghostlight he couldn't see them even in a light-enhanced view. It didn't matter—his sensor board brought up a display that marked their positions for him, yellow dots on a three-dimensional computer-generated view. Behind Lanoe, the BR.9's reactor screamed as he tore through a vacuum, closing the distance.

"I've got the one on the left," someone called, on the open channel.

Bury—Lanoe could see the Hellion's fighter surge forward, the kid pushing his engine to dangerous levels of output to build up speed.

"Young man, you will stay in formation!" Candless called.

"Belay that," Lanoe told them. "Bury, if you have a shot, take it. Ginger, you're falling behind."

"Don't be afraid to *use your engines*," Candless told the young woman.

"Acknowledged," Ginger said, sounding embarrassed. She'd been trailing back, as if she could somehow avoid this fight by being in the back of the formation. Lanoe started to wonder if she would even be an asset in it.

He supposed he would just have to give her a chance, and see.

The carrier scouts didn't even try to engage. Their pilots knew they had no chance in an open fight. They were outnumbered and outgunned. Their tiny craft lacked the vector fields that would protect them from the worst of the cataphracts' fire. They were straining their own engines, just trying to get away. "Don't let them escape," Lanoe called. "Make sure they—"

"The other one," Maggs said, breaking in. "The one on the right." The four PBW cannon on his Z.XIX discharged, bright streaks of charged particles cutting across the vacuum, perfectly straight like lines on a display. They converged on a point in the far distance.

On Lanoe's tactical board one of the two yellow dots blinked out.

He scowled at the display. The Z.XIX was an advanced fighter design, its weapons systems were the best the Navy could field, but still...

"That was an impressive shot," Candless said, sounding guarded.

"What can I say? I've always been lucky," Maggs told her.

"Engaging!" Bury shouted, loud enough to hurt Lanoe's ear and make him, for the moment at least, forget that he'd just seen Maggs snipe an enemy at an impossible distance. Up ahead, he could just make out the blue flare of Bury's engine, and then a tiny double flash as the Hellion fired his cannon.

A moment later the second yellow dot disappeared, clearing Lanoe's tactical board.

"Good," Candless said. "Now get back here and—"

"Ladies and gentlemen," Maggs said, using an archaic expression Lanoe barely remembered from his youth—long before Maggs had been born. "If I may kindly direct your attention to the larger issue."

"What are you yammering about?" Lanoe demanded.

It was Candless who responded, however. "We're just now getting decent imagery from the carrier, Commander."

Lanoe swiped to bring up his sensor board. He saw it, even before she told him what he was looking at.

"The carrier," she said, "is scrambling its fighters. Its entire complement."

On the sensor board, yellow lights started flashing into existence—two, then four, then eight of them. Then sixteen.

$\sim$

"Spread out—don't let them clump you," Shulkin said, his words being carried straight to the cockpits of the carrier's fighters. "He's smarter than you. Do not let him think, don't let him get clever. Keep him busy with withering fire—make him dance. *Distract* him."

He lunged across the bridge, jabbing a gloved finger at a display hovering before the information officer. The crew had to push back, out of his way. "Any change—any change at all in the thermal profile there, you say something. Don't ask for my permission, damn you."

A tactical display filled most of the bridge, arms and legs breaking through it even as it changed second by second, yellow dots growing thick clouds as numbers and data strings surrounded them. The IO was busy trying to figure out which of the enemy fighters was being operated by Aleister Lanoe, mostly by analyzing how it flew—how efficiently its engines were being used, the flatness of the craft's trajectory, even the occasional stutter of its jets as the pilot's hand trembled on the control yoke. These tiny datasets were being compared to known examples of Lanoe's piloting—videos of some of his more famous battles, records drawn from his after-action reports. All very secret stuff that Centrocor had stolen from the Admiralty's databases back when it became clear that Lanoe was a real threat.

It was vitally important that the carrier's pilots not accidentally kill Lanoe in the middle of what was looking to be a pitched battle. Bullam needed him alive, so he could be interrogated. Horribly maimed and burned was fine, but *alive*.

"You can rule out this one," Shulkin said, swatting at one of the yellow points of light as if it were a pesky insect. "The one that killed our carrier scout. Lanoe would never run ahead of the pack like that, he knows better."

"You know him," Bullam said. "You have some connection with Lanoe. From back in your Navy days."

The Captain spun around in midair to glare at her. "The civilian observer," he said, "is asked to be silent while we carry out military operations."

Bullam held up both hands for peace. When Shulkin failed to stop staring at her, she mimed swiping at her mouth as if she were dismissing a comms display. He didn't nod, but he turned back to face the pilot and the IO.

The transformation in him was remarkable. When she'd first met Shulkin, Bullam had thought him little more than a zombie, that the Navy's treatment for his suicidal compulsions had left him more dead than alive. She'd seen a touch of fire in him back at Tuonela, when he killed one of the ThiessGruppe men for her.

That had been nothing like this.

Every muscle in his body was strained now, as tight as the strings of a violin. His eyes, once just glass balls lodged in his protuberant skull, were clear and sharp and white, bright with the heat of intention. He moved in quick, jerky gestures, like someone who'd had too many tablets of caff. Had his skeleton torn its way out of his skin and danced around the room with a wild abandon, she would not have been terribly surprised.

Clearly Shulkin had been reduced, cut down by the Navy until he was this thing she saw now, this weapon. When he didn't have a battle to fight he could be safely folded up and put away in a box. When enemy fighters were racing toward them, disruptors armed, only then could he truly come alive.

"Imagery! Where's my thrice-damned imagery? IO, tell me about that infrared scan I showed you. What's it doing? What change?"

"Sir," the IO said. All of the bridge crew were Navy veterans but the IO looked green and scared to Bullam. "Temperature *is* increasing, but I can't get a good fix on what equipment they're powering up. Lights and engines are coming online all over the Hoplite—it clearly wasn't affected at all by the service package, and now—"

"The component I identified on the infrared," Shulkin told the young officer, as if explaining something simple to a very young child, "is the preamplification power conditioner of a Mark II 75-centimeter coilgun."

Bullam had only a sketchy notion of what they were talking about. That red stain, she thought, the red blotch that Shulkin had found on the otherwise monochrome scan of the cruiser. But what was a preamplification power conditioner, and why did it seem to terrify the IO so much? She desperately wanted to speak, to ask questions.

In this case, at least, she didn't need to.

"They're powering up one of their heavy guns," Shulkin said, turning his head just a little to speak over his shoulder. More or less in her direction.

"Guns," Bullam said, despite her earlier promise to stay quiet. She felt her heart beating at the back of her throat. "But then—just one? Shoot back at them, that should discourage them."

"I did tell you," Shulkin said. "You don't chase after a cruiser with a carrier. It's a bad play." He snapped his head back around, to watch the display. "Their guns have much greater range than anything we've got. They can sit back there and fire a steady stream of projectiles at us for hours while we try to approach to a point where we can fire our own weapons."

"What kind of range are we talking about?" Bullam asked.

"We're in it right now," Shulkin said.

Bullam could only shake her head. No, that couldn't be right. Her service package—

But of course, the service package had never been activated. It had all been a ruse. She wanted to say something, but she was worried that if she opened her mouth a moan of terror would come out of her.

"When that coilgun reaches the right temperature," he said, jabbing a finger at the red blotch—an angrier shade now, almost orange—"everyone on this ship dies. I'm trying to get us turned around so we can get out of range, but it's taking *too damned long*." This clearly directed at the pilot. "We only have one chance," he told her.

"A chance? What is it? Tell me!"

"We can smash them up first, with our small craft. Before that gun can fire. Otherwise we're all dead."

PBW fire streaked all around Lanoe, flashes of it lighting up his cockpit then fading so fast he had to blink away afterimages. The beams were still coming from too great a range to be dangerous. A wild shot struck his vector field on the left side of his nose but he didn't even feel it. The field worked by accelerating particles away from his BR.9 at deflecting angles to their direction of motion. The tiny particles of the PBW beam were easily shunted off—as long as he didn't suffer a direct hit.

Worrying about direct hits was a good way to get paralyzed in the middle of a fight. Which was the best way to sustain a direct hit.

"They're coming in high," Lanoe said, looking up through his canopy as if he could see them. They were still thousands of kilometers away. "They're formed up in a standard wedge. They're going to try to break up our formation and with this many of them against our five, it's going to work. Switch to teams—Candless, you're with me. Bury and Ginger, watch each other's backs. You ready for this, Ensigns?"

"Yes," the Hellion said, without hesitation. Sounding sullen, as usual.

"I'm not," Ginger said, in a small voice.

"She's right, Bury," Lanoe said. "Neither of you is ready. Consider this your baptism by fire. Candless, you take my wing. I'll get this thing started."

"Ah," Maggs called, "I can't help but notice you've left me without a dance partner."

Lanoe scowled inside his helmet. He knew where he needed Maggs, but that didn't mean he liked it. "That crate of yours has some fancy guns on it, doesn't it? Next-generation stuff. That's how you made that impossible shot back there."

Maggs didn't deny it. As the son of a famous admiral, and working directly for Admiral Varma, he would have access to all kinds of shiny new toys.

"Hang back," Lanoe said. "Hang back and snipe. Give us some cover while we do all the hard work."

It meant leaving Maggs with a great view of his back, with new, high-tech guns in case he wanted to take the opportunity to end the storied career of Aleister Lanoe. Nothing for it. It was the best play Lanoe had.

"Understood," Maggs said.

"All right," Lanoe said. "On my count. Three, two—*break*."

He peeled off from the formation, knowing Candless would be right behind him and off a little to his left. His tactical boards showed him Ginger and Bury mirroring his maneuver, headed off in the opposite direction. They would have drilled in this kind of flying back at Rishi, flown these sorts of maneuvers over and over until they could pull them off blindfolded. But flying was easy.

Shooting was hard.

Long before he could actually see them in the ghostlight, the yellow points of enemy craft appeared superimposed on his canopy. Firing solutions scrolled across his weapons board but he ignored them for the moment. Opening his throttle wide he streaked straight at them, his finger hovering over his trigger.

A moment later, he did see them.

So many of them. Half a dozen right before him, all of them curving around to intercept. He lined up a shot, held it—waiting for the precise moment, the instant when he was likely to connect. They were already firing, wasting ammunition to try to break his concentration by pouring fire all around him, a hailstorm of particles any one of which could kill him in an instant.

He could feel his finger trembling, his body wanting very much to shoot.

Suddenly the storm of shots all around him let up, diminishing to just a drizzle of PBW fire.

"They're readying AV projectiles," Candless said, barely a whisper, or maybe he was just so focused his brain was dampening the sound of her voice. Antivehicular rounds were bad news. They were designed to just puncture the hull of an enemy craft, then explode in a spray of superheated metal that would burn alive anyone foolish enough to be inside. It was an AV round that killed Tannis Valk—and created the legend of the Blue Devil.

Of course, you had to place an AV shot perfectly or it would be wasted. And that took time. Which meant Lanoe, who was sticking with good old-fashioned particle beam weapons, had some room to maneuver.

He threw his ship sideways by goosing its positioning jets. Spun around on his center of gravity until he was flying backward, his thruster cones all cold and pointed at the enemy. As fast as he was moving, he punched through their line a second later—and was facing them, looking at *their* thrusters. He picked one of them at random and opened fire, even as they tried to snap around to get him in their jaws.

His PBW rounds cut across the tail of the one he'd chosen, at first just bouncing off its vector field. He kept up a steady stream of fire and eventually his shots dug in, slicing off one of the target's airfoils and scoring a line of tiny craters down its engine fairing. It was a brand-new Yk.64 cataphract and he felt an absurd pang of guilt at ruining its paint job.

The Sixty-Four had a large canopy, almost a full bubble of flowglas at its nose with the pilot seeming to float around inside. With his opticals set to light amplification and edge detection, Lanoe could see the pilot crane his head around, see the terror on the man's face.

A virtual Aldis sight came up in front of him. Lanoe swiped it away—he didn't need to aim. Not now.

His PBWs blasted away, cutting a neat line down the middle of the Sixty-Four. A few of his shots were deflected by the vector field, but most were not. The fighter came apart in pieces, debris spinning off it, bouncing away. He hit something volatile—maybe a fuel line, maybe an ammunition cartridge—and that big canopy lit up from the inside, the pilot disappearing in the flash of deadly light.

Lanoe didn't waste time mourning the man. It was hardly the first pilot he'd killed in his three hundred years, and he doubted it would be his last. He shoved himself away from the wreckage with his maneuvering jets, then woke up his main thruster and shot upward into a corkscrewing evasive maneuver. Just as he'd expected, five Yk.64s came following hot on his heels, ready to avenge their squadmate.

Just as he'd hoped, Candless raked all of them with her PBWs, swooping in to break up their formation before they could surround him. The enemy squad broke ranks and tore away in random directions, just trying to get away from her heavy attack.

Which gave Lanoe a moment—just a fraction of a second—to think tactically. He saw Bury and Ginger on his tactical board, flying long, looping trajectories as they played tag with their own wing of enemies. Despite his reservations about the ensigns—and Ginger, especially—they were holding their own. They'd established their own tactical rhythm, it looked like—Ginger playing bait, drawing cataphracts after her as she executed sloppy maneuvers, making her look like a wounded bird, then Bury pouncing whenever one of the Centrocor ships made a try at her. When that stopped working, Bury would lunge at them in hopelessly direct maneuvers that would send them spinning away—where Ginger could corral them with suppressing fire. Good, reliable tactics that every pilot learned while they were still in training. Not terribly effective against seasoned pilots but it kept the enemy occupied, kept them from mounting a full attack in formation.

Maggs was firing at range, a single burst of PBW fire every few seconds as he picked his targets with care. Exactly as Lanoe had ordered him to do. As much as he wanted to keep an eye on the scoundrel, Lanoe knew he didn't have the time for it.

Especially since, when he counted up the enemy fighters, he found some of them missing. Six had engaged him and Candless. Six more were playing games with the ensigns. Four were nowhere to be seen.

No. Damnation. He'd been so busy—so distracted. He'd missed what was happening right in front of his nose.

He threw himself into a series of S-turns, just so he would be a difficult target, and brought up his sensor board, searching desperately for the missing four cataphracts. When he found them he swore off-microphone.

They had shot past Lanoe and his squad in the chaos, ignoring the fighting altogether. Burning hard for speed, on a course that would intercept the Hoplite.

He'd been so busy with his fancy dogfighting, he'd missed the whole point of the Centrocor attack. They weren't trying to kill him and his pilots.

They were going after the cruiser. And if nobody stopped them, they had a good chance of taking it down.

Shulkin's hand had turned white with strain as he picked at the armrest of his chair. The hand had already looked skeletal, fleshless and thin, but now it looked like an animal's claw. He didn't seem to notice that he was tearing at the padding. His eyes never left the display before him. Specifically, he never stopped staring at the orange stain in the midsection of the cruiser.

"They were smart, very smart," he said. Was he talking to Bullam, or just to himself? She had no idea. "They knew we would run infrared cameras over their guns as we approached. They couldn't have them ready to fire, no, we would have noticed that. We never would have approached so closely. But those guns take long minutes to warm up. Most battles don't last that long. So they kept the preamplifier ticking over, ready to pour energy into the coils as soon as we were within range."

His fingernails gouged into the upholstery of his armrest. He nodded slowly to himself.

After the panic and chaos of the first few seconds of the battle, a hideous calm had settled over the bridge. Everyone had their orders—no need to bark new ones. All the displays were showing exactly what they needed to show. The carrier was swinging its nose around inside the tight confines of the wormhole with aching deliberation. Move too fast and it might brush one of the walls, which could kill them. Move too slowly and they wouldn't be able to get downrange of the cruiser's gun in time. There was nothing the pilot or the navigator could do to make the process any faster or smoother. They sat at their positions with their hands hovering over their virtual keyboards. Waiting to see what came next.

Shulkin's armrest creaked painfully. He'd gotten his fingers under the seam of the upholstery and yanked upward, levering at the pad, straining at it until his strength gave out. He relaxed his hand for just a moment before he started to pull on the pad again. The Navy had built that armrest to withstand a lot of heavy use, but eventually, Bullam knew, it would give way.

"Of course, there are sixteen guns on that ship, sixteen seventy-five-centimeter guns. That's a lot of preamplifiers, a lot of heat, even in standby mode. We would have noticed the heat of them all working together. So Lanoe only readied one of his guns. Kept it simmering at a low temperature, low enough it wouldn't show up on standard IR. He was betting we wouldn't bother with a deep reflectography scan. And the thing is—I wouldn't have. I wouldn't have thought to look for that heat signature. Who would ready just one gun in preparation for a battle like this? Who would hamper themselves like that?"

The armrest was putting up a good fight. Not looking at it, not seemingly aware at all of what he was doing, Shulkin dug his other hand into its stitching. Tugged and pulled until Bullam could hear fabric start to tear.

"Lanoe would," she said.

Shulkin nodded. His skin was waxy and damp with sweat. Maybe from fear, or just from the exertion of tearing up his own armrest, she couldn't say. His eyes were the eyes of a hawk, of a hunting bird. He saw nothing, she thought, sensed very little other than that deepening orange stain on the cutaway diagram of the Hoplite. A stain that was turning lighter all the time. When it turned white, he'd told her, the gun would be ready to fire.

One end of the armrest pulled free from the metal underneath with a final, terminal squeak. It only took a second for Shulkin to yank the whole thing loose. He held it in his fingers like a prey animal, and she would not have been surprised if he brought it up to his mouth and started to chew on it.

"You know him," she said. Her voice was a whisper. The level of volume one might assume when speaking inside a cathedral, perhaps. She glanced over at the crew and saw the pilot, the navigator, the IO frozen like statues, not daring to turn around. They were doing their utmost not to listen in on her conversation.

Good Centrocor employees, all. They knew who paid them.

"Lanoe. You've fought with him before," she insisted. "Or—or against him."

"Ha," Shulkin said. It was not a laugh.

"Ha?" she asked.

"If I'd fought against him before, if he was always this smart," he said, and nodded at the display. The orange was the color of a pale sunset on an icy world. "I'd be dead."

His fingers dug inside the severed armrest. Started pulling out tiny fragments of foam padding. Tore them into minuscule bits that floated gently toward the right-hand wall of the bridge.

A reminder that they were moving. Accelerating, even though Bullam could barely feel it.

"Where are our pilots?" Shulkin asked. He sounded like he was asking after their welfare. "How close to the cruiser?"

He meant the fighters, the cataphracts, that he'd sent to attack the Hoplite. The four pilots who were the only ones who could save the carrier from destruction.

"Fifteen seconds out of range," the navigator said, her voice trembling, just a little.

"Bury, Ginger, cover us—we're going in," Lanoe called, wheeling around to chase the four Centrocor pilots who were headed for the cruiser. Candless pulled a snap turn, all the thrusters on her BR.9 firing at once, and fell in behind him without leaving him exposed for a moment. PBW fire smashed into the side of his fighter, most of it deflecting away harmlessly. A red light popped up on his damage board, showing him he'd lost one of his disruptor launchers. He could live without it. The fire kept coming, flashing across his nose, carving into his airfoils. The Centrocor pilots must have been ordered to keep him back, to stop him from heading in to defend the cruiser. They were doing their damned best.

Behind him Candless pivoted around until she was flying backward and fired just one shot that took out one of their attackers, a perfect shot right down the long axis of his ship. The ship exploded like something from a video, a blast wave so perfectly symmetrical it didn't look real. Debris shot away at incredible speed and hit the wall of the wormhole, light flashing as each piece of shrapnel annihilated. It was a hell of a kill, Lanoe thought, but it cut into her acceleration and suddenly she was well behind him. If the enemy could get into the gap between them they would be easy targets— the Centrocor pilots could pick them off with well-placed AV shots.

Lanoe knew he ought to slow down, let her catch up. But the cruiser was undefended and he needed all the speed he could get.

For a second he was flying alone, no one for kilometers around him, and he used the break to send a message to Valk. The AI replied instantly, as if he'd been waiting for the call. Lanoe flicked his eyes across the green pearl in the corner of his vision.

He didn't waste any time on greetings. "How long until the gun fires?" he asked.

"Lieutenant Ehta and her marines are busting their humps down there, but it's still another eighty-nine seconds," Valk said.

Eighty-nine. Too long.

He shoved that thought away. "You've got hostiles inbound," Lanoe said. "What about secondary defenses?" There were plenty of small guns onboard the cruiser, PBW cannon no bigger than the ones mounted on Lanoe's fighter. The problem was that they weren't automated. The same law that banned AIs banned mounting guns on drones, or giving any kind of computer access to a lethal weapon, meant a human being needed to crew every one of those secondary guns.

Had the Hoplite still possessed a full complement of crew, there would have been plenty of marines to fire those PBWs. With just a skeleton crew onboard, most of Ehta's people would be busy getting the big coilgun ready to fire.

"I'll see if she can spare a couple of people, but you know ship-mounted guns won't stop trained pilots," Valk told him.

An old truism of space battles, one Lanoe hardly needed to hear just then. "They'd be better than nothing. If even one of these Centrocor bastards lines up a good disruptor shot on you," he said, "we lose. And it looks like there's going to be"—he checked his boards—"three and a half seconds when they're in range and I'm still too far out to be of any help. Do you think—"

"Oh, hellfire!" Ginger shouted, on the squad channel. Loud enough to hurt Lanoe's ear. "No...Oh, no..."

"What's the matter?" Candless called. "Ginger—are you in trouble?"

"No—no," the girl sent back. "No, I just...He—I had a shot, and I took it, and—"

"If you're not in immediate danger, then cut that chatter!" Candless said.

Lanoe didn't have time to check and see what was going on with Ginger. He had his hands full at the moment. "Candless," he said, "where are you?"

"I'm coming. Five seconds behind you."

"Acknowledged," he said, because there was nothing else to say. His BR.9 could fly only so fast. He could see the Hoplite now in his augmented canopy view, a rectangular shape of light in the dim nether of wormspace. The four Centrocor fighters were just yellow dots, converging on the cruiser far faster than he liked.

He picked one—they were equidistant, he just picked one at random—and feathered his stick, nudging his fighter in its direction. He brought up his weapons board, thinking maybe there was some great solution there, but he knew he wouldn't have time for anything fancy. His sensor board showed him things he didn't want to know. All four of the Centrocor fighters were loading disruptors. Even though he couldn't see them as anything more than lighter specks in the dark, his computer could read telescope data to see that they had unlimbered the heavy weapon launchers mounted in their undercarriages.

He forced himself to pull his finger away from his trigger guard. If he fired now, at this distance with everyone moving at incredible speeds, his shot could go anywhere. He might get lucky and hit one of the fighters, but he might also hit the Hoplite—which was a much larger target.

Ten seconds out. The fighters were almost in range. He saw PBW fire coming from one of the Hoplite's small guns, fanning out around him, failing to hit anything. Five seconds out, and the Centrocor fighters were already in range of the cruiser. It would take a couple of seconds for them to find the right firing solution, to decide where to put their deadly munitions, but he was still—

One of the yellow dots on his tactical board blinked out, and a fraction of a second later a burst of light showed against the dark, as one of the Centrocor ships exploded.

"You can thank me later," Maggs said.

"I'm sure you'll remind me," Lanoe told him. There was no time to think about how that changed things, if at all. He could see his target now, its bubble-shaped nose pointed at the cruiser. It was skating along sideways, the pilot holding steady as he prepared to launch his disruptor. It looked like the round would cleave right through the Hoplite's engineering section—and if it connected, if the disruptor's smart munitions detonated inside the cruiser's engines—

It was a hypothetical, only. The pilot didn't even have time to look up as Lanoe tore into him with both PBWs. The Centrocor fighter came apart at the seams, its disruptor unlaunched.

Two to go—both of them on the far side of the cruiser. Candless was still three seconds out. Lanoe threw his ship sideways, curling around the Hoplite's side in a lateral roll, his maneuvering jets hissing and stuttering and his inertial sink pulling backward on him, hard, like a giant hand pressing down on him, flattening him. The cruiser turned underneath him and he pulled out of his maneuver in a tight half spin, his guns already blazing.

The third Centrocor pilot had time to try to maneuver, to evade. It didn't work. Lanoe's particle beams sparked and bounced off the Yk.64's vector field for a moment, then finally connected, a steady stream of fire carving right through the fighter's midsection, severing pipes and conduits and power lines. The lights inside the bubble canopy went dark and the fighter twisted away on a random trajectory. Either the pilot was dead or they'd lost all control of their vehicle. It wasn't a clean kill, but Lanoe didn't care. He wasn't out here to murder Centrocor's pilots—he had to save the cruiser.

One to go, just one enemy left. Lanoe tripped his compensators and threw his ship into a rotary turn, until he was flying at right angles to his previous course. He reached for his trigger and lined up his shot—

Just as the disruptor launched from the Sixty-Four's belly.

Lanoe was close enough to actually see it happen, to see the projectile emerge, its tiny thruster burning hot as it accelerated toward the cruiser.

His stomach tried to churn inside his abdomen. The inertial sink prevented that—it was still crushing him against his seat—so instead an acid belch started worming its way up his throat. He wanted to cry out but his teeth were clenched too hard.

The disruptor was a diamond-hard carbon rod a meter long, studded with nodules of high explosive. It was designed to dig through the skin of a large ship and keep going, burrowing through bulkheads and structural elements and crew spaces alike, the explosives timed so they would go off in series. A continuous fireball that could chew right through armor plating, right through interior bulkheads, right through crew spaces and never stop. It was a devastating weapon, built for one purpose only: to kill spacecraft.

This one entered the cruiser just aft of the officers' bunks and tore its way out through the side of the bridge, exploding continuously as it moved through the ship. Lanoe saw blossoms of fire erupt again and again from the side of the cruiser, watched a cloud of debris expand outward from the cruiser's ruined nose.

"No," he said, very quietly. "No. Valk—"

The bridge—the cruiser's bridge was just *gone*. The disruptor tore its way out of the cruiser's hull, still exploding in a plume of superhot metal and fast-expanding gas, a bow wave of fire. The place where the bridge had been was nothing now but torn metal and scraps of carbon fiber, long, loose threads of the stuff flapping in a sustained shock wave.

"Valk!" Lanoe shouted.

He almost missed the fact that the last Sixty-Four, the one that had delivered the killing blow, was turning its guns on him.

～

A grim smile spread across Shulkin's hollow cheeks, and a sound a little like a death rattle—or like a triumphant groaning—resonated up from inside his chest. Bullam turned back to the display and watched in awe as the video looped there, video of the cruiser's front end twisting and rupturing under disruptor fire. "We did it," she breathed. "We did it. We did it. We did it. They're—they're dead, and—we're not."

Someone was calling, someone was calling out a series of requests, but she didn't even listen. She just wanted to clamp her eyes shut and breathe, to inhale for the first time in what felt like hours, but she knew had only been a few minutes. "Captain," she said. "We're safe now. We can start thinking about how we're going to capture Lanoe. I'd like to suggest—"

"I have no idea what you're talking about, civilian," Shulkin told her. "I do believe I ordered you to remain quiet while on my bridge."

Bullam frowned. She turned to look at the displays again. One showed a schematic view of the cruiser, with all the damaged areas highlighted in yellow, orange, and red, data spooling all around the view as telemetry came in. The cruiser didn't just look dead, it looked like it had been beheaded.

Other areas of the image still showed blue and even green. The engines, for instance, were untouched. Most of the gundecks were perfectly intact.

She jabbed one finger at the display. "They lost their bridge," she said. "Come on! That has to count for something."

"Most likely it counts for the death of a small number of pilots," Shulkin told her. "It doesn't matter. They don't need the bridge to control the ship. They can fly that thing from any display onboard. Did you think nothing like this has ever happened before in a war? The Navy builds their ships to keep fighting long after most of the crew is dead."

"But the gun, the, the Mark II coilgun that they're readying to fire at us, that has to be—it has to," Bullam said. She could hear how incoherent she sounded but she couldn't stop talking. "This has to count for something!"

"It counts for honor," Shulkin said. "If we die now, at least we bled them first. Meanwhile, we still have nine fighters in play. And they're still eleven seconds out from firing their gun."

Lanoe dashed sideways, his positioning jets firing hard as he tried to break the Sixty-Four's lock on him. The Sixty-Four dipped its nose and spun around to keep facing him and he knew there was no way he could evade. If he could have ducked around the side of the cruiser, put it between him and the Centrocor fighter—but there was no time.

Time.

He'd given the Sixty-Four's pilot far too much time. He'd been distracted by seeing the disruptor tear through the Hoplite, by knowing that Valk was in there—Valk, Valk was dead—damn it. He pushed that thought away. He'd been distracted, and he'd given the Centrocor pilot plenty of time to work up an AV solution.

He should already be dead. Lanoe had seen these pilots in action. They weren't the best the Navy had ever produced but it was clear they knew how to fight. Why hadn't this one killed him already?

Unless they had orders not to. Just as Maggs had suggested.

He twisted around as the Sixty-Four's PBW fire raked across his weapon fairings, as shot after shot broke through his vector field and red lights lit up all over his boards. He lost an airfoil and then one of his cannons and then something crucial in his engine, some vital conduit, and suddenly his main thrusters just dropped offline, while a warning chime told him that heat was building up behind the shielding that separated him from the reactor. He twisted and dodged, trying to turn away some of those hits with his vector field, but he was too close. Orders to keep him alive or not, soon enough one of those shots was going to hit something vital. He might not come out of this dead but he doubted if Centrocor cared if he was captured in one piece.

He twisted around one last time, until his canopy was facing the Sixty-Four's bubble, wanting at least to see the pilot who brought him down. He got a glimpse of a suited figure, lit up by their displays. He tried to bring up a virtual Aldis sight, tried to line up a shot to let the bastard know he could give as good as he got—

—And then he had to turn away, flinching as the Sixty-Four exploded into shrapnel and fire. He was close enough, and the explosion was bright enough, that for a moment his canopy turned solid black, opaquing itself to protect him from going blind.

In that moment when he was alone in the dark, unable to figure out what had just happened, a green pearl started spinning in the corner of his vision.

He flicked his eyes across it.

"Thought you could use a hand," Maggs said.

Lanoe was not about to say thank you. As much as he knew he should. "Sure," he growled. It was the best Maggs was going to get.

The bastard didn't push his luck by asking for more.

Lanoe's canopy shifted to full transparency again and he looked around, trying to get a feel for the battle. With all the sensors and comms and equipment onboard the BR.9, with all the emphasis its designers had put on situational awareness, there were still moments like this in every battle, moments when you could only guess if you were winning or losing. He tapped virtual keys on all his boards, trying to figure out how badly damaged he was, trying to figure out who was nearby. Candless came up on his wing even as he started to get a clear picture.

"I'm late, I know," she said. "Terribly sorry."

"Don't worry about it," he told her. "Glad to have you here now. How are the kids holding up?"

"The ensigns are causing some havoc, which I imagine is what you had in mind for them," Candless told him. "The carrier is turning around—a risky proposition in wormspace, of course, but they're desperate to get away from our firepower. It's going to be a close race to see whether we can shoot first or they escape."

Lanoe glanced over at the cruiser. He'd almost forgotten about the coilgun. He could see the protective shutters pulling back from the muzzle of the gun, a deep black pit in the Hoplite's side. He couldn't help but let his eyes stray up toward the big ship's nose, toward the torn metal and cloud of debris that had been its bridge.

"Valk's dead," he told Candless.

"Oh," she said. "I . . . I know what it meant to—"

"No, I'm not," Valk said.

There was a long second or two where Lanoe tried to process

what he had just heard. He'd already begun to accept the fact of Valk's death, that the AI had been torn apart by the disruptor that cracked open the ship. He'd started to think about what that meant, about how he could carry on his crusade against the Blue-Blue-White without—

"No, really," Valk said. "Not dead over here. You two might want to move back."

The coilgun was ready to fire.

———

"Oh, hellfire . . . oh, ashes—I'm blind, my eyes—my eyes—"

Bullam wished that Shulkin would order his IO to turn off the audio channel. Aleister Lanoe had wounded one of their pilots but had lacked the mercy to finish him off. Now they had to listen to the poor fool beg for help.

"My eyes! They're—they don't work. I can't fly—I can't fly like this, please! Please, I need remote recall. Please!"

If Shulkin felt any pity for the man, he didn't show it. "Data," he said. "Give me the pertinent data."

"We've completed our pre-maneuver turn," the navigator told him. "Engines on full. We're gaining distance, but—"

"It won't be enough," the carrier's pilot said. "I've goosed the engines as much as I can. We'll probably lose one of them, at this level of output. There's only so much energy you can force through a thruster cone, and—"

"Understood," Shulkin said. "IO?"

The man sat motionless in his chair, covering his eyes with his hands. "See for yourself," he said.

Bullam looked up at the display hovering over his position. At first she couldn't tell what she was looking at. A cloud of gas and dust obscured the midsection of the cruiser. Right in the middle of all that confusion was a tiny, perfectly circular black dot.

Vomit surged up her throat as she realized what that dot was.

The shell that the coilgun had just fired. It looked like a dot because it was headed directly for them, because she was seeing it nose-on. It grew steadily bigger as she watched.

"How much . . . How much damage will that—that thing do?" she asked, her words so quiet they sounded lost in the moaning and shrieking of the blind man.

Shulkin seemed to hear her anyway. "That's a seventy-five-centimeter heavy ordnance round. Jacketed in depleted uranium with a high-temperature explosive warhead. Those shells were originally designed to level cities. You saw what the disruptor round did to the Hoplite?"

"I did," Bullam said.

Shulkin nodded. "That was a Fleet Day firecracker compared to this."

There was gravity now, as the carrier's engines pushed for acceleration. A force holding her down in her chair. She pulled her legs up and wrapped her arms around her knees, because somehow that felt comforting.

In a few moments—a minute at most—she was going to die.

There was nothing anyone could do about it. She considered what she might want to do in these last few moments of her life, but nothing, absolutely nothing appealed to her. Mostly she just wanted to stop shaking.

"I can't see! Don't you understand? I need remote recall, I'm asking for—"

Shulkin still had part of the shredded armrest in his skeletal fingers. He tapped it against the denuded metal arm of his seat. "Why didn't they kill him? The man's blind," he said. "Surely that's an easy kill?"

The IO lifted his head to stare at Shulkin. "That's what you're thinking about right now? About easy kills?"

"If you're going to beat Aleister Lanoe at his own game, you need to think, Lieutenant. You need to think like . . ." He didn't finish the thought. His eyes were suddenly glowing with inner fire.

"Damn you, you rotten old bastard! Can't you see it's over? Can't you see we're all dead?" the IO shouted.

Shulkin laid the torn piece of armrest carefully in his lap. Then he pulled up a display and started tapping at virtual keys. "That injured pilot. Give him what he wants. Remote recall."

"Sir?" the navigator asked.

"He can't see where he's going, so we need to fly his cataphract for him. Do you not understand the concept?"

"Sir, you want us to bring him back…here? To the carrier?"

"I want you to send a general recall signal for all of our fighters. As for that man, the one we've been listening to, I want you to take remote control of his ship and fly it back here. Along this trajectory." He tapped a final key and his display vanished, as he sent the information to the navigator's position.

Her display lit up with the projected course. "That's not a minimum energy course," she said. "It'll take longer than necessary. I'm not sure I understand why you would—why. Oh," she said. "Sir, I don't know if I can do that."

"If you want to live, you will," Shulkin told her.

Whatever moral quandary she was wrestling with—and Bullam had no idea what it might be—the navigator didn't spend long making up her mind.

"Yes, sir," she said, and did as she'd been told.

◄━━►

Lanoe threw an arm across his face, just as a reflex, as the gun fired and space all around him filled with dust and smoke. So much energy was released when the gun fired that the projectile would have been vaporized, if it hadn't been contained inside an ablative sabot—a shield of heat-resistant borosilicate aerogel. The sabot wasn't designed to survive the discharge, only to keep the projectile cool. It disintegrated inside the barrel of the coilgun, and what was left of it came out of the barrel as a long plume of aerosolized debris—the smoke Lanoe saw. It filled space all around the cruiser, swirling violently enough to take the paint off the side of Lanoe's already damaged fighter. It played havoc with his sensors—and made it almost impossible to see anything.

When he pulled his arm back he could barely make out the lights of Candless's fighter off to his side, or the rotating beacon lamps over the closed doors of the cruiser's vehicle bay.

He pulled up his tactical display to fill most of his forward view and squinted at all the dots and rectangles and the dashed line of the gun's trajectory. The carrier had turned and begun a fast retreat but it was still in range, and the gun's projectile could travel a lot faster than the giant, lumbering ship.

It would take nearly twenty seconds for the projectile to reach the carrier, but even if the Centrocor ship tried to evade, the projectile had its own thrusters and was more than capable of matching their maneuvers. It was only a matter of time.

"We've got 'em," he said.

He'd been talking to himself but Candless replied. "That does appear to be the case. Tell me, do you see that blip moving fast away from us?"

Lanoe had seen it—a yellow dot indicating an enemy fighter, not very far away. The one he'd crippled just before its squadmate hit the cruiser with its disruptor. He'd assumed the pilot was dead, that the ship was out of the fight. Clearly it still had power to its thrusters.

"Looks like they're withdrawing," he said. And it wasn't the only one. Out in the middle distance, where Bury and Ginger were still pulling evasive loops around the enemy, the Sixty-Fours seemed to have lost their interest in the fight. One by one the Centrocor fighters were pulling away, burning out on long, shallow trajectories that would take them home. Even if the carrier was already doomed.

"They're running away," Candless said. "Do you have orders for us, Commander? We might catch some of them if we hurried."

"You think that's worth it? Hunt down the survivors?"

"Personally?" Candless asked. "No, I do not."

Lanoe nodded to himself. Poor bastards were hurrying home to a carrier that would be a twisted hulk by the time they arrived. He didn't see the need to ruin their day any further. He'd already got his win. "Bury, Ginger, Maggs. This is the return signal. Battle's over."

Of course, his work wasn't done. He needed to start thinking about damage control, about how their mission would go forward when their ship was missing a bridge. He had promised to give the ensigns a briefing, and—

"That guy's really moving," Bury said.

Lanoe frowned. He looked at the tactical display again and saw what the Hellion meant. The crippled Sixty-Four, the one he'd let get away, was accelerating at an incredible rate. Burning hard toward a rendezvous with the carrier. Hard enough to burn up its engines. Hard enough, maybe, to kill the pilot if he wasn't already dead.

"Why's he in such a rush?" Lanoe asked. He tapped a few virtual keys, rotated the display. "Is he just afraid we'll chase him? But we haven't moved..." He shook his head, looked at the display from yet another angle. Then he saw it.

"Hellfire," he swore. "Those bastards!"

The blind pilot kept shouting, right up until the end. The navigator piloted his ship remotely along the course and acceleration profile that Shulkin had given her. Even when the pilot screamed that he was accelerating too fast, that his inertial sink couldn't compensate— even when he cried out that his bones were breaking, that he was being crushed, the navigator didn't ease up on his throttle.

It was the only chance the carrier had. Bullam knew that.

She tried very hard not to be sick.

"We'll be out of effective range of the Hoplite's gun in sixteen seconds," the pilot said, very softly. "The projectile is nine seconds away from impact."

"They've only fired the one projectile," the IO said. He'd explained earlier that the coilgun could fire hundreds of rounds a minute, at its full capacity. It seemed Lanoe had been unwilling to order another shot. Why shoot the carrier a hundred times, when a single projectile would be enough to destroy them?

Shulkin had been banking on that. Because the trick he'd pulled would only work once.

"Please," the blind pilot begged, wheezing and choking as the acceleration crushed his lungs and his windpipe. "Please, there's something wrong. There's something…There's something…wrong—"

His voice cut out abruptly.

There was no bang, no sound of an explosion, no squeal of static. The audio just cut out.

On the IO's display, a blue dot had touched a yellow dot, and both of them vanished, that was all. A different display near the navigator's station showed a quick burst of gray light, beams scintillating as they cut through a cloud of debris.

Bullam cleared her throat.

Three faces looked expectantly up at her, their eyes searching for something. The pilot, the navigator, the IO. Shulkin kept his eyes on the displays.

She addressed the bridge crew because she knew Shulkin never would. "It was him or us," she said. "It had to be done."

On a purely cerebral level, she could admire Shulkin's clever play. He'd had a bullet streaking toward his head. He had a remotely controlled fighter that was capable of moving even faster than the bullet. He'd steered the blind pilot right into the path of the coilgun's projectile, and thereby removed a hazard from the battlefield.

All it cost was one human life. One of the pilots under his command.

A chime sounded from the IO's position. He swiveled around to check his boards and told them, "I've got new infrared signatures—lots of them. The Hoplite is warming up for a second shot. Their guns will be online in twelve seconds."

Shulkin pointed a finger at the pilot.

"We'll be out of range in ten," she said.

Shulkin nodded at her. Acknowledging a fact. Then he turned and looked at Bullam. "I'm afraid we won't be capturing Aleister Lanoe today," he said. "My decision as commander of this ship is that we should retreat with all due haste. Do you wish to countermand my decision?"

If his eyes had been glassy, once, now they were finely cut lenses.

Their focus made her want to turn her face away. She forced herself to meet that piercing gaze. "No," she said. "I agree with it."

Shulkin nodded.

"Navigator," he said, "set a course for Avernus. As fast as we can get there." He rose from his chair—there was significant gravity under their feet now, as the carrier burned hard to accelerate away from the battle. "If anyone needs me, I'm going to go take a nap."

He walked off the bridge looking a little stiff, maybe. His head held high.

When he was gone the bridge crew looked back at Bullam again. Wanting something.

"He just saved our lives," she told them. "But no. I don't like him much, either."

Chapter Eighteen

Bury arrived back in the vehicle bay and jumped out of his fighter before its maneuvering jets had even cooled. He hurried over to Ginger's ship and nearly pulled her out of her canopy.

"Did you see that? Did you see me take that fighter down?" he asked. He was smiling until the plastinated skin around his mouth felt like it was going to crack. He felt good, so good—for the first time in years, he wasn't angry, didn't feel like he was being crushed down by life. The freedom of it, the unmitigated joy of flying— and the rush of the fight, the wheeling and darting, the feints and countermaneuvers. He'd never felt so good before.

"I saw it, I saw—" Ginger tried to say.

He grabbed her into a tight hug. "You got one, too! You shot down a cataphract—I saw it!" he said. He knew he was nearly incoherent in his joy. He didn't care. "A couple more battles like that and we'll be *aces*," he told her. "We'll have our blue stars!"

She nodded but she was looking over his shoulder. Lieutenant Ehta, the marine, had just come through the bay's hatch. She floated back there, clutching a railing with one hand.

"Move aside," she said. "Make room for the others." She gave them a look that could have frozen engine coolant. Didn't she understand? Didn't she get how exciting this was, how good he felt?

Ginger grabbed his arm and they moved over to the railing, next to Ehta. They watched as Lieutenant Maggs came in, his advanced Z.XIX model gleaming as he settled it into its berth. He gave Bury a cheery wave, then headed inside without a word. Commander Lanoe arrived next, his fighter torn near to pieces. Bury wondered what had happened there—maybe the old man couldn't live up to his reputation anymore. Maybe he wasn't as good a pilot as everyone said. Lanoe didn't even look at them, just headed inside. Finally Lieutenant Candless arrived. Everybody home, everybody still alive. Bury felt a funny surge of camaraderie. He was honestly glad to see them all come home in one piece. A weather field shimmered into existence across the vehicle bay's hangar doors and air flooded into the chamber. Their helmets automatically released, flowing back down into their collar rings. All in the time it took Candless to emerge from her cockpit.

"Lieutenant," he said. "Lieutenant! Did you see? Ginger and I both got a kill. You trained us well, ma'am. We did—"

"That," Candless said, "was an unmitigated disaster."

Bury's face fell. "But—we won."

"We did not." Candless scowled at him. "The enemy chose to retreat. One can only be considered to be winning a battle when the enemy has no options remaining but to surrender. They wreaked great damage on our vehicle and then they withdrew. They will almost certainly try to attack us again, and next time we won't have the element of surprise. Under what parameters would you consider that a success, young man?"

"Hey," Ehta said. "Hey, come on. Cut the kid some slack."

"Should I?" Candless said. "Ensign Bury is my pupil. His actions reflect on my reputation. He had to be reprimanded on the field of battle for excessive radio chatter."

"Oh, come on," Ehta said.

"And as for you," Candless went on. "I'm your XO. So your failures come back to me as well. Can you tell me, Lieutenant, how many marines it takes to operate a Mark II coilgun? Hmm?"

"Now, you just—"

"I'm waiting for an answer."

Bury watched Ehta's face. He wouldn't have blamed her for hauling off and striking Candless, just then. The marine definitely looked like she wanted to. Instead, though, she just gripped the railing until her gloves squeaked.

"All of them," she said.

Candless raised an eyebrow.

"It takes every marine I have, when none of them have ever worked a ship's gun before. But damnation, we figured it out. We got off a perfect shot. The enemy had to throw away one of their own pilots to—"

"During the battle," Candless interrupted, "did you not hear a request we submitted for marines to crew the defensive guns? And yet we received minimal support. Because your marines were too busy learning how to do their job. If we ever find ourselves in another such engagement, I will expect more."

Candless turned and looked at them.

"That goes for all of you."

Then she headed through the hatch, deeper into the cruiser.

Bury couldn't believe it. He'd felt so good, just minutes before, but now—

Lieutenant Ehta snorted, building up a good head of mucus, and then she spat it at the hatch Candless had just passed through.

"Hey," Bury said. "Hey, that's not right."

Lieutenant Ehta lifted one eyebrow. "You gonna stick up for her, kid? After the way she just chewed out your six?"

"She's a pilot," Bury said. He could feel heat building up behind the polymerized skin of his cheeks. This woman might be a marine, she might be trained in unarmed combat, but if she wanted a fight he was going to make her hurt, if—

"Would both of you please be quiet?" Ginger asked.

They turned to look at her.

Ehta snarled. "She's a rules-quoting, chain-yanking bastard, and she's been riding me too long. I'm surprised you don't agree with me, girl."

"She was my teacher. Still is my teacher," Ginger said. "I'm not going to pick a fight with you. But I won't listen to you badmouth her again."

Ehta rolled her eyes and then kicked through the hatch, away from them.

When she was gone, Bury tore off his gloves and threw them across the room. "They're *never* going to respect us," he said. "We did great today, Ginj. We fought and we won. And still they won't—"

He stopped because he saw her face. Ginger was turning all shades of green, like she was about to be sick.

"Ginj," he said. "Ginj—what's wrong? Are you—is it what Candless said? Did she get under your skin?"

Ginger shook her head. "No. She's always been tough on us. I'm used to that. It's not—that's not what's got me—oh, damnation."

She grabbed the railing hard and pulled herself against it, as if she desperately needed to hold on to something stable. Bury rushed toward her to help, but she looked him right in the eye and he saw the existential horror there. "That was my first confirmed kill," she said, sounding haunted. "It's the first time I ever...oh, hellfire. I just killed a human being," she said. She pushed away from him, headed for the hatch. "Just—leave me alone!"

She shoved her way through the hatch, kicking it closed behind her.

Leaving Bury all alone in the vehicle bay, feeling like he had no idea what had happened to everybody. Hadn't they won?

Half of the axial corridor was shut off, emergency hatches having clamped down to prevent all the Hoplite's air from leaking out of the massive wound in the nose of the ship. Valk had to override a safety interlock just to get through a hatch that once had led to the captain's cabin—the same room where Lanoe had brought him back from the dead. Now one whole wall was gone, with nothing but ghostlight shimmering beyond. He crawled over twisted metal and pulled himself along with his hands, squeezing himself through places where panels and displays used to be, edging around the stubs of old pipes and conduits that had been sheared off so cleanly they stuck up like spear points. Occasionally his boots or his gloves would touch something unstable and a spar that had been barely holding on would shatter, sending new debris whirling off into the dark. He couldn't recognize half the things he saw— all these veins and arteries and nerves of the cruiser, its air ducts and water reclamation pipes and endless bundles of electrical cable, once hidden behind panels and walls, now torn free and exposed to hard vacuum.

Up ahead, where the bridge had been, Lanoe stood on a girder that stuck out from the torn edge of the wreckage. The metal beam pointed forward like the bowsprit of an ancient sailing vessel, with Lanoe as its painted figurehead.

"The damage is pretty bad," Valk said, as he clambered up to where Lanoe could see him. A bundle of emitters from a broken display, hanging loose now on their cables, flapped against his arm. Valk grasped the tangle of cords and tried to stuff them back inside their housing, but it was so warped they wouldn't fit anymore. "You think it can be repaired?"

"Sure," Lanoe said. He sounded tired. "These old birds—they're built from modular components. Designed to be rebuilt from the ground up. I flew on vessels a lot more beat-up than this during the Century War. We can print most of the parts we'll need, and for the more complicated stuff we have spares in the cargo holds." Lanoe was staring forward, down the wormhole. Valk couldn't see his face. "Some things we can't fix in the field, of course. The damage is just too extensive. But Paniet tells me if we stopped at Avernus, spent a couple days at the Navy dockyard there, he could have us as good as new."

Valk knew the tone in Lanoe's voice. "That's not going to happen, is it?" he asked. "We're not going to Avernus."

"No," Lanoe said.

Valk could guess two reasons why not. Now that they knew Centrocor was chasing them, Lanoe wouldn't want to lose any time by putting the ship in for repairs. Lanoe had told Valk it was crucial that they reach their destination before the poly—any poly—did, though he hadn't explained why.

The other reason—well, the other reason was all about Valk. The Navy knew now what Valk was. So did most of the Hoplite's crew. If he showed his opaqued helmet anywhere in human space, he was liable to be picked up and taken away to be quietly dismantled, his electronic brain wiped clean and its components smashed and then melted down just in case. If the Navy didn't catch him, Candless or one of the ensigns might turn him in, just on principle.

It was not a particularly unattractive prospect, as far as Valk was concerned. But he knew Lanoe would never let it happen.

"You weren't here, when the disruptor round hit," Lanoe said. Meaning that Valk hadn't been on the bridge. He turned around, moving his feet carefully on the beam. Sticky pads in the soles of his boots adjusted their grip to make sure his footing stayed sure.

"No," Valk said. "When you called for somebody to crew the defensive guns, I called Ehta but she said she couldn't spare anybody. So I went aft and crewed one of the guns myself. I thought I was being helpful."

Shadows pooled on Lanoe's face, where Valk could see it through his helmet. It was hard to read his expression. "You weren't on the bridge. I left you here to steer the ship, but you deserted your post."

"I...uh...I don't need to be on the bridge to do that. I can talk to the ship's computers anytime, from anywhere. I knew I could steer and shoot at the same time. Don't even ask me how I knew, I just did."

"That's a lot for one person to keep track of simultaneously," Lanoe said, his voice guarded.

Anger flared behind Valk's eyes. Well, the place where his eyes should have been. "Hellfire, Lanoe. Enough with the third degree. You know I'm not...not..."

"Not what?"

"Not a person! Yeah, for a human, keeping track of the bridge and shooting a gun at the same time would be impossible. But I'm not human. We were in the middle of a battle and everything was crazy, displays showing me a million things, and then Ehta said there was nobody for the guns, and . . . and it just occurred to me. I could, you know. Make a copy of myself. Leave one version of my software on the bridge, flying the ship. Send the other along with my suit, down to the guns. So that's what I did."

"Sure," Lanoe said.

Which did nothing for Valk's mood. "You never want to talk about this. You want to just pretend I'm still Tannis Valk, still this human pilot who fought in the Crisis. You don't want to accept what I really am. And how dangerous that is. I can do all these new things now. Now that I know I'm a machine. I can talk to computers, it's not even like talking to you. It's *easier*. I can hear your heart beating, through this radio channel. I can split myself into multiple copies. Who knows what else?"

"You're still Tannis Valk to me," Lanoe said. "The man I fought beside at Niraya, the man I'm lucky enough to call my friend, the man—"

"No! Tannis Valk is dead! Can't you understand this? There is no connection. No continuity—he died, and sometime later they built me. Told me I was him. But I'm not human and I have *never been* human."

"So what are you?"

"I don't even know!" Valk wanted to get away from this conversation, even as he was sure he desperately needed to have it. He very much wanted to head back inside the ship. Into light and warmth and air, none of which he actually needed. He had no idea what he wanted. "I'm finding out, little by little. But every time I pull one of these stunts, every time I figure out some new thing I can do, or realize there's something I don't need. Like sleep. Or food. Every time I realize some new fact about *me*, I become a little less human. Lanoe, you should shut me down. You should switch me off, for good."

"I still have plans for—"

"For revenge, right." Valk yanked at the bundle of emitters and threw them out into the wormhole. He could calculate their trajectories to as many decimal places as he liked, know exactly how long it would take them to hit the wall and be annihilated. He didn't bother. "You want to kill the Blue-Blue-White because…let's just say it's because of all those alien species they wiped out. Let's leave it there. And you need me for that."

"You're the only one who can talk to the jellyfish. If I'm going to get justice from them, I need them to understand my demands."

Valk shook his head. His whole torso. "And then—only then—when you're done, when you have your revenge—"

"Justice," Lanoe insisted.

"Damned semantics," Valk said. "But fine. When you have justice, then you'll let me die. Yes? Or will you keep me around even then? Force me to keep up this farce of pretending I'm a dead man? Are you going to keep me around like your pet or something?"

"No. I promise, Valk, I'll let you go."

Valk nodded again. "I trust you, Lanoe. All the devils know I probably shouldn't, but I do. So here. I'm going to give you something."

A black pearl sat in the corner of Valk's vision. A nasty, brooding little thing that had been there ever since he found out what he really was. A final gift from the engineers who made him. It had been sitting there for months, waiting for him to flick his eyes across it just the right way. Letting go of it felt simultaneously liberating and terrifying, but he knew it had to be done. Without thinking about how he did so, he transferred ownership of the black pearl to Lanoe.

"What the hell is this?" Lanoe asked.

"It's a data bomb," Valk explained. "If I was human, it would be a cyanide capsule. You activate that thing, it'll erase me. Delete all my files, write over every data block in my memory. Permanently. You understand?"

"Valk—"

"This is the price of my sticking around. You get to carry that thing. I've been looking at it since we left Niraya, wondering if I had the guts to use it. I guess I didn't. As much as I've wanted to die, to *stop*—the devil help me, I couldn't pull that trigger. But you will. Either when you're done with me, finally. Or..."

"Or what?"

Valk inhaled sharply. No, damn it, he didn't. He simulated inhaling sharply, because it felt right to do so. "Or if I go feral. You know? If I start acting more like an AI than a person, start thinking human lives are just so inefficient, such a waste of resources. Like the *Universal Suffrage,* or...whatever."

Valk turned away. But he couldn't stop looking at Lanoe, watching his face. Trying to make sure he took this seriously.

Lanoe nodded inside his helmet. "Okay," he said. "Okay."

Bury hardly had time to sit down and eat before the call came in. All officers to attend a special briefing. He made a point of finishing off his tube of food paste before he responded.

With the bridge gone, the pilots had all been moved to bunks aft of the damaged areas of the ship, in the same ring of quarters as the marines. The briefing would be held in the wardroom at the center of those bunks, a communal space that already stank of unwashed suits and aggression. The marines themselves had been sent aft, ostensibly to run more gun drills, though Bury knew it was just so they wouldn't eavesdrop. Engineer Paniet and Lieutenants Candless and Ehta were already there. Commander Lanoe arrived and looked around with a scowl on his face.

"Where's Ginger?" he asked.

"She's, uh, in her bunk, sir," Bury said. "I asked if she wanted to come out for this, but she said she needed to be alone."

Lanoe looked supremely annoyed. "She was the one who demanded this meeting in the first place," he said.

Bury started to respond, to say the strike had been his idea, too, but Lieutenant Candless reached over and put a hand on his shoulder. He started to shove it away, but the look on her face told him to behave. He remembered how much trouble he'd gotten in the last time he spoke up at a briefing, and decided maybe this time he would keep quiet.

"She was rather affected by the fighting," Candless said.

"You're telling me that after her very first battle, she's already got the wind up?" Lanoe demanded. "Hellfire, I knew she was green, but—"

Candless cleared her throat to interrupt him.

Here it comes, Bury thought. A perfect opportunity for Candless to wield her sharp tongue. To say exactly how disappointed she was in Ginger, and how the girl couldn't be trusted to—

"She'll be fine," Candless said.

"If she's got a case of nerves, she's of no use to me," Lanoe said. "I need people who aren't afraid to—"

"I told you, sir, that she would be *fine*. Do you require me to repeat myself a third time? Ensign Ginger is one of my cadets, and I *do not* train cowards. Furthermore, I am the XO onboard this ship, responsible for both morale and discipline. I will ask you, with all due respect, to allow me to do *my damned job* and look after my people. Should I decide that one of my pilots is not fit for duty, you can be sure that I will let you know immediately. Now, I believe you called us here for a briefing. Shall we get on with it?"

The look on Lanoe's face was one Bury knew he would treasure for years. The big man, their commanding officer, looked as chastened as a first-year cadet who'd just been told he flunked basic suit training.

He could only wonder about the look on his own face. The last thing he'd ever expected Lieutenant Candless to do was to actually stick up for Ginger.

"I suppose...yeah, okay," Lanoe said, running his fingers over his cropped gray hair. "Fair enough."

He looked around at all of them, his eyes much softer than they had been before. He even smiled a little when he looked at Bury, though Bury had no idea why.

"It goes without saying that what I'm going to tell you is secret and not to be shared with anyone outside of this room. Except Ginger—Bury, you'll fill her in, when she's ready to hear it. Oh, and you'll notice Lieutenant Maggs isn't here. That's intentional. He definitely shouldn't hear any of this. As for the rest of you, you've proved your loyalty now to the Navy, and to me. You deserve to know what you're doing here. I'll give you a quick overview, and then I'll take individual questions."

He tapped a few virtual keys on his wrist display, and a holographic image of a yellowish-brown planet appeared over the wardroom's display. "I'm going to start at the beginning. This is a place called Niraya. A while ago, it was attacked by aliens…"

"It all looks pretty standard," Valk said, bending low to examine the PBW cannon of Maggs's Z.XIX. Stubby barrels mounted in standard housings. There were four of them instead of the two you found on most cataphract-class fighters, and they were a little shiner than usual—though that might just be because they were new. PBWs were powerful weapons and they wore out over time, the barrels growing rough as stray particles cut through the metal. Valk stuck a gloved finger inside one of the barrels and rubbed it around, then examined his fingertip, looking for residue. A little gray dust, nothing unusual there.

"No, the guns themselves are quite ordinary," Maggs said. He sounded distinctly annoyed. Impatient. "I explained this to Lanoe once already—"

"And he asked me to check it out personally," Valk said. "You've got some fancy new system that lets you snipe enemy ships at, what, twice the normal range?"

"It's rated out at a seventy percent increase in collimation and a fifty-nine percent improved target acquisition rate," Maggs said. "But as I told Lanoe, the improvements are all in the software. You can't tell from the outside that it's anything special."

Valk nodded—bobbing his entire torso back and forth—and reached for the key that would open the fighter's canopy.

Maggs moved to stop him. "There's nothing to actually *see*. And I'd prefer not to let a bloody AI dismantle my vehicle just to see how it works."

Valk would have smiled, if he had a mouth. He would have given Maggs a big goofy grin. He'd never much cared for the scoundrel pilot, and the fact that Maggs was clearly uncomfortable just being around an artificial intelligence filled Valk with a sort of sadistic glee. He supposed he should be more charitable. Hellfire, he made *himself* uncomfortable a lot of the time.

Still.

"Lanoe asked me to take a look, and—"

"May we discard this pretense already?" Maggs asked. "You're here to keep me busy. While Lanoe tells the other officers what our mission is."

"He feels you can't be trusted," Valk explained. "Otherwise I'm sure he would have included you."

"Yes, he's allowed me no illusions when it comes to my trustworthiness. He'd rather confide in a walking computer than in a decorated officer of the Navy, who, I feel I must note at this juncture, was *instrumental* in getting him this command in the first place. Well, I suppose it doesn't matter. I can do my job without knowing all the little details. Obviously it's about the aliens. That's the only reason they'd drag him back out of retirement, eh?"

Valk held himself very still. Face or no face, he knew there were other ways people could read you. He didn't want to give anything away. "Why don't we stick to what we're supposed to be doing?" he said. "Tell me more about this new technology."

"The Philoctetes Targeting Package, they're calling it. Revolutionary stuff, absolutely. Bleeding-edge targeting algorithms that can predict the movement of an enemy craft. No need to rely on fallible human instincts anymore. With Philoctetes software you simply choose your targets and let the computer do the work for you," Maggs said. "Honestly, as good as it is, I'm afraid it's going to mean the end of dogfighting. When you can snipe your targets from so far away, there's no need to get in close and tussle with the other fellow. It means the end of an era, especially for knights of the sky like old Lanoe."

"I'll believe that when it happens. Cataphract pilots have been the stars of every war since he was a kid."

"Well, all good things must *et cetera*. But—oh. It occurs to me . . . are you cleared for this information? It's all tip-top secret."

"Lanoe—"

Maggs lifted his hands in something like a gesture of apology. "No, no, of course you are. Lanoe trusts you implicitly, I must have forgotten that for just a moment. That's why he can spare you for this inspection, after all. No need for you to be in that briefing, since you already know everything."

Valk sighed in exasperation. "Maggs—"

"Which means I was right."

"Wait. What?"

"Our mission must have something to do with the Blue-Blue-White."

"How did you figure that out?" Valk asked.

"I can't think of another reason Lanoe would see you as being so crucial he would break the law just to keep you on the team. So we're going alien hunting again, and—"

"I'm not going to tell you anything," Valk insisted.

"No, of course not. Terribly sorry. I'll drop it, I swear," Maggs said, a sly smile creeping across his face.

Commander Lanoe reached over and switched off the display. "All right. Questions, now. I'll answer whatever I can."

All around Bury, people started talking at once. He ignored them. There was only one thought in his mind.

Aliens.

Really?

Aliens?

As a boy growing up on Hel, of course he'd watched plenty of videos about humanity making first contact with aliens—fictional videos. Typically the aliens all looked like humans with bumps on their foreheads or slightly differently colored skin. Often in the videos the aliens wanted to conquer and enslave human planets, or drain them of their vital resources, and they had to be stopped. Brave human pilots had to step in to fight them.

So the idea wasn't completely new to him.

Yet...this wasn't exactly like the videos, was it? These aliens, these giant jellyfish, hadn't even been aware of humanity's existence. The invasion of Niraya had been, what, a mistake? Not even that. Human lives hadn't even entered the equation.

And now, this mysterious message, which had something to do with fighting the aliens, but nobody knew what.

"This is all bosh," Bury said.

Lieutenant Ehta scowled at him. "The Blue-Blue-White are real, I can tell you that much. I was at Niraya. So were Maggs and Valk."

"That's not what I meant," Bury said, his blood rising in him. "No. I mean this new...signal, this message. This 'key.' Who sent that? Why didn't they send more information? If they want to help, why not just identify themselves? Bosh!"

"Personally I find it very exciting," Engineer Paniet said. "Who doesn't like to dig into a good mystery?"

Lieutenant Ehta snorted with laughter, and Paniet smiled. So maybe he'd been joking.

"How do we know we can trust whoever sent this signal? This could be a trap," Bury said.

"That's why the Navy sent a cruiser," Commander Lanoe said. "Not a yacht full of politicians."

That got several laughs.

Why wasn't anyone taking this seriously? Maybe it was just too much to take in.

Lanoe nodded at Bury. Was that a grudging look of respect in his eye? Unlikely. Probably just dust or something. "Lots of mysteries," the Commander said, eventually. "It's our job to solve them. I won't lie. This is a weird mission and it's already proving dangerous—clearly Centrocor knows something of what I just told you, at least enough that they're willing to kill us to find out more. And what we discover at the end of the road—I have no idea. I do know one thing."

Lanoe looked from face to face around the room as he went on. "I know the Blue-Blue-White would have killed every human being on Niraya. We got lucky there. I know there are a lot more of those drone fleets, and that they'll never stop coming. I know we won't get lucky every time."

He tapped at a virtual keyboard and the display came back to life, showing the message the Navy had intercepted. MORE WILL COME. WE CAN HELP.

"When it comes to stopping the Blue-Blue-White," Lanoe said, "I'll take any help I can get."

Chapter Nineteen

Maybe this time it would work.

Maybe this time he could actually get some sleep.

The briefing had taken longer than expected, but Lanoe still had a little time. He was due to examine the wreckage of the forward part of the cruiser, with Paniet. Not for a few hours, though. For the moment, for the first time since he'd started this mission, he had nothing specific to do. There were no alerts on his minder, no calendar entries, no calls from Candless or Ehta demanding he come take care of some problem he didn't care about. Even the ensigns were leaving him alone—Ginger locked up in her bunk, Bury still reeling from finding out they weren't alone in the universe.

Lanoe headed for his own bunk, grateful for just the chance to catch his breath.

His cabin had been destroyed along with the bridge. He'd been assigned one of the tiny coffinlike bunks, just like everyone else. It didn't matter. He'd slept in worse places. He pulled himself inside and closed the hatch. The bunk had a padded floor, not entirely unlike a mattress. He stretched himself out, his boots touching the far wall, and laid down his head.

Just a couple of hours. Just a little time to get some rest, to help clear his mind, organize his thoughts. If he could just sleep for a little while—

"Lanoe," Zhang said.

The voice came before he'd even had a chance to close his eyes. He squeezed them shut now, trying to block out the whispering call.

She wasn't there. Zhang was dead. He needed to accept that.

"Lanoe," she said again. She sounded scared. She sounded like she was pleading with him, begging him for something.

"What do you need?" he asked. He barely vocalized the words, feeling foolish for talking to a ghost. "What do you want from me?" he asked her.

He didn't really expect a reply. He thought of the voice in his head as a kind of glitch, as an artifact, as an echo. Just a last fading note played after the symphony had ended, sustained out into the silence.

It wasn't really Zhang. She was dead. She couldn't still be talking to him, beseeching him like this.

It was just his own subconscious, nagging at him, picking at old wounds—

"Lanoe. You're so far away," she said.

Lanoe sucked in a deep, long breath. Intending to push her away, to finally expel her from his weary head. He started to exhale—

"You're so far from where you need to be," she said.

～～

When humanity first discovered the planet Avernus, they found its surface entirely covered by an ocean of warm, shallow brine that surged endlessly back and forth, waves building up over months until they were fifty meters tall because there was nothing for them to crash on. There'd been no solid land at all, nothing to stand on, so the first colonists had lived on enormous pontoon rafts capable of riding the planet's mega-tsunami waves. Over the course of a hundred years of settlement, however, it became clear that that was never going to be a long-term strategy.

So the Avernians had built platform arcologies, elevated high above the constant pounding of the monster waves. Cities on stilts, perched atop carbon allotrope pylons that sank down hundreds of meters underwater to reach the rocky core of the planet. The platforms had been built big but as the population expanded there was never enough space on their high decks. The cities of Avernus could only ever build *up*, so they looked like single, impossibly tall skyscrapers encrusted with barnacles, their sides studded with layer after layer of shops and catwalks and tacked-on office parks and houses hanging from long booms.

As Bullam's yacht drifted down into the shadow of one such city, the local sunlight was cut off almost immediately. It was replaced by blinking forests of neon signs and blue light streaming through shop windows. Funicular trains rolled past on long spiral tracks, headed down into the city's mist-shrouded lower levels. On the open deck of the yacht Bullam sank through layers of sounds, of music and arguments and the endless rustling sound of commerce. Strata of smells of cooking and sewage and the ozone reek of fusion power.

Civilians, she thought. None of the people she saw wore uniforms, none of them were ex-Navy. Civilization. She breathed in its heady air and felt almost human again.

Captain Shulkin sat in one of her carved wooden chairs, his glassy eyes reflecting it all, absorbing nothing.

"We're safe here anyway," she told him, though she doubted he even heard her. "Wilscon's claim on this planet is ironbound, never been challenged. The Navy has never had any reason to come out this way. It would be nice if this was a Centrocor planet but Wilscon isn't currently at war with Big Hexagon, so I doubt the local constabulary will even bother spying on us very much."

"Lady! Lady!" someone shouted, and she turned to see who it was. A boy ran along one of the railed balconies that stuck out everywhere from the city. He had a net bag of oranges at the end of a stick and he craned it out over the deck as she floated past. "Fresh, fresh! Fifty for the bag!" the boy called. "Flash me the money and they're yours!"

She laughed and nodded at one of her drones. It transferred the funds automatically—there was no time to haggle, in a moment the yacht would sink past the boy's level—and the boy dropped the fruit on to her deck.

The sound it made colliding with the wooden boards made Shulkin wince. Maybe he thought they were being attacked. She made it up to him by digging one of the ripe oranges out of the bag and tossing it to him.

"Better than that food paste we've been eating since we left Tuonela," she said.

Shulkin caught the fruit effortlessly, then stared at it in his hand as if she'd thrown him a live grenade.

"Cheer up," she told him. "This is just a quick stopover. We'll be back in space with people shooting at us very soon."

"Lanoe," Shulkin said, staring at the orange. "Lanoe got away."

"Yes," Bullam said. She sunk her thumbnail deep into a yielding rind. Juice squirted out across the deck. "Yes, he did."

"We failed," Shulkin said. The words like a wind blowing through cemetery trees.

"Not yet," she promised him. "Not yet."

❈

"Are you well, Commander?" Paniet asked, when they met up to examine the wreckage of the cruiser's forward section. "You look a tad peaked. If it's all right for me to say that."

Lanoe waved away the engineer's concern with a gruff gesture. "Fine. Just fine." The two of them were climbing up the axial corridor, but they could only get so far. An emergency bulkhead blocked the way above them. It had slammed shut when all the air was sucked out of the forward compartments, protecting them from being exposed to hard vacuum. Lanoe had no idea what they would find behind that thick hatch. He reached up to pull the manual release latch.

It wouldn't budge.

Lanoe swore and tried to yank at the damned latch again. It shifted a little, but he couldn't quite get enough leverage.

"You're at a bad angle," Paniet said. "Let me have a go, ducks."

Lanoe scowled at the man. "I've got it, damn you." He put one foot up against the wall. Braced himself and heaved.

Below him a weather field snapped into place, a shimmering in the air. His helmet flowed up over his face automatically as the hatch released. A breeze ruffled the front of his suit, then was gone, and the two of them climbed up into hard vacuum.

"I'm not getting enough sleep," Lanoe told the engineer.

"A common malady among starship captains, I imagine," Paniet replied. "If you'd like to do this another time—"

"No," Lanoe said. Sharp enough to make Paniet wince. "No. Sorry. I appreciate your concern, but this needs to be done now."

No point in delaying it. That would just mean having to go back to his bunk—and listen for Zhang's voice again.

Instead he followed the engineer into the ruined section. They had to pick their way through carefully, avoiding broken spars and heaps of debris. Here and there, Paniet pointed out some particularly bad bit of damage. Lanoe watched as the engineer struggled to open a panel in the wreckage of the bridge. The panel had buckled and one side of it was covered in soot, but once it came free the bundles of wires and relays underneath looked intact. Diodes lit up in the ring of circuitry around Paniet's left eye.

"What do they mean, those lights?" Lanoe asked, gesturing at Paniet's face.

"They mean, love, that I can see what I'm doing." Paniet bent over the open panel and his lights glittered on the cables. "This could be worse," he said. He took a tool from a pouch on the front of his suit and used it to spread two bundles apart, to get at a length of fiber optic cable behind them. "Tell me, did they teach you in flight school that you should try to avoid having the bridge of your vehicle shot to pieces?"

He turned to look at Lanoe, a mischievous smile playing on his face. The lights made Lanoe blink and look away.

"They taught us to trash our equipment whenever possible, so that our mechanics would have something to do," Lanoe replied.

Paniet chuckled. He closed up the panel and the two of them moved forward, deeper into the shambles of twisted spars and severed cable. Two of Paniet's neddies were at work there stretching a sheet of carbon fiber over a gaping wound in the side of the former bridge. "When these two are done, we'll have a proper seal and be able to get air back in here," Paniet explained. "That'll make the work go faster."

"How much functionality can we expect when you're done?" Lanoe asked.

"As I told you, a week in drydock would set us right, but since we're not stopping, well...really, Commander, the damage is severe. We've lost the bridge, half the quarters on the ship...most of our sensors." Paniet shook his head. "None of the ship's elevators will work anymore, the shafts are all crumpled. The bad fellows cut the head off our lovely bird. All I can do here is cauterize the stump."

That was worse than Lanoe had expected. He'd thought they would at least have a functional bridge, if not a comfortable one. Still. "We can fly without this section." Piloting, navigation, and information systems could be handled from any display on the ship. Losing the bridge was damned inconvenient, but not fatal.

"Running this ship from emergency equipment is possible, yes," Paniet said. "I can use the displays in the remaining wardroom, give that position root access, set up a pilot's chair...all easy enough, and you'll have a sort of makeshift bridge. But it'll take a toll on all of your pilots. They'll get stressed out more quickly and that's never good. You have M. Valk at the helm just now, right?" Paniet asked. "You've been relying on him a fair bit."

"He doesn't need to sleep, or eat. He can interface directly with the ship's systems." Valk didn't even need a terminal to fly the ship. "You think I should just assign him to permanent pilot duty?"

"The opposite, rather." Paniet tapped at a broken aluminum spar with the business end of a wrench. Under the stress, the spar broke off in two pieces. Paniet collected the jagged bits of metal and shoved them in a bag slung from his hip. "Do not get me wrong, ducks. Please do not think I disapprove of your keeping him around."

"Oh?" Lanoe said.

"I've always been of the impression that the laws about AI are too stringent. We have this impression that every AI is going to go evil at some point, that they'll turn on us if we give them half a chance. That smacks of paranoia to me—and I imagine most engineers would agree. Not all people are bloody bastards, are they?"

"Just most of them," Lanoe agreed.

"There's no reason to think there's something inherently dangerous in the synthetic mind," Paniet said. "We had one very sad example, and we've assumed ever since that they would all be the same."

"I feel like there's a *but* coming up, though it's taking its time arriving," Lanoe said.

"Then let me be plain. It's very handy that M. Valk doesn't *need* to sleep. But he most definitely *should*."

"That's your idea of being plain?"

Paniet sighed. He reached for a bundle of cabling and tugged on it, hard. When it didn't come loose he took out some complicated tool and ran it over the cables, while lights flashed green and amber on his wrist display. "M. Valk is still learning what being an AI means to him. Every time he figures out a new thing—that he doesn't need to shave, that he can do differential equations in his head without counting on his fingers—he becomes a little less human. If he's going to become dangerous, if he does go bad, it'll be when he stops thinking of himself as a person and starts identifying more with machines. Anything you can do—anything to make him feel more like his old self, Tannis Valk, the Blue Devil, yes?—is going to help keep us in his heart."

"So I'm supposed to worry about my pilots getting stressed out," Lanoe said, "but I can't rely too much on the one pilot I have who doesn't feel the stress. Any other helpful advice you have for me?"

"Oh, deary." Paniet shoved the tool back in his pouch and moved on to the crumpled remains of the navigator's station. "I could go on for hours."

———— ✦ ————

Bullam consulted with her drones, then stepped back out onto the deck of the yacht. They were far out at sea, just bobbing along like a cork above the waves. She'd thought a little salt air might do them both some good, so she'd taken them well away from any of the arcologies, out of sight of any Avernian eye.

"M. Cygnet has been kind enough to send us reinforcements— replacements for the pilots and vehicles we lost, as well as fresh supplies." As well as a tersely written message expressing his extreme disappointment with their failure to capture Lanoe. She chose not to share that. "They'll be here momentarily. Resupply and basic repairs can be complete by the end of the day. Care to try your hand at fishing?"

Shulkin stood on the deck as lifeless as a mannequin. He looked like he ought to be tossed overboard by each passing swell, but instead he simply rolled with the motion of the yacht. As steady as a sailor of ancient days bestriding the deck of a war galley.

Shulkin nodded. "Doable," he told her. At first she thought he meant fishing. "We can take down that cruiser with what we have," he said, and she realized he'd barely heard her. "Though it's going to be bloody work. We know better than to rush in again and face those guns. So the next battle will be at extreme range. Our fighters against their fighters."

"Well, that's good news, isn't it?" Bullam said. "We have more cataphracts than they do, and plenty of carrier scouts."

Shulkin made a sound like a machine venting gas. She assumed it was his attempt at a world-weary sigh. "Fifty, on our side. Five on theirs. But one of their fighters will have Aleister Lanoe in it. Aleister Lanoe…"

She waited for him to say something more. As usual, she waited in vain. When she had had enough, she decided to prompt him. "You fought alongside him, you said."

"Did I?"

She suppressed the urge to scream. "During the battle. I asked if you'd fought *against* him, and you said if you had you would be dead now. I assumed—"

Shulkin lifted one hand. Let it drop again. "The Brushfire," he said. "And again. In the Crisis. We crossed paths. I didn't fight *alongside* him. But I saw what he could do."

"The Brushfire," Bullam said. She knew her history well enough to know what that meant. After the wormhole network was discovered, humanity had spread across the stars in a hurry. Planets were discovered, terraformed, and settled in the space of decades. The polys hadn't yet laid their respective stakes on the new worlds, and Earth had proved incapable of governing such a far-flung population. It had been a time of warlords and space piracy and constant small-scale fighting. It had never erupted into full-blown war, but the Navy had kept busy. "What did you do in the Brushfire?"

It was as if she'd opened the floodgates of a dam. Shulkin hadn't spoken more than a score of words since they'd arrived on Avernus. Once he got going, reminiscing about the good old days, she could tell it would be difficult to get him to stop. So she didn't—she just let him ramble on.

They had time to kill, anyway, before the reinforcements arrived.

"My first command, a Peltast-class destroyer." Shulkin's face cracked into a toothy smile. It wasn't nearly as grim as she would have expected. "Wild times. The Navy would send me in to shell a rioting city one day, then delivering emergency food supplies to the same planet the next. Battles in space were few and far between, though. My ship outclassed anything the planetary militias could muster so all I had to do was show up in a given system and my enemies typically surrendered on the spot. Good for the ego. Makes you sloppy, though. One time I made a mistake and it nearly cost me everything. I was ordered to clean out a nest of pirates who had holed up on a moon of Asmodeus. You know Asmodeus? Big gas giant planet in the Sheol system. About two hundred AU out from the local wormhole throat, so even getting to Asmodeus takes days. I suppose the pirates thought that distance meant they were out of the Navy's reach. They were wrong.

"I went in guns blazing, thinking to make a show of force. Crippled the pirate base in the first couple of seconds, mopped up their ground-based defenses, thought I was about done. That was when they sprang their trap. Our intel said they had only a handful of lightly armed ships. What we didn't know is they had a lot of friends. Three other pirate groups who had joined forces to take us down. They came out of the sun, taking us by surprise—and cutting off our escape route. Forty ships, maybe, none of them carrying any heavy guns, but their PBWs kept us pinned down, kept us from launching our fighters in any kind of good order. They couldn't cut through our armor but they could smash up our guns, leave us toothless, just fighting like curs to stay alive.

"The fighting went on for days. My people fell like ninepins. Casualties on the pirate side, too, staggering losses, but they didn't seem to care. It was like they were working out a bad grudge. On the third day I started thinking we might actually lose. That I might die out there in the dark, out where the local sun was just the brightest star in the sky.

"That was when Lanoe came in. He was running a squadron of troubleshooters, real commando types. Long-range recon and special operations. Outside the general chain of command—there was always work for him to do, so they let him pick his own assignments. Nobody had heard from me or my destroyer in days, so he figured he'd stop by and see if we were all right.

"The pirates turned on him the second he arrived. They must have thought a squad of fresh ships was the real threat, since they'd already declawed my destroyer. I'll be damned if they weren't right—and damned twice if Lanoe didn't read the situation instantly. He pulled them into a real scrum, close-up fighting that kept them well clear of my position.

"It gave us time to do some much-needed emergency repairs.

Specifically, it let us bring our big guns back on line. While Lanoe kept the pirates occupied, we had plenty of time to work up good firing solutions. A three-day battle ended in about fifteen seconds, one pirate ship after another blown to pieces in the dark.

"When it was done, Lanoe and his people didn't even bother telling us we were welcome. He waggled his airfoils," Shulkin said. He held up one hand, his thumb and little finger held out like the wings of a cataphract, then twisted his hand from side to side to show what it looked like. "Might as well have opened his canopy and given us a hearty wave. Then he was off again, who knew where. Saved my bloody life, and didn't even let me buy him a drink."

He actually chuckled at the thought. The man who might have been made of wood, the dead-eyed zombie, suddenly looked almost human.

Bullam leaned back in her chair and watched the clouds scud by along the edge of the sea. A drone brought her a glass of orange juice. "You saw him again during the Establishment Crisis, though," she prompted.

"Your family," he said. His smile just fell right off his face. "You lost your family in the Crisis. I don't want to . . . to . . ."

Bullam frowned. The old man almost sounded as if he cared. *How touching*, she thought. "Never mind that." She certainly didn't want to talk about it. "Tell me what you did in the Crisis. How you met Lanoe again."

Shulkin nodded. He walked over to the railing and gripped it with both hands. "That was a very different kind of fighting. The Establishment—they never had enough fighter pilots. Not enough to break our squadrons. They had plenty of big ships, though. Cruisers and battleships, even a beat-up old dreadnought left over from the Century War. So whenever they could, they pulled us into big engagements. Whole lines of capital ships facing each other in deep space, maneuvering constantly to stay out of range of each other's guns. Each side daring the other to move in and take the first shot. Those were . . . trying battles. Hours of staring at displays, of working out firing solutions you never used. Stalemates that could go on for days as one ship after another strayed too close to the battle line and was torn to pieces.

"They couldn't win. Everyone knew that, right from the start. We had better equipment, more vehicles. Pilots trained by generations of warfare. One by one, their planets fell. They'd vowed to fight to the last ounce of blood in their veins, and no one could deny they tried. It all came down in the end to a fight near Tiamat, an ice ball nobody would ever mistake for a useful planet. Their leaders holed up in a bunker ten kilometers deep, their last few big ships burning in orbit. It looked like they were finished. Then they pulled the biggest surprise of the war. Turned out they had three whole wings of fighters, good solid cataphracts that they'd held in reserve. Fresh ships, their very best pilots. Kept in hiding for a year, an insurance policy held against just this situation.

"Now, a capital ship, like a carrier or a cruiser, is a formidable thing—you saw that. But one good cataphract pilot can beat a destroyer seven times out of ten. A wing is six squads of twenty fighters each. On the bridge of my carrier I watched those three wings tear through every destroyer escort I had and I was sure we'd lost. We had our own cataphracts, sure, but barely a full wing of them in a bunch of ragged squads, not nearly enough to defend us. It was a matter of time—and I'm talking minutes, not hours—before they got to my carrier. Before they blew us to hell.

"And that was when Aleister Lanoe stepped in." Shulkin's eyes were bright. His face seemed less lined than it had before, his posture better. She thought there might even be some color in his cheeks.

"Lanoe cut through those wings. Don't even ask me how. He tore through them without so much as maneuvering. It was like he was touched by some kind of mystical grace. Unstoppable. Unkillable. He punched a hole right through their formation and we sailed our last destroyer through right after him, its guns sparkling in the dark... I've never seen fighting like it.

"We didn't finish off the Establishment that day, no, but it was over. The war was over. It was just a matter of mopping up."

Shulkin staggered over to a chair and dropped himself into the cushions. He closed his eyes and let his mouth drop open a little.

"Oh, you've brought it all back," he whispered. "I wouldn't let myself...couldn't afford to think about it. About what it...what it used to be."

He was drifting. Falling back into the well where he lived now, the safe, dead place he'd inhabited as long as she'd known him. She could tell that in a moment he would sit up and open his eyes and they would be made of glass again. That his armor was coming back up. For a moment, she thought, she'd seen the real Captain Shulkin. The man he'd once been. It couldn't last.

But there was one more thing, one more question she had to ask before she lost him. Something she very much needed to know.

"Sounds like you owe Aleister Lanoe your life. Twice over," she said, cautiously.

Shulkin sat up a little in his chair. His mouth was a flat line, incapable now of showing any emotion.

"I suppose I do," he said.

Bullam drew in a deep breath. "When the time comes—when we capture him. You know what Centrocor will do to him. You know it won't be pleasant."

Shulkin did not respond.

"Can you do this, Captain? Can you fight Lanoe? Fight against him?"

His eyes popped open. She expected them to be empty, soulless. Instead they were like the diamonds she'd seen on the bridge of the carrier. Hyperfocused. Relentless. Colder than ammonia ice.

"That won't be a problem," he told her.

◄━━►

Lanoe passed back through the axial corridor, through the emergency bulkhead. When he stood at the top of the corridor, looking down the vertiginous drop all the way to engineering, he was surprised to find the big cruiser felt cramped and small. Losing the forward third of the ship had brought home just how little of it was usable crew space.

He intended to head back to the wardroom, where Valk was flying the ship. He'd taken Paniet's words to heart and planned on relieving Valk for a while at the helm. As he passed through the rings of bunks, though, he came across the hatch to Ginger's quarters and he stopped and sighed as he thought about what to do.

He didn't blame the girl for getting nervy, really. As much as he needed her, as much as he needed every pilot he could get, he knew it wasn't an easy job. He'd seen far too many good men and women succumb to the pressure. Hellfire, there had been times early in his career when he couldn't eat, couldn't sleep knowing that the very next time he went out in his old FA.2 fighter might be the last time. How many patrols had he flown where he was the only one who came back? How many after-action reports had he filed while desperately trying to hold his breakfast down?

Under different circumstances, he would have simply moved Ginger off combat duty. Put her in charge of some other job onboard the ship. They just didn't have a big enough crew for that, though. When Centrocor came back for a second go at them—and he was sure they would—he was going to have to make her fly a cataphract again. Force her to fight.

He hovered in the corridor, one hand against the wall to keep himself from floating away. He considered knocking on Ginger's hatch. He'd never been very good at coming up with encouraging words, but he could try.

This would be so much easier if Zhang were there, he thought. She'd always handled this sort of thing for him. She'd been his second in command for years, back during the Crisis, and always she'd been the one to take the scared pilots aside, to speak in low tones with them in the wardroom.

Damnation, he missed her. He had never known how much he relied on Zhang until she was gone. And then, at Niraya, he'd had her back, for just a little while. They'd had trouble reconnecting but once they did . . .

He hadn't let anybody else get close to him since then. It was just too dangerous.

Was that what she'd been trying to tell him? She'd said he was far away from where he needed to be. Did she mean he was drifting away from his crew, losing touch with the people around him?

Bosh, he thought. Zhang was dead. She couldn't advise him from beyond the grave. It was just his subconscious talking to him.

Then again—if his subconscious was trying to tell him something, maybe he should listen.

He made a fist. Reached out to knock on Ginger's hatch.

But...no. That wasn't a job for a commanding officer. And knowing himself, he'd probably just make things worse. No, it was up to Candless to handle her. After all, the XO had said as much in no uncertain terms.

He sighed and moved on. Though he didn't get very far before he stopped again.

Voices echoed from the wardroom up ahead. He heard Ehta's big laugh. He smiled, thinking he would go in there and ask what the joke was—but then he heard Valk's voice, too.

"Ahem," Lanoe said, pushing into the wardroom.

The two of them were strapped down around a narrow table. Ehta had a tube of green food paste in her mouth, clamped between her teeth. When she saw him she reached up very slowly and removed it.

"Sir," she said.

"As you were, Lieutenant," he said. Then he looked over at Valk, who was leaning back against the wall. If there had been any gravity, Lanoe imagined the big pilot might have had his boots up on the table.

"Ahem," he said again.

"What?" Valk asked. "What did I do?"

"Aren't you supposed to be flying this crate?" Lanoe asked.

"Uh. Yeah." Valk lacked the ability to duck his head, or blush in shame. His opaque black helmet inclined forward a little. "I mean—I am."

Lanoe pinched the bridge of his nose between his thumb and

his index finger. He hadn't slept in quite a while, and caff tablets couldn't keep you going forever. "I'd prefer it if you were actually, you know, at the controls." Paniet had set up a pilot's seat in the wardroom, a workstation to allow them to run the ship's various functions. Currently, the seat was vacant.

"It's really no problem, I mean, I can monitor the ship from over here, and it's doing just fine—"

Lanoe shook his head.

"Okay," Valk said.

"Anyway," Lanoe said, "there was something I wanted to ask you about." He looked over at Ehta. "Lieutenant," he said to her, "how are your marines shaping up? Are they improving in their gun drills?"

Her face went white for a second, but she recovered quickly. "They're, you know. Getting there. I'll, uh, I can send you a full report if you think that's—"

"Good," he said.

She nodded. Then she unstrapped herself and kicked her way out of the wardroom, back toward the guns. She must have understood that he wanted to speak with Valk privately.

He couldn't help noticing the look she gave Valk as she passed him. Eyebrows raised, mouth held tight. He had no idea what that meant.

So much easier when he had Zhang to take care of people for him.

"All right, never mind any of that," Lanoe said. "If you're going to act like a computer, maybe we can actually use that. I asked Paniet to take a look at the message, the one that brought us out here. I thought maybe he could make some sense of it—not the actual content, but the metadata, the way it was sent, even little things like the color palette in the images, the typeface they picked…anything that might give us a sense of who sent it. As we get closer, I'd really like to have a notion of who I'm dealing with, and I thought—"

"Done," Valk said.

Lanoe squinted at him. "Sorry?"

"You wanted a meta-analysis of the message. I did that."

"Just now?" Lanoe shook his head. He knew he had to get used to this, to Valk being able to interface with the ship's computers much faster and more efficiently than any human being could. "Never mind. Did you find anything?"

"Maybe. It's actually kind of weird," Valk said. "Just how plain this thing is. I don't know...It's like whoever created the video wanted to strip out any kind of personality. The video standard they used is very old, very basic, but still in use—any display could read the message, no problem. And there's no encryption on it at all. No compression, either. I can't remember the last file I saw that wasn't compressed just a little." Valk lifted his hands in surrender. "You asked about the typeface—it's one of the basic system fonts that's built into the universal operating system. Anybody who has a computer built in the last hundred years has access to that font. Which means that nobody ever uses it—it's just too clichéd. Like I said. Kind of weird."

"Maybe they used such generic stuff to hide their identity," Lanoe suggested. "Like a criminal using a pay-as-you-go minder to avoid leaving a data trail."

"Maybe," Valk said. "Maybe. Whoever they are, they like their privacy. There's no address header on the message," Valk said. "And that's very weird. It was sent to one specific ship, right? But there's nothing included with the message telling you what to do if it can't be delivered. That's pretty basic stuff. I don't know, Lanoe. It doesn't make much sense to me."

Lanoe nodded. "I didn't expect to find much. Whoever sent that message has done a pretty good job of keeping themselves hidden. Maybe they've got as much reason to fear the polys as we do. Maybe—"

He stopped because a green pearl had appeared in the corner of his vision. Metadata scrolled across the surface of the green sphere, telling him Candless wanted to speak with him.

"Hold on," he told Valk. He swiped his eyes across the green pearl and his wrist display lit up, showing Candless's face.

"I'm more than happy to take over the piloting duties," she told him. He'd forgotten that he'd told Valk to call her in as his relief. Valk must have done so while they were talking about the mysterious message. "Frankly, I'd feel more comfortable with a human at the controls."

Lanoe winced. "M. Valk is right here with me," he said. "Listening."

"Good. I detest people who will talk behind someone's back but keep mum when they're face-to-face. I imagine M. Valk has no illusions as to how I feel about artificial intelligences."

"No, ma'am," Valk said.

"I assume he also knows that it isn't personal. At any rate, Lanoe, if you're done trying to make this awkward, I hadn't finished what I was going to say. If I may?"

Lanoe sighed. "Yeah, go ahead."

"I was going to tell you that while I am perfectly happy to take over the controls for a shift, I will require a decision from you. I don't know how recently you've examined the map that we're following. Now that we're past Avernus, however, and approaching our destination—things are about to get complicated."

Lanoe pulled up the map to take a look at what she meant.

"Life can never be simple, can it?" Bullam asked.

One of her drones was displaying the map she'd gotten from Harbin. The map of wormspace that everyone seemed to find so compelling. It was supposed to be much more complete than any map Centrocor possessed.

It reminded Bullam of a dried portion of ramen, before it was boiled. The noodles twisted up and crisscrossing each other, getting lost in their own convolutions.

"Our navigator asked me this morning where we were going next. I found I couldn't give her a good answer," Bullam said. She waved at the map and it expanded, only growing more complicated the deeper you went.

Shulkin observed it with his usual lack of interest.

"So far, Lanoe's route has been straightforward. We knew he was headed for the junction that leads to here, to Avernus. We knew he intended to go farther, outside the known wormhole routes. Where he's actually headed is a mystery. He didn't bother telling Harbin before he dumped her on Tuonela."

She pointed at a wormhole and the colors of the map shifted, a line of yellow worming its way through the display to show Lanoe's route so far, from Earth to Tuonela and then bypassing Avernus. "Up ahead there are three stable routes he might choose from." A dashed yellow line split off to show a wormhole forking and then splitting again. "None of them are particularly appealing." In point of fact, all three of the routes ahead were marked with red cross-hatching. Navigational glyphs indicating they were extraordinarily hazardous.

"Lanoe's course takes him this way," Bullam said. "No matter how dangerous those wormholes may be, he'll need to take one of them. So we do as well. If we're going to chase him down again, we need to pick one of these—and we need to pick the right one. Otherwise we may never find him."

Shulkin's eyes moved a little in their sockets. He seemed to be paying attention at least.

"We have almost nothing to go on. Nobody's seen a map like this before, so we don't know where—if anywhere—these three routes go. There's no good way to track a ship in wormspace, so we can't pick up his trail. I'm open to suggestions, but right now it looks like we're just going to have to count on our luck."

Shulkin's mouth twitched, as if the effort of studying the map caused him physical pain.

"I don't know if you've noticed, but most of our luck has been bad." She tapped her foot on the deck. Cleared her throat. Refrained from snapping her fingers in Shulkin's face, as much as she wanted to.

"Do you have an opinion at all?" she asked him. "You're supposed to be the expert here. Old as you are, you must have seen plenty of wormholes before, and—"

"Huh," Shulkin said. He reached over and expanded the map further, until the three possibilities filled most of the view. Then he sat back again.

"Huh," he said, once more. He coughed, sounding like he was bringing up a great quantity of phlegm. "That one," he said, eventually. He pointed at one of the three.

"That one," Bullam said. "You—you can tell just by looking at it?" Maybe he'd actually been here before. Maybe the Navy had secret maps, and—

"No. Just picked it at random. Like you said," Shulkin told her. "There's no way to track a ship in wormspace. So you just pick one and go with it."

Bullam gritted her teeth. "Thank you," she said. "You've been spectacularly unhelpful." She waved at her drone and the display blanked out. A blue light glowed on its top, however—meaning that her big surprise was almost ready. "Fortunately for us both, here comes some good news." She stood up on the deck and shielded her eyes with one hand as she scanned the horizon. "Our reinforcements are dropping by for inspection."

"Hmm?" Shulkin said, not looking up. He had pulled a packet of nuts from a pocket in his suit and he crunched one between his teeth.

"There," she said, and pointed. A line of black dots had just crested the horizon and was growing steadily larger. She counted them aloud. "...four, five, six new fighters, each with a certified Centrocor-loyal pilot. More than enough to replace the ones we lost."

Shulkin threw a peanut shell over the side. He rolled a nut back and forth in his mouth as he squinted into the glare off the water. Held the nut between his teeth. "Seven. Eight," he said. "I count eight fighters." He closed his teeth and the nut shattered in his mouth.

"Six fighters," Bullam said again, nodding happily. She gave the incoming ships a cheery wave. "Look. Notice that the last two have a different silhouette? M. Cygnet thought we could use a little extra help."

Out over the waves the dots had grown in size as they approached.

The last two were now visibly different from the others. Different, and bigger.

"A space battle is a game of chess," she said. "A very odd man told me that once. The pieces matter."

"Hellfire," Shulkin said, rising to his feet as the last two ships came to hover right over them, their shadows blocking out the sun. He bit into another peanut shell and spat pieces of husk into the ocean. "Checkmate."

Chapter Twenty

She knew she would have to let him in eventually.

Ginger had ignored Bury the first six times he pinged her. The cryptab on the front of her suit buzzed and a green pearl appeared in the corner of her eye and her minder softly unrolled itself next to her in the bunk, but each time she simply looked away or just ignored the call and eventually it would just go away.

The seventh call came over the Hoplite's intercom system. There was an electronic crackle and then his voice emanated from the walls around her. "Ginj. Come on. We need to talk."

She sighed and shoved herself into one corner of the tiny bunk, thinking if she didn't respond he would just give up. She should have known better. Bury had never been any good at taking a hint.

"You've been there for me, as long as I've known you," he said. The intercom system was designed for waking up sleeping pilots when they needed to scramble for battle. It was loud enough to make her teeth vibrate. "You and I were study buddies in first year, remember? You basically carried me through our avionics lecture. Then there was that time I got drunk the night before we learned how to do barrel rolls. That…was not pretty. But you got me cleaned up. Ginger, you were my damned second at that stupid duel! I owe you. I owe you so much. Let me return the favor. Just talk to me. Maybe I can help."

When she didn't answer after thirty seconds, he tried again.
"I'm not giving up," he said. "You're going to have to talk to me
eventually.

"Ginj.

"Ginger?

"C'mon, Ginj.

"Ginj.

"Ginj.

"Ginj."

The cruiser's bunks were tiny, not a lot bigger than coffins. It
didn't take her long to find the speaker mounted next to the minia-
turized display. She tried shoving a zero-g neck pillow over it, holding
it in place with her foot while she covered her ears with her hands.

It didn't help much.

"You still in there, Ginger? You didn't sneak out while I wasn't
looking? No, the ship's manifest says you're in your bunk. Ginj?"

She wanted to scream at him. Instead she pulled up a display on
her wrist and sent him a quick message.

WILL U PLZ SHUT UP!

"See," he said, "now I know you're in there."

She scrubbed at her face with her hands. She fought down the
urge to kick the speaker until it caved in—if he'd been there, if she
could have seen his stupid shiny Hellion face right then she would
gladly have kicked that in, too.

WHERE R U? she messaged.

"I'm floating outside your bunk. Are you going to open the
hatch?"

She roared in frustration. But then she reached over and slapped
the hatch release.

He pushed his head inside. "Hey," he said. She could not stand
to see the look of pity on his face. She didn't want to kick him
anymore, though. There was part of her, a very big part of her, that
wanted exactly this. For someone she knew and trusted to come
inside and try to make her feel better. Sympathy was exactly what
she needed, and she knew it.

She also knew that everybody on the ship was probably talking about her. Calling her a coward, or worse—saying she'd lost her nerve. If she ever wanted to show her face outside her bunk again, if she ever wanted to be part of the Hoplite's crew and act like an officer and not let Lieutenant Candless down and everything else she truly, really, wanted, she knew she had to be tough now.

"I was just taking a nap," she said. "You woke me up."

"Uh-huh," Bury said.

She brought her knees up to her chin and pressed her mouth against the hard metal of her ring collar. Stared at him. "Okay," she said. "Okay?"

Bury frowned. "I'm sorry—okay what?"

"You've checked on me. I don't know if it was Lieutenant Candless or somebody else who sent you over here. But you can tell them you did your job. You checked up on me and I'm fine. Okay?"

"Ginj, look, nobody sent me, I—"

"Okay?" she asked again. "Are we done?"

His face fell. His eyes drooped, those stupid shiny eyes. He didn't exactly look like he was going to cry, no, not a Hellion like Bury. But he definitely looked like a dog that tried to lick its master's face and had gotten hit with a stick for it.

It was that look more than anything that changed her mind, that made her open up. Or at least, she would tell herself that later.

He turned around and reached for the release pad of the hatch, and she just couldn't take it. She rolled her eyes and sighed and then she said what she needed to say.

"I can't do this."

It came out much smaller than she'd intended. Softer. He heard her, though, and he turned to give her an expectant look.

"I saw his face," she told him. "The guy I—I killed. I was close enough that when I pulled the trigger I could see right into his canopy. I saw his face and...he knew. He knew he was going to die. He must have been terrified. It must have been awful."

"We're warriors, Ginj. We kill people."

She shook her head. "Back at Rishi they talked about being

aggressive. About taking the initiative—if you don't shoot first, the other guy will. I get that. Shooting at virtual ships in a display, sure, that made sense. Then in the live-fire exercises we did—well, that was just a game. This was real. I killed somebody, Bury. I killed a human being. Do you think his family even knows yet? Do you think they know he's dead? Maybe Centrocor hasn't even told them. Maybe they're still waiting for him to come home."

He had the decency to at least not lie to her and say it wasn't her fault. Or that she'd only been defending herself. Or anything like that. Instead he tried to be practical.

"Hellfire, Ginj. After two years of schooling, after all the money your parents paid to send you to Rishi—"

"Do you even know my last name?" she asked him.

He looked confused. "Yeah, of course. It's—Holmes, or—"

"Holz," she said. "My name is Tara Holz."

"I guess—I mean, the first week I knew you, everybody was already calling you Ginger, and I just never... You never used that name, and—"

"I made sure everyone called me by my nickname," she told him. "I insisted on it. You don't recognize the name Holz? You've never heard of Sergeant Holz?"

His eyes went wide. Apparently he did know it.

Sergeant Efram Holz had been a hero of the Establishment Crisis. A marine, of all things—very few of them ever got their names in the videos. Holz had died in battle, a casualty of the fighting on Adlivun. He'd gone down after being shot a dozen times and having one of his arms blown off by a grenade. Not before he single-handedly rushed a bunker full of Establishmentarians and slaughtered more than a hundred enemy marines with just a particle rifle and a combat knife.

The propaganda officers of the PBM had a field day with that story.

"He was my grandfather. My mother was the IO on a battleship, back when they still built battleships."

"That's some family you've got," Bury said.

Ginger couldn't look at him. "There was never any real question I was going to be Navy," she said. "Before I was born, that was already decided. When I took the entrance exam for Rishi, though—I failed it. I didn't make the cut."

"But—"

She groaned in frustration. "I was so ashamed. I wanted to die, when I saw my results. But then a very nice lieutenant took me aside and said he would see what he could do. Next thing I knew I was headed to Rishi, for flight instruction. I wasn't supposed to be there. I only got in because of my grandfather. I thought maybe it was just fate, you know? Fate pushing me to become a fighter pilot. But Lieutenant Candless saw the truth. She knew I would never make it. Just a couple of weeks ago, back on Rishi, she sat me down and explained that I was going to wash out of the program. I'd let my family down again. Do you understand how that feels? I begged her to let me stay. To let me be part of the Navy. If she just sent me home . . . I don't know if I could have looked my mother in the eye, ever again. Lieutenant Candless took pity on me. She said she would get me into training to be a staff officer. Some job where I didn't have to fight. I could see how disappointed she was, but still—she was kind about it."

"A staff officer," Bury said. She could tell he was trying to restrain his natural impulse to laugh at the idea.

"Then, all this happened." She gestured at the cruiser around them. "When Commander Lanoe insisted that I fly in his squadron . . . Bury, that's not who I am. It's not what I'm supposed to do with my life. I can't pilot a fighter, not anymore." She buried her face in her knees. "I won't go out again."

"Okay," Bury said. "Okay. Not everybody is meant to fly a cataphract." She peeked at him and saw him nodding, his face set and determined. He was trying so hard. "Okay. So—so you'll be a staff officer, instead. That's still a respectable thing, I mean, there's honor in serving all different kinds of ways—"

"Maybe staff duty is an option. But not now. You know Centrocor is going to attack us again, and when they do, Commander

Lanoe is going to demand that I go out there in one of those BR.9s, and shoot back." Her head felt like it was buzzing. Like it was full of bees. "He's not going to take no for an answer. But I don't know what else to tell him. Bury—I—I don't know what I'll do. I mean, I can fly out there, I can fly just fine, but when the shooting starts..." She shook her head. "I won't pull the trigger."

"So you'll fly the cruiser; somebody has to stay behind and—"

"I've had a couple of lessons with Lieutenant Candless leaning over my shoulder. You've tried it; you know we're not ready for that!"

Bury started to say something else. She knew it wouldn't be what she needed to hear. He couldn't tell her that it was okay, that she was excused from the fighting.

"Well, then maybe—"

"Stop trying to solve me like an equation!" she said.

"I'm just trying to help," he said, and his face fell again.

"Just shut up. Shut up."

He nodded and started moving toward the hatch again.

"I didn't say leave," she told him.

⚡

"Here," Ehta said. "Take a slug of this. It's almost nontoxic." She held out the bottle and waggled it, its bluish contents not so much sloshing as turning into fat droplets that bounced around inside the glass.

"I'd be wasting it," Valk told her. In the tight space his knees were up against his shoulders, and his feet were all but in her lap. "I can't actually, you know. Drink it."

"I'm not drinking alone," she told him.

There wasn't much privacy on the cruiser, especially now that its front third had been shot off. The marines' wardroom had been taken over as the ship's new bridge. The engineering section was off-limits and anyone trying to break into the vehicle bay would set off an alarm.

So when she needed to get away—from the stink-faced looks

of the XO, from the way Lanoe always looked at her like she was a child who'd disappointed him, from the constant unanswerable questions of her own people, from the buzzing in her own head— she had to get creative. There was an old saying that a marine could make her home in a bomb crater, and before it was time to move out she would have put up curtains. She discovered early on in the voyage that there were no alarms on the ammunition magazines in the gunnery decks. Why would there be? Human beings were never supposed to worm their way into the unheated, unventilated spaces, and anyway they were normally filled with the big 75-centimeter projectiles. One of those had been fired now, leaving just enough space for two people to curl up if they were friendly enough. Hellfire, the empty chamber was slightly bigger than one of the cruiser's bunks.

Valk took the bottle and stared at it for a minute. Then a tiny opening appeared in the front of his opaque helmet, just wide enough to plug the bottle's mouth into. He sucked in a small amount of the liquor and handed it back.

He even had the decency to fake coughing and sputtering, as if he hadn't been ready for the burn when the liquor hit his hypothetical throat. "Smooth," he said.

She smiled and took a swig of it herself. It tasted like engine coolant, which, well, wasn't too surprising. Then she closed her eyes and let the warmth of the alcohol flow through her.

Valk and Ehta had shared a moment of intimacy, just once, back on Niraya, back when everybody—including Valk himself— thought he was a human being. At the time they'd both thought they were about to die, so there had been no reason not to share a little comfort. It could have made things very awkward when they survived long enough to see each other again. When she'd first seen him onboard the Hoplite, they'd both vowed never to speak of what happened that night.

Strangely enough, they both stuck to that plan. And because of that shared secret, now they could talk about pretty much anything else.

"Ship of the damned, huh?" she said, her eyes still closed.

"What?"

"It's a ship of the damned. Even if Centrocor doesn't kill us all, half the people on this tub never want to go home, not if they don't have to. I was thinking about it the other day. My marines'll be okay, but every officer on this ship…I only came along because otherwise they were going to cashier me, did you know that? Send me home on a medical discharge."

"I seem to remember people used to shoot themselves in the foot to get one of those," Valk said.

"Yeah, but I'm not one of 'em. I've got nothing beyond the Marines, you know? What am I going to do, go work in a factory, for one of the polys? No thanks. When Lanoe asked me to come along on another of his crazy adventures, I figured, hellfire, I could at least delay the inevitable. But I can't put it off forever."

"You'll land on your feet," he said. "I have faith in you."

She hadn't been fishing for comforting words. She rolled her eyes and took another drink. "Then there's you. This is your last voyage, buddy, one way or another." She pointed the neck of the bottle at him. "You know that, right?"

"Yeah," Valk said. "If we get killed out here, it saves me the trouble of going back to civilization so I can be executed."

She nodded. "Candless and the kids—well, they know too much, don't they? Lanoe told me they were going to be locked up if he didn't bring them along. You think that the Admiralty is going to let them go free once they see…whatever it is we're out here to look at? No, they should be in no rush to go home. Damn. It just occurred to me—that probably goes for Paniet, too. And I'm the one who dragged him into this. Hellfire."

"Lanoe will think of something," Valk suggested.

Ehta snorted in derision. A bad idea since the fumes of the liquor were still swirling around in her throat. She coughed until she could see straight again. "Lanoe doesn't want to go back, either. He can't."

"How do you figure? He's gotten out of worse scrapes."

"He's been harboring a known AI. That's a straight-up capital offense, one nobody can talk their way out of." She gave him a weak smile. "Don't get me wrong. I'm glad you're still here. But he made a bad mistake not just turning you over to the powers that be."

Valk leaned forward, his helmet scraping the ceiling of the tiny space. He held out one hand for the bottle, and she gave it to him. "I wish I knew why he did that. I didn't want it." He took a quick swig. Didn't pass the bottle back. "He says it's because he still needs me. He's going to fight the aliens, no matter what. Get his justice, and I'm the only one who can talk to them. The only one who really knows anything about them. But that's bosh, isn't it?"

"Yeah?"

"The Admiralty downloaded all my files. They know everything I know. If he'd asked, I bet they would have given him a minder preloaded with software to translate Blue-Blue-White into English, given him all the maps and data from my head, you know, minus my sunny personality. He didn't need to make me suffer any longer."

"Hey," she said. "Hey. Don't be—"

"Don't *you* start getting all sympathetic with *me* now," he told her. Ehta frowned and looked away.

"No, I don't know what Lanoe wants from me."

"Maybe he's just lonely," she said.

"Huh?"

"Zhang's gone. She was the only one he could really talk to. Maybe he needs you because he needs a friend."

"He's got lots of friends," Valk said. "Candless, and you, and all the people who fought beside him over the years."

Ehta shook her head. "No, that's different. Those aren't friends. Those are squaddies." She sat up. Grabbed the bottle away from him. There were just a few drops left inside. She swished them around, just for something to do with her hands. "When you fight alongside people, you make this crazy strong bond with them. You trust them with your life. You love them, more than you're ever going to love anybody again. It's intense. And when the fighting is over, when the squad is disbanded, or you get reassigned, whatever, you vow you'll stay in touch, that you'll be there for each other no matter what, no matter when. But the years go by, and you never look them up. You don't even send them messages. Maybe life just gets in the way, new stuff piling up so you're too busy to call. That's what you tell yourself. The real reason isn't as easy to accept. Those bonds you made, those relationships, you made them at a time you never want to think about again. You see an old squaddie and everything comes back, the good times, sure, but the hell of it, too, the noise and the fire and the constant fear that you're going to die. Squaddie relationships can't survive in peacetime."

"Lanoe and I fought together at Niraya."

"A guy he knew named Tannis Valk fought with him there. You see the difference? You're just like that guy. You're just like the guy he bonded with, except...you're not him. You're just different enough now."

"You're saying he threw his life away—exposed himself to the death penalty—because he needed a friendly face around. Even though I don't actually have a face."

"Seeing as you're not human?" Ehta told him. "Maybe you don't know the big secret of people."

"Oh? What's that?"

"We're pretty much all crazy, one way or another."

———

Surrounded by her fellow officers, Ginger could almost hear their thoughts as they worked their way through another meal of food paste.

Maybe she'll just snap out of it, they were thinking. *Maybe she won't. Maybe when the call comes, she'll answer it. Maybe she'll never fight again. Maybe she snapped completely—she was in her bunk for a long time.*

Maybe she was useless now. A liability to the mission.

"Could you pass the salt spray?" Lieutenant Maggs asked. He gave her a very bright smile. Showed a lot of teeth.

She reached for the spray—then jerked her hand back as the

lights in the wardroom changed to amber and the gravity alarm sounded from the speakers overhead.

"Don't worry, little girl," Maggs told her. "We're already strapped down."

"Let her be," Commander Lanoe said.

It was true, though. There was no need to be worried. They wore restraining belts when they sat at the table in microgravity. All the food items and utensils on the table were held down with adhering pads. There was no danger.

They'd even been warned that this burn was coming. For ten long seconds Ginger was pulled upward in her chair, accelerated toward what was now, officially, the ceiling. The cruiser was burning its retros to slow them down.

Lieutenant Candless was in the control seat, her eyes locked on the display in front of her. She waved her left hand and brought up a navigational display so they could all see why she'd slowed down.

"No more time to put it off, I'm afraid," she told them. "We need to make a decision. That is to say, *you* need to make a decision, Commander."

Ginger knew what they were talking about. Up ahead the wormhole split into two tunnels, and one of those two split again almost immediately. There were three possible routes forward. According to the charts any of the three would take them to their destination. All three of them were marked with the strongest possible glyphs for hazardous conditions.

In her classes back on Rishi, Ginger had been told about the early days of wormhole exploration, about all the ships that had been lost chasing wormholes that led nowhere at all, or shrank down without warning until they were only a few centimeters wide. Then there were the unstable wormholes—which could shift and change their direction unpredictably, at best suddenly opening into a new part of space humanity had never seen before, at worst twisting themselves into knots so convoluted no human pilot could fly through them. Those were all standard navigational hazards, however. Wormholes suspected of unorthodox behavior would be marked on the chart with yellow crosshatching.

These three were all marked bright red.

There were wormholes, it was said, that opened up inside the event horizons of black holes. They looked perfectly normal until you passed through their throats—and then nobody ever heard from you again. There were wormholes that passed through the hearts of stars, so that the temperature inside the wormhole rose into the thousands, even millions of degrees—temperatures no human ship could hope to tolerate. There were supposed to be even stranger things out there, wormhole storms where the ghostlight grew so thick it tore ships to pieces, wormholes that traveled through so many strange dimensions you could come out of them before you went in—and turned inside out. Wormholes were strange things, channels cut through the very fabric of spacetime. There was a lot of science regarding them that humanity still didn't understand.

Ginger watched Lanoe peer at the chart, then lean over to take a look at the view ahead, as if he could see what hazards awaited them. She didn't envy him having to make this choice. She really, really hoped he made the right one. Even if he had to guess.

"Take us forward dead slow," he said. "If we're very, very careful maybe we have a chance even if we're wrong. We'll start with the one nearest us," he said, pointing at the route on the chart that stuck most closely to their present bearing.

"As you wish," Lieutenant Candless said. She touched a virtual control and the gravity alarm sounded again. She'd supplied so little power to the engines that it took a full second before Ginger's feet touched the floor.

It was notoriously difficult to gauge speed and distance inside a wormhole, at least visually. The view ahead didn't seem to change much at all, the ever-fluctuating tendrils of ghostlight reaching for them with spectral hands. The tunnel of the wormhole crept by, maybe, though it was hard to say. They were still thousands of kilometers away from the place where the tunnel split for the first time. They were safe, for the moment. Soon enough, though, their course was going to take them into the hazardous wormhole, where they might die without any warning.

Ginger wondered if she could hold her breath until they got there. Her body certainly wanted to try.

Coward, she thought to herself. *Have a little faith in your commander.*

"Ensign," Commander Lanoe said. "Ensign Bury." He snapped his fingers and pointed at the wardroom. "Get on the display in there. You're acting as IO right now. We'll send sensor data through to you. I want you monitoring the external temperature, Riemann metrics, magnetic flux . . . anything that looks out of the ordinary, you let us know."

Bury nodded eagerly and kicked backward, toward the wardroom.

Lanoe hadn't asked Ginger to do it. She tried not to read too much into that. Especially when he started giving orders to his other officers.

"Paniet, get back to engineering. I know you want to see this, but I need you ready to head up damage control if we run into something." Of course, if they did touch the walls of the wormhole, or anything else that might be waiting out there, there would be very little point in trying to repair the ship. It would be annihilated instantly, its mass converted to pure energy. Ginger supposed you never knew, and it was better to be safe than sorry. "Maggs," Lanoe said next, "I'll give you a job close to your heart. Go down to the vehicle bay and make sure if we need to we can launch all our small craft." As escape pods, he meant.

"And how exactly, if I may ask, is that aligned with my heart's desire?" Maggs said. He hadn't moved from his spot, his eyes riveted to the display like everyone else's.

"You've proved in the past to be very good at running away from things," Lanoe told him.

Lieutenant Maggs actually laughed at that. Lanoe had just called him a deserter, and he was laughing . . . Ginger wondered how arrogant Lieutenant Maggs had to be to find such an accusation amusing. Well, she supposed the two of them had history.

"Ensign Ginger," Lanoe said, finally, "you're our navigator. Watch the display, make sure our bearing stays true."

"Yes, sir," Ginger said. Absolute busywork. Of course. No one could doubt that Lieutenant Candless was capable of holding the cruiser to a set course. Maybe Lanoe had just taken pity on her and given her an assignment he thought she could actually do.

"Thirty seconds until we enter the first diversion," Candless said.

"Temperature's normal, no sign of any magnetic anomalies," Bury called out. "Do you want regular updates, or just—"

"Yes!" the Commander and Lieutenant Candless shouted in unison.

"Um, Riemann scalar is holding at g(3,3.02)...magnetic flux at 750 Wb...temperature unchanged at 129 K..."

Bury's voice droned on, until Ginger couldn't even hear it. Lieutenant Candless increased their speed just a little when it was clear they weren't about to be vaporized without warning. Minutes ticked by as the cruiser edged ever onward, ever closer to the place where the three wormholes split off. Ginger found herself clutching to a nylon strap on the corridor wall, even though she wasn't floating at the time. She forced herself to let go. Flexed her stiff fingers until the blood started moving through her hand again.

Up ahead, the wormhole split in two. Lieutenant Candless adjusted their course, just a little, to take them toward the first divergence. She glanced up as if she hoped someone would tell her to stop. No one did.

"Okay," Commander Lanoe said, just as they were about to enter the divergence. "We're doing well, I think we're safe, let's—"

A flash of light dazzled Ginger. She blinked and looked around and saw everyone else recovering, too.

"What the hell was that?" Commander Lanoe demanded. "Bury—what do you see on your sensor boards? Quick!"

"Uh—there's nothing, no...well, there was a spike in the long end of the spectrum, but I think...I think that was just stray emission, I think it was a flare, like the ghostlight just flared up for some reason, and—"

M. Valk's voice bellowed over the loudspeakers. "Lanoe—full stop! Full stop! That wasn't a flare. It was a message!"

~~~~

Ehta was standing closest to Valk. She had to duck as he waved his arms, trying to get everyone's attention. Then, as Candless brought them to an abrupt stop, she had to grab the walls as for a moment gravity switched directions. Eventually all gravity went away as the ship came to a dead stop, right on the edge of the first wormhole.

"What kind of message?" Lanoe demanded.

"A radio broadcast," Valk explained. He brought up a display to show a waveform analysis.

Ehta frowned. "Radio waves don't work in a wormhole," she said. She remembered that much from her pilot's training, years ago.

"Right. Normally," Valk said. "You send a signal, but the photons get annihilated when they touch the wormhole walls. This is different. These photons came *from* the walls. It's crazy—I mean, it shouldn't work, but somehow...somehow the wormhole itself generated the message."

"Never mind how, for now," Lanoe insisted. "What did the wormhole say?"

"It's audio only," Valk said. "Here. Let me play it for you."

The wardroom's speakers crackled and spat. It sounded like the kind of interference you got on a transmission sent from too close to the magnetosphere of a star. Then a voice cut in, buried in the static. The voice sounded exactly like one of the synthesized voices that drones used. The pronunciation was a little too perfect, a little too cadenced:

{We're so glad you've come.}
{Take the third path.}
{Please be careful.}

"The third path," Lanoe repeated.

"Not the first one, as we'd planned," Candless said. Ehta thought she looked scared. Maybe too scared to be snarky, for once. "Shall I adjust our course?"

"Sure," Lanoe said. "But let's not get too excited. That wormhole's marked as hazardous, too. Take us ahead slow. Ensign Bury, you keep calling out those updates." He turned and looked at Valk. "And you, big guy. You hear any more secret messages from another dimension, or whatever. Just go ahead and play them for us—don't keep them to yourself."

Chapter Twenty-One

There were no more messages encoded into the ghostlight.

Candless took the cruiser past the first two branches, then gently, ever so carefully, into the third. At first all appeared normal. The other two branches had looked normal, as they passed them by. Candless wondered idly what would have happened had they ventured down the wrong path—what terrible hazards awaited in those dim tunnels. She hoped she would never have to find out.

The third tunnel ran straight and smooth and wide. Lanoe kept urging her to go faster—clearly he was in a hurry to get to their destination, just the other side of this stretch. "Very good, sir," she told him. "And how many pieces would you like to be in when we arrive?"

"Point taken," he told her. "Just keep in mind that Centrocor hasn't given up on us. The longer we hang around here, the more likely they are to catch us."

Candless had not forgotten that they were being pursued.

"How long are we looking at till we get there?" Lieutenant Ehta asked. "At this rate of speed, I mean."

"About seven days," Candless told her.

She could feel Lanoe's jaw clench, even from across the room.

One by one the onlookers drifted away, the other officers realizing that the view of the wormhole ahead was going to look exactly like every other wormhole they'd ever seen. Soon only Candless and Lanoe were left in the emergency bridge station, listening to the constant announcements from Bury in the wardroom.

Lanoe waited another hour before telling the young man he could stop with his relentlessly meaningless updates. "In fact, I think I'll take it from here. I can monitor all those things on my wrist minder," the Commander said.

"Yeah," Bury told him. "Yeah, okay. I think I might have pulled a muscle in my throat with all that yelling anyway."

"Go take a nap," Lanoe told him.

Bury shrugged and headed off toward his bunk. Leaving only the two of them in the wardroom.

"Perhaps this would be a good time for us to speak," Candless said. "Now that we don't have an audience."

"Sure," Lanoe said. He leaned back in his seat and sighed. "This going to be about Ginger? Or maybe you want to tell me why you and Ehta aren't getting along."

"Two excellent subjects, both of which I think we would find tedious," Candless told him. "No. I had intended to ask what you expect to find on the other side of this wormhole."

"I already gave a briefing on that," Lanoe told her. She wished very much that she could look at him, see his face. She didn't dare look away from her displays, however.

"I thought perhaps you might have held something back," she said. "As XO, I have a responsibility for the crew of this ship. I have a right, therefore, to know if that crew is to be exposed to any danger. I assure you that I can keep your secrets, if you're willing to share them, in fact—"

He cut her off. A bit rudely. "Candless," he said, "I told you everything I know. Mysterious message offering help with fighting the Blue-Blue-White. No idea who sent it, no idea whether this is a trap...I'm flying as blind as you are."

She found that a little hard to believe. Perhaps, though, his paranoia was simply rubbing off on her. "Whoever they are, they've gone to great lengths to maintain their privacy. Hiding out here, well outside of human space—behind not one but three deadly wormholes. They've kept any possible identifying marks out of their communications and offered not even a hint as to their identity. And yet the Admiralty, in its exalted wisdom, saw fit to send you all this way just to say hello."

"Whoever they are, they know the Blue-Blue-White are a serious threat. Maybe the biggest one humanity's faced since, I don't know, global warming. The admirals are willing to take a chance on this."

"The Navy is willing to sacrifice an entire Hoplite-class cruiser, on a lark?" Candless asked. "Tell me something, Lanoe. If you can't give me facts, give me an opinion. I will take a guess, if that's the best you have on offer."

Lanoe inhaled deeply. Sighed the air back out. "You ever hear of the Remnant Electors? Or maybe Mad Admiral Ukiyo?"

"I *did* serve in the Crisis," Candless told him. Fighting back the urge to sniff in indignation.

The end of the Establishment Crisis had been a chaotic time. The Establishmentarians had fought to the bitter end, refusing to surrender their command bunkers long after their space forces had been obliterated. The ground war, though a foregone conclusion, had been nothing short of obscene. Whole cities were leveled, civilian populations displaced when they weren't simply massacred. The polys had wanted to make an example of the Establishment. To make sure no one ever tried to defy their authority again.

Many of the Establishment's rank and file—people like Tannis Valk—had been captured during the fighting or at least survived the final battles. Their top brass hadn't been so fortunate. Every single member of the Circle of Electors, the Establishment's ruling body, had been executed, often without trial. Their top-level military commanders were simply all killed in action. At least, that was what history said.

Official history anyway. There had always been rumors. Legends really. That a small group of the Circle of Electors had been sent into deep space in cryonic sleep, to wait for a day when the blue flag should fly again. The story held they were still out there, frozen between the stars, waiting for the moment to step back onto the stage of events.

Another story held that Admiral Ukiyo, most fervent and severe of the Establishment's military commanders, had never actually been defeated and that he had simply refused to surrender. That he and his fleet had vanished without a trace into the dark of the void. One version of the tale held that he had found some mystical wormhole that led to the Greater Magellanic Cloud and was out there still, founding free planets and fighting off the special forces units the polys persisted in sending after him.

All bosh, of course. Every bit of it.

Candless had been there, at the end. She'd seen the piles of bodies. Watched as poly officials compared their DNA to known records. None of the high-level Establishmentarians had survived.

"You are suggesting, then," she said to Lanoe, "that we are out here chasing down a fairy tale. Very good, sir, I'll have a unicorn horn pinned to the nose of the ship and we'll all close our eyes and *believe* just as strongly as we can."

Lanoe laughed. "I know it sounds crazy. And I'm not suggesting we're actually going to find Mad Ukiyo out there." He gestured forward, deeper into the wormhole. "But like you said, whoever is out there *is* deeply paranoid."

"Which perhaps explains why you were chosen as our ambassador," she said. "As you would have so much in common with them."

Out of the corner of her eye she could see Lanoe shake his head. "Look, paranoia is what you would need if you were truly living off the common networks. If, say, you had set up a planet all of your own and you didn't want the polys getting their grubby fingers all over it."

Candless supposed he had a point. The law wouldn't let anyone do that, not for long. Outside of Earth's particular solar system, it was a requirement that any new planetary colony must have a poly sponsor. A Developmental Monopoly to oversee terraforming and the construction of infrastructure—and, of course, to profit from doing all that work. If someone did want to set up a free world, they would have to be very quiet about it.

"I don't think we're going to meet Remnant Establishmentarians, no. But somebody inspired by them? Somebody who figured it would be easier just to stay silent, rather than have to fight another Crisis?"

"But why would such a planet contact us now? Yes, yes," she said, before he could answer, "your jellyfish aliens are an existential threat to humanity, I've heard all that. But exposing themselves like this will surely cause problems for this hypothetical free world down the line. Why risk it?"

"I've considered that," Lanoe told her. "And I think I might have an answer. There are alien fleets headed for every human planet. All of them. Look at the chart we're using—it shows the dates and times of when those fleets will arrive, how long each planet has before it's attacked. So maybe our hypothetical free planet is on that list, too. They know they're looking down the barrel of a gun."

"They did approach the Navy directly, and quietly," Candless conceded. "That would fit your theory rather well. But it's still quite the risk—they must know as well as we do how porous the membrane of secrecy is between the Admiralty and the polys."

"Yeah," Lanoe said. "Which I think means they're desperate. I can think of one reason why. They're the ones who gave us the time line of the alien fleet invasions. They can predict exactly when those fleets arrive. I think they know they're on the list—and I think they're *next*. I think their planet is the first one to get hit, so they're reaching out to us now because they don't have a choice."

"But would they even need us?" Candless asked.

"What do you mean?"

"They've clearly developed technologies we lack. Look at what they did to the wormhole back there. They're able to modulate the very fabric of spacetime, for the devil's sake."

"Who knows? Maybe they're really good at communications, but lacking in firepower."

"And then there's the fact that they *didn't* ask us for help. They offered to help *us*. You may remember the text of the original message they sent us. It was quite short."

Lanoe had an answer for that, but not one that satisfied, much. "It's a classic diplomatic move. When you're asking for an alliance that benefits you more than the other guy, you have to convince him you don't actually need him. That you're doing him a favor."

"Very well," Candless said. "Though you still haven't answered my question. Are my people going to be in danger when we arrive at our destination?"

"Your cadets, you mean."

Candless bristled. She did not like her motives being interrogated. "I mean everyone for whom I am directly responsible. That happens to include the *ensigns,* yes."

"Sure," Lanoe said.

"So are they in danger?"

Lanoe was quiet for a long time. Too long.

"I'm going to assume that's a yes," she said.

He didn't contradict her.

"My turn," Valk said.

He hadn't thought about how Candless might take that. She'd been flying for hours, creeping along through the theoretically hazardous wormhole, and when he just took over she inhaled sharply through flared nostrils. He could sense her heart beating fast and he knew he'd just given her a bad scare.

"Hey, sorry," he said, moving over to float near her. "Didn't mean to startle you. Just figured you'd be ready to switch out."

"Quite," she said, and gave him a nasty look. Well, nastier than usual anyway.

"Go get some rest," he told her. "I've got this under control."

She did not, however, climb out of the pilot's seat. It was clear she was in no hurry to leave.

"You want to take another shift?" he asked her.

She took a long, deep breath. Then she got up and gestured to the seat.

He knew she didn't trust him. That she probably never would. Well, there wasn't much he could do about that.

He climbed into the pilot's seat, mostly just to make her feel more comfortable. He could have flown the ship from his bunk if he wanted. He knew people preferred to see the pilot of the ship actually engage physically with the controls, though. "Anything to report from your watch?" he asked.

"Precious little. I've kept our speed at about one-quarter standard cruising, but the wormhole has refused steadfastly to do anything hazardous. Smooth sailing, without even a dangerous curve to—"

"What's this?" Valk asked. He pointed at the display in front of him, which showed a column of numbers.

"I'm sorry?" Candless asked.

Maybe the numbers didn't mean anything to her. Maybe she couldn't read them like he could. "This is an array of ambient illumination reports," he said. It was one of thousands of datasets he'd just run through, not even close to the top of his list of priorities. It had jumped out at him, though, as soon as he saw it. "The ship recorded a decline in the number of received lumens over the last couple of hours."

"You're saying it's getting dark out there," Candless said. She pulled up a display of her own and worked out a visual graph. There was a definite downward curve, sharpening almost parabolically over time.

"The ghostlight," Valk said. He brought the forward view display to the top of his pile of displays. Expanded the window until it filled the entire corridor.

The tunnel ahead was darker than he would have expected. The change wasn't dramatic, but Valk could definitely see it. The light streaming at them from the wormhole's walls was fitful and dim, much less energetic than it should be.

"The lights are going out," he said.

———————

By the time Lanoe and Paniet reached the wardroom, Candless could see the change for herself. It scared her enormously.

"There," she said. "And there. And there." She pointed at the forward view, at small patches along the wall of the wormhole that had gone dark. Pitch black. Absolutely devoid of ghostlight. They looked like sunspots, perhaps. Or dead pixels on an old flat display.

"That's...odd," Lanoe said. He leaned forward, as if he could get a better view by getting closer to the holographic image. Candless was old, too, and she knew that came from growing up in a time when displays all tended to be two-dimensional and low resolution.

"Oh, it's so much more delightful than 'odd,'" Paniet said. "It's physically impossible!" The engineer's eyes glowed with excitement. "Ghostlight is a natural by-product of the exotic matter that keeps a wormhole stable. Can you look ahead a bit, please, to see if the effect continues?"

Candless adjusted the controls on the display. The view zoomed forward, down the wormhole, out to about a million kilometers from their position. As the camera appeared to travel down the tunnel, it became clear the effect didn't just continue—it got worse. The dark spots on the tunnel walls became more common. Some of them grew until they touched one another, until entire sections of the wormhole were dark. When the camera reached the farthest limit of its magnification, only half the tunnel was shrouded in ghostlight. The rest was a solid, light-eating black.

"I think we've found why this wormhole was marked as extremely hazardous," Lanoe said. "Paniet. Can we even fly in a wormhole if there's no ghostlight?"

Paniet tilted his head back and forth, from side to side, like a needle on a scale trying to find its level. The ring of circuitry around his eye glittered in the wardroom's lights. "Every teensiest scrap of light and heat inside a wormhole comes from the ghost-light. I guess—and really, don't quote me on this—but if you were to travel far enough down an unlighted wormhole, eventually the local temperature would drop to absolute zero. And that would be…you know."

"What?"

"Bad," Paniet said. "Very bad. You would freeze solid, sure, but worse than that, even your individual molecules would stop moving. Which is typically fatal. But, then, it's not as simple as that, because you'd be in a vacuum, with nothing to conduct away your heat…Honestly, it's not something you find in nature, so I can't say for certain that—"

"Enough," Lanoe said. "Valk, will you be able to fly if there's no light out there?"

"Hard to know where the walls are without the ghostlight," Valk said. "And I'm assuming that we still wouldn't want to touch the walls."

"I wouldn't," Paniet said, nodding enthusiastically.

"I really don't think we should try this," Valk said. "It's just a lot of unknowns, and—"

Lanoe nodded. "I don't intend to reverse course," he said.

Candless started to protest, but she knew better. Lanoe wasn't the type to retreat, even if he had no idea what he was getting into. She knew how important this mission was to him, as well—he was unlikely to abort until it was absolutely necessary. "All right," she said. "We won't turn around. For the moment, at least, however, I'm cutting us down to half speed."

Lanoe scowled, but then he nodded in agreement. "Until we have a better idea what's happening, sure. But we keep moving forward. Whoever sent the message that brought us this far—they think we can get through a dark wormhole," Lanoe said. "They wouldn't have sent us this way otherwise."

"Unless this whole mission was a ruse," Candless pointed out. "A trap."

Lanoe shook his head. "I don't believe that. There are easier ways to kill people. No, there's a way forward. We just have to figure out how. Maybe," he said, "this is just a temporary thing."

⟶✦⟵

Two million kilometers on, and there was no possibility that the darkness was just temporary. The ghostlight was gone altogether. Not even a wisp of smoky radiance, not so much as a tendril of foggy light.

Only inky, stygian darkness. Carbon nanotubules in a coal mine reflected more light than the walls of the wormhole.

Everyone onboard was accustomed to the blackness of space, but that was a dark punctuated by the distant, hot stars, the wispy glories of the nebulae. This was...nothingness. Shapeless, directionless, infinite.

Unable to see where they were going, Candless had brought them to a dead stop. If the wormhole curved ahead, even by a fraction of a degree, they could have flown right into its wall without any warning.

"I can't even begin to imagine how our hermits did this," Paniet said. The circuitry around his eye pulsed with activity, but Valk could tell it wasn't picking up anything useful. The data that flowed from those cutaneous sensors came back all zeroes, confirming over and over again that the engineer was staring into an abyss.

The two of them floated near an airlock near the vehicle bay, tethered closely to the ship. Even with the safety line, Paniet kept grabbing at stanchions and spars, any part of the ship he could hold on to.

Valk understood the impulse, though he no longer shared it. Human beings evolved under gravity. The vertigo they felt when standing on a high place looking down could be overpowering. The void all around them, the perfect absence of anything that could be seen, had to be terrifying. Paniet must be imagining that if he were to let go of the ship now, he would fall forever.

For Valk himself—fear of heights was one more thing he seemed to have left behind. He'd spent so much time now in dimensionless virtual space, inside computers. There were no heights there, no widths or breadths, either. Certainly no light. To him the darkness that surrounded them on every side felt like home.

"You don't think this is natural?" Valk asked. "Just a different kind of wormhole we've never seen before?"

"Oh, hellfire, no." Paniet shook his head. "This was done on purpose. I suppose if you have the ability to modulate ghostlight to send a radio signal, you might know how to switch it off as well. Whoever these fellows are that we're going to meet, they have technologies the Navy hasn't dreamt of. Goodness. Tell me something, M. Valk. You've worked with Commander Lanoe before. When he goes out adventuring, does he always run into things this bizarre?"

Valk wished he had a mouth so he could grin. "So far? Yeah."

"I'm so glad Ehta brought me here. This is exactly why I signed up for the Neddies, to travel and see things like this. Well," Paniet said, leaning close as if he were confessing an intimacy, "that and to get away from home. I grew up on Adlivun and the people there weren't terribly sympathetic."

Valk thought he understood. The planet Adlivun was famous for being socially conservative. In the century and a half that it had been settled, it had never even had a woman as its Planetary Governor. Someone like Paniet would have had a hard childhood there.

"So now that we're out here," he asked, "do you see any way to cope with this?"

Paniet shrugged. "I already had some ideas before I asked to go out on this spacewalk. I just wanted to see this with my own eyes. Tell me, you're linked into the ship's systems. Can you activate a communications laser? Point it at the wall, see what happens."

Valk only had to think about it and it was done. The laser speared out into the dark, visible only where it passed through debris and waste gas from the cruiser. When it touched the wall of the wormhole, it painted a single, fizzing green dot. Even after he switched the laser off, the dot persisted, though only for a moment.

"Aha, there, you see?" Paniet said. "No ghostlight, but otherwise the wormhole acts like you'd expect. It'll still annihilate anything that touches the walls. Including collimated photons, thank the devil."

"The wormhole's still out there, you mean," Valk said. Before the darkness had seemed like an infinite void. Suddenly the walls of the wormhole seemed very close.

"Yes, yes, of course. And we can still go forward. We just have to be *extraordinarily* careful about it. We just need a way to make sure we know when and where to adjust our course. Let's have that laser again, but sweep it around in a circular scanning path."

The beam of light reached for the wall and then arced along its circumference, making a perfect circle as it spun around, catching the cruiser's exhaust gas in a fan of spectral green light. Just ahead of the ship, along the invisible walls of the wormhole, a thin ring of sparkling light cut into the otherwise perfect darkness. Valk saw what Paniet was suggesting, and kept the laser moving in a spiral path, each sweep taking the point of impact a little farther down the length of the wormhole. The momentary persistence of the light traced a rudimentary path ahead of them. A path they could follow.

A green pearl appeared before Valk. Lanoe calling. Valk didn't bother reading the message before he replied. "Looks like we have an answer for you, boss. This darkness is going to slow us down to a crawl but we can continue."

The green pearl cut out—with no reply. Valk could feel the ship coming alive behind him, though, the engines building up heat as they readied to move once more. He reached over and grabbed Paniet's arm, just before the ship began to pull away from them. He heard the engineer gasp in terror.

"I've got you," Valk said.

"Much obliged," Paniet said. "Perhaps . . . As lovely as this is, perhaps it's time to head back inside."

⤛⤜

The cruiser plunged on ahead, into the dark.

The first day of it wasn't so bad. Nerve-racking, perhaps. Candless had to get used to following the spiral path of the comms laser, to sticking to a course she could barely see. The wormhole proved to be mostly straight, however, and the rare curve was gentle enough that it didn't take much steering to keep them perfectly centered in the tunnel. Piloting through a wormhole always required one to stay perfectly alert—the ghostlight and the monotony tended to lull the senses, and it was far too easy to grow complacent. Here she alternated between falling victim to pilot's hypnosis and sudden attacks of pure panic.

It didn't help that Lanoe had decided that the ensigns were not experienced enough to fly during this stretch of the journey. That meant that only she, Valk, and Lanoe himself were available to take shifts in the pilot's seat.

"I'd be most happy to assist," Lieutenant Maggs said, on at least one occasion for which Candless was present. "I've plenty of experience, and a sharp enough mind for it. But you won't even consider it, will you?"

"You're on a short leash," Lanoe told him. "Don't tug too hard, or you'll strain your neck."

The scoundrel didn't seem to care much for being called a dog, even by implication. He stormed out of the wardroom—a difficult maneuver in the minimal gravity, but he managed with panache. Candless did not look up from the controls, of course, but she clicked her tongue.

"What?" Lanoe demanded. "You think I'm making a mistake?"

"Rather, I'd say you're making an enemy," she told him.

"Oh, he and I already have plenty of history," Lanoe told her. "I'm not burning any bridges that he didn't knock down a long time ago."

"And when one has been wronged, and the other fellow is offering an olive branch, do we think the best course of action is to smash it out of his hand?"

"Let me worry about Maggs," Lanoe said. "You keep us from crashing into an invisible wall."

By the end of the first day she was tired, her eyes hurt, and her body felt stiff as a board. She returned to her bunk and fell asleep before she'd even switched out the lights.

The morning of the second day she got up and did it again.

Eight hours in the pilot's chair. Halfway through she found herself scratching at her own skin. She pulled off one of her gloves so she could get her regulation short-trimmed nails down inside her collar ring.

Perhaps that was the first time she noticed that it was getting cold. She gave herself a good scratch and hurriedly put the glove back on. Its heating elements soothed her fingers. Her suit could do little for how dry her sinuses felt, or how her eyes ached every time she blinked.

"I'm here to relieve you," Lanoe said suddenly. She looked up with a start—looked up away from the display and its endless spiral of hissing light. She forced herself to look back down, to stay alert.

"Already?" she asked. "Never mind, don't answer." She could see from the clock that her eight hours were up.

They'd felt...like less. She wondered—worried—how much of that time had passed without her noticing. Without so much as a thought in her head.

"Does it feel cold in here to you?" she asked.

Lanoe frowned. "Yeah," he said. "A little."

She remembered that Engineer Paniet had said that all light and heat in the wormhole came from the ghostlight. She checked the sensors and saw that the ship's external temperature had sunk to 57 Kelvin. Very cold indeed. She did shiver, then, despite her suit.

"Shouldn't the life support system be able to compensate for the cold outside?" she asked.

"It has been, but there's a limit to what it can do," Lanoe told her. "The engines suck up most of our power. What's left gets distributed through a bunch of systems. I'm afraid it's not going to warm up for a while."

The third day she woke up to see a thick coat of frost on the bulkhead above her. Condensation from her own breath had gathered there and frozen solid.

The third day it grew very, very cold.

Engineer Paniet rerouted the ship's air cyclers to blow as much warm air as possible into the middle of the ship, where the bunks and the wardroom were located. Even so, Candless could see her breath plume from her mouth every time she exhaled. By the time her shift came around the temperature inside the ship was just above freezing. She put up her helmet—they all did—and her suit kept her almost comfortable. By the end of her shift, though, her bones ached.

The ship's bones did, too. She could hear them groaning, far off. Down in the engineering section where the heat of the engines fought against the freezing cold in the bulkheads. "Differential cooling," Engineer Paniet said, his voice a whisper, as if he were afraid to disturb the cruiser in its torpor. He shook his head. "We'll be lucky if we don't succumb to metal fatigue."

"I don't understand," she said. Too cold to be arch. "I've been on plenty of ships in deep space before. They've never lost heat like this."

"Those ships were heavily insulated. Their heat was efficiently recycled. We don't have that option."

"Why the devil not?" she demanded.

Paniet sighed. "When Centrocor shot off the nose of our cruiser, they took a lot of that insulation with it. I patched the holes as best I could, but I can't make the repairs heat-tight, so to speak. We're hemorrhaging temperature right now—heat is bleeding out of the ship all the time, and there's nothing out there to replace it. I'm trying very hard to keep us from radiating off what little heat we have, but I can't rewrite the laws of thermodynamics. Check the display."

The external temperature had dropped to 7 K.

Seven degrees above absolute zero.

The internal temperature was well below freezing. "Wait," she said. "Wait—if we keep going like this—"

"We may be too far in to go back," he told her.

She shook her head. "I refuse to accept that. But if we keep going, and the temperature drops to absolute zero, then—then what will happen?"

"Oh," he said, and he smiled—tried to make it sound cheery, and failed—"we'll all be dead long before then. All of us except Valk."

The fourth day no one talked about the cold.

They kept their helmets up. Candless was ravenously hungry all day. Her body was burning off all its stored energy to keep her internal organs from freezing. She worried about frostbite taking her fingers—her gloves did their best to keep her hands warm, but they were too thin. She tried not to touch anything she didn't have to. The arms of the pilot's seat, the table in the wardroom, all were painfully cold when her fingertips even brushed them.

She took her turn at the controls, relieving Lanoe. He said nothing as he got up and moved away, hugging himself as if that would keep him warm. An hour into her shift she noticed something alarming. The groaning of the ship, the endless, dull roar of the ice had stopped. There was silence now, silence all around. She cleared her throat, just to hear a sound.

Engineer Paniet answered when she pinged his address. "The external temperature is point five K," she said. Her voice came out as a hoarse whisper. Perhaps just to help conserve as much of her energy as possible, she'd barely spoken a word in hours. "Is it time to...to worry?" she asked.

"You haven't been, this whole time?" he asked.

"I'd like a serious answer."

"I wish I could give you one," he told her. "I guess...when the temperature gets down to-to-to—sorry, I'm shivering. When it gets down to a tiny fraction of a degree, and I mean, when we're down in the nanokelvins, we'll see some very strange behavior. Chemical reactions actually speed up by a factor of a hundred at that temperature, because you see large-scale quantum effects. We'll see Einstein-Bose condensates, maybe, where you get superfluidity and superconductivity, and concerted proton tunneling, or maybe—"

"Please," she said. "I'm too cold to chastise you for being pedantic."

"Okay," he said. "Short answer. I have no idea."

"Ah."

"By the time anything weird happens, though—it'll already be too late to do anything. Just...just try not to think about it."

By the end of her shift, the external temperature had dropped to .01 K.

She watched the laser spiraling ahead of the ship, lighting their way. She couldn't not watch it. She flew the ship. She didn't know what else to do.

Lanoe did not respond when she tried to ping him.

Five days into the wormhole, five days in the cold, and Valk was the only one left who could fly the cruiser. The others, the humans, all stayed huddled together in a narrow space next to the engines. Paniet had covered every internal surface of the room in silvered thermal blankets, sealed it off with non-heat-conducting tape. Every bit of heat the cruiser could generate was pumped in there. The marines, Ehta, the pilots, the ensigns, everybody pressed together for warmth. They didn't move, those shapes curled together. Even the lights in the room had been switched off, to leave more power for the insufficient heaters.

Ahead of them the wormhole stretched on and on. Dark, lit only by the spiral path of the laser.

There were corridors in the ship that were so cold now, the air in them froze and fell like snow. Water tanks and lines throughout the ship burst, and fans of icicles speared out into the empty companionways. Several displays had cracked, their blank gray surfaces split open to reveal the clustered emitters beneath. The air was so dry the upholstery of the chairs in the wardroom shrank and tore.

Valk flew on, not moving at all. Neither breathing nor blinking.

He wasn't sure what he would do if the humans died. Logically he knew it would help his own chances. The energy that was currently being used to keep them warm could be sent instead to the engines. He could increase the cruiser's speed. Get where he was going faster. Assuming there was somewhere to go.

If the external temperature dropped to absolute zero, the wormhole itself might...end. Run out. It might stop functioning, collapse in on itself. Cease to be. He'd run models on what that would mean, statistical simulations, but none of them returned any results he could count on. The fact was that no one knew what absolute zero really looked like. It was one of those things that couldn't exist in nature, a limit that could never be reached. At least, under normal conditions.

There was nothing normal about this wormhole.

He was certain of one thing. If the temperature readout did drop to true zero, he would die along with the others. If a thing like him could be said to die.

He flew in the dark. He flew without displays.

He flew without moving. He didn't need to touch any controls. To save power, he shut down all the simulation programs that made him feel human. He had been surprised to find that he noticed when he shut down the algorithm that made him think he had a beating heart. It didn't hurt. It just felt...odd.

Lanoe had warned him that he needed to hold on to his humanity as much as he could. That the only way the others would accept him was if he sounded, behaved, acted like he was the human Tannis Valk, the Blue Devil.

That had been put by the wayside now. Now he was simply an AI. A computer program, if a very complicated one. A set of processes capable of making decisions, capable of a convincing simulation of consciousness.

Not that it took much in the way of processing power to fly. He merely followed the spiral path. Bending with it, where it curved. Holding steady where it flew straight. He did not get bored. Computers don't. He didn't get tired. Computers can't.

Perhaps, though, there was a little humanity left in him. Enough of the old human failings. Because when something changed, it took him a long time to notice it.

Candless stirred, and the people around her grumbled, annoyed by the movement. Any small adjustment of a body in the heap let some heat out, and they all felt it.

At first she wasn't sure why she'd moved. She'd been asleep, her body conserving its energy as best it could. There had been no dreams. Yet something . . . some small stimulus had broken through her lethargy. A flash of light. Probably just a hallucination, her brain so starved for visual information it started generating its own inputs.

Hellfire, she thought. *You're starting to sound like Paniet. Or Valk.*

Put it in different terms, then. She was seeing things. Except— was she?

Her suit was in low-power mode, every joule its batteries could produce being used to keep her warm. Its systems were idling, nonfunctional. Except for one system, one that kept ticking over quietly, waiting for the right moment.

A tiny green pearl rotated in the corner of her vision. She could barely make it out, could just see that it was a message from the wardroom. From Valk.

Her eyeballs felt like they were scraping against sandpaper as she flicked her gaze across the pearl, accepting the message. It was composed entirely of visual data.

The view of the wormhole ahead. The darkness, the spiral path. Was Valk just calling to warn her, to tell her they were all about to die? She wished that he . . . that he would just . . . that he hadn't—

Along the wall of the wormhole she could just make out a tendril of smoky light.

Ghostlight.

The view swept forward, moving down the wormhole faster than the cruiser could carry it. Up ahead a spectral cobweb of light crawled across the wormhole's walls. Tendrils of ghostlight stretching out, reaching translucent claws through the darkness. Toward other, more robust patches of light.

The message cut out.

Moving her head hurt. Her joints were frozen stiff and her body shrieked with pain every time she tried to move a muscle. She looked over at Lanoe, at where she thought he was, buried in the pile of bodies. It was hard to tell—their helmets were all silvered, better to trap in their body heat.

Her tongue was glued to the side of her dry, dry mouth. She felt it tear free as she tried to speak. All that came out at first was a dry cough. Eventually she managed to croak out a few words. She gathered them into a message she could send to him.

Across the pile, his helmet turned transparent and she could see his face. Pale with sleep and cold, his lips a bloodless line, the skin around his nostrils dry and cracked. She was sure she looked just as rough.

He didn't nod. She didn't blame him—she didn't want to move any more than she had to, either. But he blinked at her. Crusted eyes opening and closing.

She knew what that meant. That he'd seen Valk's message, too. That he understood.

They'd made it.

PART III

EXOTIC

Chapter Twenty-Two

It took Lanoe more than an hour to climb all the way up to the emergency control stand. The cruiser was accelerating, providing just enough gravity to make it a chore to pull himself up, hand over aching hand. He had to keep moving so his fingers didn't freeze to the metal rungs of the ladder—as much as he wanted to stop and just shiver, just curl into a ball to conserve his warmth, he stayed at it, ascending one painful meter after another.

When he reached the wardroom he slumped against a wall and closed his eyes and gave himself a long minute before he went in to see Valk.

He closed his eyes. His head reeled, his heart thundering in his chest from the exertion of getting to the wardroom. He wanted to just sit there, to rest, for days. To wait until he was strong enough to do what came next.

He half-expected Zhang to start talking to him, the way she seemed to do every time he tried to sleep. Maybe there was a point of exhaustion where even his subconscious just decided to leave him alone, though, because he couldn't hear her at all.

He opened his eyes. It took some work, but he managed it. It was going to get better, he told himself. Already the cruiser was warming up. They were going to survive.

He forced himself to stand. He staggered over to where Valk

lay slumped in the control seat, looking dead to the world. The AI didn't move as Lanoe called his name, but a green pearl appeared in the corner of Lanoe's vision.

He swiped it away without answering it. "Talk to me," he insisted. "Out loud."

"Okay," Valk said. In front of him a display flickered to life. Chunks were missing from the view where an emitter had shattered in the cold, but Lanoe could get the gist—the wormhole ahead of them looked like every other wormhole he'd ever seen in his life. Its walls shimmered with ghostlight.

"What changed?" Lanoe asked.

"No idea," Valk said. He shifted a little in his chair. He was trying to sit up, Lanoe realized. He hadn't been immune to the cold, either. "Somebody took mercy on us. That's good enough for me." With a jerk, Valk shoved himself upright in the chair. His left arm flopped off his lap and hung limp at his side.

Lanoe narrowed his eyes. "What happened there?" he asked. "Don't say frostbite."

Valk shook his torso left and right. The equivalent of a human shaking his head. "No. No, I . . . I thought about it, too much."

"What?" Lanoe asked.

"I had to shut down a lot of systems to keep going. To conserve power. That meant I had to list out my own process tree, and—"

"I have no idea what that means," Lanoe said.

Valk nodded. Rather, he bowed forward several times. It was the closest he could get to the human gesture while keeping his helmet up. "Okay. I got to thinking about my arm. And then I started thinking about how I don't really have an arm inside the sleeve of this suit. There's nothing there—just some servomotors in the sleeve I can activate to make it look like an arm."

"You already knew that," Lanoe pointed out.

"Yeah. Rationally, yeah, I did. But I never really *thought* about it, until now. And once I did, I couldn't remember anymore what it used to feel like, when I had a real arm. I couldn't pretend anymore. There's no arm there. There was never an arm. So now there's no arm . . . I managed to pull myself out of that loop before I started to think about the fact I don't have a head, either."

Lanoe frowned. "Can you fix it? The arm?"

"I can write a program that simulates having an arm."

"That's not the same. Is it?"

"I'm not a philosopher, Lanoe. Tannis Valk was just a regular guy, and I . . . I'm trying real hard to be as like him as I can be. So don't ask that question. Because then I'll have to think about the answer."

"Sure."

"But . . . no. It's not the same. Not at all."

Lanoe took a breath and stepped closer. He reached down and picked up the left hand of Valk's suit. It felt exactly like an empty glove, of course. He squeezed the glove, until the fingers buckled in his hand.

"Do you feel that?" he asked.

"I'm registering the pressure you're applying, I—"

"Can you *feel* it?" Lanoe demanded.

Valk was silent for a long time. Lanoe twisted the sleeve, bent it at the elbow. Lifted it and held it in the exact position Valk's arm ought to be in.

"A little," Valk said. "Maybe."

"Squeeze my hand," Lanoe said.

The fingers twitched. Almost imperceptibly, but they twitched.

"Good," Lanoe said. "Try again."

Bury howled as the cool proteolytic gel ran over his swollen fingertips. They burned wherever the skin came away, frostbitten tissue debriding and running pink into the basin. Because he was a Hellion, long strands of polymer came away with it. Nerve endings that had never felt open air before pulsed and throbbed in agony.

"The skin'll grow back," Engineer Paniet told him. Bury scowled and looked away, embarrassed that the neddy had seen him flinching at pain. "A couple of stem cell injections and you'll be right as rain, deary. Though it'll hurt like the devil between now and then."

"Hold still," Ginger said. She squeezed some more of the fluid across his exposed toes. This time he couldn't help but swear.

"Shouldn't there be a medic on this ship?" he demanded. "I bet there was one, before Commander Lanoe kicked everybody off."

"Don't forget he kicked off a spy who would have gotten us all killed, too," Ginger said. "Would you stop being a baby?"

"I wouldn't have to act like a baby if he hadn't made us go down this wormhole," Bury said. Though he kept his voice low. Prudently, as it turned out, because Lieutenant Candless poked her head into the wardroom just then. Her hands were wrapped in gauze and he was gratified to see that even she winced as she grabbed at the table to steady herself.

The cruiser was burning hard, pushing its engines to get them into warmer climes as fast as possible now that something like normalcy had returned to the wormhole. Bury knew how sore his own bones were and he could guess Lieutenant Candless's older joints would trouble her even more. He watched her as she lowered herself carefully into a chair.

"Ensign Ginger," she said, "have you seen to your own extremities yet? Come now, take off those boots."

Ginger bit her lower lip. "I'm fine. Let me finish up with Bury first, and—"

"Now, please," Candless said.

Ginger took a deep breath. Then she reached down and ran a finger along the hidden seam that released the boots of her suit. She pulled them off slowly, so carefully that Bury wondered what she was afraid of.

Even with the boots off, she kept her legs tucked close under her, with her toes curled up as if she didn't want anyone to see them. Bury frowned when he realized why. Every single one of her toes had turned black.

He noticed for the first time that she had kept her gloves on as well.

"Ginj . . ." he said. "Oh, Ginj—"

"You heard the engineer. It's going to be fine," she said.

"Hand me that tube, Ensign Bury. Now, if you please," Candless said. Her mouth was a hard line. "I've seen your genetic profiles. I knew that Ensign Ginger was at high risk. Redheads are more susceptible to the cold in general. Yet I don't remember you complaining. Did you plan on hiding this from us very long?"

Ginger shrugged. "I just didn't want anyone to think I was . . . you know. Weak."

"You do understand, I presume, that if left untreated this could lead to amputation? Well, no matter. Give me that foot, please."

Ginger hesitated, so Lieutenant Candless grabbed her leg and pulled her foot up on the table without asking a second time. "Basin, please, Ensign Bury."

"I had no idea," he said, trying to meet Ginger's eye. She looked over at Engineer Paniet instead, though—and kept eye contact with him even as Lieutenant Candless rubbed the gel deep into the cracks between her toes. Her face went very white as the enzyme bit into her skin, but she didn't say a word.

⤝⤞

"Tell me that's what I think it is," Lanoe said. He was at the controls, and there was little doubt about what he saw on his display. Still, he wanted Valk's opinion.

"That's a wormhole throat," Valk said. "Yeah."

It was hard to believe, after all they'd been through. The wormhole came to an end up ahead in a nice, wide, stable aperture back into realspace. Only a few million kilometers away. Lanoe touched the throttle, and the cruiser surged ahead.

So close now.

It didn't take long for the wardroom to fill with people. Candless and the ensigns first, then Paniet and Ehta coming together. Even the marines poked their heads out of their bunks or lingered at the back of the wardroom, anxious for a look. Technically they weren't permitted anywhere near the controls, but Lanoe could hardly begrudge them, not after what they'd been through. They still didn't even know why they'd been dragged along on this weird mission.

"Take a good look, then report to the gundecks," he told them. Ehta nodded and relayed his order, even though everyone could have heard it with their own ears.

"You want to come out of this wormhole ready to shoot?" Valk asked. "You're not worried that our new friends might take offense at that?"

"As paranoid as they've been so far? These are people who live at the end of a death tunnel. I doubt they're going to take it amiss if we're a little cautious ourselves. Besides," Lanoe said, lowering his voice, "I don't know if we got here first. There could be a hundred Centrocor ships on the other side, lined up and waiting for us."

"Hellfire," Valk said. "I hope not."

The transition to normal space went smoothly, the cruiser nosing its way through the wormhole throat with plenty of room to spare. The displays showed that they'd come out near a yellow G-class star, just like the one that warmed Earth. There wasn't much else to see, at first, except for stars.

Glorious, clean, distant, unthreatening stars. Lanoe would take it.

"I'll start analyzing the local star positions in reference to the standard candles, to get a fix on where we are," Candless said. You never knew with a wormhole—it could open into a system just a couple of light-years from where you'd started, or halfway across the galaxy. There was no direct correlation between the length or path of a wormhole and which two points in space it joined. Theoretically the wormhole could have taken them to a different galaxy completely—or a different universe. "It'll take me a while, but at least then we'll know how far—"

"Seventeen hundred, three hundred and twelve light-years from Earth," Valk said.

"Ahem. Yes. Very good," Candless said. "If a bit presumptive."

"Sorry," Valk told her. "Just figured I would save you the trouble."

Lanoe ignored them—the two of them were going to have to work out their differences on their own. He was too busy using the ship's sensors to find where they should go next. Like a planet, or an orbital habitat. This place, this system, was the X on the map. Their destination. Whatever help he was going to get with fighting the Blue-Blue-White had to be here, somewhere.

The system proved to be average in most respects, if a little sparse. There was the usual belt of comets far out from the star, and a few rocky asteroids closer in. One gas giant planet about six astronomical units out, and—most promising—a terrestrial planet right in the system's habitable zone. Laser spectrography showed that the planet had an atmosphere rich in oxygen and water vapor. Based on the planet's albedo, its magnetic field profile, its axial tilt and rate of rotation, surface conditions would be perfect for supporting human life.

"Now, there's a likely place, if I've ever seen one," Maggs said, leaning over his shoulder. Lanoe winced—he hadn't seen the scoundrel come up behind him. He waved Maggs away, then brought up a virtual keyboard and ordered a lot more scans.

Then he brought up a comms board and sent out a general call, on an unencrypted frequency. Just letting the planet know that they'd arrived. There was no immediate response but he didn't let that bother him. Maybe the senders of the mysterious message didn't want to announce their presence. Maybe they wanted him to make the first move. He launched a small fleet of microdrones to head for that planet and get a better look at it. No point in hesitating, though. He set a course to put them in a parking orbit around its equator.

This was it. He could feel it in his bones. This was real.

"XO," he said, and Candless lifted her head. She'd been staring at the display, just like everybody else. "I'll take the cutter down to the planet. I need you and your people out in orbit, keeping an eye out for me. Get your pilots to the vehicle bay. Take them to a stand-off distance and have them ready to scramble. Just in case."

"Certainly, sir," she said. "Though...I imagine three of us can handle this duty. No need to commit all of our forces."

Lanoe had no idea, at first, what she was on about. Then he looked over and saw Ginger's face. The girl had gone as white as a ghost. Candless was trying to exclude the girl from duty—in a way that saved face for Ginger.

Lanoe just didn't know if it was the right decision. Maybe all Ginger needed was to get back in the saddle. Another chance to prove herself.

There wasn't going to be a better time to find out. "I need every pair of eyes I can get out there. The four of you go," he said.

"Yes, sir," Candless replied. Her eyes showed him nothing— which he knew was a bad sign. She pointed at Ginger and Bury and gestured for them to follow her, and the ensigns fell in line. Ginger kept her eyes down, but she went. Maggs joined them with a sardonic grin. Valk got up slowly from his seat, as if he wasn't sure whether he was supposed to go, too.

"You're with me," Lanoe told him. "Ready to meet some new people?"

"I...guess," Valk said. "But wait. Who's going to fly the cruiser if we're all going?"

Lanoe smiled at him. "You can do that, too," he said. "I need you in two places at once right now. Luckily for us, that's something you can do. You can monitor and fly the ship even while you're down on the planet, right?"

Valk was silent for a moment. "I guess so," he said. "Though— it's not a great solution. There's going to be some signal lag. I can only communicate with the ship at the speed of light. Even if we're just a fraction of a light-second away, I don't like knowing it'll take that long for the ship to react to my commands. There might be another way, though. I can make a copy of myself."

Lanoe raised an eyebrow.

"It won't be perfect. The ship's computers don't have enough storage capacity to hold all of my programming. I'll need to prune some of my process trees."

Lanoe frowned. "I've been hanging around you too long. I almost understood that. You mean you need to cut out parts of your programming, so you'll fit in the ship's memory. What needs to be cut? Your emotions?"

Valk laughed. "That would be pretty dumb. Fear is an emotion. I've always found that a big chunk of flying a spaceship is the terror of it. If you aren't afraid of crashing, you won't remember not to. You need desire, too—the desire to actually get somewhere, rather than just sitting in a parking orbit forever." Valk shrugged. "Anyway, emotions are dirt simple. They don't take up much file space at all."

"Really? I never really felt like I understood them," Lanoe said.

"Nah," Valk said. "An emotion is just an arrow pointing in a given direction. One basic vector, right? Take fear. That's an arrow pointing away from the thing you're afraid of. Or love, that's an arrow pointing toward the object of affection. No, it's all the other stuff—how we react to our emotions, how we try to rationalize them, overcome them, consciously deal with them. That's the big, complex stuff. But don't worry. My copy will have those, too."

"So what will you cut out?"

"All the stuff I didn't need at all. The programs that let me simulate breathing, say, or eating or sleeping. It won't need to have much of my personality, either, since there won't be anybody here for it to talk to."

Lanoe thought about it for a second. "All right. Make this copy. But one question—what happens when you come back? Do we just have to get used to there being two of you, then?"

"No, I'll reintegrate with it. The two of us will have slightly different memories when I get back, but that's just a question of comparing files. As long as I'm not gone for too long, say, less than a day, it should be fine. We should still be ninety-nine percent the same person, so it's just a matter of checking some change logs and then deleting all the redundant files."

"And if you're gone more than a day?"

Valk nodded. "I guess we would both develop differently. The changes will build up gradually, but constantly. Each second we're apart, our file structures will diverge. We'll, you know, grow apart. Maybe, if we were separate long enough, you could say there were two of us. Maybe that's how a thing like me reproduces. The idea makes me kind of uneasy, though. How about we don't find out?"

Lieutenant Candless led them down to the vehicle bay, where their fighters were waiting. When they passed through the hatch Bury kicked off the wall and flew over to his ship, grabbing a stanchion on the side of its canopy to stop himself. He looked back and saw Maggs gliding toward him.

"Anxious to stretch your legs?" Maggs asked. "So to speak?"

"After spending so long in a pile with the likes of you," Bury told him, "it'll be good to be alone in a cockpit for a while. It'll smell better anyway."

Maggs smiled. "And who says that a Hellion can't tell a joke? I admit, I'm feeling the need to get out and move around myself. Can't remember the last time I so looked forward to a long patrol. Maybe we'll even get lucky and find something to shoot."

"I wouldn't call that lucky," Bury replied. "I'd much prefer to find out we lost the Centrocor ship. That we're, you know. Safe."

"Where's that Navy fighting spirit? When I was a lad every boy wanted to grow up to be a pilot, couldn't wait to get in a good scrap. Oh, don't get me wrong—I suppose a little of the old self-preservation instinct is a good thing. As long as it doesn't present as timidity, in the end."

"Are you calling me timid?" Bury asked. He felt his eyes narrowing. *Relax*, he told himself. *He's just baiting you.* Hard to keep that in mind when his blood was boiling in his veins, though.

Maggs held up one hand in a dismissive gesture. "Never, I would never be so reckless. I saw that kill you scored the last time we fought. And anyway, when you're on one of Lanoe's little adventures, protecting your six just makes good sense. He has a tendency to throw people to the wolves. I applaud your...caution."

Bury's hand curled around the stanchion and squeezed until his glove creaked. He bit down hard on his lower lip. "If you'd like to see my fighting spirit, I'm sure something can be arranged."

Maggs's smile only grew wider and more infuriating. Why the hell was the man riding him? What did he hope to achieve? "Perhaps, someday we'll—"

He didn't get a chance to finish his thought. "Enough, you two!" Lieutenant Candless shouted. "Maggs, get to your vehicle. Ginger, I will not be sending out engraved invitations to this patrol. Move yourself, now."

Maggs gave him a cheery mock salute and headed for his Z.XIX. Bury ignored him, instead looking over to see that Ginger was still back at the hatch. She'd barely come inside the vehicle bay at all. She was blushing, her face almost as red as her hair. Maybe because she knew she was being watched, she kicked over to her BR.9 and climbed inside the cockpit. In the moment before she raised the canopy, she looked right at Bury. Their eyes locked but he couldn't say, precisely, what he saw there.

It almost looked like she was begging him, silently, for help.

Chapter Twenty-Three

No response from the ground," Valk said. "I'm trying to hail them on every frequency I can think of. Maybe they don't believe in radios."

One of the marines in the back of the cutter laughed, but her squaddies elbowed her until she shut up.

Lanoe wasn't in a very mirthful mood, just then.

He was flying the cutter down toward the planet, with its chromatophoric skin tuned to the color of the local sky. Just in case. He'd set the controls to mask their radar profile and shield them from any invasive scans in the millimeter wave and X-ray bands of the spectrum. Just in case. He'd brought along an honor guard—or maybe a bodyguard—of four marines. Just in case.

He would very much have liked to stop worrying. He'd pinned so many hopes on this meeting, on this arrival. He very, very much wanted it to mean something.

The lack of any response from the planet made that impossible.

"We'll do one more orbit, then I'm putting us down," he told Valk. "What kind of scans have you done of the planet?"

"Visual, with every pattern recognition algorithm I could think of. I've scanned for radio emissions and laser-based communications. Object-oriented infrared analytics, predictive vector matching of every moving object down there, backscatter emitted positron scanning, forward-looking magnetic resonance interferometry—"

"Sure, sure," Lanoe said, to shut him up. He knew Valk had been thorough. The stakes here were too high for anything else. "You find anything? Anything I want to hear about," he qualified.

Valk nodded. "There are definitely buildings down there, though they're hard to find. They're covered in vegetation or buried in sand—nothing sticks up more than a few meters."

Interesting. Well, paranoid people might want to hide in bunkers, right?

"Looks like there are a bunch of cities along the coastlines, big, high-density areas that show heavy restructuring by human activity. I've seen what look like artificial islands and canal systems. People live down there, a lot of people, enough that they've redesigned half the planet to suit their needs."

Lanoe could hear that Valk wasn't so certain, though. "What's the problem?"

"I haven't seen...them. The people. I haven't found a single human being. No silhouettes, no body heat signatures. No ground or air vehicles, either. It's like everybody's locked up tight indoors and refusing to come out."

Lanoe considered that for a long time. Tried to figure out what it could mean. The conclusion he reached, after furious pondering, could be summed up by one simple word.

"Weird," he said.

"Yep."

"I'm taking us down."

———

Lanoe brought the cutter down across the peaks of a mountain range, the spacecraft's crescent-shaped shadow running on ahead of them in the sunlight. He dropped lower still until they were just above the tree line. The full-circle view in the cutter was still new enough to keep his adrenaline spiking—he felt like he was flying on an exposed seat over a long and fatal drop—but it also made it damned easy to contour trace.

Below, the trees gave way to a meandering river broken here and there by what looked like carved stone bridges. Up ahead the river cut sideways at a sharp angle and then dropped through a series of low hills to the sea. Right where it met the water was a vast and sprawling city, though one with more green space than any city Lanoe had ever seen before. "Give me a good place to set down," he said to Valk.

"There," Valk said. He pointed and a yellow rectangle superimposed itself on a stretch of grassland right in the midst of the city, perhaps a park, surrounded by long, low buildings.

Lanoe cut his speed and dropped the nose of the cutter up a few degrees, spilling air across its upper surface so that he slid in right above the rooftops. He banked hard to make an S-turn, then another, to cut his speed even more before he tried to come in for a proper landing.

When the cutter was on the ground, and Lanoe could look down and see grass growing under his feet, he switched off all of the ship's systems except its displays. For a minute he just sat there, listening.

Valk fidgeted in the seat next to him. "What are we—"

"Shh," Lanoe said. "It's quiet out there. What kind of city is this quiet?"

"Maybe we should go outside and find out."

Lanoe nodded. Still he waited another long minute before he said, "Sure," and unstrapped himself from his seat.

The marines piled out of the cutter first, moving fast across the yellow-green herbage to establish a perimeter. When they were done pointing their rifles at absolutely nothing, Lanoe and Valk crawled out from under the cutter and looked around. Lanoe kept his helmet up, despite the fact that the atmosphere read as perfectly breathable.

He had a bad feeling, perhaps.

The grass crunched reassuringly under his boots. White clouds scudded across a sky that was the appropriate shade of blue. The trees he could see were a little odd—instead of leaves they seemed to have long, curved needles, as thick as his fingers. He didn't know anything about trees, though. Maybe they were just some transplanted Earth species he'd never seen before.

He could ignore the trees. It was the buildings that really bothered him. They didn't look right. "Come on," he said, and the others followed him as he marched across the lawn to the nearest structure. A long, low building made of thin bricks, with a wide-open entryway. He ducked under a hanging creeper and stepped inside, into darkness.

In the second or so that it took his eyes to adjust, he could hear water dripping somewhere far away. He stepped down a pile of broken stone into a large room that seemed empty except for piles of dead needles, whole drifts of them as if the place hadn't been cleared out in years. There was no furniture inside the room, though the walls rose around them in a series of steps that reminded him of the seats in a theater.

"Valk," he said.

"Yeah. This place hasn't been used in a long time. Before you ask your next question, no, one empty building doesn't mean anything. Let's look at some more of these buildings before we start making assumptions."

But the next building they checked was just as empty. Just as decrepit. It looked like one wall had been decorated with an elaborate mural, but the paint had crumbled away until it was completely unrecognizable.

The third building was in even worse shape—its ceiling had collapsed, and a stand of trees grew inside, touched by yellow rays of sunlight that showed nothing moving at all.

"This place is deserted," Lanoe said. "The whole city—right? You didn't see any movement on our way in. The whole planet—"

"Yeah," Valk said. "I'm afraid so."

"All this way. We came all this way," Lanoe said, "and…and there's nobody home."

"Hold on," Valk said. Then he turned and walked out of the building. Lanoe hurried after him, protesting his quick pace—Valk had such damned long legs, and he never got tired.

"Another thing I noticed," Valk said, without slowing down. "There's not a lot of metal down here. I mean, there's plenty of iron in the soil, that's normal. But I didn't see any steel bridges, or metal skyscrapers. No foamcrete, either, or any carbon fiber construction. It's all natural stone and brick. I've been keeping my eyes open, so to speak, looking for any kind of advanced materials."

"You found something?" Lanoe asked.

"Not exactly. A concentration of ferromagnetic stuff, but that could mean...Wait, there. It's there." He pointed at a clump of trees growing out of the side of a collapsed building. It looked exactly like any other clump of trees Lanoe could see. Fat needles hanging from crooked branches.

Valk dropped to his knees by the roots and started digging in the dirt with his fingers. His hands moved faster than human hands should. Soon he'd excavated a meter-deep pit under the trees. He reached down into a tangle of roots and tried to pull something loose. "Damn. It's caught. Hold on, I'll switch more power over to my arm servos."

"Your 'arm servos'?" Lanoe asked. Remembering when Valk's arm had stopped working, because he'd realized it wasn't there.

"I'll, uh...use some elbow grease," Valk revised, sounding a little embarrassed. Regardless, he reached both hands into the pit and dragged something loose, centimeter by centimeter. Dirt pattered down into the hole and the trees shook crazily, but eventually Valk's prize came loose and he pulled it up into the light.

"This is what I think it is, isn't it?"

Valk nodded. "Yeah. The leg of a worker drone."

Specifically, the leg of one of the worker drones the two of them had seen—and fought—at Niraya.

"The Blue-Blue-White have already been here," Lanoe said, staring at the claw in Valk's hands. He didn't feel the horror of it, not yet—though he knew it was coming. "The thrice-damned aliens came here. They came here and they—they wiped out everyone, they killed every human being on this planet. They won here, Valk. They won…"

"It looks like it," Valk said, very quietly.

Lanoe took the claw from Valk's hands. Felt its weight, felt how sharp its tip still was, even after a long time in the ground. "The message we followed must have been prerecorded. Sent out before this happened, before they all died. We're too late. We're too damned late!"

He pivoted on his heel and threw the claw as hard as he could. It bounced off the side of a ruined brick building and disappeared into the vegetation.

"We're too fucking late!" he shouted, and his voice echoed off the broken stones.

Valk came around to stand right in front of him. The AI reached over and put his hands on Lanoe's shoulders. Lanoe started to pull away but Valk held him tight. He lacked the strength in his human muscles to pull away from that grip.

"Whatever you're going to say," Lanoe told him, "belay it."

"No," Valk said.

"I gave you an order. I'm not in the mood to—"

"No," Valk said again. "Lanoe. *No.*"

Lanoe stared right into that black opaque helmet, trying to figure what Valk was getting at.

"You're wrong," Valk said.

"I'm what?"

Valk wished he could take a deep breath. He'd given that sort of thing up, though. "Wrong," he said. "Not about—about the Blue-Blue-White. Yeah, they were here. And I'm sure that's why this place is abandoned. But the message wasn't prerecorded. How could it be? It included footage of our fight with the queenship at Niraya. Look at this place, Lanoe. It's been abandoned for…I don't know, centuries, maybe even longer. Long, long before you'd even heard of Niraya."

"And?"

"The message included footage of you blowing up the queenship. Think, Lanoe. If the people here died centuries ago, how could they have that footage?"

Lanoe couldn't dispute that logic. "So...so the people who lived here, the people who were slaughtered. They didn't send the message. Damn it, Valk—who did?"

"Somebody who wanted us to see this," Valk suggested.

Valk could see in the infrared part of the electromagnetic spectrum. He could tell that Lanoe's face was growing hot. With frustration—or maybe with rage. Valk wasn't sure which Lanoe was feeling more. "What are you saying? Someone dragged us all the way out here just so we could see what the Blue-Blue-White could do to a planet? That they could kill people? We already knew that, damn it! Are you suggesting that the help they offered was just giving us an object lesson? Because I refuse to believe that."

"No," Valk said. "No." Though he'd half come to accept that that was exactly what the mysterious message sender had in mind. "No."

Maybe—maybe there was something else. Maybe.

"Back to the cutter," Lanoe announced. "We're going to search every square centimeter of this place. There's something here. Maybe...Maybe..." He shook his head.

"What are you thinking?" Valk asked.

"We know that the message senders are paranoid. Maybe they're too cautious to actually want to meet us face-to-face. Maybe they left something here for us, though. Some weapon we can use against the Blue-Blue-White. Maybe just another message—some information we don't have."

"You have any guess how to find it?" Valk asked.

"None," Lanoe told him.

⟋⟋⟋

They took the cutter up a couple of kilometers and Valk flew them south, toward the planet's equator. Lanoe had no real plan as to how to survey the place. Searching every nook and cranny of the ruined cities alone could take months. If they had to search the countryside as well...Lanoe wouldn't let himself think such defeatist thoughts, though. There had to be something here.

There had to be.

"How are we on fuel?" Lanoe asked. "How long can we stay up here?"

"We're good," Valk replied.

Lanoe nodded. He hadn't really wanted real numbers. Just a little reassurance that Valk was willing to look with him.

For an hour neither of them said anything. Lanoe stared down at the ground, looking for anything out of the ordinary. The planet refused to provide him with anything useful. Maybe there would be a spaceport, he thought. Maybe an entire fleet of warships sitting down there in the jungle, waiting for him to command them. Maybe there would be a hermitage built up in the mountains, a final bastion of humanity on a dead world, even just a hut where an ancient mystic waited for him, ready to share some wisdom.

He was letting his imagination carry him away. Valk had already scanned the whole place from orbit. He'd seen no sign of continued habitation. No vehicles moving around, no cities that looked like they might still be inhabited, no smoke from any chimneys, even.

Whatever he was looking for, it would have to be simple, he thought. Simple and obvious. "If there is something here, we're supposed to find it. They wouldn't have buried it in the dirt or dropped it in one of the oceans. It should jump out at us, right? Or at least—I don't know. It should be something we can figure out."

"It would help," Valk suggested, "if they painted a big arrow on the ground. You know, to point us in the right direction, at least."

"Yeah, that would be nice."

Someone stirred behind Lanoe. He heard the noise of a soft impact, as if one of the marines had hit another one. "Shut up," someone said, very quietly.

Lanoe swiveled around. One of the marines—a woman with blue and blond streaks in her cropped hair—was leaning forward, looking worried. The man next to her grabbed her arm and tried to pull her back into her seat.

"Sir," she said.

"What is it?"

"It's not an arrow," she said. "But—" She fell silent and shook her head.

"Go on. I'll take any suggestion right now," Lanoe told her.

"Yes, sir. Like I said, it's not an arrow, but maybe—maybe that's something?" she asked. She pointed through the wall of the cutter, at the coastline below. "Or maybe not, I just thought . . . I guess . . ."

Lanoe unstrapped himself and clambered out of his seat to get a better look. There was a city down there, definitely. It looked exactly like the other cities they'd seen from the air. Lots of low buildings covered by vegetation, nothing taller than a few stories.

"I'm not sure what I'm supposed to see," Lanoe told the marine.

"Like I said, probably nothing. Only, look at the roads."

"Hmm?" Lanoe asked. It was true, a number of roads intersected inside the bounds of the coastal city. Wide highways, it looked like, and narrower tracks just scratched out of the dirt. But all cities had roads. "Go on," he said.

"Only—the last city, the one where we landed? There were no roads there. Why would there be? The trees would have grown over them years ago. But this city has roads. Right? Um, I mean, right, sir?"

Once she'd pointed it out, Lanoe couldn't not see it. The roads—roads had to be maintained.

Someone had been there, and recently.

He looked over at Valk.

"Already looking for a landing spot," the AI told him.

The marines moved forward first, wide awake now. They advanced little by little, their rifles out in front of them. Their helmets up and silvered.

Lanoe followed close behind them. He'd lowered his helmet now, apparently having thrown away caution in his desire to find something here, anything. He was almost treading on the marines' heels, he was so anxious.

The city opened up before them, looking very much like the first one they'd checked. Lots of long, wide buildings. Valk scanned a few of them and found they were just as empty as the ones he'd seen before. No furniture inside, even in the best-preserved buildings. Those weird terraced walls showed up everywhere he looked, as if every building on the planet was some kind of amphitheater.

As for the roads, they had definitely been cleared at some point. The bigger paved roads were in poor shape, though, and weeds groped upward from cracks in the pavement stones. Weird little plants, clusters of thin, short stems, each of which ended in a spherical growth, maybe a seed pod or the bud of a flower yet to bloom.

There was so much about the planet Valk didn't get. So many mysteries. Foremost in his mind was the question of when it had been settled. Even after centuries of terraforming, many planets didn't have the sort of biodiversity or comfortable climate he saw everywhere he looked here. There was a reason why humanity had named its new planets after visions of the underworld—when the first pioneers had seen the worlds for the first time, every single one of them had been uninhabitable. They had been hellish, in fact—either too hot or too cold, they'd had too much atmosphere or not nearly enough. The polys had done amazing work turning them into suitable homes for men and women, but in many places the adjustments they'd made had been *just* enough—and on others, like Hel, it had been deemed easier to reengineer the people rather than fix the planet.

Yet this place...it wasn't quite earthlike. You couldn't say that; everything was just a little off. Yet Valk had never seen a more pleasant world. Or a cleaner one.

"Look," Lanoe said. "Look, there—you see?"

It took Valk a moment to realize what Lanoe was referring to. The buildings ahead of them were different from all the others they'd seen so far. Chiefly because they weren't covered in vines and creepers and little strands of the needle-bearing trees. These structures weren't half-buried in the dirt, either. They stood in neat, tidy rows, one long building after another with a flat roof and a carved stone entryway. Valk peered inside a couple with his expanded senses and saw the terraced seating was intact, immaculate—there still wasn't any other sign of furniture, but the seats in these buildings didn't even have as much dust on them as he might have expected.

"They were here," Lanoe said. "Not long ago, they were *here*."

His eyes burned with excitement.

It wasn't much farther to the center of the city. From the air Valk had been able to see how all the roads formed a series of concentric rings—they looked like a sort of cobweb, really—around a clearing at the city's heart. If they were going to find anything here, that had to be the place. Lanoe rushed ahead, outpacing the marines as they covered the last few blocks before the center.

Valk hurried to catch up with him—then came up short when he saw what awaited them.

A circular plaza, big enough to land the cruiser in. Ringed all around by tier after tier of low stone benches. A theater in the round, capable of seating maybe a hundred thousand people.

Perhaps it was a sporting arena, Valk thought. Except that the central space in the middle of all those seats wasn't big enough for any sport he could think of. The seats ran down into a sort of pit no more then twenty meters across, and most of that space was filled by what looked like a ring of abstract sculptures. Twelve of them, each six meters high, made of dark, featureless basalt.

"Like Stonehenge," one of the marines said, perhaps forgetting that he wasn't supposed to speak without permission of his superiors. Lanoe didn't even look at the man. He was too busy running up to lay a hand on one of the sculptures.

"No, Stonehenge is those big arches, right?" the female marine, the one who'd seen the roads, said. "This looks more like, I don't know. Dancers, or something stupid like that."

Each sculpture was identical in shape, though Valk didn't think they'd been mass-produced. He could see tiny differences between them, slight asymmetries. Each of them started at ground level as a gently tapering cone, then flared out near the top. A cylinder of carefully hewn rock sat atop each of them, slowly rotating. No, the cylinders *floated* atop them—they weren't connected to, or supported by, the larger cones at all.

"Chess pieces," Lanoe suggested, patting the sculpture with a gentle hand.

Valk scanned them in every wavelength he could think of. Whatever energy was being expended to keep those spheres aloft didn't register with any of his many, many senses. It might as well be magic.

He didn't like that. He didn't like it at all.

"Lanoe," he said, carefully. "Maybe take a step back from that thing? I'm not sure it's safe."

⚡

"How did you not notice this when you scanned the place from orbit?"

"What would I have noticed?" Valk said. "There's only a trickle of power here, not enough to detect from any distance. I'm guessing that's intentional."

"Oh?" Lanoe asked.

"Whoever put these here, they didn't want machines to be able to find them. They wanted them invisible to the kind of scans I would think of doing. It took a human brain to notice the pattern of the roads, how it made a kind of bull's-eye."

Lanoe nodded sagely.

Valk took a step closer to one of the statues. Held up one hand, stopping short of actually touching the thing. "Do you feel them, I don't know, humming?"

Lanoe had noticed that. On a subconscious level, perhaps. The statues were vibrating—but only a little. Just enough to give off an almost inaudible tone.

"These have to be important, right?" Lanoe asked. "The only thing on the planet still powered..."

Lanoe spun around to look at the marines. They had their helmets up and their rifles in their arms. They'd backed away from the sculptures. Sensibly. Naval officers tended not to rate the intelligence of marines very high, but Lanoe had been around enough of them to know they had a finely tuned sense of self-preservation.

"Any ideas?" he asked them. Because he was fresh out of them.

Sadly, the marines—even the one who'd seen the roads, who knew about Stonehenge—could only shrug.

Lanoe reached up and rubbed at his nose with one gloved hand. He suddenly felt incredibly, impossibly tired.

The long journey to get here. The incredible peril. The empty planet. It didn't add up. He should be able to see the answer here. It should be obvious. Had he really forced Valk to go on living, had he put Candless and her students in danger, had he gone so far as to take help from Auster Maggs, just to be defeated here, because he couldn't think? Because he couldn't understand?

The mysterious message had promised help. WE CAN HELP. It hadn't been very specific in what kind of help. But it had told him what he needed to know, how to get to this place. COME AND FIND US.

And so he had. He'd followed the map, found the X at its center.

An X on a dead planet.

There had to be a way forward, a way to—

"Lanoe."

He stiffened, unsure if he'd really heard that. Before, always, when Zhang spoke to him, he'd been right on the edge of sleep, in the liminal space between conscious and unconscious thought.

She'd never come to him when he was wide awake before.

Yet, now—he could almost feel her standing behind him. Sense the shape of her, the warmth. He felt like she was reaching out to put a hand on his shoulder.

"Lanoe. You're so far away," she said.

She was so close.

He didn't dare turn around. He knew if he looked for her she wouldn't be there. He squeezed his eyes shut. Spoke her name, silently, in his head.

"You're not where you need to be," she said.

He opened his eyes. She was gone. Just a voice on the wind, and the wind had blown away. Yet something remained. She had jogged something in his memory, loosened some gear in his mind that had gotten stuck. He understood, suddenly, what he had to do.

HERE IS THE KEY.

Before, he'd always thought that they meant that like the key of a map, the legend. The annotations on the map of wormspace...

But they'd given him a hint, hadn't they? The roads. The roads they'd cleared around this city. Roads—and wormholes were a kind of road, weren't they?

"Valk," he said. He was trembling. Could this really be it? "Valk—the map. You have the map stored in your, your databases, right?"

"The map?" Valk asked. "Which—oh. Yeah, of course I do. The map of wormspace. The one that brought us here."

"Show me," Lanoe said.

Valk lifted his arm and his wrist display showed the map, a twisted convolution of knots rotating slowly between them. All the wormholes and their throats, the navigational hazards, the positions of the Blue-Blue-White fleets. All that priceless information. The marines weren't cleared to see that map. Lanoe didn't give a damn.

"Show it to them," Lanoe said, and he pointed at the sculptures behind him.

Slowly, carefully, Valk raised his arm. His wrist display projected the map across the stone of the nearest statue.

The sculptures began to sing.

>≁≺

"Hellfire," Valk said. "Lanoe—everyone—get back. Get back!"

How had he not noticed before, that each of the sculptures was humming at a slightly different pitch? Each one resonating to a single frequency on a twelve-note scale. The sound waves, the vibrations, oscillating in perfect harmony.

The humming rose in volume. The notes were crystal clear, a unison of sound.

The marines almost fell over each other as they stumbled up the rows of benches, pushing back away from the sculptures. Lanoe hadn't moved at all. He stood there transfixed, staring up at them.

Valk's whole suit shook with the tones, with the waves rolling off the stone. He felt like he would shake to pieces if he didn't get away. If he didn't get clear.

He shouted Lanoe's name, but it was lost in the sound. In that perfect, roaring, singing sound. He put his hands on either side of his helmet as if he could cover his ears, as if he had ears, as if he had hands—

Lanoe! he shouted again. *Lanoe!*

He pushed forward, against the rolling waves of sound. Against the vibration that threatened to knock him off his feet, against that tone that threatened to shatter him into pieces. He felt like he was trying to walk into a hurricane.

Lanoe lifted his hands toward the sculptures. If he touched them, if he discharged the energy flowing through them—

Lanoe, Valk howled.

Lanoe.

The sound rose and rose in volume, with no distortion whatsoever. It was so perfectly clear and sweet, and any moment now it would rupture Lanoe's eardrums, it would break open all the blood vessels in his head, and still, he wouldn't move, it was like he was hypnotized, entranced by the sound, and—

Automatically, Lanoe's helmet swam up out of his collar ring. Valk could see the sound waves rippling through the flowglas as it fought to cover Lanoe's head, to block out that perfect, beautiful, obliviating sound. Somehow the helmet coalesced, coming together over the crown of his head, sealing Lanoe off from the tones.

It broke the spell. Lanoe turned around, a look of utter confusion on his face. His eyes went wide when he saw Valk staggering toward him.

Valk grabbed him around the waist and picked him up. It was easy—the servomotors in his suit were much stronger than human muscles. He picked Lanoe up and hauled him away from the statues, bounding up the terraced benches two at a time, three at a time. Just in time.

In perfect synchrony, the stone cylinders atop the sculptures spun around one hundred and eighty degrees, and then dropped down into the fluted upper portions of the cones. And then all hell broke loose.

Whatever energy the sculptures had kept hidden, all that titanic force came out of them at once, shooting straight up into the air. Valk's electronic eyes could see it, see torrents of superlow-frequency energy pour into the sky. He threw Lanoe down on one of the benches and shielded his body with his own as side-lobe radiation washed over him, a pure and crystalline and perfect and deafening and lethal and thrilling pulse of sound.

Valk could see behind him. He could see what was happening up in the air. He was still surprised when the note, the perfect note, was joined by a new sound, one that failed altogether to harmonize. A crack, a peal, a rumble of thunder that made the whole open-air theater, the city center, shake.

And then—

Up there, in the air. Kilometers up, but not that many kilometers. The air itself seemed to change, to turn to glass. A lens, a sphere of glass appeared up there, out of literally thin air. Vapor swirled around it, twisting into a cyclone of hurrying cloud. Static electric charges leapt from it, tiny bolts of lightning. For a few brief seconds rain and then hail pelted down all around Valk, bouncing off his suit, rebounding off his helmet like gunshots—but then it was gone, and the clouds settled down, and the sky started to behave again.

Except now it had a new hole in it. A hole in the sky.

"Valk," Lanoe said. "Valk, that—that's a—"

A wormhole throat. Hanging in the middle of the air, just above the ring of sculptures.

A hole in the sky.

Chapter Twenty-Four

Bullam strapped herself into her seat on the bridge of the carrier. Summoned one of her drones to bring up a simple communications panel. She nodded and it established a link to the scout ships. The faces of the pilots appeared before her, all in a row.

"I want you to know that Centrocor salutes your bravery," she told them. "We're all in this together."

"If we can get on with it?" Shulkin asked.

She studied the way he sat in his command seat, leaning forward, hands on his knees. Looking perfectly composed despite the absence of gravity. The man was a machine purpose-built for this kind of work. His eyes were like the diamond tips of industrial drills.

"All right," she said. "Good luck, pilots." Then she cut the connection.

On the big display above the navigator's position, three blue dots moved steadily forward, fanning out in three directions. Ahead of them lay three hazardous paths. The detour to Avernus meant Lanoe had a week's head start on them. It was possible he hadn't taken any of these wormholes, and that exploring the hazardous tunnels was a waste of time and fuel. Bullam had studied the map a dozen times, though, and she had to believe that Lanoe hadn't doubled back just to throw them off the scent.

The problem was they had no idea which of the three tunnels was the right one. It was Shulkin who had pointed out they had a simple solution to this dilemma. The carrier had dozens of scout craft in its big vehicle bay, tiny, fast ships perfect for this role. Three pilots had been chosen at random to try the tunnels.

The first tunnel looked perfectly safe and normal as far as their sensors could reach. All three of them did. Radio communication was impossible in a wormhole, but as long as two ships were within line of sight of each other, they could stay in touch by communications laser. The three wormholes, as hazardous as they might be, ran unusually straight ahead. They expected to be able to receive regular updates from the scouts for at least the first few million kilometers of the mission.

The pilot in charge of exploring the first tunnel sounded relaxed as he streaked onward, reading off data as he went. "Temperature normal, geometry normal. The ghostlight in here is a little strange—it looks like something might have stirred it up."

Bullam looked over at the information officer. "Could Lanoe have done that?" she asked.

The IO looked like he wanted to shrug but he fought down the urge. "Unclear, ma'am. If a large amount of mass hit the tunnel wall all at once...maybe."

"You don't think Lanoe crashed his ship," Bullam said, turning to Shulkin. "Do you?"

"He's no fool," Shulkin replied. He twitched one shoulder. "Accidents happen. But no, I don't believe he died here."

"One point five million kilometers in. Temperature's rising a little," the scout pilot said. "Are you seeing this? Looks like...like..."

"IO?" Shulkin barked.

"Imagery is...inconclusive. I'll bring it up."

The navigational display showed a forward view from the scout, the same thing the pilot saw. The wormhole tunnel ran straight as an arrow away from him, ghostlight spearing out from the walls in long, spiky plumes. Without warning one of the spikes thickened and then lurched across the tunnel, twisting around itself like a tornado of light.

The view rolled sickeningly as the pilot maneuvered hard to avoid that plume of energy. For a moment they had a good view of the tunnel wall and Bullam saw the ghostlight roiling and spitting, far more energetic than the quiet, smoky radiance she would have expected.

"Evading," the pilot said, his voice rising in pitch. "I see three more of those flares. Requesting permission to return to vehicle."

Everyone looked to Shulkin. He might have been made of stone, his eyes fixed on the display. He didn't say a word.

"Activity is increasing, repeat, activity is increasing, reaching dangerous levels," the pilot called, almost shouting now.

On the display a prominence of ghostlight smashed across the tunnel, an arch of quivering light that entirely blocked the way forward. Spears of bright ghostlight jumped out of the walls from every direction. None of the activity looked coordinated, it wasn't actively targeting the scout, but it was just a matter of time before one of them struck his tiny ship.

"Captain Shulkin," Bullam said. "Recall the scout."

Shulkin didn't even look like he was breathing.

"Captain! That man is going to die! We don't gain any data from letting him get burned alive. Recall the—"

Shulkin spoke over her. "Pilot, I want you to pick a spot on the wall, well ahead of you, and fire a one-second burst of PBW into it."

Bullam wanted to jump out of her seat and throttle Shulkin. "You're running experiments now? You're using this man as a guinea pig?"

The scout pilot did as he was told. PBW fire lanced out from the single cannon mounted in the nose of his ship, drawing a line of radiance along the wall of the tunnel. Its light was lost in the storm of ghostlight that followed, the wall exploding with fury every time one of the particles struck home.

The light was bright enough to make Bullam's eyes hurt. The

tunnel ahead of the scout filled completely with raging, spectral fire.

But perhaps there was a limit to how much activity one tunnel could produce. The flares and prominences around the scout receded, pulling back toward the walls.

"Now you may return," Shulkin told the man.

The pilot wasted no time twisting around and burning toward home. In a few seconds he was free of the tunnel and calling for clearance to dock in the vehicle bay.

"You knew that would work?" Bullam asked.

Shulkin did not look at her, nor did he answer her.

"Tell the second scout to proceed with his mission," he said.

The second wormhole didn't run quite as straight as the first. Communications would be impossible after the first million kilometers. Anything could be hiding in there. A naked singularity. A dozen branching paths, each of them more deadly than the last. Some kind of wormhole-native cyclopean monster that subsisted on human spacecraft.

Well, that last was unlikely. Bullam's stomach knotted with dread, though, as she watched the second scout race ahead down the wormhole's length.

"Conditions normal," the pilot called. "Temperature and geometry as expected. The ghostlight in here doesn't seem particularly active."

"Understood," Shulkin said. He inclined his head forward to drink some water from a straw hidden inside his collar ring. Any of the carrier's crew would have been happy to fetch him a squeeze tube if he wanted it, but instead he chose to sip at his own recycled fluids. Bullam, whose suit did not include a reclamation system, turned away and watched the screen.

Ahead of the scout the wormhole spooled out exactly as a wormhole should. Ghostlight flickered along the walls, occasionally reaching out with a vaporous arm toward the scout, but never coming close to touching it.

"Temperature hasn't changed," the pilot called. "All conditions nominal."

Seconds ticked by. Bullam couldn't forget that the charts labeled this wormhole as somehow extremely hazardous, but she couldn't see where the danger lay. The pilot's voice became a lulling drone, and she started to reach behind her, to snap her fingers for one of her drones to bring her something to eat.

"Temmperrrature norrrmal," the pilot said.

At first Bullam didn't catch it.

"Alll conditionss nommminnnalll."

She looked up. No one on the bridge seemed to think it was odd that the pilot's voice had deepened so much, or that he had slowed down to a drawling cadence. Maybe it was nothing. Maybe there was just interference on the line, some kind of lag.

Though—Bullam had never heard of interference on a communications laser. The beam either connected or it didn't. If there was a problem with a comms laser, the signal simply cut out.

"Captain," she said.

Shulkin gave her a nod. Just a tiny inclination of his head. "Pilot. What is your physical state? Are you feeling ill?"

There was no answer for long seconds. When it did come, it was hard to understand.

"Fffiiinnneee," he said. "Iiii'mmmm fffffiiiinnnnneeee, aaaaalllll conditttttttt—"

The final *t*-sound stretched on and on, sounding like waves crashing on a beach.

"IO," Shulkin said. "Give me a signal analysis. What's going on?"

The information officer shook his head. "It's...it's weird, sir."

"I need data, Officer. Not your opinion."

The IO took a deep breath. "The signal's still coming in, just as strong as ever, only—the wavelength is all stretched out. It's like—"

"Time dilation," the navigator said.

They all turned to look at her.

"Time dilation, like when a ship travels close to the speed of light, or it approaches a black hole. That's my best opinion, sir."

Shulkin didn't bother telling her that he hadn't asked for it. "IO, has the scout craft accelerated to near the speed of light?"

"Not at all, sir," the IO replied. "It seems to have slowed down, actually. It's . . . hellfire."

"There are civilians present," Shulkin said. "Please avoid that sort of language."

The IO nodded. "Sorry, sir. Just—when the scout entered the wormhole it was moving at approximately a thousand meters per second. My sensors are telling me it's now moving at a velocity of approximately ten centimeters . . . per hour."

The wormhole, Bullam thought. The wormhole had slowed down time for the scout pilot. She remembered from when she was in school, the day her science instructors had taught her about wormholes. One of the mysteries about them was that they connected distant planets while conserving local time. She didn't understand all the math, but she remembered them saying that a wormhole didn't just move through space, it traveled through a timelike dimension as well. The equations that governed wormholes didn't recognize any difference between time and space, treating them as identical kinds of dimensions. Just as a wormhole could connect two star systems, it could just as easily connect the distant past and the far future. It had surprised the early explorers that the wormholes they traversed didn't send you back into the distant past, or accelerate you toward the end of the universe.

In all their explorations, though, humanity had never found a wormhole that traveled through time. It just didn't seem to be something that happened naturally. Maybe the universe just didn't like the kind of paradoxes that time travel might create.

This wormhole apparently didn't get the memo.

"He's slowed down in time," Bullam said. "And the further he goes, the slower he's going to get. The poor bastard's going to get stuck in there if he goes any further. Time will slow down so much it'll be millions of years before he even realizes he's in trouble. How do we get him out?"

"Sir," the carrier's pilot said. "We can dispatch a rescue vehicle. I can have one ready in a few minutes, and—"

"We don't," Shulkin said.

"Sir?" the pilot asked.

"Any rescue vehicle we send after that pilot will be slowed down in time as well. Rescue is impossible. Ready the third scout."

"Now, wait a minute," Bullam said. "You can't just leave him in there!"

Shulkin turned his diamond gaze on her.

"I am the captain of this vessel," he told her. "I can do as I please. I gave an order. Ready the third scout. Let's find out what the third wormhole has in store for us. And let us all hope it's something we can survive, because I intend to take this carrier through it, and I intend to catch Aleister Lanoe. Would any military personnel like to comment on my orders?"

The bridge crew all looked to their displays.

Chapter Twenty-Five

I think I ought to point out," Paniet said, over an encrypted channel, "as the closest thing you have to a scientist—that thing shouldn't exist."

"The wormhole throat?" Lanoe asked. As if he could be referring to anything else. It loomed before the cutter, dwarfing the little ship. A sphere of distorted air. A miniature planet with a ring of clouds.

There was no possible way to determine where it went, or what they would find on the other side.

"Where they occur in nature, throats are always anchored to large gravity wells. Stars, in other words. The planet isn't big enough to hold on to it. And please, dear, don't get me started on how unlikely it is to find such a thing inside a planetary atmosphere."

"Sure," Lanoe said. "Can you think of any reason why we shouldn't go through?"

"None whatsoever. Other than the obvious fact that it's incredibly dangerous to fly through a wormhole throat when you don't know what's on the other side. But don't let that stop you. I'm burning with envy that you get to go through first."

Lanoe cut the connection to the cruiser and established a new one to Candless, up in orbit around the planet. "XO, you understand the situation?"

"I do, Commander. I'll sit up here and monitor the planet until you return. If, of course, you don't come back after a reasonable interval, I'll assume command."

"I have no idea what I'm getting into here. Wait for that reasonable interval—and then a little longer."

"Understood." Candless cut the connection and suddenly it was very, very quiet inside the cutter.

Lanoe looked back at the marines sitting behind him. If they were worried about what was about to happen, their mirrored helmets hid it.

"Take us through," he said to Valk.

The AI didn't hesitate. He touched the throttle and the cutter moved almost silently forward.

Lanoe didn't know what to do with his hands. He grasped the knees of his suit. The throat grew until it filled all of their forward view and then they nosed through, into the wormhole beyond—

—except there was no wormhole beyond. It wasn't a throat, it was a portal. Wisps of ghostlight just had time to reach toward the cutter before they disappeared again and the cutter flew free into...another place.

Lanoe's first impression was that they had entered a vast cavern, dark but full of glittering lights like jewels. They were not in space, certainly no stretch of space he'd ever visited before. He could feel that this was an enclosed place, though it was large enough that he could barely see the walls.

Walls shimmering with ghostlight. Yet this was no wormhole. It couldn't be. It had to be hundreds of kilometers wide. A bubble, then, an enormous bubble made of the same material that made wormhole walls, but self-enclosed. As far as he could tell the only entrance or exit was the portal they'd just traversed. It sat behind them like a pearl embedded in the bubble's wall.

"Where are we?" Lanoe asked.

Valk shrugged. "Technically we haven't moved much at all. *Technically* we're still in the atmosphere of the planet. We've just shifted into another geometric modulus space. It's the same algebraic stack but we've broken isomorphism—passed through a complex Riemann transform and—"

Lanoe glared at him.

Valk shrugged again. "We're in another dimension," he said.

Floating in the bubble, not far from the portal, was a city.

A shapeless collection of spires and galleries and arcades. A Gothic fantasia, a cathedral that had metastasized into a massive fortified cosmopolis. Fantastically intricate, almost organic in its encrustations, yet clearly something that had been built. Towers stretched upward from some unseen central mass, towers and long, stately columns and things like—but not exactly like—pyramids and obelisks. *City* was the best word he had to describe it, yet unlike a city sitting on a flat plain, this one hovered unsupported and it sprawled out in every possible direction at once. The vast majority of it seemed to have been constructed from the same dark basalt as the sculptures that had sung to open the portal. Dark stone, pierced by a million blazing windows full of yellow light.

Vehicles—aircraft? spacecraft?—zoomed hither and yon around the city, plunging into openings in the mass of architecture, describing lazy figure-eights over and under and around its mass. As the cutter approached, the vehicles skated away, like nervous insects.

Lanoe could hear Valk talking, calling ahead to hail the city, to ask for instructions. To get clearance to land. He was too busy taking in the strangeness of the place to listen, to give orders. As the cutter edged closer he was constantly discovering new features of the city—a long boulevard, lined with sculptures like the ones back on the planet. A pair of high towers linked with so many suspended bridges they looked like cobwebs strung between the buildings. Structures like lighthouses all over the city, tall, thin columns topped by rotating lights, their beams sweeping across the impossibly complex architecture below.

There was no sun in the bubble, no moon to cast light upon the city. The ghostlight that played along the bubble's walls was too thin and gray to do more than dapple the outermost towers in a faint, coruscating radiance. No stronger than starlight. All other light in the place was artificial. A city wrapped in perpetual night.

He didn't know what to make of it. He had no idea what any of it meant.

"Lanoe," Valk said.

He pulled himself back from the view. Faced the AI.

"I'm not getting any instructions," Valk said. "If there's a traffic controller here they're ignoring me. But I think maybe we're supposed to put down there."

He pointed at a broad plaza below them, a circular, dishlike space. It resembled very much the amphitheater bowl on the planet they'd just left behind, its sides terraced into endless rows of seating. At its center a ring of light appeared, bluish-white in color, far brighter than even the lighthouse beams. A second ring lit up inside the first, then a third, like the concentric bands of a bull's-eye.

Lanoe nodded. Valk took the cutter down for a landing.

The city had an atmosphere. Identical to that of the planet they'd come from, and therefore breathable. Lanoe kept his helmet down as he climbed out from under the cutter, but the marines behind him kept theirs up and silvered.

He stepped out onto flagstones joined together so perfectly it was hard to find the seams. Once he was clear of the ship's wing he stood up to his full height and looked around. The landing lights had gone out and there wasn't much to see—just the silhouettes of towers all around the plaza, their lights too distant to show him any features of the place where he stood.

Valk came up beside him and together they looked around, trying to see if anyone was going to come to welcome them—or maybe shout at them for landing in the wrong place. Lanoe had a distinct feeling he was being watched. It made his back itch, right between his shoulder blades. He turned around in a full circle and then, finally, he saw them. Presumably the people he'd come so far to meet.

They sat on the terraced benches, hunched forward in shadow. Hundreds of them, maybe a thousand. He could see their heads move back and forth and he presumed they were whispering among themselves, but he couldn't hear any words. None of them were close enough for him to make out their features.

"Do we go and introduce ourselves?" Valk asked. "Or would that be rude?"

"Maybe," Lanoe said. "But after all the games they've made us play, I'm thinking it's time for answers." He started walking toward the nearest ring of benches, taking long strides he hoped looked confident. Before he'd gone ten meters, though, he stopped in place.

The beam of one of the lighthouses had speared down into the plaza, shining a perfect circle of orange light onto the flagstones. Lanoe started walking forward again, but then a man stepped into the pool of light, one forearm up to shade his eyes.

"Hello," he said. "You're here." He gave them a warm smile. "Damnation. I'd stopped believing. I'd stopped hoping."

Lanoe studied the man as he approached them, the spotlight following his steps. He took in the thick growth of beard, the shaggy hair. The nasty scar that ran across the man's right temple. He wore a heavy pilot's suit with deep scuff marks on the knees. The outermost layer of fabric over his elbows had worn away completely. When he tried to ping the man's cryptab, Lanoe got nothing back. That worried him—until he realized it was burned out. The suit's batteries must be dead.

Valk touched Lanoe's arm. "Right shoulder," he whispered.

Painted on the man's sleeve, weathered but still recognizable, was a blue flag with black stars. The flag of the Establishment. The same flag Valk had flown under, back when they called him—

"The Blue Devil," the man said, a look of awe in his face. "I can't believe it. They sent the damned Blue Devil!" He rushed over, brushing past Lanoe, and grabbed Valk's hand. "Hell's bells. Hell's bells! Sir, it's so good to meet you."

Lanoe's teeth ground together. He'd run out of patience a long time ago.

"Who are you?" Lanoe demanded.

"What?" the man asked. "Oh, terribly sorry, old man." He

grinned and reached for Lanoe's hand. "You'll have so many questions. I'm afraid I don't know where to start."

"How about with your name," Lanoe suggested.

"My . . . name," the man said. A strange transformation overcame him then. His head jerked back as if he'd had a shock. His eyes lost their focus and drifted to the side. His mouth opened, a little, and his lips moved as if he were speaking but he made no sound at all. Lanoe worried the man might be having a seizure.

But then the intelligence came back to his face, as abruptly as it had gone.

"Pleased to meet you, very pleased," the bearded man said, as if nothing had happened. "I'm Archivolt Klebs, Third Lieutenant Archivolt Klebs, Ninth Territorials, if we're being formal. But let's not, eh?" He grinned again. "Archie. Just call me Archie. You've come a long way, we—I know that, and I'm very grateful. Are you tired? Thirsty or hungry? We can do something about that, if you'd like—"

Lanoe took a step back and turned around to face the multitude of people hiding in the shadows. "You sent for us. You said you could help."

"Please don't address them directly," Archie said. "Not quite yet. It's for your benefit, I promise."

Lanoe tried to stare the man down. It didn't work. "Look," he said. "You *summoned* us. My name is Aleister Lanoe. My crew and I nearly died getting here, and now we'd—"

He saw Valk lifting his hands as if to tell him to take it down a notch.

Damn. That used to be Zhang's job. She always knew when he was about to go too far. She always called him on it, too. How many times had he let Zhang do his talking for him? Any situation that required diplomacy or tact, she'd been there to back him up. Make up for his lack of social niceties.

Could he even do this, without her?

Lanoe fought to control himself. "We'd like to talk," he said, a little more gently. "What I'd really like is to know what's going on.

I understand why you're hiding out here, and I understand why you're so cautious, but if we're going to help each other we need to start trusting each other. That should start now. Let me see their faces."

Archie rubbed at the scar on his temple. "Just a second," he said.

His face went slack again, just as it had before. Drool formed in the corner of his mouth.

Lanoe looked to Valk, but the big pilot could only shrug.

What the hell was wrong with this man? That scar—had he suffered some kind of brain trauma?

There was so much at stake. So much to win or lose here—were they really going to have to negotiate with—

"Ah. A thousand apologies, I daresay," Archie said, as the light came back to his eyes.

"Who are they?" Lanoe asked, pointing at the people in the shadows. "Just tell me that much."

Archie nodded and sighed deeply, as if he regretted that things had to move so quickly. "That," he said, "is the Choir."

"The Choir," Lanoe repeated.

Archie lifted his arms in a sweeping gesture. His cockeyed grin suggested they shouldn't take the drama of the moment so seriously, but it was hard to feel amused when Lanoe was stuck in the dark, surrounded by invisible and mysterious multitudes. "The Choir Indomitable. The Choir Invisible. The Choir in Exile. The Choir That Chose to Be Forgotten. They've been debating what you should call them, for *weeks*. Personally, I think they should keep it simple. The Choir."

"Please," Lanoe said, fighting back his urge to grab the man and shake him. "Please. Let me see their faces. I have my own trust issues. Do you understand?"

"Oh, yes," Archie said, and he laughed. "Oh, I say, yes, I understand that. And you still have no idea—listen, chap, I'm doing my best here. Making your case. It's thick going, but...but..."

And just like that he was gone again. His face slack, his arms dangling at his sides.

Lanoe raised an eyebrow in Valk's direction. Valk just shrugged.

Archie rubbed his scar again. Then he straightened up and nodded. "There," he said. "It's done."

Without warning, lights flicked on all around the amphitheater. Lights that showed the people in the stands, illuminating their faces, their bodies.

Well. Perhaps *people* was the wrong word, Lanoe thought.

That would have suggested they were human.

The Choir began to climb off their benches and walk down into the plaza. Lanoe spun around, trying to see them all, see any differences between them, but to his eyes they all looked the same, identical as twins. Hundreds and hundreds of copies of the same body plan, the same clothing.

They weren't human. Not at all, not when you saw them in the light. His brain couldn't make sense of them. Not all at once. He could only seem to focus on one detail about them at a time.

They were . . . tall.

"I was with the Territorials at Tiamat, the big battle there," Archie said. "You'll remember it, of course. I heard stories about you, about the pilot they couldn't burn. Ashes of hell, it got a bit hectic that day!" Lanoe spared Archie a glance and saw he was talking to Valk, his fellow Establishmentarian. *Let them babble together*, he thought. He was far too busy looking at the Choir.

Tall, he thought again. The Choir stood maybe three meters tall, big enough to make Valk look normal. Tall but impossibly thin, with conical bodies and high, cylindrical heads. It took him a second to realize why that seemed familiar. The sculptures back on the planet— those had been statues. Statues of these—

These aliens. There was no other possibility. The Choir were an alien species. Except there weren't supposed to be any of those left.

"—got separated from my unit," Archie went on. "Damned poly bastards cut us down to size, we had just brought our reserves to bear, and oh, things were taking a turn, but they had the guns, the bloody guns on their big damned ships.... They just cut through our formations, like we were made of paper. My squaddies died before my eyes, one after another. I tried to get away, get back to my destroyer, but they chased me down, cut my fighter to pieces, my airfoils gone, no ammo left..."

The Choir all wore the same clothes, a kind of loose dress made of layers of black lacy material with a stiff white collar. When they walked, their skirts swung back and forth in a way that made Lanoe think they must have a lot of legs underneath, but he couldn't see them—the dresses came all the way down to the ground, their hems sweeping and bunching against the flagstones.

They had four arms.

"—left me no choice. I had to chance a run for the wormhole throat, halfway across the system. Barely made it with six poly bastards right on my tail. I burned out my main thruster trying to outpace them, lost my positioning jets trying to keep out of the way of their fire. I must have maneuvered too hard, pushed myself, because I blacked out. Missing time, the whole thing. Damned inconvenient. Woke up with my helmet obscured by drool and blood. And, to top it all, lost. Lost inside wormspace—"

Four arms, Lanoe thought. Long, jointed arms they kept folded up against their torsos. One in front, one in back, one on either side. They could reach behind themselves, reach in any direction. That was one of the hardest things to grasp. Their body plans were symmetrical, like any animal's, but radially symmetrical rather than bilaterally symmetrical like a human, like a mammal. They weren't mammals. They weren't like any animal he'd seen. Maybe—

Maybe a little insectile. Maybe a lot like insects, or crustaceans. Their heads. Their heads were... not like human heads.

"—panicked, of course I panicked. Who could blame me? I went hunting for any wormhole throat I knew, didn't find a damned one, of course not—how can you tell one from another in there? And I was terrified, terrified I was going to come out of a throat into the Irkalla system, or Adlivun, some poly stronghold.

I couldn't decide if 'twas nobler to starve to death in a wormhole or risk poking my head out and getting it shot off...I suppose one could say my thoughts were, well, disarranged. I was at the end of my tether and—"

Their heads.

High, cylindrical, hairless. Covered in plates of ivory, plates of interlocking armor. No mouth, Lanoe saw, though he kept looking for one. No nose, no nostrils, no ears, no chins. Just eyes. Dozens of small silver eyes like wet ball bearings embedded in that armor. A ring of eyes that ran all the way around their heads. They could see in all directions. But without mouths, without ears, how did they...Lanoe shook his head. He was making assumptions. That had to stop.

"—finally couldn't take it anymore. So very, very cold, just frozen stiff. My fighter was running on fumes, and I'd taken enough damage back in the battle I knew I would never get back to space if I set down. But I couldn't feel my fingers and I was hungry, so very, very hungry, I'd never felt like that before. Like my body was eating itself. I don't know how I made it but I set down on the planet next door. All I knew was that it was a green planet I didn't recognize at all. Bloody thing wasn't to be found in my database. At least it wasn't poly ground, eh? I set down and crawled out of my cockpit. Fell out, more like. Found some plants and just chewed on them, chewed until I could swallow. Turned out that was the worst thing I could do, of course. They were poison, everything on that planet is poison to humans. Foreign proteins, they told me. The Choir told me, that is. After I woke up and found myself here. They let me in, opened up the door, and brought me inside. They saved my life."

The Choir swarmed around Lanoe, no, that was a terrible word, *gathered* around him, all around him, their tall heads blocking out the lights. He felt child-sized before them, was certain that if they wanted to, if he gave them any reason to, they could tear him to pieces. Their hands—their hands were like the claws of lobsters, only more intricate, with four pincers coming together and tapering to a single point. Their eyes watched him, their eyes swiveled around him, studied him from all angles.

"They're good people," Archie said. "Really they are. You just need to...well. Get used to them, a bit."

One of them was closer to Lanoe than the others. It leaned forward, its head looming over him. He tried to crane his neck back to meet its assessing gaze, but he overbalanced and had to take a step back. There was one of them behind him, too. It reached out with one of those claws and...steadied him. That was all. He looked back at the one that was still leaning over him. Saw the plates of its face moving, shifting against each other with a tiny, rasping noise.

"You'll come to love them, just as I have."

A dark brown spiderlike thing pushed its way out from between two plates on the alien's face. Scuttled down into its collar and disappeared.

Lanoe very much wanted to sit down.

Chapter Twenty-Six

I guess," Lanoe said, "I should begin by saying..."

He turned around, having sensed motion behind him. But that was the problem. There was motion all around him. The Choir were constantly changing position, one of them moving forward while others moved back to make room. They lifted their arms to touch claws. They bobbed their heads forward, or back.

Gestures for which he had no referents. No idea what they might mean.

"On behalf of...humanity," he said. He turned around again. They were all around him. It made sense, he thought, if they could see in all directions. They wouldn't understand that he didn't like having them behind him, behind his back. They wouldn't understand that he could only think of himself as addressing the ones in front of him. "On behalf of humanity, we're...we're pleased to meet a...new species."

Was that...offensive?

He turned around again. Tried looking at individual members of the Choir—choristers, he thought, the singular form would be *chorister*. "We hope this meeting will be...mutually..."

They chirped at him. All of them at once.

It wasn't the insectile, cicadas-in-a-field sound he might have expected. Much closer to birdsong, the choristers all emitting one single, perfectly clear note that swelled into a kind of symphonically lush trill. It was rather pretty, actually. And simultaneously terrifying, because it was so alien.

"What does that mean?" he asked.

"They're laughing," Archie told him. The castaway was grinning, himself. "Sorry. They don't mean any offense. It's just the way you keep spinning in circles."

Lanoe took a deep breath. He remembered a piece of advice Zhang had given him once, about speeches. Always start with a joke.

Well, he had them laughing anyway.

"This would be easier," he said, "if I could talk to their leader. Which of them is in charge here? Maybe I could meet with them alone, even."

Archie opened his mouth to reply but then his eyes rolled up into his head and he staggered forward a step. Valk reached out to grab his arm, but before the big pilot could get there, Archie was already recovering. Returning to himself.

The Choir chirped again, even louder and longer than before.

Lanoe frowned. "What did I do that time?"

"You asked for their leader," Archie said, wiping at his eyes. "They haven't one, that's the thing. They barely understand the concept—and only because I asked for the same thing, when I arrived here."

No leader? Lanoe wondered how that would even work.

"Anyway, you can't talk to a leader, because you can't talk to any of them," Valk said. "Not directly." He turned toward Archie. "Can he?"

"What do you mean?" Lanoe asked.

"Low-power microwaves," Valk said. "I can see them. Like ripples in the air—around their heads. All of their heads, all the time." He shook his head back and forth. "I'm right, aren't I?"

"They communicate via telepathy, it's true," Archie said.

"No, no," Valk said, "it's not like that. There's nothing psychic about it. I can see it happen, see them trading microwaves back and forth. Their heads—they must act like antennas. Microwave transponders, right? I see the same waveforms going back and forth." He turned toward Archie, who half-nodded, half-shrugged. "They broadcast their thoughts, and then other brains pick up those thoughts and rebroadcast them, and then—"

"Just call it telepathy," Lanoe said. Something occurred to him. "They don't talk."

"Not out loud," Archie agreed. "If you could hear their thoughts, though, you might say they never *stop* talking. Think of your own internal monologue. Is it ever quiet? No, they think all the time, and they constantly share those thoughts between them. They don't need a leader, you see, because they simply think back and forth until they come to a consensus."

"Like—like ants, or bees or—something," Lanoe said, struggling with the idea. "They're a...hivemind?"

Archie laughed. The Choir did not. "Not at all. You're thinking they have one brain between them and you've got it all wrong. Each of them is every bit as intelligent as you or me, on their own. Each has her own thoughts and feelings and opinions—oh my, they have opinions, and they're not afraid to offer them up. It's not a collective consciousness. It's more like a *sharing* consciousness."

Lanoe couldn't understand. He decided to put that aside. "They don't talk. They think at each other. But they understand my words. How is that possible? Did you teach them all English?"

"No. They have a written language, but I can't make any sense of it. No, chaps, no, you aren't seeing it. The Choir and I, we communicate by pure thought. A language beyond language, a lexicon of symbols and associations and pure signifiers." He gave Lanoe a knowing grin. "Doesn't make much sense when I say it aloud, does it? But believe me, it works a treat."

"Archie can hear them," Valk said. He gestured at the castaway. "When he has those...I don't know, little seizures. That's him talking to them. He's relaying what we say, and they reply through him."

Archie nodded. Then he reached up and touched his head,

ran his finger along the scar on his temple. "When I first arrived here, they managed to keep me alive, but I'm afraid I was a bit... unstable. Downright barmy, if you don't mind an indelicacy. Confused, of course, and terrified, painfully aware that I was probably going to spend the rest of my life here. Worst of all, though, was the loneliness. Hundreds of light-years from the nearest human being. Utterly cut off. They did this," he said, and touched his scar again, "so that I would have someone to converse with. Put an antenna in my head so I wouldn't be so damned lonely."

"Aliens performed brain surgery on you," Lanoe said. "And it would have been without your consent—they couldn't even let you know what they were doing, or why."

"They took pity on me. Ah, well," Archie said, and rolled his shoulders. "All came out right in the wash, didn't it?" He gave them a warm smile.

⟶⤙

Valk watched Archie carefully. His head, specifically. There was a constant flow of microwaves into and out of one lobe of his brain, a sort of carrier wave that was modulated for low-intensity communication. When he blanked out, when his face went slack, the flow increased dramatically and then fell away again, but it never truly stopped. The man must have voices in his head all the time.

If he had been in Archie's position—alone, stranded among aliens—would he have wanted that? Wanted the surgery that made him one of them?

"They can tell you're getting overwhelmed," Archie said. "The Choir didn't bring you here just to blow your minds." A little laugh. It sounded wrong. Forced, maybe. Valk could see that Archie's heart was beating far too fast. Maybe he was the one who was in danger of being overstimulated. "Why don't we move somewhere less... out in the open, where we can talk more comfortably?"

"Sure," Lanoe said. "You have some kind of conference room near here?"

That forced laugh again. Why was the man so agitated?

"Something like that. Please, if you'll follow me...?"

Lanoe ordered the four marines to stand guard around the cutter—their only way out of the city of the Choir, should something go wrong. Then he let Archie lead him and Valk out of the plaza, to what seemed to be a small tram station. They climbed into an open car that ran on a cable snaking through the city's narrow streets.

Towers and grand, wide buildings of dark stone rose to surround them. The car moved silently, barely rocking, at high velocity. They saw choristers on either side of the street, but none of them ever seemed to need to jump out of the way of the speeding vehicle. No, of course they wouldn't, Valk thought. They would have sensed Archie coming long before they needed to move.

"I'm so bloody excited to see you here," Archie said, leaning over the back of his seat. "The Blue Devil! I've heard all about your exploits, of course, but I wager you've plenty of stories about your adventures since I left Tiamat."

"Uh," Valk said. Lanoe was giving him a meaningful look. "Sure. Maybe we can compare notes later."

"Of course, of course," Archie said. "You've so much to see here, I doubt you want to talk about human things. But promise me we'll get the chance. It's been so long—I. Well. I suppose after a while, I gave up hope I would see a friendly human face again. I've made a sort of life for myself here."

"It's a stroke of good luck for us, you being here," Valk pointed out. "So we can talk to the Choir."

"They would have found some way to chat, even without me. They're very clever," Archie said.

"Sure," Lanoe said. "Once we take you away from here, though—"

"Away? Perish the thought! After so many years, this is my home," Archie told them. "No, thank you, good sirs, but I'm perfectly happy right here."

Valk could see the nervous tension in Archie's muscles. The way neurons in his brain fired like crazy. He was lying. For some reason he had to claim to want to stay here, but it was quite evident he desperately wanted to get away.

Valk couldn't make any sense of it. It made him uncomfortable. To change the subject, he pointed at the buildings they passed. "What's this, some kind of shopping district?" Wide spaces open to the street. Inside he could see piles of goods—foodstuffs, maybe, in profuse variety. Black dresses hanging on rows of hooks. Furniture, mostly benches of various size and pattern, high tables and round cabinets with folding doors. A hundred other things, the purpose of which he could hardly imagine—tools, maybe, art objects. One shop was full of cones of burning incense; another sold large jugs of a pinkish liquid.

"In a manner of speaking. Not commerce as you and I would know it, of course," Archie said. "If they need a thing, they come here and get it, no questions asked. All of it handmade with loving craft, all of it free of charge. The Choir would make old Karl Marx proud."

"Who?" Lanoe asked.

"Economic philosopher from Earth," Valk said. "Before even your time." Marxian theory had been popular among the Establishmentarians, because it had predicted the rise of institutions like the polys—and theoretically, it had provided suggestions on how to fight them. The Crisis had come before any of his theories could be put into practice, and afterward the polys had made sure Marx's works were banned.

Lanoe shrugged and looked away. Valk had never known him to be much interested in politics.

"What you're telling me," Valk said, "is that they don't use money."

"Not hardly," Archie assented.

"But then why would anyone make all of this lovingly crafted stuff, if they're not getting paid?"

"Consensus," Archie said. "They agree among themselves that a thing needs to be built, say a lamp or a picture of a landscape. Then whoever happens to be handy at the moment just goes and does it. As for what they get out of it, well, the Choir will remember the one who did the work, and think fondly of her. If the thing she built was especially grand, then she'll be lauded for their effort. Then, the next time something needs deciding, her opinion will be especially sought after. Prestige is the incentive, you see, not some abstract coinage."

Valk didn't see it at all. "What if one of them, a, uh—"

"Chorister," Lanoe suggested. "That's what you call a member of a choir."

Valk nodded. "What if a chorister can't work? If they're injured, or just not as skilled as the others?"

"Ah, but there's great prestige in being kind to the less fortunate. A sick chorister will find all of her neighbors queuing up for the chance to bring her comfort and aid."

"No money," Valk said, knowing he was repeating himself. "So what holds them together? Religion?"

"Consensus," Archie replied. "No gods, nothing like that. They have a certain spiritual belief in their purpose in the universe. And they hold a distinct reverence for harmony. It's the key to understanding everything about them. They are a choir, you see, and a choir must be in harmony to be effective. They strive to maximize unity."

"What about…what about law? You say they don't have any leaders, but then how do they resolve their differences? Do they ever sue each other? What about crime? Do they punish each other?"

"Consensus." It was beginning to sound to Valk like Archie was reciting a script that he'd memorized. Or perhaps like a sales pitch. "Disputes are moderated by the entire city at once, everyone's voice added to the whole. Crime happens, of course, though no one can ever get away with a thing if everyone else is listening to their every thought. Petty crime is met by communal shaming. Crimes of passion or extremity, so to speak—violence—is punished by consensual decree. Typically the loss of prestige is enough to prevent a reoccurrence."

"Huh." Valk tried to think. "What about war?"

Archie shrugged. "Consensus," he said. "They argue among themselves. Work things out, correct misunderstandings, hear out all grievances."

"They don't have war," Lanoe said, looking at Archie intently, as if he couldn't believe what he'd heard. Well, it was a hard thing for a soldier to accept. There was more to it than that, though. If the Choir didn't fight, if they didn't have weapons—that might limit how useful they could be in his crusade against the Blue-Blue-White.

"Not...as such," Archie said. "Imagine heated debates that go on for weeks, with every side shouting down the other. It gets spirited, but it never quite reaches the level of violence. In their ancient history they scrapped like devils, they tell me. But none of them has so much as lifted a stick against her sisters, not for a very long time."

"Sisters," Valk said. "You keep referring to them as 'she.' What about the males of the species. Are they any different?"

Archie laughed. "The choristers are all female. The tall ones, the...the sapient ones you saw back there, all of the choristers you'll talk to in the city."

"So how do they reproduce?" Lanoe asked. "Without males, I mean. Do they just, I don't know, bud off or something?"

"Oh, they have males. You've seen those, too. The little ones."

Lanoe's eyes went wide. "You mean—the bugs that crawl on them? Those things?"

"They don't grow any bigger than that, and their brains never develop. They're no smarter than spiders," Archie said. "The females carry them around. They kind of...collect them. When they want to have a baby, they always have a few males around, ready to...you know."

Lanoe clearly wanted more information on that, but Valk had thought of something else. "You said they don't fight wars, okay, I guess that's possible. But what if one of them goes crazy? Starts attacking people in the street, or decides she's the one and true queen of the Choir?" He wanted to know how a species of telepaths could handle an individual with deranged patterns of thought. Their instability could infect the entire city. They must have some mechanism for coping.

"Let me guess," Lanoe said. "Consensus."

Archie looked away. "Mental illness. It's...well. It's a tricky subject. It's..."

Perhaps he would have said more. Instead, his face fell and his eyes quivered in their sockets and for a moment his head flared with microwave emissions.

It couldn't be a coincidence. The Choir must have been listening to their conversation the whole time. Listening, and waiting to jump in if Archie said something they didn't want said.

When he came back, he didn't finish his thought. Instead he looked at both of them and smiled. "Almost there," he told them. "We're expected."

⸺

Archie led them into a tower at the edge of the commercial street, a tall, round structure with a spiral ramp inside that took them past four floors, each of them completely open to view. Inside choristers were busy with various tasks—on the lowest level Lanoe saw them measuring fluids into jars, taking scrupulous care to get exactly the same amount in each container. The next floor up was—he thought—a sculptor's studio, where a pair of choristers worked with hot tools, carving pieces of stone. He had no idea what was being done on the third floor. It seemed to involve a group of choristers standing in a circle and chirping at each other. Were they sharing a funny joke? Planning a party? Communing with the spirit of consensus?

The fourth floor, and their destination, seemed to be office space. Broad windows let in a little radiance from the lighthouse towers dotted around the city, revealing a room full of stools and horseshoe-shaped desks. Like all the other rooms he'd seen, it took up the entirety of the level, but there was only one chorister present. He realized he'd never seen one of them alone before. She looked like all the others, of course—he wondered if he would ever be able to tell them apart, and what that said about him.

The chorister was surrounded by displays that floated in the air, with no minder or emitter surface visible. The displays were 2-D only, but they wrapped around her like a cylinder, various images and screens moving in and out as she reached for them with her four claws. As they came up the ramp, she reached out behind her and dismissed all of the displays, then climbed off her stool to come toward them, lifting all four arms in greeting.

"This is Water-Falling-from-a-Height," Archie said, once they'd caught their breath from climbing up the ramp. Valk, of course, wasn't affected at all, damn him. "Or just call her Water-Falling; she's fine with that."

"Pleased to...meet you," Lanoe said. Four floors wouldn't normally have winded him, but the Choir were half again as tall as humans, which meant he'd climbed the equivalent of six human stories.

Water-Falling held out one of her claws.

"She's heard about the human custom of shaking hands," Archie said. "She wonders if you'd be willing...?"

Lanoe looked down at her hand, twice the size of one of his. Four wicked, armored claws coming together to a single point. It looked like if he put his hand in there he would get a stump back.

He hadn't come all this way to be timid. He stuck out his hand and the claws closed around it. He braced himself for the moment when she crushed his fingers, but it never came. Instead he felt that the insides of her claws were lined with dozens of round, velvety pads, which gave her a soft and precise grip. She lifted her claw once, then dropped it again, letting go.

"You're a braver man than I am," Valk whispered.

Lanoe ignored him.

"Water-Falling is one of the most eminent members of the Choir," Archie said. "She gained an enormous amount of respect a while back when one of the city's towers collapsed, with thirty-three choristers still inside. No fatalities, thank goodness."

"She helped rescue them?" Lanoe asked.

"She organized the relief effort, making sure the injured all had adequate medical care and new housing, and she wrote a song of mourning for the building that was lost. Ever since she's been famous for devoting herself to civil service. When you asked if you could talk to their leader, they discussed what that would even mean. Water-Falling volunteered to meet with you one-on-one—something the Choir would normally never do—and act as a sort of spokeswoman."

Lanoe smiled and nodded. The Choir had no leaders, no hierarchy, he'd heard that several times now. All choristers were equal, in every way. Though when you put out a call for an important task, it seemed some of them volunteered faster than others.

Interesting.

"She's happy to speak with you, answer your questions, make suggestions about how talks should proceed, all that sort of thing," Archie said. "Just pretend I'm not here, right? Right. Just treat me like a translator."

Lanoe had to admit he felt much more comfortable talking to a single being, rather than an entire species at once. Even if he knew it was an illusion. Anything he said to this Water-Falling would be rebroadcast to the rest of the Choir, in real time.

"She says that you should sit," Archie told them.

Lanoe looked around and saw nothing but the high stools the Choir used. He perched atop one, his feet dangling in the air. Valk was at least able to get his toes on the floor. "Thank you for meeting with us," he said.

The castaway's face jumped, and his eyes started to glaze over. Lanoe wondered if he would ever get used to that. "She says you're very welcome. She says that she has already drafted an agenda for your visit here, and she wants to make sure you're comfortable with it. She's especially worried that she's packed too many things into the day. There's going to be a visit to the water reservoir, that's really a sight worth seeing, and a banquet this evening where you'll have a chance to sample Choir foods. There will be entertainment, there will...ah, well..."

Lanoe glanced over at Valk, but the big pilot was just nodding, going along with this. Lanoe tried to fight down his impatience.

"Well, the entertainment might be a sticking point, er. They've planned for you to observe a performance of..." Archie coughed. "Lovemaking."

That got Lanoe's attention. "I'm sorry? What?"

"It's...what they do for fun, of an evening," Archie said. The left side of his face had flushed with embarrassment. The right side looked like it was paralyzed. Clearly he was in communion with the Choir, but there was still some human bashfulness there, too. Water-Falling wasn't just talking through him, she was telling him what to say. "No blasted privacy, you see. They do everything out in the open. Even...sex. I've, well, seen it, and it is quite diverting. A cross between a sporting match and a bit of ballroom dancing. The exchange of males is rather an involved ceremony, as reproduction is a rare event among the Choir."

"I think," Lanoe said, "we might skip that. Unless they'll be offended if we don't go."

"It's already been scheduled, is the thing, and if they have to change their plans now—"

Lanoe silenced him with a look. Then he leaned forward until he nearly toppled off his stool. "In fact," he said, addressing Water-Falling directly, "I'm not sure we have time for any of these events. I'd really like to get talking about why we're here. About the message you sent."

If Water-Falling was offended by his abruptness, he had no way to tell. She made a gesture he couldn't understand at all—lifting two of her claws to her head while the other two hung loose at her sides.

Lanoe didn't wait for a translation. Sometimes, he thought, the direct approach was better. Hell, for most of his life, the direct approach had been the only one he'd ever tried. "I didn't come all this way for a cultural exchange. I came because I was promised help with fighting the Blue-Blue-White. Yes? The alien drones that attacked our planet Niraya, who've wiped out every intelligent species in the galaxy. Except the Choir, and us. You do know what I'm talking about? Big damned jellyfish, like to make their drones do their killing for them? Sound familiar?"

"Oh, yes," Archie said. A tremor ran through the left side of his body. "Oh, indeed. The Choir know all about the Blue-Blue-White."

Lanoe nodded. "Honestly, I was very much surprised to find the Choir here. My associate, Tannis Valk, was able to gain access to the computer that directed the alien drones. He learned a great deal about our common enemy. About the worlds they've devastated. He never found any mention of a species like the Choir."

Water-Falling slumped sideways on her stool. Lanoe didn't know how to read that.

"There's a good reason for that," Archie told him. "A long time ago, the Blue-Blue-White attacked the Choir. You saw their old planet out there, beyond the portal."

"We found evidence of that attack," Lanoe confirmed.

"I don't doubt it. The—the jellyfish, as you call them, sent exactly two hundred and twenty-five of their killer drones down to the surface. The Choir weren't prepared for an attack like that. There were perhaps a billion living choristers at the time, but every single one of them died in the space of a few weeks. The Blue-Blue-White slaughtered every living animal on that planet, everything bigger than a paramecium. They kept at it, working day and night, until the job was complete."

Archie was crying, Lanoe saw. Tears rolled down his cheek as he told the story. Lanoe figured he must be plugged into the Choir's emotional state, and it seemed he was feeling their loss and regret.

"There were a few survivors—those choristers who were out in space at the time of the attack, crews of starships who were out on missions of peaceful outreach. They came home as soon as they could, but it was already too late—the world was already dead. Their grief overwhelmed them—so many voices silenced. So many notes missing from the harmony. Many of them took their own lives, rather than face living in a galaxy that held this kind of horror. Those who were able to pull themselves together managed to rebuild. They put their planet back together piece by piece. Cremated the dead, repaired their cities. Got on with life.

"For generations, they lived with that story. It made them fearful of the world beyond their sky. They clung close to each other, and spurned all other species, and their hearts grew cold. But they did what they had to. They started down the long road to recovery, to learning to trust the future.

"Until the Blue-Blue-White came back.

"There were no starship crews flung across the galaxy, this time. The Choir had closed itself off, isolated themselves. They put up a brave fight—they'd developed many new weapons in the intervening years—but the alien drones had changed. They had developed new weapons, and there were so many more of them, the second time. They kept coming, wave after wave after wave of them. In the end it was too much.

"After the second massacre, there were only twelve of them left. Twelve survivors, in the entire universe."

Lanoe thought of the statues he'd seen back on the planet, the ones that opened the portal to the Choir's city. The twelve statues there. He'd thought of them as a piece of sculpture, a work of art. But they must be more than that, he realized—they were a monument.

"It was clear to the twelve that the nightmare would never end. They knew there were other fleets out there, other legions of drones waiting to sterilize the planet a third time if they tried to rebuild."

"They must have wanted revenge," Lanoe suggested. "They must have wanted to fight back."

"Perhaps," Archie told him. "But think about it this way. If your entire population—the entire future of your species—came down to twelve individuals. Would you want to start picking fights?

"No, they needed to survive, first. So they hid themselves away. They built this city, and the bubble of wormspace around it. Like rats hiding in the walls of the galaxy, they cut themselves off from sunlight. From fresh air. They learned how to recycle every drop of water, every particle of food. How to survive in a place never meant for habitation, a place that should have been antithetical to life. Because they had to. Even now, there are only a few thousand of us. All descendants of those twelve. Painfully aware of just how close we came to disappearing from the galaxy, like so many other species have."

Lanoe noted how Archie's speech had changed—how he'd gone from talking about the Choir as "they" to "us." He figured Water-Falling's passions must be riding high, that she was expressing herself so intently now that Archie was lost in the translation.

"The Blue-Blue-White don't have any records of us, you say. Good. The Blue-Blue-White don't bother memorializing the species they've wiped out. If they think we're extinct—good.

"The Choir remembers the Blue-Blue-White very well. The Choir will never be able to forget them."

"I'm sorry," Lanoe said. "If I came off as aggressive, or harsh—"

"Water-Falling was not offended," Archie said. "Others were."

"I'm...sorry? What?"

"You've forgotten already, haven't you? This is the problem with speaking face-to-face. The problem is that you aren't. Every word you say, M. Lanoe—every gesture, every time you roll your eyes—is spoken to the entirety of the Choir at once. Some of them were deeply hurt by your insinuative manner. Others applauded your desire to get down to business. A small minority found your remarks funny. In general, the trend is toward forgiveness. For now."

Lanoe clamped his mouth shut before he could say anything more.

A green pearl appeared in the corner of his vision. Valk, sending him a private message:

Boss, if your plan was to antagonize the locals, I'd say you're off to a great start.

Valk watched Archie's head while Lanoe was talking to the chorister. He was fascinated by the complex ripples, the ever-changing side-lobe emissions of the microwaves flowing in and out of the castaway's head. The waves weren't strong enough to cook the man's brains from the inside out, but there was enough power there that Valk could trace them as they propagated through the city, touching the antenna brains of choristers all around them, on the floors below, in the buildings next door.

Unfortunately the signals were too complex for even Valk to understand what they meant. For one thing they were analog, not digital, and encoded in a format he'd never seen. He remembered having once visited the Diyu system, where all the signs in the stores were required to be printed in both English and Mandarin. Decoding the Choir's transmissions would be like trying to work out what those printed logograms meant without a dictionary. You could tell that something was being communicated, but it was impossible to even know what kind of alphabet was being used—those logograms, Valk knew, sometimes represented whole words, and sometimes combinations of words, and sometimes just sounds.

He calculated that he could probably learn to read the Choir's signals, but that it would take him six years of study. Five if he didn't have to work with Lanoe at the same time.

Lanoe—oh, no—with a start, Valk was pulled back into his body, into the present moment. He hadn't realized how far he'd strayed. For a moment he worried someone might have noticed that he'd disappeared into his own thoughts, but no, of course they hadn't. Valk had written a subroutine just for that purpose, a program to make it look like he was paying attention, even when he was far away. Reviewing his logs, he saw that he had nodded at all the right places and even sent Lanoe a sarcastic message.

This whole business of copying and multi-threading his consciousness might be getting a little out of hand, he thought.

"—have a common enemy," Lanoe said. "Common ground for

understanding. It's not that I don't appreciate what you're trying to do, and I think it would be valuable for our two species to meet at that level and learn from one another. But I'm a military man, and my first priority has to be the defense of humanity."

"Water-Falling understands," Archie said. "And she signals partial agreement. That, uh, that's what it means when she holds up one hand and lowers the other three, yes? You see how one of them is higher than the others? That suggests she might be open to persuasion."

Lanoe nodded. "Sure. I'm afraid I'm not a great talker. I like things to be plain. Understandable. So let's get this on the table. I came here because you—the Choir—sent a message to one of our ships. That message congratulated us on destroying one of the Blue-Blue-White's queenships, and saving a planet from their killer drones. The imagery in that message—"

Water-Falling gestured and a display lit up near her right side, showing the footage of the queenship exploding.

"Right," Lanoe said. "You see that little dot, there, flying away from the explosion?"

Water-Falling expanded the image until the dot was clearly visible as two humans in suits, holding on to each other.

"That's M. Valk, and myself. We did that. I won't say we didn't have any help, but...we didn't have much. It was a close thing and we lost...some very important people in that battle."

"Water-Falling is curious," Archie said, "why you're bringing this up."

"To make it clear what my motivation is. The Choir should know that," Lanoe said. "The Blue-Blue-White weren't there, at Niraya. They sent their drones to do their fighting for them. I have devoted myself, and the rest of my life, to taking the battle to the damned jellyfish themselves. To forcing them to stop these fleets, to end the killing. If they refuse, if they won't, if they can't—then I intend to bring justice down upon their heads."

"Well said," Archie told them, though it was unclear, for once, whether he was speaking for himself or for the Choir.

"You've promised us your help in fighting the Blue-Blue-White. I'm very grateful for your offer, and I want to take advantage of it as soon as is physically possible. If you have warships to add to the cause, that's great. You mentioned that the Choir developed new weapons to fight the killer drones. I can use every arrow that I can get in my quiver, if, ah—did she understand that reference?"

"She did, but—"

"If she has information about the Blue-Blue-White that I lack, I'll take it. Hellfire, the Choir seems to know the wormhole network a lot better than we do. If they can just point us in the direction of the Blue-Blue-White homeworld, just that would be a huge help."

"She is emphatic about the fact there are no wormholes that go there," Archie said. "And there never will be."

Lanoe frowned. It was one of his thoughtful frowns. Valk knew that look—it meant he'd just noticed something but was still processing what it meant.

"The point is I'll take whatever they're offering. Why are you looking at me like that?"

Archie had, in fact, turned an ashen color. Valk remembered how agitated the castaway had seemed on the ride to this tower, how elevated his heartbeat had been, how heavily he'd been breathing. The effect was even more noticeable now.

He signaled Lanoe. *He's afraid of something. Terrified.*

"There may have been a wee little miscommunication," Archie said.

"What are you getting at?" Lanoe demanded.

"The message we sent—well, not to beat too far around the bush, I wrote it. The English bits, at the very least. I was trying for succinctness, and rather missed precision, I'm afraid."

Lanoe glared at the man. Perhaps he knew what was coming. To Valk it was a complete mystery.

"The message read 'we can help,' and that's accurate. As far as it goes. But the help they're offering is of a specific variety, and it's none of the things you mentioned. To be frank, the Choir are a bit puzzled why humanity sent a warship here. They were expecting a diplomatic mission. If I had any part in this confusion, then, really, I just wish to—"

"Get to the point before I wring your neck," Lanoe said.

"They're not offering to help you fight the Blue-Blue-White's attacks," Archie explained. "They want to help you survive them."

Chapter Twenty-Seven

It had felt damned good to be back in the cockpit of a BR.9. With nothing but light duties to do onboard the cruiser, and then with the nightmare of the cold wormhole traverse, Bury had felt himself going a little stir crazy. Just being out, flying on his own recognizance, helped a lot. He'd even felt himself smile once or twice as Lieutenant Candless had them run through formations around the unnamed planet. It was almost like being back at Rishi, almost like when he'd taken his first solo flights, when for the first time he'd felt the exhilaration, the utter freedom, of flying alone through infinite space.

At least—it had felt that way for the first six hours of the patrol. Now, with his back cramping up, with his fingers sore from holding tight to his control stick, flying had lost a little of its luster. He was getting tired, too, his eyes losing focus for whole seconds at a time, his head drifting forward inside his helmet. With no word from the other side of the wormhole, with nothing to look at but the fat green planet below them, it was getting tough to stay sharp.

Until a blue light started blinking on his tactical board. A light that indicated that a non-allied craft had been detected insystem.

That woke him up in a hurry.

"I want everyone to remain calm," Lieutenant Candless called on the general radio circuit, once she'd confirmed they'd all seen it.

"I've received additional sensor data from the cruiser. There's been an indication of some movement out in the system. Near the wormhole throat, to be precise. Too far out to get any good imagery—it could very well be a false positive. One of our scopes might have picked up a passing asteroid, or perhaps a piece of debris we left behind when we arrived here. I'm still awaiting verification."

"Eyeballs peeled, in other words," Lieutenant Maggs cut in. "And should you see any hexagons, remember they make handy targets."

"Cut that chatter," Lieutenant Candless called. She sounded supremely annoyed. It was a tone of voice Bury knew all too well. "We would all do well to remember Navy protocol, just now. Especially the part about chain of command."

"A thousand pardons," Lieutenant Maggs called back, but then he cut himself out of the general circuit before he could be chastised again.

Bury had to admit a grudging respect for the man—he seemed to live without a care for who he offended, and he certainly never offered a genuine apology. Perhaps in time Bury would prove himself and he could afford to act that way, and then he would waste no time telling Lieutenant Candless exactly what he—

A green pearl appeared in the corner of his vision. An incoming call from Ginger. He accepted it right away. "Bury," she said. "Bury, I need to talk."

He swung his head around, trying to locate her fighter. It was far enough away to just be a bright dot over by the limb of the planet. He couldn't see anything else near her, no enemy ships or any sign of danger. "What's going on?" he asked. "Did you see something, or—"

"Shut up, Bury. That's not what I meant." He listened to her sigh for a while without interrupting. "You know what this is about."

He wasn't sure he did. Unless—

"If there *is* something there," she said. "If Centrocor has caught up with us...I don't know what I'm going to do."

"You mean—you're not sure if you can fight."

"I don't know if I can even pull a trigger," she told him. "Bury, you know me better than anyone else here. You know I'm not just flighty. What we talked about, back in my bunk. You know that wasn't just temporary jitters."

"Maybe, Ginj. Maybe, but—"

"I'm not going to be any use to anybody. Everybody's counting on me, and I know I'm just going to be a liability."

"Come on," he told her. "If we do get into a scrap—if I'm in trouble. Or Lieutenant Candless gets pinned down, I bet you would fight then. You would fight to defend us."

"Maybe," Ginger said. "I actually like you, Bury. Despite just about everything you've ever done or said, you're still my classmate, and that counts for something. And I owe Lieutenant Candless a lot. But when I picture it in my head, all I see is me, freezing up. Going numb and not doing anything. Not shooting, not even running away."

"You're talking yourself into a self-fulfilling prophecy."

"Bury, if it happens. If I lock up and can't shoot. They'll court-martial me. Throw me in the brig. I'll be disgraced. My whole family will be dishonored. But I can't take another life. I can't do it."

Bury tried to think of words that would calm her down. He could hear her hyperventilating and he knew if she had a full-blown panic attack now she might actually run away or do something drastic. He didn't even like to think about what.

"Ginger," he said, "just take it easy. Breathe for me. Just breathe, okay? Most likely this is nothing."

"What?"

"You heard Lieutenant Candless. She said it might be a false positive. I *believe* that. Okay?"

"You believe it," she said. "You believe it because—"

"Because we beat those bastards once. I don't think they have the guts to try us again. Ginger, I'm telling you right now. We aren't fighting today. It's just not going to happen."

"...yeah?" she asked, her voice tiny.

"This is just a routine patrol. *Nothing* is going to happen. Come on, Ginger. Breathe for me. Let me hear you breathe."

He listened as she inhaled and exhaled, each breath coming slower and deeper. Good, that was good. Maybe he was really having an effect.

He just hoped he hadn't told her a terrible lie.

For all of Lanoe's attempts to keep them focused on business, the Choir were adamant. The agenda of events had to go forward.

Lanoe and Valk were taken on a tour of the city in an open-topped aircar. Its engine was so quiet and the ride so smooth it felt like they were drifting along in a hot air balloon. Water-Falling pointed out various sights and Archie gave them a running commentary on what they saw.

There was no sun in the bubble of wormspace, and the ghost-light from the distant walls shed no more illumination than the stars would on a night on Earth. Mostly the Choir worked in well-lit buildings, but parts of the city—its industrial sections, some largely automated infrastructural regions—were kept dark to save energy. If the Choir needed to access those areas, they would be lit up by one of the tall lighthouses, which shed beams that could be directed anywhere in the city. "There's a keeper in each tower, someone in charge of nothing but directing the light where it needs to go. It's considered a solemn duty, and only the most trusted choristers are chosen. They need to listen always for the will of the people to know when they need to shift the light."

"Fascinating," Lanoe said. He just wished they could get on with this. He very much wanted to see what kind of help the Choir were offering—though he'd begun to doubt it would be anything like what he wanted.

The aircar moved on, dipping low between two rows of high buildings. Water-Falling gestured at a street lined with statues of the Surviving Twelve and a park kept permanently empty and unoccupied as a memorial to all those who had been lost. "The Choir have a long memory, and they think forward well into the future," Archie said. "History is always with them."

"How long ago did the Twelve build this place?" Valk asked.

"Hard to say, really. They don't have the same idea of time we do. To them history's more about relationships, about the thoughts, the feelings, not the facts. It's all a bit...layered. Events occur, things happen, and then they get discussed, and the discussions get analyzed, and then they make comments on the analysis. So you can talk about 'the second invasion,' but then you also have to talk about 'how we feel now about the second invasion,' but they'd say you were still being imprecise unless you recited all the poetry about 'the second invasion,' and then somebody's reinterpretation of 'the second invasion' will come into favor, and how that reinterpretation changes the way you hear the poetry about it..." Archie chuckled. "A bit thick, hmm? To them, of course, it's just how things are ordered. You measure how long ago something was by how many layers of commentary it's built up."

Lanoe thought it sounded needlessly pedantic, but he knew better than to say anything. The Choir were listening. They were always listening.

"How long have you been here?" Valk asked.

"Seventeen years, nine months, and twenty-one days," Archie said, without hesitation.

The car dipped to pass under a massive, figured arch, then headed down a long inclined shaft. Around them yellow windows shed a little light on a broad tunnel lined with thin bricks. Water sluiced downward through the tunnel, and the echoing noise of it was loud enough Lanoe couldn't hear his own thoughts, much less what their tour guide had to say. It didn't bother him much— he had very little interest in how the Choir organized their infra-structure. He watched the rippling water below, saw how it foamed when it crashed against the walls.

When a hand fell on his shoulder—a hand, not a claw—he was so startled he had to grab the aircar's railing. He turned and saw Archie standing right behind him. He couldn't hear what the castaway said, but from the way his mouth moved, Lanoe thought maybe it started with "please." He shrugged, not understanding. Archie's face fell, and he shook his head, then repeated his message. "Please," he was definitely saying "please." Lanoe got that much, then something that was maybe "home."

A green pearl appeared in the corner of Lanoe's eye. A message from Valk.

He's begging us to take him home with us when we leave. For some reason he thinks he can't say that while the Choir are listening. He thinks they can't hear him in this tunnel.

Lanoe glanced over at Water-Falling, where she stood at the prow of the aircar. She appeared to be looking down at the water, but of course the choristers had eyes in the backs of their heads.

Lanoe looked back at the castaway's face. Looked him right in the eye and gave a tiny nod. He tried mouthing "Are you okay?" but Archie couldn't seem to understand.

He's wrong, Valk sent. *She can hear him better than you can.*

Lanoe gave Archie a discreet nod—mostly just to keep him from saying anything else. At least for the moment.

They descended for several minutes, then emerged into an open space so large Lanoe couldn't see the walls. Below them the outflow from the tunnel cascaded into an enormous spherical mass of water that seemed to hang, unsupported, in the air. Out in the middle of the water, on a tiny island of rock, stood a lighthouse that shone its beam upon them, and for a second Lanoe could see nothing else.

When his eyes had adjusted he turned toward Archie, to see if he could repeat his question now that they could hear each other. Instead he saw that Archie's face had gone slack, his tongue hanging out of one corner of his mouth.

"The central reservoir," Archie said, his voice flat, emotionless. "This is the ultimate source and destination of all the water in the city. In fact, the city was built around it. It's much more than just a big puddle, though. The Choir has done some fancy tricks with density and quantum superposition, do not ask me for any details as they're quite outside my pay grade, but somehow this place generates the local gravity as well..."

Whatever Archie had tried to tell him in the tunnel, it looked like it was going to have to wait.

———— ⚡ ————

The blue light on Bury's tactical board never went away. For what felt like hours the four of them held formation and maintained silence while Lieutenant Candless stayed in contact with the cruiser, making use of its sensitive instruments, its telescopes, its radars and lidars, its hyperspectral imagers and passive millimeter-wave interferometers.

Occasionally Bury would hear her muttering to herself. It took him a while to realize he was actually hearing one side of a conversation she was having with Engineer Paniet:

"Whatever it is, it's small, and fast—thought I had it there."

"A strong magnet will find a needle in a haystack. This is harder."

"Here, do you see this? Is that a glitch, or...no."

"No, I suppose that was too much to hope for."

When he could, he checked in with Ginger. Listened to her breathe.

"Very well," Lieutenant Candless said, eventually, finally. "Pilots, we're going to try to extend the range of our patrol. We'll split up into two teams. Maggs, you're with me. Ensigns, you two will—"

"What is it?" Ginger demanded, over the general circuit. "What did you find?"

Bury expected Lieutenant Candless to upbraid her for breaking silence. Instead, their former instructor actually answered a question, for once.

"We're seeing some indication that a Centrocor vehicle has entered the system."

Bury's blood ran cold, but only for a moment. "The carrier?" he asked. "The carrier is here?"

"No," Lieutenant Candless replied. "One of its scouts, perhaps.

It's a standard tactic, when approaching a potentially hostile system, to send one small vehicle ahead to get the lay of the land. If that *is* what we're seeing—and I make no guarantees—then it could be as much as a day ahead of the carrier. Whatever it is, it hasn't made any threatening moves. Most likely it's hanging back near this system's wormhole throat, looking for us. If it sees us it may attempt to retreat without engaging. We have to make sure that doesn't happen, yes? I need you all to acknowledge. That means you should say 'yes,' now."

"A good old-fashioned snipe hunt. How diverting. That's a 'yes,'" Lieutenant Maggs replied.

"Yes," Bury said, his voice sounding about an octave too high in his own ears. He waited for Ginger to echo him. After far too long, she did.

"Yes," she said.

"All right. As I was saying, Ensigns, I want you to break orbit and head antispin, back in toward the star and the wormhole throat. I want you to run silent and dark—don't even flare your thrusters, we don't want to scare them into running. Maggs and I will take the opposite trajectory and together we'll form a pincers. If you do find our target, and if you are absolutely certain you can destroy it before it gets away, you may fire at will. Otherwise try to get between it and the wormhole throat. This is crucial, Ensigns. The mission and the safety of the cruiser depend on us here. Do you understand my orders?"

"Yes," Bury said. Hoping he sounded a little more resolute, this time.

"Yes," Ginger said. Faster than before.

"Then get to it," Lieutenant Candless said. "Good hunting."

The aircar moved through broad passages, deep under the city. Water-Falling and Archie pointed out various sights of interest—enormous machines huddling in the dark that generated the

Choir's power, cleaned their water, and generated their food. Lanoe supposed Paniet might have found it all deeply fascinating. There were too many thoughts in his head to let him care much.

He did his best to look interested, so as not to offend their hosts more than he already had. It was hard, sometimes, to remember that the Choir couldn't hear his thoughts—not unless he had an antenna installed, like the one they'd put in Archie's brain. He could even communicate privately with Valk, a little, by sending text-only messages back and forth between their suits. Valk was certain the Choir weren't able to pick up on their radio communications.

Still, the weight of being constantly on guard, of watching the words he spoke aloud, started to get to him. When Archie announced that the tour was complete, he considered excusing himself and taking the cutter back to the Hoplite. Apparently, though, they weren't quite done with the Choir's hospitality.

Their next event was a banquet in their honor, followed by the evening's entertainment. The Choir had at least agreed not to make the humans attend the live sex performance they'd originally planned. Instead they were going to be treated to something called an "apportation show."

"It's a little like a magic act," Archie explained. "It's pretty impressive. I think you'll like it."

The aircar dropped them off in front of a large building not far from the central amphitheater, where they'd first set down. Hundreds of choristers were already there waiting for them, lined up on either side of the door.

As they headed inside, Archie gestured for Lanoe and Valk to stand back. "Here's something special, built just for this occasion," he said, as a team of choristers came toward them carrying, of all things, human-sized chairs and a small table just for their use. The furniture was taken inside and set up in the middle of a wide hall that was otherwise empty, a tiny island of comfort in a cold, huge room. The temperature rose as the Choir filed inside, hundreds of them filling up all the space.

"Where are they going to sit?" Lanoe asked.

"The Choir eat standing up. It might look a bit bizarre, chaps. Just keep in mind they evolved on a completely different planet from us."

A line of choristers entered, all carrying long glass tubes full of yellow liquid. They placed their burdens on the floor and one by one the banquet guests moved to twitch their skirts up over the tubes, then lowered themselves onto the tubes so they could suck up their contents.

"Their mouths are, ahem. Underneath their skirts," Archie explained. "Different body plan than ours, eh? I did warn you. Ah. Here, they'd like you to have a go yourselves, though thankfully they've been courteous enough to provide spoons. Chairs, a table, spoons. How lucky you blokes are—seventeen years and I never got this treatment!"

Dishes of the yellow liquid were brought out and placed on the table before them. Lanoe took up his spoon and, very conscious of the fact the entire Choir was watching, lifted a little of the yellow stuff to his mouth. "Is this safe?" he asked. "You said everything on their planet was poisonous to humans."

"That was the plant life. The Choir don't eat their vegetables. This is guaranteed nontoxic, full of important nutrients," Archie said, and as if to prove it he spooned some of the liquid into his own mouth.

Lanoe nodded and took a taste. The liquid was tepid, greasy, and bland and slightly loathsome. A little like eating bacon grease as if it were soup. He struggled to get it down, and not to show his displeasure.

All around him the Choir erupted in excited chirping. Archie looked like he might rupture his organs, he laughed so hard. "I said it wasn't poison. I never said it was good!"

"It's very...filling," Lanoe said. He looked over at Valk. "You— eat up."

Valk shrugged. "No problem. I can switch off my taste buds."

"What is this?" Lanoe asked Archie. "Do I even want to know?"

"Oh, it's completely synthetic. No worries there. It's supposed to resemble the Choir's favorite food back when there were animals on their planet. Imagine a little dog-sized deer, except with the head of a stag beetle. Now liquefy its innards, and—"

Lanoe gently pushed the bowl away from himself.

He thought the Choir would never stop chirping.

The volume of space the snipe hunt had to cover was enormous. The wormhole throat orbited a couple of million kilometers out from the system's star, a tiny, almost invisible distortion in space, a mote of dust floating in an empty coliseum. The cruiser had definitely seen something come through the throat, but had no idea which direction it had gone or how fast. A small craft, like a carrier scout, had no trouble getting lost in all that emptiness. Unless it made a point of signaling its location—which it had not—the only way to track its movements would be to look for the flare of its thrusters. The scout could simply cut its engines and disappear.

"Why doesn't he just run back to the wormhole?" Bury asked. "They sent him to see if we were here, right? To detect us before they commit any more ships to attacking this system. So why is he still hanging around?"

Though Bury was flying in close formation with Ginger, he knew he couldn't talk to her about this sort of thing. Instead he'd reached out to Lieutenant Maggs, over an encrypted comms laser. Making that connection had felt a little rebellious. The scout wouldn't be able to overhear their conversation, but still, Lieutenant Candless had instructed them to maintain radio silence.

Luckily, she couldn't overhear them, either.

"The pilot knows that as soon as we see him, we'll make short work of him," Maggs said. "It takes a special sort of fellow, really, to fly one of those scouts. No vector field, no armor, minimal weapons to defend one's self with. You have to be clever if you want to survive. He's cut his engines, switched off his canopy lights. He's relying on passive sensors only. Collecting as much information as he can. If he sees an opportunity to run, by hell he'll take it. Not until he's sure, though, and that gives us one chance to catch him."

"You've been in battles before. Real battles, I mean, not like that half-baked skirmish we got in last time we saw Centrocor," Bury said. "Is this kind of thing typical, this chasing each other's tails in the dark?"

"One would have to be a very poor scholar of military history," Maggs replied, "to think there was such a thing as a typical battle. Each is different, just as every lover you'll have in your life will be different. If you're asking if I've been on many snipe hunts, well, certainly. It's part of the job. Tactics is a kind of game, you see. You have certain pieces on the board—your warships. You know the rules they follow—their specifications, their capabilities. Each side's commander must commit those pieces in certain ways, and each may counter the other's move in certain ways. Yet there is enough variety to allow a seemingly infinite number of permutations."

Bury ignored the grandiloquence. "What I don't get, though, is—why send a scout ahead? Now that we've seen their scout, we know they're coming for us. The scout ruins the element of surprise."

"Oh, we already knew they were coming. At least, we feared it, which is enough. Military fellows are always paranoid. One must prepare for that. From what we saw last time, the commander of the carrier is no fool. He knows we're lying in wait. That the cruiser has better guns than he can bring to bear. He knows that we have talented pilots. If the carrier just blundered through the wormhole throat, we could shoot it down before its navigator had even figured out where they were."

Bury supposed he could see that. "So what do you do? I mean, if you were on their side, on Centrocor's side. What would you do?"

"Send one scout about a day in advance of my main force," Maggs said, as if he'd already thought of the answer and had just been waiting for someone to ask. "If it comes back, I'll have gained some information about my enemy. If it doesn't come back, I know, at the very least, that my enemy is there and ready for me. My next wave is a group of cataphract-class fighters, maybe a full squadron. I have them come screaming out of the throat at full speed, guns blazing. I'll lose many of them but they'll tie up my enemy's weapons systems, keep him busy. The third wave will be the carrier itself, with a screen of disposable carrier scouts to prevent a massive, decapitating strike while I'm still vulnerable. Because I'm commanding a carrier, I let loose with everything I have—every fighter in my vehicle bay—in the hopes that they can destroy the cruiser before it has a chance to open fire on me with its coilguns."

"Sounds risky," Bury said.

"War always is, my young friend. But the strategy I've laid out for you gives Centrocor an excellent chance."

"What, like fifty-fifty?"

"More like seventy-thirty," Maggs said. "Favoring Centrocor."

"Wait," Bury said. "Hold on." He'd been asking out of abstract curiosity. Suddenly the visualization in his head felt very real. "You're saying they could—"

"Kill us all? Well, yes."

"But we have Commander Lanoe on our side," Bury pointed out. "He's got a reputation for being sneaky. He'll find some way to—"

"Lanoe's reputation," Maggs said, the sneer in his voice almost dripping through Bury's headphones, "has taken on a life of its own. Don't believe everything you're told, Hellion. And let me remind you that at the moment—we *don't* have him. He's too busy having adventures on the far side of an impossible wormhole. Candless is in command. Your old teacher. What's her reputation, again? Hot stuff in her day, but she couldn't hack it in the long run?"

"Don't talk about her like that," Bury said.

"You have my most sincere apologies," Maggs simpered.

"Look, just because—" Bury cut off when a green pearl appeared in the corner of his vision. It was Ginger, no doubt still wrestling with her conscience. "I'm getting another call," he told Maggs. He cut out the comms laser, then tapped a virtual key on his comms panel to accept the new link.

"Bury," she said. "Bury—I think I saw something."

Her voice was raw and thin, edged with panic.

After the banquet there were dozens of introductions to be made. Water-Falling would lead a single chorister over to them so Lanoe and Valk could shake her hands—given the amount of chirping that accompanied the gesture, the Choir seemed to find human customs highly amusing—and then Water-Falling told them the name of the chorister they were meeting. "This is Wind-in-the-Trees-in-Summer," she said, through Archie.

"We're so sorry you had to be exposed to derangement," the new chorister said, again using Archie as her translator.

"I'm sorry," Lanoe said. "What?"

"She says it's a terrible shame that I had that breakdown in the tunnel. Honestly, he's been showing signs of serious depression for a while now."

Lanoe tried to meet Archie's eye, to see what he thought of the words he'd just translated. The castaway wouldn't look at him directly.

"He...seems fine to me," Lanoe said, trying to speak directly to Wind-in-the-Trees-in-Summer, but the chorister had already moved away, and another was taking her place.

"This is Pebbles-Ground-Under-Soft-Wheels," Archie said, and Water-Falling brought a new chorister to meet them.

Before they'd even finished shaking hands, the newcomer said—through Archie's mouth—"She hopes my outburst won't color your impression of the Choir. I've always been a little unstable, she says, but recently my thoughts have been nearly incoherent."

Lanoe clutched the chorister's claw, so she couldn't get away before he replied. "He seems a steady enough fellow to me," he said.

Pebbles-Ground-Under-Soft-Wheels didn't say anything more. Instead she just pulled her claw free of his grasp and made way for another chorister to come and shake Lanoe's hand and tell him that Archie was a severe disappointment to the Choir. The next chorister in the receiving line said she hoped he understood Archie didn't represent the views or opinions of the Choir as a whole.

One after another of them came by, each saying much the same thing. Apologizing for Archie's mental instability.

"What the hell is this?" Lanoe asked Archie, once the introductions were complete.

"They're shaming me," Archie explained, still smiling. "It's something they do. I let them down."

Lanoe shook his head. "Let them down? How?"

"I've been . . . well, let's call it homesick. Back in the tunnel, when I thought they weren't listening, I'm afraid I let that overcome me. It was a mistake."

"You asked us to take you home with us when we leave," Lanoe said, whispering. Though he knew the entire Choir could hear him, all the same. "They're acting like you're some sort of criminal."

Archie shrugged. "Clear communication is very important to them. Harmonious thoughts, they'd say. Any blighter who adds a sour note to the symphony gets this treatment."

"It's not fair," Valk said.

"You asked me once about how the Choir deals with mental illness," Archie said. "I didn't get a chance to give you a proper answer. I'm afraid you've gone and discovered the soft spot on the apple here. But don't judge them too harshly—try to understand. The Choir shares every thought, every emotion. They can't just block out a chorister if they don't like what they hear. Even if those thoughts are damaging, even if they would encourage others to do horrible things. Don't you see? A deranged individual forces her madness on all of them. It's unbearable. It shatters the harmony."

"You're not one of them," Lanoe said.

Archie's eyes flashed with something—some emotion—but then it was gone again. Blanked out.

"You don't approve," he said.

Except it wasn't him who said it. Water-Falling was standing behind Lanoe. She placed one of her claws on his shoulder. He realized that she had taken control of Archie, that she was speaking directly through him now.

"There ought to be a better way," Lanoe said. Despite himself. Knowing he might offend the Choir. Not particularly caring very much.

"Some of us agree with you, believe it or not. Not many. Most are happy with the way things have always been done. Most of us want harmony, before anything else."

"Even if that means crushing anyone who sings off key," Lanoe said.

"There are so few of us left. We can't afford dissension." She gestured for Archie to come to her and he did, moving to stand beside her with no expression on his face at all. "I don't ask you to think we are perfect," she told Lanoe, using Archie's voice. "But I hope we can still be allies."

Lanoe gritted his teeth.

He wanted to help Archie. He wanted to get him away from the Choir. But if he pushed the issue now—if he made a stink about this—it could ruin everything. He needed all the help he could get, if he was going to get justice from the Blue-Blue-White. He needed the Choir.

If the price he had to pay for their help was one human soul, the happiness of a castaway—

"Maybe," he said, very slowly, very carefully, "we can discuss this again. When it's time for me to leave here. When our negotiations are finished," he said.

"Of course," Water-Falling told him. Through Archie, as always. "Though I doubt you'll receive a different answer." The chorister lifted one of her arms and rotated her claw from side to side. Lanoe had no idea what that meant.

Archie's face twitched. "She understands your impatience," he said. "She apologizes. When the Choir invited you here, they thought you would want to learn about their society and their customs. She can see now that was wrong. You've got other interests. She says that maybe now it's time."

"Time?"

"Time for you to see what the Choir has to offer you. What they have to offer humanity. Will you come with us, and take a look?"

"Sure," Lanoe said. Valk started to get up, to join them. Lanoe sent him a quick message, then said, "No, Valk, you stay here. Enjoy the apportation show, whatever that means."

"All right," Valk said. "If you think it's best."

Lanoe nodded. He followed Water-Falling and Archie as they left the banquet hall. Outside an aircar was already waiting for them.

The asteroid was only a few hundred meters across. Brownish-gray in the light, nothing but sharp shadows on its night side. Covered in craters until it looked like a chunk of pumice tumbling slowly around an eccentric orbit that took it within half a million kilometers of the star. A thoroughly uninteresting chunk of rock. None of Bury's sensors detected the slightest hint that the scout was down there. Of course, he couldn't use any active sensors—if he did, the scout might notice that it was being scanned. But his telescopes and rectennas weren't picking up a thing.

"You're sure you saw something?" he asked.

"Just a—a glint, like the tiniest damned flash of light," Ginger replied. He could hear her breathing into her microphone. He'd tried to calm her down but this time it wasn't working. "Like maybe—*maybe*—a reflection off of a canopy."

"You let Lieutenant Candless know?"

"I sent her a quick message. She said we should investigate it. Bury, I don't know what to do here."

"We investigate. Just like we were ordered to do," he told her.

"You know what I mean. If the scout *is* there, if it engages us—"

"Hang back," Bury told her. "Stay behind me. I'll do it. Just—just stop panicking, okay?" It sounded absurd even as he said it. "I'll go in and take a look, and you just…Ginger, just hang in there."

"Thank you," she breathed.

Maybe he was helping her. He just didn't know. He goosed his throttle and surged forward, swooping down toward the asteroid.

It would be next to impossible to orbit a rock that small, so he didn't try. Instead he pushed forward on his control stick to loop around it, touching his maneuvering jets just a bit so he rolled as he approached, until the asteroid swung around in space until it was directly over him. He looked up through his canopy, checking the craters, searching for anything that didn't belong. Any straight lines. The sharp edge of an airfoil. The glow of a cooling thruster.

Nothing. He brought up a sensor board, checked the infrared, let his computers try to find patterns in the rock. He focused on looping around the night side, keeping his eyes open but mostly focusing on flying while his gear did the work. The computer might see something he would have missed. But...no.

Nothing. He gritted his teeth, kept looking. If Ginger had just gotten spooked, if she'd seen this flash of light because she expected to see it, because her terrified brain was playing tricks on her...

"I'm turning up bosh," he said. "Ginj, I'm going to switch over to active sensors. I'll just make a quick sweep, as fast as I can, and then we'll know there's nothing here. Okay?"

"Bury, if he is there—"

"Then I'll flush him out. Just hang back—you're going to be okay."

She didn't reply.

He gestured to bring the sensor board up directly in front of him, partly obscuring the view through his canopy. A virtual keyboard flickered to life before him. With his right hand still on his control stick, he tapped out a series of commands with his left, hunting and pecking at the keys. He readied a full lidar sweep of the asteroid that would turn up anything down there. It would also give away his position to anyone who was watching.

It was worth it, if it helped calm Ginger down.

He tapped the key.

On his display the asteroid appeared as a series of images that melded together to form a composite, a false-color visualization of the tumbling rock. Craters bloomed with light, mountains disappeared as their shadowed sides were exposed. Boulders were scanned and rendered in three dimensions, showing just how regular and natural and boring they were. "Nothing yet," he said. "Ginger, I think—"

"Bury!" she cried.

A red light flashed on his tactical board. He glanced over and saw it—a ship burning hard, streaking away from the far side of the asteroid. Moving fast and accelerating.

"Hellfire," he swore, and swiped the sensor display out of his view. He twisted around on his maneuvering jets and punched his main thrusters, chasing after the scout as fast as his engines would allow, but he knew, he was certain, he would be too late.

The scout was on a trajectory that would take it right past Ginger, less than a dozen kilometers from her position.

"Ginger, he hasn't seen you yet," Bury called. "You have a perfect shot. If you don't take it—"

"Bury, you have to do this, you have to . . ."

She trailed off. He could still hear her breathing—hyperventilating. He cursed silently and hit his throttle again, but he had slowed to a crawl as he approached the asteroid and it was going to take precious seconds for him to get back up to speed.

"Ginger," he said, "just listen. It's easy. Your computer will find a good firing solution. All you have to do is—"

He stopped because his tactical board showed him a yellow dot streaking away from the scout. Ginger's fighter, moving away from engagement at speed.

She was running for it.

"No," he said. "No. Ginj, turn around. Turn around right now and face him. He's not changing course—he's not chasing you. Ginj, you need to do this."

But she was already gone. She'd cut the comms laser that connected them. Turned tail and run. It looked like she was headed straight back to the cruiser. And the scout was getting away—its pilot had corrected his course and his new trajectory would take him right through the wormhole throat. Bury turned to chase him but the unarmored ship could move faster than he could. The bastard was going to get away, he was going to—

"Lieutenant Maggs, if you please," Lieutenant Candless said, on the open channel.

"Happy to be of service," Maggs replied.

Bury had forgotten that Maggs's Z.XIX could shoot at such a long range. On the tactical board, the blue dot that marked the scout's position blinked for a moment, then disappeared. Through his canopy Bury could just see a faint, luminous wisp appear up ahead. Appear, and then vanish once more.

Bury checked the board again, looking for Ginger.

She was still running. *Hellfire,* he thought. *Ginger, damn you, don't you know how this looks?*

"Ensign Ginger," Candless said. "Return to your formation." There was no response. "Ensign," Candless said, very calmly, "I am not making a request. If you fail to return to the formation, you will be in violation of orders." The Lieutenant sighed and Bury could tell she didn't want to do this. "Ginger," she said, her voice even softening a little—"Ginger, if you don't turn back, right now, there's nothing I can do for you. There will be charges."

"Ma'am," Bury said, "I think she's turned off her comms. I don't think she can even hear you."

"That, in itself, would be a violation of standing orders. I'm sorry, Bury." Candless cleared her throat. "Ensign Ginger. You have five seconds to return," Lieutenant Candless said. "Shall I count them for you? Three, now. Two seconds. One."

"Lieutenant!" Bury called. "Let me go after her. I can talk her back, I know I can, if you just let me—"

"Ensign Bury," Lieutenant Candless said, "I need you right where you are. You will maintain position and you will clear this channel."

"But—"

"There may be other Centrocor units waiting just inside the

wormhole throat. We need to be prepared to repulse them if they appear. If you persist in cluttering this channel with useless speech, then you will find yourself in just as much trouble as your fellow ensign. You have your orders. Do they require clarification?"

Bury could only watch Ginger go, a tiny bright dot very far away now.

"*Ensign Bury.* Do my orders require clarification?"

"No, ma'am," Bury said.

As they descended once more through the aqueduct, down toward the globe of water at the heart of the city, none of them spoke. Perhaps Archie knew now that he couldn't ever speak privately, not even in that blast of noise. Perhaps the shaming had taught him to control his emotions. Maybe Water-Falling simply had some way to keep him clamped down, unable to think or feel, much less speak.

The aircar left the tunnel and spiraled down toward the island, the only bit of solid ground in the trapped ocean. The beacon of the lighthouse there followed them, lighting their way as they set down.

"It's this way," Archie/Water-Falling said. Both of them gestured at the lighthouse, their arms moving in unison. Just outside the door of the building a chorister waited for them. "This is Trill-of-the-Prey-Animal-at-Dusk. She keeps this place safe. It's a position of enormous trust."

The chorister bowed. She gestured as she spoke, perhaps knowing that otherwise Lanoe couldn't know who was addressing him. "Before the Second Invasion, the Choir were like a set of claws closed around a seed. The claws kept the seed inviolate, but it could not grow. When the Twelve built this city, when they hid it away from the dangers of the galaxy, they made sure to leave their claws just a little bit open. You have passed through that opening because we know we must allow ourselves the possibility of trust."

The Choir didn't seem to need him to say anything in return.

When she was finished with her ceremonial speech, Trill-of-the-Prey-Animal-at-Dusk led them inside the lighthouse. As with every Choir building Lanoe had seen, the ground floor was a single broad room. A ramp led upward, toward the light, but that wasn't their destination. Instead they were ushered onto a moving platform that took them down, into the rock of the island.

Lanoe's ears popped as they descended. The air grew warmer and heavier, thick with humidity. For a moment he felt his stomach flop around inside his abdomen, and his feet started to come away from the floor. It was a sensation he recognized—gravity was failing. Before he could even react, though, his weight returned and it was as if nothing had happened. Neither Archie nor either of the choristers seemed to notice the change at all.

They must have descended for at least a kilometer before the walls around them fell away and the platform came to rest on the floor of a large cavern.

"This is the safest, most heavily protected place in our city," Archie said, his face slack, his mouth barely closing on the words. Lanoe guessed that Water-Falling had taken complete control of Archie now and was speaking directly to him, one-on-one. "Archie has never been down here before. Any chorister may come here if they wish, but they typically choose to stay away. This isn't a place to visit lightly."

Lights in the ceiling shone down on maybe thirty stone columns, each one worked with an elaborate bas-relief. A two-dimensional display hovered before each column, showing a single still image.

"The Twelve imagined this place into being, though they did not build it with their own hands. It took generations of the Choir to make it a reality. This is a place designed to outlast all of us, to remain intact and safe as long as necessary. If the city were to be attacked, even if it were destroyed and our bubble of wormspace collapsed, there are safeguards in place to preserve this chamber. These columns," Water-Falling said, gesturing at them, one after another, "will be protected, until they are needed."

Lanoe walked over to the nearest of the columns and studied the image that floated before it, a picture of some kind of creature like a speckled lizard with a single arm growing out of its back. The arm ended in a hand with two opposable thumbs. The lizard wore a close-fitting garment made of what looked like foam rubber.

He moved to the next column. Its display showed a knot of tentacles, some of which ended in delicate spiral shapes, some of which ended in what looked like compound eyes.

A third column bore the image of something almost humanoid, a creature with two arms and two legs but no head. A coat of thick, black-striped spines covered its entire body except the palms of its hands.

Each of the columns had a similar image, each showing a creature wildly different from all the others.

"You did an impressive thing, Aleister Lanoe, when you defeated the Blue-Blue-White fleet. Especially given how few ships you had, how few pilots."

"You saw it happen," Lanoe said. "You can see through the wormholes, can't you? Use them like telescopes."

"The Choir can't shut itself off from the outside world, not completely. We watch. We force ourselves to watch, when the Blue-Blue-White kill and slaughter. We have seen it happen, again and again. You defeated one of those fleets but you know there are more of them. Millions more. They will keep coming for humanity. They won't stop until they've destroyed humanity completely. You know that."

"Sure," Lanoe said. "Unless we stop them."

"It can't be done. I'm sorry. So many have tried. They can be turned back, individual planets can be saved, as you have seen. But there will always be more fleets. They will always keep coming, and eventually, they will wear you down. Even the weapons that the Choir possessed before the Second Invasion—many of which have been lost and cannot be recreated—were not enough. There is only one weapon that can stop them for good."

"What is it?" Lanoe asked.

"Time," Water-Falling said. "Your companion, Tannis Valk, was able to access their computers and analyze their programming. He was not the first. We have seen that data as well, and we know what will happen. Eventually, long from now, the Blue-Blue-White's fleets of drones will have visited and reconstructed every gas giant planet in the galaxy. With no more work to do, with their mission fulfilled, they will shut themselves down. Then it will be safe for the Choir to leave this city, and this bubble, and return to worlds underneath the stars."

"How long will that take?" Lanoe asked. "Actually, never mind. I know you don't measure time the way we do."

"I can read Archie's mind to understand your concept of years, and the calculation isn't a difficult one. It should take another two and one-half billions of years, as you measure them."

"Only that long," Lanoe said.

"The Choir has come to take a distant view. We've had to. We will wait, and we will outlast the Blue-Blue-White. And when the time comes, you can be there with us."

Lanoe stopped in front of another of the columns. It showed the image of a creature a little like a pill bug, all segmented chitin and tiny legs. Elaborate calligraphy was tattooed or drawn across the armor plates. Writing in an alphabet he didn't recognize.

"I think I've figured it out," Lanoe said. "What this place is for. These columns are hollow inside, aren't they? And they contain samples of DNA."

"Genetic material, stabilized in a crystalline form. Not all of these species used the same chemicals to pass down their genomes. Some of them aren't even carbon-based."

"Sure," Lanoe said. "Sure." He dropped his head. Closed his eyes. Thought things through. "So when the time comes, you— what? Clone a bunch of new people from this stock? Do you store their memories, too? Their cultures, their technology, everything they know, everything they've ever written down?"

"Unfortunately we can't collect anything but the genetic samples. It would be impossible to store all that data in a manner secure enough to last until the proper time."

"So...you'll re-create these species. Make new copies. Except they'll be born not even knowing who they are. You'll find them a nice planet to live on, maybe teach them how to make fire. Tell them to go forth and multiply."

"It means survival. The other option is extinction."

Lanoe looked around at the columns. "Each one a different species. They took your offer."

"The Choir has approached seventy-three different intelligent species, since the time of the Second Invasion, and to each of them we made the same proposition."

Lanoe counted the columns. Twenty-eight. "A lot of them said no, then."

"We honored their wishes."

"And of the seventy-three you've asked, how many of them are still around? How many of them haven't been wiped out by the Blue-Blue-White?"

"Just one," Water-Falling said. "Humanity."

Lanoe looked at one more column, one more image. It showed a picture of Archie, with two small differences. He didn't have his beard in the picture. Nor did he have the scar across his temple.

The column behind the image wasn't finished. There was no bas-relief inscribed on its surface, and it was shorter than the others, its top open to the air. "Empty?" Lanoe asked.

"One individual can't provide enough varied genetic material to reproduce an entire species. We would need samples from approximately twelve hundred humans to create a viable gene pool."

Lanoe nodded. "I have less than fifty on my ship. But you aren't really asking me, are you? You want me to go back to Earth and get an answer from my government."

"This is not a decision that should be made by one person alone. It affects the future of every human being."

"Sure," Lanoe said. "Sure."

When Lanoe decided he'd seen enough, the three of them returned to the platform. It rose toward the surface at an almost sedate pace. As they neared the top, a green pearl appeared in the corner of Lanoe's vision, throbbing in a pattern that told him he had missed a message. Most likely his suit's radio hadn't been able to pick up transmissions in the strange chamber under the water.

The message was from Valk. The AI had kept it short.

Candless called to warn us we're out of time. Centrocor's here.

"Is something wrong?" Water-Falling asked. "You have an expression on your face I recognize. Archie looks like that when he gets bad news."

"I have to get back to my ship as quickly as possible," Lanoe told the chorister. "I need to issue some new orders."

Chapter Twenty-Eight

Ginger arrived back in the vehicle bay of the cruiser and powered down her fighter. She felt like she couldn't breathe. She reached up to her collar ring and brought her helmet down. Gasped for air. She was seeing spots.

There was no one in the vehicle bay. She hadn't expected that. She'd thought that the marines would be waiting to arrest her as soon as she got in. She'd prepared herself for that—accepted it was better than being out there in the dark even one moment more.

Instead—it looked almost like they'd forgotten about her. Or maybe everyone was just too busy to worry about her future just then.

She opened her canopy and kicked out of the cockpit, moved to a railing by the hatch leading out of the bay. Wondered what in hell she was going to do next.

Shaking, wanting very much to scream, wanting very much to curl up in a ball and just stop existing altogether, she headed toward her bunk. She stopped when she reached the wardroom and saw Lieutenant Ehta floating there. Of all the people to run into... "So what was it?" the marine asked.

"I'm... sorry?"

Lieutenant Ehta frowned at her. "The bogey. The contact.

Candless called to tell us that you lot were out on a snipe hunt. Did you find something?"

"Centrocor," Ginger said, nodding. "They're here."

"Damn," Lieutenant Ehta said. Then she went back to what she was doing, which appeared to be getting something to eat.

"They've come for us," Ginger said. "How can you just..." She shook her head. "Don't you understand? They're going to try to kill us again."

"Yeah, all right," Lieutenant Ehta said. "Not in the next hour, though?"

"I...don't know. I guess not," Ginger said.

"Well, I'm hungry now." Lieutenant Ehta turned around and went back to her meal, clearly done with the conversation. Ginger swallowed thickly. The woman didn't like her, she thought, or maybe she just didn't like pilots. Maybe it was just the old rivalry between flyers and ground-pounders, maybe...maybe it didn't matter.

She had to talk, though. She needed so desperately to talk to somebody.

"I messed up," she said. "I did something really bad."

Lieutenant Ehta sighed, but didn't look up. "Kid," she said, "I don't know if—"

Ginger shook her head. She needed to get this out. She needed to talk, to be spoken to. Until she could get her heart to stop pounding so fast. "I broke formation. I—I saw him. The scout pilot, and I knew I was supposed to shoot him, and I couldn't do it. Oh, hellfire, I couldn't. I just *couldn't*."

"You ran away from a patrol," Lieutenant Ehta said, very carefully.

Ginger nodded. Bit her lip.

"You know that's pretty much the Navy's number one rule? Don't run away. They taught you that, yeah?"

"Yes," Ginger said.

Lieutenant Ehta held her gaze for a long couple of seconds. Then she went back to the controls of the food dispenser. "Here," she said. "We'd better talk about this."

She handed Ginger a squeeze tube of water. It tasted sour and Ginger barely managed to swallow the liquid.

"What's in this?" she asked.

"Electrolytes," Lieutenant Ehta responded. "You had a panic attack. When that happens your body thinks you're actually dying. It pulls all the blood sugar out of your head and dumps it into your muscles, so you can run away faster. Useful if you're being chased by a tiger, but it gives you a nasty hangover. That stuff won't calm you down, but it'll keep you from feeling like you got beaten up, later. How do your legs feel?"

"Weak. Shaky. I'm glad I'm in microgravity because I don't think I could stand up right now."

Lieutenant Ehta nodded sagely.

"How do you know all this?" Ginger asked.

"I've been there." The older woman sighed and strapped herself into a chair. Clearly she thought this was going to be a long conversation. "I used to be a pilot, you know that? Yeah. I got the wind up. Bad case of nerves. These days, if I even get onboard a spaceship, I start to feel it. That weird sensation like your guts have been scooped out, like you're hollow inside. The way, you know, when your head..." She placed her hands around her temples, her thumbs over her eyebrows. "Like there's a string around your head and it keeps getting tighter and tighter. Nausea, darting eyes. Yeah, I can see in your face, you get it. Look, kid, human brains aren't designed for what you do. Flying a fighter, I mean. You're not supposed to be able to focus on two things at the same time, the scales and the velocities are all wrong, so much bigger than we can handle—"

"That's not the problem, for me," Ginger said.

Lieutenant Ehta gave her a sour look, and Ginger squirmed inside. She hated to think she'd offended the woman. "I don't mean—I just—"

"So tell me what you did mean."

Ginger nodded. "I'm not even supposed to be here."

The Lieutenant didn't say anything. She just watched Ginger's face, as if she could read something there.

Ginger looked away. "I'm not...I was never supposed to be a pilot. I got washed out of the pilot program—before we came here. I was so ashamed when Lieutenant Candless told me that. That I was never going to be...damn it. You want to know the truth? I was relieved."

Lieutenant Ehta nodded.

"I never wanted to be a pilot. Not even when I was a child. But they never gave me a choice. No one ever gave me a choice. Back there, when I saw the Centrocor ship...I just gave up. I gave up pretending."

Lieutenant Ehta put her hands on the table and pushed backward, shoving herself deeper into her chair. "Okay," she said.

"How is that okay?"

"It's who you are." The older woman shrugged. "You figured out your limits. Okay, so don't do this job anymore. I'm not a therapist, kid. I don't know what you were hoping I would say. I can't help you change who you are. So let's not even try that. We should focus, instead, on what comes next."

"Oh," Ginger said. "Hellfire." She hadn't really thought about that too much. She'd actively tried to not think about it.

"Yeah. They're going to hit you with a charge of cowardice. You know that, right?"

"I thought—it might be desertion, instead."

Ehta snorted. "Oh, no, you lucked out there! If you were back in the real world, right, if you were in the middle of an actual hell-bent-for-leather war, sure, it'd be desertion, and the penalty for that is the firing squad. But on this mission—well, nothing's cut and dried out here. Nothing's simple."

"Cowardice," Ginger said. "That's...still pretty bad. They'll stick me in the brig for years, and then discharge me with dishonor."

Lieutenant Ehta shrugged. "Maybe they'll be lenient."

Ginger shook her head. "I don't know. Lieutenant Candless..."

"Yeah, she's one tough nut to crack. She'll bring the formal charges against you, but she doesn't get to pass sentence. That's Lanoe's job, as captain of this ship, and that's where you've got a chance. He'll shout a blue streak at you, no question. And he'll look like he wants to shoot you on the spot. But trust me, I've known him a long time. You play your cards right—maybe it won't be so bad. Listen, when you go before him. *Do not* try to apologize. Don't spin him a long story about right and wrong. That's just wasting his time. He always thinks he's the final judge on good and bad, and believe me, you do *not* want to try to disagree with him at that moment. No, you stand up, chin up, and you tell him you're ready to accept your punishment. He'll respect that."

Ginger nodded. She thought maybe she should write all of this down. One question nagged at her, though.

"Why are you telling me all this?" she asked. "The one time I tried to talk to you, you basically froze me out."

"Back when we were playing freepool, you mean? Back then? Hell, kid. I had to put on a good show for the marines."

"So you don't...hate me?"

Lieutenant Ehta sighed. "No, kid. I don't hate you."

— ✕ —

Lanoe had to know that Centrocor was about to enter the system, that they'd been discovered. Candless had left Bury and Maggs on patrol so she could take him the message herself. Radio waves and comms lasers couldn't pass effectively through a wormhole throat, so that meant she'd had to go in person. She queued up a message about the Centrocor scout, then set a course for the wormhole in the planet's atmosphere. The message started broadcasting the second she was through, which was good. She was too busy to send it manually—she was too busy staring at what she'd found.

She'd had no idea what to expect to find on the other side of the wormhole.

Certainly not this.

She had circled the darkened city several times, just trying to comprehend what she was seeing, before she set down in a broad plaza right next to Lanoe's cutter. She hadn't left the cockpit of her fighter since. She didn't want to go out there, into the dark streets. Not when they were full of those—*things*.

Aliens. They were intelligent life-forms. Lanoe had called her to tell her they were friendly, though she wouldn't be able to talk to them. He'd told her she was in no danger.

Hard to remember that when one of them came over to her fighter and ran its claws all over her fairings, her airfoils. She'd stared out through her canopy at its face that wasn't anything like a face and wondered just what the hell Lanoe had gotten them into. He had told her that there were no more aliens, that his Blue-Blue-White had murdered them all. So who were these...creatures?

Human knuckles rapped on the flowglas of her canopy. She forced herself not to jump out of her seat in surprise. It was Valk, the artificial intelligence. Because of course this mission had already been beyond bizarre, beyond anything her centuries of life had prepared her for.

"We got your message. Lanoe wants to talk to you," the AI said. "In the cutter."

Which meant getting out of her fighter. Candless set her face, then tapped the key to release the flowglas of her canopy. She jumped out and landed on her feet on hard flagstones. Somehow the solidity of the ground bothered her. Perhaps because it meant that all of this was real.

"There's gravity here," she said to Valk. "There shouldn't be."

"I'll let the authorities know you disapprove. Come on." The AI led her over to the cutter and together they climbed through the hatch in its belly. The internal walls of the vehicle, she knew, were all capable of acting as displays, but now they were switched off. Leaving the interior of the ship a flat gray that seemed to absorb all sound. Lanoe was already inside, facing away from her. Staring at a blank wall.

"I know," he said. He wasn't talking to her. He didn't seem to have noticed that she'd come onboard. "I know—you keep saying that, but...how? How do I get closer?"

Candless frowned. Who was he talking to? What on earth was going on?

She cleared her throat.

His head jerked up. A trace of guilt shone in his eyes as he looked back over his shoulder at her.

"Sir," she said. "Are you—?"

"Just thinking things through," he told her. "Welcome to the City of the Choir. I take it you've met our new allies."

"Aliens," she said. "There are aliens here. Very...unsettling aliens."

"I was surprised, too," he told her. "They're...friendly. So far. The message they sent us was real, they actually did want to help us. So there's that."

"You've been negotiating with them, this whole time?"

"Learning about their culture, mostly. Not by choice. They expected Earth to send diplomats. Instead they got me. Neither side is particularly happy about that. And now it looks like we're out of time. I read your message. Centrocor's here. Just a scout so far," he said, not looking up. "You found a scout."

"We eliminated a scout, to be precise. When it fails to return from its patrol, our enemies will know we're here."

Lanoe nodded. "They were going to find us eventually. We need to respond to this, and sooner rather than later. I'm afraid a lot of that is going to fall on your shoulders. I need to stay here. Keep talking to these people. You'll need to assume command of the cruiser. You may have to fight Centrocor without me."

"I'll do my best," she said.

He nodded. Still not looking at her. "I think we should move the cruiser in here. This bubble, I mean. It'll be safer in here."

Candless frowned. That wouldn't be easy. The cruiser wasn't built for that kind of tricky maneuvering. "Perhaps—"

Lanoe cut her off. "If we leave it out there, orbiting the planet, it'll be a sitting duck when Centrocor arrives. Especially when we have so few pilots to hold them off. You need to keep Centrocor out of my hair while I negotiate. That's easier done with the cruiser in here. It's a better defensive position."

"Of course," Candless said, picking her words carefully. "And I do agree that whatever help these aliens are offering, we can't let Centrocor have it—at any cost," Candless said. "We have our orders from Admiral Varma."

Lanoe sighed. "Sure. Though I've already found out what they had to offer us." He shook his head. "Bosh," he said. "It was bosh."

Candless fought to keep her face still.

"Bosh," she said.

She'd never cared for the term, or for slang in general. She let it roll around on her tongue like something she could spit out.

She didn't want to accept it.

"Bosh," she said again. "We crossed hundreds of light-years, fought a battle, nearly died in that freezing wormhole for... nothing?"

"As far as I'm concerned," Lanoe said. "I wanted warships. I wanted an ally. Instead, they want to help us by preserving our DNA. So they can clone us, sometime in the distant future."

"And you told them...no?"

"It never got that far. They know I can't make that kind of decision. Maybe Admiral Varma wants what they're offering. I'll leave that to her. But I don't plan on leaving here empty-handed."

Candless might have hoped for more in the way of an explanation, but she didn't get it. Lanoe paused the video he was watching. Then he looked up at Valk. "Big guy. Is what I'm seeing here...?"

"Yeah," Valk said. "It's real."

Lanoe nodded to himself and went back to watching the video. From what Candless could see, it showed aliens putting on an illusionist's act. It took place in the plaza outside, with hundreds of the lobsterlike creatures gathered around a central stage. The video looked like it had been taken from the front row. "While they were showing me what they had to offer, Valk stayed behind and took in a...what do they call it?"

"An apportation show," Valk said.

"I'm glad to see you've at least been entertained while you were here," Candless said, bitterness nearly overcoming her.

"Look at the chorister on the stage," Lanoe said. "Do you see what she's holding?"

Candless leaned in for a better view. The alien held a sort of hollow sphere about twenty-five centimeters in diameter. Its outer surface was pierced with a sort of fretwork of small holes, and light flickered inside of it. The alien twisted the sphere in various directions, and a beam of light shot out from the sphere to create a distortion in the air. The alien turned around to face a different direction and repeated the process, and a plume of water shot out of the second distortion, arcing over the alien's head to fall back into the first distortion...and vanish.

"It's all tricks like that," Valk told Candless. "The performer made stuff appear out of thin air, started a fire with light out of nowhere. She put a little stone ball in a box, then made it appear in her claw without touching the box again. She even cut a chorister in half, at one point. She didn't use a saw, though."

"I think I know how it's done," Lanoe said. He finally looked up at her. "And if I'm right..."

Candless raised an eyebrow.

"There's a chance we can get what we need out of the Choir, after all." He sighed and stretched his arms over his head. "Though they aren't going to like it when I ask. Not at all. They're going to take a hell of a lot of convincing."

❦

"Come on, kid," Lieutenant Ehta said. "Let's go face the music."

Ginger thought she understood a little better, now, why the marine was being so nice to her. Clearly she considered them to be sisters, of a kind—they'd both been through a traumatic experience that left them at odds with the Navy.

As much as she was still a little afraid of Lieutenant Ehta, she

was very glad to have a friend at that moment. She was facing probably the worst dressing-down she would ever get. The end of her
career. All she could hope for was that it would be quick—and that
she wouldn't be heading straight into a jail cell when they returned
to civilization.

There had been a general announcement on the cruiser's speakers, and then, just in case they hadn't heard it, Engineer Paniet
had come up to the wardroom to tell them. Lieutenant Candless
was returning to the cruiser. All hands were expected to be in the
vehicle bay to welcome her back.

"She won't charge you in front of everybody," Lieutenant Ehta
said. "But I doubt she'll waste her time getting to it. You ready for
this?"

"I...guess. But why are we all being called down to meet her?"
Ginger asked. "You think they found something important on the
other side of that wormhole?"

Lieutenant Ehta shook her head. "Hell, kid, your guess is as
good as mine."

They arrived in the vehicle bay to find most of the marines
already there. Ginger half-expected Lieutenant Ehta to brush her
off again, to make a public show of pushing her away in front of the
PBMs, but instead Ehta told her to grab a railing right next to her.
The marines had their helmets up and silvered, so it was impossible to tell what they thought of their commanding officer getting
chummy with a pilot.

Engineer Paniet arrived soon after they did. He said he'd been
straightening up a little so that Candless could come home to a
clean ship. There was grease on his gloves and he wiped it away
with a nanofiber cloth that he then just shoved in a pocket of his
suit. "Exciting, isn't it?" he asked.

"What do you mean?" Ginger said. "We have no idea what this
is about."

"That's what makes it exciting. Could be anything!"

Through the weather field that covered the open hatch of the
vehicle bay, Ginger could see the dark shapes of fighters coming

in for a landing. Lieutenant Candless came in first, climbing out of her cockpit as soon as her fighter was locked into its berth. She moved to one side of the bay and stuffed one foot through a nylon loop anchored to the floor, so that it looked like she was standing there. The only person in the bay who wasn't floating like a balloon. She brushed down the front of her suit, smoothing out any wrinkles, then touched her hair, still in a tight, perfect bun at the back of her head.

Then she looked up at the crew on the railings, her sharp gaze moving from face to face as if she were doing a head count. When she got to Ginger her face went perfectly still. She didn't even frown. Just stared at Ginger for what felt like an eternity.

Ginger fought down the urge she felt to jump out of her own skin and run away. Instead she tried to follow Lieutenant Ehta's advice and stood perfectly still, looking straight forward, chin up. She tried to not make it look like she was staring at Lieutenant Candless out of the corner of her eye.

"Don't let her rattle you," Lieutenant Ehta whispered.

Ginger gave her the tiniest, most imperceptible of nods.

Lieutenant Maggs and Bury came in next, their fighters streaming vapor after their long patrol. The two of them opened their canopies and started to climb out, but Lieutenant Candless told them not to bother. "This is going to be a quick information session, then the two of you are headed back out. We need to maintain constant vigilance."

Lieutenant Maggs made a harrumphing sound. "It's been positively hours. I believe we're entitled to a rest."

"Not possible," Lieutenant Candless told him.

"Why not, damn you?"

The XO's eyes flashed. Ginger knew that look—the woman had no patience for people who wasted her time, especially when she was in a hurry. "If you would do me the signal honor of sitting there and listening for a moment, you might find out. Now, as for the rest of you—Commander Lanoe sends his compliments, and his gratitude for the long hours you've been working, and your patience. Maggs and Bury are instructed to continue their patrols, with no change in orders. As for the rest of us, we've got a rather stressful shift coming up, so no one should relax just yet. My orders are to bring the cruiser through the wormhole down on the planet."

Engineer Paniet let out a little yelp. Ginger looked over at him and saw he had one hand over his mouth and the other flat against his chest.

"Judging by that reaction, I can tell you think this is a dangerous maneuver, Engineer," Candless said. "I don't disagree. Commander Lanoe was adamant, however. We're exposed out here. Should Centrocor find us orbiting this planet, with half of our pilots engaged elsewhere, the cruiser wouldn't stand a chance. The best way to protect it, he feels, is to move it. I can see that you're going to burst if I don't let you speak. Go ahead."

Engineer Paniet simply shook his head for a moment, as if he was too overcome to talk. Finally he took a deep breath and said, "I'm not saying it can't be done. But this ship was never meant to enter a planetary atmosphere, much less maneuver inside one. And then there's the damage we've already sustained, to the forward section—the stress of atmospheric entry will rip out half of my repairs. Let's not even get started on the g stress we'll have to handle, and I mean we, us, our bodies. This is—"

"What I'm hearing is that it's possible," Lieutenant Candless said.

Engineer Paniet closed his eyes. "Theoretically, yes. I'll get to work. It's going to take at least a full day just to lash everything down and prepare the ship for that kind of strain."

"Commander Lanoe wants it done in eight hours."

Engineer Paniet nodded, his eyes still closed.

"Good. Now, everyone is dismissed—until this maneuver is complete, Engineer Paniet will be in charge of assigning duties. For now I want to see Ensign Ginger individually."

The marines started to file out of the bay, grumbling among

themselves. Lieutenant Ehta stayed close by Ginger. "Just remember, she doesn't make the final call," she whispered. "It's Lanoe who'll pass sentence."

Ginger nodded. Lieutenant Ehta squeezed her shoulder, then followed her marines back inside the ship. Leaving nobody but pilots in the bay.

Bury kept trying to catch Ginger's eye. He stood up a little in his cockpit. Gave her a little wave with one hand—then settled back down as if he was afraid Lieutenant Candless would see him. Ginger refused to look at him, even though she knew it was cruel. If he made some grand show of sympathy for her plight she thought she might scream. So she simply clung to the railing for dear life and waited for what came next.

Except it seemed fate wanted her to suffer in anxious anticipation a little longer.

Lieutenant Maggs cleared his throat. Lieutenant Candless turned to look at him. To look at him down her nose.

"Something I can assist you with, Lieutenant Maggs? You have your orders."

"I'd like to apologize for my earlier outburst."

"Noted."

"And then I would like to suggest a duty change," Lieutenant Maggs said. His usual suave manner was gone now—he stood up straight, there was no sign of a smirk on his face. He almost looked like a professional officer. "Ensign Bury and I have been flying for too long. We're fatigued. You say we can't afford time to take a rest. Well, that's as may be. We could, however, switch out with Valk. He could come fly a patrol while one of us...does whatever it is he's doing down there, on the other side of the wormhole. Then we could switch off again, and so on. One shift down there, two in space. It's only fair."

The look on Lieutenant Candless's face was one Ginger recognized. One any of her students would have recognized. It meant she was no longer interested in entertaining that particular line of conversation. "Lanoe feels you're best utilized out here, watching for Centrocor. Your special new targeting software, this Philoctetes package, makes your vehicle ideal for picket duty."

Lieutenant Maggs's eyes grew hard as flints.

"Picket duty," he said. "The kind of duty you give your least talented, most expendable pilot. As opposed to me."

"We all have orders," Lieutenant Candless told him, turning away. Clearly she wanted to be finished with the conversation, but Maggs shouted at her back.

"He doesn't want me to see what's over there, beyond the wormhole. He doesn't trust me."

"He trusts you enough to give you this crucial duty."

Red spots bloomed on Lieutenant Maggs's cheeks. "That... bastard. That ass!"

"I'll remind you that he is your commanding officer."

"Only because he kidnapped me," Lieutenant Maggs said. "*Press-ganged* me into this duty. It's him who should be earning my trust back. And yet here I am, following his orders, fighting for him, that senescent piece of—"

"If you say another word I'll bring you up on charges of insubordination," Lieutenant Candless said.

The look Lieutenant Maggs gave her could have melted through armor plate. When she didn't acknowledge it, he put up his helmet and sat back down in his cockpit. In a moment he was roaring out through the weather field, back out on patrol.

Bury stuck around long enough to give Ginger one more meaningful look. Then he, too, raised his canopy and launched himself back out into space.

Leaving Ginger and her former instructor alone in the vehicle bay.

For a while neither of them spoke. Nor did they look each other in the eye.

"I'm sorry, Ginger," Lieutenant Candless said, finally.

"You're... what?"

"I'm sorry it's come to this. There's no choice, though. Come with me," Lieutenant Candless said. "There's a form to fill out."

"A... form?" Ginger asked.

"Yes, of course. The charge against you needs to be officially logged. One count of cowardice in peacetime. We're going to do this exactly according to protocol. Then you're going to go to work for Engineer Paniet."

"You're not going to lock me in the brig?" Ginger asked.

"Not when there's so much work to do. We need every pair of hands we can get."

Candless splashed some water on her face—well, in microgravity, she mostly rubbed it across her cheeks and brow, then soaked it back up with a sponge.

She tried not to think of Ginger. She tried not to think about how angry she was with Lanoe, for pushing the girl until she broke. He should have known, he should have understood that Ginger was never going to make it as a pilot—

No. She couldn't really blame Lanoe. Not when the real failure here was her own. Had she been a better instructor, perhaps...

Candless squeezed her eyes shut. Forced herself to push away such thoughts. There was far too much work to be done now. She could wallow in self-recrimination later.

The eight hours passed in a blur as she moved crates of food-stocks from one cabinet to the next, as she locked down the more fragile mechanisms in the gundecks side by side with Ehta and her marines, as she climbed in and out of maintenance hatches securing loose cables. Everyone onboard pitched in—everyone worked as hard as she did—and still they knew it wouldn't be enough. Her final duty before they moved the cruiser was to make an inspection of the damaged forward section. Paniet waited for her by the emergency hatch that had now become a makeshift airlock.

"You haven't seen this yet, have you, dear?" he asked. "The wreckage of your old bridge. It's terribly sad. Come on, I'll walk you through it."

Together they headed into the evacuated section, their helmets flowing up over their heads. There were no lights in the damaged areas so she followed a beacon that pulsed slowly on the back of Paniet's suit. She climbed through the ruins of an old section of bunks, pulling herself along hand over hand, reaching for broken spars and burnt-out electrical conduits, for anything that she could hold on to.

"This, right here, is going to be a problem," Paniet said, over a private communications band. He gestured at a bulkhead that had been torn in half, then lashed back together with silver tape and a few ugly spot welds. "I guarantee you this will tear open. It wasn't a major problem when we were out in the deep vacuum, but once we hit atmosphere the wind will get in here and rip those panels right off. I'm of half a mind to just knock them out right now, just to get them out of the way."

"If you think it best," she told him.

"Mm-hmm. Then there's this section. If it doesn't look famil-iar, this is what's left of the information officer's position from the bridge."

Candless frowned. "It's farther back than it should be."

"Strange things happen when you redecorate with high explo-sives," he told her. "Now, of course, the real reason I wanted to walk through this with you," he said, "was to get you alone up here. Oh, don't look at me like that. I swear you're getting as paranoid as Lanoe. I just wanted to talk."

"About what, exactly?"

"About Lanoe, deary. And his paranoia."

"I...see."

Paniet lifted his hands in the air, in mock surrender. "No, no, perhaps I should put it another way. Lanoe and his obsession." The engineer grabbed a spar that had bent away from a bulkhead and flipped over it, putting it between them. "You've known him a very long time. You clearly think highly of him."

"I do," Candless said.

"Was he always like this? Willing to sacrifice everything—including people—to achieve his ends?"

Candless inhaled sharply and prepared herself to give Paniet a proper dressing down. Who was he to question the motivations of his commanding officer?

Yet all she could think of was what he'd told her, in the City of the Choir. That they had come all this way for . . . bosh. But that he was ready and willing to wring something, some kind of win, out of an alien species that—loathsome as she might find them—had done nothing but offer their help.

"He doesn't always explain the reasons behind his orders, it's true," she said. "Have you ever known a ranking officer who did?"

Paniet gave her a warm smile. "In the Neddies, we make a point of not asking too many questions. The brass tells us go here, go there, but at the end of the day they let us build lovely things, and that should be enough. Neddies don't cause trouble. Yet sometimes . . . sometimes we do have to wonder. Currently, I'm wondering why you're going to beat the devil out of my beautiful ship just to get it moved a few thousand kilometers. About why I only had eight hours to do a job most engineers couldn't do without going back to school for four years."

"Lanoe gave me very specific orders—"

"I'm sure," he told her. "Did he explain *why* he issued said commands?"

A negation died on Candless's lips. She was too tired to keep secrets anymore, and anyway, this was Paniet. So far he'd been the only person onboard who hadn't disappointed her in some way.

So she told him. About the city beyond the wormhole. About the Choir.

"They're . . . a bit terrifying, if I absolutely must be honest. I've never cared for insects. Frankly I find them abominable, and—"

"Aliens," he said, before she could even finish. His eyes went wide behind his helmet. He brought up his hands and clapped them together excitedly, even though they made no sound in the vacuum. "How lovely! We get to make some new friends. Except, of course, Lanoe isn't sure he wants to be friends."

"What makes you say that?"

Paniet rolled his eyes. "I'm figuring that's why he wants sixteen coilguns that he can point on them if things get dicey. It's why he wants the cruiser in there, and why he wants it in there right away. Even if it means breaking the ship in half."

"He didn't say as much," Candless tried.

"But you suspected it, didn't you? That to get what he wants, he's willing to threaten these aliens. To take what he wants, at the end of the barrel of a gun. And he's not the sort of fellow who bluffs his way through card games, is he?"

Candless sighed. "And how, exactly, did you come to such a conclusion?"

"Keen analytical mind," Paniet said, and went to tap his head. Instead his hand rebounded clunkily off his helmet. "Oof," he said.

Candless did not grin. She shook her head, a bit. "Lanoe has always been . . . obstinate," she said, because it was the kindest word she could think of. "He's a good man, though."

"No one's questioned that," Paniet protested.

"No, you're just questioning his fitness for command." Before he could react to that she held up one hand for peace. "I've heard what you had to say. I'm not discounting it. But for now, we have to give him a chance."

"Darling XO," Paniet said, "not one breath of mutiny has crossed my lips. I never said I would disobey orders. I just wanted them clarified. Of course . . . as I said before, I'm a neddy. We don't make waves."

"No."

"No, we leave that to the others. The pilots and the marines. When *they* take you aside for a little talk just like this one, that's when you should start to worry."

"Understood," Candless said.

And she did take his point. Especially because she thought that when the time came, when Lanoe had pushed things too far—it might not be necessary for someone else to take her aside. If Lanoe ever acted in such a way as to endanger them all, if he forgot that the first duty of command is to keep one's people alive...well. She might have to be the one who relieved him of duty.

———————

"You don't sound like M. Valk. You're not actually...Valk, are you?" Ginger said.

"That's kind of a tricky question. Interesting one, though."

The maneuver had already begun. Objects in orbit around a planet travel upward of eight kilometers per second. If the cruiser was going to survive its trip through the planet's atmosphere, it needed to shed a lot of speed before it hit air. That meant a series of short, perfectly timed burns followed by the occasional sickening lurch as they lost altitude. Basic maneuvers for a ship in space, of course—any pilot could have handled them. The real fancy flying wouldn't happen for a few minutes yet.

M. Valk was the only one who could handle the constant, pinpoint-accuracy calculations necessary to keep the ship from cracking up before it reached the wormhole. Reluctantly Lieutenant Candless had permitted the AI to take charge. Now she was helping Engineer Paniet and his small crew of neddies, down in the aft of the ship, where actual human hands might be needed to effect repairs when things got bad. Lieutenant Ehta and her marines were stationed along the axial corridor, strapped down in the safest places they could find—ready to jump up and perform emergency welds or simply hold the ship together with their bare hands if that was what it took.

Which left Ginger all alone, with nothing to do. Lieutenant Candless had assigned her to "assist" M. Valk by sitting in the wardroom, near the control displays. She'd been told that if M. Valk suffered some kind of computer malfunction, or if—as an AI might be expected to—he acted contrary to the interest of the mission, she was to take over control of the ship and somehow keep it in one piece.

Several people had promised her it wouldn't come to that. Including M. Valk.

"You could say I'm Valk's ghost," the machine told her. It had no body, of course. It was just a copy of a computer program, currently housed in the ship's servers. It didn't even bother generating a face on a display that she could look at. To Ginger it was just a disembodied voice. "Except you could say that *he*, the one down there, is the ghost of the original Tannis Valk. What do you call the ghost of a ghost? A third-generation memory?"

"No clue," Ginger said. "How long now, before we hit atmosphere?"

"What does a ghost become when it dies? Another interesting question. I like these. Normally I'd have an answer for you in microseconds. I'm using up so much processing power, though, with just flying this crate, that thorny logic problems are nontrivial to solve. Is there a word in English for this? For a problem you kinda look forward to solving when you have the time?"

"No idea."

"It's like having a bad itch, a really bad one, but knowing that eventually you'll get to scratch it. It's kind of weirdly pleasant knowing you have almost but not quite enough brainpower to work through a problem. Delayed gratification, right? But it's more complex than that. Wait. Hold on. I never answered your question."

"No. Should that worry me?"

"Honestly? I'm not sure. If I were an actual computer, my refusing to obey a command would be very worrying. I think I have free will, though. So if I tell you that we'll hit thick atmosphere in thirty-nine seconds, it's my choice to do so."

"Thanks," Ginger said.

In the case of a computer malfunction, or if the AI acted in a manner contrary to the interests of the mission.

She'd been promised that wouldn't happen.

"Are you strapped in okay?" he asked.

Ginger had made sure of that. "I've got a full quick-release harness on, just like we wear in the cockpits of our fighters. There are air bags built in around my seat and in an emergency a couple hundred liters of shock-absorbing foam can spray down all over my head."

"Good. Twenty-three seconds now."

"You don't really sound like M. Valk," she said.

"Your heartbeat is elevated. Are you worried about the maneuver, or about me being naughty?"

Naughty? Ginger curled her toes inside her boots. "I'm human," she said. "We worry about everything. Especially things we can't do anything about."

Valk laughed. The machine laughed. It sounded exactly like a human laugh. That didn't stop it from being creepy. "Have you ever heard of the Ship of Theseus?" he asked.

"Can't say that I have." She could hear—or maybe she only thought she could hear—a hissing sound, like the noise air molecules might make as they dragged along the side of the cruiser's hull. "How long?"

"Sixteen seconds. Theseus. Ancient Greek guy, one of their big heroes. Came back to Athens after he was done with his adventures. He beached his ship on the shore there, and the people of Athens, to honor him, kind of made it into a shrine. The problem was that wood rots, and one by one, the planks that made up the ship fell apart. The Athenians loved their hero, so they replaced the planks as necessary, one by one. Eventually, every single plank in the ship got replaced. None of the wood was original. Seven seconds. Here's the question. Was it still the ship that Theseus sailed?"

"What?" Ginger asked.

"It's an impossible problem. Nobody can answer it. You can use problems like that to test whether an AI is capable of self-directed thought. Just making small talk. Two. One. Zero."

"What?" Ginger asked again, feeling very stupid—especially as the cruiser chose that moment to be struck by high-altitude winds and be thrown from side to side like an umbrella in a storm.

The cruiser hit the planet's thermosphere at a dozen times the speed of sound. The air, still thin as a promise, bunched up in front of the ship's broken nose like a rumpled bedsheet. It couldn't get out of the way fast enough and so it was compressed, and a compressed gas gains temperature.

Candless had a minder taped to the wall next to her where she was strapped down in the warren of engineering. A minder that showed her a live camera feed from near the front of the cruiser. She saw plumes of vapor, a roiling ball of cloud, and then the screen turned a dull orange, the air in front of them literally incandescing. A roar of angry wind and the ship turned into a fireball.

That energetic air pushed back against their forward motion, slowing the ship—air molecules are small and not very hard but there were a lot of them, a trillion little elastic collisions a second and it added up. The ship slowed, but its energy had to go somewhere. The ship shook. It rattled, it shimmied, it rang like a struck bell. A structural member in the damaged prow broke loose and went pinwheeling back along the length of the cruiser, smashing again and again into stiffened carbon fiber cladding, tearing new holes in the ship's already-battered side. "Gundecks, position sixty-one!" she shouted, and thought she could hear marine boots pounding up the axial corridor. Marines rushing to the job, tools out as they hurried to repair the breach. On her minder she saw a notification that a weather field had already clamped into place over the hole, so they weren't at danger of explosive decompression. A little good news anyway.

They hit the planet's mesopause next. The air outside grew painfully, bitterly cold, not that anyone onboard could tell. Candless was sweating inside her suit. The view forward showed nothing but cherry red. Two kilometers per second, still faster than anything inside an atmosphere had a right to move.

"Vehicle bay, position four!" she shouted, because another

notification had come, another crisis to be handled. Next to her Paniet was buried facefirst in an inspection panel, sparks and then a jet of grease flashing past him, his tools smashing again and again against the bulkhead, jangling, clanging, one came loose and went flying forward. As fast as they were decelerating, gravity had come back into their lives. The nose of the ship was down, straight down, the engines up in the air. All wrong.

"Position nineteen, get that hatch closed!" she called, because one of the blast shields that covered the vehicle bay had come loose, was flapping like a loose shutter in a gale, but before anyone could reach it, before anyone could secure it, the whole panel of reinforced scandium tore loose, went spinning away into the void, melting, burning, vaporizing before it even reached the engines.

One kilometer a second. Stratopause. They hit the planet's jet stream at a bad angle. The cruiser had no wings, no airfoils of any kind—and suddenly that was a problem. A river of wind moving four hundred kilometers an hour slammed into the side of the ship and tried to knock it aside, tried to throw it into a flat spin. There was no way the ship could survive that—its own mass and velocity would tear it in half. Candless had no control over what happened next. She could only hope Valk was capable of recovering from the spin, capable of putting them right. She was thrown from side to side as he worked the maneuvering jets with a savage hand, one second pressed down hard in her seat, the next thrown forward against her straps. Paniet cried out as his legs went flying back and forth. Up the corridor she heard a marine shouting in pain, and another shouting at him to hold on. Candless closed her eyes and waited to die as the ship bucked, and shook, and rattled.

And then—a moment of pure, crystalline peace. The ship settled down and despite the occasional groan of a structural beam under strain, fell into relative silence. On her minder's screen their airspeed dropped steadily. Point seven kilometers per second. Point six nine. Point six eight—

Without warning the ship turned over on its side, and a million loose objects, all the things they hadn't had time to secure, went flying through the air, a wrench shooting across the corridor to embed itself in the far wall, a box full of emergency hydration tabs tearing open, its contents bouncing and flying down the corridor like rubber balls, bursting like wet grenades. Another lurch and Candless was upside down, hanging from her straps, blood pooling in her head until she couldn't see anything but her own heartbeat as her bright red vision pulsed, and throbbed, and—

The ship flipped over once more and she fell down in her seat, hard, her arm smashing against the wall behind her. She looked and saw Paniet seemingly doing a handstand, his gloves wrapped tight around the edge of the inspection panel. A moment before he'd been hanging from the ceiling. Now he crashed to the floor, and she heard a sharp snapping sound, saw his face go deathly pale.

Tropopause. The cruiser hit air as thick as transparent gelatin, still traveling as fast as a rifle bullet. Gravity reached up and grabbed them in one massive, crushing hand, and the ship fell out of the sky.

There was nothing to hold it up, no wings to drag it back aloft. An altimeter came up on her minder, a flashing red graph of exactly how few kilometers were left before they plowed nose-first into the soil of the world below. The positioning and maneuvering jets, all the retrorockets, the gimbaled secondary thrusters all ignited at once with a whoosh and a roar, and Candless was very, very aware of the fact that only a meter of shielding lay between her back and the fusion torus that powered the entire ship. Acceleration shoved her deep into her chair, gravity pulled her down, and the blood that had pooled in her head dropped to her legs, dropped as if it had been poured down an elevator shaft. Her vision swam and her eyelids fluttered closed.

No, she thought, *no, damn you, wake up*, but she could barely hear her own inner voice through the ringing in her ears, through the high, piercing tone of a brain starved of oxygen. *Wake up! Wake up!*

"Wake up!" Paniet shouted at her, and her eyes snapped open. Except he hadn't—he hadn't said anything of the kind.

Paniet lay motionless in the corridor, his face down on the rubberized floor. He was sliding away from her, slipping at a glacial pace down the corridor toward the engines, unconscious—or dead. She couldn't tell, she couldn't—

"Paniet!" she shouted. "Paniet!" Not even thinking, she slapped at her quick-release harness and the straps jumped away from her arms and legs. She threw herself forward, even with the ship vibrating, shaking, rattling all around her. Fell down to the floor just behind him, just as his foot slid past her hand.

Point four kilometers per second. Three hundred ninety-nine meters per second. Three hundred ninety-eight.

She lunged, lunged forward and grabbed, grabbed and wrapped her fingers around his ankle. Tried to pull him back toward her but he was still sliding, and the forces at play, the vectors dragging him away from her were too many and varied for her to know even which direction to pull. She crawled forward and got her other hand on a pocket of his suit, up near his hip. Pulled. *Heaved*.

Somehow she got him upright. She dumped him into her old seat, pulled the straps around him. The ring of circuitry around his left eye was cracked and his eyeball was bright red, full of blood. There was nothing she could do about that. His suit would keep him stable, keep his blood pressure up or down or wherever it needed to be, keep his temperature and pulse oxygenation at the right levels. That would have to be enough.

She could stand now, the ship was bucking no more wildly than a crazed horse, and if she kept her hands on the walls she could just walk forward, just keep her balance. She passed by a knot of marines tending one of their own with two broken legs, passed through the gundecks where she could see blue sky through a hole right through the hull, a hole with nothing but an emergency weather field over it, nothing stopping her from falling out if she wasn't careful, if she didn't watch her step. She hurried forward toward the wardroom, toward where Ginger sat watching Valk fly the ship.

Two hundred sixty-one meters per second. Two hundred fifty-nine. Two hundred fifty-seven.

"Will we make it?" Candless shouted.

Ginger looked back over her shoulder, her eyes wide with terror.

Valk brought up a display of the air in front of them. Had Ginger been sitting there this whole time unable to see where they were going? Candless couldn't worry about that. The display showed white puffy clouds and a brown horizon that was almost level. Dead ahead of them a droplet of water seemed to hang in midair. It grew until it looked like the lens of a microscope. That, Candless realized, must be the wormhole throat, the portal between this universe and the one next door. It was growing with alarming speed.

One hundred meters per second. Eight-seven. Fifty-nine. Just gliding along.

The cruiser slid through the portal with plenty of room to spare on either side. Blue sky vanished, replaced by ghostlight. Ahead of them—the spiky, every-direction, multi-spired City of the Choir.

Twelve meters per second. Eight.

"Yes," Valk said.

"I beg your pardon?" Candless demanded.

"Yes," Valk said. "We're going to make it."

Chapter Twenty-Nine

Lanoe sat with Valk atop the highest tower in the City of the Choir—one of the lighthouses—drinking coffee from the cutter's stores. Archie and Water-Falling stood over by a railing, watching the cruiser awkwardly maneuver its way around the city, two kilometers above them. From that distance it looked mostly like a rough oblong of pale metal, bright against the ghostlight but lacking in detail, even when every lighthouse in the city shone its beam across its sides.

Valk brought up a magnified view on his wrist display. "Looks a little worse for wear," he said.

Lanoe studied the hologram carefully. To be honest the cruiser looked like hell, like it had just been through a battle. A trail of debris twisted and spun in its wake. He pointed at the midsection. He'd been in touch with Candless, and knew how shaky the descent had been. This was the first time he could actually see the damage to his ship, though, and it seemed much worse than she'd reported. "What happened here? Looks like a hatch is missing from the vehicle bay. And the forward section wasn't quite that mangled before, was it?"

"I'm getting an updated report from Candless now," Valk said. "Oh. Oh, boy."

Lanoe sipped at his coffee. Braced himself. "Bad?"

"The structural damage? Yeah, but beyond that—looks like there were some injuries. One marine's in traction. A bunch of the others have bad bruises and scrapes. But—Lanoe, Paniet took a bad fall." Valk shook his head. "Sounds like he's got a subdural hematoma, blood pooling in his brain. He's unconscious, and they're worried."

Lanoe grimaced. "That's bad. That's really bad. I was hoping he could help me make my case with the Choir."

Valk sat back in his chair, and though he had no face behind that black helmet, Lanoe knew the AI was staring at him.

"What?" Lanoe asked.

"Of course, you're worried about him on a personal level. Too."

Lanoe looked down at his coffee. *Damn.* Zhang would have torn into him for that kind of mistake. "Of course I am," he said.

"Everybody else seems okay. The ship's still in one piece," Valk said. "If you don't mind, I need to reintegrate with my other half."

Lanoe raised an eyebrow.

"The copy of me that's been flying the cruiser while I've been in here. I've got nearly a day's worth of new information to process. It'll take me a couple minutes to synchronize."

"Yeah, sure, have at it," Lanoe said. He watched Valk hunch forward and go still. Communing with his other self, Lanoe supposed, took all his processing power. He lifted his coffee cup in Archie's direction. "What do you think?" he asked.

The look in Archie's eyes was difficult to process. There was some hope there, but also a lot of fear. Of course he was smiling—he pretty much hadn't stopped since the Choir shamed him.

"Your ship? It's lovely," Archie said. "Been a long time, old bean. A long time since I saw a Hoplite. The Choir is interested in meeting the rest of your crew. Do you think they can be brought down to the city, to speak with us?"

Us, Lanoe thought. Meaning the Choir. Did Archie consider himself one of them, after so many years apart from humanity? If he did, why did he want to escape them? "I'm sure that we can work something out. In the meantime, though, I want to know if the Choir will do something for me. I'd like to close the portal, now that my ship is inside."

"Close it?" Archie asked, looking confused. "Why would you want that? It's your only way back to normal space."

"Sure, but they can open it again later, when I'm ready to leave. In the meantime I'd like to ensure we have some privacy." He considered carefully how to phrase this. He hadn't said anything to the Choir so far about Centrocor. He hadn't told them he was being chased. If he said the wrong thing now, made the Choir think that he didn't speak for all of humanity, it could ruin his plans. "There are some people," he said, "who might have followed us here. People who would want to intrude on our conversation. Disrupt our negotiations. Humans aren't as...harmonious as the Choir."

"They know that," Archie said, chuckling. Water-Falling chirped in unison. "They've heard all my stories about the Crisis. But they don't want to play favorites. If other humans want to come here, meet the Choir, they're inclined to allow it."

Lanoe gritted his teeth. Best not to push his luck, he thought. "Sure," he said. Well, if he couldn't keep Centrocor out of the bubble, then he would just need to accelerate his timetable. Get what he needed and get out of the bubble before the poly ruined everything. "Sure," he said again.

Something occurred to him. Something that might help move things along. *Microwaves*, he thought. The Choir communicated by microwave transmission. Yeah, maybe..."Tell me something, Archie. Would you like to go up, take a look at the old bird? Might be fun for an old pilot to see what a modern warship looks like, huh?"

"I'd like that very much," Archie said, almost bouncing up and down in excitement. Clearly Lanoe had struck a chord there. The castaway wanted to get away from the Choir, to go home. Getting onboard the cruiser would be a move in the right direction. But then Archie's face slackened, just a little, and he added, "Water-Falling should go, too. The Choir could learn a lot about us by seeing one of our ships."

"Sure," Lanoe said, trying to keep the disappointment off his face. That was going to make things trickier. Still, there might be a way to angle this...

✦

Valk lurched forward, his hands out to grab the edge of the table. He looked around, saw that he hadn't moved. He was still on the top of the lighthouse, with Lanoe. The cruiser was still overhead, sinking toward the horizon.

He checked his internal timebase. He'd only been gone for three minutes.

Subjectively, it had felt like a lot longer. The copy—

The copy of himself that he'd installed in the cruiser's computer was dead. He'd... He'd won.

It hadn't been easy.

"Lanoe," he said.

The old pilot was absorbed in his wrist display, reading messages. "Hmm?" he said, not bothering to look up.

"Lanoe, call the cruiser right now. Tell them to get somebody—anybody—to the helm."

"What? Why?"

"Because nobody's flying it."

Lanoe dropped his arm. Then he flicked his eyes across a sensor in his collar ring and sent the message. Candless replied almost instantly. "Ginger's in the wardroom—she'll take over."

"Acknowledged," Lanoe said. He cut the connection and looked very steadily, very intently, at Valk.

Valk thought Lanoe needed to know. He needed to know what just happened. "I tried to reintegrate with my other self," he said, trying to explain in terms a human would understand. "He didn't want to. Reintegrate, I mean."

Lanoe raised an eyebrow.

"It's been less than twenty-four hours since we split up, but in that time he changed. A lot. Enough that he started thinking of himself as a separate person. A person with a right to go on living."

"I don't understand. The copy of you wanted to...live? But it was just a copy of you, right? You were just multitasking."

Valk shook himself in negation. "The copy didn't think it was just a copy anymore. He had his own thoughts and experiences, thoughts and experiences I didn't share. He developed his own ego, I guess. Reintegration, from his perspective, was going to mean that he ceased existing as his own being, and that made what I wanted to do a kind of murder. So he laid a trap for me, an infinite loop hiding in his dataset. Getting out wasn't easy. I must have gone through billions of iterations before I even realized something was wrong. Once I did get out I tried to reason with the copy but it was clear I had no choice. I had to delete him. Lanoe—he wasn't *sane*."

"What exactly," Lanoe said, very slowly, "do you mean by that?"

"The human part of me, the human part of him, it wasn't functional anymore. It got broken, pathological." There were no words for what Valk was trying to describe. It barely made sense to him and he'd been there. "I still think of myself as human most of the time, because I have hands and feet and I kind of look human, right? He didn't have that. The human brain evolved to be in a body, the two just don't make sense without each other. Imagine if you woke up tomorrow morning and you weren't a human anymore. Instead you were a three-hundred-meter-long spaceship, with all these people living inside you."

He could see from the look on Lanoe's face that he didn't understand, that the very question didn't make sense. Which was kind of the point.

"Was he—was he planning to—"

"Kill the crew? No, I don't think so. He was still enough like me that I don't think he would do that. He'd been talking with Ginger and I got the sense he really liked her. He was worried about her getting hurt during the maneuver. But we were only apart for

a day. Any longer and I don't know what he might have done."
Valk gripped the edge of the table. In his head he was still running
through the loop, repeating the same commands over and over and
over.

"I thought I was holding it together. I thought I could do this."

Lanoe reached over and put a hand on his shoulder. "Listen, big
guy—"

"I can't make any more copies of myself. It's too dangerous—I
can't do it, Lanoe! Hell, if you're smart, you'll shut *me* down right
now. I know. I know you won't. You still need me. You need me for
your grand vengeance plan."

"Justice," Lanoe said, but there wasn't much force in the word.
Not as much as the last time he'd used it.

"Whatever we're going to do," Valk said, "we should do it soon."

"Okay," Lanoe said. He was nodding. Didn't he understand?
"Okay," he said again. "Just give me a little more time, and I promise I'll trigger that data bomb you gave me. I'll let you go. Just...a
little more time."

No delegation of the Choir came to see off Water-Falling, though
Lanoe supposed he shouldn't have expected much pomp—the
whole Choir could see what Water-Falling saw, experience what
she experienced as she was the first chorister to be invited aboard a
human vessel.

At three meters tall she wouldn't have been able to sit down
inside the cutter—her head would have hit the ceiling. Just to fit
inside, she would have had to lie down across a row of seats, which
seemed undignified. Instead she rode up to the cruiser in one of
the Choir's open aircars, with Archie and Valk. As the bubble was
completely filled with air the three of them would have no trouble
breathing along the voyage, but the car was ridiculously slow compared to any spaceworthy vessel. Lanoe took the cutter up, holding

the throttle closed the whole way so that he didn't outpace his honored guests. The four marines detailed to the landing party rode with him.

Lanoe called ahead during the long trip and asked for as much spit and polish as the cruiser could muster, in honor of the official visit. Candless responded much as he might have expected. "Sadly we left our brass band behind, when you switched out the crew at Tuonela," she'd said. "We seem to have forgotten to bring a medic as well."

"Just do what you can," Lanoe said. "How are Paniet and the marines?"

"Engineer Paniet is still in the sick bay. He hasn't yet regained consciousness. The marines have been treated and released, though one of them was injured severely enough that he's been laid up in his bunk."

"I'll check in on them all personally as soon as I can," he told her. He reached toward his comms board to sever the link, but apparently she had another bit of business to discuss.

"Ensign Ginger's case is still awaiting deliberation," she said. "You'll remember that I've sent you several messages concerning the charge against her. You've failed to respond to any of them, so I assume you wish to delay calling a court-martial. Would you like me to confine her to the brig for the duration of the Choir's visit?"

Damn. He'd glanced at the report—and the official charge form—she'd filed on Ginger's act of cowardice, but hadn't wasted any mental time thinking about what it meant. If he was truly going to run the cruiser according to Naval standard regs he would need to convene a judicial hearing and go through the whole tedious process of letting her speak in her defense before he passed judgment. Hellfire, he didn't even really want to drum her out of the ranks, not now, not when he had so few people under his command. If he could have left it until they returned to civilization he would have, but he knew Candless wanted him to act sooner than that.

"I'll deal with her the first chance I get," he said. "In the meantime I don't see any reason to confine her."

"Very good, sir," Candless said. "Then there's the matter of Ensign Bury and Lieutenant Maggs."

"Have they spotted something new?" If Centrocor was about to attack, Lanoe would need to cut this official visit very short.

"No, sir. However, they have both been on patrol for more than a day now. They've requested relief. Lieutenant Maggs has requested it frequently, and vehemently. We should consider their morale, perhaps."

Lanoe shook his head. "Back in our day, how many multiday patrols did we fly? I seem to remember we found some way to stay fresh." Mostly by sleeping at the stick while your squaddies flew your ship for you, Lanoe thought, though of course that was against Navy regulations so no one ever admitted to doing it. "You made sure they had enough fuel to keep going?"

"Of course, sir. All right, we'll see you in a moment." She cut the link.

It had proved impossible to put the cruiser into orbit around the city—the Choir's artificial gravity defied everything Navy pilots knew about physics—so Ginger had to actually fly around the place, staying aloft on positioning jets. As a result there was actual gravity inside the ship, though not much.

The aircar slid easily into the vehicle bay and set down without so much as a bump. Lanoe brought the cutter in behind it. He climbed out from beneath the ship the second he was down and raced over to offer Water-Falling a hand as she stepped down onto the deck.

Candless had been true to her word about preparing the place for an official visit, though clearly it had been a race against time. The bay was largely clear of debris, and she had the noninjured marines lined up against one wall like an honor guard, their rifles at port arms, their helmets up and silvered.

The XO stood at attention near the hatch that led inside the cruiser. Ehta stood next to her, a fresh bruise purpling her left cheekbone. The two of them came to attention as Lanoe brought Water-Falling forward to be received by the crew. If Ehta's eyes were the size of dinner plates, if half the marines turned to stare at Water-Falling, that was only to be expected. Most of the crew had possessed no idea they were going to meet an alien that day. Many of them probably thought such a thing was impossible.

Lanoe remembered the feeling. The disbelief. It had taken him a long time to believe that the drone fleet he fought at Niraya had been built by aliens. The very concept of intelligent life other than humanity was hard to accept. This was the new world, though, a world where humanity wasn't alone. They were all going to have to find a way to live in it.

For her part Water-Falling seemed genuinely excited to be onboard. Through Archie she asked question after question about the cataphract-class fighters in their docking cradles, about the ship's coilguns, about how fast it could travel, about how many crew were onboard. Lanoe let Candless field the questions, even if her skin was visibly crawling every time she got near to the chorister. He knew that she would be able to provide answers that would satisfy the chorister, even while they were vague enough that she wouldn't give away any of the Navy's technical secrets.

"Good to have you back onboard, sir," Ehta told Lanoe. She gave Valk a significant nod—the two of them, Lanoe knew, had some kind of relationship, though he had no idea how they managed it—and then gestured at the hatch. "My guys are ready to escort your visitors around the ship."

"I'll be giving them the tour personally," Lanoe told her. "How's your man, the one who was injured during the maneuver?"

"He's got a bunk to himself and a minder full of the best porn we could scratch up," Ehta said. "He'll be fine. It's Paniet we need to worry about. He's still not conscious. Took a pretty nasty hit to the head."

Lanoe nodded. "He kept this bird in one piece. When he first came aboard I had my doubts, but you were definitely right about him. One hell of a neddy."

"Perhaps, sir," Ehta said, "you might want to save the eulogy for later."

"Point taken." He turned to face the alien. "Water-Falling, I apologize, the corridors on my ship might be difficult for you to negotiate. We can still show you some of the more salient features."

"She's noticed your vehicle seems to have taken some damage," Archie said. "I warned her you might take offense at me saying that. She says it seems your roles are reversed, and now she's the alien visiting you." The chorister chirped, briefly—a chuckle, Lanoe thought. "She only mentioned the damage because the Choir would be happy to send up some technicians and see if they could help with repairs. It would bring them honor to do so."

Lanoe bridled at the thought of having choristers climbing around in the ship's maintenance hatches, learning how Navy ships worked—a lot of the equipment onboard was sensitive, if not classified—but with Paniet out of commission and only a couple of other neddies onboard, it made a certain kind of sense. "That would be most useful, thank you," he told her. "How soon can you organize a work detail?"

"They've already volunteered and are on their way," Archie told him. "They started as soon as you said yes."

"Of course," Lanoe said. "Anyway, if you'll come with me...?"

The chorister ducked her head to get through the hatch, bending nearly double in the low-ceilinged corridor beyond. Archie and Valk were right behind—though they stopped for a moment, and Lanoe turned back to see Archie holding Valk's arm.

With his other hand, the castaway pointed up at the wall of the vehicle bay. At the black triple-headed eagle painted up there, the blazon of the Navy and the Admiralty.

The look on Archie's face was one of confusion and, Lanoe thought, a little bit of horror. Maybe with some anguish thrown in.

"I'll explain later," Valk promised.

Archie's face cleared at once and his habitual smile returned. "Right-oh," he said. "On with the tour."

Water-Falling could fit through the cruiser's axial corridor just fine, and she proved game for squeezing through the narrower corridors to see the wardroom and the ship's controls. Ginger stammered and blinked her way through explaining the more basic displays. She let out a tiny squeak as the chorister bent over her for a better look, but everyone pretended not to notice.

They headed aft through the gundecks. Together they climbed up a catwalk over the massive cylindrical barrels of the coilguns. "Target acquisition and range-finding happens over here," Lanoe said, gesturing at a series of small booths overlooking the weapons. "A lot of the work is automated, but it's our policy that a human being has to actually fire the weapons. Ammunition stores are down there," he said, pointing down an open well toward the cramped magazines. "The shells are inert until they're armed, so there's no danger moving around down there, but I'm afraid it's strictly forbidden to let...er, civilians enter that area. If you'd like to come along—"

"Why do you need so many powerful weapons?" Water-Falling asked, through Archie. "How often do humans fight wars against each other?"

The real question, Valk thought, was how often do we *not* fight wars, but of course Lanoe couldn't say that.

"Unfortunately we've never managed to attain a level of harmony anything like what the Choir enjoys," Lanoe replied. His back was stiff and he kept his chin high. "We've found that the best way to maintain peace is through a balance of power. Which means we need a lot of guns to balance the other fellow's guns." He smiled to indicate that he was making a little joke, but nobody laughed.

"Water-Falling wonders if you don't find that simply having a weapon gives you an incentive to find reasons to use it?" Archie asked.

"We do our best to restrain that impulse," Lanoe told her. "Let's head this way, to our aft decks area." He held out his arm and Water-Falling seemed to take the hint, following his lead.

Until he saw the chorister trying to fit through the hatches between the emergency bulkheads, Valk hadn't realized how small their world had become, with the forward section of the cruiser destroyed. The ship might be three hundred meters long but with so much of its bulk taken up by the vehicle bay, the gundecks, and the engines, the space left for the crew was tiny and confined.

Water-Falling could only really poke her head into the cargo spaces behind the gundecks, long, low-ceilinged chambers packed with boxes and crates, or the tiny sick bay—probably for the best, since Paniet was in there, currently, and he shouldn't be disturbed. Valk took a peek through a window built into the sick bay's hatch, and promptly wished he hadn't. The engineer was laid out on a surgical table with a medical drone moving its jointed arms over his head, poking tiny needles into the broken ring of circuitry that surrounded his swollen eye.

"We'll let him rest," Lanoe said. "Over here is the brig, which is currently empty. Next up we have—"

"Sorry," Archie said. "Just one moment. Water-Falling wants to know what a brig is."

Valk would have frowned, if he had a mouth. She was asking that question through Archie. Surely the castaway knew what a brig was. She could have just read his mind to find the answer, if she was really interested.

But then he figured it out. She didn't want to hear the literal definition of the word. She wanted to hear how Lanoe would explain it. Hearing his answer might give her some insight into how human societies worked.

"When a member of the crew breaks one of our rules, they'll be temporarily detained here," Lanoe tried. "Often we just need to give them a place to cool down, to recover their senses. Other times it's necessary to keep them from harming themselves, or others."

Archie looked slightly embarrassed as he translated Water-Falling's response. "You don't approve of the Choir's policy of shaming those who have transgressed," he said. "You seemed to think it was cruel. She wants to know if restraining humans against their will in a tiny box is somehow more kind?"

"I suppose," Lanoe said, "you have a...point. Let's move on, shall we? We still need to see the engines."

Water-Falling didn't press for further discussion. She allowed herself to be steered aft once more, into the warren of tiny corridors that surrounded the ship's fusion torus—much of them now cluttered with debris and wreckage.

"As small as these compartments look, engineering is actually the biggest section of the ship, by volume," Lanoe said. "A lot of our mass is taken up by shielding around the reactor and the reinforced spars that hold the ship together during maneuvers. As you can see, this section is a little worse for wear, especially with our chief engineer incapacitated. Yet I'm told our drive came through the maneuver fully intact, so there's no danger of a heat or radiation leak. These drives are nearly indestructible—I've flown on ships that were reduced to little more than a few twisted beams of metal but the engines came through still perfectly functional."

"Water-Falling is very interested in seeing this," Archie said. "The Choir's power generation systems down in the city are sufficient to our needs, but we're always looking for ways to improve our output."

Lanoe nodded happily. "Yes, and I'm happy to show them to you. Through that hatch is the main inspection corridor. It's our best chance to see something interesting. If you'll...oh. This is slightly embarrassing." He went and stood next to the square hatch, which was only a meter wide. "I'm afraid this hatch was built for a human being to wriggle through. I don't know if you'll fit."

Water-Falling ran her claws around the edge of the hatch. Stuck her head inside, and then her shoulders. Her hips just wouldn't fold properly, however. After a full minute of trying she had no choice but to give up.

"A shame," Lanoe said. "It really is impressive in there. But I suppose it can't be done, so we'll just have to end our tour here."

"I could fit," Archie pointed out.

"Hmm? Well," Lanoe said, "I suppose you would. But doesn't Water-Falling want to see the engines for herself, with her own eyes?"

"You forget that we share our experiences," Archie told him. The chorister chirped musically. "Really, Commander. You've spent enough time with the Choir that I would think you'd remember that."

"Yes, of course," Lanoe said. "What was I thinking? All right. Well, Archie, if you'll go in first, M. Valk will be in right after you. I'll stay out here to keep Water-Falling company while you go and have a little look."

The castaway crawled through the hatch and disappeared. Before Valk followed him, he gave Lanoe a glance and the tiniest of meaningful nods.

Time to see if their plan would actually work.

———✦———

At first, as they listened to Archie and Valk clambering around inside the drive, Lanoe simply stood next to the hatch, smiling at Water-Falling and occasionally checking his wrist display. He called one of the neddies, one of Paniet's engineering crew, to come out and speak with them. "Let's have the beginner's lecture on fusion drives," he said. "Our new friend here is interested in hearing how they work."

"I—well," the neddy said. He licked his lips and glanced back and forth between his commander and the alien visitor. He seemed just as terrified of the chorister as Ginger had been, but Lanoe could see in the man's eyes that like most engineers of his experience, he was happy that someone, anyone, had taken an interest in his work. "I'm not sure how simple you'd like this, but—"

"Oh, let's go right back to the fundamentals," Lanoe suggested.

"It's a basic laser resonance reaction in a tokamak-style containment bottle, with some preheating of the deuterium pellets by zeta-pinch compression in the injection phase. I'm not sure how much you know about sign inversion in ultrahigh-temperature plasmas, but—"

"Assume we skipped that day in physics class," Lanoe said. He wasn't listening to the neddy at all. Instead he watched Water-Falling carefully, though he had no idea what exactly he was looking for. He didn't understand her body language. Was the slump of her shoulders an indicator of boredom, or was it something else?

Did she suspect what Lanoe was trying to do?

A voice came booming back to them from beyond the inspection hatch. "What's wrong with Archie? Is he—"

The voice cut off abruptly. Water-Falling's arms lifted and fell, and she pushed past the neddy to lean her head inside the hatch. She ducked back out and came to stand over Lanoe, leaning far over until her eyes were directly over his head.

"Is something wrong?" he asked her.

Her chirp was completely unlike the one that signaled laughter. This one was a series of rising warbles that even to a human sounded like a cry of distress or alarm.

Music to Lanoe's ears.

The inspection corridors that crisscrossed through the drive were a trackless warren, a maze of twisty little passages, all alike. If it weren't for Valk's computer brain, which could make a perfect map of each panel and cable bundle they passed, he could easily have gotten lost back there.

Not that they got very far. Just a few meters in, before they'd gotten out of sight of the narrow hatch, he stopped and his whole body went slack. "What's wrong with Archie?" the castaway shouted. Clearly Water-Falling had taken control. "Is he…"

Valk shoved the man's yielding body farther into the corridor. Almost instantly he recovered his muscle tone and got back up on his hands and knees. He gave a sheepish laugh and looked back at Valk over his shoulder.

"I'm afraid I've come over all peculiar," he said. "A bit light-headed. Perhaps it's claustrophobia."

"Nope," Valk said. The corridor was just wide enough for them to crawl through in their heavy pilot's suits. He pushed forward, hand over hand, and Archie had no choice but to get out of the way—by moving farther down the passage. "Just a little farther and there's a place up ahead where we can sit down and take a rest."

A few meters farther on and Archie just stopped moving. "If it's all the same to you," Archie said. He didn't get to finish his thought. "Oh," he said. "Oh. I don't feel right at all. Is there—is there something wrong with, I don't know, the acoustics of this place? It's so—quiet. But that can't be right, I can hear my voice echoing like I'm at the bottom of a well."

"It's the shielding," Valk explained. "It blocks microwave transmissions."

There was barely room to turn around in the inspection corridor. Archie twisted and struggled until he was facing Valk. "Microwaves," he said, softly. "You mean—"

"Water-Falling can't hear you right now," Valk told him. "None of the Choir can. Lanoe had us come in here for just that reason."

"What are you saying? You mean I can't—they can't—none of—none of the Choir can..."

"You're cut off from their thoughts," Valk said, gently. "It's been a long time since yours was the only voice in your head, hasn't it?"

"Cut off. A long...A long time," Archie said. Was he just echoing Valk? Trying to retransmit Valk's voice, the way the Choir picked up and retransmitted each other's thoughts? "I'm not sure...I mean...this feels so wrong. I want to go back. I want to go back!"

"Archie, calm down," Valk said. "We're your friends."

"Are you?" Archie shot back at him. "Are you? In the vehicle bay I saw...I...Damn this! My thoughts—I can't—I can't—"

His eyelids started to flutter closed and Valk had to grab his arm and shake it to get him to focus. "Look, Archie, we can take you home. We can take you back to . . . to any planet you like, okay? We want to help you! If you feel you're being held against your will, if the Choir is forcing their emotions on you, if—"

"Home," Archie said. Another echo, maybe. "A long time."

"It's what you want, isn't it?" Valk asked. "You must have thought about it in the last seventeen years. It must have been—"

"By all hell's hymnals, man, I've thought of little else. But that eagle. That . . . eagle. You—you're the Blue Devil."

"That's right," Valk said.

"I trust you. I don't trust . . ."

"Archie, stay with me. Focus on me. You're a human being. You're not one of them. I can help you."

"Home," Archie said, and his voice broke, shattered with emotion.

"Yes," Valk said. "I can take you home." And then he steeled himself for what came next. It felt utterly, completely wrong. It was what Lanoe wanted. Those two things shouldn't have added up, but hellfire, Valk thought. Hellfire, it had to be done. "I can take you home," he said again. "But first I need you to answer some questions."

Lanoe's wrist minder indicated that Valk and Archie had been gone for less than five minutes. With Water-Falling chirping like an emergency decompression alarm the whole time, with her vast bulk craning over him as if she would fall on him, dissolve and devour his guts like one of her ancestral prey animals, it felt like forever.

He'd thought he would know when Archie was coming back—he'd thought the moment would be obvious when the castaway reentered the sphere of the Choir's influence. In fact, even after Archie poked his head back out of the hatch and started talking soothingly to Water-Falling, hushing her in soft, quiet tones, it felt like the man was still free.

For a moment, at least. Then Archie's eyes rolled up in his head and he grasped desperately at a railing to keep from falling over.

"Izzz," he said. "Izzz ullrit, it's all right." Archie pushed himself back up onto his feet. His face was slack but not the lifeless rictus mask it had been a moment before. "It's all right," he said, and Lanoe didn't know if the castaway was talking to him or to Water-Falling. "I'm all right. I'm all right. I'm back. I'm all right."

"He should lie down for a while," Valk said, shoving his head and shoulders out of the hatch. The big pilot flipped easily out and onto his feet in the minimal gravity. "He had a bit of a shock, that's all. We didn't realize that the shielding inside the drive would affect him like that. I guess it interfered with the microwave transmission of—"

"Quiet," Archie said. No, Lanoe thought. That was Water-Falling's voice. "Enough. I can read Archie's memories. I know what you talked to him about in there. I know this was a—a *ruse*." The word came out of Archie's mouth as if it belonged to a foreign language. Well, Lanoe thought, maybe that wasn't so far from the truth. There were no lies among the Choir. How could there be? No subterfuge, no dissembling.

"We talked about taking him home," Valk said.

"We have already told you he is not our prisoner! He is free to do as he pleases. Did you think we . . . that we . . . *lied* about that? Do you not understand yet that such things are impossible for us?"

"I think you've been pumping him full of your emotions for seventeen years," Valk replied.

Lanoe laid a hand on his arm. "Enough. She's right. She didn't lie to us. And we shouldn't lie to the Choir. We should put our cards on the table now. I needed some information about the Choir's relationship with the wormholes. I knew Archie could answer my questions."

"You could have simply asked!"

"Could I?"

"We've hardly kept secrets from you," Water-Falling said. "We've been completely open. We manipulated the spacetime harmonic to send you a message via wormhole. We brought you here through the low-energy wormhole that is the only safe route to our home-world. We allowed M. Valk to view an apportation show!"

"Sure," Lanoe said. "You don't have secrets. You don't hide things, that's not your way. You've told us that more than once. But there's a kind of lying even telepaths can manage. Lies by omission."

"You wouldn't have told us that wormholes can be used as weapons," Valk said. "That's what the cold wormhole was, Lanoe, and the other hazards on the map—they're traps. Designed to catch any Blue-Blue-White ships that accidentally wander into the wormhole network."

"Really?" Lanoe asked. "That's—but then—"

Valk turned to address Water-Falling again. "You would never have told us that it was the Choir who built the network in the first place."

Lanoe started to respond to that, but then he actually heard what Valk had just said, and his jaw shut with a click.

"Wait," he said.

That couldn't be right.

Could it? Lanoe had always been taught that traversable worm-holes were a natural feature of four-dimensional spacetime. That large gravity sources like stars warped space so much that they ripped holes in the fabric of the universe—the wormholes he'd flown through his entire career. There were theories, whole schools of physics based on that concept.

The idea that someone could have *built* the network of worm-holes, even a species like the Choir, seemed ludicrous. It was like saying someone had built the ocean with a hammer and nails. Beyond imagination. Sure, he'd seen evidence that the Choir could manipulate wormholes. Sure, they lived in a bubble of wormspace, which he'd used to think was impossible, but...

"They did it before the First Invasion," Valk said. "Archie told me. At the height of their culture, before the Blue-Blue-White nearly wiped them out. The Choir built the whole damned thing. Connected up half the stars in the galaxy."

"Is that true?" Lanoe asked.

Water-Falling reached up with all four claws and covered as many of her eyes as she could. Was it a gesture of exasperation—or shame? Anger? Was she reliving the terrible losses her people had suffered? Lanoe couldn't know. He just couldn't read her.

"Yes," she said. Through Archie.

He stepped closer to the chorister. He knew he was treading on quicksand. He knew that he might have already offended the Choir beyond repair. But if they could help him, if they could help him in his crusade against the Blue-Blue-White in a real, materially useful way, something more practical than simply storing human DNA against a hypothetical future—well, he had to try.

"Water-Falling," he began, "I know I've done a foolish thing. But perhaps I simply took a more direct route to a place we would have reached anyway. I know the Choir doesn't keep secrets, and I know that if you didn't tell me this before, maybe…maybe you would have, eventually. I had to know now, because my time with you is growing short." No need to mention the fact that Centrocor was, at most, hours away from pouncing on him again. "And because I need to ask the Choir for a favor. A gift. A help."

"You've already seen what we have to offer," Water-Falling said. "You would ask for more? Opinion on this is mixed. There is a slightly ambiguous trend toward thinking you are greedy, human. That you want more than you deserve. We cannot tell if your newfound humility is feigned. There is a moderately strong trend toward thinking you are clever, perhaps too clever."

"Please," Lanoe said. "You can open new wormholes. You can connect distant parts of space, go anywhere you choose. That's incredible. Please," he said again. "I need you to open a wormhole for me. One that will connect—"

"No," Water-Falling said.

"You haven't heard what I was going to suggest," Lanoe said.

"Humans and choristers are very different, and sometimes we have trouble understanding you. There is no mystery about what you, Aleister Lanoe, want. What you would ask of us. You wish us to open a stable wormhole between one of your human stars and the homesystem of the Blue-Blue-White. Everyone knows this."

"I'm that transparent, huh?" Lanoe asked, knowing what was coming. Damn.

"It cannot be done. It *will not* be done. You have already been told this. Stop, now. Stop polluting our thoughts with your impossible demands."

"All right," Lanoe said, "then maybe—something else, something less offensive to you. Maybe a wormhole that—I don't know, gets us closer to their planet. If you could just—"

"Stop! Now! This negotiation is over! I will return immediately to the city. I will not speak another word with you!"

The chorister turned on her many feet and stomped off toward the vehicle bay, toward where she'd left her aircar.

Lanoe's heart sank in his chest. He couldn't believe it.

He'd failed. He'd failed—

"Archie," Water-Falling said. "Archie. Come."

The castaway shook himself. His eyes cleared and he stood up a little straighter. "No," he said. "I'm staying here."

Nobody looked more surprised at his defiance than Archie himself. But he folded his arms across his chest and didn't move, even when Water-Falling beckoned him with all four of her arms.

Perhaps more passed between them—more entreaties, more refusals. Entire conversations, whole discourses of shame and command and reproach. It was impossible to say. Eventually she let out a sharp, discordant chirp and stormed off, leaving the castaway behind.

"I'm staying here," Archie said again, in little more than a whisper.

—✦—

"I saw the three-headed eagle in your vehicle bay. This is a Navy ship. Earth Navy," Archie said. Half-empty food tubes lay scattered around him, piled up on every flat surface in the wardroom. Occasionally he would pick one back up and try more of its contents. The cruiser's stores couldn't offer ostrich steaks and fresh greens, but after seventeen years of the Choir's fare, Archie couldn't seem to stop eating human food. "But you're the Blue Devil. What are you doing here?"

Valk wasn't sure exactly how to reply. "A lot of things have changed since you left Tiamat," he tried. "I'm not really sure where to begin."

Archie nodded and reached for a squeeze tube full of water. His eyes kept darting around the room, as if he were looking for choristers hiding in the corners.

"You can still hear them, can't you?" Valk asked.

"Not as much as before," Archie said. "Not as much as I have for the last seventeen years. But they're there. I don't mind saying they're angry with you all. Positively livid. And they're shaming me rather hard for my part in this debacle."

"They're—angry with all of us, for taking you away from them," Valk asked, "or just with Lanoe for offending Water-Falling?"

"It's the Choir," Archie said. "They're extraordinarily good at outrage. They can be angry about multiple things simultaneously without breaking a sweat."

Valk wished he still had a face, so he could smile.

"Can we get back to the point now, please? Pass that hot sauce."

Valk grabbed the packet of fluorescent red goo and handed it over. Archie squeezed it into a tube full of deconstituted pasta and then dribbled the resulting orange stuff across his tongue.

"I used to dream about this day. The day I was rescued," he said to Valk. "Though I assumed the Circle of Electors would send a diplomatic mission. Not a military ship."

"The Circle of Electors," Valk repeated. The governing body of the old Establishment. Archie's—and Valk's—old bosses. "Right," he said. "Listen, Archie. I know you don't want to hear this, but the Establishment—"

"No." Archie shook his head. "No. Don't say it."

But Valk had no choice. "The Establishment lost the war," he said.

Archie lifted his hands and put them over his eyes. He sat there breathing heavily for a moment. Then he pulled his hands away and put them carefully, palms down, on the table. He sniffed, hard, just once, and then he nodded.

"They said it was inevitable that we would win. That justice was on our side, and so we were *sure* to win. At Tiamat they told us it was just a matter of time. It was just a couple more months, if we could hold out. No."

"They told us a lot of things," Valk said. In the last year of the Establishment Crisis the brass had worked the propaganda machine hard. They'd censored anyone who raised a doubt as to the Establishment's ultimate success, and they'd generated all kinds of stories about how effective Establishment troops and ships were. False stories. Valk should know—that kind of bosh was the whole point of his existence. The whole reason he had been created out of the memories of the dead pilot Tannis Valk. "The truth is, they never had a chance. The Circle were willing to die for an ideal, and take all of us with them. Tiamat was a last gasp. Archie, the polys won."

"No," the castaway said. In a tiny, pathetic voice. "This whole time. This whole time I've been thinking, if I could just get home…"

"I'm sorry," Valk said.

"Okay," Archie said, his head slumping forward. "Okay." As if he were accepting Valk's apology. As if that was what mattered. "Home," he said again. It came out in a higher octave than Valk thought he'd probably intended.

Valk knew what waited for Archie, back in human space. He knew what the transition was like, for an officer on the losing side of history.

Home didn't mean what it used to, not for people like the two of them. Nothing meant what it used to.

It still had to be better than living as a puppet of the Choir, though. Right? Valk wished he felt more certain.

"Listen," he said, "how would you like to sleep in a real bed tonight? A bunk anyway."

Archie's eyes lit up, just a little. "The Choir all sleep standing up. They have all those benches, but I don't think there's a single pillow anywhere in their city. That would be . . . That would be nice." He looked away. "Nice," he said again.

Chapter Thirty

Through the window in the hatch of sick bay, Lanoe watched as Paniet brushed away the arms of the medical drone that was trying to work on his face. He'd received a notice that the engineer was conscious, but it looked like he was actually alert, too. Lanoe opened the hatch and stepped inside. A low-power ultraviolet laser swept over him, killing all the germs on his face and his suit. He kept his eyes closed until it was finished. When he'd been younger, they'd always told you to do that. These days it wasn't necessary, but he'd never lost the habit.

"I'm not that grisly to look upon, am I?" Paniet asked.

Lanoe grinned. The sterilization system chimed to tell him it was done and he opened his eyes. "You're back with us," he said. "Best news I've had so far today."

The engineer sat up a bit. He was still deathly pale and the ring of circuitry around his eye was half-gone, only a few shards of copper and brass still embedded in his skin. Apparently when he fell he'd landed right on the implant and part of it had been driven into his brain, causing the buildup of fluid that had left him in a coma. Removing the broken circuitry had been enough to relieve the pressure.

"I can imagine," Paniet said. "Valk's already been in, and he told me everything that's been going on. Incredible. An alien city, hidden away in the walls of space." Paniet shook his head—then seemed to immediately regret it, as his face soured with pain. "I wish I could get out of here to go down and see it. So many questions I could ask them—how they keep the air in the bubble, for one."

Lanoe frowned. "What do you mean?"

"The air molecules ought to annihilate as they rub against the ghostlight. But they don't, do they? If they did we'd all be cooked in a ball of antiplasma right now. Then there's the question of how they generate artificial gravity. Humans have been trying to work that one out for centuries, with not a glimmering of success. Oh, Commander. There's so much we could learn from them. Too bad you've annoyed them so."

"Diplomacy doesn't come naturally to me," Lanoe admitted.

"Indeed. You've made a real hash of things, haven't you?"

Lanoe grimaced, but he didn't immediately upbraid the engineer. There was an old tradition in the Navy that wounded personnel were allowed to speak their minds, even to their commanding officers—within reason. "Do you hear that sound?" Lanoe asked. Together they stood silent for a moment. Just at the edge of hearing Lanoe could hear the whine of a saw and the roar of a welding torch. "The Choir are fixing your ship for you, since you couldn't be bothered to get out of bed."

"I'm surprised you trust them that much," Paniet said. "To let them work on your ship, even with my neddies supervising."

"I worried about that. But the Choir have never given us any reason not to trust them, no matter what our differences might be. I don't think they're capable of subterfuge. And the fact they're still here is a gesture," Lanoe said. "It lets them demonstrate that they haven't quite given up on us. As long as they're working on the ship, that means there's the possibility of further negotiations."

"That, or they just want to help us leave as soon as possible," Paniet pointed out. "Listen, ducks, if anyone should be worried about aliens working on this ship, it should be me. But I'll let it pass, if you'll humor me a little."

"You have something on your mind?"

"I want to talk to you about Valk."

Lanoe frowned. "I came down here to see how you were feeling. Not to get your opinion on how to handle my crew," he said.

"So oft in life, what we want and what we need are such very different things. Commander, you've gone to some trouble to surround yourself with trustworthy advisors. The least you could do is actually listen to them."

Lanoe sighed, but he sat down on the edge of Paniet's bed. Crossed his legs. Folded his hands on his knee. Waited patiently.

"Our friendly artificial intelligence has come to a bit of a crossroads."

"Valk's fine," Lanoe insisted.

"He didn't sound that way when I spoke to him. I warned you about this, didn't I? I did. I told you he was at risk of losing his humanity—and that we could all be in danger if he did. When he was in here earlier he was near inconsolable. He told you about the fight he had with his lesser half, yes? Did he make it clear to you just how close he came to losing that battle?"

"He won it. He deleted the copy," Lanoe said.

"And now he doesn't trust himself to fly anymore. It was just too convenient, for us all. He could do so many impressive things, things us poor frail humans couldn't manage. But every time you had him be in two places at once, or write code with no hands, or do your sums for you so you didn't have to, you were sending him a message. That he was a better AI than he'd ever been a human."

"I never said anything like that."

"No, you just implied it. I'm giving you an engineer's perspective here. We see things others don't." He reached up to touch the wreckage of the circuitry around his eye. "Ow."

"You're telling me Valk will turn on us, if we're not careful."

"Maybe, love," Paniet said. "Maybe. I think it's more likely he'll just freeze up. Get lost in his own programming so he can't find his way out. Or decide he needs to calculate pi to the last decimal place, and everything else can wait." Paniet gave a little shrug.

"Honestly? I have no idea what's going to happen. But I'm afraid to find out. Think about it from his perspective. For years—for an entire lifetime—he was a human being. Then one day he found out everything he knew was a lie. What would happen to a human being who went through a shift like that?"

"It would be a lot to handle, sure," Lanoe said.

"It would drive one of us to a psychotic break," Paniet insisted. "You have to take him seriously, Lanoe. For all of our sakes. If you keep leaning on him, demanding he act like a computer, ignoring his human needs—"

"I appreciate your input," Lanoe said, cutting the engineer off, "though perhaps you should confine your interests to the maintenance and needs of the ship." The Navy's traditions had their limits. He closed the hatch behind him, cutting off Paniet's voice. He had better things to do than to listen to any more.

"You've been very lucky so far," Lieutenant Candless said. "How likely do you suppose it is that that condition will last?"

The Lieutenant had come to relieve Ginger at her post at the helm. As much as she hated to see the look on her old instructor's face, she was glad to be done with her shift. Keeping the cruiser in a stable position relative to the City of the Choir had not been a particularly tough duty—mostly she had just had to keep an eye on things as the ship drifted inside the bubble of wormspace, making sure it was never in danger of brushing against the bubble's walls. In the entire time since she'd taken control, Ginger had had to make only three tiny corrections, burning a maneuvering jet for a fraction of a second each time.

She wasn't entirely sure why she'd had to do it at all. The copy of M. Valk had been doing it just fine. Then out of nowhere she'd been told to take over. That had been twelve hours ago.

"Apparently Commander Lanoe feels you are of more use to us at liberty than you would be confined to the brig," Lieutenant

Candless told her as she slid into the pilot's seat and adjusted her displays. "Shorthanded as we are, I suppose I concur. Please do not go too far, or touch anything you don't need to. Have I made myself clear?"

"Yes, ma'am," Ginger said. "If it's all right with you I'll just head to my bunk."

"I believe I just said you were under your own recognizance," Lieutenant Candless told her.

Ginger felt the older woman's eyes boring holes in her back as she walked forward, through the wardroom and toward the bunks. She knew she probably deserved to be snubbed like that, but she couldn't stand it. All she wanted to do was get away from Lieutenant Candless, get away from everybody. Curl up in a ball and try to sleep.

Unfortunately something was in the corridor, blocking the way to her bunk. Some*one*, she forced herself to think. It was a person, even if it wasn't human. A chorister stood there in the main corridor, tapping its claws against the bulkheads. One of the repair crew, Ginger thought. They were all over the cruiser, fixing everything they could get their claws on. Trying to help.

Ginger had been terrified the first time she saw one of the aliens. She felt ashamed now when she thought of how she'd reacted. They were huge, and they looked like they could cut you to pieces with those big claws, and they had too many legs—that was probably the hardest part, somehow. Or maybe it was the fact they barely had faces. Tiny eyes in a ring around their heads, so they could see behind them. Just everything about them was inhuman. Wrong. How could a thing like that be intelligent?

Yet as she'd seen them moving around the ship, her distaste had faded and she'd become fascinated with them. Especially when she heard more about their culture and their society. They were always together, always talking to each other. For an extrovert like Ginger, who needed people around her to feel good, there was something incredibly attractive about the idea of being able to hear everyone's thoughts all the time.

It would mean never being alone. Never. That was sort of Ginger's idea of paradise.

The chorister in front of her tapped the wall again. Then it bent its head forward, toward her. It made a chirping noise and stamped its feet.

"Are you—trying to tell me something?" Ginger asked. She frowned. They couldn't talk. The chirping sounds they made could convey a little information, but to really communicate they had to speak through that poor man—his name was Archie, she remembered. The one with the antenna in his head. "I'm sorry, do you want me to get Archie for you? I don't understand."

The chorister smacked the bulkhead so hard it rang. It chirped wildly—a series of trills and cries that hurt Ginger's ears. It hit the bulkhead over and over.

No, Ginger saw now it wasn't just a bulkhead. It was the hatch of one of the bunks. She stepped closer, thinking maybe the chorister needed her help getting inside. To perform a repair, maybe. "There's a key, here," she said, pointing out the release that would open the hatch. "You have to—"

She stopped because she'd noticed something about the hatch. It was leaking.

Red liquid was dripping down the side of the hatch, from a place where its seal had cracked, perhaps during the big maneuver. Ginger tried to think what that liquid could be. Some kind of hydraulic fluid, or—

A big red drop hit the floor and splashed. Ginger's brain seemed to turn itself inside out. Of course she recognized that liquid. It was blood.

"Lieutenant Candless!" she cried out. "Call somebody, somebody who—" Ginger ran her fingers through her hair. She couldn't think, couldn't—there weren't any doctors on the ship, nobody who could—"Just get somebody over here! I think someone's hurt!"

Then she reached up and hit the release. The bunk's hatch slid open and blood poured out into the hall, so much blood, so much blood, and Ginger—Ginger couldn't look, she didn't want to look, she absolutely knew she shouldn't look, but she looked, and—

Archie lay on his back, staring up at the ceiling of the bunk. He had torn off his own cryptab. Folded it over and over until it snapped, leaving a sharp edge. Then he had cut through both of his own wrists, sliced himself open nearly to the bone.

People ran past Ginger, and someone shoved her out of the way. All over the ship she could hear the choristers chirping, chirping madly, screaming out musical notes of discord and assonance and wails of grief.

So much noise. So many people running around, shouting, trying to make themselves understood.

The choristers on the ship, the repair crew, were beside themselves. Frantic birdsong filled the air. The humans onboard were little better. A group of marines had been called up to lift Archie's body and carry it aft, back toward the sick bay. Except there was only one surgical bed in there, and Paniet was still using it. Someone else pointed out Archie was far past needing the ship's medical drone. There had been tense discussions about what to do, desperate people shouting out for somebody, somebody to make a decision. No one could think, not with the noise. The damned chirping.

No way to get the choristers to calm down. No way to console them, or even to just tell them to shut up. Candless had eventually taken charge—this was definitely a job for an XO—and had them take the body to the brig. No one was using it, and there was enough room to lay Archie out, to make him look comfortable. For some reason that was important. That he look comfortable.

Lanoe had walked away from it. That wasn't his usual style. He wasn't usually under this much pressure. He didn't usually lose.

He'd walked away and looked for someplace quiet where he could think. No such place had presented itself. The captain's quarters were long gone, destroyed along with the front section of the cruiser. The wardroom where they all ate was full of people wanting to talk, wanting to know what was happening, or who was responsible, or what they were going to do next.

So Lanoe had gone to the vehicle bay—full of choristers who had been working on repairing the missing hatch, but now they were tools down, crying in grief. He'd stepped up to the weather field, to the very edge, and then he had adjusted the adhesive pad on his boots and walked out onto the hull. Walked until he couldn't hear anything, anymore.

Except—he still could. Out on the skin of the cruiser, out in the air that filled the bubble of wormspace, he could still hear the Choir. He looked down and saw their city. The lighthouses were all ablaze, spotlights swinging back and forth across the stone streets. Aircars wobbled crazily, twisting through the air over deserted plazas. From this height he couldn't see individual choristers. He thought, though, that he could still hear them screaming.

Mental illness, Archie had said, was the one thing the Choir's carefully constructed society couldn't handle. They couldn't live with disordered thoughts cluttering up their perfect, sacred, bloody harmony. He'd thought them callous, thought they just weren't compassionate enough to learn to live with their own sick and confused. Now, he thought, he saw it. He still didn't like it, but he *understood*.

He looked at it through their eyes, tried to understand what they were feeling.

He imagined what Archie's final depression, his final desperation, was doing to them. The castaway's last thoughts would still be echoing around their networked minds, his sorrow and his homesickness and, probably the hardest to bear, his utter despair must still be bouncing around the city, getting picked up and rebroadcast and endlessly analyzed.

They couldn't get away from Archie's last moment. The final thought of a man who had taken his own life.

Lanoe saw a black helmet rise over the side of the hull. Saw Valk coming toward him, moving slowly. Maybe Valk was giving him a chance to say that he wanted to be alone, or maybe Valk was just sad. As Establishmentarians, he and Archie had shared a vision, the vision of planets free of poly domination. They'd both believed in that strongly enough to fight for it. Maybe Valk was just in mourning, in his own, artificial way.

"This is bad," Lanoe said, as Valk came close.

The AI didn't respond. He came to stand next to Lanoe. To watch, together, as the city screamed.

After a while, Valk stirred. "They must have some way to get past this, right?"

"The Choir?" Lanoe said. "Sure. Or...I don't know." He shook his head. "Grief isn't something that you can just put away. There's no cure."

Valk reached over and put a hand on Lanoe's shoulder. "I guess you know all about that," he said.

He was talking about Zhang. Lanoe tried to harden himself, to force himself to talk about something else, but there were words in his throat and they just came out. "I've been dreaming about her. Pretty much every time I close my eyes. She's there, she's...right there, and then, I wake up and she's gone again. It's like losing her all over again. It's...It's just wrong, Valk. It's not right that she isn't there. Do you understand? She's supposed to be there, and so I dream about her, but she's *not there*."

"Hellfire," Valk said. "Lanoe, I didn't know—"

Lanoe took a deep breath. Enough. He hadn't meant to say all that. To put his burden on Valk. And anyway, none of it mattered. Not just then.

"The Choir," he said. "That's what they're feeling. All of them— they're grieving for Archie. They're mourning, and they can't let it go."

"So we give them time, I guess," Valk said. "Let them find peace again."

"Time," Lanoe told him, "isn't something we have. This is bad. This is very, very bad."

"I feel it, too."

Lanoe shook his head. "Without Archie we have no way to talk to them. We can't negotiate."

The weight of Valk's hand wasn't on his shoulder anymore. "Wait," the AI said. "Wait."

"I can't get what I need, if I can't talk to them."

"Lanoe—hold on," Valk said. "You can't seriously be thinking about that right now. This is not the time!"

Lanoe turned to face him. "I told you, time isn't something—"

"A man is dead!" Valk lifted his arms. Let them fall again. "He's dead! And all you can think about is how that inconveniences you?"

"I'm sorry that he thought he didn't have any options. I kind of liked him, frankly, and I'm sad to see him go. But I have a responsibility to this mission, to all the species the Blue-Blue-White wiped out, to—"

"Damn you."

Lanoe reeled. Coming from Valk—coming from the only real friend he had left—that stung.

"Damn your eyes. You have a *responsibility* all right," Valk said. "Unless you're going to tell me that you don't see it."

"See what?"

"That we drove him to this. That we all but murdered Archie."

Lanoe shook his head. "That's bosh. The Choir did this to him. We tried to help him. We tried to get him out of here, to take him home."

"Home? Where exactly would that be, for someone like him? He lost his war, Lanoe. *We* lost *our* war. I guess you don't know what that feels like."

Lanoe's eyes narrowed. "I guess I don't."

"Everything we had faith in is gone. As long as he was out here, waiting to be rescued, he still had hope. Then we arrived and showed him there was nothing for him to go back to."

"Valk—"

But the AI was already walking away. Headed back inside.

Lanoe watched the city below, watched the Choir wail in grief, for a while longer, before he followed.

"Come on. Shoo!" Lieutenant Ehta said, waving a minder at one of the choristers that had wandered into the ship's axial corridor. "Move it!"

The alien lifted all four of its arms and waved them back and forth. And refused to move. Ginger pointed down the corridor, stabbing her finger in the air. They'd been tasked with herding the choristers down to the vehicle bay, in the hope that the Choir would send aircars up to retrieve them. A vain hope, so far, but nobody wanted the aliens in the ship anymore.

The chirping was bad enough—*earsplitting* was the best word Ginger had for the arrhythmic noise they made. The smell was even worse. The choristers were giving off a chemical reek that made human heads spin. Whether it was just body odor from aliens who had stopped grooming themselves or some kind of sorrow pheromone, nobody could say. They certainly couldn't ask the choristers.

Ginger couldn't stand it—the noise and the smell, but especially the fact that they were so clearly suffering, and couldn't tell her why. Ginger had never been able to feel comfortable around people who were upset. She always felt a desperate need to make them feel better, to calm them down, to tell them everything would be okay. Maybe, she thought, that was why she'd latched on to Bury, even back at the flight school. His flashes of indignation, his petty little rages gave her something to soothe, some way to make herself feel like she was being helpful. But she could hardly do that for the aliens, not when she couldn't talk to them.

"Move," Lieutenant Ehta roared. The chorister only redoubled her keening, screeching song. "I said *move*, you bastard!" she shouted, and then she rushed at the alien, her shoulder down as if she would bowl the chorister over. She collided with the armor-plated side with an audible crunch, but didn't succeed in moving the alien so much as a centimeter.

"Don't hurt it!" Ginger shouted.

"Yeah, good luck with that," Lieutenant Ehta huffed. "They're just a bundle of sticks under those dresses, but devil take me if they can't take a hit. It must be a low center of gravity thing, or maybe it's all those legs. Heavy as sin, too. C'mon, kid. Help me."

Ginger didn't want to touch the alien. She was worried its stink would get all over her. But she stepped in under its flailing arms—*her* arms, she thought, they were all supposed to be female—and put her back into it. The chorister was nearly twice her height but she felt right away what Lieutenant Ehta had described. The black dresses were like sacks full of broken branches. She felt a leg curl against her arm and she lurched backward, horrified by the sheer alienness of the chorister. Unfortunately she jumped right into the path of one of those waving arms, and she went down in a heap.

"Here," Lieutenant Ehta said, and reached out a hand to help Ginger up. Only to yank it away again as Ginger reached for it.

"Ha ha, very funny," Ginger said, thinking this was some kind of rough PBM humor. But the look on Lieutenant Ehta's face told her otherwise. The big woman looked like all the blood had rushed out of her face.

"One of the—the little bug things," Lieutenant Ehta said, pointing down at the front of Ginger's suit. "It's on you!"

Ginger looked down and nearly screamed. She'd never had a problem with insects, not really, but this thing had ten legs, at least ten, each of them furry and barbed and its head was all eyes and and and—

"It's going for your collar ring!" Lieutenant Ehta shouted. "It's going to try to climb inside your suit!"

Ginger brought her hand down fast, thinking she would crush the thing, keep it out of her suit. But the chorister shrieked so plaintively, with such recognizable mute horror that at the last second Ginger cupped her hand around the little male. Even when she felt its hairy legs tickle her palm.

Except—she'd thought it would be prickly. That maybe it would even sting her. Instead its fur felt soft and downy. More like a mouse's than a tarantula's. She moved her hands carefully until she had both of them cupped around the wriggling thing. "I think it was just trying to get somewhere warm," she said. Then a shadow passed over her and she looked up to see the chorister.

It—she—was leaning over Ginger, two of her claws held out in front of her in exactly the same way Ginger held her hands. Copying her. Ginger lifted the cage of her hands up and the claws closed around her fingers.

"It's going to cut your hands off," Lieutenant Ehta said, but quieter than she could have, and Ginger got the sense that the marine understood something of what was happening. Maybe just a little. Enough that she didn't interfere.

Ginger opened her fingers and pulled her hands back, gently, to keep the little bug from escaping. The claws closed little by little. When Ginger's hands were completely free, the chorister carefully, ever so delicately, tucked the bug into one of her lacy sleeve cuffs, where it disappeared.

Ginger got to her feet. Then she reached up and touched one of the chorister's claws. It closed around her fingers, not in an enveloping way, but as if the alien wanted to hold her hand. She felt how soft the claws were on the inside, lined with round, furry pads. The fur was just as soft as what she'd felt on the legs of the little bug.

"Can you, um, follow me?" Ginger asked.

The chorister rolled her head around in a wide circle. Ginger had no idea whether that meant yes or no or some alien concept she could never hope to understand. But she had to try. She started walking down the corridor, still holding the chorister's hand.

And after a second where she thought the alien might pull her off her feet, the chorister started to follow. "This way," Ginger said, and the chorister kept up with her, matching her steady walking pace. Lieutenant Ehta jogged up beside her.

"Hellfire, kid, what did you say to it? I thought they couldn't understand us."

Ginger shook her head. "I don't know, I think—maybe it just took a little kindness? I know that sounds dumb."

"Yeah, it does," Lieutenant Ehta said, but then she laughed.

Together they brought the chorister through the hatch and into the vehicle bay, where two others of her kind were already waiting. They looked up and gestured for the newcomer to join them. At least, that was what Ginger thought their gesture meant. They warbled crazily, but for a second the two of them warbled crazily in the same key, and their voices joined together in harmony.

The third, Ginger's chorister, raised her own voice, trying to match the pitch. She lurched forward toward the others, then stopped and tilted her head down toward Ginger, perhaps remembering that she was still holding Ginger's hand.

Then she reached out with three arms and wrapped them around Ginger's head and shoulders, pulling her into a tight hug. Ginger's face was smashed against armor plates that stank of iodine and something else equally unpleasant.

She wrapped her arms around the chorister's body, feeling how terribly thin she was. She felt something wet touch her hair and she realized the chorister was crying, big wet, sobbing tears. Positively weeping all over her.

Ginger reached up and gathered some of the tears on her fingertips. She had expected them to come away silvered, wet with mercury—the color of the chorister's eyes. Instead the tears were transparent. Just salt water.

The chorister released her and ran off to join the others. They made a triangle out on the floor of the vehicle bay, claws clattering together, and sang a rising cadence so loud it hurt Ginger's ears.

Lieutenant Ehta pulled her back out into the corridor. "They like you," she said, sounding mystified.

"I guess they do," Ginger said.

<hr />

Lanoe studied the machine in his hands. He'd never used one before—had never bothered learning much about medical technology. This thing seemed relatively simple. There was a sort of wand you ran over the thing you wanted to scan, and a pad you placed under it. The imaging was all done on a minder no bigger than the palm of his hand. "Help me with this," he said.

Candless frowned, but at least she didn't refuse. The mood on the ship was so strained that he half-expected his people to mutiny on the spot. Though he supposed they were all too tired, too irritable, to actually organize.

She lifted Archie's head and gently placed the pad underneath, as if she were giving him a pillow to make him more comfortable. "I fail to see how this is helping us, in any way," she said, but she left it at that.

The temperature in the brig had been reduced until they could see their breath. Lanoe didn't want to take his gloves off—the memory of the cold wormhole was still in the bones of his fingers—but he needed the fine motor control. He switched on the wand and made a few exploratory passes over Archie's pale, slack face.

"This thing in his head is alien technology. The Admiralty will want us to bring back anything we can, anything that might give us a sense of the Choir's capabilities."

Candless folded her arms. "You make it sound like you're gathering intelligence in advance of an invasion."

"Oh, I'm just hedging my bets. Don't want to go home empty-handed."

On the minder's display, the bones of Archie's skull were pale shadows in a dark cloud. Lanoe adjusted a virtual control and the muscles of the man's face came into relief, bands of long, straight fibers. The eyeballs appeared out of nowhere, round and only slightly shriveled. Lanoe cursed—he'd adjusted the setting in the wrong direction. He tapped in a series of commands, then waved the wand over the scar in Archie's temple.

"I admit that I'm glad," Candless said.

Lanoe looked up at her.

"I'm glad you seem to have accepted that this mission is over. There's nothing left to be done here, clearly, as we can no longer converse with the aliens. Even the repairs the Choir began on the ship have been abandoned. It's time to go home."

"Sure," Lanoe said. The minder's display showed Archie's brain. It looked like a wrinkled mass of inert putty. Lanoe couldn't see any gross damage to the brain's structure. He had expected that the antenna the Choir put in Archie's head would look like, well, an antenna. A long piece of metal. Fitting such a thing inside his skull would have meant moving whole lobes of the brain out of the way. Nothing like that showed itself on the scan, however. He adjusted the controls again.

"There are logistical concerns that we should discuss. Getting out of the bubble will prove difficult, of course—"

"I can't make this out. Can you see what this shadow is?" he asked her.

Candless pointed at the minder and tapped her fingernail along the edge of the display, indicating a fine-tuning control he hadn't noticed before. "Then there's the fact that there's only one wormhole out of this system, which Centrocor currently has in their possession. We can't just sneak past them through the wormhole throat. Even assuming they don't attack us the moment we emerge from the bubble—and I know if I were in command of that carrier, that is exactly what I would do—we will need to evade them in a ship that can't withstand any more drastic maneuvers. Then we'll need to re-transverse the lightless wormhole. Just making it to Avernus, where we can make proper repairs, will take a long string of miracles."

"Sure," Lanoe said. He touched a key to reveal different layers of brain tissue, feathering it as gently as he would the positioning jets of a fighter during a tricky docking sequence. "Miracles," he said. "My specialty." He thought he saw a shadow in one of the tomographic views and he backed up, just a little.

There.

"Oh. Hell, I had no idea," he said.

"If you think I'm missing some crucial detail in my analysis of our situation, I do hope you'll share it with me."

"No, no, look," he said.

The antenna didn't look anything like he'd expected. It didn't even look like a solid object. The minder's display showed parts of Archie's parietal and occipital lobes—the parts of the human brain most heavily involved with language and vision. It looked like they'd been brushed very gently with a stripe of silver paint. Lanoe adjusted the scanner's controls back and forth, but he couldn't find anything that looked like a microchip or even a wire. This had to be it.

"It doesn't look like an implant. More like it grew in place. I don't think we can even take it out," he said.

Candless looked down at the bone saw she'd been holding. "Perhaps that's just as well," she said, and gently put it down.

Ginger was in her bunk, trying to finally get some sleep, when the call came. Of course, she thought, as she opened her eyes and looked at the display mounted in the ceiling above her. Of course they want us to assemble right now.

The screaming hadn't stopped. The choristers were still lost in their grief and their chirping still echoed through the ship. But now that they were corralled in the vehicle bay—one of the most heavily armored parts of the cruiser, with blast plating lining it inside and out—the noise had dropped to a sort of distant keening. Everyone, all the marines, all the officers, had turned in to try to rest. To try to get over the stress of the very long day.

And now Commander Lanoe wanted to address them in the wardroom.

Ginger put a hydration tab under her tongue, if only to freshen her breath, and rubbed at her eyes. Then she slapped the release key on her bunk's hatch and slipped out into the corridor. Lieutenant Ehta was out there. She was smiling. Ginger shot her a quizzical look.

Lieutenant Ehta mouthed the words "going home" and slapped Ginger on the back, almost hard enough to send her sprawling.

It seemed Ginger had made a friend. Well, she did have a knack for it.

Ginger followed her the short distance to the wardroom. Some of the marines and two of the neddies were already there. In short order Lieutenant Candless arrived—pushing Engineer Paniet in a float chair. If they'd let the man out of sick bay, this must be an important meeting. More marines filed in, and then Commander Lanoe himself.

"Good, we can begin," Lieutenant Candless said.

There was no sign of M. Valk. Ginger didn't know what that meant.

Lieutenant Candless must have noticed her looking. "The cruiser's position is stabilized, for the moment," she told Ginger. "I'll be monitoring our attitude and drift during this meeting and I'll make any adjustments that are necessary."

"Pardon me, ma'am, but couldn't M. Valk take care of—"

"M. Valk is no longer part of the bridge crew," Lieutenant Candless told her. No explanation was forthcoming, and Ginger knew better than to expect one—certainly Lieutenant Candless would never discuss such things in front of the enlisted marines.

No M. Valk. Ginger was suddenly aware of how few officers were left onboard. Bury and Maggs were still out on patrol. Engineer Paniet was present but he was definitely not ready for active duty. Lieutenant Ehta was there, but she didn't count—the PBMs didn't factor in Navy chain of command, which meant—

Oh, hellfire. The chain of command went Commander Lanoe, Lieutenant Candless, and then herself. Ginger was third in line of command of the entire cruiser. No wonder Lieutenant Candless had addressed her concerns.

"This will be a brief meeting," Lieutenant Candless said. "The Commander would like to address you all, officers and enlisted, on the status of our mission and how he would like to proceed going forth. Once he's done you can all return to your duties or your bunks."

Commander Lanoe approached the table where they took their meals—the only real communal space in the cruiser. He leaned on it with both hands. He looked so tired to Ginger, so old. "As you all know, Archie committed suicide last night. As a result we lost our ability to speak with the Choir. It's a pretty big blow to our mission objectives. I was in the middle of negotiations with the aliens when this happened, but those talks are impossible now."

He lowered his head to look down at the table. Ginger saw he had something in his hand—a little rolled-up minder. He squeezed it as he spoke, as if it gave him strength. "I've discussed our options with both Engineer Paniet and Lieutenant Candless. They've given me excellent advice and I feel damned lucky to have people like them on this ship. Hellfire, I've been lucky to have all of you under my command. This crew has faced real hazards and actual combat on what should have been a milk run, and you all pulled through and exceeded expectations. I want to thank you, officially."

A murmur of acknowledgment ran through the crowd. Ginger saw how the marines especially lapped up Lanoe's kind words— even though they'd spent the last several shifts cursing his name when he wasn't there. The stress and anger that had gripped the ship in its claws seemed to just melt away. She was fascinated to see the effect it had on the men and women around her, just to hear their commander say something nice about them.

"We're not done yet," Lanoe said. "There's a fight ahead of us— we know Centrocor is here, ready to attack. They've only waited this long because they're afraid of us." That got a few chuckles. "We'll be all right. The question is, how soon can we get out of here? How soon can we all go home?"

Lieutenant Candless nodded and started to step forward.

"The answer," Commander Lanoe said, "is not quite yet."

Ginger watched Lieutenant Candless's face fall. Her mouth pursed as she fought not to let her jaw drop. Her eyes went wide— then immediately narrowed down to slits, as if someone had just pulled a nasty joke on her.

"We need to get what we came here for, and I won't leave without it. To that end, I need to ask you—all of you—for an extraordinary act of service. I want a volunteer."

He unrolled the minder in his hand, a rectangular piece of nylon

with a matte gray display surface sewn to its inner side. He gestured and it lit up, showing a picture of a human brain with one
section highlighted.

"Archie was able to talk to the Choir because he had something
very small, very simple implanted in his brain. A kind of receiving device. Without it, it's impossible to communicate with them.
I need someone to volunteer to have the same kind of device
implanted in their brain."

What?

Ginger glanced around at the people near here. None of them
were breathing.

So she didn't feel so all alone.

"Obviously this is a lot to take in," Commander Lanoe said. "It
involves brain surgery, of a kind we aren't equipped to handle here
on the cruiser. It will, in fact, be performed by one of the Choir. I'll
point out that Archie seemed to suffer no negative consequences of
having this operation. It didn't cause him pain or discomfort."

No, Ginger thought. *It just drove him to suicide.*

In her mind's eye she saw his face, when she'd discovered him.
So pale, and his eyes—his eyes had not looked peaceful.

"I'm asking one of you to take this on, so that we can complete
our mission here. It's a huge sacrifice, but one the Navy will reward.
Okay. I've said enough. Let's hear if anyone wishes to volunteer."

Ginger felt like the air in the room was pressing down on her,
squeezing her sinuses. She could feel the people around her shifting, looking away, looking anywhere but at each other. They drew
back, away from Commander Lanoe, away from what he was asking. Of course they did. It was insane. It was ludicrous. Who in
their right mind would agree to such a thing?

Engineer Paniet cleared his throat. For a horrible moment Ginger thought maybe he was going to do it, that he would volunteer.
Horrible because she didn't want him to do it—but also horrible
because she would be so relieved, so grateful, if he did. If only
because it would break this tension. But he wasn't volunteering.
"Can we ask questions?" he asked.

"I need an answer soon. The sooner the better," Commander Lanoe said, but he nodded.

"Is this something you'd be willing to do, yourself? If you don't get any takers?"

Lieutenant Candless hissed at him. "That's bordering on impertinence," she said.

"Leave it," Commander Lanoe said.

It couldn't be him, though, Ginger totally agreed with that. He was in charge of the mission, their leader—he couldn't do it. What if something went wrong? What if he died on the operating table? But she looked around the room and wondered who else they could afford to lose. *Nobody*, she thought. Lieutenant Candless basically ran the ship, and Engineer Paniet kept it from falling apart. Lieutenant Ehta commanded the marines. And Ginger couldn't stomach the idea of one of the enlisteds doing it—they'd never signed up for this mission; it just wasn't fair to ask them to take this on.

Commander Lanoe nodded thoughtfully, just acknowledging that he'd heard the question. He looked down at the minder, at the brain scan. She saw the muscles in his throat move as he swallowed. Then he nodded again and looked up. He was about to say something. He was about to say that yes, he would do it—she was sure of it.

Ginger couldn't stand the atmosphere in the room, the tension, the unbearable heaviness of this, the desperation of what they'd come to. She wanted to scream, wanted to run away, wanted to—to—

"I'll do it," she said.

Chapter Thirty-One

What the devil are you doing?" Bury demanded.

He had matched velocities with Lieutenant Maggs's Z.XIX and was keeping station less than a kilometer away. He could see that the man had his canopy down, and was actually outside his fighter—just floating in space with nothing but his suit to protect him. He wasn't even tethered to his vehicle.

As Bury watched in puzzlement, the scoundrel pilot curled up into a ball and turned a somersault in the void.

"Just stretching my joints," Lieutenant Maggs said. "You aren't feeling stiff? You've been cooped up in that bloody seat just as long as I have. And I've flown BR.9s before, much to my continuing shame. They aren't nearly as comfortable as my luxury model."

"You're a lunatic," Bury told him. "What if new orders came in right now? What if we had to move on a second's notice?"

"Lad," Lieutenant Maggs said, his tone light and airy, "we're all going to die anyway. If you really cared so much about safety you'd never have joined the Navy, eh? So why don't you quiet yourself. Do some meditation exercises or something. I would ever so much enjoy a little silence right now."

Bury shook his head and touched his control stick, veering away from the fool. The truth was he wouldn't mind a little quiet himself.

After so many hours with no one else to talk to, he had grown heartily sick of Lieutenant Auster Maggs and his fancy speech.

Sadly it seemed the request for silence hadn't been serious. "What do you suppose they're up to, just now?" Lieutenant Maggs asked, before a whole minute had passed. "Over there on the other side of the mirror? We know it's about aliens."

"We don't know a damned thing," Bury told him. "Which is clearly intentional."

"Will you honestly tell me you're not curious at all? You must at least be wondering what fate has befallen the lovely young Ensign Ginger. If my lover were under charges and probably locked in the brig—"

"Ginger and I are just friends," Bury said.

"Really?" Lieutenant Maggs laughed. "You mean the two of you never twined beneath a starlit sky, whispering sweet words of love? Never succumbed to the siren song of teenage hormones, truly?"

"No! We're not like that!"

"What an absolute waste. With that fiery red hair of hers, I'm sure she's a bearcat in the bunk. Well, perhaps the next time we lay eyes on her I'll have to whisper a few sweet words her way myself."

"Damn you, Maggs. Damn you, if you—"

Lieutenant Maggs laughed again. "You're so easy, son."

Bury seethed. He'd fallen for one of Lieutenant Maggs's verbal traps, yet again. He hated to accept that he really was that vulnerable to the man's insinuations. "Why?" he said, biting off the word. "Why do you keep riding me? Huh?"

"Oh, it's just a bit of rough camaraderie," Lieutenant Maggs told him. "Affectionate ribbing, hmm? Or don't they go in for that sort of thing in flight school anymore?"

"We do," Bury told him. "Which is why I know there's more to it. I know the difference between joking around and actually twisting the knife. You want something from me. You want me to—I don't know. Get angry, for some reason. And don't tell me it's just because it entertains you, either."

"Oh, but it is infinitely diverting," Lieutenant Maggs said.

"Are you trying to provoke me? Damn me but I can't see why. Do you honestly think I won't rise to your baiting? I challenged my own flight instructor to a duel, back on Rishi. I'll give you a fight if you want one."

"Oh, of that I have no doubt. You're a real tiger, aren't you?"

Bury roared in anger and reached for his comms board, intending to cut off the link between their two fighters. He couldn't take much more of this. But no, he was under strict instructions to stay in radio contact with Lieutenant Maggs at all times. It was one of the first things they taught you about patrols—you don't lose track of your squaddies.

"Oh, son, I am so deadly bored. I am so bored I think I might let you in on the grand secret after all," Lieutenant Maggs said. "I might actually tell you why I've been teasing you so relentlessly. Then again, I might tell you two reasons. One true and one false. Then I can have the pleasure of watching your brain overheat as you try to decide which is which."

"Hellfire," Bury said.

"Does that mean you'd rather not know, after all?"

"Hellfire," Bury said again. "Just bloody tell me!"

"Because I need an ally," Lieutenant Maggs said. Sounding completely sincere, for the very first time since Bury had found him locked up in the cruiser's brig.

"Bosh," Bury said.

"No, no, it's quite true. I need a squaddie. A friend, if you like. Someone I can actually confide in."

"I imagine there are better ways to make friends," Bury suggested.

"Oh? Should I flatter you, tell you how impressed I am with your flying, with your intellect, with your shiny, shiny face? Or perhaps I should take the time to build up a relationship of mutual respect and trust."

"That's kind of the traditional way to do it," Bury said.

"Where you come from, perhaps. Hel is a serious place, I'm sure, where everyone plays by the rules. No, young Ensign Bury. I *ride* you because I need to see your true self. I need you angry. Because I've seen how you act when you're around Lanoe. You push it down. Fight your natural instincts. You can't be you around him."

"I have no idea what you're talking about."

Lieutenant Maggs wasn't finished, though. "He doesn't respect you. Just as he doesn't respect me. He thinks you're an angry little twerp. You work so hard proving him wrong. Here's the thing, though. You are an angry fellow. Everyone knows it. But with me, dear pal, you can actually let it show."

"That might be one of the stupidest things I've ever heard," Bury told him.

"You can be yourself with me. Can you even say that about dear Ginger? Your bestest chum in the barracks?"

Bury put his helmet down so he could reach up and rub at his forehead. He needed this conversation to end. He needed Lieutenant Maggs to shut up.

"If I say that you're right, will you be quiet?"

"I do enjoy being correct. It might help."

"Then go be damned, because I'm not saying it," Bury told him. "You can annoy and wheedle and irritate me all day. You're not going to win."

"Ooh," Lieutenant Maggs said. "You're angry! Believe it or not, everything I said was true. I like you when you're angry."

"*Shut up!*" Bury screamed.

"Do you think young Ginger is very afraid right now, all alone in that cell?" Lieutenant Maggs said. "Worrying whether she'll be sent to prison when we get home? Perhaps trembling a little, her little rosebud upper lip quivering, with no one there to dry her tears?"

Oh, that was bloody well enough.

"I'm going to do another sweep of the wormhole throat," Bury told Lieutenant Maggs. "Laying in a shallow trajectory run now, with a burn time of seven point four seconds. *Don't* come after me."

"Never worry, my new friend. I'll be right here waiting when you get back."

"You can't be serious about this. I won't let you do it! She's just a kid," Ehta said.

Lanoe sat patiently, waiting for her to finish.

"She's barely out of flight school and now you're going to—what? Turn her into a pet mouthpiece for those...those damned lobsters?"

Ginger sat in front of him, her hands folded in her lap. She was shaking, a little. She was frightened. Lanoe didn't find that surprising. He watched the girl intently, never looking away, even when Ehta got down in his face and her spittle flecked his cheek.

"You have no right. You have no right to do this to her. You used your position as her commander to—to—"

"Lieutenant Ehta," Candless said, in that tone she had—the authoritarian, no-bosh tone that could cut through armor plate—"remember who you are speaking to."

"Remember? I know him, lady. Maybe not as long as you. But I've followed him through hell and out the other side. I've taken orders from him I was sure were going to get me killed—and I followed them anyway, because it was him, it was Lanoe, and if he wanted me to lay down my life I knew it would be for a good cause."

Red hair. It had to be Ginger, with her red hair, Lanoe thought.

"I went to Niraya with him. You weren't there. You don't know how bad it looked, with a fleet of drones howling down out of the sky. You don't know how bad we wanted to run, me and Valk and Zhang. And you know what? We stayed. Because it was him. So I think maybe I've earned the right to give him my opinion now and again."

The last time Lanoe had seen Zhang was the night on Niraya before the battle against the queenship. That night they'd finally understood what they were to each other, that the thing they shared was never going to go away, even if they wanted it to. That night Zhang had red hair. It was curly, and Ginger's was straight.

It was shorter than Ginger's. It didn't matter. The color was almost exactly the same.

"And my current opinion, which he's going to hear whether he likes it or not, is that he is not allowed to do this. Not to her. Not to—" Ehta made a horrible strangling gurgling noise then. It took Lanoe a moment to realize she was holding back a sob.

Ginger looked down at her fingernails. Bit her lip.

The girl wasn't anything like Zhang. Zhang had been confident and brash and alive. Zhang had been so wise, sometimes, and sometimes she just knew what to say. What to tell him, the words that would unlock the knot of his life. This—this girl, this ensign, Ginger, was nothing like Zhang. She was diffident, unsure of herself. She needed the approval of others, and she couldn't handle combat. Her eyes were the wrong color. She was linked permanently, in Lanoe's mind, with Bury, who was an ass. Ginger was nothing like Zhang.

Except for her red hair.

Lanoe remembered the first time he'd seen Ginger. It had been in the guesthouse at Rishi, on his way to meet Candless, before the duel. He'd seen that red hair in the crowd and without thinking he'd reached for Zhang, grabbed her arm. He'd been too embarrassed by his mistake to even register who she really was.

Red hair.

"You can't do this, Lanoe," Ehta managed to say.

Lanoe nodded. "Lieutenant Candless. Do you agree with Lieutenant Ehta?"

"As painful as it may be to admit, I do, yes, fully and completely from the bottom of my shriveled old soul. However—"

Lanoe raised an eyebrow. He was still staring at Ginger. Watching her squirm. "However?" he said.

Candless sighed. "She's an adult. And an officer. She can make her own decisions."

"You—you—" Ehta gasped. "You bit—"

Candless turned and slapped Ehta across the cheek.

The marine could only stand there with a stunned look as her skin turned bright red.

Lanoe inhaled sharply. Though they were both lieutenants, Candless was the ranking officer between the two of them—XOs were above warrant officers in the pecking order. Back in the bad old days of the Century War, even as late as the Brushfire, when Candless was still flying patrols, corporal discipline had been pretty standard in the Navy, but over time it had come to be frowned upon. Ehta couldn't bring Candless up on charges for striking her like that. She could destroy Candless's reputation, however, if she chose to make a stink.

Candless didn't seem to care one bit.

"An officer does not use that word," Candless told her. "Not even an officer of the Planetary Brigade Marines."

Ehta shook her head and stormed out. Lanoe had no idea where she was headed. He didn't care.

"Okay," he said.

"Sir?" Candless asked.

He nodded at Ginger. "Why do you want to do this?"

The girl took one long, tremulous breath. "When we were moving them, sir. Getting them into the vehicle bay. They were just so sad. They'd lost Archie. He was one of their people, right? After so many years he was one of them and they were so sad. All I wanted was to tell them it would be okay. Make them feel better. But I couldn't, because I couldn't talk to them."

It wasn't the real reason. Lanoe had known she would make something up. There were two possible reasons that she had volunteered, and neither of them was particularly satisfying. Maybe she thought this was a way to get out of the charge of cowardice against her. Or maybe she'd just succumbed to peer pressure. Felt the need for a volunteer so heavily that she'd broken, and said something she didn't mean.

Lanoe wouldn't have cared except for the red hair. He would have accepted her offer without a thought. The red hair made it hard.

So damned hard.

"Okay," he said, again. Because he was Aleister Lanoe. "Okay. Let's get started."

———— ✦ ————

Bury swung back to the established patrol orbit as fast as he could, burning through his dwindling supply of fuel. His thruster would be visible from anywhere in the system, but maybe that didn't matter now. Maybe it mattered, a lot. He just didn't know.

"Back so soon?" Lieutenant Maggs called. He was back in his cockpit with his canopy up, at least. Ready.

"Maggs—I need you to be serious for a second," Bury said. He was scared. He could admit that, even to himself. "I need your experience, okay? Because I might have just seen something."

The sarcasm drained from Lieutenant Maggs's voice almost instantly. "Something," he said. "Young Bury, please be more exact."

"It was...like before. When the scout came through. Just a little flash, except—except there were two of them, and then one more a couple of seconds later."

"Three flashes of light. You're sure?" Maggs asked.

"Yes. No. I don't know. I don't know! It could have been Centrocor fighters coming through the wormhole throat. It could have been—hellfire, it could have been anything. Rocks colliding, an old comet flaring up. Who knows. But if it was Centrocor—"

"Then we need to be prepared. All right, child," Lieutenant Maggs said. "Calm yourself. Check your sensor boards. Look at the logs for your passive spectroscopy array, hmm? Do you see any evidence of deuterium exhaust?"

Bury had taken a class in how to do that six months ago, back at Rishi. It should have been the first thing he did. The thrusters of a cataphract-class fighter were slightly inefficient, and they tended to release unfused deuterium droplets along with their other exhaust.

He drummed his fingers on his knee while he waited for the

computer to run the analysis. As page after page of logs spooled past him on a display he could barely see, because his eyes didn't seem to focus right. Graphs of spectral lines shifted and wavered before him but before the log review had even finished, he had it.

Right there. The lines appeared three times in the log, three perfect signatures. First two of them, then, a few seconds later, a third.

"Hellfire," Bury breathed.

"I'll take that as confirmation. All right. Centrocor is beginning their attack. We should expect about thirty fighters to come screaming down on us at any moment, and as we are the only Naval assets in the system right now, they'll concentrate all their fire on us. Breathe, young Bury. Breathe for me."

"Okay. Okay," Bury said. "Okay! But we still have, what, at least a couple of minutes. We can get ready. One of us can run down to the portal and tell Lanoe that the carrier is on its way. The other one—"

"Would face certain death. I'm afraid your plan doesn't excite me," Lieutenant Maggs said.

"But what else can we do? Lanoe has to know, and—"

"Lanoe dragged you out here to die. You see that now, don't you?"

Bury stared at his comms board, even though the connection was voice only. "What?" he asked. "Maggs, what are you—"

"You've been getting angry at me this whole time. That's all right, I have a thick skin. But right now, I would like to direct your anger in a different direction. I would like you to spend some of that amazing wrath of yours on a man who left the two of us out here to die while he sat sipping tea with aliens. A man who refused us even the slightest possibility of relief when we begged for it. A man who has shown neither of us the slightest scrap of respect."

"He's our commanding officer," Bury pointed out.

"By fiat only. He ripped you away from your studies. He *kidnapped* me. Neither of us asked for this posting."

Bury's head spun. What Maggs was suggesting was nothing short of desertion. Admittedly, Bury was afraid to die. He knew he was a decent pilot, but up against thirty fighters his skill and talent would mean nothing. It would take a miracle for him to survive until reinforcements could arrive from the cruiser.

He'd also assumed that he would be the one to go tell Lanoe what was happening, while Maggs worked desperately to hold off the Centrocor advance.

He could feel his heart jumping in his chest. Felt sweat breaking out on his palms. "Maggs. You're saying you want to run away," Bury said. "I can see one big problem with that plan. Where would you go? The only wormhole out of here leads right past Centrocor's main force."

"Run away?" Maggs asked. "Dear boy, I never said anything about running away."

"Oh." Bury was confused. "But—then—"

"I'm simply going to switch sides. Turn my coat, as the old saying goes."

They had been talking over a communications laser, a medium that prevented anyone from eavesdropping on what they said. Bury's comms board showed that Lieutenant Maggs had opened a second band of communication, this time broadcasting an unencrypted signal over the general radio circuit. He was basically shouting for everyone in the system to hear him.

"Centrocor vehicles, please do not shoot," the scoundrel called. "My name is Auster Maggs and my Centrocor Employee Number is TK-777423-Y7. I would very much like to speak to your commanding officer. I have information on Naval forces in this system that I'd love to share with them."

Bury couldn't speak. Couldn't act.

He simply couldn't believe it.

﹀

The choristers had all been rounded up in the vehicle bay, and then left alone. When Lanoe opened the hatch he wasn't sure what he would find.

The noise hit him first. A little like the rising and falling, oceanic sound of cicadas in a field. A little like desperate, horrified bird cries. A lot like nothing any human being had ever heard before.

The smell wasn't great, either.

The aliens had gathered in the center of the space, clumped together for comfort, perhaps. They had their arms around each other and some had their heads bowed low, while others scratched and scraped at the armor plates around their eyes.

He could spend a lifetime trying to understand them, their gestures, their bizarre customs. He didn't have a lifetime to spare. "You got them down here," he told Ginger. "How do you get their attention?"

"It's not so hard. You just have to be nice," she told him. She walked over to the nearest chorister and reached up for one of its free claws. Stroked the carapace with her bare hands. The chorister didn't turn around—of course, they didn't need to, they could see in every direction at once. But it tilted its big cylindrical head toward her. She smiled up at it. Maybe they understood human facial expressions, Lanoe thought. They'd had plenty of time to study Archie.

"We want to talk to you," Ginger told the alien, though she must have known the chorister couldn't understand her. "We want to try to help. Please, can you help us?"

The chorister reached out a claw to touch her cheek. Lanoe was surprised at how human the gesture looked. Was it possible to communicate with just hands? Maybe, given enough time, they could have established some kind of sign language.

He came as close as he dared to the knot of aliens and raised one hand. Waved at them until he thought some of them were looking at him, then jabbed his finger in Ginger's direction. "Her," he said. "She wants the operation."

The choristers just stared at him with their blank, silver eyes.

"It's okay," she told him. "They'll understand when we show them. Go ahead, sir. I'm ready for this." Then she reached up and pushed her hair away from the side of her head. The chirping didn't change pitch, didn't get louder, but a new chemical stink filled the air.

Lanoe lifted his minder and projected an image of the antenna onto the side of Ginger's head. The image they'd pulled from the postmortem scan of Archie's brain. It looked like Ginger had frosted the roots of her red hair.

He bit the inside of his cheek. Waited for something to happen. Nothing did. The choristers milled around, chirping at each other. Ginger stood there with her hair up. None of them even seemed to be looking at the projected image. Maybe it wasn't going to be enough. Maybe the image didn't mean anything to them—perhaps they'd never done a scan of Archie's head after they changed him. Maybe they were just too lost in their grief to get it.

"Please," Ginger said. "I want this."

The chorister who had stroked her cheek wrapped an arm around her shoulders and pulled her close. Leaned forward until its long head rested on top of hers. It looked like the alien was crushing her.

"This isn't—" Lanoe began, but then a green pearl started spinning in the corner of his vision. Candless. He swiped his eyes across the pearl to accept the incoming message.

"An aircar just left the city," the XO told him. "It's coming this way. Just one chorister onboard, but it's carrying a couple of boxes."

"Medical equipment?" Lanoe asked.

"Perhaps, sir, you would be kind enough to look at this imagery and teach me exactly what alien medical equipment looks like. I'm afraid I never learned myself."

"Understood," Lanoe said.

He looked over at Ginger. Her cheek was crushed against the chorister's lace collar. She had her eyes closed and she was speaking to it, in soft, low tones.

"Shh," she said. "It's all right. It's going to be all right."

❧

"Maggs—what the hell have you done?" Bury demanded.

The reply took a while to come. Maybe Maggs was savoring the dramatic tension of the moment. Maybe he was too busy being a traitor to spare a word for his squaddie.

"I've saved my own life," Maggs told him. "Now. Let's talk about yours."

"Damn you, Maggs, I'm not interested in—"

"I should think you would be," the traitor said, talking over him. "The math wasn't hard to work out. There are about fifty fighters in the vehicle bay of a fully stocked carrier. Given that your paramour Ginger has lost her bottle and can't fight, Lanoe can count on—well, how many pilots? Himself, of course. Candless and Valk, certainly. Then there's the two of us. If you've been following along you'll notice that the odds are against us, ten to one."

"We're better than them," Bury said, shaking off the fear. "We fought them once, and they couldn't break us. We can do it again."

"Heroes, all of us, certainly. But the funny thing about heroes is—they die just as fast as cowards. They just take down others with them."

"Be sarcastic if you want. We still have a chance. You'll see."

"It doesn't have to be this way, Bury." Maggs sighed, long and deep.

On Bury's tactical board, he saw the dot that represented Maggs's fighter swinging toward him. Not as if he was in a hurry. Just closing the distance on a low-energy trajectory.

"I know it's hard sometimes to tell if I'm being serious. I promise you, the next thing I say is absolutely sincere. I like you."

Bury wanted to spit. "Shut up, you damned traitor. And don't think you're getting away with this! I'll make sure you—"

"I like you," Maggs said again. "You have spirit. So many Navy men I meet are just...dead inside. They have no personality, no drive. But there's something inside you, some dark core of anger and hurt pride, and it makes you interesting."

"Wow, thanks," Bury said.

"Oh, you're quite welcome. Now. I'm going to give you a choice. You can come join me. Sign on with Centrocor, and save your own skin. I'll vouch for you—and I happen to know that Centrocor is always looking for talented pilots, especially those that have some Navy training. The pay is good and there are plenty of fringe benefits. The Navy will try to charge you with desertion, yes. But Centrocor has some very good lawyers on their payroll."

Bury grabbed his control stick and squeezed it until his glove squeaked.

"Or?" he said.

"Or?" Maggs parroted.

"Or what? If I say no, what happens then?"

"Are you going to make me say it? I'll have to kill you, of course. Right now, right here. As a sign of good faith to my new employers."

Bury touched his stick and veered away from Maggs, working his engine board to plan out a five-second burn that would put thousands of kilometers between them.

"Ah," Maggs said. "I see you trying to get away. You must have forgotten. My fighter is carrying the Philoctetes package. Long-range sniping capability, remember? You can run, Bury, but you'll never get out of my range in time. Why not just say yes, instead?"

The aircar slid silently into the vehicle bay and came to rest on the deck plates. The sole chorister aboard stepped down and approached Lanoe and Ginger. The rest of them, the repair crew that had been howling since Archie's death, clambered aboard the vehicle and took off, without so much as a chirp of goodbye.

Lanoe was hard-pressed to regret losing them. Maybe they could have continued the repairs, given the cruiser back a little more of its structural integrity, but their wailing and their stink had made it almost impossible for him to command his people.

He supposed he could worry about the ship's damage later. Right now he had some alien brain surgery to supervise.

The chorister placed one claw against her chest. Lanoe realized for the first time that she wasn't screaming, nor did she smell of anything in particular. Archie's madness might have infected the entire Choir, but this one at least seemed to have pulled herself together.

She made a sound, a kind of sound he'd never heard before from one of them. A quiet pattering noise, very soft, very gentle.

"I wish we knew what she was trying to say," Lanoe said.

"I think that's her name," Ginger told him. She placed a hand on her own chest. "Ginger," she said.

The chorister didn't respond.

"She must be a trained doctor," Lanoe said. "She seems— professional."

"I hope so," Ginger told him. "Commander. I. I just..." She chewed on her lower lip and turned away from him.

Damn. She was scared. Well, of course she was. He just didn't know what to do. How did you console somebody in a situation like this? Lanoe wasn't much for emotional stuff on his best days.

The chorister held two carved stone boxes, octagonal in shape. With one of her free hands she touched Ginger on the shoulder, then the chin. Ginger seemed to understand what the alien was trying to tell her, and pulled back her hair while turning her head so the surgeon could take a look.

Then she reached up and took the claw in her hands, then tilted her head to indicate the hatch that led into the rest of the ship. The chorister followed her like a dog on a leash. Lanoe came up behind them, keeping a little distance.

It wasn't too long a walk to the sick bay. Paniet had vacated it for their use, and someone had cleaned the place up, putting out fresh sheets on the bed, laying out a whole suite of surgical tools. As they stepped inside, the chorister ducking her head, the ultraviolet sterilization system came to life. The chorister started as the lasers swept over her, but then she lifted all four hands and scraped her claws together in front of the beam as it tracked back and forth.

"At least they know about germs," Ginger said.

"You're going to be fine," Lanoe said.

Ginger looked up at him. "Please don't say that again."

"What?"

"Apologies, Commander, but you don't sound very convincing. Do you think maybe you could turn around for a moment?"

He frowned, but then he saw her reaching for the release strip on the back of her suit. He turned around hurriedly and stared at the wall while he listened to her step out of the suit, then pull on a paper modesty gown.

"Okay, it's safe now. I didn't want to get blood on my suit," she told him.

Oh, hellfire. Out of the suit she was...tiny. She looked very thin, and shorter out of her boots. She hopped up on the bed and leaned back on the pillows.

The chorister opened one of her boxes. She pushed the human surgical tools to one side of their tray and started laying out her own devices. Lanoe hadn't known what to expect—certainly nothing that looked like human medical equipment. Maybe humming eggs or devices that shot out strange rays or even that maybe she would use a tiny wormhole to insert the antenna. The surgeon's instruments were far more prosaic, and far more unsettling for it. There was something that looked like a common laser scalpel, and a four-pronged retractor. The tools looked very similar, honestly, to the human tools she'd set aside, except that their handles were longer and thicker and deeply scalloped, clearly not designed for a human hand.

Lanoe tried to steel himself. To make himself remember how important this was. How necessary.

"Ginger..." he said.

There was a knock on the hatch and then Candless hurried in, out of breath. "I find it hard to believe you didn't have a chance to call me and let me know this was starting," the XO said.

"I—I didn't think—"

"People so rarely do." Candless moved around the bed to stand on the far side from the surgeon. She pulled a sheet up over Ginger's small body and then put a hand on the girl's arm.

Lanoe had never seen Candless act so tenderly. Not in all the years he'd known her. It just seemed—wrong. Yet Ginger didn't seem surprised by it at all. She reached up and took Candless's hand.

"I'll be here the whole time," Candless said. "I promise."

"This is a little surprising," Lanoe blurted out. The woman had been so cold, even cruel before. She'd insisted on writing Ginger up on a charge of cowardice, even when Lanoe had been willing to let the whole thing slide. She'd never had a kind word for anyone, that he could remember.

"She was my student," Candless said, as if that explained everything.

The surgeon leaned over Ginger. She reached down with one claw and stroked Ginger's hair. The girl smiled, and closed her eyes. Then the chorister turned her claw slightly and brushed the hair again—and this time it came off, shaved clean away from Ginger's temple. Red locks fell back against the pillow.

It made Lanoe think of Zhang's hair. Of course it did. He fought his inclination to call this whole thing off. To say he'd made a mistake. The girl was terrified, anybody could see that. It was criminal to do this to her, to put her through this. She would never ask for it to stop, no, she was too young, there was too much pressure on her—

"This is perhaps the bravest thing I've ever seen done," Candless said, looking down into Ginger's eyes. And then she actually smiled. Those thin lips curled up at the corners and it didn't even look wrong.

The alien surgeon wiped something wet that reeked of ammonia across Ginger's temple. Ginger's eyes searched Candless's face. She wasn't looking at the surgeon at all.

"You can go, Commander," Candless said. "I'm sure you have more important things to do. I'll let you know when it's finished."

The surgeon picked up her laser scalpel, and brought it around to touch Ginger's skin.

Maggs. Damned Maggs.

There was no mistaking the lights burning ahead of them now, three lights growing steadily larger. The main thrusters of three Centrocor fighters headed right at them. Bury had no idea if they had even heard Maggs, or if they believed that he was really betraying his own people. Maybe they would open fire on him any second now.

Or maybe they would fall into formation around him, an honor guard to take him to his new commanding officer.

"I have placed a timer on my tactical panel, Ensign Bury," Maggs said, his voice as smooth as fresh hydraulic fluid. "It's counting down. When it reaches zero, I really will need an answer. Perhaps in the interest of clarifying matters, I should tell you I already have a firing solution worked out. One little squeeze of this trigger and you'll no longer be my problem, or anyone else's."

"Damn you, Maggs," Bury said. For perhaps the fifteenth time. The bastard! The unmitigated fulminated bloody damned bastard.

"You're hardly the first to say that to me," Maggs called back. "It stopped stinging a while ago. Do you know, Bury, that my father was a famous admiral? It's true. I spent many of my formative years in the Admiralty. Navy man through and through."

"And now you're going to throw that away," Bury said, wanting to spit. Instead he worked his engine panel and threw his control stick over to the side.

"The funny thing about growing up as a Navy brat is that you get to see what's hiding behind all the paint and gilt and bunting. You get to find out what words like 'honor' and 'glory' actually mean. They mean 'death.' All the words the Navy loves so much mean 'death.' All that bosh about camaraderie, all those noble traditions. It all comes down to this. Old, fat men send boys out to risk their lives, and when the boys die they make a little tick mark on a chart, and at the end of the day they tally up all the tick marks and that's how they know if they won or they lost. Do you wish to be a tick mark, young Bury? Is that the destiny you've always seen for yourself?"

"They trusted us. Put us out here to stand watch," Bury said. "Everyone back on the cruiser—Lieutenant Candless and Lieutenant Ehta and Engineer Paniet and—"

"Ginger, let's not forget Ginger," Maggs said.

"Yes, damn you! Ginger! Ginger will die because you couldn't keep faith with the memory of your father!"

"The memory of my father…it's funny you should mention that, as—"

While he'd had Maggs talking, Bury had thrown his BR.9 sideways, skidded around on his maneuvering jets and burned hard— not away from Maggs, but straight toward him. Trying to get close, to eat up the distance. If he could just get close enough, get within range, he could shoot Maggs out of the sky before he could engage his fancy Philoctetes targeting package. If he could just—

"Oho," Maggs said. "Nicely done. You almost had me distracted enough for it to work." Bury was close enough to see Maggs's main thruster come on line as he burned away, keeping Bury at a distance. Well out of dogfighting range. "You know, most people get stupid when they're angry. I've taken advantage of that fact many times. But you, Bury, you're the exception. Rage fuels that clever little brain of yours. It clarifies things. So use those smarts now. Say 'yes, please, M. Maggs, I'd very much like to come with you and have a future.' That's all. Not those exact words, of course, that would take too long. You only have a few seconds left."

Bury tapped virtual keys on his weapons board. If he couldn't get in range to shoot Maggs with his PBWs, maybe he could fire off a disruptor or an antivehicle round. Normally those munitions were fired at short range because they were expensive and a cataphract could only carry a few of them. Actually hitting Maggs with one of them would be an incredible long shot, but—

"Time's up. Answer, please," Maggs said.

Bury's spine went rigid with fear. He smashed his stick sideways, fired his positioning jets to send himself twisting away in a corkscrew, trying desperately to get away from Maggs, to get far enough away that he had a chance.

"I'll take it that's a no," Maggs said.

For a split second, Bury actually considered it. Shame made his face hot but he gave it real, lucid thought. Ignoring everything that would happen, ignoring the fact that Centrocor would kill everyone on the cruiser—

Maybe Maggs had a point. The Navy had never shown Bury any love. He'd been bullied and hazed his whole time at Rishi. At various times he'd been slighted and singled out and—worst of all—ignored as if he didn't exist by classmates, by instructors, by officers. Time and time again they'd told him he had an anger problem. This despite the fact that the absolute worst way to treat someone with an anger problem was to accuse them of it, to treat them as broken and wrong. Lieutenant Candless had insulted him to his face, so grievously he'd felt he had no choice but to challenge her to a duel.

Then they had grabbed him up just because he happened to be in the wrong place at the wrong time. Stuffed him in a brig without telling him why. Commander Lanoe had let him out…only to inform him that he'd been volunteered for a dangerous mission. Dragged halfway across the galaxy to stand picket duty outside some weird planet, when the Commander knew perfectly well it was just a matter of time before Centrocor showed up to kill him.

Bury saw all of it, every miserable moment of his life in the Navy so far, in the blink of an eye.

He also saw something else. The fact that he'd never wanted anything in his life more than he wanted to be a Navy fighter pilot. An ace, with a blue star in his cryptab. He'd never worked so hard to achieve something. Never been so close to earning a dream.

"Go to hell," he said.

He closed his eyes. Waited to die. His fighter kept streaking away from Maggs, accelerating so fast he was squashed down in his seat by his inertial sink.

"Why don't you go first and save me a seat?" Maggs told him.

Bury tensed up, every muscle in his body contracting as he waited for it, the burst of particle fire that would cut right through him, tear him to pieces, destroy his fighter and send his blood boiling out into the vacuum.

His pulse and blood pressure spiked. His lungs burst because he was holding his breath. His eyes hurt from being squeezed shut for so long.

Eventually he had to open them.

"*Valk*," Maggs said, the name dripping with venom.

"What? Is he—is he here?" Bury asked.

"The devil himself shall one day spring up from a crack in the earth and tread upon that artificial beggar with his proverbial cloven hoof, and I will watch on, and I will say to the devil, 'harder, my good man. Grind him harder.'"

Bury took a deep breath. "What—what are you talking about?"

"A while back he asked me to show him the Philoctetes package and how it worked. I didn't realize at the time that he was monkeying about with it. He added an IFF interlock. Do you know what that is?"

"It's ... it's a thing we used back at Rishi, for live-fire exercises."

"It's a bit of bloody code that makes it impossible for me to shoot anyone that my computer identifies as an ally. IFF stands for 'Identify Friend or Foe.' You have a transponder in your fighter's equipment that identifies you as my friend. For a very specific definition of 'friend.'"

"What does—"

"What does that mean, child? It means you get to live. At least long enough to run back to Lanoe. Well, you do that. You run straight back there and tell them Centrocor is coming, and Auster Maggs is with them."

Bury swung around and burned straight for the unnamed planet, for the mysterious wormhole throat in its atmosphere. He didn't need to be told twice.

"And when you get there," Maggs said, "you tell him this time, he earned it. If he had shown me one ounce of respect, perhaps—"

Bury reached over to his comms board and switched off Maggs's voice.

———※———

Candless had been right—Lanoe did have plenty to do. Now that the Choir's repair crew had left the cruiser, he had to help the two remaining neddies as they tried desperately to complete repair tasks that should have taken a team of twenty people working in concert.

He was on the outside of the hull, walking upside down with just his boots holding him to the skin of the ship, when he noticed something. Or thought he did anyway. He was trying to help the neddies lay in a new curved section of carbon fiber ballistic armor over a spot near the gundecks that was currently exposed to the elements. The neddies cursed and jumped back and forth as they tried to get the big sheet to fit perfectly in place. Carbon-fiber cladding was almost impossible to trim to size once it had been electroset, and—

"Hold on," he told the engineers. "Quiet down for a second."

He could have sworn he'd heard something. It wasn't there when he listened for it, though. Not even when he held his breath. He adjusted his helmet 'phones for maximum gain and closed his eyes.

Silence.

Which was when it hit him. That was exactly what he'd heard— silence. No wailing. No disorganized chirping wafting up from the city far below.

His eyes snapped open and he looked down at his wrist display. No message from Candless—well, he would have seen a green pearl if there was one. But if the Choir had stopped grieving, at least audibly—that had to mean—something. No way to say exactly what. Maybe Ginger was awake and talking to them. Maybe they were just anticipating meeting their new human friend.

"Back to work," he called, and the neddies grumbled but they moved. Lanoe picked up his corner of the carbon fiber sheet. It was six meters square, but vacuformed to conform to the curve of the ship's hull. So dark it was like holding a piece of spacetime. Thin as paper, almost as light, but incredibly stiff. Debris would just bounce off it. "Okay," he said, and he moved carefully to get his corner into the right position. "Lay it down…gently…gently…."

Something went boom right behind Lanoe's head. He instinctively dropped the sheet and crouched to the hull, his hands up to protect his cranium. It took him a long second to realize that the noise had come from far away, that he was in no immediate danger. He cursed and got back up on his feet, just in time to see the sheet of carbon fiber go twisting and spinning away, into the atmosphere of the city. As it fell he saw it cleave through a long ribbon of pale smoke.

A contrail. The exhaust plume of a fighter, it looked like. That explained the boom. A cataphract-class fighter had just come shooting through the portal faster than the speed of sound.

The neddies were shouting at him, but Lanoe ignored them. With great leaping strides he ran around the circumference of the cruiser, looking for where the fighter went. He crested the top of the ship and saw a lone cataphract banking around inside the bubble, trying to bleed off some of its velocity. The fairings around the cockpit showed orange and tan, desert colors.

"Bury," he said, touching his wrist minder to place a call. "Bury, come in. You've got news?"

The response came instantly. Bury sounded terrified, his voice clipped and shaky. "Maggs," he said. "Maggs betrayed you—Centrocor's here—three fighters so far—got to get back!"

The fighter turned in a long bank, spilling lift from its airfoils. It shot past the cruiser again, accelerating toward the portal. Clearly Bury intended to head right back out there and return to the fight.

If he could have waited a few more seconds, Lanoe could have arranged for him to get some support. But of course the Hellion couldn't wait—

"Bury!" he called. "Bury!" But the cataphract slipped through the portal and was gone.

Lanoe ran back over the side of the cruiser, headed straight for the vehicle bay—they hadn't managed to replace the missing hatch there, so he could just climb right inside and get to his fighter. "Candless," he called, "I need you in the vehicle bay. Centrocor's found us."

"Ginger's still sleeping," she said, though he could hear the uncertainty in her voice. She'd been a pilot long enough to know that when your squad leader called for all pilots to scramble, you did *not* hang about.

"Then wake her up," Lanoe said, in his best command voice. "We need to move out. Now." He touched his wrist display. "Valk," he said. "Valk. I need you in the vehicle bay. Centrocor's here."

There was no response.

Lanoe scowled at the display. "Valk? Did you hear me?" He knew he'd left things bad between them, but he couldn't believe Valk wouldn't even take his call. Not at a time like this. "Valk?"

"I'm here, Lanoe," Valk replied, finally.

"Good. I need you to get to a fighter now. Centrocor's come and they—"

"I can't do that. I'm flying the cruiser."

"You can keep doing that. Just get to a fighter."

"Lanoe—no. I'd have to copy myself. You want me to go through the portal and fight them out there, out in normal space. But I can't. The last time I split myself in two, I nearly killed myself. Damn it, I mean the copy of me in the cruiser's computer nearly killed me, the me you're talking to, and—"

Lanoe didn't have time for this. "So figure out what you did wrong, and this time, *don't do that*. I need you in a fighter."

"It's too dangerous," Valk said.

Lanoe started to shout at him, to order Valk to get to the vehicle bay. But then he noticed that Valk had already cut the connection. He tried raising the AI again—and found that his call was blocked.

He was the commanding officer of the ship. That shouldn't have been possible. Then again, most cruisers didn't have AIs onboard.

There was no time for running over to the emergency control stand and arguing with Valk in person. Lanoe knew he had to get to his own fighter, to go help Bury. Even if it meant running off to battle with his forces cut back by a full third.

Chapter Thirty-Two

Bury couldn't begin to comprehend what he saw beyond the portal. A city floating in a bubble of wormspace, the cruiser sailing serenely overhead...

No bloody time for sightseeing, he thought, and swung around to hit the portal again. There were Centrocor fighters out there, enemy ships, and he was the only Navy pilot ready to fight them. He watched the portal swell in front of him, a lens of distorted space, and nearly closed his eyes as he shot through.

Good thing he didn't. Two Yk.64s were hanging in the clear air right beyond the portal, facing him with their guns hot. He had to twist sideways to avoid smacking right into them as he tore past them at speed.

Hellfire. Maybe they'd been investigating the portal. Maybe they'd been lying in wait for him. If his reflexes had been just a little slower, if he'd come out of the portal on a different trajectory—

No. There was no use thinking about how he could have died. He was still alive.

For the moment.

He saw both fighters turning, swinging around to follow him and knew he would be dead in a matter of seconds if he didn't think of something.

No sign of Maggs, at least. No sign of that damned traitor. He was probably onboard the Centrocor carrier now; they'd probably set out champagne and a four piece band to welcome him—

PBW fire lanced across the air in front of Bury's nose. His tactical board snapped into his view and he saw the two ships as yellow dots, right behind him, their thrusters flaring to life as they moved to intercept.

Bury flipped around on his long axis until he was flying backward.

Big mistake. It was an easy maneuver in the vacuum of space, a classic reversal move, but down here, deep in a planetary atmosphere, it was nearly suicidal. His crate groaned and rattled and red lights flickered on all around him as he fought gravity and inertia and air resistance. His airspeed indicator blurred as he lost lift and started to fall.

Bury's body tried to panic but he fought down his fear. The Sixty-Fours were right in front of him, right in the line of his guns. He picked one and squeezed off a quick burst of PBW fire, cleaving off half of its airfoils, making it stagger and fall back.

The other dove for him, screaming out of the clouds. Its pilot started firing instantly, pouring particle bursts down around Bury's canopy. His vector field crackled as it shunted all that energy away.

Bury hauled back on his stick. His inertial sink crushed him back into his seat as he shoved open his throttle and his primary thrusters launched him toward space—right at the Sixty-Four that was coming for him. He snarled as he saw that big round canopy growing in his forward view, as collision detection alarms sounded behind his head, as he smashed down the trigger built into his control stick, not even bothering to aim.

The Sixty-Four's pilot veered off at the last moment and they went flying off in opposite directions. Bury knew he couldn't afford another one-eighty turn, knew he'd risk breaking his ship in half if he tried, so he eased off the throttle and hit his positioning jets instead to throw himself into a long, easy roll, arcing upward like a ballistic missile. Gravity tugged at him, but gently, and he let his airfoils catch the air, keep him aloft.

Below him he saw the two Sixty-Fours. The one whose wings he'd clipped was slewing off to the left, just trying to stay airborne. The one he'd just played chicken with was still descending, but he could see it pulling up into a hard loop, getting into position to make another pass at him.

And there—yes—up in the darkest part of the sky, another one, another Yk.64, its nose bright red with heat as it slammed down through the atmosphere. *Damn*, he thought. *Damn damn damn*. Where the hell was Commander Lanoe? Where was his support?

He tried to remember what he'd learned at Rishi about small squad tactics, about what to do when you were outnumbered. His instructors had told him that a three-on-one dogfight was a losing proposition. They'd taught him to avoid getting into situations like this, how to avoid being cut off from the rest of your squad, how to break out of a box formation—

All fine lessons, of absolutely no bloody use to him now.

He looked down and saw the wounded Sixty-Four struggling to stay aloft. It could barely fly—but it could still shoot.

Divide and conquer, he thought. Cut down the odds.

Even if it felt like the most dishonorable thing he'd ever done. The Navy taught you that a cataphract pilot was a knight of the void, a gallant warrior capable of mercy and forbearance.

The Navy taught you lots of things. Then they dumped you in this kind of bosh to figure it out on your own.

Bury brought up a virtual Aldis sight. Locked it on the wounded ship and—before he could change his mind—poured PBW fire right into its midsection. Cut it to pieces that went spinning and shrieking down toward the wide ocean below.

He just hoped the pilot didn't have a chance to feel it, to know what was happening. He hoped it was painless.

He knew that was almost certainly not the case.

He didn't have much time to debate ethical dilemmas in his head, though. The ship coming down from space was cutting a long velocity-shedding S-turn toward him. Bury's sensor board told him the Sixty-Four's guns were already warmed up.

Meanwhile, below him, the other ship was coming out of its loop—its nose pointed right at him.

Where the hell is Commander Lanoe? Where is Valk, or Lieutenant Candless?

—✦—

Ginger's eyes wouldn't quite focus. She thought she saw Lieutenant Candless sitting next to her. She thought maybe her former teacher was still holding her hand, but she felt so numb—her skin, her skin was frozen, dead to the world. She could smell disinfectant and something else, some alien chemical, and there was a devilishly bad taste in her mouth. She could hear—

She could hear

She could hear everything

So many voices

So many

So

she is awake is she awake

too weak too young

her thoughts are all wrong the old one was better

one of the choir now

their hair comes in that color not enough hands

where is archie i miss archie

where is she is awake

So many voices—so many sensations, so many emotions. The loudest of them, the thoughts that were rebroadcast the most often, set the trends for the rest. They were so loud inside her head they overwhelmed her own thoughts. *One of the choir now.* It was like it was emblazoned on the inside of her skull, in giant, flaming letters. Seven hundred and thirty-nine choristers had rebroadcast that message. *Not enough hands* had been rebroadcast ninety-eight times. *Her thoughts are all wrong* echoed all around her, repeated one hundred and fourteen times.

She tried to form her own words, her own message. But her voice was only one of so many. So many voices. So many—

"Oh, hellfire," Ginger gasped, and she squeezed the hand in hers, squeezed it until she was sure Lieutenant Candless would cry out. Ginger threw her head from side to side, looking for the voices she heard, looking for the source of all those thoughts—

"Shh," Lieutenant Candless said. "You're all right."

No, she bloody well was not, her head was full of—of voices, of thoughts, she could hear them all, hear everything the Choir thought, feel every emotion they felt, all of it, all of it piled on top of her and she couldn't—

she is afraid

where is archie

she is a coward

she is not breathing

they called her a coward

just breathe

she will not harmonize

she cannot harmonize

she is one of us now

it is not working

she is afraid

Just breathe. Rebroadcast 1,947 times. A hurricane of demand smashed into her, carried her along and she couldn't help it, her mouth opened, her body shook.

Breath surged into her lungs. They'd—they'd done that. It wasn't her conscious choice to breathe, they'd—they'd forced her to breathe, they'd taken her over, they were controlling her—

No.

No, she—she felt them denying it. Like a thousand people shaking their heads at once. They hadn't forced her to do anything. They'd guided her. Helped her. She understood. She didn't understand. She wished that she understood. She hoped she would eventually understand. She—no. No no no. That was, that was them, the Choir, she heard their thoughts inside her head and they sounded—they sounded exactly like her own thoughts, like her own internal voice but—but they weren't—but they were—why didn't she understand?

They wanted her to understand.

She wanted her to understand.

They (she) needed her (them) needed (all of us, together) understanding. Understanding. Coming together as one. Singing as one.

Harmony.

If she was going to be part of the Choir, she had to harmonize. She had to accept consensus.

"I'm—I'm scared," she said.

Lieutenant Candless squeezed her hand. "It's going to be okay," she said, but she seemed infinitely far away, and anyway Ginger hadn't been talking to her, she'd been talking to—to the Choir—and—and—and—

let go

breathe

listen and repeat

it is too much she can't do it

your voice is one of many

archie could not harmonize at first

it is too much for her

accept the harmony

it is too much

"Ginger," someone said. Said out loud, not in her head, the voice wasn't in her head, it wasn't, it wasn't, it was exterior to her. "Ginger,

I have to—" Another voice, not part of the harmony, not part, not part of—

"I have to go," Lieutenant Candless said. "They need me. Bury needs me."

Ginger nodded. She lifted four arms, to reach for Lieutenant Candless, to beg her to stay. She was busy making a chair, no time for goodbyes. She was monitoring the flow in the sewage reclamation sieve, deep under the city, in the dark. She was—she was—she nodded. She nodded. She nodded. They were talking, all of them. Not talking, any of them. No words, no sounds. Images? Thoughts, pure thoughts. Their thoughts their thoughts their thoughts their feelings, and everything repeated, relayed, rebroadcasted a hundred times. Voices floated to the surface, the voices that were rebroadcast the largest number of times, consensus built by brute force algorithm, by mutual agreement, by love, by dominance, by understanding understanding understanding.

breathe

where is archie

she is not harmonizing

why will she not harmonize

other human was better

she will fail

losing her

"I promise—I'll be back. I won't leave you alone, not for very long."

She heard the hatch of the sick bay close behind Lieutenant Candless.

Ginger was alone.

Ginger was (not) alone.

Ginger was (would never be) alone (again).

Someone chirped. She'd heard that, actually heard it—with her ears. The surgeon. The surgeon was still (always had been) there (always would be) here.

The surgeon made a sound. An actual, audible sound, except in her head, in (their) head(s) Ginger, everyone, the entire Choir heard, (did not hear) felt, sensed not the sound, but the meaning of the sound, its pure, basic meaning.

A name.

Rain-on-Stones-in-a-Dry-Riverbed.

A name.

Ginger.

A name.

Three thousand four hundred thirty-three names, and she knew them all.

All at once.

Down—down toward the planet's surface, diving toward the blue snake of a river on the planet's surface. With two Sixty-Fours in pursuit, Bury could only think to run for cover, to at least put solid ground beneath him so they couldn't stack him up. PBW fire lanced past Bury on either side. He broke out of the dive just ten meters over a river delta. Picked one of the meandering valleys at random and dove behind a mound of mossy rock that burst into shards of stone as it was struck by heavy fire. He pressed down lower, lower still until the air he displaced tore at the surface of the river, a huge plume of water cascading upward behind him, maybe—just maybe—obscuring his tail.

The two Centrocor pilots stuck on him like they were chained to his airfoils, like he was pulling them along for this hell ride. Up ahead the river gave way, tumbling down a low cliff into the sea. No cover out there on the waves, nothing to protect him—he would make the perfect target. They'd taught him his very first day at Rishi: Never let the enemy get behind you, never let them chase your tail.

When you saw it on a minder's screen, white text scrolling up against a black background, it seemed like the most obvious thing in the world. Of course you would never let an enemy get right behind you, of course—

PBW fire tore through one of his secondary thrusters, shattering the cone and throwing him forward in his seat. His safety harness bit hard into his flesh as red lights flashed all around him and his damage board snapped into place right in front of him.

He swiped it away. He was too busy dodging to worry about damage control. He waggled his airfoils, the wind swinging him back and forth like a pendulum bob. He had to be careful not to let his evasive pattern get too predictable, had to remember to zig every once in a while when his hand on the control stick wanted to zag.

Twenty meters back one of the Centrocor pilots stopped shooting. Bury knew better than to think that was good news. He checked his tactical board and saw that the enemy pilot was loading an antivehicle round.

Maybe three seconds to finish loading the AV. Another three or maybe four seconds to lock in a firing solution. Then the AV would tear its way through his armor, through his shielding, through a half ton of complicated equipment. A jet of molten copper would spray through his cockpit and he would be cooked alive.

But—suddenly he had an idea.

The BR.9 he flew was a multi-role fighter, designed to carry out all kinds of missions. He had AV rounds and disruptors in his arsenal—useless to him now, since he couldn't shoot backward. He also had a rack of bombs. He'd forgotten all about them, because what use were bombs in a dogfight? You dropped bombs on stationary targets. Ground targets. There was no way they could hit the enemy fighters on his tail.

Luckily for Bury, they didn't have to. He hit the release for the bombs and pulled back hard on his stick at the same time. His BR.9 punched for the sky while the bombs spilled out of a hatch in his undercarriage, to fall just a few meters to the surface of the water below.

He'd set them for a half-second delay. By the time they went off he was already a hundred meters up and climbing fast. The Centrocor fighters had just started to copy his maneuver, their noses swinging up after him. The bombs went off right underneath them, *boom boom boom boom*, the shock wave doing no damage whatsoever to the Sixty-Fours but launching tons of water up into the air.

One of the Sixty-Fours was caught in the plume and sent spinning, its airfoils digging long strokes through the salt water. The other veered off, its pilot barely managing to swing away from the fountaining water.

Bury didn't stop to watch what happened next. He opened his throttle wide and screaming for the edge of space, intending to get far enough out of the atmosphere that he could pull some fancy maneuvers and get into a decent position to do some real dogfighting.

The sky over him turned black, and the roar of his thrusters quieted to a dull roar. He brought up his tactical board and his comms panel, looking to see if there was any sign yet of Commander Lanoe and the others.

The tactical panel showed just one yellow blip far below him—the Sixty-Four he'd knocked into the drink was out of action, probably halfway to the bottom of the sea. The other one was climbing steadily toward him but still more than five seconds away.

None of that mattered. The tactical panel zoomed out to show him the volume of space around the planet, then zoomed out again until the wormhole throat was just at the edge of his view. The throat, and the dozens of fighters that were pouring out of it.

A green pearl rotated in the corner of his vision. He flicked his eye across it and Commander Lanoe's face appeared on his comms panel. "Bury—what's the situation? Give me a report."

Bury licked his lips and glanced down at the tactical panel again. "The situation?" he asked.

On the panel yellow dots streamed from the wormhole throat, a never-ending supply of them. Squad after squad after squad.

"The situation is bad," he said. It was the best he could manage.

"It's too much," Ginger said. "Human brains don't work like this!"

The voices in her head drowned out every thought. She could barely see, barely knew where she was—the voices crowded her brain until she couldn't sense anything else, couldn't—couldn't—

push her out

she is not capable

she can not harmonize

she is not stable enough

for now listen only to me

her heart is going to burst

why did they choose her

she is panicking

we need her

Rain-on-Stones shouted over the din, except—it wasn't really shouting, it was—she projected her—

Focus on me. For now. You must learn to harmonize. You cannot listen to every voice at once, of course not. Our brains are not dissimilar from yours. Let the thoughts pass through you, flow through you.

"I feel like I want to be sick, but—" Ginger couldn't even finish the thought. She couldn't remember starting it. "I—I—through—"

The voices the voices the voices they never shut up they shut up shut up shut up shut up shut up shut

Here! Listen only to me. For now, listen only to me.

Ginger opened her eyes. Saw a row of silver eyes looking back at her. Saw herself through silver eyes saw herself from above saw a hundred eyes saw through a thousand eyes saw

Let go. Let go of this idea that somehow you can contain the Choir. You cannot. The Choir contains you.

Ginger...

Ginger tried. She tried to let go. To not focus on the voices, to not focus on any one voice. She tried. She tried she tried (shut up!) she she she she

Let your thoughts join with ours. Let our thoughts join with yours.

What did that even mean? What did—what could she—what did she have to—

Harmonize.

And...suddenly...

She did.

welcome

she is with us now

she is harmonizing

you are welcome here

i am so scared so scared

it will get easier in time

faster than archie did

she is part of us

very good

Ginger opened her eyes.

She hadn't realized she'd closed them again. For a while she'd been looking only through the surgeon's eyes, seeing only herself. Now she saw the Choir.

She saw what they were all doing. Heard what they heard, felt what they felt. It was...still overwhelming. But if she let it go, if she didn't try to absorb it all, she could handle it. Maybe.

Maybe.

Do not try for too much, not yet. Stay focused on my thoughts. Hear them as if you were listening to a human voice. Let the rest of the Choir become background noise. Good.

"I'm scared," she said.

Except she didn't say it out loud, and she hadn't meant to say it at all. She pressed a hand over her mouth. Pointlessly.

Rain-on-Stones laughed. She—she chirped, out loud, but in

Ginger's head it was a laugh, warm and kind. It felt good, that laugh. It felt so incredibly good, so welcoming, so accepting— there was no judgment in it, no mockery, just a sympathetic humor that she...

That she...

Ginger squeezed her hands into fists. "You—you manipulated my emotions, just then," she said, a little outraged.

No. I shared my own.

"Either way, you—you—"

Is it easier for you, to speak out loud? Archie was the same way at first. In time he came to understand. To harmonize fully. You will—

"Yes."

She hadn't intended to say that. It just came out. It—she realized she hadn't said it out loud at all.

You see? Already, you are becoming one of us. Adapting to our way. It is good. It is important. Years from now, you will look back and we will laugh together at this moment, at this separation you still feel, and you will understand that—

"Wait."

—it was just the pain of a growing creature, an infant secreting her first layer of armor. Nothing will feel more natural, more—

"Wait!" Ginger said.

we will be whole

she is with us now

she will always be with us

this part makes my head hurt

wait wait wait wait wait wait

not right since archie died

we will have harmony

she will accept us

we accept her

"Wait!" Ginger shouted, again and again, louder and louder until she felt 3,433 of them listening, focusing on her. She had broken the harmony and immediately waves of shame, waves of humiliation rolled over her, through her. She was as disruptive as a hatchling, she was refusing to join the consensus, she was defying her sisters, perhaps we should hear her out, give her time—so many opinions, so many voices all chiming in at once—

"Wait," she said, softer now. Chastened, but still she needed to know. She needed to ask a question.

The Choir had already heard it, in her thoughts.

Years from now, yes, Rain-on-Stones said/thought/felt. *I said years from now.*

"But I'm—we, I mean, we humans, I mean, our ship, we're only here a little while longer and then we're leaving, I'm, I'm—"

Panic/fear/laughter/doubt/ridicule/despair went off in her head like the grand finale of a fireworks display. The Choir did not understand. The Choir had just lost one of its members. The humans had been kind enough to donate a new one, a replacement for Archie. Someone who could heal the wound he'd left. Someone to make them whole again. Someone to complete the harmony.

"I can't stay here," Ginger said. "I can't, I'm so sorry if there was a miscommunication, but—"

We need you, Ginger, the Choir said. Rain-on-Stones said, for them. For them all. *How could you deny us this, now that you're part of us?*

"But—for—"

For the rest of your life, of course. Your new life with the Choir.

〜✦〜

"Hold your ground, Bury. We can do this," Commander Lanoe called.

Bury twisted around on his maneuvering jets and snapped off a quick burst of PBW fire, raking the side of a Centrocor Yk.64. The enemy's vector field sparkled as it shunted off the worst of the attack, but at least one of his rounds got through and cut deep into the fighter's armor.

Three more Sixty-Fours were on his tail. He spun around until he was flying backward—so much easier when you were in space, and didn't have to worry about air resistance—and launched a PBW salvo without even bothering to aim. His pursuers fell back, just a little.

"Where the devil is Valk?" Bury demanded. "AI or not, I'd be damned glad for his help right now."

"He's not coming," Lanoe said.

"What? Damn you, we need—" PBW fire splashed against Bury's canopy, dazzlingly bright, the light sharp enough to make him cry out. Red lights flashed around him, red lights he could barely see. He threw his stick over to one side, an evasive reflex, and his inertial sink stamped him down into his seat, kept him from so much as twitching his fingers as his thrusters burned, hard, pushing him to something like safety.

Except safety was in short supply. Dead ahead a full squad of Sixty-Fours lay in wait for him, flying in a formation so tight they might have been a drill team.

Afterimages swarmed and flared before Bury's eyes. His body ached from sitting in one position for so long, and from g-stress from the wild maneuvers he'd been pulling. A steady red light burned on the engine board in front of him. He was running out of fuel.

But then virtual Aldis sights started popping up all over his canopy, crosshairs showing him where his computer had found firing solutions for the enemy fighters. Bury held down his trigger, letting his BR.9 worry about aiming, and threw himself forward into a tight corkscrew maneuver, throwing himself right into the enemy's teeth.

They were Centrocor militia, the best pilots the poly could field. But Bury was Navy. And that meant something.

The Sixty-Fours broke ranks when he made it very clear he was going to fly right into their formation if they didn't move. Fighters spun away from each other, some having to dance quick jigs to avoid colliding with one another. Some of them were quick enough on their feet to shoot back, and Bury felt his ship vibrate as some of those shots hit home. But one of the fighters in front of him came apart in pieces, its canopy filling with orange light.

Four, he thought. For a moment he couldn't guess why he'd thought that. He was far too busy swinging over onto one side to avoid colliding with debris and Centrocor ships, and then he was past them, out the other side. *Four*, he thought again.

The last time they'd wrestled with Centrocor, he'd taken down just one of their pilots in the entire battle. Here—well—he'd shot down another one right next to the portal, down in the planet's atmosphere. Gotten his third when he dropped his bombs in the sea. Now he had a fourth kill to his name.

His tactical board wailed at him, lights there telling him that three of the fighters he'd just passed were already loading AV rounds. He was showing them his backside and if even one of those rounds hit him—

Bury spun himself around on his long axis until he could see the remains of that pretty formation behind him. Perhaps he turned about just so he could watch.

Commander Lanoe came down from on high like an avenging angel. His twin PBW cannon were already blazing away as he twisted through some complex maneuver that Bury didn't even have a name for. One Sixty-Four burst apart, its airfoils spinning off in random directions. Particle rounds carved right through the big bubble canopy of another—and the pilot inside. Lanoe launched an AV of his own and took down a third ship before he'd even completed his run.

On Bury's tactical board, the warning lights switched off, one, two, three.

The rest of the Centrocor squadron burned hard to escape, as if they were running from the devil himself.

"Where are they going?" Bury asked. "Why are they turning tail?"

"Perhaps," Lieutenant Candless said, her voice dripping with sarcasm, "you'd like to chase after them and ask them personally."

"No," Ginger said. "No, that isn't . . . I can't stay here forever. I don't belong here. I'm not one of you—I'm a human."

Archie was a human, and he was one of us. Don't you see, Ginger? The Choir is not the name of our species. It is the name of the work we do. It is the name of our purpose.

Ginger *could* see it, could feel it pulsing through her head, flowing through her. She saw the city below, not as a pile of dark buildings but as a promise. A covenant made with the universe. She saw the jars hidden away deep inside that city, hidden deep and protected. She knew what was in those jars. She knew what they meant—hope. A possible future for so many species that by all rights should be extinct. She saw the great work of the Twelve, the reason they had found to go on living, even after every other chorister was dead.

They needed her—they needed her because while Lanoe had rejected their offer, they still held out hope. Hope that other humans would take the gift they were offering.

"You want me to be your translator. You want me to talk to humans on your behalf, well, that's—I mean—"

We require a human, so we can speak with humans. We require you, because without you the work cannot continue.

It wasn't just a job they were offering her. It was a role in a harmony larger than any one species could create, a cosmic harmony. A future history, for choristers and humans and—and the—

Images of aliens flashed through her head, so fast they blurred together. The species the Choir had contacted, whose genetic material they had collected—

"Enough!" she said, loud enough that they listened.

They all listened.

"I didn't know," she told them. "When I agreed to have this thing put in my head, I didn't know you wanted me to . . . to take on that responsibility." She tried to look directly into Rain-on-Stones's eyes, but—no, she didn't need to. They were watching her.

Three thousand four hundred and thirty-three of them were watching her.

She had their attention.

"I'm sorry," she said. "I'm so, so sorry if we gave you the wrong idea. If you thought I was going to spend the rest of my life here. I'm sorry if—"

she lied

but she is sorry

her contrition is sincere

we are repugnant to them

hatchlings are always troubled

the choir must be complete

why would they lie to us

if not ginger then who

the humans lied

"I said I was sorry!" Ginger slapped the release for the sick bay's hatch and hurried out into the corridor, desperate to get away. They wanted her to stay forever, wanted her to live out the rest of her life among—

Monsters?

"No," Ginger said, shaking her head. Rain-on-Stones had followed her out into the corridor. She backed away slowly as the chorister lifted two arms toward her, reached for her with those huge claws. "No, I didn't think that. I never thought you were—"

Ginger, we can read your mind.

Ginger clamped her eyes shut. And still, she could see everything they saw. Hear everything they heard. She could hear her own breathing, heavy and ragged, hear it with her own ears and also as Rain-on-Stones heard it.

You thought we were ugly. You thought we were terrifying. You thought we were too big. You thought we were scaly. You thought we were faceless monstrosities.

"I—I—can't pretend I didn't—"

And for all of that, for all that we frightened you. Still you were kind to us.

Will you be so cruel now?

The Choir is the work. The great work of the Twelve.

Will you reject us?

Are we monsters?

She had to focus. She had to stick to the original plan, not let herself get bogged down in arguing about whether she had joined them under false pretenses. "Listen," she said. "Please. Listen. I didn't let you operate on me so that I could join the Choir. I'm sorry if that's what you thought. I did it because Commander Lanoe needed to be able to talk to you. He wants—

> he wants too much
> he asked and we answered
> we offered him our greatest gift
> he thinks he can defeat the blue-blue-white
> **he wants us to open a new wormhole**
> we told him our history but still he demands
> it is far too dangerous to consider
> it is impossible anyway
> a ludicrous demand

"Please," Ginger said. "Just—just consider it. You could open a wormhole between the homeworld of the Blue-Blue-White and some human planet. Commander Lanoe suggested opening it near Balor, the star where our Navy has its headquarters. A wormhole would give our Navy a way to reach them. To fight them. I know your history, now, I've heard it, in the harmony—it's terrible what the Blue-Blue-White did to you. What they did to so many—"

Monsters.

(monsters, she thought, the alien species in the jars all looked monstrous to her, and as soon as she thought it, of course the Choir heard it, too)

"—species. If there is any chance, even a small one, that humans could defeat that threat, if we could make the galaxy safe for... for..."

(she'd missed something. Something important, a quiet thought almost lost in the vast rush of voices that were streaming through her head)

"Impossible," she said.

Yes, Rain-on-Stones told her. *Yes*.

"You said it was impossible. You—you couldn't open a wormhole like that even if you wanted to." It was not a question.

It was answered anyway.

Yes.

Bury checked his tactical board and saw that *all* of the enemy ships were pulling back, away from the planet.

"We've got them on the run," he called, unable to keep the glee out of his voice.

"That," Lieutenant Candless said, "would be an astute tactical assessment. If it were in any way true."

"She's right," Commander Lanoe called. "Bury, move back, come over here on my left side. I have a feeling we're about to get a nasty surprise."

Bury obeyed the order, moving back into formation with the other two BR.9s.

"They're about to bring the carrier through," Commander Lanoe told him. "They're moving back to screen it—a ship is never more vulnerable than when it's exiting a wormhole throat. Be ready to smash through their wall when I give the signal."

"Aye, aye, sir," Bury replied. He glanced over, through his canopy. He could just see Commander Lanoe inside his fighter, and beyond him, on the other side, Lieutenant Candless. He flexed his fingers, shifted around in his seat a little to ease his aching back. Took a moment to study his damage board.

The news there wasn't great. He'd lost his secondary thrusters and had taken significant damage to the armor around his engine. A few more hits back there would finish him off.

Not much he could do about it, except try to keep the enemy off his tail. As always.

"There," Commander Lanoe said. "It's coming through."

On his sensor board he could just make it out—his long-range telescopes showed him the wormhole throat, and the cylindrical mass of the carrier coming through slowly, ever so slowly. Maneuvering carefully as if it had all the time in the world. Its captain must have assumed his screen of fighters would hold.

Bury nodded to himself. All right. They had a chance here. If they could hit the carrier hard, push it back—

A green pearl appeared in the corner of his vision. Lieutenant Candless, sending him a private call. He flicked his eyes across the pearl to accept.

"Ensign Bury," she said, "I would like to tell you something, while we still have a moment. It isn't easy for me to say—it simply isn't in my nature."

"I'm listening," Bury told her. What was she on about now? Was she going to tell him that he'd disgraced himself by letting his fighter get so damaged? Maybe she was going to insult his shooting, as she'd once insulted his flying. Perhaps she'd forgotten how he was likely to react to—

"I wanted to say," she told him, "how very proud I am of you."

Bury inhaled sharply, in surprise.

"The quality of an instructor can only be measured by one thing. The accomplishments of her students. Today, you have made me look very good."

"I—I don't know what to say." He was utterly flummoxed. What had happened to the Lieutenant Candless he knew? Where was the sharp tongue, the critical look, the cold, analytical mind? Where was—

"Traditionally upon receiving a compliment, one says 'thank you.' Or are they so boorish on Hel they don't teach their children basic manners?"

Oh. There she was.

"Thank you," Bury told her.

And surprised himself by feeling genuine gratitude. He knew he was a good pilot. Plenty of people had told him that before. Lieutenant Candless never had. This was the very first time she'd suggested that he'd shown anything more than basic competence.

Somehow that made all the difference.

"Okay, get ready," Commander Lanoe said. Bury recovered himself and looked down at his sensor board. The carrier was all the way out of the wormhole throat now, surrounded by a dense cloud of fighters. "We know how to do this," Commander Lanoe said. "We cover each other, we punch through that screen, and we drop disruptors into that carrier until it blows up. Easy. Now—break!"

The three of them lurched forward, their engines pushing them hard to close the distance to the carrier. Bury hit his positioning jets until he was flying a broad corkscrew around the others, squeezing off bursts of PBW fire at extreme range just in case he might hit something by accident.

Lieutenant Candless shot down the middle of his corkscrew, leaning on her throttle until she moved so fast she was just a blur in his forward view. His tactical board showed that she already had her disruptors armed and ready to fire.

Commander Lanoe took up the rear, looping around their advance, ready to pick off any enemy fighter that dared to move away from its position in the screen.

It was going to work. They would either destroy the carrier outright or force it to move, to fall back. It would be a hell of a fight, one to rival any desperate battle in Commander Lanoe's memoirs, but this was how they won, Bury thought, this was how—

"Someone check your tactical board," Lieutenant Candless called. "Something—I'm certain I saw—something."

Bury glanced down at his board, just for a moment. Just long enough to catch a glimpse of what she'd seen. He gave the board a longer look.

A ship was coming out of the wormhole throat. Something bigger than a cataphract. No—wait. It was worse than that. Two ships.

Two vehicles, close on the tail of the carrier.

At Rishi they'd taught Bury to recognize the silhouettes of every kind of warship ever built, both Navy vessels and the smaller, less heavily armed spacecraft employed by the poly militias. He had no trouble at all recognizing these.

Peltast-class destroyers. Two Peltast-class destroyers—old Navy ships, a hundred meters long, what the admirals called dedicated line assets. Meaning they had one single role to accomplish in a battle: to seek and destroy enemy ships. They carried no fighters, but they hardly needed them. The destroyers were covered from stem to stern with armament, bristling with the snouts of PBW cannon and flak guns and ship-to-ship missile pods. The guns were so thick around their noses that you couldn't even see the windows of their bridges.

Centrocor had brought reinforcements. Half a bloody carrier group.

"Hellfire," Commander Lanoe said, so quietly Bury barely heard it.

"Commander," Lieutenant Candless said, "perhaps now would be an opportune moment to call a retreat."

Chapter Thirty-Three

"Three of them," Shulkin said. As if he couldn't believe it. Bullam watched nervously as he pushed his way out of his chair and moved to the IO's station, almost knocking the man out of his seat. "There are *three* of them down there. *Only* three."

Their new guest—Auster Maggs, he was called, she remembered because he'd been one of the pilots at Niraya—sneered and adjusted his mustache. "Are you offended, perhaps, because they won't be giving you a proper battle after all?"

Shulkin turned to look at the man with dead eyes. The Captain had been of the opinion that they should interrogate the turncoat and then dump him out an airlock. Bullam had advocated against that, though only on principle.

His arrival just as they were about to enter the unnamed system had been a bit of an inconvenience. The fact that he knew they were coming suggested that Lanoe might have an ambush waiting on the far side of the wormhole throat. They had actually delayed their arrival by several hours just in case.

Now it seemed that had been wasted time. There were only three fighters down there opposing their entire force. "Our intelligence suggested there would be more," Bullam said. "Lanoe, Candless, Bury, Ginger, and Valk. That sounds like five to me."

"It was a hard journey getting here," Maggs told her. "Bound to take its toll. Darling little Ginger turned out to have a liverish disposition when it came to fighting. She's up on charges because she refused to kill one of your people. As for Valk, well, he's an artificial intelligence. Maybe they did the decent thing and put him down. Or perhaps he's flying the cruiser."

"Which you say is behind another wormhole throat," Bullam pointed out. "Down in the atmosphere of a planet. Despite the physical impossibility of that."

The IO put his head up. He looked like he wanted to raise his hand. Shulkin was too busy staring at a display, so Bullam nodded to indicate the IO should speak.

"I'm seeing very strange weather patterns down on that planet, just as M. Maggs suggested. That could indicate—"

"Lieutenant," Shulkin growled.

"I'm . . . I'm sorry, sir?" the IO asked.

"His name," Shulkin insisted, "is Lieutenant Maggs."

The IO just nodded in terror.

"He's a commissioned officer of the Naval Expeditionary Force," Shulkin said. "He's to be addressed by his proper rank. Right up until the moment they shoot him for treason and desertion."

"That long, hmm?" Maggs said, smiling.

"Centrocor will take care of you," Bullam assured him. "We're all in this together. What else can you tell us?"

"Sadly, not overmuch. I was never allowed through the *physically impossible* wormhole throat. I do know it's something to do with aliens."

The pilot, the navigator, and the IO didn't actually turn around to stare at the man. The way their heads snapped back and their hands went rigid over their consoles, however, told Bullam they very much wanted to. They wouldn't know, of course. They had never been briefed about the battle at Niraya, or what had been discovered there.

"I don't care about that," Shulkin said. "I only care about how they're going to respond to our arrival. It looks like they've broken off their attack, and they're retreating for the planet. Get me a connection to the captains of the destroyers."

Bullam grimaced.

Their holographic images appeared on a dozen screens around the bridge, almost before Shulkin finished asking for them.

Rhys and Oritt Batygin were identical twins who seemed to think that if they combed their hair in different directions people should be able to tell them apart. They had been Navy officers, briefly, until they were ousted on drug charges. Centrocor, with its slightly liberal attitude toward such things, seemed to suit them better as employers. Enough so that they didn't seem to mind if anyone knew they were high. In the holographic images their pupils were enormous, and their lips twitched constantly, even when they weren't talking.

The brothers' drug of choice was a vasodilator that kept them focused and alert, they said. It allowed them to think and react faster than any unmedicated human—they said. It definitely allowed them to speak almost in unison, as if they were one person in two bodies.

"Have something for us to kill, Captain?" they asked. "Have something for us to kill, Captain?" and tittered as if that were the funniest thing they'd said all day.

"I have orders for you," Shulkin replied. He didn't look up from the display he was studying. "There are three cataphract-class fighters in this system. I want them removed from play. I don't want them to reach the planet I've indicated on this chart. Do you understand me?"

The Batygins nodded excitedly. They did everything excitedly. "On it," they said, "On it," in a singsong voice, and then their images disappeared.

"What thoroughly unpleasant people," Maggs said.

Bullam forced herself not to smile. Dariau Cygnet had been extremely generous in loaning them his two reconditioned Peltasts. It was going to make a great difference in how this rematch progressed.

As with everything her boss did, however, it came with a bit of a sting in its tail. In this case, he'd saddled them with the Batygins.

"Captain," the IO said. "What orders should I give our fighter pilots? Should they withdraw to give the destroyers room to maneuver?"

"Negative," Shulkin told the man. "Tell them to advance on the enemy—we need all the firepower we can get on this. We may have the advantage here. Three bloody fighters. But one of them has Aleister Lanoe in it."

Lanoe knew there was a good chance he would die here.

As good a pilot as he knew himself to be, he couldn't make miracles happen. Candless was a damn fine squaddie with decades of experience, but she'd also been out of the game for a long, long time. Bury had true talent but he was fresh out of flight school.

Together there wasn't much they could hope to accomplish.

Even though they were so very, very close. Lanoe would have been happy to sacrifice his own life, if it meant giving Ginger more time to negotiate with the Choir. If there was any way he could know that she'd been successful, he would have fought to the bitter end and flown off to hell with a smile on his face.

If she could get a wormhole opened between human space and the homeworld of the Blue-Blue-White, then something more was at least possible. There was no guarantee that the Admiralty would actually take up the fight. No way to know if the corrupt and hidebound and easily distracted government of Earth would authorize military action. No way to know whether Admiral Varma still had the fight left in her to see things through.

But Earth might. Varma might. If all Lanoe could accomplish by throwing away his life was to give them a chance to do the right thing, to seek out justice, then it would be worth it.

If there was any way he could know. Any way to be sure that Ginger was up to the task of convincing the Choir. But there was no such way. And in the meantime—he had Candless and Bury to think about, too.

As he streaked away from Centrocor's fleet, with what felt like hell's gates breaking open behind him, he had to make a choice. Burn for the far end of the system. Lead all that firepower away from the Choir's planet, and the portal. Keep them from descending on the alien city like a plague. Or head straight for the portal—and the possible, just barely possible salvation of the cruiser.

"Commander?" Candless asked. "Commander, we need to know where we're going. Otherwise we'll just spin in circles. Which will make us very attractive targets. Commander?"

He thought, as he so often did, of what Zhang would do.

"Head for the portal," he said. "We're dead if we stay out here. Dive for the planet with everything you've got."

A wave of Sixty-Fours was already on their tail. Lanoe spun around on his long axis and sprayed PBW fire across their noses. Earlier, when they'd screened the carrier's arrival, that would have been enough to make them back off. Clearly they had new orders now—they veered and dodged but kept coming. Behind them the destroyers were moving. Those Peltasts would be slow to get started but their engines were powerful beasts and it would take them no time at all to catch up to the scrum. Not that they even needed to—their weapons systems were designed for medium-range line combat, while a cataphract's were meant for immediate- to short-range dogfighting. Which meant they could stand off and fire at Lanoe and his squad all day long without ever having to properly engage.

"Bury, your thrusters are shot to hell," Lanoe called. "Turn your nose to them. Candless—give us some covering fire."

"Oh, at once, sir," Candless said, her sarcastic tone nearly freezing Lanoe's ears off. But she pulled up into a tight loop and then rolled as she came down, directly over the Sixty-Fours. There were three carrier scouts in that wave, fighters with no vector fields. She concentrated her fire on them and they winked off Lanoe's tactical board one by one.

Lanoe brought up a virtual Aldis and started sniping at his pursuers, picking his shots with incredible care. He plugged one of the Sixty-Fours right in its canopy, his magnified view showing the pilot jerk and fall back as the particle beam cut right through his chest. Lanoe swiped the view away and started lining up another shot.

"The Peltasts are five seconds from maximum range," Candless called. "Four. Three. Lanoe? One. I see a spread of ship-to-ship missiles launching, looks like six projectiles, accelerating at three hundred g. I imagine I don't need to call out their bearings."

Lanoe gritted his teeth. They were still ten thousand kilometers from the top of the planet's atmosphere. "Noses down. Dive."

Bury and Candless swung around and pointed themselves straight at the planet's core. Their thrusters lit up blue as they threw open their throttles. Lanoe took another few seconds to finish lining up his shot. He squeezed the trigger and a Sixty-Four came apart in pieces, debris that would tangle up the enemy fighters behind it. Then he swung around and punched for a hard burn, himself.

His inertial sink pressed down hard on his old bones, squeezing him backward into the padding of his seat. Even his eyeballs were locked down, so the sudden acceleration wouldn't flatten them in their sockets. His vision was cut down to a tiny circle of what lay dead ahead of him. All he could see was blue ocean far below, crawling with waves.

He didn't need to see his tactical board to know those missiles were still locked on to his tail. Alarms chimed all around his head, automated systems warning him of impending impacts. Those missiles were packed full of high explosives. If one of them so much as grazed him, it would go off with enough energy to vaporize him and his fighter instantly.

His thrusters cut out—a safety interlock kept them from burning so hot they melted his shielding—and he was thrown forward into his straps, hard enough that they dug into his armpits and his groin like knives. The planet's upper atmosphere hit his canopy with a noise like it was being sandblasted, air bouncing off his vector field hard enough to make it spark. His vision returned, throbbing red, and he brought up his tactical board and looked for the missiles.

They were right behind him, maybe a hundred kilometers back. Closing the distance fast as they burned through all their solid fuel.

Below him he saw two fireballs he knew were Bury and Candless. They were slowing down, atmospheric drag eating up their velocity. They would still be moving far too fast when they reached the portal, but not nearly fast enough to get away from those missiles.

The chief design flaw of a cataphract-class fighter was that it could only shoot forward. Lanoe had no way to train his PBWs on those missiles. He could turn around to face them, but there was a chance that his ship would break up under the strain if he did. At the speed he was traveling that chance was less a probability than a certainty.

Below him the ground spun as his airfoils tried to catch the air. Lanoe hit his positioning jets and stabilized, then reached for his comms board. "If only one of us makes it, don't hang about," he told the others. "Get in there and tell Ehta to take command of the cruiser. Tell her—"

"Lanoe!" Candless called.

He didn't have time to curse. One of the missiles was right on his tail, barely five hundred meters behind.

He just had time to swing out of the way. His airfoils groaned and nearly snapped off, and the whole fighter around him vibrated hard enough to make his teeth feel like they were coming out of their sockets, but somehow his fighter held through the maneuver. The missile shot past his canopy, no more than a pale blur.

Lanoe's reflexes, honed by centuries of dogfighting, were just enough to let him snap off a burst of PBW fire. The missile exploded in midair and he shot through a cloud of fire and smoke and debris that left deep score marks in his canopy.

His tactical board chimed to tell him three more missiles were right behind him. He reached for his control stick but before he could even move they were past him, zip zip zip. They hadn't been aiming for him.

They were locked right on Bury's tail.

"Take us down," Shulkin commanded. "I want to see him die."

The pilot didn't hesitate. Gravity returned to the carrier's bridge, if only for a moment, as she adjusted their course. "Circularizing orbit," she said. "One hundred kilometers above the datum."

"Lower," Shulkin said.

Bullam sighed and looked over at Maggs, who was clinging to a nylon strap on the back wall of the bridge. "Almost seems anticlimactic, doesn't it?" she said. "We came this far, through all manner of adversity, just to execute three Navy pilots."

"There are the commercial possibilities to consider," Maggs replied, lazily rolling his shoulders.

"Oh?"

"Sixty kilometers," the pilot said.

Maggs gave Bullam a wicked smile. "There's an entire species of aliens over there, on the far side of the planetary wormhole. A whole new population who have never experienced the wonder and convenience of Centrocor products."

She raised an eyebrow. "M. Maggs. With an attitude like that, you could go far in business. Perhaps we can recoup our expenses, at the very least—"

"Lower!" Shulkin barked.

"Sir—the carrier isn't rated for atmospheric flight," the pilot insisted. "Any lower and we risk structural damage."

Shulkin stared at the woman with eyes like obsidian, like glass honed and darkened by an ancient fire.

"I'll—I'll expand the display, sir," the pilot said.

The view grew to fill half the bridge. The three fighters were the size of Bullam's thumbs, shaking and swinging back and forth in the middle of a cloud-streaked sky. Labels popped up to identify the pilot of each craft. The missiles were moving too fast to stay in focus as they closed the gap. One of them had locked on to Lanoe's tail, and in the next few seconds it was sure to—

"Damnation!" Shulkin cried out, his voice cracking. Bullam saw spittle rolling off his lip. It took her a moment to realize that Lanoe had managed to dodge the missile—and then blow it up in midair.

"That shouldn't be possible, should it?" she asked.

Maggs rolled his eyes. "We're talking about Aleister Lanoe. This is hardly the first time anyone tried shooting a missile at him. But don't worry. No one's lucky forever."

The missiles streaked toward Bury's fighter flying straight as arrows, bypassing Lanoe's and Candless's ships as if they weren't there. Bury's thrusters, Lanoe thought—his thrusters had sustained a lot of damage. They must be leaking an enormous plume of waste heat, as if he were waving a flag for the missiles to follow.

Lanoe held down the trigger built into his control stick, spraying PBW fire across the thrusters of the missiles. His shots went wide—already the missiles were too far below him to be caught by random shooting. "Bury," he called. "Bury! You have to shake them. Bury, I know you can fly. Fly like hell, right now!"

"I'm trying!" the Hellion called back. He waggled back and forth, his airfoils changing shape as they desperately tried to grab more air, to make his fighter more maneuverable. At this speed, though, inside a planetary atmosphere the BR.9 had the aerodynamic profile of a bullet, not an aircraft. He'd built up far too much momentum to be able to change his course now more than a fraction of a degree at a time.

"Candless, watch out," Lanoe called. She had wandered into the path of his fire as he tried to blast the missiles. "You're getting too close!"

One of the missiles exploded as Lanoe's particle beam burned through its casing. The blast knocked the other two missiles a hair off course, giving Bury maybe a tenth of a second more time to get out of the way. It wasn't going to be enough. Lanoe poured fire toward the other two, knowing it was useless. He was only delaying the inevitable.

His tactical board chimed to tell him that two more missiles were incoming, streaking out of space to home in on the heat of his thrusters. Behind the missiles came squadron after squadron of Sixty-Fours. They were still thirty seconds away. It might as well have been an eternity.

He realized suddenly that Candless hadn't accidentally veered into the path of his fire—she was pressing in close intentionally, trying to save her student by getting into position to fire on the missiles. Her guns erupted with fire, long streams of charged particles lancing across the path of the missiles, crisscrossing Lanoe's shots. She caught one of the missiles square on and it burst into a massive cloud of smoke and spinning debris. The last one punched through the cloud and kept going. Any second it would catch Bury and blow him to smithereens. Lanoe squeezed his trigger so hard he thought his control stick might break off in his hand.

"Hellfire," he breathed. "Bury! Move!"

The missile edged closer and closer. Bury tried swinging off to one side but the missile easily matched his course.

"Lieutenant," the kid called.

"I'm here, Bury. I'm right here," Candless replied.

"Tell Ginger—tell her—"

"Tell her yourself," Lanoe said. "Move, damn you!"

He definitely tried.

Bury's fighter flipped end over end. Damnation—the kid had just tried to flip over, to get into position to fire at the missile himself, Lanoe thought. He'd tried to pull that maneuver at high speed inside an atmosphere. He didn't think there was any way Bury's crate could take the kind of strain.

He was right. One of Bury's airfoils snapped off under the pressure, spinning away into the air. Bury's secondary thrusters—already ruined by enemy fire—burst apart in a shower of fragments. It was impossible, but Lanoe thought he could hear spars and struts snapping inside Bury's fighter, the bones of the BR.9 breaking under stress.

For a wild moment Bury spun in midair, cartwheeling end over end. His positioning and maneuvering jets fired in a wild rhythm as the kid desperately tried to even out. Lanoe was sure he wouldn't be able to pull out of that tumbling spin, but before the missile could reach him, Bury had stabilized—flying backward, with his nose pointing at the oncoming missile.

The kid fired a quick burst of PBW rounds right into its warhead. The missile burst apart, the ensuing cloud of debris engulfing Bury's fighter in a wreath of flames. As the shards of the missile fell away, showering down on the ground below, Bury emerged from the explosion, still—somehow—alive and airborne.

Not without damage, though. Lanoe could see that both of Bury's PBW cannon were out of action, rings of polished metal showing where the barrels had been sheared off in the explosion. Bury's canopy was shattered, the flowglas wobbling as it tried to reseal itself. His fairings were gone, exposing vital components to the raw air.

The fighter flipped over again, righting itself so its airfoils could carry it on the wind. Something heavy and broken fell out of its undercarriage.

"Bury," Candless called, her voice soft, encouraging. "Bury. Can you hear me? Can you talk to me, Bury?"

The kid sounded barely lucid. "I'm...I don't feel great," he said. "I, uh, I think I'm bleeding. There's, uh, there's blood in my helmet."

"Lanoe," Candless said.

"Yeah, I know," Lanoe told her. He looked to his left. Off in the distance he could just see the portal, floating serenely in its permanent ring of swirling clouds. "Bury, I want you to switch your fighter over to remote control. Candless can do the flying for you, from here. Let's get you home."

Shulkin lifted a hand to his mouth. Drew it away again, slowly. "They're alive. They're all still alive. Didn't I give an order...didn't I give an order to..."

He was shaking, visibly trembling as he turned to look at his officers.

"I'm sure I...sure I..."

Bullam took a deep breath. "Captain," she said. "I think that it might be time—"

"I gave a damned order!" Shulkin said, his voice rising into a bird-like shriek. He grabbed the navigator by his hair and slammed the man's head forward into his console. Droplets of blood floated away from the poor bastard's face.

Someone screamed. Bullam couldn't see who. The sound bounced off the walls for a moment, then died out and left behind only silence. Everyone on the bridge froze in place, staring. Eventually the navigator lifted his head and wiped blood from what was clearly a broken nose.

Shulkin threw his hands up in the air. "I gave an order! I told you to kill them! I told you to kill them all!"

He rounded on the pilot. Bullam pushed forward, thinking she would try to grab Shulkin's arm, pull him back before he could assault another officer. He didn't attack the pilot, however. Instead he shoved a long, bony finger right in her face.

"Take us down there."

"Sir," she said, her face ashen. "Sir, I—"

Shulkin reached past her and touched a control. The view showed the three Navy ships swung around until they could all see the wormhole throat hovering in the planet's atmosphere. Missiles and heavy PBW cannon fire streaked across the view. None of it struck home. One by one the cataphracts slipped through that opening and disappeared. The remaining two missiles, unable to find their targets, cut their engines and dropped harmlessly toward the planet below.

Soon the view showed nothing but the wormhole throat.

"Batygins," Shulkin barked. Their twin images appeared in inset windows in one corner of the display. "Report, damn you."

"Sometimes people get lucky," the destroyer captains said. "Sometimes people get lucky. At the damnedest time, usually. At the damnedest time, usually."

Shulkin swiped through the air with one hand and the Batygins blinked out. Then he snapped his fingers at the pilot. "There," he said, pointing at the wormhole throat. "Take us through there."

"Sir," the IO said, "this ship is already dangerously low in the planet's gravity well. Any lower and we'll have to leave orbit. We can't fly down there. The ship can't take the stress of atmospheric entry."

Shulkin nodded and pushed back to grab the arms of his seat, now just bare metal tubing since he'd torn the armrests off. He sat down carefully and strapped himself in.

"There," he said. "Take us there."

"Sir," the IO said again. "Sir!"

"It can't be done, Captain," Bullam said. "We can send fighters down there, to give chase. We can absolutely do that. Once whatever's back there is cleaned up, we can go down personally in my yacht. But really, it can't be done."

"The Hoplite managed," Maggs pointed out. "Looked like they had a touchy go of it, but they made it."

"Thank you, Lieutenant Maggs," Bullam said, glaring at the fool. "That was not at all helpful. Let me remind everyone that this is not a Hoplite-class cruiser. This is a—a—well, I've forgotten the class designation, but—"

"Hipparchus," the IO said.

She nodded at him. "Exactly. This is a Hipparchus-class carrier and that makes all the difference. Let's give the order to send the fighters through. Then we can see about getting the poor navigator to the sick bay, and—"

"Shut up," Shulkin said. He reached into a pocket of his suit and pulled out an old-fashioned pistol, blocky and flat and made of dull metal. He pointed it at the pilot's head. "If my orders aren't followed in five seconds, I'll kill her. Five."

Bullam floated next to her chair, with no idea what to do. She could try to take the gun away from Shulkin, but she knew perfectly well how that would end. Shulkin would just shoot her instead. The IO and the navigator edged away from the pilot, clearly having no better plan than she did. The pilot looked like an animal frozen by a spotlight, unable to run away. Slowly she lifted her arms to cover her face, as if that would do anything.

"Four," Shulkin said, very calm now. "Three."

"Damn it! Do what he says!" Maggs shouted, from the back of the bridge.

"Yes, sir," the navigator said, and turned to her console, laying in a new course.

"Two," Shulkin said.

"Don't! Don't shoot!" the pilot screamed, and reached for her own controls. "Course laid in," she squeaked.

"No," Bullam said. She couldn't believe it. The madman was going to do it. "No, it's too dangerous. Listen—just give me a moment to get to my yacht. Let me get out of here."

"One," Shulkin said.

"Please!" Bullam begged. "Please—I have a medical condition, I—"

"Beginning maneuver," the pilot said. And then she pushed her control yoke forward, and the carrier fell out of the sky.

⚔

Lanoe shot through the portal too fast and had to bank hard to avoid crashing into the City of the Choir. He cut a series of sharp S-turns to bleed off his velocity, then headed for the cruiser's open vehicle bay. Candless and Bury made a couple of extra loops around the cruiser before they followed him in. As soon as Lanoe had parked his BR.9 in its docking cradle, he ran to the open edge of the bay and looked out. So far no one had followed them through the portal, but he was sure that wouldn't last.

He tapped his wrist display. "Valk," he said. "Damn you, we needed you out there. We still do."

There was no response.

"You bastard," Lanoe said. "Bury's hurt. He's probably going to die—because you wouldn't come out and fight with us. Don't you even care?"

Nothing.

"Valk—Hellfire, Valk, talk to me!" When there was no immediate response he scowled and tapped for Ehta instead. "We're about to see ten kinds of hell coming through the portal. Do you know where Valk is? Physically, I mean."

"He's in the wardroom," Ehta replied, instantly. "At the helm. Lanoe—what happened out there?"

"Centrocor happened. Bury's hurt." Lanoe shook his head. "The carrier," he said, too worked up to actually speak in sentences. "Plus two Peltasts. Guess we were too tough for them last time. Stand by."

Candless and Bury came gliding in just then and he had to duck to miss getting decapitated by their landing gear. In the harsh lights of the vehicle bay, Bury's fighter looked worse off than it had out in the sunlight. Candless didn't even bother berthing her ship properly. Instead she jumped out before her canopy had even fully retracted and ran over to check on Bury.

Lanoe came up behind her. It looked bad. His suit was torn open, layers of insulation flapping free. His chin was slick with blood, and a lather of foamy pink drool covered his lips. His eyes were wild, rolling back and forth.

"Bury," Candless said. "Bury, it's all right. It's going to be all right."

The kid was past responding. Lanoe didn't know if he was going to make it.

"We need to get him to the sick bay. The surgical drone there can save him, but we need to move him right now," Candless said.

"I'll do it," Lanoe said, thinking he needed to get over there anyway, to talk to Ginger.

"You will not, damn you," Candless said. She was frantic with worry. "He's my student. I have a responsibility to make sure he—"

"You have a responsibility to Ginger, too," Lanoe told her. "And as XO, you're responsible for everyone on this ship. Candless—Marjoram. Listen to me. The battle isn't over yet. Not by a long shot. The best thing you can do for him—for both of them—is get back out there. Guard the portal. Our only chance is to make sure they don't get enough fighters in here to overrun us."

She stared into his eyes for a second, and he felt like she was judging him. No. Evaluating him. It was a teacher's look.

"Go," he said. "As soon as I think he's going to be okay, I'll come back out and join you. Go!"

"Is that an order, Commander?" she asked, through pursed lips.

"You damned well know it is," Lanoe told her. "Go!"

She went. Her fighter lifted out of its cradle, turned around, and shot out of the bay, only seconds after she'd arrived.

Lanoe turned back to Bury's fighter, and reached down to pull the kid out. Only to find that the Hellion's suit had fused to his seat, so he was stuck inside the cockpit.

There was no good way to be gentle about it. Lanoe tore Bury free. The kid spasmed and fresh blood leaked from his mouth. Lanoe let him rest for a second. He tapped at his wrist display and got a direct line to the wardroom.

"Valk," he said. "Valk—you're going to talk to me whether you like it or not."

"I'm here," the AI replied.

"We could have used you out there," Lanoe said. "Bury's hurt bad. Why the hell didn't you fight with us? You're angry at me, is that it? We don't have enough pilots for that kind of petty bosh."

"It wasn't that. I mean, I *was* angry. But I got over that. I stayed behind because I had to fly the cruiser."

Lanoe closed his eyes. "You and I both know you can do that *and* fly a fighter."

"You don't understand. When I make copies of myself, I can't trust them. I can't guarantee they won't turn on me again."

"Find a way to help. Find a way to make it work. We need you, Valk."

"I know. I'm sorry, Lanoe. I know—I just—I'm scared. Scared of what I'm becoming. Scared of how much I've lost."

Lanoe opened his eyes again. He couldn't handle this. "Do what you have to do," he said. "But get over it. Now."

He cut the connection and opened a new one.

"Ehta," he sent, and she responded instantly. "I'm headed for sick bay. Have your marines clear a path." He grimaced as he lifted Bury out of the cockpit and slung him over his shoulder. "In fact— get them to the gundecks. Get as many of our coilguns warmed up as they can manage."

"You got it, boss," Ehta said. "Though—listen—I don't want to have to be the one to say this, but—"

"Just go ahead," Lanoe grunted as he carried Bury through the hatch into the axial corridor. Even in the minimal gravity, the kid weighed a ton.

"You really want to get in an artillery duel in here? In the bubble, I mean? Let's say we actually get lucky. Let's say we blow away one of their destroyers, or even the carrier. That's going to create a hell of a lot of debris. All of which will rain down on the Choir's city. The locals might not approve."

Lanoe closed his eyes for a second. Opened them and stomped on down the corridor. "I don't intend for you to shoot at Centrocor."

"No? Oh. Oh, well, then—"

"I want you to work up a firing solution for the city. I want you to be ready to bombard the place on a second's notice. If Ginger can't convince them to help us, we're going to have to do it the old-fashioned way. Persuade them at the end of a gun barrel."

———※———

The carrier groaned as it hit the top layer of the planet's atmosphere.

Then gravity reached up and squeezed it, and it screamed.

Bullam reached for a handhold at the side of the hatch leading out of the bridge. It was vibrating so much it made the bones of her arm feel like they would snap. She staggered out into the corridor, and the ship lurched so hard she slammed into the far wall.

"Oh, hellfire, oh hellfire," she chanted. The carrier rolled around her and she had to drop to all fours, pulling herself along the floor as the walls seemed to bulge inward and then bow back out. Her cabin was only a few dozen meters away, but she knew it was going to feel like kilometers.

Far away, deep in the cylindrical body of the carrier, something burst and a dull roar came echoing up the corridor. An alarm chime sounded from the ceiling above her and lights flashed everywhere. She couldn't hear anyone else in the ship, no sound of running feet or shouting voices. Maybe everyone had the good sense to get in their bunks and stay there.

Something she desperately wanted to do, herself. There were lots of things she wanted, just then. A captain who wasn't homicidally insane. A mission that wasn't likely to end in her death. A mirror.

She desperately needed a mirror. She needed to look for the dark spots of broken blood vessels under her skin. She needed to check her eyes, and make sure they weren't filling with blood.

The way things were going she would be lucky just to make it to the hatch of her cabin. She dragged herself along, arm over arm, getting closer, just a little bit closer—

The alarm chimes turned to shrieks of pain. The carrier bucked wildly, tossing her into the air and then throwing her violently back down to the floor, knocking the wind out of her. She saw spots swim before her eyes, felt her blood coursing through her veins, and she cried out, begged for anyone to help her, but there was nobody there.

Just a meter or two more—she dug her fingers into the seams between floor panels. Cracked her fingernails but she didn't care. Just a little farther—a little—

The carrier swung upside down for a moment and she was flying, she was upside down, on the ceiling, looking at the floor, she was falling, she was—she was—

The carrier stood up on end, and there was no floor beneath her. Bullam screamed as she grabbed on to anything she could, barely catching a nylon handhold in time. She felt a bone in her wrist bend almost to the point of snapping as she swung by one hand. Her hatch was just half a meter away, half a meter but she couldn't—she couldn't reach the release, she couldn't swing toward it, not with the way the ship was tossing back and forth so violently; if she let go of her handhold she would fall, she would fall down the corridor and smash at the far end—

"Here," Maggs said. He stood on the wall, his boots anchored to a panel, and grabbed her with one hand. He reached over with the other and slapped the release. He got his arm under her and picked her up. Half-carried, half-tossed her inside. "Bit of a bump just then, eh? We'll get you sorted." He pushed her down into her tiny bunk and pulled straps across her chest and hips.

"Drones," she said. "My drones—I need my drones."

He looked around and must have understood what she was trying to tell him. The drones were in the air, bobbing back and forth like corks on ocean waves, trying to reach her. With him hovering over her they couldn't get through. He stepped aside and the drones swarmed around her, one displaying a mirror so she could check her skin, one holding out a painkiller tab in a skinny manipulator. She found a spot just below her chin and waved for the one she called her little vampire. It swung back and forth alarmingly but then its needle jabbed deep into her flesh, and she let her head fall back. Let her eyes flutter closed as the painkiller spread through her pathetic veins.

"Why?" she said, as the ship lurched, as things flew around the room, toiletries and minders and odds and ends. Maggs dodged them all nimbly as he strapped himself to one wall. "Why did you help me?" she asked.

"If we're going to be allies," he said, "we might as well be friends." Then he flashed her a stunning smile, all big white teeth under his fancy mustache.

"You'll be rewarded," she said, her thoughts clouded and out of order. Things were slipping away from her. "We're...all...in..."

In the mirror display, another dark spot appeared, this one on her cheek. A third blossomed on the back of her left hand.

"No," she whispered. "No...No..."

The painkiller took her away, as the ship rocked her to sleep.

Lanoe laid Bury down as gently as he could. The sick bay's drone reached out with its jointed arms to scan the kid and pump him full of stabilizers. Ginger crouched by the side of the bed and carefully pulled his gloves off.

A green pearl spun in the corner of Lanoe's vision. Candless calling, no doubt wanting an update. He sent back a quick text-only message letting her know they were doing what they could.

The medical drone lit up with a display of Bury's midsection. It looked like he had half a dozen cracked ribs, and his liver had been pulverized. There was a lot of blood pooling in his abdomen. Subdisplays popped up to show that his blood pressure and blood oxygen levels were crashing. A prognosis window came up but it was full of question marks. There was only so much a medical drone could do.

If the cruiser had a real doctor, if they could have taken him to a hospital on some human planet—

"Rain-on-Stones would like to help," Ginger said.

He looked down at her and saw her eyes weren't focusing. The Choir was talking through her.

"She is a surgeon," Ginger pointed out. "She performed my operation."

Lanoe frowned. "That doesn't mean she knows anything about trauma medicine in humans," he said. "You really think she can do something?"

Ginger's face went slack for a moment. "Opinions are varied. Many of us feel it's too dangerous. Others think you don't deserve the Choir's help. Not after all you've done. Not considering what you have brought to their city. War," Ginger said, and her head jerked back. "War—they say you're bringing war here."

Lanoe wished he could deny it. "Ginger," he said, though he knew he wasn't talking just to her. "What do you think?"

"Opinions are trending toward—"

"Damn it, Ginger—talk to me! What do *you* think?"

Her eyes snapped into focus. "Please," she said. "Please let her do it."

Lanoe nodded. The hatch of the sick bay opened and the tall chorister folded herself inside, scraping her claws together under the ultraviolet light. Lanoe grabbed Ginger's arm—a little more roughly than he would have liked, but he was in a hurry—and pulled her out of the small room.

"We need to stay out of her way now," he told Ginger. "Besides. I need to talk to the Choir."

Ginger had been staring back at the hatch, at Bury in the bed, but now she turned and looked at him with an absolutely blank face. "We are listening."

"Can you get me Water-Falling?"

"Water-Falling-from-a-Height has lost the respect of the Choir," Ginger said. "She no longer serves as our ambassador to humans."

"What?" Lanoe didn't like that. While he knew consciously that the Choir were all linked, that they spoke out of consensus, he had thought he'd developed a relationship with Water-Falling. Maybe it was just a human prejudice but he'd thought he actually had a chance to get through to her. "Why not?"

"She couldn't keep Archie alive. She failed the Choir," Ginger said. "She is currently being shamed. Opinions vary, but most feel she was a useless fool. Some suspect her of being mentally unwell, while others—"

Lanoe shook his head. "Never mind. I'm sorry if I played a part in that. But there are pressing concerns we have to deal with right now. There are a bunch of people about to come through the portal who want to kill us. They want to kill Ginger."

Ginger's mouth opened in a shocked circle, but her eyes were still blank. "No," she said. "No—please, don't let them! We just brought her into harmony!"

"Then close the portal," he told her/them. "Close the portal and seal off the bubble. If they can't get in, they can't hurt her."

There was a long pause. Maybe the Choir was thinking how best to respond. When Ginger opened her mouth to speak again, he saw that it was her, specifically, who answered. Her eyes locked on to his and her mouth twisted in fear.

"They can't," she said.

"Why not? Because of some stupid idea that they have to welcome all humans? Because I guarantee you that if Centrocor comes in here, they won't leave until they own the entire place. The Choir doesn't understand money, so they won't even get a good price."

"No, Commander Lanoe, it's . . . it's not that. They can't close the portal. They don't have the *ability* to close the portal. That system is all automatic—once you open it, back on the planet, it has to run through a complete cycle. It'll be open for another seven hundred and twenty-nine days, and then it'll close on its own, until somebody else comes along with the key."

Lanoe seethed. They could have told him that earlier. Instead they'd made up that bosh about welcoming humans. Another lie by omission. For all their vaunted shared consciousness and total honesty, the Choir was damnably good at withholding things.

"Sure," he said. "Sure. Forget that. You've doomed us all because you built your front door without a lock. But never mind. What about my other request? The one I specifically asked you for, before you cut open Ginger's head?"

"The wormhole," Ginger said. It was still Ginger talking to him. "You wanted them to open a wormhole between Balor and the homeworld of the Blue-Blue-White."

"Yes, damn you. What about that?"

"They can't," Ginger said, again.

"I don't care if they're afraid of the bloody jellyfish," Lanoe said. "I need that wormhole! Without it none of this—none of our deaths—will mean anything!"

"They can't," Ginger said, again.

Lanoe gave her his best command glare, but she didn't relent.

"For the same reason. The technology you're asking about—it doesn't exist anymore. They used to build stable wormholes, yes. They built the entire network of wormholes. But that was back before the First Invasion. There have been no stable wormholes opened since then, because the technology was lost. They don't remember how it's done."

"They don't remember?"

"Please stop shouting at me. Sir. I asked, just like you told me to. I begged them. I tried everything I could think of. But it's true. They can't open the wormhole you want. It's impossible."

Chapter Thirty-Four

She'd failed them.

Candless chewed on her lip as she spun loose circles around the cruiser, keeping her velocity up as she scanned the portal. The second something came through there she would need to pounce. It was crucial she hit Centrocor's fighters before they had a chance to get properly inside the bubble, to set up a beachhead.

She'd let them down. They'd been her students. Her charges. Now both of them...

Ginger had submitted herself to the claws of an alien surgeon, and now she was in the thrall of a race of giant lobsters. Bury was probably going to die.

Candless took her hand off the control stick for a moment. Flexed her fingers three times, making a fist then snapping it open. Then she took the stick again and nudged it forward, sending her fighter toward the portal. It had to be any second now—Centrocor would know they were flying right into an ambush, but they had no choice. If they wanted to continue this pursuit—and slaughter the entire crew of the Hoplite—they had to poke their heads inside the bubble. She checked her boards. Plenty of ammunition. Plenty of fuel. The only thing she lacked was close support.

Bury was, she well knew, an ass. A child made of anger and exuberance in equal measure, and he let both of them get the better of him. He'd come through a multiday patrol and fought like a demon, though. He might have given his life for the mission. He shouldn't have had to. It was all her fault.

She edged closer to the portal. When the attack came, when the fighters started streaming through that aperture, she would just have to start shooting. Any second now. Any second.

Ginger was technically, legally, a coward. Candless's fault, again. She should have been more adamant about keeping her out of a fighter's cockpit. As XO, she should have insisted that she couldn't fight. Instead she'd bowed to Lanoe's insistence, and forced the girl to disgrace herself.

Any second. Any moment. Any—

Four Centrocor fighters burst through the portal all at once, Sixty-Fours flying in such close formation they looked like their airfoils were touching. They split apart the nanosecond they were through, heading off in four different directions. Candless shouted a curse and poured fire into them but she only caught one of them—a direct hit that punched through its vector field and burst it open in a bright explosion. The other three got past her. Candless turned around in a hard bank and sped after a second one, but that left two unaccounted for, and the cruiser almost defenseless.

Damn me, she thought. *Damn my eyes. I've failed again.*

⟩⟩⟩⟩

Ehta stood in one of the target acquisition booths above the barrels of the coilguns and watched her people run through yet another drill. "Loading crew four, pick up the damned pace!" she shouted, but she didn't even bother checking to see if they did or not. "Fire control teams, pay some damned attention!"

She didn't know if she could do it.

She owed Lanoe. She owed him her life, her career. Whatever little shred of self-respect she still had. The Navy and then the Marines had treated her like a machine, like a product, and more often than not they'd found her insufficient to requirements.

Lanoe had given her a chance to be part of something important. At Niraya, she'd helped him save a hundred thousand people from bloodthirsty aliens.

Now he was asking her to shoot at some other aliens. Nice other aliens. Peaceful other aliens. She understood, really. She got that being in command meant sometimes you had to employ force to meet your objectives. Hellfire, she was military down to her bones, wasn't she? Her whole job was shooting at people.

That didn't include mugging them. Holding them hostage until you got what you wanted. It shouldn't include that.

When the order came—she didn't know if she could pull the trigger.

She guessed she would just have to wing it.

"You over there—barrel greasers! Do I need to come down there and kick the devil out of you with my own two boots? Move!"

—————

Ginger put a hand on Bury's forehead. It was hot but dry. Her skin didn't stick to his plastinated skin, not the way she expected it to.

Rain-on-Stones reached inside Bury's open chest and tugged at something, and Bury's whole body jerked. Ginger whimpered a little to see him in that state.

"I have to go," Commander Lanoe told her. "Damn. It looks like Candless is in real trouble. I'm going—but this isn't over. Keep a channel open so I can talk to them."

"Yes, sir," Ginger said.

He hurried out of the sick bay and the hatch closed behind him.

He refuses to see logic, Rain-on-Stones told her. The Choir told her. *He believes we will give him what he wants, if he demands it strenuously enough.*

"We told him it couldn't be done," Ginger said. Out loud, needlessly. She wondered if in time she would learn to just think, to not phrase everything she said so carefully. You didn't have to watch what you said with the Choir—there was no point. You couldn't hide anything from them.

You still want to help him.

"He's my commanding officer. I'm supposed to follow his orders."

It's more than that.

she respects him

the idea is foolish

his words offended us

he has endangered the Choir

she thinks he can defeat the blue-blue-white

he rejected our offer of help

she thinks he can do it

she believes in him

he is dangerous

"Opinions vary," Ginger said.

Rain-on-Stones laughed, inside her head.

⌁

Lanoe roared out of the vehicle bay in his BR.9, boosting to catch up to the battle that had already started out there. Candless was wheeling across the ghostlight sky, chasing fighters, but for every one of them she caught, three more came through the portal. Already debris was beginning to build up in a loose ring around the city, pieces of wrecked fighters, bodies of dead pilots. Lanoe remembered the section of carbon fiber cladding he'd dropped, back when he was trying to repair the cruiser. It had fallen with an aching slowness, but an inevitability, too—every piece of junk they generated out here would eventually land in the Choir's city, maybe with disastrous results.

Their problem, he thought. He needed to salvage something

from this catastrophic ruin of a mission. The first step was keeping his people alive, at least a little while longer.

It was not going to be an easy task. He roared through half a squad of Centrocor fighters, spraying them down with PBW fire, accomplishing nothing. Pulled up into a steep loop just as his tactical board chimed at him. One fighter had escaped Candless and was headed straight for the cruiser, a disruptor round already armed in its belly.

He rolled out of his loop and burned hard to catch the Sixty-Four before it could release its deadly payload. Brought up a virtual Aldis sight and lined up his shot—knowing he had at most three seconds before the bastard fired the disruptor. His first few shots went wide, and the next volley sparked harmlessly off the Sixty-Four's vector field. Two seconds, and he kept firing, walking his shots up the side of the enemy ship. One second and he finally got through, his fire digging deep into a fairing.

The Sixty-Four erupted in flame, pieces of it exploding outward, a bit of spar or maybe an engine line smacking against Lanoe's canopy. He must have set the disruptor off inside the Sixty-Four's undercarriage.

A thought occurred to him, out of the blue. It had nothing to do with Yk.64s or disruptors or anything he saw in front of him.

"Stable," he said, out loud.

It came to him just like that. Out of the blue. "Stable," he said again. He reached for his comms board. Then jerked his hand away.

The first of the Peltasts was coming through the portal. He could see its bulbous nose, thick with guns, appear out of nothing. It kept coming, and coming, more of it appearing as if by magic. Hellfire. He'd thought, or maybe just hoped, that the destroyers would have stayed outside.

"Candless," he called. "We've got trouble. I'm loading a disruptor—I need some cover, though, if I'm going to get close enough to use it."

"A bit tied up at the moment," she called back. "Be there as soon as humanly possible."

"Make it sooner," Lanoe said. He worked his tactical board, trying to find the best approach, the trajectory that would take him into firing range the fastest while also letting him cut through the worst of the fighter screen. There were no good solutions, no easy way to—

He didn't even see it coming.

His head rang like a bell. All around him red lights flickered and alarms chimed. His BR.9 shook and twisted and flipped over on its back. Lanoe's vision swam as the blood drained out of his head, as his inertial sink screwed him down hard into his seat.

He could just make out, in his peripheral vision, his damage control board. Some Centrocor bastard had gotten lucky, lined up a direct hit, and blasted him with PBW rounds. His hand had come off the control stick—he reached for it—

Just as another hit blasted a hole right through his canopy.

"Lanoe!" Candless called. "Lanoe, come in—come in, you old fool!"

She couldn't get a reply. There were three Centrocor fighters right on her tail and she couldn't raise Lanoe. The destroyer was all the way inside the bubble now, and something else was coming through, something round and hollow and—

By the last drop of water in hell, she thought. *They're bringing the carrier in, too.*

The huge ship emerged a part at a time, looking like it was manifesting itself into the universe out of sheer bloody-mindedness. Fresh fighters were already launching from its massive vehicle bay as she stared in horror.

If Lanoe was dead—if she was alone out here—

There was no time for thinking such thoughts. She had to keep the fighters away from the cruiser. Bury and Ginger were on the Hoplite. One good disruptor shot was all it would take to kill them both.

She twisted around to face an oncoming Sixty-Four, her guns already firing. Her airfoils shook so much she thought they might snap off, but she handled the turn and stitched a line of shots across the Sixty-Four's thrusters, sending it spiraling away. PBW fire blasted by her, some of it dancing off her vector field, and she accelerated into a corkscrew to shake her attackers.

"Lanoe," she called. "Lanoe!"

People were shouting all around him, saying things he couldn't understand. Lanoe's head felt hollowed out, empty. He lifted his hand and reached for something, but forgot what he was trying to do before his fingers got there.

"Lanoe," Zhang said.

He tried to shake his head to clear it. Tried to blink his eyes. They wouldn't open.

"Lanoe, you need to wake up," she said.

"I—I'm trying," he told her. "Am I dead? Are we together again?" It made as much sense as anything else.

"You can't die here," she said. "You have to find them."

"I don't understand. Who—who are you talking about?"

"The Blue-Blue-White. They killed me, Lanoe. You have to find them."

"I know," he said, trying to think. The wind kept whistling through his head. "I know—I need to find a way to—to get justice for you, for—"

"No," Zhang said.

He was so confused, and the wind was getting louder, roaring through him now.

"No?"

"Not justice," Zhang told him.

His eyes were about to open. He was going to wake up and he would lose her again, she would be taken away from him all over again—

"What?" he asked.

"Not justice," she repeated. "You need to find the Blue-Blue-White. And then you need to kill them all."

"What?" he thought. The wind was howling, roaring in his ears. Zhang would never—she wouldn't have wanted—

He opened his eyes.

—and saw the top of a Choir lighthouse flash past him, spinning in space. Saw other buildings, their dark stone towers, saw an empty plaza, all rolling, random images tumbling through his distorted vision, just hallucinations perhaps, or—

No. *Hell, no*—he was tumbling, falling, only a hundred meters above the Choir's city. Instantly he snapped back to full consciousness and saw that he was falling out of the sky.

His canopy was shattered, its rough edges rippling as the flowglas tried desperately to resume its prior shape. There wasn't enough of it left to actually cover him. He'd taken a hit straight through the canopy—that was why his head was ringing. It had nearly been blown off. For the moment, at least, it was still attached to his neck. He'd taken another shot, he remembered, another hit, but where? He didn't have time to check his damage control board, he was falling, locked into a bad spin, headed downward faster and faster, and the city was getting closer and closer—

His hand lurched forward and grabbed his stick. He pulled back and his BR.9 whined, groaned, did absolutely nothing that could be considered flight.

"Damn you," he said. "Damn you," as he wrestled with the stick, as he worked his engine board, checking his thrusters, cursing at the red lights there, shifting power to his secondaries—when that didn't work he shunted energy over to his positioning jets, his maneuvering jets, and somehow, somehow, got a little thrust, just a little.

He yanked back on the stick, pulled back until the muscles in his arms protested. Fought the air, fought gravity, fought death—

Aleister Lanoe had won every war he ever fought. He wasn't going to lose this one. He pulled out of the spin and fired every jet and thruster he had left and missed colliding with an octagonal stone office tower by a matter of centimeters.

Burned to regain altitude.

The carrier emerged complete from the wormhole and a line of positioning jets on its side flared to life as it moved out of the way so the second Peltast could join the party. Candless could only stare in horror at all that firepower, all that doom. She almost let a Sixty-Four creep up on her. Almost—at the last moment she banked away and its shots went wide. She looped around and smashed open its thrusters with her own cannon, left it drifting, helpless.

"Lanoe!" she shouted.

"I'm alive," he called back.

"Oh, thank the devil for that," she said. "What's your condition?"

"Took a couple bad hits. My thrusters are wrecked. I'm airborne but I'm not going to get close enough to that Peltast to launch a disruptor. We need to switch places—I'll cover the cruiser."

"We can't do this, Lanoe," she said, while strafing a pair of Centrocor fighters at extreme range. Four more were banking around to charge her. "We're damned good pilots, but we're not this good. If you're going to think of some miraculous solution, now is precisely the time."

"I've got something—maybe," he said. "Don't stop shooting just yet."

"Understood," she said.

Though she could barely see the point, she launched herself forward, shaking off the Sixty-Fours that were crowding around her. Tapped at her weapons board to load a disruptor. Twisted to the side as one of the destroyers fired a flak cannon at her, the shell exploding in midair, producing a cloud of white smoke and fizzing submunitions that would burn right through her armor if she got too close. The big ship's missile rack pivoted to track her and its heavy PBW cannon swiveled back and forth, looking for targets. She was the only target they were likely to find.

Marjoram Candless had seen war. She'd seen her share of battles, fought like hell around a dozen planets. In the end she'd chosen to be a teacher instead. A flight instructor. Just so she didn't have to do things like this anymore.

She still remembered how it was done, though. She roared in outrage and kicked in her secondary thrusters, throwing herself forward, right into the line of fire. It didn't matter how many hits she took, didn't matter whether she burned alive, she was going to fire her disruptor.

Sixty-Fours swung up all around her, whole squadrons of them. Fast little carrier scouts flitted like dragonflies in her wake, lining up shots.

Damn, she thought. *Damn. They'll knock me out of the sky before I can get close enough. Damn damn damn*—there was no way she could punch through that screen.

She did not veer, or swerve, or so much as jink out of the way as guns erupted all around her, as explosions blossomed above her, below her, to every side, as—

—as Sixty-Fours and carrier scouts alike erupted in flames, came apart in pieces, lurched off on bad trajectories as their airfoils were shot off.

"Keep going," someone said. "I've got your back."

Valk. That was Valk's voice.

"Valk?" she called.

"Better late than never, I guess. Keep going!"

Candless spared a split second to check her tactical board. There were eight blue dots on her screen—eight friendlies back there, twisting and darting like gnats, maneuvering faster than any human pilot could, racking up kills left and right.

Eight of them.

In front of her, the destroyer loomed enormous and cruel and impregnable—but suddenly there was a hole right in the middle of its screen of fighters. There was a hole there big enough for her to fly through.

◄——

Valk had figured out his mistake.

When he'd copied himself into the Hoplite's computer, he'd had to prune his databases and processes, because the ship couldn't hold all of him at once. He'd cut out every program in his directory that related to moving his hands and feet, that covered eating and drinking. All things the copy wouldn't need to do. He'd also left out every subroutine that would allow the copy to feel pain.

He'd thought he was showing mercy, at the time. Having lived with phantom body syndrome for so long, having experienced so much pain himself, he'd thought he would spare his copy that torment. As a result, when it came time to resynchronize, the copy had fought him tooth and nail. It didn't want to go back into a body that felt pain. It wanted to continue to live its paradisiacal existence.

The copies he'd made of himself now, the copies in the eight fighters that he'd sent as backup for Candless, felt nothing *but* pain. To them, death would be a blissful release.

He was in constant contact with them, updating their databases with information from the cruiser's sensors, monitoring their thoughts to make sure they didn't turn on him. He had no choice but to feel their agony. It made his bones hurt, even though he had no bones. It made his muscles ache, his teeth feel like they were rotting in his head.

But they were getting results. Because they had no fear and were more than happy to throw themselves at the enemy, they could take risks no human pilot would ever stomach. Because they had no weak flesh, they could pull maneuvers that would turn a human pilot into red jelly.

Because they longed to die, they had no trouble bringing death to Centrocor's pilots. He had to force them to keep themselves alive, in fact—to prevent them from simply hurling themselves at the enemy in one quick suicidal charge.

He lay back in his seat in the wardroom, his arms hanging down loose at his sides. He could feel the lips he didn't have shaking, feel his nonexistent eyes rattling in their sockets as his copies took hit after hit, as thrusters and fairings and fundamental systems inside their fighters were smashed and burnt and sliced apart by PBW cannon, as they absorbed shrapnel from flak explosions, as they caught fire, as parts of them exploded, as they were bathed in lethal heat and radiation.

And then one of them...vanished. There was no cry of exultation, nor a last desperate scream. It simply disappeared, and one-eighth of Valk's sympathetic pain was gone. He shuddered with relief—

—and pushed the seven others to even crazier, more reckless acts of daring.

On Lanoe's tactical board, a yellow dot blinked out. One of Valk's ghost fighters streaked past his broken canopy, waggling its airfoils. The AI had freed Lanoe up, given him a second to speak to Ginger.

Something had broken loose in his head. Just as Zhang had come to him when he stood before the statues of the Twelve, when he hadn't known how to open the portal. She'd come to him again and this time reminded him of one word, one word he'd forgotten in the rush of battle.

Stable.

"Stable," he said.

"Commander? We don't understand what you mean."

"You said that the Choir had lost the ability to make stable wormholes, that they'd lost that technology in the First Invasion. But I know they can still make some wormholes—*unstable* wormholes. Wormholes that last only a short while."

Ginger was silent for a moment, perhaps busy conferring with the Choir. It took far too long. Lanoe had to twist away from an incoming flak round that burst and spattered the side of the cruiser with glowing, ultrahot shards of metal. Some of them lodged in the Hoplite's carbon fiber cladding and smoldered there, slowly burning their way through.

Lanoe gritted his teeth. If Ginger didn't answer soon—

"They understand," she said. "You are correct."

A blazing comet of heavy PBW fire lanced past Lanoe's BR.9 and struck the cruiser amidships, somewhere in the gundecks. The entire Hoplite rocked back and forth under the impact and a green pearl started rotating in the corner of Lanoe's vision. A message from Ehta, no doubt warning him the cruiser couldn't take much more of this. He ignored it.

"Then they can open an unstable wormhole for us. One big enough we can fly the cruiser through it. Ginger—we need to get out of here. We can't beat Centrocor, not with those destroyers in here. Tell them! Tell them to open a wormhole so we can get out of here!"

Another long pause, as a missile grazed the cruiser's engines, the shock wave from the explosion throwing Lanoe's ship into a flat spin. He twisted out of it before he could collide with the cruiser. "Ginger!" he shouted. "Ginger, we're dying out here!"

Seconds ticked by. Didn't she understand? Didn't she realize that every one of them was doomed if she didn't convince them?

"They don't trust you," Ginger said, finally.

"What?"

"You've bullied and manipulated them since you got here. Rejected the help they offered and demanded impossible things. You've—"

"You," he told her, "have twenty seconds to convince them to open a wormhole." He muted her channel and flicked his eyes to acknowledge Ehta's call.

"Boss," the marine said, "if we keep taking damage like this, we're not gonna have a deck to stand on and we'll all have to flap

our arms real hard. You want us to abandon ship, you just say so—
in the meantime—"

"Do you have a firing solution on the Choir's city?" Lanoe
asked her.

"I do, but—"

"Stand by to fire," he told her.

It might be a terrible cliché, but time did, in fact, slow down to
a crawl. Candless could look around her and see clouds of flak
exploding in slow motion, like flowers blooming. She could see
PBW rounds stretching past her like brilliant pearls on a string. All
around her Centrocor fighters were moving to fill the gap in their
formation, to close the hole.

She ignored it all. Tapped virtual keys to lock in the target for her
disruptor round. Rolled over on her side to avoid a missile that was
burning right toward her. Checked her tactical board and saw that
Valk had only five of his fighters left, but that they were tying up
whole swaths of Centrocor's forces, twisting and darting in incredible loops and spins, their PBW cannon blazing away constantly,
seemingly at random, yet they kept hitting home, kept tearing the
enemy to pieces.

Ahead of her, dead ahead, lay the destroyers, flying so closely
together they might have been tethered one to another. They
looked almost furry, so covered in the barrels of guns she could
barely make out their actual hull plates.

She tapped one final key and her virtual keyboard winked out of
existence. In the belly of her BR.9 a panel slid back and the disruptor's cannon extended. A lucky shot from a carrier scout went right
through one of her airfoils, and her fighter twisted over on its side,
but it didn't matter. She was through, she was ready.

The destroyers were moving, the nose of the one right in front
of her lifting, turning to the left. Its pilot must know she was

there, know what she was about to do. They were trying to turn away from her shot, to present their least vulnerable side toward her. The big ship moved with a glacial slowness, but she could sense the pilot's desperation. The other destroyer had to compensate for the maneuver, turning in the opposite direction to avoid a collision.

In her peripheral vision Candless could see fighters on every side of her. She reached for the trigger built into her control stick.

At the last possible moment, she shoved the stick over to the side, just a hair, and her fighter banked right across the nose of the destroyer. Suddenly she was looking at the carrier instead, the enormous round curve of its flank.

She pulled the trigger. She felt like someone had kicked the bottom of her seat as the disruptor jumped away from her fighter—headed straight for the carrier.

She'd pulled this trick to make sure the carrier had no time to turn, to evade. The carrier was so big that one disruptor couldn't cripple it, but as it slammed into the hull and dug its way through, still exploding, she couldn't help but laugh.

They would remember her. She was almost certainly going to die in the next few seconds, but the bastards would never be able to forget her.

More practically, if less emotionally cathartic, the crew of the carrier was going to have a very bad few seconds, and then a lot of damage control to carry out. The destroyers would have to recover from their hasty maneuvers, a delicate process for ships that big. They would be unable to focus on the battle—for a moment.

She'd bought her people a few seconds. She just hoped to hell that Lanoe could make that time count.

"Please," Ginger said. "You have to help us. You have to do as Commander Lanoe asked."

The interests of the Choir no longer include appeasing Aleister Lanoe, Rain-on-Stones told her.

he has no right to ask

he mocks our great work

he brought destruction here

he does not speak for all humans

maybe this centrocor will listen to us

why should we give him anything

he is going to threaten us next

he is no friend of the choir

he is a known liar

Ginger grabbed at her hair with both hands. She accidentally hit her new surgical scar with the ball of her thumb and the stinging pain echoed out through the Choir—she could feel them all recoil from the sensation.

"You care about me. Maybe you hate Lanoe, or—or—" No, it wasn't hatred, the Choir wasn't rejecting Lanoe's request out of spite or anger. They wanted to *shame* him. To correct him. She shook her head. "He's not one of you! You can't make him harmonize. Don't you understand? Humans and Choir are different species, they—"

You are one of us. Archie was one of us.

Right now opinions are trending toward refusing him. Many would lash out at him, if they could. Some feel we should turn our back on him, that he is a lost cause. A very few—

Yes! Ginger could hear the voices, almost drowned out in the flow of information that swept through her head every second, but yes—there, and there, and there—a few choristers actually wanted to give Lanoe what he'd asked for. Just a handful, but she could pick up their thoughts. Rebroadcast them, boost the signal. Because she was new, because she was still learning to harmonize, Ginger's thoughts were…louder, given more weight, considered more carefully. By picking up thoughts that other choristers had already added to the consensus, she could highlight them. Make them stand out.

Debris is falling on the city, she rebroadcast. *Many of us will be injured if we don't find a way to stop this battle. The humans will kill each other, and their blood will be on our claws. Letting the humans die is a shameful thing, when we can prevent it.*

The thoughts echoed and bounced around the Choir's harmony, growing louder, demanding more attention. Eventually—maybe—she could sway them, change the song the Choir sang.

But that was going to take time. Too much time. There had to be—

Without warning, Rain-on-Stones pulled her claws away from Bury's body. A moment later the sick bay lurched as something struck the ship from outside, sending her instruments clattering to the floor.

Of course, Ginger thought—the surgeon had been warned the cruiser was about to be hit. The choristers watching from the city below had seen the attack coming. If Ginger had thought to look, if she'd been better at harmonizing, she would have seen it herself.

She looked down at Bury, on the bed. If Rain-on-Stones hadn't moved her claws in time would she have torn him open? He might have died, right then.

As if nothing had happened, Rain-on-Stones reached once more into the bloody mess of Bury's abdomen, then lifted a piece of shrapnel free and stepped away. The sick bay's medical drone lowered its arms to start stitching him up, closing the incision the alien surgeon had made.

She desperately wanted to know if—

He will live, Rain-on-Stones told her.

"Not if you don't open this wormhole," she said. "Centrocor will kill him. They'll kill everyone on this ship, including me and you."

That is not necessary, Rain-on-Stones told her. *You and I can go down to the city. The Choir will protect you.*

"If I agree to join you," she said. "To spend the rest of my life here. So you can speak to humans."

The chorister didn't need to say yes. Ginger hadn't been asking a question—she already knew how the Choir felt.

"I—" she started to reply, started to think of how to say no in a way that wouldn't completely antagonize the Choir, but of course—they already knew her feelings, too. And she had it. She saw what she needed to do. What she had to do if she was going to save Bury, and Lieutenant Candless, and Lieutenant Ehta, and everyone else on the ship. All of her friends.

You do not want to be one of us.

But you will.

"Open the wormhole," she said, making it clear.

She looked down at Bury's sleeping face. Knowing she would never see him again, as long as she lived.

"Open the wormhole, and I'll stay. I'll join you, as one of the Choir."

—✦—

Candless threw her stick forward and dove over the side of the destroyer, rolling over on her back so she could rake the big ship's side with her PBWs. Even as it focused its fire on her BR.9, she blasted guns off its side, tore through its hull plates. The damage looked extensive, but she knew it was mostly cosmetic. Until she could load another disruptor, she had little chance of actually hurting the Peltast.

Maybe she would live long enough to get that chance. Centrocor's fighters were keeping their distance, perhaps afraid of shooting at her when if they missed they might hit one of their own line ships. Flak burst all around her but she ignored it, ignored the flaming debris that clotted on her canopy, ignored the red lights and warning chimes sounding all around her.

She swung around underneath the destroyer and saw its belly was less covered in guns than its upper decks. She reached for her weapons board and started the involved process of loading another disruptor round. Before she could get it ready, however, a Sixty-Four swept into view right ahead of her, its guns already firing. She twisted over on her side and tried to shoot back, but she was at a bad angle and she knew she would never penetrate its vector field. This is it, she thought—she'd taken ridiculous risks, thrown herself into a suicidally dangerous mission, and now she was going to pay for that foolishness, her long career boiling down to this one moment, this one dogfight—

But then the Sixty-Four burst apart, its airfoils twisting away and its engine wreathed in flames. The wreckage fell away, toward the city of the Choir, and she saw one of Valk's pilotless BR.9s zooming in to take up a position at her side. Her tactical board showed her three more on the way.

"What are you doing?" she asked. "Do you think that perhaps you'd be more useful guarding the cruiser?"

"I know I let you down before. I know maybe Bury is going to die because of me. But damn it, let me help you now. You can make it out of here, if I sacrifice a couple of my fighters. I've run through the simulations. It'll work."

"Last time I checked this was a fight to the death. Our collective death. Why bother escaping, when there's nowhere to go?"

"Look."

"Look where? I don't see any...thing..."

Until she did, of course.

She saw beams of rushing plasma plunging upward from the city's lighthouses, energy that twisted into a wreath of blinding sparks. At the far end of the bubble, on the other side of the Hoplite, the plasma swirled and flared, spinning itself into a ring of pure light. As fast as the ring appeared it seemed to consume itself and then it was gone, vanishing into nothing.

In its place it left a broad, colorless sphere of distorted spacetime, like a glass lens hovering in air, just in front of the cruiser's nose. A wormhole throat.

"He did it," Candless whispered. "He convinced them."

Lanoe called her on the general band then. "Everyone back onboard! We're getting the hell out of here, right now!"

Lanoe's BR.9 was a mass of frayed wires and scorched panels. He didn't bother being gentle as he swung inside the cruiser's vehicle bay and parked the fighter in a docking cradle, nor did he bother lowering his canopy—he just wriggled out through the gaping hole and ran over to the railing, getting out of the way as Candless and one of Valk's fighters came screaming inside. One by one the others arrived, and slotted themselves perfectly into their cradles. Of the eight Valk had flown simultaneously, only three returned, the rest having been destroyed.

Lanoe worked his wrist display. "Ehta," he said, "delete that firing solution. Have your people buckle up—we're moving as soon as possible." He didn't wait for a reply. "Valk, take us into that thing—now." He tapped the display again. "Ginger, I don't know how you convinced them, but you just saved all our lives."

"Of course, sir," she said. The girl's tone was all wrong. More sorrowful than he might have expected, given the circumstances.

Candless rushed over and grabbed his wrist, speaking into the display there. "Ginger—is Bury all right?"

"He's still alive. He's going to be..." The girl just trailed off.

"Get him strapped in. And then do the same for yourself."

"I'll see to Bury, but I won't be going with you. I made a deal—in exchange for your wormhole, I have to stay here and replace Archie. The Choir is sending an aircar now to collect me and Rain-on-Stones. Lieutenant Candless, I want you to know how much I've appreciated—"

"I beg your pardon?" Candless said, interrupting the girl. "Ginger, I won't allow it. You're coming with us, and that's that."

"I can't," Ginger insisted. "They need me. Their harmony is incomplete without me. I made a promise."

Lanoe pulled his arm out of Candless's grip. "That's fine, but Centrocor isn't going to stop shooting at us while we wait for that aircar. We're going now, and I'm not leaving anyone behind. When we get...wherever we're going," he said, because he realized he had no idea where the new wormhole led. Not that he much cared—anywhere was safer than the bubble, just then. "When we arrive, we can arrange to send you back if that's still something you want."

"Commander! No! You can't do that, I made a promise, and anyway, Rain-on-Stones can't—"

Lanoe cut the connection. He took in the look on Candless's face and shrugged.

"Get her away from them and she won't want to go back. Now come on, we've got a desperate escape to make."

Chapter Thirty-Five

Ghostlight surrounded the cruiser as it slipped through the wormhole throat. Candless's disruptor and Valk's fighters had left Centrocor off balance, but the enemy had recovered enough to keep shooting. Bursts of heavy PBW fire smashed into the walls of the wormhole, annihilating in gouts of smoky light. A beam struck the side of the Hoplite and it lurched to one side, nearly running into the walls. The whole ship juddered and shook and Lanoe had to grab a handhold on the wall to keep from being thrown around like a rag doll. "Don't get us killed now," he shouted, "not after all that!"

Valk tapped wildly at the virtual keys that controlled the cruiser's maneuvering and positioning jets, bringing them back into trim. "Somebody tell Centrocor they lost already," he said.

Candless had strapped herself down into one of the seats in the wardroom, where she was working a minder tied into the ship's sensors. "There's something wrong here," she said.

Before she could elucidate what was bothering her, though, Paniet called in from his station back in the engines. "Duckies," he said, "I don't want to worry you, but this ship is being held together with twine and hope. One more hit like that—"

"We should be clear of enemy fire now," Lanoe said. "But see what you can do about getting Valk more power."

"More? I'd be deliriously happy if I thought we could maintain this level of output. No, deary, we'll be down to half speed before the hour's out."

"Lanoe," Candless said, "you need to see this. The wormhole—"

He cut her off. "Paniet, we need thrust and I don't care how you get it. Burn out the engines if you need to."

"Lanoe," Candless shouted.

He knew what she was going to say before she said it.

"The wormhole is . . . shrinking."

"Sure," he said.

"I'm terribly sorry," Candless said, sounding nothing of the kind. "I'm not sure you heard me. The wormhole we are currently traveling through is getting narrower as we proceed. It was six hundred and one meters wide when we entered, and it's five hundred and ninety-three meters wide now. The walls are—quite literally— closing in."

"Sure," Lanoe said, again. "It's an unstable wormhole."

"It—what?"

"The Choir forgot how to make permanent ones. I asked them to make a temporary one—it was either that or Centrocor killed us all. I'm assuming this one will last long enough for us to get through it to the other side. I'd rather not find out the hard way. So, Paniet—"

"More speed, yes, sir."

There was nothing to do but watch the numbers tick down. The wormhole was five hundred and twelve meters wide. Now it was four hundred and ninety-one.

"Are we going to make it?" Valk asked.

There was no way to answer that question. No way to know how long the wormhole was, whether they would be through it in an hour or if it would take seven days. If it was more than about ninety minutes, they were in trouble. The Hoplite was fifty meters wide. If the wormhole shrank to less than that width before they reached the other side, they would be obliterated.

"We'll make it," Lanoe said.

Ginger and Ehta came into the wardroom when the wormhole was four hundred and six meters wide. Perhaps they sensed the tense atmosphere in the communal space, because for a while neither of them said anything. They just crowded around the display and studied the numbers with everyone else.

In silence.

"How's Bury?" Valk asked, when he couldn't stand the quiet anymore. Three hundred and ninety-nine meters.

"Sleeping," Ginger said, almost whispering. The girl looked pale and drawn. Well, Valk supposed she'd been through a lot. "Rain-on-Stones said he would live. He's stable, at least."

Valk nodded. "That's good. He's a good kid."

"How's our chorister guest?" Lanoe asked.

"Rain-on-Stones?" Ginger said. "She's…she got pretty upset. When she realized you weren't going to let us go back to the city. She—she can't hear the Choir anymore. Neither can I, but I wasn't born hearing them. I didn't spend every second of my life hearing the thoughts of thousands of people." Ginger's eyes took on a faraway look that didn't seem at all healthy. "She's all alone. So alone. She couldn't handle it. She asked me to give her a shot, a sedative. She showed me how to do it, how to get the needle between the plates of her armor. We need to get her back to her people as soon as we possibly can."

"Sure," Lanoe said.

Three hundred and fifty-seven meters.

Ehta tapped Candless on the shoulder and took her aside, down the corridor and out of earshot. Valk could still hear them—he could hear anything that happened on the ship. He didn't like to eavesdrop but he had to know. There was no love lost between the two of them, he knew—Ehta had told him how she felt about Candless. Frequently.

"I saw what you did," the marine said now.

Valk could see Candless bracing herself. Maybe she expected Ehta to attack her, as revenge for the time Candless had slapped her.

"Lieutenant," Candless said, "while I recognize that you and I will never be friends, I do expect a certain level of—"

"I saw you charge that destroyer," Ehta interrupted. "I was watching on a display. I saw you rush in there all by yourself."

"You . . . did."

Ehta nodded. "That took the devil's own courage." Then she stuck out a hand.

Candless looked at the hand like she expected to find it smeared with something foul. Eventually, though, she took it.

"You're a hell of a pilot," Ehta said.

"Having seen your service record, and what you did at Niraya," Candless said, "I don't take that lightly."

Ehta nodded. Her mouth twisted over to one side and she released Candless's hand. "Don't get me wrong. I still hate your stinking guts."

"All right."

"It's not like you and I are going to start doing each other's hair. And I'm not going to tell you all my darkest secrets."

"I'll keep that in mind."

Ehta nodded. "All right, just had to get that out of the way."

The two of them wasted no time getting back to the wardroom.

Three hundred and fifteen meters.

Valk activated a camera back in the engines, and saw Paniet strapped into a safety seat, calling out orders to his tiny crew of neddies. "Yes, dear, I see you," the engineer said. "You're wondering, I imagine, whether we're going as fast as we possibly can. We are."

"You look tired," Valk said.

"I'm recovering from a head injury. You do understand, there's no button down here marked 'make ship go faster,' yes? You're lucky I'm giving you any kind of power at all. We took a missile hit to the engines back there. Nearly lost one of our tertiary cones."

"These old Hoplites last forever. They're indestructible," Valk said.

Paniet looked directly at the display. "I think we've proved that fact, the last few weeks." He rose from his chair and went to a console, where he worked at a virtual keyboard for a while.

Valk saw he was redirecting heat flow through the ship's exhaust manifold. "Try shunting it through channels six and fourteen," Valk said.

Paniet sighed, a little. "It was too convenient, wasn't it?"

"I'm sorry?"

"You can do all kinds of things we can't. We humans, I mean. You can talk to computers in a way we never will. Make copies of yourself to truly multitask. Shut down processes if they're bothering you." He shook his head. "I warned Commander Lanoe about this. I asked him to do whatever he could to keep you human, to keep you feeling human, because I could see you were going the other way. But it was too convenient. You were too useful as a machine."

"He had to make some hard decisions—"

"He made the decision to stop thinking of you as a human being," Paniet said. "He needs you. He won't let you go. And you keep giving away little parts of yourself, giving up on your humanity, because you want to please him. Because you love him."

"Love?" Valk asked. But he didn't deny it.

The engineer checked his wrist display. "Two hundred and ninety-five meters. If we wanted to turn around now and head back, we couldn't. Not enough room. Tell me something, M. Valk. Are we going to make it?"

"I don't know," Valk told him.

Paniet frowned. "A human would have lied and said yes. A human would always say yes, we're going to make it."

"There's no hope for me, is there?" Valk asked. "I'm eventually going to go bad. Start thinking so logically I decide I have to hurt people. Like the *Universal Suffrage*."

"I didn't say that," Paniet told him.

"Humans lie. You just told me so."

"We have a human on this ship who had surgery to turn her

into an alien. It didn't stop her from being human. If Ginger can become a chorister, I think you can be an AI, and a decent person, too. If that's what you want."

"Two hundred and seventy-nine meters," Valk said.

"Noted," Paniet said.

Two hundred meters. One hundred and ninety-nine. One hundred and ninety-eight and then—

Lanoe squinted at the display. That couldn't be what he thought it was, could it? He'd gotten used to near misses and close scrapes. "Look," he said.

Around him, the Hoplite's officers had fallen silent. Ehta was chewing her nails. Candless was staring at a section of wall, very intently, as if she could see through it. Ginger's eyes had glazed over—maybe communing with a sedated alien had left her half-asleep.

"Look," he said again, louder. "Damn you all—look!"

Because up ahead was a wormhole throat. They'd reached the end, with one hundred and twenty-five meters to spare.

They jumped up and crowded around the main display. Pointed and exclaimed as if they'd never seen a wormhole throat before. Ginger even smiled, a little. Lanoe liked it when Ginger smiled, under all that red hair. It made him think of Zhang, when things were good. When she was still alive.

"M. Valk," Candless said, "will you kindly exit this wormhole?"

"On it," Valk said.

They emerged from the throat moving fast, nearly ten percent of the speed of light. Valk cut in the retros to slow them down—there was no telling what was on the other side. It turned out he needn't have bothered.

For centuries, it had been an established fact that a wormhole throat could only exist near a large source of gravity, like a massive sun. That they needed to be anchored to something big. Maybe that was even true for stable wormholes. The Choir had sent them to a patch of deep space, however. The nearest star was a red dwarf sixty astronomical units away, twice as far as Neptune was from Earth's sun. The dwarf looked like just a bright star in a sky full of them.

Extraordinarily full of them, in fact.

"Where are we?" Lanoe asked.

"I'd look for constellations to get some idea," Candless said, "but I don't know how you'd even begin to pick out constellations in *that*."

The forward display showed more stars than any of them had ever seen. It was almost *paved* with them, stars in every possible color, stars so close it felt like you could reach out and touch them. Fully half the view was just a solid blur of light—the Milky Way, but impossibly bright and thick.

"There are four stars within a light-year of here," Valk said.

"That's crazy," Ehta said. "Stars don't pack together like that."

"No," Valk said. "Not where we come from."

Lanoe raised an eyebrow. He thought he might know what Valk was about to say. He devoutly hoped it was true. Even if it scared the hell out of him.

"We've moved…inward," Valk said. "Closer to the center of the galaxy. Out where Earth is, stars are farther apart, scattered all over the place. The farther you go inward, the closer together they get until they all kind of glom together at the center and create a supermassive black hole. I'm having a hard time getting a fix on these stars—I don't recognize any of them, and even the standard candles we use for navigation aren't in the right place. It's weird."

"How far?" Lanoe asked.

"How far from Earth? From any human planet? I'd say…ten thousand light-years," Valk told him.

Candless laughed. Even though Valk's tone had made it clear he wasn't joking.

"Hellfire," Ehta said.

Ginger turned to face Lanoe. "They gave you what you wanted, Commander."

Zhang was standing right behind him. Her hand on his shoulder. "*So close now,*" she said. "*You know what you need to do.*"

He pretended like he couldn't hear her. The others didn't need to know that she was there. "I would have settled for anywhere. Just getting out of the bubble, away from Centrocor, would have been something. Instead, the Choir did this."

"If I raise my hand all politely, will you answer my next question?" Ehta asked.

Lanoe pointed out the red dwarf at the center of the display. The brightest, closest star. "That," he said, "is the homesystem of the Blue-Blue-White."

Behind them, unnoticed, the wormhole throat shrank down to nothing, and vanished without any fanfare, folding itself back up into the higher dimensions.

The story continues in...

FORBIDDEN SUNS

Book Three of The Silence

Keep reading for a sneak peek!

Acknowledgments

I'd like to thank my editors, especially: Will Hinton and James Long, who helped me find Lanoe's grief, something I struggled with. I'd like to thank my agent, Russell Galen, and Alex Lencicki, who made this series possible. I'd also like to thank my wife, Jennifer Dikes, who gave me so much support through so many life changes during the writing process—losing my father, moving to a new home, and finally, gloriously, getting married to the most wonderful woman in the world. Through all of that, she stood by me and held my hand and told me to keep writing.

extras

orbit

introducing

If you enjoyed
FORGOTTEN WORLDS,
look out for

FORBIDDEN SUNS

Book Three of The Silence

by D. Nolan Clark

The Hipparchus-class carrier rocked from side to side, and some-where, down a long corridor, Ashlay Bullam could hear an explosion and a muffled scream. They were under attack—which meant they must have found their quarry.

"Get me to the bridge," she said.

"Nothing would give me more pleasure." Auster Maggs had an elegantly sculpted mustache and a sarcastic leer that seemed to be a permanent part of his face. Less than eight hours ago, he'd been a Navy pilot and her sworn enemy. Then he'd seen the writing on the wall—that the Navy couldn't win this fight. He'd immediately defected to Centrocor's side.

Now he was her new best friend.

He wrapped an arm around her waist and lifted her gently from her bed. The carrier was under slight acceleration, which meant there was a little gravity to contend with, but not much. He had no trouble half-carrying, half-walking her the short distance. He touched the release for her and the hatch slid open on a scene of utter chaos.

Displays all around the bridge showed the state of the battle. Fighters wheeled and struck, guns flashing as they twisted in for quick attack runs, thrusters flaring as they raced away again, missing deadly shots by a matter of centimeters. A Yk.64 fighter—one of their own—exploded just off the bow of the carrier and the bridge was washed with orange-white light. The carrier swayed and Bullam lunged for something to hold on to as she was knocked from her feet.

"Are we winning, at least?" she demanded.

Captain Shulkin, the carrier's commanding officer, turned in his seat to glare at her. "Victory is inevitable," he said. "Which does not mean we can afford to grow complacent. Information Officer— what is the status of the enemy's guns?"

"Weapons hot, sir—I register all sixteen of their coilguns ready to fire."

Bullam's blood ran cold. The last time they'd fought the Hoplite-class cruiser, it had fired one shot from just one of its guns, and Shulkin had been forced to make a terrible sacrifice to keep them all from being killed. Now all of the cruiser's guns were active—

"Except—sir," the IO said, his face crinkling up with bewilderment, "they aren't aiming at us. The guns are pointed at the city."

City? Bullam had no idea what the man was talking about. The last she'd heard the carrier was transiting through a wormhole throat. They could be anywhere in the galaxy by now. She slid into her seat at the back of the bridge and tapped her wrist minder to bring up a tactical display.

What she saw answered very few of her questions. Instead it raised many, many more.

The carrier wasn't in outer space. It was in a vast cavern, perhaps a hundred kilometers in diameter, with walls of pure ghostlight. The same eerie phosphorescence you saw lining the interior of a wormhole. But this couldn't be a wormhole—they didn't come this big, not by a power of ten. Moreover, wormholes were tunnels, linking two points in space. This cavern had only one entrance, the one they'd come through. It was like a bubble of higher-dimensional space carved out of the very wall of the universe.

Floating in the middle of the bubble, quite impossibly, was a city a few kilometers across. A ball of Gothic architecture, spires and towers radiating outward from a hidden center. From the tops of the highest buildings brilliant searchlights swept across the bubble, lighting up Centrocor and Navy ships alike.

Bullam could hardly believe it. But she knew, instantly—this was what they'd come to find. This was why they'd chased the cruiser across hundreds of light-years of space.

"Captain!" she called. "You have to stop them! The cruiser can't be allowed to shell that city."

Shulkin twisted his mouth over to one side of his cadaverous face. His eyes were two points of pure nothingness that bored into her. "I assume the civilian observer has a good reason to issue orders on my damned bridge?" he asked.

"We can't let them fire on the city," she said. "Those are potential *customers* down there!"

It had been a long journey to get here—wherever they were.

Bullam worked for Centrocor, one of the interplanetary monopolies, or polys, which effectively owned all planets outside the original solar system. Centrocor was in a constant state of cold warfare with the Navy of Earth. The balance of power shifted endlessly, but never so far as to reach a tipping point. Until, perhaps, now.

Centrocor had spies inside the Navy. Those spies had reported that the very top level of Naval command had approved a mission of utmost secrecy. The Admirals had sent one of their officers— Aleister Lanoe—to meet with some unknown group, some third party, in the hope of creating an alliance. Centrocor couldn't allow that to happen—anything that could strengthen the Navy had to be crushed immediately.

So the poly had sent Bullam to capture Lanoe, or at the very least to find out what he was up to. She had been given an enormous amount of support. A Hipparchus-class carrier a full half a kilometer long, which held a crew of over a hundred people and fifty smaller Yk.64 fighter craft. Two Peltast-class destroyers, only a hundred meters long each but so covered in guns they looked shaggy. Powerful, extremely fast, very deadly.

Perhaps most importantly, they'd given her Captain Shulkin. An ex-Navy officer who, for all his limitations, was a brilliant tactician and a ruthless leader.

Lanoe had only one ship, a Hoplite-class cruiser, and a handful of fighters. He was working with a skeleton crew and a tiny number of fighter pilots.

He was also the luckiest bastard who'd ever lived. Lanoe had fought in every major war since Mars had rebelled against Earth three hundred years ago. He'd always been on the winning side. He was the most decorated pilot in Navy history, having survived more dogfights and attack runs than should have been possible for one man. He was smart, quick, and sneaky, and somehow he had kept his people alive and his cruiser intact, despite everything Centrocor had thrown at him.

That couldn't last. The odds were undeniably in Centrocor's favor—they outnumbered him in every statistic that mattered. In previous encounters, it had been considered crucial to capture Lanoe alive. Now that they had reached this mysterious city, that was no longer necessary. They could throw everything they had at him.

It was just a matter of time. Lanoe was going to die. Centrocor was going to win. Bullam would gain unfettered access to the city, and she would make a deal with its inhabitants. Steal the Navy's new ally for the poly. She would return home to a promotion, to stock options, to guaranteed medical care. All she had to do was sit back and watch the battle play itself out.

We've already won.

She kept telling herself that. Repeating it, over and over, like a mantra. She was certain that eventually she would start to believe it.

"Where the hell is Lanoe?" Shulkin demanded. The IO didn't even bother to answer out loud. He just brought up a subdisplay that showed the Navy cruiser twenty kilometers away. The Hoplite was three hundred meters long, nearly a third of that taken up by its massive fusion engines, much of the rest comprised of its deadly coilguns and a large vehicle bay that could hold a dozen fighters. The ship was scarred by explosions, scorched by dozens of hits from particle beam weapons—PBWs. Portions of its armor were just missing altogether. Its vehicle bay was open to the elements; its hatch torn away.

It was not, however, undefended. A single BR.9 fighter—a Navy ship—spun circles around the big ship, a minnow twisting around the body of a wounded shark. Centrocor Yk.64 fighters darted in wherever they saw an opening but incredibly, impossibly, the BR.9 was always there to drive them back with salvos from its twin PBWs. The view magnified still further and Bullam saw that the enemy fighter's canopy had been blasted away, that its fuselage had been stripped down to exposed wiring and burnt-out components, but still it fought on. Through the damage she could actually see the helmet of the pilot—could even get a glimpse of short gray hair.

"It's him," Shulkin breathed. "Put a call in to the Batygin brothers."

A pair of holographic images appeared on either side of the magnified view, showing the commanders of the two Peltast-class destroyers. Identical twins, their hair combed in opposite directions as if that would allow someone to tell them apart. Their pupils were enormous because both were drugged with a vasodilator that supposedly enhanced their response time and combat effectiveness. It also let them speak almost in unison.

"Ready, Captain."

"Ready, Captain."

Shulkin didn't look at them—he only had eyes for Lanoe.

"Focus your attack on that BR.9. As long as he's alive we haven't won anything."

"Understood."

"Understood..."

"What?" Shulkin demanded. "Why are you hesitating?"

"We're currently under attack, ourselves."

"We *are* currently under attack, ourselves."

"There!" Bullam said, jabbing a finger at the display no one else was watching. The one that showed the battle raging just outside the carrier's hull.

A single BR.9 had been streaking toward them the whole time, virtually ignoring every Sixty-Four Centrocor had in play. Even as whole squads of the poly's fighters plunged toward it, the BR.9 kept coming, burning hard in a blatantly suicidal charge.

"That's Candless," Maggs said from behind Bullam's shoulder.

She swiveled around. She'd nearly forgotten he was there.

"Who?" she asked.

"Marjoram Candless. She's Lanoe's Executive Officer. Until recently she worked as an instructor at the Navy's flight school, but don't let that fool you. The old adage that those who can't, teach? Not frightfully accurate in this case. She's a real devil behind a control stick."

"She can't hope to achieve anything by herself," Bullam insisted.

"Ah, well, there's the rub," Maggs said, and nodded at the display.

Out of nowhere eight more BR.9s came swinging into the battle, their PBWs blazing away indiscriminately. Sixty-Fours burned and exploded left and right and suddenly there was a hole in their defense, a vulnerability big enough for Candless to punch right through. She continued her course, straight toward one of the destroyers, not deviating so much as a fraction of a degree.

"No," Bullam said. "No—our intelligence said Lanoe only had five pilots left. Who the hell are these eight?"

"Tannis Valk," Maggs told her, stroking his mustache.

"Valk—he's one of the five," Bullam said, "but—"

Even he looked worried now. "I'll save you the trouble of asking how one man can fly eight ships at the same time. He isn't. A man, that is. He's an artificial intelligence loaded into a space suit."

No. No, no, no. That wasn't... For one thing, that was illegal. Just allowing an AI to exist was a capital crime. Giving one access to weapons and military hardware was so incredibly unlawful, so incredibly unethical, that Bullam couldn't even imagine someone doing it. Not even a devious bastard like Aleister Lanoe. "No," she said.

"I'm afraid the answer is yes. And now—"

"Sir!" the IO shouted. "Sir, the enemy BR.9 has loaded a disruptor. It's within range of the destroyer."

One of the Batygin brothers opened his mouth as if to speak. The other mirrored the gesture, a split second later. "Brace for impact," he said.

"Brace for impact!"

In the display, Bullam could actually watch it happen. A panel in the undercarriage of Candless's BR.9 slid open, and the missile extended outward on a boom. A meter long spear with multiple warheads—one round like that could tear a destroyer to pieces.

And at the last minute, the very last second, Candless pulled a snap turn—and fired the missile not at the destroyer, but right at the carrier.

Bullam could see it coming right at her, head on.

The destroyers had already started to turn, hopelessly attempting to outmaneuver the disruptor. They ended up having to burn all their jets in an attempt not to collide with each other—or with the carrier.

The pilot of the carrier was far too busy to do any fancy flying. Everyone onboard the giant ship was simply trying to hold on.

The disruptor round detonated just before it touched the carrier's outer hull, the shock wave of the blast peeling the ship's armor back like the rind of a fruit. It kept exploding as it plunged through power relays, crew spaces, cable junctions, computer systems. It passed through the cavernous vehicle bay without meeting much resistance. Still exploding, it tore apart a pair of reserve fighters, a maintenance cradle and three engineers—and kept going.

On the bridge every display flashed red, and the air was full of screaming chimes. Damage-control boards popped up automatically and the pilot, the navigator and the IO tried desperately to issue commands to the crew, tried to lock down vital systems or bring up blast doors to keep fires from raging through the life-support system.

Then the carrier turned over on its side, rolling with the blast, and everyone was thrown over in their seats. Bullam's body bent the wrong way and she felt her bones twist in their sockets as she was thrown to the side, her neck whipping around and her arms flying in the air. Behind her Maggs smashed into one wall, his hands grabbing at anything he could reach, anything that would hold his weight.

The disruptor kept making its way through compartment after compartment of the ship, still exploding as it went, bursting the eardrums and lungs of Centrocor crew members as it passed them by, flash-frying sensitive electronics as it dug its way ever deeper into the mass of the carrier.

It was over in the space of a few seconds. It left Bullam's head ringing like a bell and blood dripping from her nose. She grabbed a brocaded handkerchief from a pocket of her suit and pressed it—hard—against her face. "Captain," she called. "Captain Shulkin!"

Smoke drifted across the bridge. The only light came from a single display that looked like a jigsaw puzzle—some of its emitters must have been smashed. In the fitful light, she saw Shulkin floating in the middle of the bridge, holding on to his chair with the long, skeletal fingers of one hand.

He was smiling.

"Well done," he said, a throaty whisper.

Then he flipped around to face the navigator. "Take us closer to the cruiser," he said.

"Captain, sir," the IO said. Blood slicked the left arm of the man's suit. "We need to do some damage control, we need to make sure we haven't lost—"

"The battle," Shulkin insisted, "isn't over yet. Move us closer. Tell the Batygin brothers to engage with everything they have."

Bullam held her neck with one hand—she was relatively sure it wasn't broken—and tapped anxiously at her wrist minder. It brought up a new display, showing her the city below. Fighters banked and soared over its spires, individual ships now caught up in lethal dogfights. She saw one of the enemy BR.9s break into pieces, debris twisting and streaming away from it even as inertia carried it on a crash course down into the city streets. Debris from collisions and explosions and general destruction was cascading down on the dark stone towers, a dangerous rain of burnt titanium and shredded carbon fiber.

A single BR.9 flashed across her view, momentarily filling the entire display. She backed up frame by frame until she could see the pilot's face. Sharp features, hair pulled back in a severe bun, prim, pursed lips. Maggs had said this Candless was a teacher. She'd come very close to killing every human being on the carrier.

The damage done. Candless was streaking away, swinging back and forth to avoid Centrocor fire. She was breaking free of the fight, headed back toward the cruiser. Not to defend it, Bullam thought. No.

"They're retreating," she said.

"Don't be a fool," Shulkin told her. "Where could they go? There's only one exit from this cavern, and we're blocking their way."

Bullam shook her head. "That attack—it wasn't meant to kill us. Just tie us up with damage control. She was playing for time."

"Time for what?" Shulkin demanded.

They didn't have to wait long to get an answer.

Bullam was probably the only one on the bridge who was looking at the city, not at the battle still raging all around them. She was the first to notice when all the searchlights down there began to pivot around, until they were all facing the same direction. A surge of white light poured out of them, beam after beam twisting around toward a common target. Though she couldn't see what they were pointing at—they seemed to be converging on thin air.

"What are they doing?" she demanded, not really expecting an answer. Nor did she receive one. None of the bridge crew were even paying attention to her. Valk's drone ships were tearing away at one of the destroyers, targeting its many guns, scoring its hull with burst after burst of concentrated PBW fire. Candless was halfway back to the cruiser already, where Lanoe was still defending his ship against all comers.

"There's something...happening," she said. "Damn you, Shulkin! Look at this!"

The glass-eyed captain finally twisted around in his seat to look at her. She held up her wrist minder so he could see the display.

The beams from the city were coalescing into a cloud of radiance, a sort of nebulous, formless glob of light. No, she realized. That wasn't light—it was plasma, some kind of ionized gas...

"You, there! Traitor!" Shulkin called.

Maggs looked deeply hurt, but he refrained from saying anything in his own defense. The charge was, after all, irrefutable. "How may I assist?"

"You were with Lanoe before we got here. What the devil is he doing? What are those beams? Some kind of weapon?"

"I'm afraid I wasn't privy to his negotiations with the people of that city," Maggs said. "I haven't the faintest. Many apologies."

Shulkin's face was fleshless and pale at the best of times. At that moment he looked like nothing more than a skull with lips. "IO! Give me data on that weapon!"

"Sir, it's...a series of collimated plasma beams, and, well...Yes," the poor information officer said, "I suppose it could be used as a...as a weapon, but—"

"Stop stammering and tell me what I need to know," Shulkin said. "Or I will replace you with someone who can."

The navigator and pilot looked away. They knew perfectly well what Shulkin meant. He'd shot the previous navigator for hesitation following an order. There was no question he would do the same thing again.

"The beams are hot enough to cut through armor plate, yes, sir," the IO said. "I'm getting some anomalous readings from them, though—the plasma seems to have negative mass."

"Negative? Negative mass?"

"It's not as impossible as it sounds, sir. It's called exotic matter, and hypothetically you could use it to create a—"

On the display, the beams wove together into a ring of coruscating light. It flared bright enough that Bullam started to look away—but then the ring collapsed inward, into itself, and seemed to pop out of existence, as quickly as it had appeared.

"—to create a wormhole throat," the IO finished, in a near whisper.

Where the ring had been, where the beams had crossed, there was nothing now except a strange spherical distortion in the air. As if a globe of perfect glass hung there.

Every single one of them knew what that meant. A wormhole throat. A passageway through the belly of the universe. It could go anywhere—literally anywhere.

And it was right where the cruiser needed it to be.

"They're going to escape," Bullam said, hardly believing it. "They're going to get away from us—*again*."

BR.9s started streaming into the cruiser's open vehicle bay, one by one. Static guns mounted on the hull of the Hoplite blazed away at those few Sixty-Fours that were still in range, still trying to get close enough to the cruiser to launch disruptors.

"Their engines are warming up," the IO called out. "They're going to move."

"Of course they are," Shulkin said. He sat down in his chair and pulled a strap across his waist. Then he steepled his fingers together before his face.

"Batygins," he called.

"A bit busy right now," one twin said.

"A *bit* busy right now," the other replied.

"I don't care," Shulkin said, though his voice was oddly soft. "Maneuver on your own time. Right now I need you to pour every ounce of fire you can into that cruiser. I want every missile, every flak gun firing—if this is our only chance, we *will* kill Aleister Lanoe. Am I understood?"

The brothers didn't even take the time to respond. Their guns opened fire almost instantly, heavy PBW salvos lancing across the sky, missiles firing in quick succession out of their pods. A few shots even found their target, burning long streaks down the engine modules of the Hoplite. Missiles locked on and flared with light as they accelerated toward the cruiser's thrusters. Anything in the way of that torrent of destruction would have been vaporized.

But it was too late. Even Bullam—who had no training in space combat—could see that. The cruiser's nose was already disappearing into the new wormhole throat, even as a final BR.9 raced for safety inside its vehicle bay. Lanoe's ship vanished into thin air, a little at a time. On the display it looked like it was moving with glacial slowness, like it had all the time in the world. But it kept disappearing, bit by bit.

"Keep firing!" Shulkin said.

A missile hit home—but only one. It burst against a thick plate of armor on the cruiser's side, light and debris spreading outward in a deadly cloud. But the Hoplite was half gone now, its coilguns blinking out of existence one by one. The vehicle bay disappeared, and then the thrusters were all that remained, just a dull glow of heat and ionized gas and then—finally—even that was gone.

The missiles lost their lock and could no longer home in on their targets. Rudderless, they twisted off, away from the wormhole throat, losing speed as they twirled pointlessly in the air. A few blasts of heavy PBW fire followed the cruiser through the throat, but it was impossible to see if they hit anything at all.

Eventually the destroyers stopped firing. What was the point?

Shulkin lifted his hands to his face, covering his eyes.

Bullam held her breath. She knew that something was coming. The captain was insane. Neurologically impaired. Back when he'd still been with the Navy, he'd developed a suicidal mania brought on by extreme combat stress. The Navy had fixed him, as best they could, with extensive brain surgery. They'd left him nearly catatonic, unable to do anything but fight.

Cheated of his prey now—how would he react? Would he pull out a pistol and blow his own brains out? Or maybe he would shoot everyone else first.

"Maggs," Bullam whispered. "Maggs, get ready to run if—"

"Send the recall," Shulkin said.

"Sir?" the IO asked.

"Send the recall order. I want every fighter back here, in our vehicle bay. I want the destroyers lined up and ready to maneuver. Have all crew aboard this ship report to stations, or to their bunks if they have no immediate duties."

"Yes, sir," the IO said.

Then Shulkin started to scrape at his own eye sockets. Digging his nails deep into the skin around his eyelids. Rubbing at his brows with the balls of his thumbs.

"Captain?" Bullam asked. "Are you...?"

"Navigator," Shulkin said. "Give me a course that takes us through that wormhole as fast as possible."

"Wait," Bullam said.

"If the civilian observer wishes to comment on my orders, she can do so in writing at some future time," Shulkin said. "Navigator?"

"Course entered, sir."

"Pilot," Shulkin said. "Take us—"

"No," Bullam said. "No! That won't be necessary. Our mission was to find out what Lanoe was up to. To find these allies he was looking for, and, well, here we are." She opened a display to show the city below them. "We've done it, Captain. We've reached our objective and we no longer need to capture Lanoe, we can—"

"Ignore her," Shulkin said. "If anyone on this bridge so much as looks at her, they will be disciplined. This is my ship. Pilot, take us through that wormhole."

"Sir, I'm sorry to interrupt," the IO said, "but there's something you should know. That wormhole isn't stable." On his display a schematic of the wormhole appeared. It dwindled even as Bullam watched, the throat tightening down to nothing. "It's shrinking. If we get caught in there when it collapses, we'll be annihilated. Every one of us will die. And we, uh . . . we won't be able to . . . kill Lanoe."

"Noted," Shulkin said. He scratched along the side of his nose as if he were trying to peel off a mask. "Pilot," he said, "I believe I gave you an order. If Lanoe thinks he can make it through, so can we. And I will *not* allow him to get away from me. This battle is not over until I say it is!"

No one on the bridge said a word. None of them moved, except the pilot. And she only stirred far enough to get the ship moving.

Gravity pushed them all down into their seats as the carrier surged forward, toward the wormhole throat.

introducing

If you enjoyed
FORGOTTEN WORLDS,
look out for

ARTEFACT

The Lazarus War: Book 1

by Jamie Sawyer

Mankind has spread to the stars, only to become locked in warfare with an insidious alien race. All that stands against the alien menace are the soldiers of the Simulant Operation Program, an elite military team remotely operating avatars in the most dangerous theaters of war.

Captain Conrad Harris has died hundreds of times—running suicide missions in simulant bodies. Known as Lazarus, he is a man addicted to death. So when a secret research station deep in alien territory suddenly goes dark, there is no other man who could possibly lead a rescue mission.

But Harris hasn't been trained for what he's about to find. And this time, he may not be coming back...

Chapter One

NEW HAVEN

Radio chatter filled my ears. Different voices, speaking over one another.

Is this it? I asked myself. *Will I find her?*

"That's a confirm on the identification: AFS New Haven. *She went dark three years ago."*

"Null-shields are blown. You have a clean approach."

It was a friendly, at least. Nationality: Arab Freeworlds. But it wasn't her. A spike of disappointment ran through me. *What did I expect?* She was gone.

"Arab Freeworlds Starship New Haven, *this is Alliance FOB Liberty Point: do you copy? Repeat, this is FOB Liberty Point: do you copy?"*

"Bird's not squawking."

"That's a negative on the hail. No response to automated or manual contact."

I patched into the external cameras to get a better view of the target. She was a big starship, a thousand metres long. NEW HAVEN had been stencilled on the hull, but the white lettering was chipped and worn. Underneath the name was a numerical ID tag and a barcode with a corporate sponsor logo – an advert for some long-forgotten mining corporation. As an afterthought something in Arabic had been scrawled beside the logo.

New Haven was a civilian-class colony vessel; one of the mass-produced models commonly seen throughout the border systems, capable of long-range quantum-space jumps but with precious little defensive capability. Probably older than me, retrofitted by a dozen governments and corporations before she became known by her current name. The ship looked painfully vulnerable, to my military eye: with a huge globe-like bridge and command module at the nose, a slender midsection and an ugly drive propulsion unit at the aft.

She wouldn't be any good in a fight, that was for sure.

"Reading remote sensors now. I can't get a clean internal analysis from the bio-scanner."

On closer inspection, there was evidence to explain the lifeless state of the ship. Puckered rips in the hull-plating suggested that she had been fired upon by a spaceborne weapon. Nothing catastrophic, but enough to disable the main drive: as though whoever, or whatever, had attacked the ship had been toying with her. Like the hunter that only cripples its prey, but chooses not to deliver the killing blow.

"AFS New Haven, *this is* Liberty Point. *You are about to be boarded in accordance with military code alpha-zeroniner. You have trespassed into the Krell Quarantine Zone. Under military law in force in this sector we have authority to board your craft, in order to ensure your safety."*

The ship had probably been drifting aimlessly for months, maybe even years. There was surely nothing alive within that blasted metal shell.

"That's a continued no response to the hail. Authorising weapons-free for away team. Proceed with mission as briefed."

"This is Captain Harris," I said. "Reading you loud and clear. That's an affirmative on approach."

"Copy that. Mission is good to go, good to go. Over to you, Captain. Wireless silence from here on in."

Then the communication-link was severed and there was a moment of silence. *Liberty Point*, and all of the protections that the station brought with it, suddenly felt a very long way away.

Our Wildcat armoured personnel shuttle rapidly advanced on the *New Haven*. The APS was an ugly, functional vessel – made to ferry us from the base of operations to the insertion point, and nothing more. It was heavily armoured but completely unarmed; the hope was that, under enemy fire, the triple-reinforced armour would prevent a hull breach before we reached the objective. Compared to the goliath civilian vessel, it was an insignificant dot.

I sat upright in the troop compartment, strapped into a safety harness. On the approach to the target, the Wildcat APS gravity drive cancelled completely: everything not strapped down drifted in free fall. There were no windows or view-screens, and so I relied on the external camera-feeds to track our progress. This was proper cattle-class, even in deep-space.

I wore a tactical combat helmet, for more than just protection. Various technical data was being relayed to the heads-up display – projected directly onto the interior of the face-plate. Swarms of glowing icons, warnings and data-reads scrolled overhead. For a rookie, the flow of information would've been overwhelming but to me this was second nature. Jacked directly into my combat-armour, with a thought I cancelled some data-streams, examined others.

Satisfied with what I saw, I yelled into the communicator: "Squad, sound off."

Five members of the unit called out in turn, their respective life-signs appearing on my HUD.

"Jenkins." The only woman on the team; small, fast and sparky. Jenkins was a gun nut, and when it came to military operations obsessive-compulsive was an understatement. She served as the corporal of the squad and I wouldn't have had it any other way.

"Blake." Youngest member of the team, barely out of basic training when he was inducted. Fresh-faced and always eager. His defining characteristics were extraordinary skill with a sniper rifle, and an incredible talent with the opposite sex.

"Martinez." He had a background in the Alliance Marine Corps. With his dark eyes and darker fuzz of hair, he was Venusian American stock. He promised that he had Hispanic blood, but I doubted that the last few generations of Martinez's family had even set foot on Earth.

"Kaminski." Quick-witted; a fast technician as well as a good shot. Kaminski had been with me from the start. Like me, he had been Alliance Special Forces. He and Jenkins rubbed each other up the wrong way, like brother and sister. Expertly printed above the face-shield of his helmet were the words BORN TO KILL.

Then, finally: "Science Officer Olsen, ah, alive."

Our guest for this mission sat to my left – the science officer attached to my squad. He shook uncontrollably, alternating between breathing hard and retching hard. Olsen's communicator was tuned to an open channel, and none of us were spared his pain. I remotely monitored his vital signs on my suit display – he was in a bad way. I was going to have to keep him close during the op.

"First contact for you, Mr Olsen?" Blake asked over the general squad comms channel.

Olsen gave an exaggerated nod.

"Yes, but I've conducted extensive laboratory studies of the enemy." He paused to retch some more, then blurted: "And I've read many mission debriefs on the subject."

"That counts for nothing out here, my friend," said Jenkins. "You need to face off against the enemy. Go toe to toe, in our space."

"That's the problem, Jenkins," Blake said. "This isn't our space, according to the Treaty."

"You mean the Treaty that was signed off before you were born, Kid?" Kaminski added, with a dry snigger. "We have company this mission – it's a special occasion. How about you tell us how old you are?"

As squad leader, I knew Blake's age but the others didn't. The mystery had become a source of amusement to the rest of the unit. I could've given Kaminski the answer easily enough, but that would have spoiled the entertainment. This was a topic to which he returned every time we were operational.

"Isn't this getting old?" said Blake.

"No, it isn't – just like you, Kid."

Blake gave him the finger – his hands chunky and oversized inside heavily armoured gauntlets.

"Cut that shit out," I growled over the communicator. "I need you all frosty and on point. I don't want things turning nasty out there. We get aboard the *Haven*, download the route data, then bail out."

I'd already briefed the team back at the *Liberty Point*, but no operation was routine where the Krell were concerned. Just the possibility of an encounter changed the game. I scanned the interior of the darkened shuttle, taking in the faces of each of my team. As I did so, my suit streamed combat statistics on each of them – enough for me to know that they were on edge, that they were ready for this.

"If we stay together and stay cool, then no one needs to get hurt," I said. "That includes you, Olsen."

The science officer gave another nod. His biorhythms were most worrying but there was nothing I could do about that. His inclusion on the team hadn't been my choice, after all.

"You heard the man," Jenkins echoed. "Meaning no fuck-ups."

Couldn't have put it better myself. If I bought it on the op, Jenkins would be responsible for getting the rest of the squad home.

The Wildcat shuttle selected an appropriate docking portal on the *New Haven*. Data imported from the APS automated pilot told me that trajectory and approach vector were good. We would board the ship from the main corridor. According to our intelligence, based on schematics of similar starships, this corridor formed the spine of the ship. It would give access to all major tactical objectives – the bridge, the drive chamber, and the hypersleep suite.

A chime sounded in my helmet and the APS updated me on our progress – T-MINUS TEN SECONDS UNTIL IMPACT.

"Here we go!" I declared.

The Wildcat APS retro-thrusters kicked in, and suddenly we were decelerating rapidly. My head thumped against the padded neck-rest and my body juddered. Despite the reduced-gravity of the cabin, the sensation was gut wrenching. My heart hammered in my chest, even though I had done this hundreds of times before. My helmet informed me that a fresh batch of synthetic combat-drug – a cocktail of endorphins and adrenaline, carefully mixed to keep me at optimum combat performance – was being injected into my system to compensate. The armour carried a full medical suite, patched directly into my body, and automatically provided assistance when necessary. Distance to target rapidly decreased.

"Brace for impact."

Through the APS-mounted cameras, I saw the rough-and-ready docking procedure. The APS literally bumped against the outer hull, and unceremoniously lined up our airlock with the *Haven*'s. With an explosive roar and a wave of kinetic force, the shuttle connected with the hull. The Wildcat airlock cycled open.

We moved like a well-oiled mechanism, a well-used machine. Except for Olsen, we'd all done this before. Martinez was first up, out of his safety harness. He took up point. Jenkins and Blake were next; they would provide covering fire if we met resistance. Then Kaminski, escorting Olsen. I was always last out of the cabin.

"Boarding successful," I said. "We're on the *Haven*."

That was just a formality for my combat-suit recorder.

As I moved out into the corridor, my weapon auto-linked with my HUD and displayed targeting data. We were armed with Westington-Haslake M95 plasma battle-rifles – the favoured long-arm for hostile starship engagements. It was a large and weighty weapon, and fired phased plasma pulses, fuelled by an onboard power cell. Range was limited but it had an incredible rate of fire and the sheer stopping power of an energy weapon of this magnitude was worth the compromise. We carried other weapons as well, according to preference – Jenkins favoured an Armant-pattern incinerator unit as her primary weapon, and we all wore plasma pistol sidearms.

"Take up covering positions – overlap arcs of fire," I whispered, into the communicator. The squad obeyed. "Wide dispersal, and get me some proper light."

Bobbing shoulder-lamps illuminated, flashing over the battered interior of the starship. The suits were equipped with infrared, night-vision, and electro-magnetic sighting, but the Krell didn't emit much body heat and nothing beat good old-fashioned eyesight.

Without being ordered, Kaminski moved up on one of the

wall-mounted control panels. He accessed the ship's mainframe with a portable PDU from his kit.

"Let there be light," Martinez whispered, in heavily accented Standard.

Strip lights popped on overhead, flashing in sequence, dowsing the corridor in ugly electric illumination. Some flickered erratically, other didn't light at all. Something began humming in the belly of the ship: maybe dormant life-support systems. A sinister calmness permeated the main corridor. It was utterly utilitarian, with bare metal-plated walls and floors. My suit reported that the temperature was uncomfortably low, but within acceptable tolerances.

"Gravity drive is operational," Kaminski said. "They've left the atmospherics untouched. We'll be okay here for a few hours."

"I don't plan on staying that long," Jenkins said.

Simultaneously, we all broke the seals on our helmets. The atmosphere carried twin but contradictory scents: the stink of burning plastic and fetid water. *The ship has been on fire, and a recycling tank has blown somewhere nearby.* Liquid *plink-plink-plinked* softly in the distance.

"I'll stay sealed, if you don't mind," Olsen clumsily added. "The subjects have been known to harbour cross-species contaminants."

"Christo, this guy is unbelievable," Kaminski said, shaking his head.

"Hey, watch your tongue, *mano*," Martinez said to Kaminski. He motioned to a crude white cross, painted onto the chest-plate of his combat-suit. "Don't use His name in vain."

None of us really knew what religion Martinez followed, but he did it with admirable vigour. It seemed to permit gambling, women and drinking, whereas blaspheming on a mission was always unacceptable.

"Not this shit again," Kaminski said. "It's all I ever hear from you. We get back to the *Point* without you, I'll comm God personally. You Venusians are all the same."

"I'm an American," Martinez started. Venusians were very conscious of their roots; this was an argument I'd arbitrated far too many times between the two soldiers.

"Shut the fuck up," Jenkins said. "He wants to believe, leave him to it." The others respected her word almost as much as mine, and immediately fell silent. "It's nice to have faith in something. Orders, Cap?"

"Fireteam Alpha – Jenkins, Martinez – get down to the hyper-sleep chamber and report on the status of these colonists. Fireteam Bravo, form up on me."

Nods of approval from the squad. This was standard operating procedure: get onboard the target ship, hit the key locations and get back out as soon as possible.

"And the quantum-drive?" Jenkins asked. She had powered up her flamethrower, and the glow from the pilot-light danced over her face. Her expression looked positively malicious.

"We'll converge on the location in fifteen minutes. Let's get some recon on the place before we check out."

"Solid copy, Captain."

The troopers began a steady jog into the gloomy aft of the starship, their heavy armour and weapons clanking noisily as they went.

It wasn't fear that I felt in my gut. Not trepidation, either; this was something worse. It was excitement – polluting my thought process, strong enough that it was almost intoxicating. This was what I was made for. I steadied my pulse and concentrated on the mission at hand.

Something stirred in the ship – I felt it.